Mr Blackwood's Fabularium

Mr. Blackwood's Fabularium

by
Stephen Lycett

Illustrated by

Talya Baldwin

Stephen Lycett asserts his moral right to be
identified as the author of this book.

Published by Stephen Lycett
Copyright © 2018 Stephen Lycett

Mr Blackwood's Fabularium paperback edition
ISBN: 978-1-9995853-3-4

Designed, typeset and printed by Riverside Publishing Solutions Ltd

Wel nine and twenty in a compaignie
Of sondry folk, by aventure yfalle
In felaweship and pilgrimes were they alle,
That toward Caunterbury wolden ride.
Chaucer: *General Prologue to the Canterbury Tales*

'Talking of Exhibitions, World's Fairs, and what not,' said the old gentleman, 'I would not go round the corner to see a dozen of them nowadays. The only exhibition that ever made, or ever will make, any impression upon my imagination was the first of the series, the parent of them all, and now a thing of old times – the Great Exhibition of 1851 in Hyde Park, London. None of the younger generation can realise the sense of novelty it produced in us who were then in our prime.'

Thomas Hardy: *The Fiddler of the Reels*

Contents

Cast List

At the Ebenezer Temperance Hotel

Percy Blackwood, proprietor (also on the train)
Serafina Blackwood, his wife
Palmerston, the parrot
On the Train
In the 'Tub' or Third Class carriage

The Reverend Francis Culpepper, Chaplain
to the Ebenezer Temperance Society

Nan Foxley, parlour maid at the Ebenezer Temperance Hotel
Miss Violet Osgood, Secretary to the Ebenezer Temperance Society
Mr Albert Turpin, an inventor
Mr Hector Beamish, a phrenologist
Stumps, a railway navvy
Corporal Costello, a Waterloo veteran
George Costello, his son, a bugler in the East Kent Militia (the Buffs)
Mr Humphrey Ezard, a daguerreotypist
Mr Cyril Purselove, an out-of-work actor
Miss Aurora Lark, a governess
Mr Gilbert Meek, a tripe dresser
Mr Charles Breeze, an advertising copywriter and Chairman of the
Canterbury Glee Club
Gabriel, a boot black
The Saturnine Stranger

In the Second Class Carriage

Dr Erasmus leGrove, the Diocesan Exorcist
Mr Bartholomew, a watchmaker
Mr Alfred Malachi Brown, the eminent pteridologist
Mrs Anne Malachi Brown ('Mrs Alfred'), his wife
Mr Dacre, an ecclesiastical architect
Mr Jocelyn Critchley, a bookbinder
Mme Emily Fontana, a medium and adept
Miss Binnie, a novelist and friend of Mme Fontana
Mr Henry Scudamore, butler to Lady Rippledale (outward journey only)
Maud Gowlett, a musical artiste who performs under the name of the Duchess of Croydon

In the First Class Carriage

Lady Rippledale,
Miss Tintsford, companion to Lady Rippledale
Mr Henry Scudamore, butler to Lady Rippledale (return journey only)

Employees of the South Eastern Railway

Mr Albert Sturdee, engine driver
Mr George Bowles, Station Master at Canterbury West

In the Crystal Palace

The Duke of Wellington
Lord Palmerston, the Foreign Secretary
Augustus Welby Northmore Pugin
Lord Tennyson, the Poet Laureate
A choleric American patriot
Mr Joseph Burch, an inventor and exhibitor

Part One

Extract 1

6 October: Today I re-enacted the Judgment of Solomon and snapped a locomotive in half. Since neither of the mothers (both elderly clergymen) was willing to back down, I divided the baby (dark green boiler, red under-frames) between them. Oh you should have seen their faces when I handed one the engine and the other the tender! Instantaneous uproar! How could I, how dare you. Etc, etc. But by then I was past caring. The decision to dissolve the Stour Valley Railway Society may have been unanimous but it wasn't exactly harmonious, the various factions blaming each other for the failure of the project and all of them blaming me, as chairman, for not dividing the spoils fairly. If only such a thing had been possible! There wasn't a bridge, a station, a carriage that wasn't a joint effort, and as for those marvels of research and engineering, the locomotives, who wouldn't have wanted to fight for them? If I hadn't had my eyes on a larger prize, I might have joined the fray myself. Gentlemen, I said, when the uproar had died down, you will notice that I have claimed nothing for myself, nothing material, that is. I shall therefore reward myself by taking over the blog for my personal use. Since I have been keeping it on behalf of the Society for the last two years, I can't see that anyone can object. Yes? No? Motion carried.

So, for those of you chancing on this blog for the first time, a word of explanation about what you will no longer see, though you are free to rummage in the archive. The Stour Valley Railway Society was formed in

1996 to mark the 150th anniversary of the South Eastern Railway's arrival in Canterbury. Our intention was to build a model, accurate to the last rivet, of the branch line that connects Canterbury to Ashford and, where possible, run trains as scheduled in Bradshaw. In the end we were defeated not by engineering but by scholarship. Progress was halted by squabbles over cap badges, coach bolts and gas mantles – and the smaller the detail the bigger the row. It didn't help that many of our members were clergymen and when clergymen fall out, they do so with a fervour all their own. As the line inched towards Ashford, the disputes became ever more bitter, with the result that fewer members attended meetings and fewer still met deadlines. This led to a permanent state of unfinishedness. We had trucks without wheels, locomotives without nameplates, clocks without dials. Even the station hoardings were left blank when no-one could agree when particular brands of soap or tobacco first appeared.

I wasn't sorry to see the back of the Stour Valley Railway project. And not just because of the quarrels. To be frank, I was bored by it. On a model railway, only the trains move. The people don't. Ever. They have no past, no future. Of them there are no stories waiting to be told. Those waiting on the platforms never get on the trains, those on them never get off. Guards never blow their whistles, porters stay rooted to the spot. There are no seasons, no sun and showers. In other words, the perfection of model railways is sterile. It's a version of pastoral with porters and passengers instead of nymphs and shepherds. In my nightmares it is how I imagine the afterlife to be: an eternity of watching the same exquisite trains going round and round and feeling the magic go stale without ever being able to run away.

So farewell to all that. What then of future blogs? Well, that has still to be decided. I have recently been approached, as a retired medievalist, to write a booklet for the St Dunstan Press about Chaucer's Canterbury. Some of my findings might well end up on these pages. As might my wife's guests. (My wife keeps a B and B by the way – Garlands. Check us out on Trip Advisor.) We get all sorts – tourists, weekenders, film crews – but this being a university/cathedral city a fair few academics and clerics as well. Take last week for example. We had a director who wanted to make a film about Dickens and the Staplehurst railway disaster of 1865. Ten people dead, countless injured, ten coaches in the river. CGI would take care of all that, freeing up more rehearsal time for the characters. Then there was a software designer who was convinced that he had cracked the problem of computer-generated storytelling, together with a philosopher who was convinced he had done no such thing. They argued late into the night, the one insisting that all mental acts were replicable, the other that for a computer to write a half-decent story it must first want to do so and it would only want to do so if it had had real-world experiences beforehand. Or take the PhD student who was trying to Marxify Victorian ghost stories by suggesting that spectres represent the occluded presence of labour in manufactured commodities. Something like that anyway. With guests like these my blog will not be short of material. I wonder what Chaucer's pilgrims would have made of it.

7 October: One door closes, another opens. I have found the perfect retirement project for a Chaucer anorak and a train anorak. A new party arrived at Garlands today, a team of data miners engaged by the Church to customise theologies for communicants based on their shopping preferences. It's part of the C of E's Bespoke Beliefs Programme which I happen to know is run by an ex-SVRS member, a liberal cleric with flexible views on everything except the Stour Valley Railway. Of all my tormentors, he was the most pitiless.

– Beware of Geeks bearing gifts, said one of the new arrivals, handing me a parcel. Found it at the end of your drive.

– Couldn't you have left it there? said my wife shooing away a spider which had crawled out of the brown paper. Or at least dumped it in the porch.

(She hates untidy guests and festoons the house with DO NOT notices in 48 point Ariel.)

– But it's got your address on it, said the geek.

– In fountain pen, too, said his colleague. So last century.

– I don't care if it's in poker work, said my wife. I don't want it in the house. Jonathan, get rid of it.

Holding the parcel at arm's length for fear of other insect life, I made for the cellar door.

– How intriguing, said one of our guests. I wonder what's in it.

What indeed? I wondered, as I descended to the cellar stairs.

Percy Blackwood could not have entered our lives at a worse moment, and entering as a badly wrapped parcel was particularly embarrassing, for there are no customers my wife values more highly than clerics and academics, even untidy ones. Left to her own devices, she would probably have taken the parcel down the garden and burned it.

In the cellar, which is part workshop, part office, I cut the string and let the contents spill out on the table. It was obvious at a glance that these were someone's foul papers – foul in the everyday sense of having been nibbled by mice, and foul in the scholarly sense, of being drafts of a work that had never been completed or perhaps – who knows? – scarcely begun. To make matters clear, let me open the parcel, brush away the spiders and lay the contents before you. There they are, spread out across the table as I write – notebooks, letters, loose sheets of Pitman shorthand, press cuttings, a printed story from Blackwood's Magazine. What the author intended to do with this material is hard to say. It was clearly intended for publication, either as separate items or as a collection. My guess is that he wanted to publish separately, but, having failed to do so, rolled all the items into a huge omnium gatherum which he hoped would be more than the sum of its parts.

October 13: Most of the stories in the collection seem to have been written up as if for publication, though a few exist in a fragmentary state and one or two are unattributed. We shall probably never know the reason that the author failed to complete his task. Perhaps it was beyond his strength, perhaps he lost heart. Over the coming months I shall prepare the papers for publication in a way that I hope he would have approved.

So who was our mysterious author? His name was Percy Blackwood. He was a teller – or, more, accurately a collector – of tales, most of them, as far as I can tell, unread until I opened the parcel. But that was not how the world knew him. When we meet him in the following pages he is the proprietor of the Ebenezer Temperance Hotel in St Margaret's Street, Canterbury, and organiser of an excursion to the Great Exhibition of 1851. With his wife's health failing and the Ebenezer losing money, he resolved to stake everything – money, prestige, hope – on that trip to London, though at what cost and with what success I shall leave the reader to decide.

Two questions remain unanswered: who delivered the papers to my doorstep and where had they been until our guests discovered them? Neither question can be answered with any certainty. The only clue – if it is even that – lies in the words YOU WIN scribbled on the outside of the parcel. What they might mean I hope to discover in the course of my labours.

[Editor's Note: In what follows most of the ordering is mine and therefore conjectural. I shall confine my editorial comments to indicating where I have made decisions on the author's behalf, and in an appendix will add such facts about his life and times as will make more sense in retrospect. Here then, published for the first time, are the foul papers of Percy Blackwood, proprietor of the Ebenezer Temperance Hotel in St Margaret's Street, Canterbury, in the middle years of the nineteenth century, and occasional contributor to that quintessential Victorian publication, Blackwood's Magazine.*]*

1

CANTERBURY TO ASHFORD

Prologue

The Reverend Francis Culpepper rose unsteadily to his feet and watched the roofs and towers of Canterbury disappear round a bend in the iron road. For those who had never strayed far from home this was the most solemn of moments. There was an exchange of anxious glances as the bandsmen, who had been playing temperance hymns in the rearmost wagon, fell briefly silent.

"Man," announced Culpepper, who was known to Cathedral wags as the Rev. Felix Culpa, "is born unto trouble as the sparks fly upward."

Far from flying upward, the sparks from the locomotive struck the underside of a bridge and rained down upon the open trucks, or 'tubs', as I am told they are called. The poor excursionists, whose holiday finery was already black with soot, shrieked in horror as the fiery particles settled in the hollows of hats and shawls. A straw bonnet, belonging to Nan Foxley, our parlour maid, began

to smoulder and would surely have burst into flame had not her
neighbour plucked it from her head and pinched out the blaze with
her fingers. Miss Violet Osgood, who was Secretary to the Ebenezer
Temperance Society, was known to disapprove of straw bonnets, her
own being a rather grand affair of maroon bombazine, which she
had borrowed from an aunt in Hastings and complemented with a
matching cape and ruffles.

"What were you thinking of?" she scolded. "Travelling third class
with linen flowers in your bonnet is simply to invite disaster. Now be
a sensible girl and place it under the bench."

The Rev. Culpepper, from whose mind conflagrations – or one
in particular, at least – were never very far away, resumed his seat
and was clearly about to opine on the subject, when a man with luxuriant side whiskers leant forward and offered Nan his card.

"Excuse me, miss," he said, touching the brim of his hat, "but I
cannot help pointing out that anyone with a headpiece like mine
need have no fear of sparks. Permit me to introduce you to the
Turpin Travelling Topper, soon to be available in bonnet form for
ladies."

Everyone turned to look at him. He was not a member of the
Ebenezer Temperance Society, which, although it had organised
the excursion, had been unable to secure tubs exclusively for its own
use and was therefore scattered throughout the train. Why no-one
had remarked upon him before – or why, having done so, had kept
it to himself – was hard to explain, for he was indeed remarkable.
Not just for his side whiskers, magnificent though they were, but for
the headpiece to which he had drawn our attention. At first sight it
resembled a top hat, a little higher than the normal article perhaps
but otherwise unremarkable until one noticed a band of rivets
which ran round the circumference about half way up the cylinder.

I took the card from Nan, who was struggling with the unfa-
miliar script, and read: 'Albert Turpin Esq. Bespoke Inventor and
Engineer. Satisfied customers include JPs, Ministers of Religion and
Fellows of All Souls.'

*A straw bonnet belonging to Nan Foxley, our
parlour maid, began to smoulder*

"Scientists have told us," continued Mr Turpin, "that fifteen per cent of the body's warmth is lost through the head and, in travellers exposed to the elements, as much as twenty-five per cent. Why, in inclement weather that's as good as a death sentence. Or would be," said he, tapping the barrel of his hat, "were it not for the Turpin Travelling Topper."

He removed the Turpin and placed it on his knees.

"Now what do you suppose is in here?" he asked, turning the hat upside down.

"Why, it's a metal cylinder!" remarked Miss Osgood.

"A water cylinder," agreed Turpin, "and more to the point, a hot water cylinder."

"But does it not burn your head?" I asked.

"Not a bit of it," he replied. "The insulation is sufficient to release the heat slowly. By the time we reach London, I expect it to be still warm."

"Why," marvelled Miss Osgood, "you should be represented in the Crystal Palace."

"Never fear, madam," replied Turpin, "I am. Several times over, in fact. You will find me among both the industrial machinery and the domestic conveniences. The Turpin Travelling Topper is not, alas, among the exhibits, being something of a last-minute inspiration."

Whilst Turpin had been speaking, Nan had quietly retrieved her bonnet from under the bench and had got as far as tying the ribbons under her chin, before Miss Osgood noticed what she was about.

"Unbonnet, child, unbonnet!" she scolded. "Do you want your linen flowers to be the death of you?"

Poor Nan! For her, as for many girls of her class, a visit to the Crystal Palace was both an opportunity to view the exhibits and, for a few glorious hours, to become one herself. To achieve which, she had been denying herself soap, snuff and other small luxuries these three or four months past.

"If Nan wishes to set herself alight," I told Miss Osgood, choosing my words carefully, for I could not afford to offend her for reasons which will shortly become clear, "then she must be allowed to do so. After weeks of self-denial she has surely earned the right."

I caught a look of reproach in Nan's eye and was relieved when Culpepper, never one to let slip an opportunity to talk about fire, warned her that, unlike lightning, sparks always fell in the same place twice. Such, he added, was their nature. The look in Nan's eye had been intended to remind me of an occasion earlier in the year at a time of mounting Exhibition fever when she had asked Serafina, my wife, for a temporary increase in her wages. An 'Exhibition supplement, if you please, mum,' was the phrase she actually used, an Exhibition supplement such as would put her on a level with all the other parlour maids in Canterbury. Serafina could scarcely believe her ears. It was most unlike her. She had clearly been put up to it by servant girls from other establishments – Garlands, for instance – who were in the habit of answering back and getting away with it. But my wife was not angry. Such was the excitement that The Great Exhibition had created in all classes that requests for a little something extra were neither surprising nor unreasonable – or would not have been had our circumstances, for reasons that will shortly be made clear, not been so straitened.

For several seconds Nan hesitated between vanity and prudence. Oh, how she longed to show off her precious plumage, and how, at the same time, she dreaded arriving at Hyde Park with her feathers blackened and burnt! What was she to do? To whom was she to turn for impartial advice? First, she untied the ribbons, then, thinking better of it, tied them again defiantly, but, at the first tut! of disapproval from Miss Osgood, snatched the bonnet from her head altogether. She would have continued to tergiversate had not a gentleman with dazzling white cuffs who until now had been concealed behind the Turpin Travelling Topper leaned over the back of the bench and congratulated her on going bareheaded – a state, he said, on which both God and Nature smiled.

"As you can see, I myself go bareheaded and wish others would do likewise. And now, my dear", he said, turning to Nan, "since you removed your bonnet, I have been admiring the bumps on your cranium. I wonder if, in the interests of science, you would allow me to measure them with my callipers." – From a leather case he drew what looked like a pair of giant brass sugar tongs – "The procedure is quite painless."

The bareheaded gentleman I knew by sight. He had recently opened a consulting room on St George's Street with the words 'Hector Beamish, Consultant Phrenologist' blazoned on the window in gold. It was said that his services were much in demand by clergy after he had saved one of them from an unfortunate marriage by investigating the bumps of his intended. Culpepper, however, was adamant.

"Miss Foxley," he declared, "is a member of my flock. What you propose is quite out of the question."

"Forgive me, sir," replied the bareheaded gentleman, holding out his hand and exposing his white cuffs, "you have the advantage of me. I do not think we have been introduced."

"The Reverend Francis Culpepper, Chaplain to the Ebenezer Temperance Society."

"Hector Beamish, consulting phrenologist. You may have seen my premises in St George's Street."

It soon became clear clear that Beamish was much more interested in his fellow excursionists than in the object of their excursion. Whilst others meant to feast their eyes on silks and shawls, pumps and ploughshares, the phrenologist meant to feast his on their cranial peculiarities. But Culpepper saw only too clearly what he was at and determined to thwart him. Would Beamish, I wondered, admit defeat gracefully, or would he, like a wolf shut out of the fold, pounce on unattended bumps elsewhere? Before the question could be answered, however, there was an unexpected intervention.

Next to Beamish sat a giant of a man wearing a calico jacket, plush waistcoat, green neckerchief and a felt hat with a turned-up brim. During the conversation between Beamish and Culpepper, he had been paring his nails with a clasp knife, apparently indifferent to what was being said. Suddenly he turned to Beamish and demanded:

"Do hands count?"

Beamish looked baffled.

"You know. Hands. Two palms, ten fingers – or in my case eight and a half."

Beamish smiled indulgently.

"No, my friend, hands do not count. Not to me, anyway. The business of phrenology is confined to heads. To me the human cranium speaks of character, whereas the hand, with its calluses and broken nails, speaks merely of toil. I make an exception, of course, for the ladies, whose cuticles are perfect."

"That," said the giant, "is because they never done a hard day's work in their lives."

The man in the calico jacket was a railway navvy, who went by the name of Stumps. (In my experience navvies rarely go by the names they are christened with.) Earlier I had seen him, like the Ancient Mariner, at the station, inflicting on passengers the story of how he had lost his fingers during the construction of the line. Of course, there was no reason why a navvy should not enjoy the fruits of his labours by travelling on a train with honest folk. But navvies were not popular. Their drunkenness, their boorishness, the squalid living conditions in their tents and shanties led to their being regarded as a race apart. It was widely believed that they held their wives in common and that prize-fighting and poaching were popular pastimes among them. Against the general tide of lawlessness the magistrates seemed powerless. Riots had erupted across the country, the North bearing the brunt, though even closer to home there had been skirmishes between the navvies and the young gentlemen of Tunbridge School.

It was clear to me that, whatever his claims to our sympathy, the navvy should not be allowed to spoil our conviviality. A digression was called for. Without further ado, I removed my hat and offered up my scalp to Hector Beamish, informing him that he could wield his callipers to his heart's content.

"My dear sir," he said, "I can see you are a man after my own heart. A man of vision, a man of science. But first, whom do I have the honour of addressing?"

"My name, sir," I replied, "is Percy Blackwood. I am the proprietor of the Ebenezer Temperance Hotel in St Margaret's Street and President of the Ebenezer Temperance Society, to which Miss Osgood and the Reverend Culpepper are Secretary and Chaplain respectively."

There was a groan from Stumps.

"As soon as I heard them hymns from the band," he said, "I might have known that you lot was temperance. Seven years building the line, pestered every inch of the way by missionaries, all of them temperance, and I ends up on a train full of 'em."

My diversionary tactic was clearly not working. I had offered my head to Beamish in the hope of silencing Stumps and here he was, more garrulous than ever.

"Have you anything to report, Mr Beamish?" I enquired loudly, praying that, phrenologically speaking, my head was yielding untold riches.

"I believe I have, sir," he replied. "I believe I have. Benevolence, sobriety, integrity – these I expected to find. But they are not all I have found. You have, I believe, hidden depths, Mr Blackwood. Unless I am much mistaken you are something of a writer. A poet perhaps."

I shook my head.

"Or a light essayist?"

I shook my head.

"Or perhaps you are related to the proprietor of that excellent publication, *Blackwood's Magazine*. Come now, admit it."

Unseen by Beamish, Violet Osgood blushed deeply. Knowing that Violet was not the blushing sort, Nan Foxley looked alarmed and asked her if she felt unwell.

"Of none of these am I guilty," I said loudly, hoping to divert Nan's attention from Miss Osgood.

"Now that is strange, unaccountable even," pondered Beamish. "The lobes of language and eventuality" – he ran his fingertips in the area above my right eyebrow – "are strongly developed – abnormally so – which would suggest an inclination towards literature. Well, if you have not yet set pen to paper, I suggest you do so, since nature has been generous in her gifts. A career in letters surely awaits you."

"I thank you sir, but I consider it most unlikely."

It said little for Beamish's skill as a phrenologist, I reflected, as he returned his brass callipers to their case, that he had not discovered how little developed was my cranial lobe for truth. No sooner had the thought crossed my mind than I caught the ghost of a smile on Miss Osgood's face and knew that the same thought had crossed hers.

By now, dear reader, you must be thinking that I have been less than frank with you and that I owe you a fuller explanation. Very well. Let me start by admitting that Beamish was correct in his surmise: I am indeed a writer, though less out of inclination than necessity. The story of how and why I became one must now be told. For the moment, then, let us leave the members of the Ebenezer Temperance Society and their fellow passengers, with banners flying and band playing, speeding towards the Great Exhibition of the Industry of All Nations on the morning of Monday the 6th of October 1851 at an average speed of a little over thirty miles per hour.

One morning in May, my wife Serafina had remarked over breakfast that our income from the hotel had dwindled to five pounds per week with little prospect of improvement. A curate from Leeds, whom we had looked forward to accommodating for two weeks, had cancelled his booking, pleading extra parish duties.

"Which leaves us," she said, "with no bookings until the French polisher arrives next month."

"And the French polisher's family, Serafina, my love," I replied. "Let us not forget them."

"With or without them, we cannot go on like this. I have Nan and the cook to pay, the laundry has impounded our sheets and the butcher will accept only cash. What has happened to us, Percy? The Ebenezer used to be such a thriving establishment."

I recognised the anguish in her voice. Her constitution, never strong, had of late been further enfeebled by fear of failure. Strange as it may seem, money was not her first concern, though heaven knows she mentioned it often enough. What fretted her most was letting down the Cause. Serafina's family were veterans of the Temperance Movement. Generations of them had carried the fight into gin shops and public houses, where, if they had not always bested their foes, they had at least retreated with dignity. But if the Cause was dear to her heart, it was rather less so, I confess, to my own. To be sure, I supported her loyally in her endeavours and no drop ever passed my lips within the four walls of the hotel – or even within the bounds of the city. As for the world beyond, well, I confess to discreet lapses from time to time.

"Do you hear me, Percy? What has happened to us? And what, if anything, is to be done?

"What has happened, Serafina, is that Garlands is thriving at our expense."

And indeed it was. A newcomer to the city, Garlands Temperance Hotel had seduced our customers, not with softer beds or larger portions, but with rail excursions to places of local interest, such as Ramsgate and Tunbridge Wells. But that was only the start. In January it had delivered its master stroke. Inspired by Mr Thomas Cook, it had opened a Shilling Subscription Club, the purpose of which, according to the notice in the Kentish Gazette, was 'to enable persons of modest means and sober habits to be amongst the first to visit the Great Exhibition of All Nations in May of this year.' In vain did we try to compete. We formed a Pleasant Sunday Afternoons group for working men; we allowed the Band of Hope to meet in

our dining room; we installed a harmonium in the parlour. But it
was to little effect. Our customers continued to desert us. All this
Serafina knew – or said she knew, though I was convinced that she
clung to a secret hope that our rival would simply disappear and
leave us masters of the field.

"But what are we to do, Percy?" pleaded Serafina. "Surely there
must be something we can do."

And it was at this moment that Nan, with exquisitely bad timing,
had entered the morning room, and, after making a show of dusting
the ornaments on the mantelpiece, demanded a little extra something on her wages, which, unbeknown to her, we could scarcely
afford to pay her anyway. Of course we sympathised. We were all too
well aware, we said, of the interest that the Exhibition had created
in all classes of society; indeed, we were not immune to it ourselves.
Had we not been shackled to the Ebenezer, we would have taken
the trip too.

"But now is not the time to discuss it further," I said to Nan. "Your
mistress looks pale and faint. Please would you show her to her room
and draw down the blinds. Her strength is easily overtaxed."

Nan escorted Serafina to her room where, no doubt, she spent
the rest of the day on her chaise longue, fretting about the problems
of the Ebenezer, reading *The Lay of the Last Minstrel* and communing
with Palmerston, the parrot. To her anguished refrain of "What are
we to do, Palmerston, what are we to do?", the crotchety old bird,
whose feathers had long since lost their tropical splendour, would
reply, "Nothing to be done, nothing to be done."

It was fortunate for Serafina, as well as for Nan and the cook,
that I was made of sterner stuff. With the help of Miss Osgood and
the Rev. Culpepper, I had formulated a scheme that would, I hoped,
save the Ebenezer and show Garlands that we meant to stand our
ground. If the latter could organise an excursion to Hyde Park, then
so could we. Only ours would not be near the start of the Exhibition
but near the end, when Exhibition fever had had time to spread like
a contagion. To this scheme Serafina had agreed, though without

much enthusiasm or faith in its success. She gave the excursion her blessing, but refused to grace it with her presence. Her health, she insisted, would not be equal to it. To please her, I engaged a band to serenade us on our way with temperance hymns, omitting to tell her that once we reached Ashford the bandsmen were to be let off the rein and allowed to play what they pleased. Culpepper had agreed to this only in return for a promise that he would be permitted to read out extracts from The *Pilgrim's Progress* during the journey.

But that was only part of my scheme. There was another part, to which only Miss Osgood was privy, though Beamish in his blundering way had come close. My name, you will recall, is Blackwood and although I am not related to the owners of *Blackwood's Magazine*, I had pretended to them that I was and, pleading kin, had persuaded them to publish some stories, for which they paid handsomely. Thus for some months past it had been *Blackwood's* rather than our paying guests who had supported the Ebenezer. But *Blackwood's* had published barely a dozen of my stories – and those little more than re-tellings of tales our guests had told me – before the supply of guests dwindled and, with them, my inspiration. (As you can see, although I was not telling Beamish the strict truth when I denied being a writer, I was not far off.) Then one day I had an inspiration of a different kind.

One Sunday, at a meeting of the Ebenezer Temperance Society, Miss Osgood announced that she had been learning Mr Pitman's Stenographic Soundhand and asked the Rev. Culpepper if he would object to her taking down his sermon by way of practice. He readily agreed. As I watched her scribbling away on her pad, it came to me that if on the journey to London I were to coax tales out of my fellow passengers, she could notate them in shorthand and I would work them up into stories for *Blackwood's* at my leisure – and if not for Blackwood's, then for any publication that would take them. Of course, it would mean taking her into my confidence, but she was a person on whose absolute discretion I could rely. My secret, I was confident, would be safe. To my relief she raised no objection to my proposal and was happy to put her notebook at my disposal. And that, dear reader, was why Miss Osgood, who was not given to blushing, had blushed deeply at the mention of *Blackwood's Magazine* and why Nan Foxley had had to comfort her.

I decided at an early stage that the Ebenezer Subscription Club should be open to all. For one thing, the railway company would not provide an excursion train for fewer than three hundred passengers, and the Ebenezer Temperance Society, even at full strength, fell far short of that. There was also the desire to do better than Garlands, who had simply booked their members on to the first train they had found in Bradshaw. Theirs had been a one-day excursion, whilst ours was to be a three, thus allowing a full day in the Exhibition itself. And then Serafina had set her heart on a band at the rear of the train, bands having been a popular feature of Mr Cook's excursions. Such provision, we were informed by the railway company, would be possible only on a 'special'. Thus it was that Ebenezer members found themselves cheek by jowl with the likes of Beamish and Turpin, an intermingling which was repeated in the second class coaches, to whose passengers I shall introduce the reader in due course. Miss Osgood and I had purchased second class tickets, so that we could move freely about the train, which I had arranged to stop at Tunbridge to pick up members of our party who, for one reason or another, could not start easily from Canterbury.

At last the great day arrived. Even though she was too unwell to travel to London, Serafina accompanied me to the station, where we were greeted warmly by Mr George Bowles, the stationmaster, who had dressed for the occasion in silk hat and frock coat. Furthermore, he had paid us the compliment of wearing the white rosette with which the Ebenezer party was to identify itself once it reached London Bridge Station. The platform awnings were decked with bunting, and the band, its silver instruments glinting in the sun, was already at work beneath a Temperance Society banner in the rearmost wagon. Mr Bowles was clearly proud of his handiwork. He invited Serafina and me to inspect the 'special', trusting that it met with our approval. "And where better to start," said he, "than with the locomotive?"

Where better indeed? The locomotive was a dark green beast which delighted in the name of *Hengist* and boasted a huge brass dome and copper-topped chimney. Serafina, who had never before seen a locomotive at close quarters, declined the driver's invitation to step up on to the footplate. I, on the other hand, accepted gladly, eager to gaze into the fire which gave the beast its thrilling potency.

"Sturdee is the name, sir," said the driver clasping me by the hand. "Albert Sturdee, driver first class. Not temperance myself, but happy to drive them that are. Have no fears: not a drop on dooty and no more that a pint of porter when off. You're in good hands, sir. When anyone books a special, I'm the one as gets to drive it. The Company trusts me, see. None more."

Like the station master, Sturdee had dressed for the occasion. He had brought a (somewhat scuffed) top hat to wear when the train was standing in the station, and a driver's cap to wear when it was in motion. His neckerchief was clean at the collar, though he had been unable to resist wiping his oily hands on the ends, which rested on the lapels of his blue pea jacket.

Sturdee was about to introduce me to the fireman, when Culpepper arrived and, apologising for being late, insisted on blessing the locomotive.

"As you know, Blackwood," he said, "I am not one for blessing everything in sight, but in this case I am troubled by the name of the locomotive. You may recall from Bede that Hengist was a pagan. A careless oversight on the part of the railway company, no doubt, but one might have expected better, especially as one of their directors is related to Mr Alford, the Dean."

From a small leather case he took a stole and, placing it round his neck, blessed *Hengist* in the name of Father, Son and Holy Ghost. Sturdee, who was looking on from the footplate, removed his top hat and gave a loud amen at the end. *Hengist* hissed restively.

The ceremony completed, we resumed our inspection of the train. Since most of our subscribers were people of modest means, there were five times as many tubs as second class coaches. If the former, as we have seen, were somewhat Spartan, the latter were, in truth, little better. An extra five shillings may have brought the traveller a roof, but the sides were still open to the weather and the benches still made of varnished wood. Those on the windward side were just as likely to be soaked as those in the tubs. Fortunately, the glass was high and, with a fine day in prospect, the excursionists were able to keep their umbrellas furled, though many, fearful of autumn chills, had already spread tartan blankets across their knees.

By now the train was filling fast. Serafina and I greeted the subscribers, some of whom we knew but most of whom were strangers, until Serafina's strength began to fail and I escorted her to the hired brougham, which was waiting in the station yard.

"God speed, Percy," she said, as I handed her into the carriage. "When you return we shall go though the Exhibition catalogue together and you shall describe all the items in as much detail as you can remember. Look after Nan and makes sure you bring her back safe and sound."

I kissed her hand, signalled to the driver and the brougham rattled out of the yard.

As the hour of departure drew near, all was bustle, noise and bewilderment. Porters in dark velveteen jackets, their shoulders worn white with repeated loads, hurried to and fro, some with carpet bags and portmanteaux, some clambering on to the roofs of the second class coaches to secure the luggage. The fireman hurled more coal into the fire. Clouds of black smoke poured from the locomotive and drifted along the platform. Taking their cue from Mr Bowles, all the gentleman took out their pocket watches and held them at arm's length. The last doors slammed. The station master removed his hat and waved it at Sturdee, who waved his at the guard in the front coach, who waved his at the guard at the rear, who, after a frantic search through his pockets, found his whistle in a forgotten fob and blew till he was red in the face. *Hengist* hissed; the carriages creaked in readiness; and then, with a rattle of connecting chains and a fanfare from the band, the Ebenezer 'special' eased out of the station.

And now, dear reader, let us re-join our friends on their journey, which has already taken them past Harbledown on the outskirts of Canterbury. A glance at our pocket watches tells us that five minutes have elapsed since Mr Bowles waved his silk hat. In our absence, the other passengers have embraced phrenology with enthusiasm and are queueing to offer Beamish their bumps, which they all hope are rich in unsuspected genius. Given the design of tubs on the South Eastern Railway, this is not always easy. For those of you not familiar with them, let me explain. On each side of a tub are three doors opening into three compartments, across which benches run from side to side. Since there is no central gangway, the only way of changing compartments when the train is in motion is to climb over the seats. In their haste to reach Beamish, who was seated (or rather standing) in the central compartment, this was what the gentlemen now did, much to the annoyance of Culpepper, who, in an attempt to stop them, clambered up on to his seat and began reading from *Pilgrim's Progress*.

"'As I walked through the wilderness of this world,'" he declaimed in a loud voice that must have been audible in the adjacent tubs, "'I lighted on a certain place, where was a den; and I laid me down in that place to sleep: and as I slept I dreamed a dream. I dreamed, and behold I saw a man clothed in rags, standing in a certain place, a book in his hand, and a great burden on his back. And as he read, he wept and trembled, saying "What shall I do?"'"

But the answer – if any – to his question was lost in the press of bodies converging on Beamish. First across the bench were Corporal Costello and his son George. The Corporal's Christian name, if he had ever had one, had long since been swallowed up by his rank. To the world at large, including to his wife and son, he was known simply as 'the Corporal'. A boot maker by trade, he was a veteran of Waterloo and the Peninsular Campaign and was never to be seen without his medals, even in his workshop. Few were the conversations with him that did not, by devious twists and turns, end up at Waterloo, by way of Torres Vedras, Salamanca and Badajoz. In an abandoned pigeon loft, he had built dioramas of the battles, on whose anniversaries he would don the red jacket and stovepipe shako of the 27th Inniskillens and charge the public 2d to watch the silent cannonading and hear him dilate on the niceties of the conflict. Small wonder, then, that Beamish discovered on his head the bumps of 'Constancy, Courage and Combativeness'. Or that he found them, too, on the head of his son George, who had just taken the Queen's shilling and enlisted as a bugler in the Buffs. Replacing his pillbox cap on his chestnut curls, the boy looked relieved that Beamish had found nothing that might diminish him in his father's regard. If he looked every inch the soldier with a few inches to spare, that was because his red tunic was too big for him, the regimental quartermaster presumably having decided that the boy still had plenty of growing to do. His bugle, which he had brought at my request so that I could marshal my troops once we reached London, was polished to mirror brightness and hung round his neck on a lanyard of braided silk.

The Costellos were followed by a stream of supplicants, many of whom – though by no means all – were members of the Ebenezer Temperance Society. Nan Foxley was delighted to learn that she was rich in Conscientiousness and Ideality, without, I suspect, having the faintest idea what they were. Mr Humphrey Ezard, the daguerreotypist from Broad Street, had a right forelobe symptomatic of Imitation, as did Mr Cyril Purselove, an out-of-work actor who had played Banquo to Macready's Macbeth in Drury Lane. (Like most of profession, he would scarcely have wished to join the Ebenezer.) Then there were Miss Aurora Lark, governess to the Latimer children at Devaux Lodge, who inadvertently revealed a pair of dainty ankles in clambering over the seat (bumps of Amativeness and Cautiousness); Mr Gilbert Meek, a tripe dresser from

Lower Bridge Street (ditto Alimentiveness and Acquisitiveness); Mr Charles Breeze, an advertising copywriter for the *Kentish Gazette* and chairman of the Canterbury Glee Club (Mirth and Suavity); Albert Turpin, whom we have already met (Constructiveness and Self-Esteem); and finally Gabriel, the boot black who was generally to be found most mornings outside the railway station and most afternoons outside the Christchurch Gate, hoping to catch worshippers on their way to Evensong. His most prominent bump was identified by Beamish as that of Vitativeness. Finally, Beamish relented over Stumps and, after a cursory examination, declared his head devoid of interest.

I shall not dilate further on the cranial peculiarities of Miss Lark, Mr Ezard, Mr Purselove and the rest. Readers may infer their characters from the stories they told rather than from the pronouncements of Hector Beamish. In vain did the phrenologist try to talk Culpepper into removing his shovel hat and Miss Osgood her bombazine bonnet. The former distrusted anything that smacked of science and Miss Osgood of anything that might expose her collusion in my authorial project.

So far I have accounted for all my fellow passengers save one. The exception was the Saturnine Stranger. He had wedged himself tightly into the corner of the tub, barricading himself in with a long black box whose key he wore on a chain round his neck. Men who wear black generally do so with a certain dash. Purselove, for example, sported under his black tail coat a floral waistcoat and a silver watch chain with enamelled seals. Our man, on the other hand, admitted no colour of any kind. With the exception of his shirt, he was dressed from head to toe in black; even his key chain was tarnished, the links shading off into the folds of his waistcoat. A black muffler, which he had wrapped several times round his neck, hid the lower part of his face, whilst a pair of green-tinted spectacles hid the rest. From his high-crowned bowler hat, I had him down as a bookmaker or a publican, perhaps even a horse dealer or a boxing promoter, though these designations scarcely explained the black box which he clutched so fiercely. Far from being indifferent to the rest of the company, he watched us closely, from time to time making notes in a small black pocket book.

Attempts to draw him into conversation, however, were unsuccessful. At one point, talk had turned to the things that people most longed to see in the Exhibition. For Nan it was the Koh-i-Noor Diamond, the so-called Mountain of Light. When, last year, it had been presented to Her Majesty the Queen, she had talked of little else for days. Did it shine in the dark? she had wanted to know. How big was it, what was it worth and was it true there was a curse on it? And now she returned to the subject, her enthusiasm greater than ever. It must be, she said, brighter than any lamp, brighter than the moon and stars, brighter than the gates of the New Jerusalem. As for the others, their aspirations were less transcendent. Mr Meek, the tripe dresser, had set his heart on seeing a particular vase.

"A vase?" scoffed Breeze. "Do you mean that you have foregone the pleasure of a day's tripe dressing just to see a vase?"

"But this is no ordinary vase," explained Meek. "This vase is six foot high and sculpted in lard."

"You astonish me," said Turpin. "I understood that no foodstuffs were to be exhibited."

"But this vase is not foodstuff," protested Meek; "this vase is art."

"A vase may be art, I grant you, but I fail to see why anyone would want to sculpt one in lard," I objected.

"There is virtuosity in all things," opined Meek. "Every profession has its Franz Liszt."

"Including tripe dressing, no doubt," remarked Breeze.

"Perhaps not in tripe dressing," interjected Culpepper, "but virtuosity exists in more fields than we imagine." Although he was too modest to mention preaching specifically, it was clear what he had in mind, for he identified as his personal Koh-i-Noor a pulpit that was connected to the pews via a series of gutta-percha tubes for the benefit of the deaf. Others were less predictable in their tastes.

Turpin, the very spirit of modernity, was eager to visit Mr Pugin's Mediaeval Court, Miss Lark to the section devoted to heavy engineering. For Miss Osgood, journey's end was the Osler brothers' Crystal Fountain which stood at the intersection of the nave and transepts, and for Gabriel wallpaper, which he'd heard about but never seen on account of never having set foot in a house that had any. Of all these heartfelt desires, none was as poignant as that of Stumps, who desired nothing more, he said, than to find among the artificial limbs a couple of digits to replace the ones he'd lost. Find those, he said, and he'd die a happy man. As for the Saturnine Stranger, if there was a lard vase or a gutta percha tube amongst his deepest wishes, he kept it well hidden and resisted all attempts to draw him into the conversation.

Having introduced my fellow passengers, it is time now to hear their stories. We are well on the way to Chartham and I see that Miss Osgood's pencil is poised in readiness. With whom shall I start? Not with Culpepper, who will simply deliver a sermon, nor yet with Stumps, whose tales, if he has any, are likely to be indecent. Purselove's offerings may prove to be profane and Turpin's boastful. My eye lights on Corporal Costello. Who better than a military man, especially one who, when fitting me for a pair of boots, once told me that he had met a man who thought he was God? It was, he said, a remarkable story and asked if I should like to hear it. I had declined his offer, pleading urgent business, but afterwards regretted it, for by that time I had begun my connexion with *Blackwood's Magazine* and was eager for all the stories I could pass off as my own. It had always been my intention, when I had an hour or two to spare, to remind him of his offer and a train journey to London seemed as good an opportunity as any.

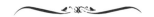

[Editor's Note: To prevent inverted commas nesting inside each other like Russian dolls, I have adopted two separate typefaces, one for Blackwood's outer narrative and the other for the stories with which his fellow excursionists whiled away the journey to London.]

"Corporal Costello," I said, glancing at Miss Osgood to check that she had her notebook and pencil at the ready, "you once offered to tell the story of the man who thought he was God. At the time I had a pressing engagement elsewhere, but I am sure we should all be in your debt if you were to tell us now."

Now Costello was a man who could not pass the time of day or sell a pair of bootlaces without mentioning the Peninsula War or remarking on the shoe leather of Wellington's armies. So when he began his tale with 'I started the war as a humble private in the Inniskillens and ended as a Corporal', I realised that I had made a terrible blunder. As battle followed battle, I sensed that the passengers were hoping that Culpepper would rescue them with a chapter of *The Pilgrim's Progress*. It was Beamish, however, who saved the day. He had been much struck, he said, by the mention of a man who thought he was God. Would that he had that man's skull under his fingers! How he longed in the name of science to identify the protuberances that accommodated such a delusion! Or even, he joked, such a deity! Flattered by Beamish's interest, Costello abandoned his battles and sieges and plunged into his story.

The Corporal's Tale of A for Augustus

The story starts with a body in a river, he said. Two privates of the 27th Regiment of Foot, who were hurrying back for roll call after a night on the town, found it between the Pont Neuf and the Pont au Change. What made it worse was that it was a British body. Even in their befuddled state they could make out the red coat, so they knew it wasn't a Prussian grenadier or a Napoleonic officer. Had it been a Parisian body – and there were plenty of those in the river after Bonaparte's defeat – they could have ignored it and hurried on their way. But it wasn't. It was unmistakably, obstinately British. "The divil take it," said one. "If we stop to pull it out, we'll miss roll call and have our pay docked, and if we let it go, we could be depriving a comrade of a dacent Christian burial." "And that would be a mortal sin," said his comrade, "whereas the other would merely be a crying shame." So saying, he pulled off his coat and plunged into the river.

There were plenty of officers who would have ordered stoppage of pay for missing roll call and one or two who might have gone as far as a flogging. But our two privates had no need to make excuse. The dripping corpse excused all. When Colonel Power interviewed them next morning, he was full of praise for their heroic action.

"The Seine is such a filthy river," he said. "God knows what horrors lurk in it. You're a plucky pair, I must say. No doubt of that. But are you trustworthy, I wonder? Can I count on you?"

"To the death, your honour."

"And beyond."

"Then listen carefully. The man you brought in last night may have been wearing a private's uniform. But he was, I regret to say, no private."

"Might we be so bold as to ask who it was then, your honour?"

"No, you may not. And if you're wise you'll say nothing of this to anyone in your billet. I tell you this because rumours are already circulating. If you're asked what you saw, you will tell your comrades what they already know: namely, that you found a corpse, you did your duty and brought it home for burial. That is all anyone needs to know. Is that clear?"

"As the day itself, your honour."

"Good, because if I hear that tongues have been wagging, I shall know who to blame and have you flogged. Dismissed."

Well, tongues did start wagging and Colonel Power kept his word and had them flogged. Which was unjust and unwise – unjust because, having been flogged before, the privates had been in no hurry to repeat the experience and had obeyed the Colonel's orders to the letter; unwise because the privates' ordeal set tongues wagging harder than ever. Rumour quickly connected the privates' silence and the disappearance, at about the same time, of a regimental chaplain named Catchpole.

The Reverend George Catchpole DD was, on the face of it, ill-suited to the army. He was never without a Greek New Testament from which he would quote constantly, and he always wore a wig, long after wigs had ceased to be fashionable. Yet the men loved him. In the thick of battle, he was a familiar figure in his wig and gown. He carried the wounded to safety and comforted the dying; and when the fighting was over he would drink with the men and play dice with them as if they were his equals, even if it meant borrowing from the officers to pay his debts. So trusting was he that it never occurred to him that the men played with loaded dice and even when warned refused to believe it. For a man of God he was remarkably ill-equipped to resist temptation, especially if temptation took the form of drink and drink took the form of brandy. And brandy was, as you will hear, the undoing of him.

According to rumour, it was Catchpole that the two privates had dragged out of the river. Of course, the Colonel denied it, but the more he did so the faster the rumour ran. In the end he was forced to admit that the body was indeed that of the Rev. Catchpole, who had thrown himself into the Seine in an inexplicable fit of despair. No mention was made of his drinking and gambling, and no mention was made of the private's uniform. Foul play was not suspected.

At about the same time as the Colonel's announcement, a second scandal shook the regiment. In what everyone assumed to be a drunken outburst, a private named Nolan accused his company commander of cowardice. Now this company commander, Captain O'Hare, was known to be something of a buck who spent more time heating his curling irons than sharpening his sword. He could dance, it was said, the best waltz in Wellington's army and had been the last man to leave the Duchess of Richmond's ball on the eve of Waterloo. Any young lady there who fancied herself as a beauty simply had to be seen on the dance floor with him. This was the man that Nolan accused of cowardice, of always leading his men from the rear. He was, in the language of the men, a 'go on officer' rather than a 'come on officer'. In battle after battle, at Vimeiro, at Oporto, at Talavera, at Ciudad Rodrigo, at Badajoz ...

"If it's all the same to you, Costello," said Beamish, "I think we are all eager to hear what became of Private Nolan."

"He was shot," replied Costello.

"For insulting a man who sounds as if he richly deserved to be insulted?" demanded Purselove.

"Wouldn't a flogging have been more merciful?" asked Mr Meek, who, as a purveyor of dressed tripe to the East Kent Militia, considered himself an expert on military matters.

"You've obviously never had a flogging," said Costello.

"Have you?" demanded Purselove.

"No," replied Costello, "but I've given a few and was to have given one to Nolan. But he broke out of gaol before the sentence could be carried out and headed for Calais. That was why he was shot. A court martial convicted him of desertion."

"Never mind about this Nolan, what about the man who thought he was God?" persisted Beamish.

Nolan didn't escape alone. He flew the coop along with another private named Dodds. Once they were outside the gaol, they quickly separated. What became of Dodds no-one could discover. There were rumours, of course. Rumours that he'd escaped to Spain, where he'd a wife and child; rumours that he'd gone to ground in Paris; rumours that he had made it back to England and joined a circus. But there was no evidence and enquiries failed to produce any. Tapsters, card sharps and – begging your pardon, ladies – whores denied all knowledge of him. Eventually word reached us that in the Hospice de la Salpêtrière, there was an English soldier who, though answering to no name, answered to the description of Dodds. How he came there nobody knew, but it was generally thought that alcohol had had a hand in it, as had the mercury cure which had driven so many men out of their wits.

"I have heard people speak of this mercury cure", said Miss Osgood innocently, "though I have never been able to learn the ailment for which it is the remedy."

There was an uneasy silence as Costello looked at me, who looked at Beamish, who looked at Culpepper, who seemed to be captivated by the way in which the River Stour meandered through the water meadows, now on one side of the train, now on the other.

"Saving your presence, ma'am", drawled Purselove, "mercury is the cure for ... for, well ... dammit, help me someone."

His appeal went unheard, the men having joined Culpepper in a close scrutiny of the landscape.

"Mercury is the cure," Purselove continued, gathering his courage, "for the French pox, though from what I have heard it is worse than the disease. Mercury, if you ask me, is a quack's remedy for an incurable affliction."

"Oh speak not ill of mercury," protested Mr Ezard, the daguerre-otypist, who until that moment had scarcely spoken at all. "Mercury is the most subtle of metals, being neither solid nor fluid, neither animate nor inanimate. Out of its vapour one can conjure the most delicate of pictures. I have spent some of my happiest hours envel-oped in it, watching it summon pictures from plates of silvered copper. To me mercury is the essence of life itself."

We all looked at him closely, sharing, no doubt the same thought: that if mercury was indeed the essence of life, it had been very sparing in its gifts to Humphrey Ezard. His hair was thin, his skin pale and flaking; his hands trembled as he spoke. I feared that he was about to describe to us the whole chemical process of making daguerreotypes, but his impassioned speech seemed to have exhausted him and he sank back in his seat, tugging fretfully at the black armband which he had tied tightly round his sleeve like a tourniquet. From his appearance one might have concluded that he was a man consumed by an over-whelming grief.

So persistent were the rumours, continued Costello, that Colonel Power despatched Captain O'Hare and me to investigate. Well, you could see that the Salpêtrière wasn't to O'Hare's refined tastes, for he took one look at the cells and ordered me to search for Dodds whilst he presented his compliments to the governor. It wasn't easy finding Dodds and in the end you might say he found me. I had searched every cell and was about to report back to O'Hare, when a wild-eyed figure wearing military cross belts over his asylum clothes, seized my sleeve and beckoned me to follow. He led me to the corner of his cell, where he had built a nest of rags, among which I could see a battered shako and a scattering of military buttons. For several minutes he rummaged around in this foul-smelling heap, before producing a bottle, which he pressed into my hands. At first I thought he was offering me a drink. I refused, but again he pressed the bottle into my hands. From the weight of it I could tell that it was empty. Perhaps, I thought, he wants me to fill it, but even had I been willing to oblige, there was nothing to fill it from, so again I refused. Still he pressed the bottle into my hands until it dawned on me that what he wanted was for me to keep it. So I tucked it under my arm and thanked him profusely, after which he crawled into his corner, covered himself with rags and sobbed loudly.

I made my way back to O'Hare, who was sharing a glass of Madeira with M. Pinel, the governor. The decanter on the table between them was already half empty and neither seemed particularly pleased to see me.

"Well," asked O'Hare, "did you find him?"

"Yes, sir."

"And what did he have to say for himself?"

"Nothing, sir."

"Nothing?"

"Not a word. But he did insist I take this."

I placed the bottle on the table. O'Hare picked it up and shook it.

"Empty," he said and replaced it on the table.

"Here, let me see that," said M. Pinel. "Why, it has the Emperor's - forgive me, the Tyrant's - coat of arms moulded into the glass. See here. The crown and the eagle."

O'Hare took the bottle from him and inspected it carefully.

"Is that important?" he asked.

"It means that the bottle came from the Tyrant's cellars."

"You mean it was looted?"

"I wouldn't go that far. The Tyrant guarded his cellars well. Not only that, but they were well hidden. At Fontainebleau it was said that there were cellars within cellars. The bottles in the innermost one were said to carry a special mark."

"And is this one of them?" asked O'Hare tapping the crown and eagle with his forefinger.

"I couldn't say. Only the Tyrant's inner circle could tell you that."

"And where would I find them?" asked O'Hare.

"You won't, my friend," chuckled M. Pinel. "Not easily. Ils sont tout dispârus. These days no-one owns to having been a friend of Bonaparte. The wonder is he got as far as he did with as few friends as he now appears to have had. Now, about my patient. Will you take him with you or do you wish to leave him to our tender care?"

"For now, I shall leave him with you," said O'Hare, "until such time as Colonel Power decides to send for him."

It was clear from the outset that Colonel Power had no intention of sending for Dodds.

"Let him stew in his own filth," he said. "The less attention he receives the better. It's bad enough having a deserter and a suicide in the regiment without having a lunatic as well. What interests me more is this bottle of his. You might be interested to know that identical ones were found amongst the belongings of Catchpole and Nolan. Three members of the regiment dead, disgraced or demented, each possessing a brandy bottle bearing Bonaparte's coat of arms. A curious coincidence, is it not? What are we to make of it, I wonder? Well?"

"Completely baffled, sir," replied O'Hare.

"Perhaps if you waltzed less and thought more, you might come up with an answer. What about you, Costello?"

"If anyone can solve the mystery, sir, it must be Bonaparte's cellarer".

"And how to do you propose we find him?"

To that, of course, I had no answer. But as it happened, finding Bonaparte's cellarer proved easier than any of us had thought. A few days after this interview, the wife of Colonel Power invited the wife of a certain Colonel Campbell to tea in the villa which the Powers had occupied in one of the leafier suburbs of Paris. Now this Colonel Campbell had been the British officer chosen by the allied powers to escort Bonaparte to Elba in 1814. On the journey south he had struck up an acquaintance, not only with the Tyrant himself, but also with members of his entourage, among them his cellarer. The Colonel's recollections, as related by Mrs Campbell, became the topic of conversation over tea. When asked about the cellarer, Mrs Campbell replied that her husband had thought him a sly fellow and wasn't it odd that Mrs Power should ask because her husband had heard only recently that the man in question had set up an establishment in St Denis from which he was said to be dispensing the Tyrant's choicer vintages.

Since it was I who had suggested finding the cellarer, Colonel Power appointed me to the search party that was to scour St Denis, along with Captain O'Hare and two French National Guardsmen, commanded by a Major d'Orlan. Discreet enquiries by the Major had identified a liquor shop called Le Tourbillon as a likely hiding place for our cellarer. We found it in a narrow street of tenement houses, where limbless soldiers played cards or slept in doorways and children floated paper boats on an open drain. At the tramp of marching feet, the inhabitants scurried indoors and watched suspiciously, no doubt wondering what we had come to seize or whom we had come to arrest.

Our cellarer, whose name was Vervier, made no secret of his trade. Inside Le Tourbillon notices advertised wines and spirits of all kinds 'as drunk by the Tyrant but now for sale at modest prices to the people'. Another notice described them as 'purchased from the choicest vineyards', only to be contradicted by a third which boasted that they had been 'rescued from the cellars of Fontainebleau'. M Vervier had obviously been busy elsewhere in Bonaparte's palaces. Half a dinner service (somewhat chipped), some china figurines, a marble urn, a bust or two, an ormolu clock were all for sale, each with a label identifying the palace from which it had been rescued. These items Major d'Orlan seized in the name of His Majesty King Louis XVIII. As to Vervier there was some debate as to who should lay claim to him. O'Hare wanted to drag him off as a prize to Colonel Power, whilst the Major wanted to lock him up for stealing the property of the state. In the end it was agreed that Major d'Orlan should have his way, but that he should be made available to the British on request.

So it was that for several days running, Captain O'Hare and I would collect Vervier from Major d'Orlan for questioning by Colonel Power. Convinced that Vervier was a man with a talent for disappearing, the Colonel insisted I stand by the door, musket poised, to prevent his escape. The only other person present was Mrs Power, who acted as interpreter. And what a story it was that she translated, the story of a man who for a brief time believed that he was God.

"At last!" exclaimed Beamish. "I was beginning to wonder if we were ever going to make his acquaintance."

Unlike yourself, Mr Beamish, the Colonel was a patient man. For the first few interviews they discussed Vervier's service with the Tyrant. No mention was made

of Catchpole, Nolan, Dodds or the brandy bottles with Bonaparte's coat of arms
on them. Then one day, in the middle of a conversation about life on Elba, the
Colonel offered a drink, which Vervier, his guard down, happily accepted. From
behind his chair the Colonel produced one of the three bottles and started to pour
the contents into a glass.

"Why do you start, monsieur?" he asked when Vervier, taken completely by
surprise, gasped aloud.

Vervier tried to laugh off the question.

"Was there something about the bottle that alarmed you?"

No, there was nothing about the bottle that alarmed him.

"Then what about these?" asked the Colonel, producing the other two bottles
and placing them on the table.

Vervier looked at the bottles for along time before answering.

"Where did you find them?" he asked at last.

"Among the belongings of three of my men who either died or disappeared,"
replied the Colonel. He went on to describe the fate of the two privates and the
chaplain and asked Vervier if he remembered them.

Oh yes, he remembered them very well. They had taken shelter in his shop
during a thunderstorm. They were drunk, of course, like most of the British
soldiers one saw in Paris. Perhaps that explained why they were drawn to the
notice advertising the treasures of the Emperor's cellars. He offered them this
or that vintage, leading them on an imaginary journey from cellar to cellar, from
rarity to rarity, until they arrived at a cellar so secret it been known only to the
Emperor himself.

"And what did it contain?" asked Colonel Power.

Why, the three bottles in front of them, of course.

"Just those three?"

Just those three.

"And what was so special about them?"

What was special about them was suggested by the mark on them. No, he didn't
mean the coats of arms. He meant the other marks. Surely, monsieur le colonel had
noticed the other marks? No? Then with monsieur le colonel's permission ...

Vervier turned each bottle upside down. Painted on the underside was a
different letter – L, F and A. L stood for Louis XVI and F for Frederick the Great.

And the reason? Well, monsieur le colonel must understand that the Emperor was, despite appearances, a whimsical man, even on occasions superstitious. Before he left Elba on his last and most reckless enterprise, he had asked M. Vervier to acquire three brandies, each corresponding to a likely outcome of his great gamble. " 'For if I am captured and condemned to death,' he said, 'I wish to drink brandy from the cellar of Louis XVI, who was captured at Varennes and faced the guillotine with dignity. If I am defeated and in despair resort to suicide, I shall first drink brandy from the cellar of Frederick the Great, a man who knew both victory and defeat and who died hating the world and despising his own achievements.'

"And that, monsieur le colonel," concluded Vervier, "is the story of the bottles in front of you."

"On the contrary, M. Vervier," retorted the Colonel, "it is the story of only two of them. You have not explained the third bottle, the one marked with the letter A, and I believe you have deliberately avoided doing so."

Ah yes, the third bottle. How could he have forgotten? – especially as the third bottle was the one His Majesty would have most liked to have drunk. After all, who but a fool would wish on himself execution or despair? Very well. Monsieur et madame would recall that the Emperor had once occupied Rome and expelled the Pope, in gratitude for which a sympathiser had made him a curious present. It was a Roman amphora full of wine, its wax seal still unbroken, and it was said to have been found in the ruins of a villa belonging to the Emperor Augustus. And Augustus, the sympathiser had reminded him, was not just an emperor: he was also the Deified Augustus, a god. This was the wine that had gone into the making of the third brandy. 'For,' said the Emperor, 'if I triumph I shall be as a god and will drink to the health of the god Augustus and, in so doing, invite him to drink mine.'

"So there you have it, monsieur le colonel: three brandies, three consolations – for defeat, despair and for triumph such as no man has ever known."

"And which of my men took the bottle containing the wine of Augustus the god?" asked Colonel Power.

"That I cannot tell you. They paid for the brandies – every sou they had; I made sure of that – and went away. The one in the perruque said they would throw dice for them. It would be, he said, the greatest cast since the soldiers played for the robe of Christ at the foot of the Cross."

"Then it looks as if poor Catchpole drank from the bottle of Frederick the Great," remarked Power.

"And Nolan from the bottle of Louis XVI," added his wife, "which must mean that it was Dodds who drank the liquor of Augustus."

"If he did," said Power, "then the form his godhead took was pretty damned odd".

"Drinking, gambling, whoring," observed his wife, who was no stranger to the vices of soldiers, "are how most deified Roman emperors celebrated their godheads. I suppose they thought they could indulge in every imaginable human vice and get away with it."

So that was how our three comrades-in-arms met their untimely ends. For them death came not in the form of shot or shell but in the form of a bottle containing the essence of three great men – for Catchpole Frederick the Great, for Nolan Louis XVI and for Dodds the god Augustus.

Or that was what we thought when M. Vervier had finished his story and it is what Colonel Power thought to his dying day. Of course, I was sworn to secrecy and it's only today that I have broken my promise. Well, the Colonel is long dead, so is O'Hare and so are the privates who fished Catchpole out of the river and so, too, are Dodds and M. Pinel. But there's another, deeper secret that I didn't even share with the Colonel.

A few weeks later, the regiment received orders to return home. Mrs Power held her last tea party; Captain O'Hare waltzed his last waltz; the regiment paraded for the last time on the Champs de Mars. As one of the last to depart, I was ordered to search our quarters in the Bois de Boulogne for anything of military value that the men might have overlooked.

"And was there?" asked George Costello. From the look on his face it was clear that this was a story of his father's that he had not heard before, a story that had not dulled the edge of hearing by endless repetition.

Not of military value, no. But there was something else. The very last place I searched was the makeshift chapel in which Catchpole had held his services. The altar was an ordinary kitchen table covered with a white cloth. The cloth had been removed, but the table was still there. Not expecting to find anything, I opened the drawer and found a letter with an unbroken seal. I have it still.

"And do you have it with you?" asked George.

It's at home, tucked into the lining of my shako. No matter, for I can quote it word for word. Catchpole starts by describing how he and the two privates played dice for M. Vervier's bottles. Colonel Power was right about Nolan. He had drawn Louis XVI's bottle. Very well, he said, if he was going to be arrested and shot, he would make sure it was for a good reason and would start by telling Captain O'Hare exactly what he thought of him. But he was wrong about Dodds and Catchpole. Dodds had drawn the Frederick the Great bottle and fallen into an instant despair, which he tried to cure by embracing all the vices Paris had to offer.

"Then it was Catchpole's cerebellum that I should have been examining," remarked Beamish. "Do you know where he is buried? Perhaps the French authorities would allow him to be exhumed."

"But if Catchpole thought himself a god, then why did he throw himself into the river?" I asked.

Because the pain was too great to bear, said Costello. "'I awoke next morning,'" he wrote, "with great lightness of spirit. The sun shone with dazzling splendour; the Seine was a river of light; the very smoke from the chimneys rose to my nostrils like incense. In this state of ecstasy I persisted for some days. These wonders, I began to realise, were not something offered for my delight; these wonders were something I had conjured out of pure thought. What I beheld was not part of creation; my very beholding was the act of creation itself. Thus I began to glory in my work. The stained glass in Notre Dame, the voices at the opera, the fountains in the Tuileries – I beheld them and saw that they were good. I thanked God for leading me to the right bottle and found, of course, that I was thanking myself. But then a dreadful thought occurred to me. If I had no-one to thank, then I had no-one to blame. Those limbless soldiers outside Le Tourbillon, those children floating paper boats on an open sewer: they, too, were my work. So were the drunks, the whores and the beggars. Then I remembered the late wars. All those redcoats whom I helped to bury in the Peninsula and at Waterloo; all those soldiers of the late Emperor who had frozen to death in Russia; all those many thousands who had died at Trafalgar, at Austerlitz, at Borodino, at Salamanca, at Marengo: all had died cursing God, but I who am the object of their curses have no-one in turn whom I can curse. I did not ask to shoulder this burden: I have ordained it for myself and find myself unequal to the task. If I could have a respite from immortality at weekends or have the power to set aside omnipotence once in a while, that at least would make my condition bearable. To atone for the horrors I have wished into being, especially among the soldiers who once accounted me their friend, I intend to don the coat of a private soldier, since it is the private soldier who has suffered most, and throw myself in the Seine. Whether or not a god can die I have yet to discover, but whoever finds this letter will surely know the answer."

There was an uneasy silence after Costello had finished his tale. George squeezed his father's hand. For a while most were lost in contemplation of the autumn stubble fields. As we approached Wye, a small boy ran alongside the train, trying to attract our attention, whereupon The Saturnine Stranger lowered the notebook in which he had been writing, aimed an imaginary rifle at him, fired silently and returned to his reading. The boy lay on his back in the dust, his legs kicking theatrically.

"It seems to me," said Mr Ezard, "that Catchpole was suffering from what Mr Tennyson calls a 'divine despair'. And that, alas, is something that even laudanum cannot cure."

"Perhaps, Corporal Costello," said Culpepper, who, far from being outraged by the story, seemed surprisingly subdued by it, "it would have been wiser to have kept the letter secret. For that is what Colonel Power, had he known about it, would surely have wished."

"Perhaps you're right," replied Costello. "Apart from anything else it has made me digress. Now where was I? Oh, yes, I had taken you up to the siege of Badajoz and left you poised in the breach. At that moment our artillery began a furious barrage ..."

Costello's reminiscences proved contagious and were soon joined by Stumps's tales of pick and shovel. Instead of Salamanca and

Badajoz, we were given Woodhead Tunnel and Chat Moss, but where Costello had been magnanimous to his enemies, Stumps was positively vindictive and to none more than the missionaries, who, according to him, had harried the navvies every inch of the way with their reiterated injunctions to keep the Sabbath holy, praise the Lord and love their neighbours. "Which ain't so easy," he said, "when you're sleeping eight to a tent and they all snore." Even worse, though, were the prohibitions.

"Don't drink, don't swear. Why, they'd drive a man to both. Don't gamble. Is a man to be denied his hard-earned pleasures by a bunch of interfering busybodies who want to save his soul? And why pick on his soul? Why not the souls of gangmasters and shareholders, directors and engineers? Don't they swear? Don't they ever have a flutter? O' course they do. So why pick on the working man? Why deny him his drink and his baccy, his fancy women and his snuff? Why? To make him obedient, that's why. Keep him sober and he'll mind his ps and qs. Get him to love his neighbour and he won't down tools to black his eye. Get him to praise the Lord and he'll get out of the habit of answering back. If you ask me, they was put up to it by the bosses to get the job done quick."

"When Our Lord commanded us to Keep the Sabbath Holy," observed Culpepper, "I scarcely think it was because He wished to expedite the construction of railways."

"I'll tell you what," said Stumps, "I'd like to meet this Vervier character. Get him to mix me up a few drops of Robespierre. Go down lovely, they would. Is he still in the liquor line?"

"The last we heard," said Costello, "he was peddling the Empress Josephine's perfumes."

"How too, too delicious," said Purselove. "How one longs to meet a woman with the courage to wear a dab or two of Pompadour or a soupçon of Cleopatra."

But Stumps was not to be deflected by Purselove's sardonic whimsy. Now that he had the subject of missionaries in his sights, he was loath to point them elsewhere.

"You don't believe me, do you?" he demanded. "All this stuff about missionaries, you think I'm making it up. Admit it."

"I am simply suggesting that you are wrong to impugn the motives of those who devote themselves to rescuing others from error," replied Culpepper. "What you must learn to accept is that there are those who know better than you."

Now Culpepper was undoubtedly sincere in believing that he knew better than Stumps – and, for that matter, than the rest of us – but he was ill-advised to say it, since Stumps was equally convinced that he had a duty to tell people home truths they did not wish to hear. In Culpepper's defence, it must be said that though he was censorious, he was no hypocrite: moral rectitude was not something he enjoined on others and neglected himself. He led by example and, perhaps surprisingly, by kindness. No widow or orphan was sent away empty-handed, no penitent sinner unblessed. This was a side of Culpepper that few saw and those who did – with the possible exception of Miss Osgood, who thought him too forgiving – esteemed him for it. Needless to say, it was a side invisible to Stumps, whose anger showed no sign of abating. In a voice that could be heard in the adjacent tubs, he accused Culpepper of turning a blind eye to the faults of those who made it their business to correct the faults of others.

"Hypocrite," he shouted. "'Cast out the mote from yer own eye before you cast out the mote from yer brother's'. That's what yer scripture says, isn't it?"

Culpepper, who liked to think he had the monopoly on quoting scripture, was clearly nettled.

"It is not your place to quote scripture at me," he insisted.

"And why not?" replied Stumps. "You don't own it."

"Very well. Prove to me that the people whom you complain of act in bad faith and I will concede your right to quote scripture."

"Then I'll tell you a story you won't want to hear, a story of murder and drink."

"How thrilling!" exclaimed Miss Lark.

"There's no bad language in it, I hope," said Miss Osgood.

"If it's a story about navvies", remarked Beamish. "I cannot see how it can fail to have bad language in it. They have the bumps for it, most of them."

"Oh, it isn't a story about navvies," said Stumps. "It's a story about preachers."

Stumps's Tale of The City on a Hill

It is not possible, alas, to tell Stumps's story in his own words, partly because Miss Osgood refused to transcribe it and partly because Culpepper kept protesting vociferously against a story that showed such scant respect for the cloth. At one point, both rose to their feet, Culpepper trying to make himself heard and Stumps, who had the louder voice, shouting him down. It was Nan, our parlour maid, who shamed them into silence by reminding them – with an accusing glance at me – of the sacrifices they had had to make to pay for their tickets. Culpepper resumed his seat with bad grace, whereupon Stumps took the floor and proceeded to tell his tale. In what follows, I can only offer an emasculated and somewhat more polished version of the original.

Imagine, then, a rain-swept hillside inhabited by sheep and curlews. Look closer and discover a small town of shacks and canvas shelters, of smithies and forges. Leading up to it across the moor is a track churned to a muddy porridge by innumerable hoofs and wheels. On the top of the hill, first a horse gin, then a small steam engine are erected to raise and lower buckets into a shaft that has been sunk into rock below. Other shafts soon follow. To the North West the sky is dark with the smoke of Manchester and the mill towns; to the South East the night sky glows with the furnaces of Sheffield. Hundreds of feet down men are blasting away the rock to connect the two. Day and night, weekday and Sabbath, the work continues without stop. The Mayors of Manchester and Sheffield have been promised that on such and such a day they will shake hands under the moor and the Mayors of Manchester and Sheffield must not be denied. A doctor visits once a week, a parson rarely if ever. In the early days of tunnelling, this world of tommy shops and tally women is lawless and remote. There have been deaths, too, mostly below ground from rockfalls and careless use of explosives, but one or two in the open air. One man is struck by the flailing arms of a capstan; another, too drunk to stand, falls face down in a peat bog and drowns. Such is the fearsome reputation of the navvies that the clergymen of Glossop, to the West, and Penistone, to the East, are reluctant to venture on to the hilltop to bury them.

But others are not so timid. For ambitious young preachers the encampment above Woodhead Tunnel is the place to prove their worth in the eyes of the Lord. Succeed here, they are agreed, and you can succeed in darkest Africa or among the cannibals of the South Seas. Many of the navvies are Irish; some are Catholic; most are godless. None takes kindly to being harangued from the pulpit. One Sunday a young preacher from Oldham is interrupted in mid-peroration by a deep roar beneath his feet. The congregation sniggers. Undeterred, the preacher continues. There is a second, deeper roar. The congregation guffaws. Almost immediately there is a third roar which shakes his makeshift pulpit. 'It's Old Nick,' shouts one of the navvies; 'he don't like having his rest disturbed of a Sunday.' The preacher flees, to be replaced by doughtier spirits amongst whom there is sharp competition for the cure of souls. One day a Wesleyan from Rochdale and a Moravian from Salford come to blows in front of their congregations, who cheer on their own men and even start laying bets on them.

This was the state of affairs when the Rev. Enoch Ingle, a Primitive Methodist from Glossop, first appeared on the moor. He chose his time well. Not only had potential rivals disappeared in disgrace, but blasting had stopped for the day because of a fatality below ground. Ingle was able to give the victim a Christian burial, the first for many months. This disposed the navvies to look kindly on him and hear his sermons in respectful silence. For a week or two, Ingle had the place to himself, time enough to dismiss the tally women and shame the liquor sellers, time enough to set up a Sunday school in an empty tool shed and a reading room in the lamp cabin. Men drank less, swore less, even beat their wives less. As the tunnel inched out from its central shafts towards Glossop and Penistone, so the encampment on the windy hilltop inched towards godliness. He looked at the rosy-cheeked children learning their letters, at the women pegging out their washing, at the men whitewashing the inside of his own cabin and knew, like Abraham, what it was to be a father to his people. From time to time rivals took advantage of the Pax Ingleana, and established congregations of their own. Ingle resented them, but wisely kept silent, calculating that, if left undisturbed, they would disgrace themselves as earlier preachers had done and engineer their own departure from the city on the hill.

His judgment was quickly vindicated. Soon the rivals were in full retreat, pursued by the jeers of their erstwhile congregations. All, that is, except one. Among the spoil heaps at the eastern end of the workings, Father Cuthbert Stringer, a Catholic priest from Warrington, had established a loyal following which showed no sign of turning against him. Ingle would not stoop to outright denunciation; instead he would wait. Time would surely bring about the desired result. But Time did not oblige. The rival remained fast, a very barnacle. Worse, he seemed to be attracting lapsed Catholics, especially amongst the Irish, back to the fold. At first the drift was scarcely noticeable, but when whole families absented themselves, Ingle began to feel alarmed, and when, one Sunday, he found that his congregation had shrunk to little more than a dozen, he gave way to rage and resentment. He prayed to rise above such base feelings. What, he asked himself, would Wesley have done? Or Whitfield or Knox? Why, they would have preached as they had never preached before. They would have preached by day and by night; they would have preached indoors and out; they would have preached without ceasing until their rivals had crept away in shame. But how to reach the heights of a Whitfield or a Wesley? Ay, that was the question.

Seeking inspiration, Ingle took himself to Manchester to consult the sermons of Wesley and Whitfield. The first bookseller he found was unable to oblige, as were the second and third, but the fourth directed him to a narrow-fronted shop in Primrose Lane, an alleyway where two could scarcely pass abreast. He entered the shop and there on a table in front of him were the works he sought. Greedily he opened the books, but, alas, words which in their author's mouth had been tongued with fire lay cold and lifeless on the page. His disappointment must have been all too visible, for he found himself confronted by a curious looking individual who seemed to have emerged from a crack between two bookshelves.

"The Rev. Enoch Ingle?"

"How did you know my name?"

"Who does not know your name, sir? In preaching circles the talk is all of the great work you have accomplished on the barren hillside."

"And whom do I have the honour of addressing?"

Ingle's interlocutor stepped out of the shadows. Nose, chin and elbows all seemed to have been sharpened to a point, the better perhaps to negotiate the narrow ravines between the tiers of bookshelves.

"My name, sir, is Wesley. I take a certain pride in it, though I am not entitled to. And since you are sure to ask, yes, I am descended, somewhat circuitously, from the great man. But forgive me, I disturbed you in the perusal of my ancestor's works."

"Not at all. I have seen what I came to see."

"But not found what you came to find?"

Ingle hesitated before replying.

"Well no," he said at last. "I confess to finding myself a little disappointed. Take away the fiery delivery, and your ancestor's work seems curiously cold and unimpassioned."

Wesley chuckled.

"'Twas ever thus. You are not the first to find it so, you are not the first. But do not despair: I think I may be able to help you."

He rummaged round in his pockets, of which his threadbare black coat seemed to have a good many and, plunging his arm up to the elbow in one of them, produced a slim volume wrapped in hessian, which he handed to Ingle.

"This should answer to your purpose. My ancestor held some of his sermons back from general publication on the grounds that they were too strong for the palate of his regular congregations and had them privately printed instead."

Ingle accepted the book gratefully.

"How can I ever repay you?"

"By continuing the good work and when you have completed it, by returning the book to me personally here in the shop. Day and night you'll be sure to find me. I am always here."

Meanwhile, Father Stringer had not been idle. He had sent for wooden benches from Penistone so that his congregation did not have to sit on the wet grass, and had made an altar out of a crate, adorning it with a velvet cloth and a pair of tall brass candlesticks. Such trumpery Ingle despised, especially as Stringer himself had taken to draping himself in lace-trimmed cassock and stole. Ingle would not wait for Sunday: he would strike at once. Clutching the precious volume in his hand, he climbed into a bucket and had himself lowered into the tunnel. There amid the glare of the torches, the rattle of chains and the roar of gunpowder, he set to work. He did not excuse himself, but launched straight into his text. "Thus saith the Lord God of hosts," he began, quoting from Jeremiah, "Because ye speak this word, behold, I will make my words in thy mouth fire and this people wood and it shall devour them." One by one the men set down their barrows, their stemmers and their shovels and came to listen. Even the overseers, who should have prevented such idleness, were silenced. At the end of half an hour, Ingle knew that he had won his congregation back, former lapsed Catholics having lapsed once more. Thanking the men for their attention and, enjoining them to be sober and upright in all their doings, he summoned his bucket and rose to the surface.

For the next few weeks Ingle was master above ground and below. But Stringer was not yet ready to admit defeat. His first response was to send to Penistone for more chairs and when that did not do the trick, he sent for a large tent. In this Fortune (or, as he would have seen it, Divine Providence) favoured him. On St Swithun's Day the weather, which until then had been warm and dry, changed for the worse. Words that had stirred the men below ground and the women above lost their fire and fizzled out. In the rain the unpublished sermons of John Wesley proved no match for a canvas tent and the extra chairs from Penistone.

Ingle was first angry, then dejected and, finally, having reminded himself that God was a stern taskmaster, resolute. If Stringer could win a temporary victory for Rome by sending for more chairs, then he, Enoch Ingle, would win a decisive one for God by sending for more Wesley. Early one morning he set off for Manchester and made his way to the narrow-fronted shop in Primrose Lane. It was early evening when he arrived. Wesley seemed to be expecting him and had another volume, wrapped in oilskin against the weather, waiting for him. Ingle declined his offer of refreshment and returned to the city on the hill, arriving weary but exultant shortly after dawn. For the next two or three days he busied himself getting Wesley's text by heart. Again he descended by bucket to the tunnel workings; again he harangued the wives and families, excoriating drinking, gambling and whoring – all, according to Stumps, the pleasures that made life bearable for the working man – and enjoining upon his congregation the virtues of restraint and sobriety.

Now whether it was the persistent rain (and the consequent attraction of Stringer's tent), or whether it was that the new volume did not possess the force of the old, he could not say, but such success as he had was modest at best and at worst scarcely perceptible. This time Father Stringer had no need to send for more chairs: his congregation, after a brief contraction, remained steadfast. And so, for the second time within the space of two weeks, Ingle found himself starting at dawn for Primrose Lane. The nights having started to draw in, he did not arrive until after dark. To his horror the shop was empty. Wesley had disappeared. The only light in the alleyway came from a single gas lamp at the end, but by its yellowish glow Ingle thought he could discern a slip of white card at the bottom of the window. He screwed up his eyes, pressed his nose to the glass, tried looking first with one eye, then with the other, and eventually made out the legend: 'The Word of the Lord has moved elsewhere. Urgent enquiries to No1 Ashpit Lane.'

Ashpit Lane was but a short step away. No1 stood in a large nettle patch beside a cinder track which wound between mounds and pits of ash, some cold, some still glowing. Wesley seemed to be expecting him and had even prepared him a modest supper of boiled mutton and potatoes. Ingle, who was hungry after his walk, was about to say a hasty grace, when he was interrupted by the entry of four men from an inner room, men who, Wesley informed him, were eager to make his acquaintance. If they were eager, however, they did not show it. They sat silently whilst Ingle ate his supper and Wesley explained that the shop in Primrose Lane had become a hazard to life and limb. Towering shelves with narrow ravines between them had never been easy to negotiate, even for the slimmest of customers, and when one day a corpulent clergyman had become wedged between them, defying all conventional means to extricate him, he, Wesley, had realised that more suitable premises must be found. The clergyman, he added, had borne his sufferings with Christian fortitude.

"Now, Mr Ingle," continued Wesley, "I had anticipated your visit and have taken the liberty of consulting my four associates about how best to proceed." – The four associates bowed their heads gravely. – "But please first accept my apologies for providing you with a volume that was simply not up to the task you required of it. I misjudged the difficulty of your situation up on the moor. The fault is mine entirely. To make amends I have, with my associates' agreement, decided to lend you my most valued possession."

From one of the four associates he took a package wrapped in black silk.

"This," he said, placing it on the table in front of him, "is the most powerful sermon my illustrious ancestor ever composed. It was never published and never delivered. What you have here" – he touched the silk-clad package – "are the words of John Wesley in his own hand, a hand that was guided, I doubt not, by Holy Spirit Itself."

On hearing these words, Ingle felt a fierce rush of joy and reached eagerly for the package, only to find his hand arrested in mid-progress by Wesley.

"You will understand, Mr Ingle, that I let this precious notebook out of my keeping only with the greatest reluctance. I warn you that you might find yourself surprised, even alarmed, by the contents. You may be tempted to modify what you read when you climb into your pulpit. This you must on no account do. I must therefore ask you to swear an oath in the presence of these four gentlemen that you will neither read the sermon before you deliver it, nor alter one single word whilst you deliver it, so help you God."

Now Ingle was an old-fashioned puritan who believed that his yea should be yea and his nay should be nay and who did not, therefore, care much for oaths. But such, he felt, was the overriding importance of his work on the hilltop that he set scruples aside and swore.

Refusing Wesley's offer of accommodation for the night, he slid the silk-clad book into a pocket next to his heart and declared his intention of returning immediately. God's work, he declared, would not wait. So saying, he bade Wesley and the four gentlemen farewell and hurried back to the moor. Tomorrow was Sunday and he wished to deliver his broadside before Stringer was astir. Nonetheless, the journey home tested him to the limits of his strength. When he saw the sun rise above the summit of the moor whilst he was yet at the foot, he feared that he was too late and that Stringer would have started mass before he arrived. But God was with him and forced his limbs up the steep ascent. He arrived in Stringer's tent to find the congregation gathered whilst Stringer was still robing himself in the engine house that served as a vestry. Casting aside the brass candlesticks and the velvet cloth, Ingle clambered on to the makeshift altar, opened the precious notebook and began:

[Editor's note: A scribbled note in the margin of Blackwood's manuscript indicates that it was at this point that Miss Osgood, ever zealous in the cause of temperance, refused to transcribe Stumps's narrative any further. Culpepper, he notes, had long since pulled up his collar about this ears and buried himself in The Pilgrim's Progress.*]*

"My text is taken from St Paul's Epistle to the Ephesians, Chapter 5, Verse 18: 'Be not drunk with wine, wherein is excess; but be filled with the spirit.' When Jesus attended the wedding at Cana of Galilee and changed the water into wine, he was following the custom of the country, for wine was what the people of Cana drank at weddings. But what if he had attended a wedding in France or Kentucky, would he still have turned water into wine? No, my friends, Our Lord would have known better than that. He would have changed the water into eau de vie or moonshine. Or in Greece into raki, in Hungary into palinca, in Romania into tuica, in Italy into grappa, in Russia into samogon and in faraway Brazil into Crazy Mary. And had he attended a wedding in Cork or Connemara, he would have turned the water into poteen."

By now Ingle was beginning to feel alarmed at what he was reading. But bound by his oath and driven by a sense that his congregation was hanging on his every word, he continued:

"Yes, he would have taken the water of the flesh and changed it by miracle into the poteen of the spirit."

Ingle breathed more easily: Wesley was clearly talking in parables.

"Take a forty gallon copper pot with a wooden lid and connect it to a spiral of copper enclosed in a barrel of cold water. – Remember, I am speaking in parables. – And when you have done all this, seal all the joints with a paste of oatmeal and flour lest the precious liquor escape, for that which is distilled must all be consumed."

A few days earlier a bucket has broken free of the windlass and plunged into the depths of the shaft, carrying a man with it. By some miracle the rope had stopped short of the floor of the tunnel and the man was saved. Ingle felt himself to be that man and prayed fervently that his rope, too, would turn out to be too short.

"Pour the fermented mash of potatoes and water – about eighty-four pounds of the one to a hundred gallons of the other should do the trick – into the still and beneath it, light a fire of turves, but beware lest the smoke from it does not betray you, for there are those that will persecute you for distilling the gifts of the spirit."

Dear God! what was he saying? This was no parable. This was a recipe for poteen. Just when the bucket was about to hit the floor, the tent flap opened and Stringer, holding aloft a monstrance which he had walked all the way to Sheffield to purchase the day before, stood there, his face black as thunder.

"Judas!" he roared. "Whoremaster! Spawn of Satan!"

Walking up to the remains of his altar, he took a prayer book from his pocket and began to read what Ingle, who knew no Latin, guessed to be the Service of Commination. Now the Service of Commination – especially the part which called upon the Lord to rain down snares, fire and brimstone on sinners – was a favourite of Ingle's and he would have been happy to trade curses with the enemy, but found that the words would not come. Instead he found himself babbling something about a hundred gallons of water, eighty-four pounds of potatoes and six stones of sugar.

"Paleas autem conburet igni inextinguibili," intoned Stringer. "And the chaff he will burn with unquenchable fire. Matthew Three Twelve."

To which Ingle, struggling to find a suitable riposte from the Book of Common Prayer, also found himself quoting from St Matthew: "'Seize him! Bind him! Loose him not!'"

At this point the congregation, which until a few minutes earlier had belonged to Stringer, went over to Ingle in a body. They rose menacingly to their feet and advanced on the hapless priest, who, sensing their hostility, turned and fled. They drove him out of the encampment, mocking his lace-trimmed surplice, his crossings and his genuflectings; then someone picked up a stone and threw it. Once the first stone had been thrown, whole volleys quickly followed. To escape which, Stringer ran out on to the moor, clear of the encampment, and plunged into a peat bog which was reputed to be bottomless and which the navvies' children were forbidden to approach. His ankles secured by the bog, he raised his hands to protect his face, though the real danger came not from above but from below. He began to sink, his surplice first billowing out round him and then, as he slid from sight amid the lichen and cotton grass, forming a brief rosette of white linen above his head before it, too, was sucked into the depths. The last missile to strike the departing pastor was the handwritten sermon of John Wesley. As

the notebook landed in the peaty water, Ingle, to his horror, could have sworn he
heard a hiss as of escaping steam.

This tumultuous episode had a curiously banal conclusion. Ingle and his
congregation (for such we must now account them) made their way back to the
tent, where the preacher, having achieved his ambition of reigning undisputed
on the hilltop, preached a temperance sermon, to which his new flock listened
in sullen silence. His words lacked fire, as if he were reciting something that he
had learned off by heart long ago, and after a hasty blessing he made his excuses
and left. As to the congregation, no-one spoke, no-one accused his fellows of
murderous mockery or blamed Ingle for instigating it. Indeed, no-one referred to
the episode again. Work on the tunnel was, in any case, coming to an end, and
the navvies had started to drift off in search of work elsewhere, so by the time the
winding gear was dismantled few who had been present on that fateful Sunday
remained. In Warrington, Stringer's absence was not much remarked, it being
generally assumed that he had joined the migration of the navvies and taken up a
cure of souls somewhere down south.

On a snowy day in December, a train of twenty carriages containing the local
gentry, the directors of the railway company and the mayors of Manchester and
Sheffield passed under the moor from east to west and, later in the day, from west
to east. On both occasions, the train paused in mid-passage, their worships shook
hands, and the Rev. Enoch Ingle, famous for his sterling work amongst the navvies,
was invited to pronounce a blessing on this miracle of progress and ingenuity.
Although he tried to infuse his words with a solemnity befitting the occasion, his
mind was elsewhere, for he was certain he could hear, above the hissing of the
locomotive, the scratching of fingernails against the roof of the tunnel.

Stumps's tale was not well received. Turpin and Beamish thought
it self-evidently false, Miss Osgood found it blasphemous and
Culpepper thought it both. Stumps, whilst insisting on the truth of
his story, damaged his case by claiming, first, that he had heard the

poteen sermon himself, and then, a few minutes later, by claiming that had had the story from a friend. When this was pointed out to him, he became extremely agitated. What did it matter where it came from? he demanded. They only disbelieved him because he was a navvy. If it had been a swell like Blackwood or Purselove who'd told it, no-one would've raised a murmur. ("Too kind," murmured Purselove.) But he stuck by his story, which was gospel truth, every word.

The bad feeling between Stumps and his fellow passengers was casting a shadow over the whole excursion. Nan looked miserable, Miss Osgood embarrassed. Purselove and Breeze looked mildly amused, but since they never took anything seriously that was only to be expected. Most humiliating of all, passengers in the tubs behind, taking their cue from the Saturnine Stranger, cupped their hands to their ears the better to savour Stumps's invective, one wag even shouting to him to speak up. It was Miss Aurora Lark, the governess from Devaux Lodge and a woman used to settling quarrels between fractious children – usually, I suspect, by telling them a story – who took it on herself to restore the festive mood with which we had started our journey.

"My father," she began, "was an officer in the Indian Army attached to the Ordnance Survey. His mapping expeditions took him the length and breadth of India, where, from nawabs and fakirs, Brahmins and merchants, he heard enough tales to fill a new Arabian Nights. When he died, we returned to England, to my mother's home town of Margate, where she supplemented her widow's pension by taking in sewing. Our existence was bleak and cheerless. The sea mists seemed to penetrate the very house. For three years we lived thus before my mother contracted influenza and died in an unheated bedroom where the water had frozen in the wash stand. Her death cast me on my own resources. Like so many young women in my position, I became a governess, but, unlike so many governesses, my experiences in that particular station have been happy ones. The first family to whom I applied

asked me what qualifications I could bring to the post. Without hesitation I replied, 'I can tell stories.' 'Then tell us a story,' said the
eldest of the children, 'and let it be a sad story with a happy ending.'
'With a tiger,' added the next child. 'And a witch,' requested a
third. 'And a long lost manuscript,' concluded a fourth. No story of
my father's met these requirements, but with a little ingenuity I was
able to marry one of his tales to one of the Brothers Grimm's and
even managed to throw in the Bengal Lancers on the way. The children were enthralled, the parents delighted. I was offered the post
and for the first time in several winters enjoyed the comfort of a
fire in my bedroom. Since then I have held other posts, all of them,
including my present one at Devaux Lodge, highly satisfactory.

"Although it may not contain the Bengal Lancers, the tale I shall
tell, like all the best tales, is a sad one with a happy ending. It even
contains a witch of a sort and, as for the tiger, well, the best I can do
is to include him as a rug."

"And the long lost manuscript?" asked Purselove.

Miss Lark thought for a moment.

"I shall do my best," replied Miss Lark, "but, yes, I think I
can promise you it will be there. I will not claim that the story is
true, though it was told me as if it were. There was indeed a Miss
Biddlecombe's Academy for Young Ladies in Margate until fairly
recently, though whether the circumstances attending its closure
correspond to those in the story I cannot say."

*[Editor's Note: Miss Biddlecombe's Proprieties is something of a puzzle in that
it is the only tale, apart from the printed ones, that does not appear in Percy
Blackwood's handwriting. To complicate matters further, it is not written
with his pen or with his ink, which is always mid-blue and often shows
signs of having been watered down. The hand in which MBP is written is
compact and the ink violet. I offer two suggestions, both entirely speculative.
One is that at some stage Percy Blackwood let Serafina into the secret of his
secret authorship and suggested that she become his amanuensis. (There is
some evidence in the Blackwood Magazine archives that editors were often*

exasperated by the untidiness of Percy's manuscripts.) The problem with this hypothesis is that no other story exists in this hand as it surely would have done if Serafina had acted regularly as copyist. The other suggestion is that Percy 'gave' this story to Violet Osgood as a reward for taking down all the tales in Pitman and promised to offer it on her behalf to Blackwood's for publication. The problem here is that no such story was published by them. Either Percy failed to keep his promise or for some reason Blackwood's rejected it. Although Freud's discoveries lay half a century in the future, would it be fanciful to suggest that they found the end troubling in ways that they couldn't quite identify and for which they had no name?]

The Governess's Tale:
Miss Biddlecombe's Proprieties

Miss Biddlecombe's Academy for Young Ladies was generally referred to as The Proprieties, because the proprieties were what it prided itself on. At table, in conversation, in church, at balls and garden parties, Miss Biddlecombe's girls were famous for them, and since the proprieties were known to attract husbands of the better sort, Miss Biddlecombe's services were much in demand. Six girls were under her tutelage at any one time, with at least another six on the waiting list.

The Proprieties was situated at the highest point in Margate with a fine view of the sea. Now Margate is famous for its bathing machines, and from their perch on the cliff top, the girls eyed them longingly. But that was as far as their interest was allowed to go. The girls, insisted Miss Biddlecombe, were free to enjoy the sea as watercolourists, but not as bathers. No, she would brook no argument: her decision was final. And with that they had to be content, until one of them read in a newspaper of the Queen's fondness for sea bathing at Osborne. Was it not unpatriotic, she asked, to condemn a pastime in which Her Majesty took such delight and did not Miss B's reproofs smack of republicanism? Although the question was not addressed to her directly, Miss Biddlecombe got to hear of it and was so eager to avoid the taint of anything incendiary that she relented. So every morning, just after dawn, the young ladies were escorted to the beach, where each was ushered into the bathing machine assigned to her. Miss Biddlecombe would not hear of them sharing. The proprieties, she declared, were every bit as important in the ocean as at the dining table. What applied to bathing machines applied also to dress. The young ladies were covered from head to toe in black – black bathing dresses with skirts and bloomers, black mob caps and black bathing shoes. Had the proprieties demanded black parasols, no doubt Mrs Biddlecombe would have insisted on those as well.

But what about Miss B herself? asked the girls. Would she be joining them in the sea? Miss Biddlecombe was horrified by the suggestion. The very idea! She was too old, too set in her ways. What was acceptable in young ladies was not becoming in matrons of mature years. The girls looked at her with renewed interest. Set in her ways she most certainly was. But whether she was too old, or even old at all, was a different question. Although she had been spared crow's foot and greying temples, there was a stateliness of manner and a prominence of feature – "like well-made door furniture," quipped one girl – that suggested that she was not in her first youth, nor even in her second. Some girls inclined to a lower estimate of her years, some to a higher. Among the former was a girl named Clarissa Pond.

"She is more youthful than you think," she would say to her friends. "Why, I had it from Dixon" – Dixon was the housekeeper – "that she has her own bathing machine set apart from all the others and swims every evening after supper in a bathing dress of blue gingham."

Dixon, who was fiercely loyal to Miss Biddlecombe, denied it utterly.

"I don't know where she heard that," she said, "but she never got it from me. Anyway, gingham is a fabric Miss Biddlecombe abhors."

But Clarissa persisted with her story. "So what if she does deny it? I had it of Tadpole, too." – Tadpole was the carrier's boy, who helped bring up the girls' trunks from the station – "He says he saw her with his own eyes."

"What a lot of taradiddle!" said Dixon when she heard of Clarissa's latest outburst. "And more fool her for believing anything Tadpole says. Anyway, he should have been ashamed of himself for looking. Not of course," she added hastily, "that there was anything to look at."

And there the matter rested, the girls divided evenly between those who believed Tadpole's story and those who would have liked to but did not dare. Indeed, it would have been quietly forgotten had not an alarming incident brought it back to everyone's attention. The business of Miss Biddlecombe's Academy was, as we have seen, the proprieties. Miss Biddlecombe inculcated good table manners, insisted on correct elocution, supervised her girls' reading habits, corrected their grammar, refined their posture and generally improved their prospects of making a good match. In all of which endeavours she was conspicuously successful. Of all her achievements, however, none was dearer to her heart than turning out fine needlewomen.

"Call it a weakness," she would say, "but cross stitch is as close as I get to a grand passion. A girl who is good with her needle cannot fail to be a good wife. A girl who can create a beautiful sampler will always possess a corresponding beauty of character."

The walls of the Proprieties were hung with triumphs of the girls' art. Miss Biddlecombe would proudly show them to prospective parents, indicating how this hunting scene had secured a master of Fox Hounds, that sailing ship a tea merchant, those butterflies a fashionable portrait painter and a verse which read,

'Tis religion that can give
Sweetest pleasure whilst we live
'Tis religion must supply
Solid comforts when we die,

a rural dean from Monmouthshire.

One day, when the sea bathing rumour had died away, Clarissa Pond found herself once more the centre of attention. She had been engaged on a sampler which featured recumbent stags within a leafy border. With much labour – for she was the first to admit that she was no poet – she had completed a verse which Miss Biddlecombe had approved for inclusion in the finished work:

All you my friends who now expect to see
A piece of work perform'd by me
Cast but a smile on this my mean endeavour
I'll strive to mend and be obedient ever.

On the morning in question, Miss Biddlecombe unlocked the schoolroom cupboard and handed the girls their samplers. She was about to hand Clarissa hers, when her eye fell on a text where, as yet, there should have been none. It read: 'I rave in a most exquisite delirium.' The stitching was exemplary, the sentiment anything but. There was uproar. The girls were horrified, none more than Clarissa who found herself accused of desecrating her own work.

"You wicked girl!" accused Miss Biddlecombe. "If word of this gets out, it will destroy the reputation of the entire Academy. Had you thought of that, Pond? When you crept downstairs in the night to commit this outrage, did you stop to think of the injury it might do to your friends' good name and marriage prospects? I very much doubt that you did."

"But Miss Biddlecombe," objected Clarissa, "I never crept down in the night. I never perpetrated this outrage. As for this" – she indicated the offending phrase – "I don't even know what it means."

"What it means, Pond," retorted Miss Biddlecombe, "is that you are given to lewd thoughts and lewd thoughts in one girl beget lewd thoughts in others. Indeed, I should be very surprised if they had not done so already". She looked round the room accusingly.

"But," began Clarissa.

"No buts, if you please. You will go to your dormitory and pack your trunk. The carrier will remove it – and you – first thing in the morning."

The other girls watched in horrified silence as Clarissa was bundled from the room, her marriage prospects damaged beyond repair. Her fall from grace had been so rapid, so spectacular, that none of the girls could be sure that it would not happen to her. Clarissa's name was expunged from the records of The Proprieties and, though not specifically forbidden to do so, the girls understood that it was not to be mentioned within the hearing of Miss Biddlecombe. Soon all that remained of Clarissa Pond was a faint perfume which lingered in odd places and surfaced at odd times but never entirely went away. No-one could say exactly what it was, but all agreed that there was something exciting, even dangerous about it. Its persistence after Clarissa had left was odd; odder still was the fact that no-one could recall her wearing it whilst she had been a pupil at the Academy.

Her place was quickly filled from the waiting list. Sewing classes resumed, so too, after a brief suspension, did sea bathing. It was as if Clarissa Pond had never existed. As to the offending sampler, no-one dared ask what had happened to it, despite a feeling, quietly voiced by Clarissa's friends, that it should have been returned to her with the offending message removed. After all, even Miss Biddlecombe had admired the recumbent stags.

Then to everyone's horror, disaster struck a second time. The words 'Do you think because I am poor, obscure, plain and little, I am soulless and heartless?'

appeared on a sampler beneath a picture of a parish church. This time there could be no doubt as to the identity of the culprit. Not only was she obscure, plain and little, but a search of her writing case revealed a letter from Clarissa Pond, who was now in service in Maidstone, and who had written, shameless creature, to beg the recipient to protest her innocence to Miss Biddlecombe.

"There!" exclaimed Miss Biddlecombe triumphantly. "What did I say? One girl with lewd thoughts may taint a dozen innocents. One must always be on one's guard. One must not relax one's vigilance, not for one single moment."

A second prophylactic expulsion followed. Girl Number Two was despatched without ceremony and replaced by another girl from the waiting list, who, as it happened, was also obscure, plain and little. By now the other girls were thoroughly alarmed, for after two expulsions who could feel safe? Evading Miss B's scrutiny – for she insisted on reading all the girls' correspondence, ostensibly to check their grammar – several girls managed to get word to their fathers, who approached Miss Biddlecombe in a body and demanded that something should be done.

"And what, pray, had you in mind?" demanded Miss Biddlecombe, who did not take kindly to being confronted.

"A private detective, ma'am," replied one father.

"With experience of such cases," added a second.

"But there have been no such cases," said Miss Biddlecombe. "Ours is surely unique. That being so, you will struggle to find your detective, gentlemen."

Nonetheless, a private investigator was found and he presented himself at The Proprieties without delay. Mr Arthur Henstridge had been chief clerk to a firm of private investigators in Folkestone and had only recently set up shop on his own, so recently in fact that this was his first case. No-one would have guessed it from his manner, however, which was commanding and ingratiating by turns. Henstridge prided himself on his understanding of women, whom he always referred to quaintly as 'the sex' and was delighted that his first case was to be an all-female affair. From the outset, however, it was clear that this was going to be a difficult investigation. Dixon, who received him at the front door, had had instructions from her mistress to say that she was indisposed.

"Then I shall have to interview you instead," he replied. "And for that I shall need a comfortably furnished room with a view of the sea."

"Why with a view of the sea?"

"Because I like looking at the sea. I find it accelerates the mental processes."

"I shall have to ask Miss Biddlecombe."

"Before you do so may I ask you what perfume you are wearing?"

"I am not wearing perfume, Mr Henstridge; I never wear perfume."

"That's odd. I could have sworn ..."

"We do not swear in this establishment, Mr Henstridge. Miss Biddlecombe does not permit it."

Recognising that he had got off to a bad start, Henstridge assumed a business-like manner.

"I shall, of course, need to see both the offending samplers."

"That, I am sure, can be arranged, though I fear you will be disappointed."

"Why so?"

"Because the offending messages were unpicked within a short time of their being discovered. Miss Biddlecombe was afraid of contamination."

"Well, at least you can show me the cupboard where the samplers were kept."

Dixon led the way to the schoolroom. She took a key from the bunch on her belt and was about to open the cupboard when Henstridge stopped her. Taking out a pocket lens, he examined the keyhole carefully.

"There are no scratches round the keyhole," he said. "The lock has evidently not been forced. How many keys are there?"

"I know only of Miss Biddlecombe's. Of course, there may be others, but on the whole I think it improbable."

Henstridge proceeded to cross-examine the housekeeper. Where did she keep her keys at night? On her person. Had she heard anything untoward on the nights in question? She had not. Had she any explanation as to why the culprits should have committed these particular acts of folly? Girls were foolish creatures who sometimes did foolish things.

"Mr Henstridge," interrupted Dixon after a while, "I must be about my work. Girls have to be fed, rooms dusted. Do you have any urgent questions for me?"

"Just one, Miss Dixon."

"Well, Mr Henstridge?"

"Will you marry me, Miss Dixon?"

"Certainly not."

"In that case, will you please tell the girls that I should like to see them one at a time here in the schoolroom. Good morning, Miss Dixon."

There was a brief interval before the girls arrived in which Henstridge had time to compose himself. He had not come to The Proprieties in a marrying mood. In fact, he had surprised himself by his own question, though it was by no means the first time that it had happened. The question usually slipped out without his intending it and so far he had always been lucky enough to have been refused. (To have fought a breach of promise case would have ruined him.) This occasion, however, had been slightly different. Marriage had been on his mind of late. Now that he had a brass plate on his door and calling cards in his pocket, he felt the need of a wife. When he had faced Dixon across the threshold – he thickset, florid-faced and heavily whiskered, she plump, apple-cheeked and lightly moustached – it had occurred to him briefly that she might do very well. He had put the thought to one side whilst he was examining the cupboard, then, suddenly, there it was, no longer an unspoken thought but a question. Perhaps, he reflected, Dixon's non-existent perfume had had something to do with it.

For the rest of the morning Henstridge interviewed Miss Biddlecombe's flock, demanding to know what they had seen and heard and, in particular, how they accounted for the actions of the two black sheep. The girls had seen nothing, heard nothing and, though shocked by the actions of the black sheep, were quite unable to account for them. And perfume, asked Henstridge, did any of them wear perfume or know of anyone who did – Miss Dixon perhaps? Oh no, Miss Dixon never wore perfume; she wasn't the sort. With that, Henstridge concluded the interview, having decided that the whole morning had been a waste of time. None of his questions had met with a satisfactory response and he was no nearer either to solving the mystery or to finding a wife.

His morning was not to be entirely wasted, however. As he climbed into the dog cart, Dixon reappeared on the front door step and informed him that Miss Biddlecombe's headache had eased and that she wished to speak with him before he left.

"Miss Dixon," he said, climbing down from the dog cart, "should you wish to reconsider, my recent offer is still on the table."

"And so, Mr Henstridge, is my refusal," she replied.

She led the way to the back of the house, where the floors were newly polished and the gas jets burned low. Henstridge was ushered into Miss Biddlecombe's private sitting room, where what could be covered was covered and what could not was polished. Thus lamps were draped, ferns crammed into Wardian cases, the wax flowers on the mantelpiece squeezed into a glass dome, whilst the fireplace, together with the poker and coal tongs, had been freshly blackleaded and the chiffonier polished to mirror brightness. Behind the piano, a full-length curtain hung from a brass rod which terminated in two enormous finials like hyacinth bulbs. A parting in the folds revealed a slice of varnished door which led, presumably, to her innermost chambers. A tiger skin rug, its snarl intact, guarded the threshold. Miss Biddlecombe, who had put on the silk turban in which she normally greeted visitors, put her beadwork to one side and looked up when he came in.

"Mr Henstridge," she said. "I will not pretend you are a welcome visitor. You were wished upon me by parents, and when parents act in a body they cannot, alas, be ignored. You need pursue your investigations no further. A foolish girl gave way to lubricious imaginings and has since infected others. That is the truth of the matter. You will oblige me by writing to parents with your conclusions and charging an exorbitant fee to discourage them from engaging private investigators in the future."

Before Henstridge could object, she rang the bell.

"Good day, Mr Henstridge. I trust we shall not meet again. Dixon will show you out."

But they did meet again, sooner than either had foreseen. Some days later Henstridge received a telegram at his office in Folkestone which read: COME IMMEDIATELY STOP FURTHER LUBRICIOUS IMAGININGS STOP DIXON. Henstridge was eager to oblige. The Biddlecombe affair had not gone as well as he would have wished. He had to confess that he was baffled. Was Miss Biddlecombe right in saying that there was no case to investigate? Was she right in concluding that one girl with lewd thoughts could infect a second and even, by the look of it, a third? Somehow Henstridge doubted it. But if not Clarissa Pond, then who? His reflections were disturbed by a knock at the door. It was the postman. From somewhere in the bundle of letters which he handed to him, Henstridge thought he could detect a familiar perfume. Taking his lion-headed paper knife from the desk he slid it beneath the perfumed flap and teased it open, fibre by fibre. He read the letter quickly, frowned, then crossed to the window as if he needed a better light to be sure of what he was reading. "How could I be expected to know that?" he exclaimed aloud "How could any man be expected to know that?"

Later that afternoon Henstridge found himself facing an audience of fathers and daughters in the schoolroom. Even Miss Biddlecombe, resplendent in purple turban, was present. On the table was a sampler, which bore the text: 'Are you in earnest? Do you truly love me? Do you wish me sincerely to be your wife?' Henstridge had decided to dispense with preliminaries and proceed straight to naming the guilty party.

"And the culprit is ...," he began.

At that moment, the door opened and Dixon entered the schoolroom with a jingling of keys.

"The lady in front of you," he concluded.

"Dixon?" gasped Miss Biddlecombe.

"Me?" echoed Dixon.

"Yes, Miss Dixon, I name you as guilty party."

"Don't be ridiculous," said Dixon. "And now if you would like to come through to the dining room, ladies and gentlemen, tea and cucumber sandwiches await you."

"One moment, Dixon," said Miss Biddlecombe. "I think we should hear the case against you. Mr Henstridge, if you would be so kind."

Henstridge set out his case, which was entirely circumstantial. First, the lock had not been picked; second, it had been opened with a key; third, Dixon had the only spare; and, fourth, as the person who darned the girls' stockings, often as many as half a dozen pairs in an evening, Dixon possessed the requisite skills.

"The case," concluded, Henstridge, "is overwhelming."

The case, of course, was nothing of the kind, but it satisfied Miss Biddlecombe, who, in matters concerning The Proprieties, was both judge and jury.

"Dixon," she announced, "you will leave tomorrow by the earliest train. In the circumstances, I am sure you will agree that it would not be possible for me to provide you with a character reference."

Dixon flung down her keys and flounced out of the room, slamming the door behind her, only to re-appear a moment later to remind them that tea was on the table, adding:

"And if any of you doubt that I am innocent, I shall prove you wrong so conclusively that you will be ashamed you ever suspected me. You have my word: proof is on its way. Good day, Miss Biddlecombe. As for you, Mr Henstridge, I wish your future clients, assuming you have any, better success than your present ones."

There was a shocked silence as she strode from the room. Miss Biddlecombe, Henstridge, the girls and their fathers all stared at the floor as if they found ink stains the most engrossing sight in the world.

"Mr Henstridge," said one of the fathers, a rural dean from Barnstaple, "let me congratulate you on clearing up this most unfortunate business. It is a comfort to know that Miss Biddlecombe can now get back to the proper business of educating young ladies in their Christian duties."

Miss Biddlecombe set to work with a will and soon her girls were hard at work on the rudiments of social intercourse and the niceties of deportment, though, as it transpired, the respite was a brief one. A week or so after the dismissal of Dixon, Henstridge was visited in his office by the rural dean from Barnstaple.

"Mr Henstridge," he began. "We were badly mistaken in you. Far from solving the crime, you have, in removing Dixon, abetted a far greater one."

"I am distressed to hear it," replied Henstridge.

"Miss Biddlecombe has disappeared; another sampler has been tampered with; and, worse, new ones with the most lubricious messages have appeared on the walls. The girls were left unsupervised for twenty-four hours before they decided to call the police. It hardly bears thinking about."

"And what do you wish me to do, especially as my conclusions were erroneous and the police are now investigating the case?"

"You must return to Margate with me. My daughter wishes to speak with you. She says she has an urgent communication which she insists on delivering to you personally. It is most irregular, but she can be very stubborn, and I have, on this occasion, decided to give way. I have a fly waiting outside. We can catch the 1.30 and be in Margate by early evening."

The communication turned out to be a letter which had been entrusted by Dixon to the rural dean's daughter with instructions that it was to be given to Henstridge, and to Henstridge alone, in the event of Miss Biddlecombe's disappearance.

"It seems that Dixon knew in advance that Miss Biddlecombe was going to disappear," said the girl handing him the letter. "Clever old Dixon!"

Henstridge held the letter up to the light, sniffed it suspiciously and laid it on the schoolroom table. On the envelope was written: 'To be given to Arthur Henstridge Esq. in person and to be read aloud if he sees fit.'

"Well, aren't you going to open it?" asked the girl eagerly.

"In due course," said Henstridge. "First, though, I should like to see the latest samplers. Since the police are now in charge of the investigation, I suppose I ought to ask their permission. Where are they?"

"Searching the beach. They think Miss B may have thrown herself over the edge of the cliff."

"Then if you would be so good as to gather all the samplers together and ask everyone to gather in the dining room, I shall read Dixon's letter to you. Although I have yet to read it myself, I am confident that it will shine some much-needed light into this strange and unsettling affair."

Whilst he was waiting for the girls to assemble, Henstridge examined the latest batch of defaced samplers. 'Wait for me! Oh, I will come', ran one text. 'What sweet madness has seized me?' ran another. Henstridge examined them carefully, wondering if the rural dean's description of them as 'lubricious' was not perhaps a little overexcited. Soon his audience began to gather and faced him nervously across the table. It was clear to him that they feared he might inculpate some innocent party a second time. And given that his last dénouement had been so disastrously mistaken, who could blame them? He put away his pocket lens and smiled in his most ingratiating manner.

"First let me reassure you," he began, "that Miss Biddlecombe is perfectly safe. I am confident that no harm will come to her. I am happy to announce, ladies and gentlemen, that the Biddlecombe case has been solved." – There were gasps of astonishment from the girls and a questioning look from the rural dean – "But it was not I who solved it: it was Dixon. I have here a letter from her which I trust will explain everything. I have not yet read it, though I am privy to its contents, having been in correspondence with her since her dismissal a week ago. I shall now read it to you. *Dear Mr Henstridge, I imagine you are reading this aloud to the girls and, who knows, perhaps to a father or two as well. By now I can confidently predict that Miss Biddlecombe will have disappeared, much to the surprise of everyone except me. After our first meeting, I wrote to you to draw your attention to a clue you had overlooked, namely, that all the 'lewd thoughts', as Miss Biddlecombe called them, that had appeared on the samplers were quotations from a recent novel entitled 'Jane Eyre' by one Currer Bell. That Miss Biddlecombe knew of the work is certain, since she ordered me to seize any copies of the book I might find amongst the girls' belongings. It was, she said, a work that might have incendiary consequences if placed in the wrong hands. Needless to say, I found no copies amongst the girls' belongings, though my curiosity was so piqued by her warning, that I procured a copy for myself and read it avidly. I am convinced that Miss Biddlecombe feared the book's effects because she had read it herself and, unable to contain the feelings it aroused in her, expressed in cross stitch what she dared not express in speech. But why, you will be asking, has she disappeared? Because she has fled to embrace her own Mr Rochester. I do not know who he is or how she met him, but clearly the passions aroused by him and by Currer Bell have led to her abandoning the proprieties for ever.*

Girls, I hope you will forgive me for suggesting to Mr Henstridge that he should expose me as the culprit. Please believe me when I say that I acted in your own best interests. It was important to hurry events to a crisis to prevent more girls from being expelled for entertaining lewd thoughts.

Now that you have all read this letter, I suggest that you proceed to Miss Biddlecombe's private quarters. Under the wax flowers on the mantelpiece you will find a key to her inner chamber. I was told that on no account was I ever to enter it and in this, as in all others things, I obeyed her behest. I cannot know for certain what you will find there, but I should be astonished if you did not find a copy of Jane Eyre on the bedside table and on the wall another sampler, the text of which I leave you to guess."

Henstridge led the way to Miss Biddlecombe's immaculate outer chamber where, as instructed by Dixon, he removed the key from beneath the wax flowers, drew back the heavy curtains from the hidden door, stepped carefully over the tiger skin rug and inserted the key. Neither the rural dean nor the girls were prepared for the scene of wild disorder that lay before them. The bed was a chaos of twisted sheets and blankets, some torn, some wine-stained, all thrown this way and that, as if Miss Biddlecombe had been fighting with some unknown assailant in them. Clothes, including intimate undergarments, had been flung with promiscuous abandon across the chaise longue. The bowl in the wash stand was full of soapy water, already congealing to a grey paste round the rim. A window had been flung open and the wind had caught the curtains and wrapped them round the pole. And over everything hung the perfume that Henstridge had smelt when he first entered the Proprieties. He sniffed the unstoppered bottles on the dressing table, but none seemed to be the source. Sandalwood, said the rural dean. Musk, said the girls. Tom cat, thought Henstridge.

"Well, here's part of Miss Dixon's prophecy come true," said the rural dean, leafing through a book full of pencilled underlinings. "'Jane Eyre' by Currer Bell. Would that be a woman or a man, I wonder?"

"A woman," said one of the girls. "Most definitely. No man could have written anything half so fine."

"How do you know?" asked Henstridge. "Have you read it?"

"We all have," the girls said. "Tadpole had a copy and used to hire it out to us for a penny a day. He must have made a fortune."

"And look," said one of the girls, "there's the other sampler that Dixon predicted. Clever old Dixon!"

And there indeed, hanging over the bed, though hanging slightly awry, was the final sampler. The text was the shortest to date. It said simply, 'Reader, I married him.'

Mr and Mrs Arthur Henstridge sat side by side smoking cigars on the terrace of a hotel in Eastbourne. Though it was late in the season, the air was balmy and other honeymooning couples were taking advantage of it, too.

"To think," chuckled Henstridge, "I used to pride myself on my understanding of the sex."

"Well, I hope you've learned your lesson," said his wife. "In future, I'll do the understanding for you and you can just pretend that you did it all by yourself."

"If you say so, my dear. And we shall have to change the brass plate. What shall we call ourselves – Dixon and Henstridge, Henstridge and Dixon – Private Investigators?"

"No, just Henstridge and Henstridge. That way people will assume it's father and son or brother and brother. It's a way of hiding the truth without actually telling a lie. Like Currer Bell. Most people still think he's a woman. But that of course was exactly what he wanted them to think. Give it time, though. Truth will out, the same as it always does."

Henstridge gazed intently at the Belle Tout lighthouse on Beachy Head.

"I wonder," he said.

Further along the South Coast, enjoying the last of the sun from the steps of their bathing machine, sat Mr and Mrs Edward Grantchester. She, dressed in blue gingham bathing dress with matching turban, sat on the lower step, trailing her bare feet in the water; he, dressed in mauve bathing drawers, cradled her head on his knees and blew cigar smoke in the direction of the Isle of Wight.

"Are you sure you don't keep a mad wife in the attic?" she asked, rubbing her cheek against his knee.

"Only junk in the wildest disorder imaginable," he laughed. "One your first tasks as mistress of Thorneycroft will be to take it in hand and make the attic as presentable as the drawing room."

"Good heavens, no," she said, gazing across the Solent at the Needles. "I've done with the proprieties for ever."

2

ASHFORD TO TUNBRIDGE

The Tripe Dresser's Tale of the Nizam and Uncle Jack
The Advertising Copywriter's Tale of The Retrospective Destinator
The Daguerreotypist's Tale of the Midlands Mona Lisa
The Bugler's Tale of Red Spangle and Mr Henry (Part One)

As the train approached the new carriage works at Ashford, the band launched, somewhat prematurely, into a selection of popular airs, which they played with shameless abandonment.

"I was under the impression, Blackwood," said Culpepper, "that they were to continue playing temperance hymns until we had passed through the station. What the good people of Ashford will say when they see Canterbury passengers being serenaded with glees and catches, I dread to think."

"As Chairman of the Canterbury Glee Club," said Mr Breeze, "I can tell you what they'll say. They'll say, 'Thank God for the people of Canterbury, thank God for people who know how to enjoy themselves.' That's what they'll say. 'Let us take a leaf out of their book and do likewise.'"

"Ah, how little you know the good people of Ashford," sighed Culpepper. "Not only – with the encouragement of the diocese – did they persuade the railway company to build a chapel next to the carriage works, but a mechanics' institute with as fine a library as one could wish."

The peace which Miss Lark had so artfully restored now seemed to be threatened again, especially when Stumps, no doubt still thirsting for a drop of Robespierre, announced that Ashford was the birthplace of Jack Cade and that if ever a man deserved to be honoured with a statue in his home town it was Good Old Jack. In this proposal he found an unexpected ally in Purselove, who, it turned out, had played the mediaeval rabble rouser in a revival of *Henry VI Part Two* at Drury Lane some years earlier.

"Rum play," he said, "not one of the Bard's finest, but it kept me in work for a few weeks, which is more than can be said for most plays. So hurrah for the Bard and hurrah for Jack Cade. Statues all round, say I."

"Do you know," remarked Breeze, "I shouldn't be at all surprised if our friend here hasn't been a bit of a Chartist on the sly."

"There warn't nothing sly about it," said Stumps. "I *wos* a Chartist and proud of it. I waved my banner on Kennington Common in '48, though I might as well have stayed at home for all the good it did."

Now to Englishmen no subject is as combustible as that of Chartism, and under my breath I cursed Breeze for having mentioned it. I was about to appeal to Miss Lark for another story, when Nan Foxley suddenly screamed and grabbed hold of Gabriel, who had leaned over the side of the tub to touch the freshly painted carriages on the adjacent track. In so doing he had overbalanced and, but for the prompt action of George Costello, would have plunged to his certain death beneath the wheels of the train. For several seconds he hung suspended by his ankles until eager hands hauled him to safety and handed him to Nan.

"Oh Gabriel!" cried Nan, hugging him tightly. "Whatever possessed you?"

What had possessed him, apparently, was wet paint. Up to the wrists he was smeared in the green of the South Eastern Railway Company. He would have preferred wet cement or even wet putty, he said, but they were harder to come by and paint was the next best thing. Only to sniff, mind. Not to lick. He wasn't stupid.

By this time the train was trundling through Ashford Station and the bystanders, seeing the boy's raised hands, assumed that he was waving to them. A little girl in a navy blue dress waved back enthusiastically, despite her mother's efforts to prevent her. A sporting type in a check jacket touched his cap, a soldier saluted. Glad of an excuse to pause in their work, a pair of porters, who were loading mail sacks on to a barrow, threw their caps in the air as we passed. Only a rather grand gentleman in a top hat – presumably the station master – seemed to recognise where Gabriel's hands had been and wagged his finger in admonishment. As to the oompahing of our band, the good people of Ashford – to the evident disappointment of Culpepper and Breeze – showed no inclination either to join in or to disapprove.

Once we had left the station and Gabriel had been returned to his seat by Nan, Mr Meek, the tripe dresser from Best Lane, prompted by Miss Lark's earlier reference to her father's Indian adventures, now came forward with a tale of heroic deeds enacted under a tropical sun – in short, the kind of tale for which *Blackwood's* were known to pay generously. Miss Osgood and I exchanged glances, so that when Meek began his narrative, her pencil was at the ready.

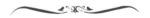

"Look at me, ladies and gentlemen," he said. "Look hard and tell me what you see. Speak up. Don't hold back, don't spare my feelings. I can bear it. Well? Yes, you, sir – your verdict, if you please. A tripe dresser? Worse still, a tripe dresser born and bred. That's harsh indeed, but all too true, alas. Now shall I tell you what I see when I look in the mirror? I see a soldier, someone, I admit, who never quite got round to taking the Queen's shilling, but a soldier nonetheless. And that's not all I see. Sometimes I see a fur trapper, a lighthouse keeper, a balloonist and a dozen such. An operatic tenor, a steeplejack, I could go on. That's the poetry of imagination for you. But real life is prose and the prose of it is that I am a tripe dresser.

"I inherited the business from my father and he from his father before him, both of them, as it happens, Gilberts. Surely, you must be thinking, no family can be that dull. Is it possible that none of them distinguished themselves? Might not my grandfather have been Tripe Dresser-in-Ordinary to King William IV, or my father Master of the Worshipful Company of Tripe Dressers with a seat at the Lord Mayor's table? Alas, no. They served, as I have served, behind the same counter every day of their working lives. No tales are told of them and their like, because there are no tales to tell. But to every Gilbert in our family there has been a Jack, a younger brother who has flown the flag in some far-flung corner of empire, sometimes as merchant, sometimes as missionary, sometimes as desperado – and, in the case of my own brother, a combination of all three. And it is through these Jacks that we Gilberts have lived. From the safety of our counters we have braved the dangers that they have braved, shot the savages they have shot, forded the rivers they have forded. Imprisoned in our shop we have roamed free in our thoughts. We have shared the glory but left them the risk."

The Tripe Dresser's Tale of
The Nizam and Uncle Jack

My tale is not of my own brother, madcap though he is, but of my great uncle, Jack the First, generally known to the Meeks as Jack the Great. When he was nineteen he went to Calcutta as a clerk in the East India Company. All the things that Englishmen usually die of out there – cholera, snakebite, debauchery – he managed to avoid, so that when his colleagues succumbed, as they did regularly, he was ready to step into their shoes. Up he climbed – clerk, chief clerk, auditor, examiner, up and up – and soon, having mastered the local tongues, was appointed as Secretary to the English Resident in Mandrapur. There he caught the attention of the Nizam himself and was made tutor to his son.

"It is a great honour," the Resident told him, "but not without its dangers. Tread carefully."

Has it ever occurred to you to ask how we rule India, how the few govern the many? The answer is that we don't, not directly. Most of it is ruled by native princelings, who have their own armies, and very pretty they are. To each native state the Governor General appoints a Resident to keep an eye on things, but on the whole we let them go their own way. We even let them fight wars – sometimes even encourage them to do so – and, if they fight themselves to a standstill, we send in the East India Company regiments to impose a peace on our terms and in our own interests.

One of the Nizam's ancestors was said to have married the sister of the Mughal Emperor Akbar and to have received Mandrapur as a dowry. Although my uncle Jack owed everything to the Nizam, he had no very high opinion of him. He was a weak man who lived mainly for pleasure, whilst trying to pass himself off as a warrior. He loved nothing more than to sit in his pleasure garden and listen to the nightingales. He loved to hunt gazelle with cheetahs, to go hawking with the court ladies, to show guests round his menagerie, to consort with astrologers and calligraphers. But perhaps his greatest pleasure was to sit on his war elephant and have his armies parade before him. He took a keen interest in their uniforms, frequently altering the colours of their turbans or of the tassels on their lances. No button, no pleat was too small to attract his attention. His soldiers were amongst the best paid in India. Morale was high, desertion low. All they lacked was a war.

From time to time he was tempted to provide one. To the north and east the Marathas had been chipping away at his borders. Oh, nothing much to speak of – a patch of jungle here, a swamp there – but provocation enough should he wish to rise to it. That he didn't was partly because it seemed a shame to waste such splendid uniforms on a battle and partly because he doubted whether his son would have the will to carry on should anything happen to him. Ah, his son. There was the spider in the cup of his contentment. Jahandar Bahadur showed no interest in military matters, preferring instead to mope in his apartments and play the sitar. Nothing less than the threat of having it removed would induce him to join his father on the parade ground. So exasperated was the Nizam that he confided his feelings, perhaps ill-advisedly, to Sir William Ingoldsby, the English Resident.

"Why not," suggested Sir William, "get him an English tutor, one who would read Caesar's Gallic Wars with him? It works wonders for our chaps. Half of the officers in the East India Company's regiments can quote Caesar at you. And, as it happens, I know just the man. My Secretary speaks Urdu like a native and can quote Caesar with the best of them."

A word about my Uncle Jack's education. The truth of it is that he had none. Whatever he knew he had taught himself. It had simply never occurred to Sir William that a chap who could speak Urdu like a native wouldn't be able speak Latin like one, too. It was quite unthinkable. Not that this mattered to Jack. Never one to shirk a challenge, he accepted the post eagerly.

"I should be honoured," he told the Nizam. "But I shall need a month to settle my personal affairs before taking up the post."

To this the Nizam readily agreed, whereupon Jack hid himself away in the Residency with a copy of Kennedy's Latin Primer. Within a week he had mastered the grammar, within a fortnight he had struggled through Caesar and by the end of the month was swapping quotations with Sir William himself, who had once won a prize for Latin verse at Harrow.

Caesar's Gallic Wars proved a great success. Within a short time Jahandar Bahadur, who had been indifferent to military matters, was pestering his father with impertinent questions. Why, he wanted to know, were the sepoys armed with outdated muskets? Why were the lances of the cavalry shorter than those of the neighbouring Marathas? Why was there no camel corps, no commissariat? Had his father considered equipping the elephant regiments with Congreve rockets? Or the artillery with twelve pounders? In short, ought not his father to face up to the fact that his army was simply an enormous fancy dress party?

At last the Nizam could stand it no longer. He dismissed Uncle Jack from his post and banished Jahandar from the parade ground. To cheer himself up he ordered his diwan to organise a large hunting party, from which Sir William Ingoldsby and Uncle Jack were excluded. Led by a detachment of sepoys, followed by noblemen on horseback, courtesans in their ivory palanquins and, finally, the Nizam on his hunting elephant, its tusks newly gilded, the procession took over an hour to pass through the palace gates. Jahandar remained in his quarters, reading Livy.

And it was there, later in the same day, that they brought him news of his father's death. A hunting accident, gasped the officer who been sent as messenger. His father had been thrown from his elephant and savaged by one of his own cheetahs. The astrologers had warned him of this, but he would not listen. He was too proud, too great of heart. "A lion of a man," sobbed the officer, "a very lion."

"Stop blubbering," ordered Jahandar, "it is unmanly to a fault. Now go fetch me Meek Sahib from the Residency. No, wait. What must you do first?"

The officer looked at him blankly for a second and then prostrated himself on the floor.

"Long live Your Highness," he said.

"That is a bit more like it," replied the new Nizam. "Now go and tell Meek Sahib that I want him immediately. On occasions such as this one feels the need to read Livy."

When the officer had gone, Jahandar paced the room for a while before picking up his sitar and, after playing a few notes, broke the finger board over his knee and threw the tangled remains into the corner.

Jahandar buried his father beneath a massive granite slab, which he enclosed in a mausoleum with heavy bronze doors to which he alone had the key. Though he claimed to have it on his person at all times, no-one had ever seen it and there were those who said that he had thrown it down a well. His father disposed of, Jahandar turned his attention to the army. Out went the egret-plumed turbans, the antiquated muskets, the gold sashes. In came a camel corps, muskets with rifled barrels, Congreve rockets, a commissariat, longer lances and compulsory study of Caesar's Gallic Wars. And, at last, after several months of ruthless modernisation, along came a war. Everyone agreed that one was long overdue and that the old Nizam's failure to defend his swamps and jungles had been humiliating. "Shameful and intolerable," was Jahandar's verdict and the durbar thought it best to agree.

To everyone's surprise, the war was over almost before it had begun. The Marathas, who had always regarded the Nizam's army with contempt, turned and fled. Jahandar was elated. Not only had he recovered his ancestral territories, but had decided to seize a few extra towns, one of which he made the capital of a new province. His generals applauded enthusiastically.

"And now," he explained to Uncle Jack, "it is time to celebrate. A Roman Triumph is called for. Prisoners in chains, trumpets, elephants as far as the eye can see. And a triumphal arch, Meek Sahib – oh, how my soul yearns for a triumphal arch."

But Uncle Jack, who had been reading ahead in Livy, pointed out to Jahandar that he had only won a battle and that to earn a triumph he must first win the war. His enemies had been taken by surprise, but they would be back. And indeed they were, though thanks to Uncle Jack's advice, Jahandar's army was waiting for them. Time and again they were beaten off, Caesar and Livy pointing the way.

"For a certainty Caesar is worth another fifty elephants," said Jahandar. "These Marathas are ignorant fellows who know nothing of the splendour that was Rome."

Nevertheless, the war dragged on. Weeks passed, months, a year. Between battles, Jahandar and Uncle Jack studied the defeat of Hannibal and the campaigns of Alexander the Great. At last, outside the walls of his new provincial capital, with Uncle Jack in the howdah beside him quoting Caesar, Jahandar directed his army to victory from the back of his war elephant. The Marathas were crushed. At a peace conference called by the Governor General, the new borders were ratified by treaty and guaranteed by East India Company troops.

This time Jahandar could not be denied his triumph. For the parade he dressed his soldiers in brilliant silks, not unlike those worn in his father's day. Jewelled aigrettes reappeared in turbans; elephants were encased in ceremonial armour and camels' necks hung with gold tassels. Wearing a laurel crown on top of his turban, Jahandar led a mile-long procession through a wood and plaster copy of the Arch of Titus, engravings of which Uncle Jack had found in the Resident's library. When the procession was over and the Maratha captives who had been marched through the streets in chains had been freed, Jahandar summoned Uncle Jack to the palace. His mood was subdued, his manner peevish.

"The triumphal arch," he said, "was not up to scratch."

"But it was a faithful copy of the Arch of Titus in Rome, Your Highness," protested Uncle Jack.

"In appearance only," said Jahandar, "but the substance was lacking. Is the Arch of Titus made of wood and plaster? Does it tremble when elephants pass beneath it? Consult the classical authors. I think you will find it otherwise."

"No doubt," replied Uncle Jack, "but it wasn't possible to build the real thing in the time available."

"But now the time is available, Meek Sahib, and I wish for the real thing. Time and cost are no object. Build me the Eighth Wonder of the Ancient World. Such a one that in years to come men will say, 'That is Jahandar's arch and it is fully up to scratch.'"

"I once marched through Bonaparte's triumphal arch in Paris with an entire army," interrupted Corporal Costello. "Cavalry, infantry, artillery, the British in scarlet, the Prussians in black, Wellington and Blucher at the head: you've never seen the like. The only thing that spoiled it was that the arch had no roof."

"Whatever had happened to it?" asked George.

"Nothing," said his father. "It's just that Bonaparte never finished it. We finished him before he could finish it, if you see what I mean. And once he'd gone no-one could be bothered with it. Louis XVIII even wanted to pull it down."

"Well, there's a roof on it now," said Purselove. "I know because I've sheltered under it from the rain, along with several hundred pigeons and a delightful Parisienne with a scarlet umbrella."

The masons had started digging the foundations when the old Nizam appeared to Jahandar in a dream to tell him he was building the arch in the wrong place. Or that, at any rate, was what Jahandar told Uncle Jack.

"But it is where it was on the day of your triumph, Your Highness," replied Uncle Jack.

"My triumph," said Jahandar. "Such a paltry affair! I shudder when I think of it. Next time we shall have the pukka thing, true Roman, and I look to you, Meek Sahib, to organise it."

"And where do you propose to put the new arch, Your Highness?" asked Uncle Jack.

Where Jahandar proposed to put it was on swampy ground near the river. An altogether better place, wouldn't Meek Sahib agree? Meek Sahib would not agree, pointing out that the ground was liable to flooding and that the foundations would be spongy.

"In that case," replied Jahandar, "you will just have to build the foundations deeper."

It was obvious why Jahandar had changed his mind. The new site was close to the old Nizam's tomb, inviting passers-by to compare the achievements of the son with those of the father. By now Uncle Jack knew better than to challenge his former pupil. Jahandar had taken to imitating Caesar in peace as well as in war and would not be gainsaid.

So the digging began all over again on the new site. Cartloads of stone were tipped into the foundations and disappeared without trace. When Uncle Jack drew Jahandar's attention to the problem, Jahandar dismissed him irritably, saying, "Did Caesar beat the Gauls by worrying about niceties? Did Alexander become the Great by fussing about the small?" To which the answer, as Jack well knew, was yes, but he said nothing, knowing that nothing he said would make any difference.

"Be off with you," said Jahandar. "Just build the damn thing."

For a while Jahandar reverted to his old self, shutting himself up in his father's pleasure gardens, where he entertained a succession of noble ladies, from whom he selected one, Zeenat Begum, as his consort. Other wives, he declared, would surely follow, but one was enough for now. By day the courtiers gathered in the marble pavilions to play chess, fly pigeons and watch dancing girls. By night they composed poetry and observed the heavens. This pleasant idyll was brought to an end by a letter from the Governor General. On receipt of it, Jahandar dismissed the sirdars from the garden, shut up the pigeon house and sent for Meek Sahib.

"What do you think has happened?" he asked. "We have been elevated. Such an honour! And so richly deserved, if I may say so. Here, read and savour."

He handed Uncle Jack a letter from the Governor General. In it His Excellency, Marquess Wellesley KG PC, was pleased to inform His Highness that following His Highness's recent victory over the Marathas, he would in future be greeted at Government House by a fifteen gun salute as against the nine to which his father had been entitled.

"Such an honour!" he kept repeating. "And from no less than Marquess Wellesley KG PC himself – and in his own hand! You too have played your small part in this part in this triumph, Meek Sahib. No, don't deny it, you have. To show you that Jahandar does not forget his friends, I am going to make you my secretary, my munshi. Now is that not generous?"

Uncle Jack wanted to refuse, but Sir William Ingoldsby decided to refer the matter to Calcutta first. The Governor General was adamant. 'On no account,' he wrote, 'should your man refuse this offer. With the Company on the brink of war with the Marathas, we need all the influence in the Mughal courts we can muster. Your man must do his patriotic duty.'

Uncle Jack cursed the Governor General under his breath, though it was not long before he had cause to curse him aloud – and with good reason. The new munshi and his master had ridden out to inspect the progress on the arch. Jahandar was particularly keen to see the newly sculpted battle scenes in which his own victories alternated with those of Julius Caesar.

"Sadly I have to tell you," said Jahandar after a careful tour of inspection, "that this is not the noble work I had in mind. Oh, the sculptures are very fine, no doubt. But there has been a new dawn. Mandrapur in now a fifteen-gun state. This I do not see. Where are those extra guns? Where is that extra glory? I must have both, Meek Sahib. I must have both."

"But every surface has already been filled, Your Highness," said Uncle Jack.

"Every surface but one. On top there is room for one thing more – a statue of me on my war elephant leading my troops to victory. Four times life size, of course."

"I will order the stone this very day," replied Uncle Jack.

"Who said anything about stone? I am talking about bronze. And let it be solid bronze. It must not be said of me that I am a hollow man."

"But ..."

"But me no buts. Find the bronze. Build a foundry. Do the needful."

With that, Jahandar turned his horse's head and rode away. After a few yards he turned and shouted, "Did I say four times life size? Make it five. Larger if possible."

It was not possible, any more than four times or even three times had been possible ...

"It would have been perfectly possible using a steam crane," interjected Mr Turpin. "A Fairbairn can lift six tons, and bronze, if I remember rightly, weighs approximately nought point two seven pounds per cubic inch."

"But steam cranes had not then been invented," replied Mr Meek.

"So what did they do?" asked Miss Lark.

"They built a ramp of sand and dragged the statue up it on a wooden sledge. It was Sir William Ingoldsby who suggested it. He was something of an antiquarian and said that that was how the Pyramids were built."

"Assuming a slope of no more than fifteen degrees and a height of fifty feet, that would mean a ramp of about a hundred and eighty feet," said Mr Turpin.

"Never mind the size, what about the cost?" asked Miss Lark. "How on earth did they pay for it all?"

"Taxes, forced loans. Everyone was expected to give something."

"Now let us assume a width of fifteen feet," continued Turpin, writing on his cuff with a pencil, "that would make a total of approximately two hundred and fifty-eight thousand cubic feet of sand."

"That's a lot of sand," said Stumps. "How much did they pay them?"

"Not nearly enough, you may be sure," replied Mr Meek.

"Never mind how much they paid the navvies or how much sand there was," said Miss Osgood. "Did they manage to place the statue on top of the arch?"

"Oh, yes", replied Mr Meek. "After a great many delays they did."

"And what happened then?" asked Mr Beamish.

"The arch began to sink."

"To sink?" echoed Culpepper.

"Is that so surprising?" asked Mr Meek. "After all, it was built on swampy ground."

"And when did anyone first notice it?"

The trouble began with the opening ceremony. Uncle Jack had been ordered not just to organise the parade but also to instruct the people how to cheer.

"A very rousing British huzzah when I ride through the arch would be most welcome," said Jahandar.

Had Jahandar, who led the procession, decided to ride his favourite elephant, the problem would have become apparent in a way he couldn't ignore. But he hadn't, having chosen instead to be carried on a silver throne by four bodyguards. Behind him came the lancers, whose plumes cleared the arch by a hand's-breadth, as did the pennants of the camel corps who followed close behind. It was the elephant regiments which ruined the parade. As they passed beneath the arch, their howdahs, whose finials had been specially gilded, scraped the roof in a spray of gold. When Jahandar heard the sound he reined in his horse. Instead of blaming the mahouts, he turned on the crowd, who, under Jack's guidance, had been practising British huzzahs since early morning.

"You have no business being here," he said angrily. "This is only a rehearsal. Perfection does not grow on trees: it must be practised first. Be off with you. But make sure you come back again this time next week, when you will surely see something worth seeing."

When the crowd had dispersed, Jahandar berated the mahouts for their carelessness. They in turn blamed the carpenters for making the howdahs too high. 'These are no howdahs,' they complained; 'these are palaces.' Jahandar had the carpenters arrested.

The following week, the elephants, minus their howdahs, passed beneath the arch to loud huzzahs from the crowd. Everything was going splendidly until the lancers passed under the arch. Their weapons, which as everyone knew had been lengthened on Jahandar's orders, scraped along the roof in a shower of sparks. This time the officers tried to blame the armourers and farriers. But Jahandar would have none of it. He ordered the officers to be thrown in gaol, where, to their disgust, they were forced to share a dungeon with the carpenters. Uncle Jack, who had warned all along about the lack of foundations, retired first to the Residency and then, pleading urgent business, to Calcutta, where he spent a pleasant few months carousing with the clerks of the East India Company with whom he had once shared an office.

Jahandar, meanwhile, sulked in his pleasure garden, where he surrounded himself with calligraphers and poets. He even took up the sitar again. Never, said the toadies with whom he had surrounded himself, never had music sounded so enchanting. No-one mentioned the arch; no-one referred to the triumph or even to the war it celebrated. Uncle Jack thought it safe to return from Calcutta and, on sending his greetings to Jahandar, was told that his services as munshi were no longer required. With some relief he reported his dismissal to Sir William Ingoldsby, who reported it to the Governor General who wrote to Uncle Jack ordering him to restore himself to the Nizam's favour without delay. "It is imperative," he wrote, "that I have my eyes and ears in the Mughal courts."

An opening soon presented itself. Some months after the failure of the Roman triumph, Zeenat Begum presented Jahandar with a son, whose arrival awakened the Nizam from his torpor. A parade was called for. Camels, elephants, fireworks, cheering crowds, whatever was needed to make a spectacle. Soldiers, too, whole regiments of them. "And animals from the royal menagerie, for did not Caesar include tigers in his processions? Meek Sahib will know. Where is Meek Sahib, by the way? He should be here at my side, organising things. Fetch him, someone, quickly." Uncle Jack was fetched, forgiven and set to work immediately.

Orders flowed ceaselessly from the Palace. Every blade and barrel, every tusk and tassel was the subject of detailed instructions. Regiments were required to perfect their marching drills and the British, who were quartered in a tented cantonment outside the city, were invited to supply the fifteen gun salute of which Jahandar was so proud.

Since the last procession Jahandar's triumphal arch had settled further into the swamp. It was impossible to march or ride beneath it without ducking. Lancers sloped their spears; infantrymen marched with long loping strides which, as the arch continued to sink, looked more and more like a Cossack dance; mahouts and camel drivers had to steer their beasts round it. Since no-one dared tell Jahandar the truth, they decided to ask the British to tell him. "Let the British enter the lion's den," they said to each other; "let the British feel his wrath."

And feel it they did – none more than a certain Lieutenant Elphinstone, who had pointed out jocularly that the arch was sinking so fast that they would soon be able to ride over it like a bridge. "Pardon me for mentioning it, Highness," he said. "Thought you ought to know. Bad show, can't be helped, but that's the way it is."

"That is very far from the way it is, actually," shouted Jahandar. "Get out of my sight. You are all conspiring against me. I should never have trusted Meek Sahib. He has betrayed me. Well, tomorrow, you can pack your tents and go. I am beginning to see that I was wrong to fight the Marathas when I should have been fighting the British. Go."

It was the elephant regiments which ruined the parade

Lieutenant Elphinstone was astonished by the outburst and reported it to the Resident. Sir William was alarmed. "This must not be allowed to happen," he said. "At all costs the army must be prevented from leaving." There was no time to seek instructions from Calcutta, no time to obtain the Governor General's endorsement for what he proposed to do. He hurried to the Palace, where he found the doors shut in his face. It required more bribes than usual to get him into the royal presence.

"Your Highness," he said, "I have this morning received a letter from his Excellency the Marquess Wellesley KGB PC, authorising a seventeen gun salute to mark the birth of your son."

"A letter, you say, from Lord Wellesley himself?"

"In his own hand."

"That is a true mark of favour. Give it me. I should like to hold it."

Sir William caught his breath. This was awkward, deuced awkward. Of course, no such letter existed. But if it was urgently required, then it must be produced and Uncle Jack was just the man to do it.

"It shall be in Your Highness's hands shortly," he promised.

"See that it is," said Jahandar. "You may go. And tell Lieutenant Elphinstone that I forgive him. You may wish to have him flogged, of course, but that is entirely up to you."

"In the British army we do not flog officers."

"Do you not? Take my tip: try it. I find it works wonders. I have only to threaten it and I get what I want every time."

Relieved that he would not be transferred to Calcutta in disgrace, Lieutenant Elphinstone was nonetheless alarmed to hear that the procession was to go ahead as planned.

"But that d~d arch is sinking fast," he told Sir William. "The procession will be a catastrophe. The laws of nature aren't going to suspend themselves just to please some seventeen-gun princeling."

"Provided that he rides at the head of the procession," replied Sir William, "it won't matter, because if anything goes wrong..."

"Which it will."

"Which it will, he won't be able to blame it on anybody else."

"But how do we persuade him to ride in front? The traditional place for nawabs is on their elephants in the middle."

"We'll persuade him that it's what the Romans did. We'll present him with one of your cavalry horses, call it Bucephalus and tell him that it's a gift from the Governor General."

The deception worked perfectly. Jahandar was overjoyed by what he saw as a new token of Lord Wellesley's favour and promised to ride it at the head of the procession.

At last the great day, feared by all but Jahandar, arrived. The procession began to form up before dawn. In the citadel camels and horses were groomed and caparisoned; the beasts from the menagerie were transferred to their travelling cages. Close to the arch the ladies of the zenana, Zeenat Begum among them, assembled behind screens of woven reed. Opposite them, on a low knoll crowned with tamarisk trees, the British gunners, watched by Sir William Ingoldsby and Uncle Jack, rolled seventeen artillery pieces into place and stood to, linstocks at the ready. The huge gathering waited in silence. The sun rose and burned the mist off the swamp. Soon it was beating down mercilessly on man and beast. The elephants in the citadel grew restive; the tigers growled in their cages. Not until mid-day, when the sun was at its hottest, did a groom appear at the Palace door with Bucephalus. Drums beat, trumpets sounded. Jahandar appeared, mounted his horse and signalled to the huge procession to follow. All along the route, the crowd huzzahed loudly, just as Uncle Jack had taught them. As they approached the arch, trumpeters appeared amongst the bronze figures on the top. Lieutenant Elphinstone raised his sword. The trumpets sounded. Elphinstone's sword dropped and seventeen cannon crashed out in rapid succession. In the still air, the arch was quickly enveloped in smoke. Jahandar, who had been seen entering the cloud, vanished from sight. When the smoke cleared again, he seemed to have disappeared without trace. Everyone stared at the empty space within the arch. Could the earth have swallowed him? Could he have been gathered up into heaven? If the cannon had been charged with grapeshot, his disappearance could not have been more complete.

Then, as if from nowhere, Bucephalus, eyes wide, nostrils flared, appeared among the crowd, lashing out with his hoofs. Several lancers seized his bridle and led him away. From everywhere – among the soldiers, the crowds, the women of the zenana, the British gunners – rose the buzz of excited voices, though no-one actually moved from their places. So used were they to taking orders that none of them knew what to do when there was no-one to give them. They might have remained there all day had not the trumpeters on the ach blown a ragged fanfare to announce their master's return.

The Jahandar who now appeared was very different from the one who had led the procession. Very different, too, was the procession he now led. Here were beggars, cripples and ex-sepoys in ragged uniforms. Everyone watched in silence as they approached the arch from the other side, dropped on all fours and crawled beneath. As they emerged, the crowd, which had been taught to huzzah at the sight of uniforms, huzzahed loudly. It was not hard to guess what had happened. At the sound of the guns, Bucephalus had shied, hurling Jahandar over the arch. In the smoke his landing had gone unnoticed. Dazed by the impact, he had wandered off among the hovels by the marsh, where army veterans, many of them blind or crippled, eked out a miserable existence as beggars or pimps. This was Jahandar's new durbar and it was clear that he was leading them to the Palace.

"You'd better follow, Meek," said Sir William. "The Governor General will want a detailed report of what's going on."

Uncle Jack joined the procession, feeling conspicuous in his gold epaulettes, brocade waistcoat and lace cuffs. He was followed at a distance by a group of sirdars, who feared losing their position at court. Though Uncle Jack was just in time to squeeze through the Palace doors before they closed, the sirdars were not so lucky. Denied access, they immediately began to plot in the courtyard outside. Jahandar was mad. That was obvious. If he was mad, then he would have to be replaced. That, too, was obvious. But replaced by whom? Why, by his son, course. Which meant there would be a regency and with it the possibilities for endless intrigue. All this the sirdars saw quite clearly. So, too, when they had had it explained to them, did the officers. Summoning an elephant, they goaded it to kick the Palace doors down.

So ended the brief and troubled reign of Jahandar. He was confined to the pleasure garden with his durbar of beggars, on whom he bestowed titles and medals. From time to time he issued declarations of war which were copied by Uncle Jack and passed through the gates in exchange for food, paper and birdseed. In between games of chess and pigeon racing, he composed despatches to the Governor General and bribed the guards to send them to Calcutta. When he ran out of money, he plundered the silver buttons and gold braid from his court dress and when, at last he was reduced to the same ragged state as the beggars, he ceased to write altogether.

Not that it would have made much difference. Unknown to him the world beyond the pleasure garden had changed beyond recognition. In the Palace, Zeenat Begum, mother of the young Nizam, had taken charge. Supported by the anti-British sirdars, she had shut down the cantonment and expelled Sir William Ingoldsby. In Calcutta, too, there was upheaval, Lord Wellesley having been replaced by Lord Cornwallis, who, on learning of the fate of the Resident, wrote to the Begum to inform her that henceforth Mandrapur would be rated as a nine-gun state.

If Uncle Jack was forgotten, so, too, was Jahandar. Provisions to the pleasure garden were irregular. The beggars ate the pigeons and cut down the cypress groves for fuel. One evening Uncle Jack found one of them putting Jahandar's sitar on the fire. There was a tussle in which he was knocked senseless. By now he was desperate to get away. He persuaded Jahandar that, as a conqueror in the mould of Caesar and Alexander the Great, he deserved a larger palace, at the same time as getting word to the Begum that her husband wished to move into one of the empty cages in the royal menagerie. The Begum, who wished to restore the pleasure garden for the use of her son, readily agreed.

A grand ceremony was prepared. A military band, lancers and a war elephant escorted Jahandar from the garden to the menagerie, where a cage had been prepared with fresh straw. Whilst the Begum and her sirdars were busy installing Jahandar in his new quarters, a detachment of sepoys stormed the pleasure garden and drove out the beggars. With his last silver button, Uncle Jack persuaded a dhobi wallah to sell him her clothes. Dressed as a washerwoman, he escaped from the Palace and, after many adventures, made his way back to Calcutta, where he resumed his old place as a clerk in the East India Company.

As for Jahandar, he was happy in his cage. He held audience twice a week and reviewed imaginary troops through the bars on alternate Thursdays. The Begum and her son were regular visitors and fed him Turkish delight on the anniversary of his great victory over the Marathas, despite the fact that the Marathas had long since recovered their lost territories without a shot being fired.

Nor was Jahandar entirely forgotten amongst the people who had huzzahed him on his last ride. In time, the arch finally reached the bedrock beneath the swamp. Cast in bronze, Jahandar with Uncle Jack beside him reading Caesar was still visible above the mosquito-infested water, not far from where the mausoleum of the old Nizam was perched on a rocky knoll. As Jahandar had intended, passers-by could take in both at a single glance and compare the achievements of the father with those of the son.

Publishers pay handsomely, I am told, for oriental tales, so when Mr Meek had finished his, I longed for someone else to continue the theme. Alas, none obliged. Instead, Mr Breeze, who earlier had taken a keen interest in Miss Lark's tale of the Proprieties, now returned the conversation to the point at which she had left it just as we were approaching Ashford.

"I suppose I ought to be grateful to this Currer Bell," he said, "for starting the craze for mad wives in the attic. In my former line of business I was called on to supply several. True, most of them only existed on paper, but one or two were required to appear in the flesh, but since I knew an out-of-work actress who was willing to oblige, this was not an insuperable difficulty."

"And what in heaven's name was your former line of business?" demanded Culpepper.

"And more to the point, Breeze, was it business or was it merely trade?" joked Purselove. "Supplying mad wives in quantity sounds very much like trade to me."

"Business or trade, it scarcely matters which," replied Breeze. "Either is better than talking up cod liver oil and cocoa like a common huckster. God knows how many aches I have eased or locks I have curled. Or for that matter how many waists I have corseted or collars starched. And for none of these have I ever received one word of thanks. Not one. An advertising copywriter is the most despised of creatures. When they see me approaching their shops, most tradesmen lock themselves in their store rooms; when they see me coming down the street, they cross over to the other side. But I have known better days, when clients beat a path to my door and paid good money for my services."

"I'll wager it was still trade," said Purselove.

"On the contrary, it was every bit as much of a profession as Beamish's here, albeit one of my own making. I had a brass plate on my door and consulting rooms in Sydenham."

"And what was this profession of yours?" asked Beamish suspiciously.

"I was a retrospective destinator," announced Breeze, "one of only two such in all England."

The Advertising Copywriter's Tale
of the Retrospective Destinator

Why is it, he began, that men of destiny are always statesmen or generals? Why does one never meet tobacconists or muffin men of destiny? Why are green grocers never summoned by Mercury to open shops in far-flung continents or upholsterers to fill oriental palaces with sofas?

"Never mind green grocers," remarked Nan. "Why are men of destiny always men? Whey are there never any women of destiny?"

"What about Good Queen Bess? Was she not a woman of destiny?" asked Corporal Costello.

"Not to mention our own dear sovereign," said Culpepper, "who, if you recall, was summoned from her bed to be told by the Lord Chancellor and the Archbishop of Canterbury that she was Queen. Was that not Destiny?"

"I think you will find," opined Beamish, "that it all comes down to the right bumps. Destiny visits those who have the right endowments and that, alas, does not include many women."

Well, at least we can agree that Destiny has no use for the little man – or woman – and reserves its favours for the great, said Breeze, resuming his story. This is the wrong I spent the best years of my life in righting. For my efforts I can claim a dozen successes and, as you will hear, one disaster. I found my vocation by accident, for, like Nan, I began life in service and expected to end it there, too.

One day at Egham races – for I was a regular visitor to the turf – I met a fellow manservant named Joe Hancock, whom I had not seen for some time.

"Well met, Joe," says I. "You've been making yourself scarce. I missed you at Epsom and Goodwood. You're not a man to scant his pleasures – what's been keeping you?"

"What's been keeping me," he said, "is locks and bars. I've been in prison, Charles. I don't mind admitting it."

"You?" said I in astonishment.

"For theft," he added.

"You astonish me, Joe," I said. "I would have trusted you with my last farthing."

What had happened was that on his deathbed Joe's late master had asked for a posthumous favour. Having never married, he intended to leave his estate to his nephew, who was a clergyman with High Church proclivities. There had been, he told Joe, some wild passages in his youth of which he was now ashamed and by which the nephew might be embarrassed were he ever to find out about them. More to the point, they might impede his progress to the bishopric he had set his sights on. For many years Joe's master had conducted an illicit liaison with the wife of a well-known politician. There had been an incautious exchange of letters, and, although he had burned those which he had received, he feared that the lady in question still retained hers. And now came the posthumous favour. Would Joe on some excuse or other introduce himself to the lady's maid and either persuade her to steal them or allow him access so that he could steal them? And anyway 'steal' was hardly the *mot juste*, for to 'steal' was to appropriate that which had never been one's own in the first place. That could hardly be the case with letters, to which the writer had as much claim as the recipient, though that was not how the judge saw it when Joe, having bungled his one and only attempt at robbery, appeared before him and was sentenced to two years.

Shortly after this encounter at the races, my own master, who had been ill for many years, took a turn for the worse and, to my alarm, asked me to render him a posthumous service. Like Joe's master, mine had never married and had a nephew for an heir. But there the similarity ended, for the two nephews could hardly have been more different. Where Joe's master's had had his heart set on a mitre for his heir, my master's had had his set on nothing in particular, unless it was the gratification of the present moment. The curious thing was that my master did not object to his heir's dissolute habits; on the contrary, he was proud of his nephew and enjoyed a vicarious participation in his various scrapes.

"Now listen to me, Charles," said my master one day, summoning me to his bedside. "I have a confession to make."

I must have looked surprised, for in between bouts of coughing, he chuckled and said:

"That surprised you, didn't it? Well, my confession is that, to my shame, I really have nothing to confess."

This time I must have looked relieved, for he went on:

"Don't look so pleased. It's nothing to be proud of. The truth is, Charles, I have been a dull dog all my life and though it is too late to do anything about it now, you can at least ruin my reputation when I am gone. My nephew thinks that I have a whole cupboardful of skeletons, whereas you know only too well that all my cupboards are bare. Now I really do not want to disappoint the boy. He thinks the fortune he is about to inherit is ill-gotten and I wouldn't want him to think it wholly untainted. Do you think you could arrange for a mistress or two and a few unpaid gambling debts? Among my papers you could easily plant receipts for a luxurious apartment in Belgravia tenanted by a mysterious Mme de St Victoire and a letter from a non-existent gambling syndicate demanding payment for huge losses at whist and chemin-de-fer. I've been a good master to you, haven't I, Charles? Surely you won't refuse me this last request?"

Of course I wouldn't – and didn't. Unlike the favour demanded by Joe's master, this one exposed me to no danger. I was not required to purloin anything or to corrupt a lady's maid; I merely had to supply the means to sully a hitherto untarnished reputation. I had no regrets and set about my task with relish. As a result my master sleeps easily in his grave and his nephew was – and is – delighted. Far from having an uncle who was a dull dog, he now has one who proved to be a dark horse, tempering debauchery with discretion. And as such, the nephew tells his friends, an example to us all.

My master rewarded me generously for my services with the result that I was able to go into partnership with Joe Hancock as a maker and mender of reputations. I forget which of us first came up with the title 'retrospective destinator', but that was how we thought of ourselves and how we described ourselves to our clients. But how were we to find our clients? How were our clients, assuming that there were any such, to find us? In the early days of our partnership those were pressing questions. Using the money left us by our late masters we took a lease on consulting rooms in Sydenham and drew up an advertisement whose wording we reached only after much discussion. 'Retrospective destinators,' it read. 'Messrs Hancock and Breeze offer a discreet service as makers and menders of damaged or incomplete reputations.' We ran the advertisement for five consecutive days in *The Times*, *The Morning Chronicle* and *The Manchester Examiner* and sat back to await the response.

Our first client was the Rev. Dr Theodore Moon, a fellow of Balliol College, Oxford, who asked us if we would do him the honour of calling on him at our earliest convenience. He was, he explained to us, an epigraphist – that is to say, an expert in Greek and Roman inscriptions. In a long and scholarly life he had spent a good deal of time in Italy, deciphering the messages with which the Romans had adorned their monuments. During the many long and glorious summers he had spent in Rome, Pompeii and Herculaneum, he had led an exemplary life such as befitted a Protestant clergyman in a Catholic country. But although Italy had offered him many temptations, he had resisted them all, believing foolishly that celibacy and scholarship were their own rewards. Well, they were not and it was now too late to do anything about it.

"Or at least that is what I had supposed," he concluded, "until I saw your advertisement in *The Morning Chronicle*."

"And what precisely do you wish us to do?" asked Joe.

"I wish you to re-visit all my lost opportunities, so that my colleagues here at Balliol will think that they were not lost but embraced wholeheartedly. Amongst my papers, which naturally I shall leave to the College, I wish there to be scores of billets doux from amorous signorinas which suggest that my summers in Italy were not wholly devoted to scholarship. Although I can speak Italian tolerably well, my hand, as you will have observed from my letter, is no longer vigorous and could by no stretch of the imagination pass for that of an Italian woman in the prime of life.

Nor have I any notion of what a billet doux from a hot-blooded signorina might actually sound like. And there is a further requirement. When my funeral is over and my will published, I should like the Master of Balliol to receive a letter from Italy from someone describing herself as my donna amata and demanding to pay for a memorial tablet in the Chapel on which will be inscribed the words: PLVS INERAT QVAM VIDERI POTERAT, vidilicet There Was More To Him Than Met The Eye. Well," he concluded, "do you think you can do it?"

"It will be an honour," replied Joe.

"Oh, this will set tongues wagging and no mistake", he chuckled, "and not just in Balliol. Just imagine the sly glances at high table as all the dons start wondering whether I was the only one living a double life. Do you know, I begin to think of myself as a public benefactor. It is not given to every man to create a climate where his fellows can bask in reflected infamy."

Joe and I did our work well. At Balliol Theodore Moon is remembered both as an epigraphist of note, as well as a man of prodigious appetites, a combination that eluded him during his lifetime but which we were able to furnish after his death. At Evensong in the college chapel many is the don whose eye still rests enviously on his memorial tablet. How curious, they think, that an epigraphist who had revealed the secrets of so many inscriptions should have failed to conceal the secret of his own. And that, of course, was precisely what Theodore Moon, a man whose secret was that he had no secret, had wanted them to think.

The Moon case was followed by a string of others which we brought to more or less successful conclusions. There was the case of the Dorset corn chandler who wished it to be known posthumously that in a drunken rage he had sold his wife at Weyhill Fair. We supplied more than one country parson with a mistress and, in one case, two. And then there were Mr and Mrs Henry Bellinger, an elderly couple to whom the best and worst of fates had befallen. They had gone to Epsom, where he backed an outsider at 40 to 1 and she bought a half share in a lottery ticket. Both of them won and they went home twelve thousand pounds better off. But what had at first seemed a blessing soon seemed a curse. The Bellingers were over eighty, he with rheumy eyes, she with swollen ankles. Can you imagine anything worse than being invited to life's feast but having no teeth to chew the viands? Henry Bellinger had been a clerk in the East India Company and had supplemented his modest income by acting as pew opener to the local squire and his family. Had he never wondered, I asked, what it would be like for someone to open the pew for him? His eyes shone. Frequently, he said. And so were born Sir Hector and Lady Bella Burton-Bellinger of Bucks, a gentry family whom Joe and I inserted into the crevices of history by means of a few additions to the documentary record. We found an expired family – the Burtons – in a part of the country where the Bellingers were unknown and grafted a forgotten cadet branch on to the main stem. Of course, twelve thousand pounds could not restore the Burton-Bellingers to their former glory. What it could buy them, however, was a little swank – an entry in Debrett's, a family pew in the church, a new escutcheon over the Burton almshouses (now, of course, the Burton-Bellinger almshouses), a lapdog for Lady Bella. In a final posthumous flourish, Joe and I commissioned at their expense a new east window for the parish church, in which their coat of arms sits alongside those of the diocese and His Excellency the Duke of Wellington, whom they claimed as a personal friend.

The Burton-Bellingers went to their grave – a rather splendid affair guarded by four beefy angels – posthumously fulfilled, or, as Joe and I preferred to call it, 'retrospectively destinated'. For Joe and me, however, the Burton-Bellinger case did not end happily. Not to put too fine a point on it, we quarrelled. By the time our clients had shuffled off their mortal coil, they were beginning to acquire expensive tastes which could only be afforded if we waived our fee. This I was happy to do. I had greatly enjoyed conjuring a fictitious family out of the omissions of history; moreover, I could see possibilities in the Burton-Bellinger case which we had scarcely begun to realise. Why not, I suggested to Joe, invent a complete identity – town house, coat of arms, liveried footmen, the lot – and hire it out to self-made men anxious for a little pedigree. To be sure, we would have to borrow, but there must be armies of Manchester cotton kings or Staffordshire potters who would enjoy slipping on the mantle of gentility for a few days. Why, Joe, I said, there is a fortune in it. Joe, still smarting from the fact that I had allowed the Burton-Bellingers to squander our fee, disagreed. I accused him of having no sense of poetry, of being in it simply for the money. To which he replied it was a good job somebody was, because if it had been left to me we should be bankrupt. Tempers flared. He called me a day dreamer. To my eternal shame, I called him a gaolbird. Thus ended a fruitful and invigorating partnership. Joe helped himself to half the petty cash, for which he insisted on a written receipt, threw his keys on the table and walked out, saying he was d___d if he would ever work with me again. To my everlasting regret he has kept his word.

Without Joe my schemes came to nothing. Not only did I need the money he had withdrawn from the partnership, but I missed his help and – yes, I freely confess it – his comradeship. Perhaps Joe felt the same about me, for I learned that he had returned to his old trade – that is, the mending rather than the making of reputations. That, of course, left me free to pursue mine, though on a more modest scale than I would have wished.

And that is where the mad wives came in ...

The mad wives, however, were delayed by an unscheduled stop at Pluckley. The train came to a halt between white clapboarded buildings, beyond which the rooks rose in a great clamour from the trees by the gravel pits. From our tub we could see porters assembling a goods train in the siding, a fly waiting in the station yard, its owner fast asleep on the box, and the station master's wife trying to cut chrysanthemums from a flower bed with a pair of nail scissors. A man reading the *East Kent Gazette* frowned when the band struck up with 'Elsie from Chelsea' and positively glowered when Stumps jumped up on the seat and joined in the chorus.

"Does no-one wish to hear about my mad wives?" asked Breeze plaintively

"Of course we do," replied Miss Osgood.

"Stumps doesn't," remarked Purselove, "or he wouldn't be singing that ghastly tune. Do shut up, there's a good fellow."

"Well, I most certainly do, Mr Breeze," I declared, "but before you proceed, I must find out why we are delayed. Our first scheduled stop was to have been at Tunbridge."

I jumped down from the tub and walked along the platform to the head of the train. Anxious faces peered from the second class carriages and one or two choleric gentlemen waved their pocket watches at me. Sturdee, by contrast, seemed quite unconcerned and was using the opportunity to polish Hengist's name plate with an oily rag.

"Will we be delayed for long?" I asked. "We have a steamboat to catch to Pimlico Pier."

"That depends on signals," he replied.

"And what do signals depend on?"

"Who knows?" he replied. "Signals is signals."

Beyond that he had nothing to say. To him it was a sufficient explanation that a higher providence acting through pulleys and wires had halted the train and that nothing was to be done except polish the brass and admire the flower beds. For his part, he said, he had preferred it when there were men beside the line with flags. At least you could look your man in the eye when you passed. Sometimes he'd wave, sometimes he'd swear. But whichever it was, it was more human – or, as he had it, 'yooman' – than wires and pulleys, which were anything but. I sensed that Sturdee was warming to a theme on which had a great deal to say, none of which would indicate how long we would be delayed. I walked back along the platform.

By now many of the passengers had alighted from both the tubs and the second-class carriages and were stretching their legs on the platform, some admiring the chrysanthemums, others shouting encouragement to the porters rolling the trucks in the siding. The single first class carriage at the head of the train, however, remained sealed, its blinds – at least on the platform side – lowered. Culpepper, who had been deep in conversation with a fellow clergyman and his friend, called me over to introduce them.

"Blackwood," he said, "let me introduce you to Dr Erasmus leGrove, the diocesan exorcist, and his friend Mr Samuel Dacre, the ecclesiastical architect and follower of Mr Pugin." Dr leGrove was an imposing figure with ruddy cheeks, heavy eyebrows and huge hands; his companion, by contrast, was compact and elegant, almost dandyish, with eyebrows so fair that it seemed at first glance that he had none at all.

"My apologies, Dr leGrove," I said. "It was no part of my plan to stop at Pluckley."

"I am, sir," replied Dr leGrove ponderously, "no stranger to Pluckley. Would it surprise you to learn that it is the most haunted village in England? At the last count there were ten manifestations and that does not include the poltergeist in the village inn."

"If I were the landlord of the village inn," remarked Mr Dacre, "I should very much want my poltergeist to be included in the total."

"No doubt you are right," conceded Dr leGrove. "From a professional point of view, however, poltergeists are very small beer. A broken teacup here, a banging door there. A poltergeist may haunt one's premises, but an apparition who knows his business haunts the imagination as well. I can purify bricks and mortar of their taint, but the human imagination is proof against my prayers and perhaps that is as it should be."

"I sometimes wonder," observed Mr Dacre, "whether our understanding of ghosts is not entirely mistaken. What if they are not visitors from the past, but from the future? What if someone in the future, near or distant, were to visit us in imagination, to populate our own time with figures conjured out of thin air – might they not appear to us as ghosts? And what if we – you, me, everyone on this train – were to be merely a reservoir, a set of possibilities from which future imaginings may be drawn, what then?"

"Ignore my friend," declared Dr leGrove; "he does not mean these things seriously. Many are offended by his speculations – Mr Alford, the Dean, for one – but I find they soothe the tedium of a long journey."

Prompted by a whistle from Hengist, the two guards began to usher people back on to the train.

"Ah, I believe we are being summoned to join our travelling companions," said Dr leGrove. "I should have liked to introduce you to those in my carriage, Mr Blackwood, but time, it seems, will not permit."

"As organiser of this excursion," I replied, "I can claim a certain privilege in being able to move freely between carriages. At Tunbridge, where we are to make a scheduled stop, I shall join you and you may introduce me to whomsoever you please. Until then, I shall join my travelling companions in the tub. One of them has reached a climax in the story he has been telling us and is about to plunge his hero into misfortune. I would not miss it for the world."

"Stories, eh?" said Dr leGrove. "I could tell you a tale or two, believe me."

"And so could I," added Mr Dacre.

"Then I shall most definitely join you at Tunbridge," I replied.

As I climbed aboard the tub, I thought of Serafina, reciting *The Lay of the Last Minstrel* to Palmerston in the gloom of the upstairs sitting room and wished I could telegraph her the news that my treasury of stories was filling up and that the future of the Ebenezer was a little less uncertain as a consequence. But then, I reflected, she was not privy to my design and I must hug my stories to myself in secret.

Where were we? Ah yes, the mad wives, I believe, said Breeze, after the train, with a rattle of connecting chains, had resumed its journey. After the publication of *Jane Eyre* mad wives were quite the thing. Where men like Theodore Moon had yearned for Italian signorinas, my clients now yearned for mad wives in the attic, or cellar, or, in one case, an abandoned coal barge on the Shropshire Canal. No-one suspected that these cackling relics were anything but what they seemed. It never occurred to anyone that they might be, as it were, authored. Until, that is, two of them turned up on the same spot.

Two years ago I was visited in my consulting room by a Smithfield poulterer named Lionel Stagg. Now I always prided myself on having a rapport with my clients, but with Stagg I had none. He was a clammy man, with pale cheeks, heavy eyelids and a handshake that felt like a freshly plucked chicken. Without any preliminaries he stated the details of his case. He had, he explained, spent a good deal of his fortune on trying to recover his estranged wife Elfrida, who had put herself beyond his reach by fleeing to Baden-Baden with her son by a previous marriage. This son, this viper on whom he had showered every affection, was the cause of all his misfortunes. The youth had never reconciled himself to his mother's second marriage, fearing perhaps that it would lead to his being disinherited. After only a few months he had persuaded his mother to embrace exile in Germany rather than perform her duties in the marital home. Those were the very words he used, and I could not help shuddering in distaste.

"And now," he concluded, "to the crime of desertion she has added that of infidelity. Some months ago she yielded to of one of those gallants who do the rounds of the fashionable spas – Baden-Baden, Marienbad, Aix-les-Bains – in a never-ending whirl of seductions and bad debts. She thinks I don't know, but I have my spies, Mr Breeze, I have my spies."

"So what do you wish me to do?" I asked, desperately trying to think of an excuse for refusing his commission.

"Since she flaunts her lover in my face," he said, "I wish for one to flaunt in hers. My health is not good, Mr Breeze. I suffer from occlusion of the arteries and my doctors tell me that I have not long to live. Time is, therefore, of the essence. You have heard, I take it, of *Jane Eyre*, an absurd romance by someone with the unlikely name of Currer Bell?"

Well, you may guess the rest. The monster wished me to supply a mad wife, not in the abstract, but in the flesh. At his funeral he wanted her to appear at the graveside amongst the mourners and, once the interment had actually taken place, jump up and down on his coffin. And the point of this? To make his estranged wife jealous, to make her realise that the man whom she had cast aside like a worn-out glove was a man to whom the passions were not unknown.

"But how can you be sure," I asked, "that your wife and stepson will attend the funeral, for without them there would surely be no point in the deception?"

"I have already written a letter," he said, "in which I forgive them both and promise them a generous settlement in my will. On my death you will send it to them. You may be sure that either greed or shame will compel their appearance at the graveside. Name any fee, you like, Mr Breeze. And remember that you will also have the satisfaction of righting a great wrong."

I accepted.

Amongst the mourners at the graveside, it was not hard to identify Mrs Lionel Stagg and her son. They were marked out by their red hair, hers peeping coyly from the edges of her bonnet, his erupting in fiery side whiskers which he smoothed continually with his black-gloved hand. Somehow one always expects burials to take place on wet days. Black umbrellas and mud on the parson's gaiters are as much part of the English funeral as goose is of Christmas dinner. But Stagg's did not oblige. It was too hot for grief. The undertakers and mourners were perspiring heavily beneath their top hats and veils; even the horses' black plumes seemed to wilt in the heat. Stagg's relict remembered now and then to dab her eyes with a handkerchief and her son to grimace dutifully. As for the rest, eminent men, most of them, in the poultry trade, they looked on unmoved as the coffin was lowered into the grave. Then, suddenly, on to this scene of enervating heat and emotional torpor burst the mad wife.

Clad entirely in black, bareheaded and barefoot, she burst through the throng of mourners and threw herself into the grave. The suddenness of her appearance took me by surprise, as did the language in which she poured forth her pent-up griefs. From the depths of the grave came a torrent of what sounded like Spanish. This was odd, because the actress whom I had coached was to vent her feelings in French. I had no time to reflect on her departure from the script, for no sooner had she disappeared into the grave and started drumming on the coffin lid with her fists, than a second figure burst through the mourners and followed her into the pit. She, too, was bareheaded and barefoot, though her dress was more ragged and her hair was decked with scarlet ribbons. This was the actress I had trained and, to do her credit, she was playing her part splendidly.

But where had the first figure come from? I looked across the mouth of the grave and saw the stepson grin broadly. Could he, I wondered, have had the same idea as his stepfather? But that was absurd. What possible motive could he have had for doing such a thing? Meanwhile the sounds of mock grief which had come from the grave gave way to sounds of tearing cloth and yelps of pain. This drama was by now attracting a crowd of onlookers. Mourners at a funeral in a neighbouring plot had quietly abandoned their own obsequies to join ours. And one could scarcely blame them. After all, it isn't every day that the coffin of a Smithfield poulterer attracts such controversy. The vicar appealed for calm and, being ignored, disappeared into the pit, followed by one of the undertaker's mutes. Between them the two men dragged out first one mad wife then the other.

I began to feel alarmed for my safety. Although I was standing at a little distance from the funeral party, I was still close enough to be recognised by my own mad wife. I sidled away, taking refuge behind a large cedar tree. To my surprise the space into which I crept was already occupied. I was about to apologise when a familiar voice said: "Charles!"

"Joe!"

"What brings you here?"

"I might ask the same of you."

"I came to watch my mad wife."

"And so did I!"

And so it came out, this tale of the two mad wives. Mine had been commissioned partly to spite Mrs Stagg and partly to restore my client's reputation amongst his colleagues, by whom he wanted to be remembered as the devil of a fellow. Joe's, on the other hand, had been commissioned by the stepson to mend his mother's reputation. As a runaway wife she had been an object of suspicion; as the victim of bigamy she would, he reasoned, become an object of sympathy. Now, with her reputation restored, she might hope to make a respectable third marriage. Of course, Elfrida had known nothing of this scheme. It was the son, he of the fiery whiskers, who had approached Joe with a view to making his mother a respectable woman.

After this hurried exchange of stories, Joe and I thought to make ourselves scarce. A glance round the trunk of the tree revealed that hostilities at the graveside had ceased and been replaced by animated discussion. Doubtless the truth would soon be revealed and fingers pointed.

Joe and I parted on good terms and I have neither seen him nor heard of him since. Whether or not he acts as a retrospective destinator, I do not know. Somehow I doubt it. After the tragicomedy of Lionel Stagg's funeral I did not feel it safe to continue. I removed the brass plate from the door, abandoned my consulting rooms and set myself up as an advertising copywriter. Whereas I used to clothe unremarkable people with a glamour they did not possess, I now do the same for anything from patent medicines to chutney. Fossett's Electuary, Dean's Relish – how they have poured out of my pen! You might even say that I am plying the same trade.

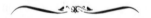

Since his spirited defence of mercury, Mr Humphrey Ezard had contributed little to our conversations. After it he had lapsed, exhausted, into the sickly torpor which seemed to be his natural state. Culpepper concluded that he was in mourning and that it was grief rather than sickness which inhibited his intercourse with the other passengers.

"Might I enquire if your loss was a recent one?" he asked

Ezard looked up startled. His face was deathly pale and as he spoke I noticed that he had several teeth missing.

"July, Mr Culpepper," he replied, shaking his head sadly. "Barely three months, yet the remembrance is still green."

"Was it a close relative you lost"?

"Not a close relative, no. More, I should say, a kindred spirit. I speak, of course, of the late M. Louis Daguerre, who left us in July, his great work scarcely begun."

From the exchange of baffled glances which followed this remark, I could see that the name of M. Daguerre was unknown to all but Turpin, who nodded in sympathy.

"And what was his great work precisely?" I asked.

"To impress on plates of metal a record of the phaenomenal world more complete, more accurate than any engraving."

"But how," enquired Turpin, "does one get the phaenomenal world to attach itself to a metal plate? Pray do not spare the details. We men of science can never have detail enough."

The same cannot, of course, be said of readers, who are quickly surfeited. I shall hurry, therefore, over Ezard's account of how he prepared silver-plated sheets of copper with an alarming mixture of chemicals, chlorine and cyanide among them, and how he released the final impression from the plate with fumes of mercury. This, declared Ezard, was the most miraculous part of the process, the part that most resembled alchemy, where blind chemicals reassembled themselves into a simulacrum of the world. In loving detail he described how he would heat mercury in a shallow dish and how he would immerse himself in the rising vapours the better to see the impression emerge from the plate.

His explanation was briefly interrupted when a gust of wind blew a dense cloud of black smoke from the locomotive over the passengers in the tubs. Ezard was the first to emerge, coughing violently and wiping his eyes with a rag which looked as if it had been used to mop up chemicals in his studio.

"So what kind of impressions do you take, Mr Ezard?" asked Mr Meek.

"Those of you who have visited my studio will know that I specialise in portraits, both family and funerary," he replied, when he had recovered his breath. "Grieving parents and deceased children are something of a speciality. But my great ambition is to produce a work of art worthy of M. Daguerre and worthy, too, of my late father."

"You surely can't pretend," said Meek incredulously, "that daguerreotypes are art."

"That's rich coming from a man who thinks that a lump of lard can be called a sculpture," scoffed Purselove.

"Not only are daguerreotypes art," persisted Ezard, "it is my fervent belief that soon they will be the only art of any consequence."

"Well said," nodded Turpin. "The march of science sweeps all before it."

"Tell us about your great work, Mr Ezard," said Miss Lark, "and tell us about your father. You evidently thought highly of him."

"My father," began Ezard, "was a drawing master with ambitions to be a portrait painter, an ambition in which he never succeeded, either because his sitters were bad payers, or because they neglected to recommend him to their friends and acquaintances."

"Or could it have been," suggested Purselove, "that he simply wasn't up to the job? I think that's what you're trying to tell us, isn't it, Ezard?"

"I think that is what I am trying to avoid telling you," replied Ezard, "though I fear that what you say is true. All the same, the baldness of your statement is exquisitely painful to me. A man of feeling would not have said such a thing."

"Shame on you, Mr Purselove," rebuked Miss Lark.

"In order to support his wife and, in due course, his son, he was forced to take in work as an engraver. Much as he disliked such drudgery – he once described himself as a bee who pollinated the blooms of others but stored up little honey for himself – he was good at the work and soon established a reputation as an engraver of skill and delicacy. But the work was exacting and his sight, never strong, began to suffer. Within a few days of finishing an engraving on which he had laboured with more than usual care, he went blind and, though with rest, the optic nerve recovered sufficiently to admit a little sight, his engraving days were done."

"But what was the tale that so occupied his thoughts and devoured his sight?" asked Miss Lark.

"It was," sighed Ezard, "an illustration to the tale of Orlando Piper, a painter who, like my father, had been reduced to taking in engravings and lost his sight as a consequence. Here it is."

The Daguerreotypist's Tale of A Midlands Mona Lisa

Piper, an ambitious young painter with a studio in the shadow of Nottingham Castle, bought his wife a lace collar for her birthday. It was of local make and, on the chance of securing a commission, he wrote to the manufacturer, saying that he would esteem it an honour to paint his portrait. To his surprise he received a reply by return, instructing him to call at the offices of Mr Joshua Brinklow in the Lace Market at his earliest convenience. Since Piper had little work on hand, he hastened to comply.

"My daughter Arabella", explained Brinklow, "attends a finishing school on the South Coast. Like any dutiful father, I wish her to marry well. A brewing or banking heir would be acceptable, a Leicestershire squire with leafy acres even more so. I need a portrait to hang on the drawing room wall to whet the appetites of rich suitors. Will you do it?"

"Gladly," said Piper.

"Then I shall send her to you when she is next home on holiday. At present she is with her schoolfellows on a sight-seeing tour of Paris. Now if I might have your signature on this contract."

Piper hurried home to tell his wife, who was decoupaging a screen with pictures of bridges and viaducts.

"I am delighted for you, Orlando," she said. "Where Brinklow leads others must surely follow. This commission will be the making of you. Now tell me. Here I have an empty corner. Should I fill it with the Menai Straits Bridge or the Maidenhead Viaduct?"

Bella Brinklow proved to be a timid creature with downcast eyes and mousy hair; she deferred to her father in everything and showed little excitement at being married to a bank or brewery, let alone a portion of leafy Leicestershire. On the other hand, she was the perfect sitter: she did not fidget, nor did she distract the painter with empty chatter. All the same, Piper was dissatisfied. It was a maxim of his that sitters in good portraits always look as if they are about to get up and leave the canvas. Yet Bella refused to oblige. Despite his best efforts, she remained resolutely chair-bound.

"What she lacks in spirit, you must make up with frills and furbelows", advised his wife. "Why don't you dress her in the lace collar you bought me and borrow a few trinkets from my dressing table? I think you'll find they will make all the difference."

She was right. Almost immediately, he sensed a living presence taking shape beneath his brush. It soon became clear, however, that it would take more than a collar and a trinket or two to fatten up this silly little goose for her Leicestershire squire. She needed jewellery more brilliant than anything his wife could supply and backgrounds grander than his studio could furnish. So without telling his wife, he began to borrow items from the house – a tortoiseshell comb here, a Chinese vase there – and, when they proved insufficiently splendid, to borrow items from friends in return for autographed sketches of their children and pets. As Bella bloomed, the demands she made, though silent, grew ever more clamorous. There came a day when he needed a ruby brooch and none of his friends could – or would – oblige. He had no alternative but to hire. He found a jeweller in Long Row. The fee was extortionate, the deposit atrocious, but he reasoned that the brooch was the finishing touch and that when, on account of the portrait, Bella made her brilliant marriage, some of the credit would belong to him and his future would be assured.

When Bella arrived for her next sitting, she resumed the previous day's posture with her characteristic indifference. Watching her carefully, he removed the brooch from its velvet case with a flourish and held it up to the light.

"Magnificent, is it not?" he asked, scarcely expecting a reply.

"On the contrary," she said, "it is hideously provincial. Take it away."

Piper gazed at her in astonishment. Not only had she spoken for the first time, she had spoken as one unused to being contradicted. On the easel in front of him the canvas seemed to shrink and fade.

"And now we will continue if you please," she said, "though not before you have changed the flowers on the mantelpiece. The blooms are fading. I marvel that you did not notice for yourself."

Stuttering an apology, Piper rang the bell and ordered the maidservant to send out for fresh flowers.

"These sittings have already lasted far too long," she continued. "If the picture is not finished within the next two weeks, I shall go elsewhere. I have already instructed papa to make enquiries."

Next day he received a letter from her in a strong, masculine hand, informing him that in future she intended to wear green velvet and expected him to provide the emeralds to go with it. According to the contract, dresses and fabrics were to be at her father's charge, baubles and furnishings at his. "You will find it," she concluded, "in the last paragraph." And when he came to examine it, there it was, as plain as could be.

A wise man would have found an excuse to free himself from such an engagement. But Orlando was no longer wise. He was infatuated. She was suddenly both desirable and beyond desire. What she wished for herself, he wished for, too. And in this, he realised, he had come to resemble her father, whose aspirations she embodied as fully as if they had been her own. If she wanted to marry a Leicestershire squire, then no sacrifice, no hardship would be too great to help her.

The next day he took the first step on the road to ruin by visiting the jeweller in Long Row. The jeweller would not agree to an exchange of brooches, insisting that an emerald brooch would be a new transaction and would therefore incur a new fee, not to mention a new deposit. Until now Piper had always been a man who kept his affairs tidy and regarded the whole business of bills and promissory notes with horror. Yet this was the very expedient to which he was now reduced. He persuaded a friend to put his name to the back of a bill for a hundred and fifty pounds at six months' date and took it to a money lender.

That evening he returned the studio, lit a candle and gazed at the portrait. To his astonishment he found himself staring at his wife's lace cuffs and sapphire engagement ring, all painted in meticulous detail. He must surely be dreaming. He lit a second candle, then a third, only to find that on the mantelpiece behind the sitter was his wife's linnet in its cage. And there, by the door, was the screen with Maidenhead Viaduct. As for Bella herself, she looked more radiant, more imperious than ever. After supper, during which he and his wife sat in silence, Piper made his excuses and went in search of the magically transposed items. None was in its accustomed place. The ring he found in the scullery, the lace cuffs between the rollers of the mangle and the cage, door open and occupant flown, in the cupboard under the stairs. What had happened to the screen, he never discovered.

This pattern soon repeated itself. Valuables would be, as it were, sucked out of the Pipers' private quarters, squeezed dry and then cast aside in some neglected corner of the house, faded and exhausted. And for every such depletion an added brilliance appeared in the person of Bella. Her lips grew fuller, her eyes brighter and the curl that fell in front of her ear was so soft, so lustrous that he could scarce restrain himself from stroking it.

Although he managed to conceal the changes in the picture from his wife, it was impossible to hide the trail of destruction in the house. At first she blamed the maidservant and he, to his shame, allowed her to do so; later, her suspicions alighted on him and were met with evasiveness.

"Only a few more days, my love," he told her. "That is all I need to finish the work. Then all the secrecy, all the mysterious disappearances will be explained and you will see that it has been worthwhile."

So proud was Piper of his work that he did not doubt that Bella would accept it. Why, it seemed no longer an imitation of the original but an extension of her very presence. She could not but be ravished by it. No other painter could have done anything half so fine. All the same, to ensure Bella's acceptance, Piper persuaded a fellow portraitist to put his name to a bill of two hundred pounds with which he purchased a gilt frame of such exuberance that she could not, he reasoned, but be won over by it.

She was not. When he presented the finished work, she refused to examine it until he had removed the frame. "I have no intention," she said, "of being the subject of a painting where the frame – especially a frame of such hideous vulgarity – outshines the sitter." With sinking heart, Piper obeyed and watched as she scrutinised the picture. For a long time she remained silent, examining the canvas inch by inch. As her eye travelled over the picture, the light seemed to go out of it. The jewels lost their brilliance, the velvets their bloom and the kissing curl above her ear its irresistible tactility.

"When I was in Paris," she said at last, "I was introduced to a salon where the women wore turbans in memory of Mme de Stael. I was only a schoolgirl, but the women, some of whom remembered Stendhal and Byron, accepted me as one of their own. My father knew nothing of this and would not have understood if I had told him. He wishes me to become the wife of a booby squire, so that he can brag of it to his fellow tradesmen. I shall, of course, consent. For me there is no Parisian salon, only a corner of leafy Leicestershire. That is to be my portion in life. I embrace it with a ready smile and an inward shudder. My father sees only the ready smile. You, too, saw only what you wanted to see. That is why I reject your portrait."

There was worse to follow. Not only did Bella refuse the picture, but his wife, who had observed the little drama unobserved from the doorway, rejected her husband, declaring that she could no longer stay with a man who had squandered his prospects so recklessly. She would pack what was left of her belongings and throw herself on the mercy of her sister in Derby, who shared her taste for bridges and viaducts.

"And should she refuse to take you in, my dear," said Bella, smiling odiously, "then I am sure my father would find work for you in his mill."

Orlando's wife fled weeping. Bella, insisting that her offer was kindly meant, followed her out of the studio. Piper was left alone.

Here Ezard paused and seemed to be fighting for breath.

"I think we may guess what happened next," said Miss Lark. "He was forced to take in engravings, was he not?"

Ezard nodded.

Though he was indeed forced to pawn the frame, he refused to let the portrait out of his sight. Whatever Bella may have thought, he knew it to be his finest work and vowed never to part with it. This obstinacy cost him dear. Work came in irregularly. He quickly discovered that one of the oddities of poverty is that needy tradesman are less likely to be paid than prosperous ones. Little by little he pawned the few belongings he had, starting with the gilded frame and a silver pocket watch with fighting cocks enamelled on the dial. When they had gone, he abandoned his studio and took rooms in one of the poorer parts of the city. He ate the bread of adversity, which contained more sawdust than flour, and drank the waters of affliction, which issued in a rusty trickle from the pump in the yard.

On the day he pawned his last pearl button, he was visited by a servant of Bella, who, having married her Leicestershire squire, now went by the name of Lady Stirrup. It was a year since she had refused his portrait. Now, it seemed, she wanted to borrow it.

"Naturally," said the emissary," she is prepared to pay twenty guineas for the privilege. Quite a temptation for a poor man, I imagine."

"Leonardo never let the Mona Lisa out of his sight," replied Piper." It travelled with him wherever he went. And so shall my painting with me. I will not part with it."

"Then I am authorised to increase my offer to thirty guineas. Think how many engravings you would have to do to earn thirty guineas. Come now, you cannot afford to refuse."

"But why is she willing to pay so handsomely to borrow a picture that she disliked so much in the first place?"

"Ah," replied the emissary, "now we come to the heart of the matter."

The heart of the matter was that Lady Stirrup was to have her portrait painted as a wedding present from her fox-hunting husband, who, although he professed to know nothing about pictures, had thought it would be a fine thing to see her hanging above the mantelpiece. Bella had thought so, too, and suggested that it would be even finer if, within the new painting, there appeared on the wall behind her the earlier portrait by Orlando, the one picture, as it were, framing the other. The new painting was all but complete: all it lacked was Orlando's as the finishing touch.

"Such a delicious caprice, is it not?" chuckled the servant." And so very like her. As for your beloved picture, it will be back before you have time to miss it."

With heavy heart Piper agreed. Anticipating his consent, the servant had come armed with brown paper and string. Soon the portrait was trussed up and handed into Arabella's carriage. Clutching the purse of guineas, Piper watched as the brougham and its precious cargo disappeared into an opaline Nottingham smog.

A week went by. He toyed desultorily with other work, but his thoughts were elsewhere. He took to counting the days and, as the fortnight drew to a close, the hours. When, finally, it expired, he kept vigil by the window, watching for the brougham to return with the picture on the back seat. But the brougham did not come, not that day, or the next. He wrote a frantic letter to Bella, who did not reply. Unable to wait any longer, he engaged a local carrier to take him into Leicestershire with a view to recovering his property, if necessary by force.

Stirrup Hall was a modest country seat with a rookery behind and a croquet lawn before. In the carriage sweep stood a line of vehicles, two landaus prominent amongst them. Their drivers looked on disdainfully as Piper climbed down from the cart and marched up the front steps, only to be told by a footman that the servants' quarters were round the back.

"Fancy not remembering that," scoffed one of the coachmen, when Piper, propelled by the footman's boot, landed at his feet.

Preceded by the carter, Piper made his way round the side of the house, where he heard, coming from an open casement, the sound of well-mannered applause. He paused to watch as a polite company gathered before a portrait which hung above the fireplace.

"May I propose a toast?" said a man in a double-breasted scarlet waistcoat. "Would you please raise your glasses to Augustus Derby, the painter, who, having finished with my wife, is about to set to work on my dogs. Take whatever liberties you like with my wife, I told him – pull her in here, plump her out there – but have a care with my dogs. Get them wrong and I'll set the whole d——d pack on you."

The company tittered politely and raised their glasses, whereupon Augustus Derby stepped forward in dazzling white linen and velvet necktie and protested that he was merely pursuing his vocation.

"The toast," he added modestly, "rightly belongs to the sitter, whose merry company made light work of my task. Would that all my subjects were so easy to please."

At this point, Bella, wearing the same green velvet and emerald choker that appeared in the portrait, stepped forward. But it was not her finery that attracted Piper's attention: it was his own masterpiece – or rather the hideous travesty of it that hung above the fireplace in Derby's picture. It was a crude paraphrase, an image deliberately debased in order to lend brilliance to the painting which contained it.

"You will notice," said Bella, pointing to the portrait, "that I appear twice –
first as you see me now, as mistress of Stirrup Hall, and secondly as I was until oh
so very recently, a lump of wet clay waiting for the potter's hand. In Charles" – she
laid her hand on the scarlet waistcoat's arm – "I have found my potter." And at
that moment Piper could have sworn that her face assumed the faintest of smiles.

He crept away. His picture had been appropriated by a rival and fed to the
hostile canvas, like a moth dropped into a Venus fly trap. His only desire now was
to recover his own work. No matter that it was the ruin of his fortunes and his
marriage, he wanted it by him, asleep and awake, at work and at rest. But when
he asked in the servants' quarters, no-one could recall it. The servant who had
collected it from him was fetched and, irritated at being summoned from the
splendid company in the drawing room, feigned ignorance, but, when pressed,
remembered vaguely that he had seen something of the sort in the tack room.

"If you're lucky, it might still be there," he said; "if not, someone will have fed
it to the bonfire. Skip along now, look smart."

Piper needed no second bidding. There in the tack room was a package, the
string loosely knotted, the brown paper streaked with pigeon droppings. He seized
it eagerly and handed it to the carter, who wedged it between two boxes in the
back of his cart. During the long journey back to Nottingham, Piper resisted the
temptation to tear off the brown paper and look at his masterpiece, partly because
it had begun to rain and partly because he did not wish to share the moment
with anyone else. Once he was home, however, he lost no time in tearing open
the package. What he found was not the picture he had surrendered a fortnight
earlier, but the picture as quoted by Augustus Derby. The fabrics had lost their
gloss, the brilliants no longer scintillated, the linnet in its cage was a dull speck and
the flowers on the mantelpiece were curled and brown. As for Bella herself, she
was neither the mousy creature who had first sat before his easel, nor the disciple
of Mme de Stael, nor the mistress of Stirrup Hall. And yet, when he looked closely,
she was all three at once and perhaps many more besides. The same went for the
Mona Lisa smile she had somehow acquired. Was it mocking or triumphant or
self-pitying? Or indeed all of them simultaneously?

A few weeks later Piper received a letter from Lady Stirrup thanking him for
the loan of his picture and inviting him to Stirrup Hall to make drawings of the
new portrait with a view to engraving it. Needless to say, he declined, dedicating

himself to the recovery of his masterwork, his very own defaced Mona Lisa. By the light of a tallow candle, he strained his eyesight and memory to the uttermost to yield up all the intricacies of the lace and the jewellery but, since he could no longer afford either paint or canvas, he had to engrave them and, in so doing, brought upon himself the darkness in which no artist can work.

"And it was engraving this picture that cost your father his eyesight?" asked Miss Lark.

"It was as if a curse had leapt like an electrical spark between the two pictures," replied Ezard, "and it is that curse that I intend to exorcise. One day I shall produce a daguerreotype that captures the beauty of Orlando's original portrait. And for that I shall need frills and furbelows which I cannot at present afford. You may, however, rest assured that I shall not resort to issuing notes of hand or pawning my watch. All shall be earned honestly. Every last button and bauble shall be paid for. And then ..."

He paused.

"And then, Mr Ezard?" asked Miss Lark.

"Then all I shall need is a sitter. Would you care to oblige me, Miss Lark? I think you would do very well."

"I am flattered," she said, "but you will find in me neither a doormat nor a bluestocking and you will need someone who is both. Moreover, you will need a reliable sitter, someone who will be there whenever you need her. Alas, I can offer no such guarantee."

"Such a shame," said Ezard. "I can picture myself peering through the mercury fumes waiting for your image to emerge and for the curse to lift."

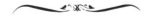

Before I proceed to George Costello's tale, I must say a little about how he came to enlist in the Buffs. It was widely believed that the

Corporal had wanted George to join his old regiment, the 27th Inniskillens, whilst George would have preferred to join no regiment at all, having set his heart on becoming a bandsman, like the ones he saw in the Old Palace Gardens. For months the father had insisted and the son demurred. Now the Corporal was not a man to threaten his son, but as a veteran of his country's wars, he felt it his due that his son should wear the Queen's uniform. In the end a compromise was reached, by which George became a bugler in the Buffs and moved to the barracks on the Margate Road. He still frequented the Old Palace Gardens, where in his scarlet uniform he cut a striking figure and was rarely seen without a girl on his arm and, not infrequently, two. But such companions were no more than passing flirtations, for according to rumour, George's heart was set on the daughter of a lieutenant in the —— shire Regiment, an unattainable beauty on whom he lavished trinkets and poetry of appalling ineptitude.

When his father urged him to tell the company something stirring, something manly – in other words, something as unlike Mr Ezard's tale as possible – , it was his own story, or a disguised version of it, that George now chose to tell. He tried to excuse himself by pretending that he had heard it in the barracks and insisting that the chaps there thought it manly enough, even though there was no actual fighting in it.

"Admit it," interrupted his father, "it's a love story, isn't it?".

"It is indeed a love story," confessed George, adding hastily, "though one that contains cockfighting, the bloody details of which I shall spare the ladies."

"Then why mention it at all?" asked Stumps. "Cockfighting is a bloody business."

"Which has now been made illegal," said Mr Beamish, "and rightly so."

"But a love story, nonetheless," said Miss Lark, "and so far that is something that we have been lacking."

"Bravo, George!" said Purselove. "Blood and feathers to please the Corporal, the tender passion to delight the ladies. A tour de force. Or would be were it not that what attracts the one repels the other. Proceed, and let us see who is delighted or repelled the most."

The Bugler's Tale of Red Spangle and Mr Henry

Howgill Senior, began George, named his firstborn Tertius after a pedigree fighting cock. When the boy was seven years old, he had a vision which haunted him for many years. Riding his pony across the Cat Bells, he crossed an unfamiliar beck and found himself in a valley where there should have been no valley at all. No doubt the mist was to blame, though he thought it odd that he should lose his way when, mist or no mist, he had never lost it before. For lost he most certainly was. More curious than fearful, he followed the stream into the valley. There a sudden squall of rain sent him running for a sheepfold, from which he saw a patch of sunlit turf hollowed out of the mist on the opposite bank. Into it rode a hunting party consisting of man in a tricorn hat and lace ruff, a girl of Tertius' age in a riding cloak and another man, possibly a servant, also dressed in tricorn hat and long riding boots. Each man was dressed in red and green and bore on his wrist a hawk, hooded and tethered, whilst the girl held aloft a gyrfalcon of silvery white. As he watched, she released the bird, which circled three four times over their heads before returning to her hand. Soon after, the rain swept across the beck and invaded the hollow space. For a moment the hunting party composed themselves into a tableau, the girl with the white falcon at the centre, the men in red and green on either side, before the rain thickened and hid them from view.

All this he remembered as a dream, though when, many years later, he told his father of it, he was soundly cuffed for his pains.

"One, it was no dream," growled his father; "two, you wasn't alone; four, you wasn't lost; three, you read too many damn novels, for which I blame your late mother; and, sixth, I was there, too."

"And the white gyrfalcon?" ventured Tertius.

"The gyrfalcon I grant you," replied his father. "It might have been. Or a hawk. One of the two, though I doubt it was white. Up in the hills there are still

people who think they can sit out the modern age in wigs and knee breeches. And
if there are still a few falconers among them, well, that couldn't surprise me."

Tertius was too young to recognise the irony in this verdict and his father
too dull-witted. Howgill Senior – 'The Sportsman' to his cronies – was as much
in danger of being overtaken by the modern age as the wig wearers of the hills.
A horse breaker by trade, he was well known in cockfighting circles. Not only
was his own bird, Red Spangle, the latest in a long line of champions to bear the
name, but the birds he supplied to the miners of Whitehaven were famous as far
afield as Barrow and the Solway. Challengers tried in vain to match them and in
tournaments of sixteen cocks and more (and on one celebrated occasion thirty-
two), Howgill's was always the last bird standing. For those who followed the sport,
he was a man one could simply not afford not to know. He was sought out by the
fishermen of Maryport, as well as by claret-faced squires who thought nothing of
staking half a year's rents on the latest Red Spangle. But it could not last. A wise
man would have seen that cockfighting belonged to a coarser age and would one
day follow bear baiting into oblivion. Bills had already been laid before Parliament
and failed. Had The Sportsman moved in anything but sporting circles he would
have known the respite was only temporary and returned to horse breaking.

When his son expressed distaste for the whole vile business, The Sportsman
urged him to remember where his bread came from and told him that if he wanted
to starve with a good conscience, then he was welcome to try. At other times, when
spirits had made him maudlin, he would take the boy into his confidence, telling
him how at his school in Grange-over-Sands the boys had paid 'cockpence' to the
master who bought and trained fighting cocks on their behalf. "Oh the excitement
of them Shrove Tuesday matches, Tertius," his father would say. "Those boyhood
moments, what can equal them? – when the desks were pushed back and the
classroom turned into a cockpit? How the feathers flew! How the boys cheered! Oh
youth, youth, whither art thou fled?" Then he would place his head in his hands
and sob loudly.

When he was sixteen, Tertius re-entered the secret valley. He had delivered a
pair of fighting cocks to a knife-grinder in Workington and, returning to Keswick
late in the day, found himself in a place strangely familiar. The day was bright
and there was a promise of frost. Dismounting from his horse, he watched the
stream wind between boulder-strewn slopes towards a tarn, on the far side of

which was a low manor house of dark stone. As he stood watching, the selfsame hunting party emerged, the men in tricorn hats, the girl – now a young woman – in velvet riding cloak, falcons poised on gauntleted hands. From the shelter of the sheepfold he watched them ride briskly along the valley, making towards the open fell. Before they reached it, they stopped opposite his place of concealment for the servant to adjust the master's stirrup. During that brief pause, the young woman glanced in his direction, as if she were aware of his presence – had indeed been expecting it – before releasing her gyrfalcon, which circled the sheepfold once and returned to her wrist. For a moment he half-hoped that he had been discovered. But if he had, she gave no sign and, spurring her horse, led the way out of the valley.

Once Tertius had found his way back into the valley, that second encounter had quickly been followed by a third and then by a fourth, in which he had no longer tried to conceal himself. After that it was easy to contrive a meeting with her on her own, for she was a fearless horsewoman who loved to fly Mr Henry, her gyrfalcon, unaccompanied. Anything, she said, to escape the tedium of life at Urmiston New Place. "Was ever a house so ill-named?" she asked. "There isn't a square inch of panelling that isn't green with mould or a window that doesn't look out on to that dreary tarn."

Her name was Artemis Temple. Her great-grandfather, having been one of the first to welcome the Young Pretender into Carlisle during the '45, was one of the first to be blamed when he retreated north of the border with the redcoats at his heels. He had found it prudent to retire to Urmiston New Place and shun county society. But what had been an expedient for Artemis's great-grandfather became a settled way of life with his descendants, who rarely ventured beyond the valley's end. That they ever attracted wives to this monastic solitude was remarkable, but manage it they did and somehow the Temple line struggled on, culminating in Artemis, the only child of the present Master of Urmiston. Of her mother she had little to say other than the fact that she had been enfeebled by childbirth and finished off by boredom.

When he was eighteen, Tertius Howgill proposed marriage to Artemis Temple and was refused. She had, she said, no intention, of being poor. Never again did she wish to live in a house with moss on the front steps and mildew on the bed linen. If he could offer her something better, there was no-one she would rather marry. It was an impossible condition. Instead he offered her a beautifully bound book on falconry which he had bought in Carlisle, having first sold a pair of his father's fighting cocks. The Sportsman was convulsed with rage when he found out, and, had he been sober enough, would have knocked his son down on the spot, but had, instead, to content himself with shooting songbirds in his neighbour's orchard.

Though hurt by Artemis's refusal, Tertius was unsurprised by it. For over a year he stayed away from Urmiston New Place and busied himself about his father's business, which, despite growing opposition in Parliament, continued to prosper. Affluence and infirmity – brought on, of course, by drink – softened The Sportsman. Instead of treating his son as an unpaid servant, he began to treat him as a partner. For the first time in his life Tertius found himself with money in his pocket and resolved to renew his suit to Artemis. He sent a letter to Urmiston New Place, inviting her to meet him at the sheepfold where he had first seen her.

The news she brought was bad. In the year since she had last seen him, her father had fallen ill and let it be known that he wished to see her married before he died. It was his dearest wish to see her provided for.

"And has he decided on a suitable candidate?" he asked.

"Oh yes, it is all arranged."

"May I know who it is that you are to be married to?"

"You must find that out for yourself," she replied and, turning her horse's head, began to ride back up the valley.

"Is there nothing I can do to persuade you to abandon this match, or even delay it for a year, a month, a day?" he shouted after her.

The answer to his question came next day in the form of a letter which was brought to him in Keswick by Gilpin, the steward. *Mr Henry is dead,* she wrote. *Although he had not flown for several years, I take no pleasure in riding the fells without him. My husband-to-be has offered to send him to a London taxidermist who, he assures me, will make him as good as new. It is to be my wedding present from him. Is not this kind? Is not this generous? What could you offer that would induce me to abandon this paragon among men? Well, there is perhaps one thing. If you can find me another bird to match Mr Henry, then I agree to embrace the squalor you have to offer me. You have no time to lose. The banns have already been called; Mr Henry is already on the train to London. Ever – or, if you fail, never – yours, Artemis.*

"Tell me, Gilpin," said Tertius, "when is your mistress getting married?"

"In a week from now," replied Gilpin.

"Then my hopes are at an end," said Tertius.

And seeing that he no longer had anything to lose by concealment, he plunged into his story, starting with his childhood encounter with the falconers and ending with Artemis's refusal of his offer of marriage.

"And so, Mr Gilpin," he concluded, "if I am not myself today, that is the reason and neither you nor anyone else can do anything to mend it."

"On the contrary, Mr Howgill, there is someone," said Gilpin, "but you have already lost two days and it may be too late."

"Do you mean that a successor to Mr Henry might still be found?"

"Mr Henry," replied Gilpin, "was not bred in captivity. He was caught in the wild shortly before Artemis was born and named Henry after the son both the parents expected her to be. The bird catcher who trapped him lives still. But he is an old man and may be unwilling to risk life and limb on the crags as he once did. And if he is, well, you may find his price too high. He was never an easy man to bargain with."

"Where may I find him?" asked Tertius.

"It is best if I speak to him on your behalf. Meet me at The Albion in two days' time."

Two days passed during which Tertius imagined the mysterious cragsman scaling impossible peaks and clinging with his finger nails to the narrowest of ledges, never doubting that Gilpin would arrive at the appointed hour with Mr Henry's successor. Tertius arrived at The Albion early. An hour passed, two hours, and there was still no sign of Gilpin. Diners came and went. The Ambleside coach disgorged its passengers, most of whom crowded into the parlour and tried to engage him in conversation. It was early evening before the steward arrived. He carried neither bird nor basket.

"Well, Mr Howgill," he announced, "we may be in luck."

"You have the bird?"

"I have the promise of a bird. As I feared, he will not settle for less than fifty guineas."

Tertius's blood froze. He struggled to find his voice and was both horrified and reassured to hear himself say:

"Tell him that he will be paid, but that I require two days to raise the money. He will receive his fifty guineas when I collect the bird. In three days from now, Artemis will be married. That leaves me one day in which to deliver the bird to her and save her from a man who thinks to please her with a carcass in a glass dome."

By now the train had left Marden and Paddock Wood far behind and had plunged into the first of the cuttings which mark the approach to Tunbridge.

"Mr Costello," I interrupted, "in a few minutes we shall be stopping in Tunbridge where I have promised to join passengers in the second class. Not for the world would I miss the end of your tale. May I beg you to hurry?"

Very well, said George, I shall spare you a detailed account of how Tertius raised the money, of how he found his way to the bird catcher and received from his hands a gyrfalcon, which he named Endymion, and of how, on the day appointed, he rose to find the fells thick with mist and lost his way.

There was a gasp of anguish from the ladies, and an admonition from Turpin never to travel without a pocket compass, a design for which he had, at great personal expense, recently patented and a sample of which he happened to have on his person, would they care to see it? The ladies made it abundantly plain that they would not.

Yes, continued George, he lost his way to Urmiston New Place in a mist as thick as the one in which he had fancied himself lost all those years before. When, at last, he crossed the beck and made his way into the valley, it was late afternoon. With sinking heart he rode round the edge of the tarn and through the gate. Clutching Endymion, he ran up the moss-covered steps and through the open door into the great hall. He found himself in a vaulted chamber, down the length of which ran a massive oak table, overlooked by the mounted heads of badgers, otters, martens and other creatures of the chase. On the walls old portraits dimmed by smoke sat alongside breastplates, crossbows and ceremonial swords.

"You may omit the details of the furniture," said Miss Osgood urgently. "Was he too late? Was there anybody there? Had the wedding party left?"

Of the occupants, continued George, there was no sign. Tertius shouted until he was hoarse and had almost given up hope of a reply when Gilpin appeared.

"Why, Mr Tertius," he said, "I was not expecting you. I had thought that by now you would have waylaid the party on the way to Carlisle."

"Would to God I had," said Tertius, "for now I see that I have lost everything."

"You have lost Miss Artemis for sure."

"That is indeed the worst blow, but it is not the only one. I have ruined not only myself, but my father as well."

"How come?"

"To pay for Endymion I sold his most treasured possession. I sold Red Spangle for fifty guineas. I sold the most famous fighting cock in Cumberland for the price of a pair of donkeys."

"Could you not have held out for more?"

"How was I to know that the buyer would haggle so? I had no time to drive him down. I had to settle or lose the sale. I should have known better than to deal with one of my father's customers. But he had so often admired the bird that I thought he would pay me whatever I asked."

"Was he a gentleman?"

"A tradesman in a good way of business. A ropemaker named Alfred Norris."

Gilpin looked horrified.

"Mr Howgill," he said, "you have sold the best fighting cock in Cumberland to the very man Artemis is to marry."

In the depths of the house a clock struck three.

"Whom Artemis," he corrected himself, "will by now already have married."

"Mr Costello," protested Miss Osgood, "I must confess to feeling cheated. This is not the ending we had a right to expect."

"On the contrary," interjected the Corporal, "it's the ending the boy deserved for disobeying his father."

"Hard as it may have been for the boy," opined Mr Meek, "it was eminently satisfactory from the girl's point of view. She gained a husband who, on her own admission, was kind and generous and presumably lived happily ever after in a house without mildew or moss."

"And what about young Romeo?" asked Mr Purselove. "Let me guess: he took to drink or laudanum – or both, if he had any sense – and was admitted to the local bedlam, where he was visited every Sunday by his father who had renounced liquor and devoted himself to good works."

"How can you all be so cruel?" protested Nan between tears. "Can you not feel the emptiness in Artemis's heart as she dusted Mr Henry's glass case on the mantelpiece?"

"But this," announced George Costello, who had been struggling to make himself heard, "is not the end. There are tragedy and triumph still to come."

"I hope that does not mean the boy is going to be rewarded with the girl after all," remarked the Corporal.

"Or that he is going to escape from bedlam and keep chickens," said Purselove.

"Mr Costello," I said, "I am sure that we are all eager to learn what happened to Tertius and Artemis …"

"Not to mention The Sportsman," interjected Stumps.

"Or indeed The Sportsman," I continued, "and none, I can assure, you, is more eager than I. In view of the fact that I am expected in one of the second class carriages, I must beg you – beseech you – to delay the ending until we gather again in London – on the steam boat, perhaps, or in our lodgings at Pimlico."

My request was greeted by loud protests from my travelling companions, most of whom were clearly hoping for a reversal of fortune, by means of which the lovers were to be reunited. The exceptions to this general wish were Stumps, whose interest in the story, as I have already indicated, lay elsewhere, and Turpin, who hoped that the undelivered portion of the tale would contain details of the rope making trade into which Artemis had married. At this, I noticed, The Saturnine Stranger nodded vigorously.

"Why do you not each invent an ending, sad or happy according to your inclination?" I suggested. "And perhaps, Mr Beamish, you might care to reflect on whether their continuations confirm your own phrenological conclusions."

"A most excellent suggestion," replied Beamish. "I shall give you a full account when we meet again in London. And who knows but that I might make it the subject of a scientific monograph when we return to Canterbury."

3

TUNBRIDGE TO REIGATE

All Change at Tunbridge
Fraud is Committed under our Very Noses
The Diocesan Exorcist's Tale of The Tethered Goat
The Pteridologist (and his Wife's) Tale of Strickland and Flowerdew
The Bookbinder's Tale of The Library of Lost Books

Consult Mr George Measom's admirable *Illustrated Guide to the South Eastern Railway* and you will see that Tunbridge boasts a gas-lit main street, a mechanics' institute, four dissenting chapels and two good inns. It also possesses a fine grammar school, though Stumps, hearing its praises sung by Beamish, who was an alumnus, growled that he still bore the scars of the pitched battles that had taken place between the schoolboys and the navvies during the building of the railway.

As the train entered the station, the band was cheered by the crowds on the platform, whilst those of us in the tubs were greeted by shouts of "Pauper!" and "Workhouse!" from a pack of urchins on the footbridge. Breeze and the Corporal shook their fists, Miss Osgood wagged an admonitory finger, whilst Purselove rose to his feet and gave a stately bow. "Take a tip from an old actor," he said. "The louder the abuse, the deeper the bow."

Accompanied by Miss Osgood, who carried the list of new-comers to our party, I greeted the white rosettes and directed them to their seats, most of which were in the second class, with only a few in the tubs. When I had finished, my arm was seized by Dr Erasmus leGrove, the diocesan exorcist whom I had met at Pluckley, and was dragged bodily towards his compartment. Whispering to Miss Osgood to follow, I allowed myself to be hauled into a second class carriage and inserted between two gentlemen wearing ulsters of identical check. Seeing my evident discomfort, Dr leGrove, who had appointed himself master of ceremonies, decided on a wholesale rearrangement of the passengers in his immediate vicinity.

"Mr Bartholomew," he said to the ulster on my left, "would you be so good as to step into the seat behind me, next to the newly arrived gentlemen and his wife, whose names I have yet to learn."

"Mr and Mrs Alfred Malachi Brown," replied Mr Alfred, the gentleman in question.

"The eminent pteridologist," added Mrs Alfred.

Since none of us had any idea what a pteridologist was or how one became eminent in that profession, the description went unchallenged. I had a notion that pteridology was something in the plant line – orchids, perhaps, or cacti. Whatever it was, Alfred Malachi Brown had not grown rich by it. The nap of his hat was thinning and Mrs Alfred's fingertips were peeping through the ends of her gloves.

"Samuel Bartholomew, watchmaker," said the gentleman in the ulster whom I had displaced, extending his hand to the pteridologist and his wife as he settled himself beside them. In the meantime, Miss Osgood had seated herself on my left, opposite Mr Dacre.

"Ah, another newcomer," said leGrove to a figure who now presented himself at the carriage door. "Come, sit here, next to Mr Dacre and me. Mr Dacre, if I may take the liberty of speaking for him, is an ecclesiastical architect and follower of Mr Pugin. And may I in the interests of good fellowship ask your name, sir?"

"Mr Jocelyn Critchley, bookbinder and fellow of the Society of Antiquaries."

"Ah, a scholar after my own heart, I see," said leGrove. "Are you familiar with the Cathedral Library in Canterbury?"

"I have had the honour of binding some of their most precious volumes," replied Critchley.

"Then you must be familiar with their Edward VI Prayer Book," said leGrove.

"Most certainly," said Critchley.

"I will let you into a little secret," said leGrove in a loud whisper: "I have on several occasions borrowed it – unofficially, of course – to help me in my professional duties. Stubborn manifestations yield to it very readily, I find. And now, ladies and gentlemen, it is my pleasant duty to introduce you to Mr Percy Blackwood, the proprietor of the Ebenezer Temperance Hotel in St Margaret's Street, without whose efforts this most agreeable excursion to the Great Exhibition of the Industry of All Nations would never have occurred and we would all have found ourselves on a train plucked from Bradshaw without a band to serenade us."

There was a polite round of applause.

"And may I in turn," I replied, "introduce you to Miss Violet Osgood, who, as Secretary to the aforementioned Society, has done all the hard work for which I have received the thanks?"

Miss Osgood flushed crimson as her bombazine bonnet.

"You are too kind, Mr Blackwood," she murmured. "Yours was the vision; I am but the instrument."

LeGrove's presence, like that of the sun, illuminated those around him. His beams warmed the inner planets – that is to say, those sitting on the benches in his immediate neighbourhood – but fell short of Uranus and Neptune at the further end of the carriage. The inhabitants of those cold and distant planets were out of earshot and therefore play no part in this narrative.

"And what about us?" said a voice from the bench opposite the eminent pteridologist and his wife. "Do we not deserve an introduction?"

Facing the Malachi Browns and Samuel Bartholomew were two women who now introduced themselves as Miss Binnie and Mme Fontana, or, to use their own designations, 'Miss Binnie, though Plain Binnie will do' and 'Mme Emily Fontana, Medium and Adept.' The latter threw out the title defiantly as if challenging anyone to who dared question her respectability. From the look she exchanged with leGrove I suspected that the two had at some time in the not-too-distant past crossed swords professionally. It would be hard to imagine a greater contrast than that between Mme Fontana and Miss Binnie. The one was an exotic bird of paradise with a great deal of turquoise about her – a turban surmounted by feathers of that colour was particularly striking – whilst the other was a drab Scottish sparrow – Edinburgh by the sound of her – with tight auburn curls and tiny claw-like hands. Though they had exiled themselves to the margins of the company, they nonetheless felt themselves entitled to feel aggrieved about being ignored by the rest of us.

In this they were not alone. The gentleman on my right now pointed out to Dr leGrove that he, too, had been excluded from the round of introductions and had every right to feel aggrieved by the omission.

"Forgive me, sir," said Dr leGrove with barely concealed sarcasm, "I failed to introduce you to the newcomers. Ladies and gentlemen, this is Mr Henry Scudamore, butler to Lady Rippledale, who is travelling in the first class carriage with her companion, Miss Tintsford."

"As indeed I should have been doing," added Mr Scudamore bitterly, "had not her companion overruled her ladyship and demoted me to the second class."

"You will have, therefore, to treat him with respect, ladies and gentlemen," said leGrove, "since we are not the company he was expecting or, indeed, thinks himself entitled to. Demoted indeed!"

It was, as even Mr Scudamore must have realised, an unfortunate choice of phrase. However, he was rapidly restored to favour by the arrival of one of the footbridge urchins who had been working his way along the train bawling, ''Freshments, Tea, Iced Buns. 'Freshments,

Tea, Iced Buns.' Several passengers at the other end of our carriage had already climbed down and were making their way to the coffee stall and, among my own neighbours, Mr Bartholomew and Mr Dacre were about to follow when Mr Scudamore advised against it.

"On what grounds?" asked Mr Dacre.

"On the grounds that you might get less than you paid for," said the butler. "Follow my advice. You will not regret it, I promise you. Just sit back and observe carefully."

We did not have long to wait. Hardly had half a dozen passengers been served with their tea than Hengist gave a piercing shriek, whereupon the guard at the front of the train waved to the guard at the rear who raised his whistle to his lips, thus offering the crowd at the coffee stall a stark choice between their beverages and their train. With cries of anger they rushed across the platform and climbed into their seats with moments to spare.

"You will see now why I urged you to desist," said Mr Scudamore to Mr Dacre. "What you have witnessed was not an accident but a deliberate deception and one for which Tunbridge is notorious. When a train is within a few minutes of departure, passengers are enticed to the coffee stall, relieved of their money and then, before they have time to drink what they have paid for, are summoned back to the train, leaving the tea and coffee to be sold a second time to passengers on the following train. If you consult Bradshaw, I think you will find that the Folkestone train is following hard on our heels."

It would be hard to say who was most outraged by this episode. Some proposed writing to the *East Kent Gazette* until Mr Scudamore pointed out that that was where he had learned of the practice in the first place; some proposed writing to the directors of the South Eastern Railway on whose property, some to the Member of Parliament in whose constituency and some to the Archbishop of Canterbury in whose diocese the offence had occurred. One way or another everyone was agreed on the need to write to someone.

Once initial outrage had been exhausted, however, talk turned first to crime in general and then to crimes in particular. Everyone, it seemed, had his own tale to tell. Mr Dacre's concerned the removal of a silver chalice during communion, Mr Critchley's of an illuminated missal from a chained library. Not wishing to be left out, Mme Fontana began a tale of crimes committed from beyond the grave, but was prevented from completing it by Miss Binnie, who reminded her of a duty of confidentiality towards her clients. Had it been a prize competition, however, I should have awarded the palm to Mr Bartholomew, the watchmaker, for his tale of the man who was swindled on his own doorstep by someone who offered to sell him the right time.

"Surely not!" exclaimed Dr leGrove..

"Time," rejoined Mr Bartholomew, "is one of the marvels of the present age – or one of the great tyrannies, depending on your point of view. For that we have to thank the railways. It was they who carried London time on guards' watches to parts of the kingdom where time followed local custom. Now when we hear our clocks strike we know that, wherever we are, we are sharing the same seamless garment as the prisoner in Millbank Penitentiary or the Queen in far-away Balmoral. We take it for granted. But it was not always so. Which was why the man handed over his pocket watch to the stranger at his door to be purged of impurities."

"How on earth does one purge a watch of impure time?" asked Dr leGrove.

"By taking the watch and its owner to the top of a distant hill so as to be free of contaminating influences – church clocks, misaligned sun dials and the like – and immersing it in a casket of pure London time."

"And did it work?"

"Not only did it not work, but when the man got home again he found that the stranger's accomplices had broken into his house and robbed him of everything he possessed."

"How shocking!" cried Mrs Malachi Brown. "It quite makes one afraid to leave one's home.

"Intruders take many forms," remarked Dr leGrove. "In my profession one can never feel safe inside a house, however tightly bolted the doors and windows."

"Do you have a particular case in mind? I asked.

"Several," he replied, obviously hoping to be invited to share them with the company, "several."

"Oh, please tell us", said Mrs Alfred.

"Are you sure?" said Dr leGrove with an unconvincing show of reluctance. "Oh very well. Know, then, that I began my career as a curate in Lincolnshire, where I was neighbour to Charles Blomfield, then rector of Quarrington, and now Bishop of London."

[Editor's Note: Blackwood's narrative stops abruptly at this point, though it is clear what must have come next. He had agreed to join Dr leGrove at Tunbridge, eager for any crumbs that fell from the diocesan exorcist's table, especially if they took the form of ghost stories, for which magazines such as Blackwood's *and* Bentley's Miscellany *would pay handsomely. Neither leGrove's tale nor Miss Osgood's shorthand notes have survived, presumably because Blackwood used them as the basis for the following story and then discarded them. The Tethered Goat is, as far as I know, the only piece that Blackwood had published in his namesake's magazine, a copy of which he placed among his foul papers, along with the notes and drafts of the other tales. Its uniqueness is a puzzle. At some stage his editors must have discovered that Percy Blackwood was no kin of theirs and out of pique refused to accept further work from him. (As to how that discovery came about, I offer an explanation in the Epilogue.) Which is a pity since* The Tethered Goat *is no worse than most of the stories in* Blackwood's Magazine *and a great deal better than many. How much of the credit is due to Erasmus leGrove and how much to Percy Blackwood we shall never know, since the Ur-text of the tale, as notated by the indefatigable Miss Osgood, has long since disappeared.]*

The Diocesan Exorcist's
Tale of The Tethered Goat

Marblewood Hall had been one of the great houses of Lincolnshire. With its back to the wolds and its face to the fens, it had, so the local saying went, one foot on land and one in water. Its owners, the Earls of Fritton, had once been amongst the most lavish entertainers in the county. Scarcely a week had gone by without a wildfowling expedition or a ball or a dinner party on the grandest scale. Out on the marshes wayfarers would marvel at the lights in the dusk, tier upon tier of them, blazing like a great chandelier on the edge of the fen. Such was the fame of Marblewood in the days of the first three Georges. In the days of the Prince Regent, however, its fortunes fell into decline. The war, the fall in agricultural prices, a disputed succession – all took their toll. Reed beds advanced towards the centre of the lake; mould grew on the inside of the ice house. Then, in the year of the Great Reform Bill (though surely unconnected with it), a fire swept through Marblewood, leaving it first a blackened shell, and, within a very few years, an ivy-clad ruin. The cause was never ascertained, though there were theories aplenty. According to some, negligent servants were to blame; and to others, a disaffected heir, whose depraved habits had led to angry words with his father.

What little could be saved was moved to the dower house on the eastern edge of the park. A tolerable Rubens was salvaged from a flap of burnt canvas, likewise a presentable tapestry of Actaeon and Diana, some decent furniture, a complete set of the Waverley novels, a harpsichord, a canteen of silver cutlery, a Chinese vase or two – all these, together with such exiguous furnishing as the dower house already possessed, were packed into the downstairs rooms in a crazy profusion of periods and styles. Lord Fritton, his health broken by the calamity, tolerated it for a month or two, before quitting Marblewood for ever. Thereafter the dower house was rented to a succession of tenants, most of them unmarried daughters or sisters who had been abandoned to a lingering spinsterhood by their families. Of these the latest and most enigmatic was a Miss Henrietta Adwick, and it is she, who, in the autumn of 18__, begins this story by advertising in The *Morning Post* for a lady's companion.

Information about Marblewood was easy to come by. Letters to friends, a surreptitious visit to my employer's library, produced the facts I have assembled above. About Miss Adwick herself, however, my researches were less fruitful. Few of my correspondents had heard of her, though one mentioned a rumour, gathered from a friend of a friend, that she had reverted to her maiden name and title, her husband having died or disappeared some little time ago. That Miss Adwick, alone in her fenland retreat, should require a companion, ought to have surprised no-one. What *was* surprising was that her requirements should have been so precise yet at the same time so undemanding. The companion was to be in robust health, of medium height, have a high forehead and dark hair, ringlets preferred, and be somewhere between thirty-five and forty. No mention was made of the usual genteel accomplishments, such as French, or petit point (both of which I could supply), and none at all of the duties she was to perform. What kind of companion was it, I wondered, who had ringlets but no powers of conversation, or the right stature and no store of accomplishments with which to while away the fenland evenings? Why, none – or none worthy of the name. And yet I was tempted, tempted despite familiarity with the fen country and its huge skies and bitter winds; tempted, too, because my present position as governess to five unruly boys, who screamed profanities and broke my pencils, was drearier than any fenland winter. So I decided to write to Miss Adwick, hoping that her reply might ease my doubts and point me, one way or the other, in the direction I should take.

Dear Miss Adwick, I wrote. *My name is Florence Pentiman. I am governess to the five sons of Colonel and Mrs Standish of Imber Lodge in the neighbouring county of Cambridgeshire. Although my duties are exacting, I endeavour to discharge them to the satisfaction of my employers, who are pleased to tell me that I have a natural affinity with my delightful charges ...* (This was a flat lie. My employers never remarked upon my efforts, either by way of censure or approval. As for my delightful charges, they were little better than savages, on whom my civilising endeavours had left no mark. To my complaints their parents were deaf. When I reported to the Colonel that his sons had introduced a fox cub into the schoolroom and invited the groom to set the hounds on it, he declared it was just the sort of trick he'd got up to at that age. It was what boys did and thank God for it.) *I find my present duties satisfying in every way, save one: namely, a want of adult company, the which, I am confident, would be supplied by the post you offer. You may, of course, refer to Colonel and Mrs Standish for a character. I fulfil your requirements as to age, stature and complexion and claim in addition some knowledge of French, music, petit point and drawing. I await your reply with eager anticipation. Faithfully yours, Florence Pentiman.*

Whether Colonel and Mrs Standish would supply a favourable character – or indeed any character at all – was somewhat doubtful, as was their willingness to grant me leave of absence should Miss Adwick summon me to Marblewood. But Fortune seemed to favour me. On the day I received Miss Adwick's letter, the Colonel and his wife received an invitation to a regimental gathering in London. What was more, they decided to take the boys with them, since the boys were eager to see the lions in Regent's Park. In their absence the Colonel enjoined me to tidy the schoolroom and to put the books in the Library into some kind of order. "I find colour works as well as anything" was his parting shot. "Or size. Something of that sort."

Miss Adwick's reply was as cordial as I could have wished. She looked forward to seeing me at my earliest convenience and enclosed two guineas for my expenses. I could scarcely believe my luck; indeed, I began to question whether it was luck at all and to think of it, half-jokingly, as my destiny. Thus it was that a few days later I boarded a train – the first I had ever set foot in – to Wisbech, whence I was driven in a hired dog cart through a flat expanse of reed and water to Marblewood. A few early stars dusted the sky. Once I caught a fiery gleam where a workman was tending one of the new steam pumps that kept the waters in check. How I envied him the light and warmth of his brick cabin, for by now I was chilled to the bone. At length the dog cart turned through a pair of lofty gates, and the lights of the dower house swung into view. Modest though they were, the most brilliant chandelier could not have been more welcome to me at that moment. The dog cart stopped before the front door, I paid off the driver and rang the bell. The maidservant who answered told me that I had been expected earlier and that I was to be shown in to Miss Adwick directly. She pointed to a door on the other side of the darkened hall and hurried off down the corridor, leaving me to make my own introduction.

The Miss Adwick who welcomed me was very different from the one who had written the letter. The handshake was perfunctory, the smile wintry. She said she was pleased to see me and immediately took to calling me Pentiman, as if she had engaged me already. Although she asked a few routine questions about my present situation, about governessing in general and even about my journey from the station, I doubt whether she listened to the answers, since she spent most of the time breaking macaroons into small pieces and feeding them to her lapdog, whom she addressed as Frolic. Suddenly she stood up and looked into the mirror above the fireplace.

"Come here, Pentiman," she ordered. "Stand beside me."

I stepped on to the hearthrug.

"Now look into the mirror and tell me what you see."

What I saw were two faces, mine reddened with cold from the journey, hers pale and drawn.

"I see two faces, Miss Adwick. Three," I joked, "if you count the dog."

"And if I were to ask my maidservant to arrange your hair in ringlets like mine, what might you see then?"

For a fleeting moment I glimpsed what I was being invited to see. It was an inchoate likeness. Had Miss Adwick been fuller in the face or her complexion less deathly – was she, I wondered, consumptive? – or had we been dressed similarly, we might have passed for sisters. Where I wore a grey woollen dress, she was dressed in brilliant red with a shawl of deepest burgundy. Her hair, which was fashioned into heavy ringlets, was secured with scarlet ribbons. And now I looked about me, I saw that she had swathed herself and her immediate surroundings in red of every shade and texture. Round the fire, which was banked up high against the chimney back, she had built an enclosure of screens in red and orange silk, patterned with dragons and salamanders. Inside were a chair in embossed velvet, a side table, a footstool, cushions, a rug, lacquered boxes, a pile of leather-bound books, a spray of wax flowers in a glass dome, all of them aflame with scarlets, vermilions, carmines, maroons and damasks. Even Frolic's basket was lined with red velvet.

I must have made some involuntary sign of recognition, for she said more to herself than to me, "It is true that our dresses are different: our persons, though, are remarkably similar – or with a little contriving might be made so. Now take this candle, Pentiman. Sit over there and let me look at you."

The place she indicated was in the far corner of the room. A clock in the hall struck the quarter. There, beyond the reach of the fire I was made to sit in a hard chair by an ill-fitting lattice. Small wonder, then, that by the time the clock struck the half I was numb with cold and thinking fondly of my five charges in the schoolroom. In the meantime, Miss Adwick had settled back among her cushions, a Titania in her flame-coloured bower. For a time she gazed at me, then seemed to lose interest, picked up a book and began to read. The clock struck three quarters. The maid came in to stoke the fire. When it was blazing up the chimney again, Miss Adwick put down her book and said, "Did you hear a sound, Pentiman?"

"I heard nothing, Miss Adwick."

"Indeed? There we differ. Open the window and lean out."

I did so.

"Further, if you please."

I leaned forward, so that my upper body was angled forward out of the window. The outside air was cold, the moonlight flecked by scudding clouds.

"Well?"

"I hear only the usual night sounds."

"Enumerate them."

"The wind in the creeper, a distant owl. There is nothing else, I assure you. My hearing is very sharp. May I close the window?"

"No. Leave it. The sound may return."

She picked up her book, pulled her shawl around her and began to read. This was intolerable. I could restrain myself no longer. I protested loudly – too loudly, I fear – about her want of hospitality, about her presuming to call me Pentiman before she had even engaged me, about her thrusting me out in the cold, about the way her letter had raised my hopes only to dash them so cruelly. In saying this, I knew that I had sentenced myself to that hateful schoolroom, where my five charges, reinvigorated by their encounter with the lions, would be ripe with new mischief. No mistress on earth would tolerate such an outburst from her companion, not least the glacial Miss Adwick. But I was wrong. In an instant the ice thawed and she was all smiles.

"Why, Pentiman," she cried, springing to her feet. "How thoughtless of me! Come here. Sit on the footstool beside the fire. I shall give orders directly for a room to be prepared and supper brought up to you."

I was speechless with astonishment. Here, for the first time since my arrival at Marblewood, was the Miss Adwick of the letter, the Miss Adwick whose companion

I had craved to be. Was her treatment of me, I wondered, some kind of test? And in that case was she about offer me the post in which I had invested such hopes?

"No doubt you are wondering," she said, as if reading my thoughts, "whether I am about to employ you as my companion. Well, I will not deceive you: I am as yet undecided. But this I promise. You shall have my decision first thing in the morning." I must have looked somewhat crestfallen, because she continued, "I might add that my first impressions are very favourable, very favourable indeed. But it is not my custom to make hasty decisions. I should like to reflect overnight. Now, would you care to ring the bell? Thank you. Now tell me about yourself."

I obliged by telling her about my charges, about life in the household of Colonel and Mrs Standish, a narration which she interrupted frequently with questions about the children, their pets, their servants, the furniture, even about the hunting trophies in the hall – all the minutiae, in fact, which close friends enjoy sharing about each other's domestic arrangements. Whilst the maid brought tea, she prattled light-heartedly – and often indiscreetly – about the Lords Fritton and the rise and fall of Marblewood Hall, now a sad ruin, which she promised she would show me on the morrow. Here was a change indeed! What was I to make of this transformation from ice to fire, from indifference to intimacy? When at length we had finished tea, she rang for the maid and ordered her to show me to my room.

"Goodnight, Pentiman," she said, clasping me by the hand. "You shall have my final answer in the morning."

The room to which I was shown was a modest affair at the end of the second floor landing. A small fire burned in the grate with enough coal beside it for a single replenishment, after which I should be forced to take to my bed to stay warm, though the bed itself promised little by way of either warmth or comfort. It had once been a handsome four-poster, but the side curtains were missing and those at the end were thin and frayed. The blankets – there were only two – did not reach to the extremities of the mattress and were, like the curtain, the worse for wear. One of the sheets had a large scorch mark on it, the result, presumably, of an encounter with a warming pan. Of the warming pan itself, there was, alas, no sign. With a cold night in prospect, I rang repeatedly for the maid, but no-one answered. I was reluctant to approach Miss Adwick, since a want of stoicism might make an unfavourable impression on her just when I most wanted to impress. No, for this night at least I would do without creature comforts, the absence of which was surely an oversight. If Miss Adwick decided in my favour, such matters could be attended to on the morrow.

I ate a solitary supper and glanced at the books on my bedside table. Tillotson's *Sermons* and Bunyan's *Grace Abounding* I rejected as insufficiently companionable; Byron's poems, on the other had, were ideal for driving away autumn chills. I threw the last shovelful of coal onto the fire and began to read. I was half way through *The Bride of Abydos* when I heard strange harmonies coming from the depth of the house. Unable to identify them, I opened my door and ventured on to the landing. It was some minutes before I recognised the source of the ghostly tinklings as a harpsichord. Nowadays such instruments are rare. Even Colonel and Mrs Standish possessed a Broadwood, so that I could play to them during their interminable whist parties. I crept to the head of the stairs and listened. Miss Adwick, if indeed it was she, was playing a medley of popular airs, interspersed with – and how odd they sounded on a harpsichord! – polkas and gallops. For some fifteen minutes the sounds welled up from the drawing room, then stopped as abruptly as they had begun.

I returned to my room and the remains of my fire. I had just begun to close my curtains when I saw, or fancied I saw, a metallic glint on the grass outside. I was about to dismiss it as a trick of errant moonlight when it appeared again. There! And again there! At first I thought it the flash of a silver blade, but on its second reappearance I saw that it cast a human shadow. What could it mean? Although I stood at the window for ten minutes or more, those three glimpses were all that the moon vouchsafed. It was as if the figure had been attracted by the sound of the harpsichord, had stood for a while to listen and then, the music having ceased, had started to return whence it came. Such was my fancy as I stood by the window. But whence had it come? I had obviously caught it on the wing, as it were, since the glimpses I had seen were separated by several yards and in each its shadow was differently configured.

I wondered whether to venture downstairs and tell Miss Adwick, but decided against it, reasoning that if the figure was moving away from the house, then we were in no danger. In any case, what was I to report? A trick of the light, a play of shadows? No, I would need more than that to convince her. So I went to bed, having said my prayers with unusual fervour. That I was not entirely convinced by my own reasoning was demonstrated by the fact that I bolted my bedroom door and left the candle burning.

As you may imagine I slept little that night. For one thing it was cold and I lay under the meagre blankets fully dressed; for another, my mind could not help returning to Miss Adwick's erratic behaviour and, above all, to the mysterious figure outside the window. Towards dawn, however, I must have drifted off, because I was awakened by the maidservant bringing me a breakfast tray and a message that the mistress wished to see me directly. Before I had collected my wits sufficiently to ask her about the events of the night, she had hurried from the room. All subsequent attempts to engage her in conversation proved equally futile. Whenever I tried, she pleaded domestic duties and hastened away to some other part of the house. It was clear that the maid had no wish to be questioned and had quite possibly been instructed not to allow herself to be so.

I dressed quickly and went downstairs, having decided to tell Miss Adwick what I had seen on the previous evening in as unemotional and matter-of-fact a way as possible. To my astonishment she clapped her hands and laughed. Far from being vexed by my foolishness, she seemed delighted. She clasped my hand; she hugged me; she picked up Frolic and kissed him on the nose. When at last she managed to compose herself, she sat me in her chair and explained that what I had seen was almost certainly the gardener, who was attracted to music like a moth to a candle flame. She was often aware of him at the window winter or summer, she said, as she played of an evening.

"And now I have some good news, Pentiman," she said. "I promised you a decision and I have reached one. Can you guess what it is?"

"I scarcely dare to hope," I began.

"Then let me put you out of your misery. You are to be my companion and you are to begin today. This very minute, in fact. Does that please you? Will you accept?"

"Dear Miss Adwick," I replied, "I hardly know what to say. Of course I accept. I am almost speechless with joy. I shall write to Colonel and Mrs Standish without delay and offer my resignation."

"There is no need," she laughed. "It is done. I took the liberty of writing on your behalf. It was obvious from your manner last night that you were eager to accept, so I thought to save you the trouble of writing a letter. I have also written to my cousin in Wisbech and asked him to arrange for your trunk to be collected. The gardener, whom you saw in somewhat unusual circumstances last night, was despatched early this morning to take the letters to the carrier. Until your trunk arrives, you will have no fresh clothes, so I have arranged with my maidservant for you to have full use of my last year's wardrobe. There, do I not think of everything?"

That morning – how shall I ever forget it? – passed in a blur of reds and crimsons. I was dressed, undressed and dressed again by Miss Adwick as if I were a favourite doll, and, under the expert hands of her maidservant, my hair was spun into ringlets and trussed up in scarlet ribbons.

"Now, Pentiman," said Miss Adwick, when the maid had finished. "Stand beside me in front of the mirror and tell me what you see."

What I saw was not the fleeting resemblance of yesterday but a fully achieved likeness. Not only were we now alike in dress (including, I am ashamed to say, décolletage) and ringlets, but either she had lost her pallor or I had lost my ruddy cheeks or we had lost and gained a little from each other.

"Why," I exclaimed, "we might be sisters."

"Then sisters we shall be," she beamed and gave my ringlets a playful tug.

Sisters we may have been, since it pleased her to call us such, but I could not help remarking that she did not invite me to call her Henrietta or take to calling me anything but Pentiman.

After lunch, Miss Adwick ordered the maid to bring shawls and bonnets, for she wished to show me the grounds. We began with the lake. On one side the reed beds had advanced far into the water, rendering the boat house inaccessible, but on the other, nearest the house, the shoreline was clear, apart from a huge weeping willow, which formed a green cave with its branches. According to Miss Adwick, who led me inside, it was one of the wonders of Marblewood. Generations of children had picnicked inside it, sons had hidden from tyrannical fathers and, on summer evenings, boats, their sterns hung with Chinese lanterns, had hovered like fireflies before it, drawn by musicians who played, unseen, inside their verdant cage.

The tree was obviously not a favourite of Frolic, for he struggled out of his mistress's arms, raced round the enclosure, yapping loudly, before pushing aside the willow fronds and escaping into the park.

"Such an adventurous little fellow," she said. "Too adventurous for his own good. Quick, Pentiman. We must follow. There are foxes in the grounds."

Our search took us past the ruin of the great hall. Its lower floors were covered in nettles, its tumbled walls with wild clematis. Amid the weather-stained masonry, vestiges of grandeur remained – a marble fireplace or two, a stretch of plaster cornice, even a flight of steps leading up to a buddleia-choked front door.

From somewhere round the back of the hall, we could hear the sound of Frolic yapping excitedly.

"Off you go, Pentiman," ordered Miss Adwick. "Remember, the first duty of a lady's companion is the safety and comfort of her mistress's dog. Here, take a macaroon. Frolic finds them wonderfully soothing. I shall wait here."

Behind the ruined façade were the remains of a terrace with a blackened balustrade complete with urns and beyond that an overgrown lawn. I forced my way through waist-high grass and docks, fearful of damaging my borrowed finery. When at last I found Frolic, he was growling at a beehive-like structure hidden in a tangle of overgrown bushes. The ghost of a path led up to a pair of metal doors, which, though secured with a padlock and chain, were slightly ajar. Into the crack between them, Frolic had wedged his nose and was growling with what sounded like a mixture of fear and murderous hatred. I bent down and, calling him by his name, offered him a macaroon. He took no notice. I leaned forward to drag him away and in so doing brought my own nose up against the crack in the doors. The air was intensely cold and tasted bitter, like charred wood. I pulled Frolic away from the doors and carried him back across the overgrown lawn to his mistress. To my surprise, she was not there. In the fading afternoon Frolic and I had the ruins of Marblewood Hall to ourselves.

I returned to the house to find her seated before the fire. She took Frolic from me without a word of explanation, kissed him on the nose and dropped him in his basket.

"Shame on you, Pentiman," she teased. "Look at that dress. It is covered in green stains. Ring for the maid. I must have you looking your best at all times."

So I submitted to a second change of dress that day. My dress of the morning was replaced by a gown of even deeper décolletage. When I protested, she laughed aloud.

"Why, Pentiman," she said, "I had no idea you were such a prude. Have done with this old-maidishness. Enjoy your good fortune while it lasts."

"I am obliged to you for your kindness," I replied, "but I shall feel more comfortable when my trunk arrives and I can wear my own clothes again."

"Well, that will be as it may," she said enigmatically. "And now I have a little surprise for you. Open up the screens and see what I have hidden behind them."

I did as I was bidden and there, as I had expected, was the harpsichord, a splendid baroque affair painted in red and gold.

"I feel invigorated by my turn round the park," she said. "I wish to play and you shall be my audience. You play yourself, do you not? Well, one day perhaps you shall play and I shall listen. But not today. Today you must indulge me, so please be seated."

Judging that our intimacy was sufficiently established for me to sit in her chair by the fire, I settled myself in it only to be ordered out peremptorily and told to sit by the window. Perhaps sensing my dismay, she tried to make light of it by saying she often pretended she was performing to a roomful of people, to create illusion of which she needed me to sit at some distance from the instrument.

So I sat by the window as I had the day before and indeed as I was to sit in the days that followed. By the time her recital was over, I was feeling cold and hoping to be invited back to the fire and fussed over as before. Alas, no such invitation was forthcoming. When she had finished, she slammed down the lid and dismissed me.

"I am tired, Pentiman," she announced. "I should like to be left to myself. The maidservant will show you to your room. This one, I believe is grander than the one you had last night. Your supper will be brought up to you."

Grander perhaps, but not warmer. Though the bed was more comfortable and the choice of reading more varied, the fire was as undernourished as ever. The deepest chill, however, came not from the damp sheets or the mould on the wainscot but in the realisation that Miss Adwick's cordiality was a matter of whim, or, worse, a play in some game whose rules were unclear to me. But for all her caprices, I was in no doubt that life was better here than in the schoolroom and that I had done the right thing in resigning as governess.

Or so I sought to reassure myself at the end of that first day. As the weeks passed, however, doubts began to grow. Take my resignation, for example. It had been snatched from me without a by-your-leave, thus depriving me of the satisfaction of vexing Colonel Standish myself, and, secondly, of the chance, however remote, of changing my mind at the last minute. Then there was the matter of the missing trunk. Miss Adwick assured me that her cousin had sent for it and that its failure to arrive must surely be the fault of the carrier. It will come, she said; be patient, it will come. But it did not come and as the days lengthened into weeks I resented more and more being imprisoned in someone else's clothes. In fact the sense of being a prisoner *tout court* grew ever stronger. I was the prisoner of an unvarying routine – of turns round the garden, of listening to Miss Adwick's harpsichord recitals (I was never, despite her offer, invited to play), of solitary suppers in my room. I was a prisoner, too, in the most literal and intolerable sense of the word. My salary was to be paid half-yearly in arrears, so until the spring I could not afford leave Marblewood and go elsewhere. Only for me there was no elsewhere. Without a situation to go to, without close family to whom I could turn, there was no question of my leaving Marblewood. A prison, I reflected bitterly, was no less a prison for having no walls.

I have said the days were unvarying. In my case, this was undoubtedly true, but not, I came to realise, in Miss Adwick's. One evening as I sat reading by the fire in my room, I heard the sound of carriages. Here was a strange turn of events: Miss Adwick, who gloried in her solitude, was receiving guests. From below came the chatter of conversation, followed shortly after by snatches of song and the jangle of the harpsichord. How I longed to join them, partly out of curiosity and partly, I must confess, because I did not wish my mistress to share her favours with others. But no invitation to join the company was forthcoming, either on that or on any subsequent occasion. The most I could hope for was to share the gossip the next day, but there, too, I was disappointed. When we were alone together, Miss Adwick made no reference to her guests and I did not think it my place to ask. How large a company she entertained I never discovered, nor whether it always comprised the same people, though one voice – that of a man with a fine operatic tenor – always seemed to be present. His soaring arpeggios could be heard far into the night, long after the others had departed.

There was another visitor, too, a silent partner in these musical soirées. From time to time I caught sight of the elusive shadow I had glimpsed on that first evening. Miss Adwick's explanation – viz. that it was the gardener indulging his musical tastes – was clearly disingenuous, not least because I had never seen such a person by daylight. As autumn deepened into winter I found myself sharing more of my evenings with this mysterious companion, especially when Miss Adwick was entertaining guests. This was no trick of the moonlight. This was a tangible presence which had established itself under my window and not, as I had at first deluded myself, outside hers. For a long time I had tried to convince myself that it was not so. But one evening in early December, when the lake had frozen and the trees were furred with frost, I glanced out of my bedroom window and found that my attendant shadow had knotted itself into a kind of grimace. But that is to mislead, for a grimace requires a face and this had none. I might call it a stare, but a stare requires eyes and this had none. And when I write that I *saw* whatever it was, that, too, is to mislead because I *felt* this presence every bit as much as I saw it. It struck me like a blow. I needed to rush from the room, to tell someone there and then. But Miss Adwick was entertaining guests. The operatic tenor was in full flight. I simply could not gatecrash the concert party to demand an explanation for what most of them would dismiss as the delusion of a half-crazed (and probably drunken) servant. There was no alternative but to wait and confront Miss Adwick on the morrow.

But the opportunity never arose. Next morning the maidservant, who normally brought up my breakfast tray, told me to join the mistress and her guests in the dining room, adding that I was to dress as cheerfully as my borrowed wardrobe would allow and to prepare myself for a day on the ice.

"On the ice?" I echoed.

"Miss Adwick and her guests are going skating on the lake and she particularly wants you to be present."

My heart leapt. So my mistress had not abandoned me after all.

"I ought to warn her that I am a very poor skater," I laughed, "and am likely to prove an embarrassment to her in front of her guests."

"Oh she doesn't mean you to skate, miss."

"Not skate? What does she want of me then?"

"She wants you to look after their coats."

Of that day by the lake, I can remember little save the beauty and the terror. How many comprised the skating party or what their names and titles were, I cannot now recall. As to beauty, they were all dressed in silvery grey and glided across the ice like wraiths, now merging with the ice, now emerging from it, as the sun veiled and unveiled itself. Miss Adwick herself did not skate. Some of the

*They were all dressed in silvery grey and
glided across the ice like wraiths*

gentlemen having carried her harpsichord on to the ice, she confined herself to singing and playing, in which she was joined by the operatic tenor, whom I was now able to observe for the first time. Though not in his first youth – his hair and beard were greying and his face lined – there was something of the former dandy about him. To the applause of the skaters, they sang a duet from *Fra Diavolo* and then waltzed across the lake and back whilst one of the guests played. A table with refreshments had been set up on the ice, as well as smaller tables for whist, should any of the skaters feel sufficiently warmed by their exertions to take a turn at cards.

So much for the beauty. As for the terror, it glided up so stealthily that I failed to notice anything until it was too late. I had been advised by Miss Adwick to wear red, the better, she said, to identify me as I stood at the edge of the lake to receive her guests' cloaks and shawls before they ventured on to the ice. At the last moment – at least that was how it seemed at the time, though I think now that she had planned it beforehand – she decided, on the advice of the operatic tenor, to hide me away behind the fronds of the willow tree. The red dress, she said, was an error of judgment on her part, a blot on a carefully modulated design of silver and grey. If it pleased her guests to play the part of phantoms, it would be discourteous to ruin the effect with discordant colours. She said it kindly enough, though some of her friends' remarks, falling within my earshot, were less polite.

"Do not pull a long face, Pentiman," she said. "I hate a long face. These friends are not for you. They are far above your station. You would not thank me for including you in the party. Now goodbye, Pentiman, and thank you for being so obliging. I hope you do not regret it. With all my heart I do." She kissed me and caressed my ringlets with her gloved hand. "Now off you go. And Pentiman, you are not to leave your post until I give you leave. Is that clear?"

So within a few minutes of arriving at the lakeside I found myself within the willow cage. In a place where children had picnicked and lovers kept tryst, I found myself a mere cloakroom attendant. A table and chair had been provided, which confirmed my suspicion that Miss Adwick's decision to banish me there was no afterthought. I heaped up the shawls and coats on the table and over the course of the next hour there was a brisk trade as her guests took to the ice. Most of them remarked on the beauty of the crystal cage, though few stayed long enough to experience the cold. It froze my hands and numbed my face, so that when the maidservant brought me a bowl of hot broth, it was all I could do to hold the spoon. Of capes and mufflers there was no shortage; they lay heaped on the table before me. Even so, I could not bring myself to touch them. Even when half-frozen, servants do not wear their betters' clothes unless they are bidden.

As the day wore on, I settled into a kind of torpor in which I was neither asleep nor awake. One by one the skaters reclaimed their coats, and by early afternoon I found myself staring at an empty table. By now all sounds had ceased. The skaters had departed; the harpsichord was silent. And it was at that point that the terror started. By then I was almost insensible to my surroundings. It is, I suppose, even possible that I had fallen asleep, for I awoke with a jolt to find a hand burrowing into my ringlets. My immediate thought was that Miss Adwick had returned to release me from my confinement. But when I put up my hand gratefully to clasp hers I received a shock as if I had been riven by lightning. The fingers I clutched were not merely icy: they were burning with cold and as white as death. I leapt up, but the hand was quicker yet and withdrew to the other side of the frozen curtain. At that moment I knew that my nocturnal companion was waiting outside, knew that I could not leave the willow cage nor yet find safety within it, knew that Miss Adwick had intended this to happen all along, for why else would she have forbidden me to leave until she gave permission? There was no point in calling for help, since the skaters had long since disappeared. Instinctively I began to walk round the inside of the enclosure keeping myself at a diameter's length from where I sensed my assailant to be. This circular dance lasted for some minutes. I soon began to tire and do not know what would have happened had not salvation appeared from the most unlikely of quarters. It announced itself in a volley of barks. The persistent yapping I used to find so irksome was suddenly the most angelic of voices. Dear Frolic! I could have burst out of my cage and hugged her; indeed, I would have done so had not she pushed through the willow fronds and pawed eagerly at my dress. I picked her up and kissed her on the nose. Cautiously we ventured outside. Of my shadowy attacker there was no sign. Nor was there any sign of Miss Adwick, the operatic tenor or any of the skating party. The harpsichord and whist tables rested on the ice, together with an abandoned muff and some empty wine glasses.

Clutching Frolic tightly, I made my way back to the house – not to my room, for that I now associated with danger, but to Miss Adwick's refuge by the fire. She, I was now certain, had sought safety by the fire and had deliberately exposed me to danger by leaving me in the cold. When Frolic and I reached the sitting room, the fire was out. I rang for the maid, but, unsurprisingly, she did not reply. But in the hearth there were logs and coal and soon I had a reassuring blaze to protect me. Drawing the screens round me, I sank back into her chair hugging Frolic whilst I took stock of my situation. I was hungry and thirsty, but with night coming on I dared not venture out into the unheated and unlit part of the house. Whilst I was considering my plight, my eye fell on a letter which had been addressed to me in Miss Adwick's hand and left in Frolic's basket. I tore open the envelope and read:

How does it feel to sit in my chair at last? Your instinct serves you well. In your present predicament it is, I suppose, as a safe a place as any. Well, as you can see, the cage is open and the bird has flown. Did you not admire the ease with which my friends spirited me away? It was exquisite, was it not? – and what a stroke of genius to manage it all under the guise of a skating party! Far from being in the wings – as you no doubt thought at the time – you were at the very heart of our little drama. My greatest regret is the loss of my beloved harpsichord, which I cannot bear to think of floating in the lake.

Oh Pentiman, with how small a quantity of affection did you allow yourself to be bought – so small that I could feel guilty were I so inclined. To make amends I leave you Frolic – a silly, yapping creature of whom I am happy to be rid – and for whom I no longer have any use. She will at least keep my late husband at bay – or at any rate that unexpended portion of malice that yet survives him. Cling to the warmth – avoid unlighted places – keep Frolic with you at all times – in a few days he will tire, leaving you free to go where you choose. I am not so completely heartless as to leave you without means – on the overmantel you will find two guineas and a testimonial which should enable you to find employment. As for your trunk – it is still, of course with Colonel and Mrs Standish. I have, needless to say, no cousin in Wisbech.

Do not think to find me, Pentiman. Those who effected my escape – my new husband chief among them – have also ensured my permanent erasure. If they succeed – as they surely will – you will never hear of, yours sincerely, Henrietta Fritton – née Adwick – again.

What devilry there was in that last sentence! For if my mistress was Lady Fritton, then her husband must surely have been the madcap lordling who had burnt down Marblewood. It was he, then, who had been the silent companion of my evenings; it was he who, having first sensed my presence in the window, had attached himself to me in mistake for – perhaps even in preference to – his wife. I have read that in India it is the custom to tether a goat in order to lure tigers into the range of the guns. That had been my role at Marblewood, but with this difference: that once they had flushed out the tiger, the hunters had turned and fled, leaving the goat to its fate. And in my case that fate was a terrible one. I was more a prisoner than ever and, though tormented by hunger and thirst, dared not stir from the fireside. There I remained for the rest of that day and half the next, but when at last the coal ran out and the pangs of hunger – both mine and Frolic's – became unbearable, I had no choice but to move. Summoning the last dregs of my courage and clutching Frolic tightly, I set off to find the kitchen. Sealed rooms, pregnant with menace, pressed in on me. At any moment I expected doors to fly open and release unimaginable horrors into the corridor. It had been Miss Adwick's express wish that I confine myself to my own quarters in the evening and to the music room with her during the day. Although she had promised to show me the rest of the house, she had always found some reason to postpone our tour. Now that I was free to pry as much as I liked, I was too afraid to do so. In the kitchen I remained only long enough to gather up such scraps of food as I could find before hurrying back with them to the music room. A second trip, and indeed a third, was needed to fetch sufficient coal to renew the fire. Fortunately, there were several buckets' worth beside the range; had there not been, I should have had to venture into the coal cellar, through whose open door I could see steps descending into total darkness. Sooner than venture there, I knew I would rather freeze or take my chance out of doors.

For four days I remained in the sitting room. By day I played patience; by night I dozed fitfully in Miss Adwick's chair. Without Frolic, who seemed to have transferred her affections wholly to me, I think I should have gone out of my wits. On the fifth day, when I knew that I would either have to descend to the cellar or let the fire out, I awoke to the sound of icicles dripping. It had begun to thaw. And there was another sound, too: the sound of voices, human voices. Putting on my bonnet and shawl, I hurried outside with Frolic under my arm and walked towards them. They were coming from the direction of the lake, which lay on the opposite side of the ruin. I turned the corner to see five scarecrow-like figures – local urchins most likely – throwing stones at what at first I took to be a boat half submerged in the lake and then, to my horror, realised was the harpsichord. Already the keyboard end had broken through the thinning ice and was sinking fast. Summoning my courage – after all, these were creatures of flesh and blood – I was about to shoo them away, when a burly figure in a black coat and John Bull hat appeared on the landing stage and bellowed across the lake at the intruders. For the best part of a minute, the two parties hurled insults at each other across the melting ice. But when the man left the landing stage and strode towards them, they turned and fled. Nonetheless, he continued to move in my direction, curious to see what the boys had been stoning.

"Good morning," I called when he came within earshot.

Frolic wriggled out of my grasp and ran up to him, jumping up and licking his hands.

"Why, it's Frolic," he said, picking up the dog, who seemed quite happy in his embrace. "And who," he asked, noticing me for the first time, "might you be, miss?"

"I am Lady Fritton's companion," I replied. "My name is Florence Pentiman."

"It's news to me she had a companion. Have you been with her for long?"

"Three months. But who, may I ask, are you?"

"Name of Arthur Bannerman. I'm Lady Fritton's gardener."

"Her gardener!" I laughed aloud. So Lady Fritton had had a gardener after all! In this, then, if in nothing else, she had been telling the truth. I must have laughed hysterically, for his manner changed and, coming closer, he examined me carefully and asked:

"Are you sure you're all right, miss? If you'll pardon me for saying so, you don't look well."

"I'm a little weak," I said. "It will soon pass." Unable to check myself, I continued: "I haven't eaten – not properly eaten – for five days. Nor slept, nor ..."

On the threshold of my story I hesitated. What stranger would believe such a tale? And what servant would believe such a tale of his mistress? Sensing my distress, Bannerman pulled a chair off the ice and placed it on the bank.

"Sit here," he said. "The dog cart is at the lodge gate. You don't look up to walking that far."

"Dog cart?" I echoed in alarm. "Where are you taking me?"

"I'm taking you home, so my wife can feed you."

As we drove along between the frozen dykes and meres, Bannerman, at my prompting, told me a little of himself. Of how he had been a gardener at Marblewood; of how, after the fire, he had become a fenman, servicing the steam pumps which were then coming into service; of how the last Lord Fritton, on bringing his new wife home to the dower house, had paid him to keep an eye on the park; of how he had continued to serve Lady Fritton after her husband's disappearance.

"And what kind of man was the late Lord Fritton?" I asked.

"Charming when sober, ill-tempered – even violent – when drunk, especially towards his wife, of whom he was insanely jealous. A man had only to look at her and he would lose all control. After that he was the very devil. Once, perhaps more than once, he struck his wife in public."

"And then?"

"Well, he disappeared, no-one knows where exactly. All her ladyship would say was that her friends had arranged a permanent separation, whatever that might mean. Fled in shame, most likely, perhaps to the colonies, where most young gentlemen of that sort are sent to reflect on their excesses."

"He does not sound like a man who would flee in shame."

"Then perhaps he's still there."

At this point we left the road and turned on to a track leading to a brick building which housed one of his steam pumps. Beside it was a low-roofed cottage with a large vegetable patch along one side.

If he was still there – and I presumed by 'there' he meant Marblewood or its environs – then where was he exactly?

"One of the cellars maybe, for you can still get to the cellars in the ruin, or at the bottom of the lake, or even in the icehouse."

"Ice house?"

"It's the small beehive-like building behind the terrace of the main hall."

Over the next few days Bannerman and his family restored me to health and spirits. Mrs Bannerman fed me and washed my clothes; their children fussed over Frolic. Bannerman even invited me – a rare privilege according to his wife – to warm myself by the steam pump, joking that winter had got such a grip on my bones that it would take more than the kitchen range to shift it.

Both he and his wife tried to coax my story out of me. The memories were still painful and in any case I very much doubted that I could make Bannerman and his wife believe them, so, omitting all mention of Miss Adwick, I told them that I had been engaged by Lady Fritton, that she had suddenly and inexplicably disappeared and had left me in sole possession of the dower house. Of the sinister revenant, the musical soirées and the skating party, I made no mention.

As I warmed myself by the steam pump, I had time to take stock. My belongings, such as they were, remained with the Standishes and if, with the help of Miss Adwick's testimonial, I was to start anew, I needed to recover them. Two guineas were all I had to show from my sojourn at Marblewood, but among my other possessions were a few items I could pawn and these sums would, I hoped, see me through until I could find new employment. At first the Bannermans would not hear of my going, but after a extracting a solemn promise that I should return if no situation materialised within a few weeks, they agreed to let me go. Mrs Bannerman gave me some potato cakes wrapped in a cloth; the children reluctantly surrendered Frolic; and Bannerman offered to drive me to the station. It required the utmost self-control not to look back. With Miss Adwick's testimonial in my pocket and the Bannermans' promise of a refuge should the need arise, I resolved to be cheerful, and in this robust state of mind steeled myself for the encounter with the Standishes.

From the moment I alighted from the train, I felt my courage ebb away. Christmas was coming on. In all the windows there was a great show of baubles and evergreens, and for the first time it struck me that until the festivities were over no-one would want to engage me as governess, lady's companion or anything else. This I had quite failed to foresee. My courage underwent a further loss when, opening the Standishes' front gate, I caught sight of five heads peeping out of the landing window. Although I could hear nothing, I could sense the explosion of excitement inside the house. I had scarcely raised the knocker, when the door flew open and I was greeted, not as I had hoped by the maidservant, but by the entire family. As I stood on the step confronting my former employer and his wife, the five boys spilt out of the door on either side of me, closed in from the rear and propelled me into the house.

"Where the devil have you been, Pentiman?" demanded the Colonel.

"And where was the three months' notice to which we were entitled?" protested his wife.

"And whatever kind of dog is this?" scoffed Standish Major, trying to wrest Frolic from me.

"Did you see that?" shouted Standish Secundus. "It bit him."

"Vicious!" observed Standish Tertius.

"Decidedly," added Standish Quartus.

"Then it must be taught a lesson," squeaked Standish Minimus.

"Speaking of which," continued Mrs Standish, "do you realise that these children have not had a single hour of instruction since you left? Governesses are a scarcer commodity than one had supposed – at least, at a price one is prepared to pay."

"It would d___d odd if some kind of moral atrophy hasn't set in," observed the Colonel.

In vain did I try to explain that whilst it was true I had not given formal notice, I had believed that Miss Adwick had informed them and that my trunk had been collected by her cousin; that I was sorry for any distress my actions might have caused; that they were under a misapprehension that I was reporting for duty, for I had come merely to collect my belongings, after which I meant to trouble them no further. They ignored me completely, making it plain that they intended me to serve out my notice whether I would or no. When I protested, the colonel and his wife, followed by the pack of hounds at their heels, marched me upstairs and locked me in my old room. No sooner had they turned the key on the outside, than I heard Frolic yelping on the landing. I beat with my fists on the door and begged them to let me keep her. "Please, please," I begged. "I will serve out my notice if you allow me to keep the dog."

Frolic's barks grew fainter as their footsteps receded down the corridor.

Dec 20?: Frost at nights. The maid who brings me my meals is ordered to tell me that lessons are to resume after the festive season. I shall use the interval to set down my story from first to last. And I shall begin with Miss Adwick's advertisement in The Morning Post.

Dec 21?: Lessons have still to resume. I must presume the moral atrophy of the boys continues unchecked. Today I took up my pen.

Dec ?: I have lost all count of the days. Christmas must have passed. The church bells have stopped, but in the street I hear horses, passers-by, the sounds of everyday life returning after the festive season. Work progresses.

Dec ?: Cold, so cold. My narrative is nearly complete.

Dec ?: Tomorrow I return to the schoolroom. The boys, I am assured, are eager to be at their studies.

Dec ?: Lessons resume, moral atrophy checked. An uneasy peace in the schoolroom. The fire smokes, the young wolves are sly, hatching some scheme no doubt.

Dec ?: I am summoned by Mrs Standish who waves a document under my nose. It is Miss Adwick's testimonial. Lies, she says, lies from start to finish and throws it in the fire. Claims she has a duty to protect future employers. Then a wonderful thing happens. Frolic appears, leaps on me, upsetting Mrs Standish's silver tea tray. We are banished to my room. Was ever such joyful banishment?

New Year's Eve: Church bells from six different parishes. A frosty sky. Frolic restless in the night. Woke several times to find her alert, ears bristling. I fear, I very much fear ... but I dare not set down what it is I fear lest uttering bring it on. What if everything returns?

New Year's Day: High words in the schoolroom. The uneasy truce breaks. An exchange of wolvish grins. Oh they knew what they were doing from the very start. First the hounds are introduced into the schoolroom. And then Frolic.

Jan ???: No fire in my room. We must save coal, says Mrs Standish. By candlelight I read my narrative twice through from beginning to end. I stand by it, every word. I pick up the tumbler of water from my bedside table. From top to bottom it is full of ice.

The unasked question which had been hanging over us since Tunbridge found an answer somewhere between Penshurst and Edenbridge. I refer, of course, to the question none of us had dared put to the Malachi Browns: namely, 'What is it that pteridologists actually do?' It was Mr Dacre who blurted out the answer. "Ferns!" he exclaimed, voicing a thought that must have occurred to the rest of us at more or less the same time. "Pteridology is the study of ferns."

What had prompted him was an involuntary action of Mr Alfred. Miss Binnie and Mme Fontana had shown a conspicuous lack of interest in Dr leGrove's tale whilst he was telling it and a marked lack of appreciation after he had finished. Both were engrossed by their books, Fontana by, of all things, Sir Charles Lyell's *Principles of Geology*, Binnie by a novel of George Sand. At one point as Binnie turned the page, a pressed fern slipped out and fell to the floor, whereupon Mr Alfred picked it up and, saying "Ah, *Polypodium dryopteris* – most likely from Scotland or the Lake District", returned it to Binnie.

"How did you know that?" she asked suspiciously.

"I should be a poor pteridologist if I did not," he returned.

And it was at this point that Mr Dacre exclaimed: "Ferns! Pteridology is the study of ferns."

"Indeed," assented Mr Alfred, "though it is not to be confused with pteridomania which denotes the present frenzy for collecting them."

"Not a term that Mr Alfred and I care to use," continued Mrs Alfred, "since many of the enthusiasts to whom he supplies rare specimens might be said to be suffering from it. After all, one does not offend one's clients, especially when one has, as yet, so few of them."

"Of course," sighed her husband, "it is not how I began in life."

"Indeed no," confirmed Mrs Alfred.

"Ferns," he continued, "crept in, as it were, by the back door, though that makes them sound like weeds, which, until people began cramming them into Wardian cases and conservatories, I suppose they were. I began life as a geologist and indeed knew, if only slightly, the great Sir Charles Lyell, whose book you see in Mme Fontana's hand. It was as fossilised imprints in coal seams that I first made the acquaintance of ferns, together with the acquaintance of those foolish enough to believe that those imprints had been left there by the Noachian flood."

"Oh spare us the Noachian flood, Alfred," exclaimed wife, who clearly felt that her marriage had been irrigated enough by it already. "Tell us one of your stories about the great fern collectors."

"As you wish, my dear," said Mr Alfred stiffly, "but the Noachian question is far from settled. The diluvianists ..."

"Diluvianists?" queried Mr Bartholomew.

"Those who believe in the existence of Noah's Flood."

"Then as a clergyman," remarked Dr leGrove, "I must confess to being something of a diluvianist myself. It is rather expected of one."

"Shame on you, Dr leGrove," said Mme Fontana.

Dr leGrove looked startled.

"Why, Mme Fontana," said he, "I should have thought that you of all people would have conceded that there are more things in heaven and earth than are dreamt of in our philosophy."

"I think no such thing," she replied, "and you have no right to assume that I should."

"But your profession must surely incline you to the view that there are mysteries too profound for our comprehension."

"You will oblige me by leaving my profession out of it," rejoined Mme Fontana.

"Emily!" said Binnie sharply.

"But what do you say to your clients," persisted Dr leGrove, "when they ask you whether you are in touch with the Beyond?"

"Why, whatever comes into my head, of course," replied Mme Fontana.

"Emily!" repeated Binnie.

"If my clients are foolish enough to part with their hard-earned money...."

"Emily!"

"... then naturally I give them what they paid for."

"Even if it means telling them something that you yourself do not believe?" asked Dr leGrove.

"Particularly if it means telling them something that I do not myself believe."

"Emily," interjected Binnie, "these confidences are ill-judged. You will come to regret them."

"But what about séances?" asked Mr Scudamore.

"Hocus pocus."

"And manifestations?"

"Mere trumpery. You look surprised, Dr leGrove. Yes, I confess to taking advantage of the gullible, but since I bring them comfort, where is the harm in it? If I dispense illusions, in what way is that different from Mr Malachi Brown's selling what, on his own admission, are merely exotic weeds? In either case, no harm is done and some good, at the level of the individual, may come of it."

Binnie, who had given up all pretence of reading George Sand, now joined the fray.

"Has it occurred to you, Dr leGrove," she said, "or indeed to any of the gentlemen present, that being a medium or clair-voyant is one of only three ways a woman can establish her inde-pendence? Unless she inherits money – in which case she will be plagued by suitors – or stoops to becoming a governess, like Miss Pentiman, she faces a choice of slaveries: namely, marrying or throwing herself on the charity of others. The mediums one now encounters everywhere may or may not be frauds, but they are at least women of independent means. There is, of course, a fourth choice, the Great Evil, the existence of which polite society simply refuses to acknowledge."

Polite society in the form of Miss Osgood and Mr Bartholomew looked decidedly uncomfortable and were relieved when Mr Malachi Brown returned the subject to the Noachian Flood, from which, in his view, it should never have been diverted.

"The catastrophists," he said, "whilst granting that fossils are indeed the traces of living creatures, hold that they were transported to where we now find them by Noah's Flood and there turned into stone by some kind of lapidifying juice, a convenient fiction which enables them to maintain that our planet is no more than a few thousand years old. Gradualists, of whom I account myself one, hold this to be erroneous. A universal flood would have scattered the remains of living creatures thinly over the earth's surface and not into the earth's depths which is where we commonly find them."

"Your vehemence does you credit," said Mr Dacre, "but why would a man who feels so keenly on this subject abandon it for the study of mere ferns?"

"In a word," replied Malachi Brown, "money. It is hard to support a wife by the study of rocks alone. In ferns, about which I had acquired a useful stock of knowledge, almost, as it were, by accident, I saw a chance of securing a steady income. I was wrong. Hence the lamentable state of my hat and of my wife's gloves."

"But it has been worth it, has it not, Alfred?" asked Mrs Malachi Brown sweetly.

Mr Malachi Brown affected not to hear.

"Tell them one of your tales of the great fern hunters. Tell them the tale of Strickland and Flowerdew. This was the tale, ladies and gentlemen, by which I was wooed and won."

"Very well," said her husband, "since it obviously pleases the company to listen to idle tales rather than to scientific argument, I shall, with great reluctance, oblige."

The Pteridologist's (and his Wife's) Tale of Strickland and Flowerdew

Albert Pryce named a collier brig after his infant daughter and later had her carved, several times larger than life, on the figurehead. From the outset the *Albertine* was a lucky ship. Though confined to the Severn Estuary, she was never short of a cargo. The growth of the railways, with their insatiable appetite for coal, saw to that. Over the next few years, she was joined by so many sister ships that it was said one could not stand on the shores of the Severn without seeing at least two sailing in opposite directions. Soon Albert Pryce set his sights on higher things. Wishing to become a transatlantic shipping magnate, he sold his brigs, moved his family into Albert Court, a grand house overlooking the Mersey, and launched the *Princess Albertina*, a side-wheel paddle steamer modelled on Mr Brunel's *Great Western*. "No more floating coal scuttles for us," he said on the day that the *Princess Albertina* set off on her maiden voyage to New York.

Bigger and better steamships followed, enabling Pryce to indulge Albertina more than ever. When her governess remarked that she had rarely met with such a bookish child, her father built her a library; when she expressed an interest in the night sky, he built her an observatory; and when she began to show early signs of pteridomania, an affliction then unknown on Merseyside, he built her a conservatory. In general these enthusiasms were short lived. In the library the books remained unopened and from the observatory the stars largely unobserved. But the pteridomania raged unabated. In her sitting room Wardian cases full of rare specimens filled every available surface, so much so that, as one of her friends remarked, one almost expected to hear the roar of dinosaurs, dinosaurs then being the novelty du jour. Yet in the conservatory itself the dinosaurs refused to oblige. The cathedral of iron and glass was so vast that it swallowed up everything placed inside it. The ferns which Albertine and her friends brought back from Anglesey and the Lake District were lost in the splendour of it. If it was hints of the Jurassic she wanted, she would have to look elsewhere.. Someone, she decided, would have to pay a visit to the tropics on her behalf.

This was the state of affairs when Albertine's brother, down from Cambridge, invited two friends to stay at Albert Court. Strickland and Flowerdew were rivals of long standing. Thomas Strickland was a foundling, who had been taken in by a military tailor and re-fashioned as a gentleman by Dr Arnold of Rugby. Henry Flowerdew was the son of a down-at-heel country squire, who, though poor and getting poorer, could at least boast sixteen quarterings in his coat of arms. It was hardly surprising, therefore, that there was friction between them. The one envied the other his income, the other the one his quarterings. At Cambridge this rivalry had stayed within bounds, Flowerdew and his cronies toasting the martial spirit of the Royal Tailoring Corps, Strickland offering to pass round the hat for indigent country squires. What ended this pleasant chaffing was their first encounter with Albertine. It was love at first sight, not on her part, to be sure, though she was amused by their attention for a time before becoming irritated by it. Flowerdew urged his sixteen quarterings, Strickland his father's overseas contracts. These arguments quickly became counter-arguments when they changed hands. "Trade, mere trade", scoffed Flowerdew, unaware that Albertine had started life as a collier brig; "Snobbery, pure snobbery," sniffed Strickland, ignorant of the fact that Albertine's father, like his own, had applied to the College of Heralds for a grant of arms. Finding that these calumnies met with little success, the two rivals changed tack. Flowerdew declared himself a bibliophile, whilst Strickland acquired a passion for stargazing. A few months earlier these enthusiasms might have endeared themselves; now they left Albertine unmoved.

"Well, you can imagine what happened next," said Mrs Alfred, taking up the thread. Far from being irritated by having his wife appropriate the story, Mr Alfred asked if he might borrow Mme Fontana's copy of Sir Charles Lyell and was instantly engrossed by it.

On the same day, continued Mrs Alfred, almost at the same hour that Flowerdew became an ardent pteridologist, Strickland revealed to Albertine that he was one, too. "And have been for some considerable time," he said, adding, "Of course my interest is largely scientific. Flowerdew's – insofar as he has one – is confined to Flowerdew Hall. So damp are the rooms I am told that ferns flourish in the most unexpected of places. Rumour has it that Old Squire Flowerdew found one growing in his shaving mug."

Albertine liked the sound of Flowerdew Hall.

Together they made the tour of the conservatory, a vast tank of humid air in which a few commonplace ferns struggled towards the light. In such a place it was impossible to imagine the dinosaurs thriving. She confessed as much to Strickland.

"Hardly surprising," remarked Strickland, "what you need are tree ferns, *Dicksonia Antarctica* perhaps. Or even ..."

"What was the word, Alfred?" asked Mrs Alfred.

"*Dicksonia Squarrosa*," said Mr Alfred without looking up from his book.

"*Dicksonia Squarrosa*," said Strickland, who had put in a couple of hours in the library before Flowerdew was astir, unaware the Flowerdew had done the same the previous evening after everyone else was abed. "Only then will you hear the dinosaurs roar."

"*Dicksonia squarrosa?*" echoed Flowerdew dismissively. "In Amazonia you could do better than that."

Seeing in this exchange an opportunity to be rid of her suitors, by whom she was now thoroughly bored, Albertine proposed a challenge. Whoever was the first to present her with a new kind of fern, she said, would win her hand – and, in the case of a tie, the larger specimen would prevail. With that she dismissed them and, within a few days, had forgotten all about them. That they might take her challenge seriously never occurred to her. It was a caprice, a jeu d'esprit, nothing more. And, if God forbid, they were to arrive on her doorstep with a fern as high as a house, well, she could always say that she had seen bigger ones at Kew. Suspecting nothing of this, Strickland and Flowerdew hurried away to make their plans.

Three months later Flowerdew disembarked at Para, the port of entry to the vast region watered by the Amazons. The steamer was greeted by bells and fireworks and the passengers, as they stepped ashore, by a military band in splendid scarlet uniforms. Flowerdew scanned the crowds on the quayside anxiously for signs of Strickland. Though it was unlikely that his rival had preceded him, he could not be sure. With Strickland one never knew. He might even have persuaded the military tailor to charter a steam ship for his excusive use. And why not? Surely all was fair in love and ferns. Had his pater had the money, he would have done the same himself.

For the moment, however, there was no sign of his rival, so Flowerdew was able to look about him with satisfaction. Para was a city of red roofs and white walls, of towers and cupolas hemmed in on three sides by towering vegetation. With luck he might not have to stir far beyond the city boundaries to find what he sought. But if that were the case, he reflected, might not Strickland have succeeded already – and if not here, then in some other corner of Amazonia? With this alarming thought in mind, he hurried ashore, entrusted his trunks to two mulattoes and directed them, in halting Portuguese, to the house of a Mr James Urquhart, an eminent botanist to whom he had been given a letter of introduction. A mutual friend had agreed to recommend him as an enthusiastic fern collector who wished to extend his knowledge of tropical species. Nonetheless, Flowerdew was nervous. So formidable was Urquhart's reputation that he feared being quickly unmasked as a sham. But he need not have worried. All Urquhart required was a willing listener. After years in the wilderness, he was desperate to share his carefully hoarded knowledge of forest flora. No sooner had Flowerdew set foot in the house than he launched into an exhaustive account of his various expeditions up the Amazon tributaries and scarcely drew breath till lunch time.

After lunch, he reappeared wearing a tam o' shanter and a kilt in the Urquhart tartan. "I never go out dressed in any other way," he said. "The natives relish a pair of fine knees, and mine, I'm told, are among the best." He proceeded to take Flowerdew on a guided tour of those parts of the forest which encroached on the edges of the city. Mangoes and palms with their luxuriant crowns towered above white-walled houses, and beyond the orange and lemon plantations, the forest rose up like a wall. In the tree tops there were flashes of brilliant plumage as macaws and parrots went about their business, adding their voices to the cacophony of frogs and monkeys that welled up from below. Seeing Flowerdew put his hands to his ears, Urquhart shouted, "You'll get used to it. When you've been here as long as I have, you hardly notice it." Flowerdew somehow doubted it and wondered how anyone ever managed to sleep during expeditions into the interior.

"Well, there you have it," said Urquhart, as they returned to the house towards the end of the afternoon. "After supper I suggest we take a montara – that's a native canoe, by the way – and visit one of the islands. I can guarantee you a fine display of fireflies if nothing else."

"If it's all the same to you," said Flowerdew, "I am rather tired. I have had a long day and should welcome the chance to turn in early."

"Of course, of course. How thoughtless of me. Till tomorrow then."

A second day of botanical sightseeing ensued, by which time Flowerdew felt that he had done his duty as a guest. Urquhart made no mention of Strickland, so Flowerdew felt confident that he was ahead of his rival, unless, of course, his rival had decided to search elsewhere. This, he judged, was a good a time as any to broach the subject of ferns.

"Ferns?" said Urquhart. "There's no shortage of ferns in these parts. You've but to step outside the city and you'll find plenty; the trouble is that I've not yet set eyes on any I couldn't find back home in Cromarty. From what I hear the best specimens are to be found on the lower Tocantins river system and to reach that you'll need a vigilinga."

A vigilinga turned out to be a two-masted vessel with an awning thatched with palm leaves. It took two days to agree a price with the owner and a further two to recruit a crew of mamelucoes and to provision the vessel for a return voyage of ten days. The mouth of the Tocantins, though only forty miles as the crow flies, was some eighty or more following the bends of the river.

"Good luck!" shouted Urquhart as they cast off. "Don't go further up the Tocantins than the first rapids. There's no need. You should find what you're looking for near the mouth of the river. Three days should see you there. Four at most."

It took a week. There was little wind and the mamelucoes were obliged to row against the current, at which they grumbled excessively. The only way to appease them, Flowerdew found, was to allow frequent stops at the towns and villages along the water's edge. Here a second hazard presented itself. Once the word got about that an English botanist was making his way upriver, everyone wanted to meet him. Merchants, sawmill owners, government clerks, mining engineers all turned out to greet him. One wanted to know about the latest in jute manufacturing, another about Little Nell. Was it true, he asked, that she was dead? How could Senhor Dickens be so heartless? A third had heard that screw propulsion was taking over from paddle wheels. How was this possible? And if possible, how long before they appeared on the Amazon? At first Flowerdew enjoyed their attention, but quickly discovered that with every successive stop it was harder to retrieve his crew. Some drank themselves into a stupor with cashiri, a liquor fermented from berries by the Indians; others disappeared up-country to visit relatives. In the end he had to restrict stops to uninhabited islands, much to the chagrin of the mamelucoes who retaliated by demanding more breaks than ever.

A week after leaving Para they entered the network of narrow channels at the mouth of the Tocantins. It soon became clear that the streams were too shallow for the vigilinga, so leaving it in the charge of one of the mamelucoes named Joaquim, they proceeded in the montara which they had been towing behind them as far as the Guaribas rapids. Here the river was about a mile wide and choked with rocks, between which the currents twisted themselves into numerous eddies and whirlpools. At the rapids themselves, they took to the bank and dragged the canoes along the forest path until they reached the upper level of the river. There the stream ran broad and deep between palm-fringed woods of brilliant green. Beyond the shoreline they could see groves of Brazil nut trees, in and out of which flew flocks of hyacinth-blue macaws. But what caught Flowerdew's eye were not the trees or the jewel-like birds, but the ferns. Here at last were tree ferns, ferns of a kind that Flowerdew had not seen before, in unimaginable profusion. As he stepped out of the canoe to examine them, he fancied he could hear the roar of dinosaurs and with it Albertine's voice issuing her challenge. It was a trick of the forest, no doubt, howler monkeys perhaps, or the noise of rapids further upstream. Selecting a vigorous plant that would not overhang the canoe, he severed it at the base with his machete.

"I name this fern *Dryopteris Albertina*," he announced holding it aloft.

The mamelucoes clapped loudly.

"We rest now," they said. "Have drink, celebrate."

"Certainly not," replied Flowerdew in alarm, fearful that Strickland might appear round a bend in the river at any moment. "We carry canoes over rocks now."

But the mamelucoes were adamant. They had triumphed; Senhor Flowerdew had triumphed; they must celebrate. So Flowerdew fumed quietly whilst they drank themselves senseless with cashiri, which they had acquired from Indians on their various stops along the river.

It was late the next day when they reached the vigilinga. With more grumbling than usual, the mamelucoes allowed themselves to be bullied and bribed into turning round the vessel and threading through the myriad waterways of the Tocantins and out into the Amazon, whose strong current bore them quickly back to Para.

On the quayside, the military bandsmen, who, since Flowerdew had last seen them, had added silver epaulettes to their scarlet uniforms, were celebrating the Feast of San Thome with vigour. Pausing only to claim the golden sovereigns Flowerdew had promised them, the mamelucoes quickly clambered ashore and disappeared in search of cashiri to drink the saint's health. Flowerdew was left to carry his *Dryopteris Albertina* back to Urquhart's house on his own. Urquhart was not impressed.

"*Dryopteris Albertina*, you say? I'm no pteridologist, but I'd say that was a common or garden *Dicksonia Fibrosa*. As I recall, there's a particularly fine specimen in the Botanical Gardens in Edinburgh. Not that it matters. It won't be with us for long. See here, the fronds are beginning to die back already. You weren't too canny when you cut it off at the roots. I should have thought you would have known your business better than that."

Flowerdew had returned to the house in Para to find Urquhart packing his trunk. All that talk of ferns, he said, had made him homesick for his native glen and it would give him great pleasure to introduce Flowerdew to its botanical delights. Could he count, therefore, on the pleasure of his company for the voyage home?

Needless to say, Flowerdew was tempted, sorely tempted. But the thought of returning to Albertine empty-handed, or, worse, finding Strickland triumphant was too much to bear. He would stay. Or rather, he would stay if Urquhart would lend him enough money to make a second attempt. The sad fact was that he was down to his last few golden sovereigns. Not that there was anything new in that: it was, indeed, his normal state. Even at Cambridge he was always short of funds and was for ever writing home for money which he knew his father did not have.

Urquhart was reluctant to oblige, not because he was ungenerous, but because he recognised a consuming obsession when he saw one.

"If I'm to lend you money," he said, "I want to know the real reason you're here. You're no pteridologist, that's for sure."

Flowerdew admitted that he was not.

"And unless I'm much mistaken, there is a young lady somewhere at the back of all this."

Flowerdew admitted there was.

"You'll regret this," said Urquhart. "Whether you return empty-handed or whether you don't, believe me, you'll regret it. Very well then. Call me a sentimental old fool, but I'll lend you fifty guineas, payable with interest on your return, which may be next month or, who knows, never."

Urquhart counted out fifty guineas from his strong box and handed them to Flowerdew.

"And you're to telegraph me the moment you get back to Liverpool. I want to know my money's safe – and you with it, you damn fool."

Flowerdew handed back one of the fifty guineas to Urquhart.

"If I am not back within six months," he said, "I want you to do something for me. Find a florist in Liverpool and order the largest fern you can find and have it sent to Albert Court."

Flowerdew escorted Urquhart to the quayside and saw him safe aboard the steamer. The sky was overcast, and the military bandsmen, with black sashes over their scarlet tunics, were playing a dirge, the bishop of this vast Amazonian diocese having died some days previously. With a blast of its whistle and an eruption of black smoke from its funnels, the steamer edged out into the river.

"I'm in good hands," shouted Urquhart, pointing to a brass plate which bore the name of a Clydeside ship builder. "I would to God that you were."

Flowerdew's second expedition was a desperate affair. Unable to afford a vigilinga, he was forced to borrow a montara. Of the original mamelucoes, only Joaquim and one other agreed to accompany him, but not beyond the Guaribas. That, they insisted, was the domain of the Curupira, the spirit of the forest, who, though slow to anger, could be terrifying when roused. Flowerdew decided not to contest the point, hoping that his companions could be persuaded when the time came. But his powers of persuasion were never put to the test, for he lost both mamelucoes in quick succession, Joaquim to a boa constrictor, which unlooped itself from an overhanging branch and pulled him out of the canoe, the other to the Guaribas rapids themselves into which he fell whilst trying to clamber up the rocks beside them. As he watched the body churning in the water below, Flowerdew knew that the only sensible course was to turn back. But even as he hesitated, the voice of Albertine urged him on. "Only a little further," it seemed to say. "You must not give up now."

Making sure that the canoe was safely moored, he shouldered his rifle and pack and set off upriver, attended by clouds of cabouri fly. Alert to the dangers that might lurk in low-hanging branches, he picked his way though the forest, cutting a path with his machete and trying, unsuccessfully, to banish all thoughts of the Curupira from his head. Just when the vegetation had become all but impenetrable, he emerged with a cry of surprise into a large clearing with a narrow opening on to the river. Crimson flowers ran up tree trunks and across the forest floor, whilst overhead flew tanagers, flecking the branches with scarlet. What had caused him to cry out in astonishment were not the flowers, nor even the birds, but a hut. Festooned in crimson blossoms, its roof had partly collapsed and its door hung limply on one hinge. It was built on low piles, one of which seemed to have been gnawed through by ants, so that the edifice looked as if it were about to topple over. Machete at the ready, he crept slowly forward and freed the door which had wedged itself half open against the tilting floor.

Inside were a table and chair, their legs reduced to thin sticks by the ants, an oil lamp and in the corner a wooden cot in which lay the body of a man covered in a soiled blanket. Flowerdew hesitated on the threshold, unsure whether the man was alive or dead. Suddenly the man shuddered and sat bolt upright, reached out a quivering hand to the newcomer and cried out "Aqua!" Flowerdew poured a few drops from his water bottle between the man's lips, whereupon the stranger tried to grab the bottle, but, exhausting himself in the attempt, fell back upon the pillow. Cautiously, Flowerdew drew back the blanket and looked at him. From his dress it was clear that he was a European and from his confused mumblings he was able to pick out a few words of Portuguese.

Flowerdew now faced an agonising choice. He could leave the man to his fate – and by the look of him that was not far off – or he could nurse him back to health. There was no sign of a canoe, so escape by water was impossible. The only way out of the clearing was the way he had entered, and if he lingered more than a few days the path he had cleared would have grown over again. Every rational consideration urged retreat. And yet Flowerdew hesitated. Old Squire Flowerdew, his father, never turned a beggar from his door and something of the father's generosity had descended to the son. Try as he might, Flowerdew could not bring himself to abandon the man in the cot.

He lit a fire, boiled water in a saucepan and washed the man's hands and face. Amongst the latter's belongings he found a razor and so was able to shave him. He removed the man's shirt and washed it in the river. Later, he shared his scanty rations with him, telling him of how, having lost two companions, he had moored his canoe below the Guaribas and proceeded alone, of how he had been on a previous expedition and even, as he warmed to his theme, of his reasons for coming into Amazonia in the first place. The man allowed himself to be fed and, having stopped his confused ramblings, turned his yellow eyes on his saviour and appeared to listen intently. Afterwards, Flowerdew tucked the man into his cot. When he placed his hand on the man's forehead, it seemed to him that the fever had abated a little.

That night Flowerdew slept little. By now had had grown used to the forest noises, but the passage of ants over his hands and face was a persistent irritation, as were the scufflings of rats beneath the piles. It was hardly surprising that he felt listless next day. The stranger, on the other hand, was showing signs of recovery and, by afternoon, was able to leave his cot and take a few steps across the uneven floor of the hut. That evening they ate the last of their provisions. Tomorrow, thought Flowerdew wearily, he would have to summon his strength and go hunting in the forest. After tucking up his patient, he spread his blanket on the floor and, ignoring the ants, fell into a profound sleep.

He was awakened by the sun streaming through the open doorway. Outside he could see the crimson tanagers flitting between the tree tops and smell the heavy scent of the crimson flowers. Wearily, he pulled himself to his feet and looked about him. The hut was empty. The stranger had gone. So, too, had his rifle and machete. He rushed outside and called frantically, creating uproar amongst the howler monkeys and macaws. When, at last, it died down, he strained his ears for the sound of an answering voice. There was none. Worse still, the voice of Albertine, which had never ceased to urge him on, had fallen silent. For the first time in his life Flowerdew knew what it meant to be utterly, terrifyingly alone.

Malachi Brown shut Sir Charles Lyell with a loud snap and looked about him.

"Where are we?" he asked.

"Flowerdew has just been abandoned," said Mrs Alfred. "Betrayed by the man for whom he had sacrificed everything to save."

"That was not what I meant," remarked Mr Alfred. "I wanted to know if we had reached Reigate yet. But since you mention Flowerdew, I wish to make it clear that I have no sympathy with him whatsoever. It does not do to trust complete strangers or tell them everything on the mistaken assumption that they speak no English. Strickland was far more sensible."

"I'd forgotten all about Strickland," remarked Mr Critchley. "What happened to him? We haven't heard from him for some time."

What happened to Strickland? laughed Mr Alfred. Why, he was loafing in his club in St James's. Whilst Flowerdew was toiling through the jungle, Strickland spent most of the time playing whist. That may seem a coward's way out, but Albertine had said nothing about going to Amazonia in person. She had wanted a rare fern and did not seem to care how she got it. So why should he expose himself to danger, when he could pay someone else to do it for him? And, as it happened, he knew just the man. His adoptive father, the military tailor, had recently won a contract to supply uniforms to the Brazilian army. He even had a man at Para to supervise their distribution. Imagine the latter's surprise when he received a letter from his employer's son offering him a generous reward to go fern hunting. Well, you can guess the rest. Taking his own montara, he made his way into the Tocantins river system, where he knew there were huts in which miners rested on their journeys into the interior. It was in one of these, between the Guaribas and the next set of rapids that he contracted a fever and fell into the delirium in which a pair of passing miners found him. Denied the use of their hut, they took his canoe, rifle and machete in lieu of rent. When he recovered, he exacted the same penalty from Flowerdew, telling himself that it was merely the custom of the country. Once in the forest he was able to follow his predecessor's tracks. Pausing only to gather a choice specimen – some kind of *Cyatheales*, no doubt – he made his way back to the Guaribas, where he found the canoe and, surrendering himself to the current, was carried swiftly back to Para.

Here Mrs Alfred, who clearly did not care much for Strickland, intervened to bring us news of Albertine.

Albertine, she continued, was surprised to receive two ferns on the same day, the one a splendid tree fern which she placed in the conservatory, the other a humble *Polypodium dryopteris* in a Wardian case which she placed on the mantelpiece of a little used parlour.

What my wife has omitted to mention, said Mr Alfred, is that the ferns were an embarrassment. By now she had completely forgotten about Strickland and Flowerdew and had become engaged to the son of a shipping magnate. The last thing the parents wanted was for this cosy arrangement to be disturbed by the arrival of a couple of unsolicited ferns and the glutinous notes of affection that accompanied them. Hence their banishment to obscure corners of the house.

"So what happened to Strickland and Flowerdew?" asked Mme Fontana.

Strickland got over it quickly enough, said Mr Alfred, and married an heiress with enough quarterings to satisfy the military tailor. Not a happy marriage, I'm told, but then what marriage is? As for Flowerdew, I have no idea what happened. Still marooned in the jungle for all I know.

Don't listen to him, said Mrs Alfred. He only says these things to vex me. With help from the local Indians, Flowerdew made his way painfully back, village by village, to Para. For a time he lived there as a beggar, but was eventually rescued by Urquhart, who, having had no news of him for over two years, had returned to the Amazon to look for him.

"And there you have it," concluded Mr Alfred with a yawn. "A romantic tale for those of you who care for that sort of thing; a tale, not unworthy, I imagine, of George Sand herself, eh, Miss Binnie?"

Not if that really was the end, said Mrs Alfred. But it isn't. The true end involves the ferns. One day a maidservant ran screaming to Albertine's father that she had found huge spiders in the conservatory. They had legs a foot long and were covered in reddish-grey hair.

"Almost certainly *Heteropodidae* or crab spiders," said Mr Alfred. "Common in the Americas. Ferocious looking beasts to be sure, but harmless to humans. They make quite good pets I am told. I have often been tempted to keep one myself."

"Don't you dare, Alfred. Whatever they were, it was obvious they'd come from the tree fern."

"Which they threw on the bonfire without first having it properly identified it," interjected Mr Alfred bitterly. "What would I not have given to have catalogued it!"

"And what about the other fern?" asked Miss Binnie. "Did I understand you to say that the end involved both ferns?"

Indeed I did, replied Mrs Alfred. One day after an argument about the wedding arrangements with her husband-to-be – an argument which revealed a brutal and mercenary side to his nature which she had not observed before – she fled weeping to the little-used parlour to which she had banished Flowerdew's gift. Fearful of being pursued, she slipped inside and turned the key. To her surprise the room seemed to be full of foliage. Flowerdew's fern had burst through its glass walls and overflowed into the room. Great fronds soared towards the ceiling and the sun, shining through them, threw lattices of greenish light across every surface in the room.

"From a scientific point of view, I feel bound to point out that this is highly improbable," observed Mr Alfred.

Improbable or not, she felt that Flowerdew was somehow miraculously present. Every frond and fibre vibrated with the sight and sound of him. His voice, his struggling moustache, his quarterings, his ancestral home where ferns grew in shaving mugs – all came flooding back. And when, from the depths of the house, she heard her husband-to-be's voice summoning her, she pressed a cool frond to her cheek and wept.

Mr Alfred snorted disapprovingly and re-opened *The Principles of Geology*.

"Now that," said Miss Binnie, re-applying herself to her novel, "really is an ending worthy of George Sand."

With a hiss of displeasure our train drew to a halt within sight of Reigate Junction, causing Mr Scudamore to shake his head in exasperation.

"We must now expect a delay," said he, consulting his pocket watch, "whilst a train from Brighton takes precedence at the station, where it will waste ten minutes of our time by taking on water."

"In that case," said Mr Jocelyn Critchley, the bookbinder from Tunbridge, "let me divert you by recounting a conversation I once had with Lord Monson, whose seat at Gatton Park lies not two miles from here as the crow flies. From time to time his lordship has been pleased to commission a number of bindings from me, mostly of collected works – the Despatches of the Duke of Wellington, Lives of the Archbishops of Canterbury, sets of The Rambler, that sort of thing. Indeed, so generous has been his patronage that he used to joke that my work, laid end to end, would probably fill a cricket pitch stump to stump."

"I am pleased that his lordship is a connoisseur of fine bindings," observed Mr Dacre, "but does he ever read what is inside them? In my experience gentlemen who are connoisseurs of the one are rarely connoisseurs of the other."

"Alas, no," replied Mr Critchley, "but he was always a friend of true scholars and never refused them access to his library, whatever the inconvenience to himself. Indeed, it is with one of these scholars that my story is concerned. One day I chanced upon him in the library talking to Father Eustace Shirley, a Catholic priest who was something of an expert on early printed Bibles and Tudor crypto-grams. Was his lordship aware, he asked, that in Psalm 46 the for-ty-sixth word from the beginning was 'shake' and the forty-sixth word from the end 'spear'. His lordship had to confess that he was not. And would it surprise his lordship to know that in 1610, the year that the King James version was completed, Shakespeare was forty-six years old? This was surely no coincidence. Knowing that Father Shirley was capable of finding ciphers in Elizabethan laundry lists – had, indeed, actually done so – I changed the subject, by asking them how many libraries they could see in front of them. "Why one, of course," said Lord Monson. "Now that is strange," said I, "for I see two." "How come?" he asked. I explained to him that within the cover of a book the boards were often wrapped in old paper or parchment before being sealed within the outer skin of leather. This old paper often consisted of discarded galley proofs or, in the case of older books, of hand-written parchment, which may have been rescued, some of it, from monastic libraries. Within every book, I told him, there lies the possibility of a secret book and within every library, therefore, the prospect of a secret library. The thought that every work has a silent partner, to which it is both liter-ally and metaphorically bound, should give us pause. Who can fore-tell what fate lies in store for our own most treasured productions? Who dare guess the final resting place of Sir Walter Scott or Lord Byron? – or even Mr Dickens and Mr Carlyle? Eheu fugaces!

"Our talk turned by degrees from secret libraries to lost ones – to the English monastic libraries, to the royal libraries of Constan-tinople and Matthias Corvinus and, above all, to the great Library of Alexandria. Such loss, such grief! By the time we had finished enumerating the lost works of Aeschylus and Sophocles, of Aristotle and Pythagoras, we were feeling not a little glum. Lord Monson remarked that it did not do to have such a conversation too often, whereupon Father Shirley observed that we should be grateful for what had survived – and, in any case, he added mysteriously, perhaps more had survived than we realised. From his face I could see that he was not wholly serious, yet at the same time I suspected he had something he wished to confide to me."

"And did he confide it?" enquired Mr Dacre.

"Oh yes, and it forms the substance of my tale, a tale which, you may be flattered to learn, I have never told anyone else."

[Editor's note: Although the Bookbinder's preface exists (see above), his tale does not – at least not in publishable form. What survives are notes, which were probably transcribed by Miss Osgood from her shorthand record, then passed on to Blackwood to be used as the basis of a continuous narrative. No doubt most, if not all, of Blackwood's tales passed through this intermediate stage. All the others have been lost; the Bookbinder's alone remains. By a delicious irony it survives thanks to the very mechanism that Jocelyn Critchley described to Lord Monson and Father Shirley: namely, by being used as a wrapper. Among Blackwood's foul papers there are a number of engravings of Old Canterbury, including a unique image of the Ebenezer Temperance Hotel before St Margaret's Street was bombed in 1942. The ink from engravings often stains adjacent sheets in any bundle or pile of which they are a part. To prevent this, Blackwood had folded the handwritten transcription in half and used the sheets as wrappers for the engravings, thus preserving what might otherwise have been lost. Here then is the tale – or what remains of it – told by Jocelyn Critchley in words that are more nearly his own than those of any other teller.]

The Bookbinder's
Tale of The Library of Lost Books

Father Shirley. Chaplain to old Catholic family. Discreet, sensitive even. Hardly surprising given all those centuries of persecution. Trustworthy? Oh highly. Expected it of others too. – Wanted me to swear an oath. Mum's the word. Not I. Good Protestant. Not keen on oaths – let your yea by yea and your nay be nay. Epistle of St James. – So did I swear? Yes I did, shame on me I did. Swear. I swore. – Never could resist a secret. Desperate to know. Mind you never could keep a secret either. Which is why I'm telling you now. Well, who's to know? Father Shirley long dead, God rest him, as are the cardinals, but more of them anon.

So what was the secret? Be patient, sir, be patient. – Do you know Romney Marsh? No, neither did I. But that's where we went, depths of, Fr Shirley and I. – Fly waiting at the station. Off we go. Clip clop, cracking pace. – Drove us to an old priory. Gothic, you know. Mullioned windows, draughts, that sort of thing. And *mirabile dictu* a chained library. – Stuff that dreams are made on. Couldn't believe my eyes. I reached out – well, one would – may I? No, no, says he. By no means. First you must swear. – Again? – Yes, again. The rules. Not mine, the cardinals'. – Cardinals? – My little joke, says he. My name for the Senior Scholars. Not a word to them. No sense of humour, dry as a biscuit. Follow me.

To, as it happens, the penetralium of the cardinals. Greying, whiskery. Hands ripe with knuckles. – May I introduce? Mr Jocelyn Critchley. Dr This, Mr That, Rev Something or other. – So, Mr Critchley you are a bookbinder, we hear. – I have that privilege, gentlemen. – The privilege is ours. You are the very man we need. All these – sweep of the hand indicating the books – rescued from oblivion but not alas from the ravages of time. – Well, that much I could see. But what were they, these chained treasures? – Survivors, Mr Critchley, survivors of fire, flood and conquest. Each and every one a nonpareil.

What would you say if we told you we possessed the Margites of Homer? asked the knucklesome cardinal.

Or the complete poems of Sappho? asked the whiskery one.

Or the forty plays of Aeschylus the Athenians lent to Ptolemy of Alexandria?

Or the comedies of Menander, thought to have perished in their entirety?

Or the Life of Alexander the Great by Callisthenes?

Or St Paul's lost letter to the Corinthians?

Or the Commentaries of Origen?

The Histories of Bede?

Not to mention later works.

Chaucer, for instance. Unsuspected Canterbury Tales, some from the outward journey, some from the return. Oh very different the latter.

Vernacular lives of the saints.

Unknown miracle plays.

And more, much more.

But how ... ? - How did we come by them, Mr Critchley? Rescued, most of them, by Catholic families from the monastic libraries. - Hidden, hoarded, never talked about. And finally assembled here in the Library of Lost Books. - A unique collection. No item replicated here or elsewhere. A Noah's Ark of the written word and known to none but ourselves.

The Margites of Homer! The lost plays of Aeschylus! Unsuspected Canterbury Tales! - Small Latin I had and no Greek. But what would I not have given to tread where so few had trod before? - Did I? Was I allowed? No. - That was the business concluded. Good day, Mr Critchley. The fly is at the door. When we have need we will write. Or perhaps even telegraph. After all - scholarly chuckle - this is the nineteenth century. - Not such a dry biscuit after all.

Weeks passed, months. Began to think it a dream. - Then yes - O the thrill of it - a telegram. HOMER AND AESCHYLUS DETERIORATING STOP. BRING TOOLS COME IMMEDIATELY STOP. - Packed a bag and caught the next train. Fly waiting. Clip clop, off we go. Not a moment to lose. - Cardinals waiting, oaths at the ready. Swear. God forgive me I swore.

For the sake of posterity, Mr Critchley, save this treasure. Patch it up until it can be published. - Enter Arthur Havelock. May we introduce? Scholar of distinction. Fellow of St John's, Oxford. Have you read him on the Iliad? Organist, too. Fine voluntaries of a Sunday. A respite from his scholarly labours. And what labours! The Margites of Homer no less. Just think of it. The blind bard's first work, of all things a comedy. Rapture! Now we must leave you. Scholarship never sleeps. Adieu. - Havelock enthusiastic, keen to expound. Margites a fool, a dupe. No Achilles he. Quite the contrary. - Let me quote you, says he, a scene. - Long passage of unintelligible Greek. Havelock guffaws, slaps his thighs. Ho ho. Prime is it not? says he. - Now let me quote you another. Long passage of unintelligible Greek. Hee hee. Are not these scenes worthy of Aristophanes? - No doubt if one could understand them. - You don't? - Small Latin, less Greek, apologies. - Oh, says he crestfallen. Oh, oh. Then let me tell you about the style. Which he does. And the metre. Ditto. After which he removes the book from the shelf and lays it before me.

A moment to savour. With trembling fingers I open it and find ... well, a blank. The first page is blank. And the second and the third. - A Byzantine copy of a Roman codex, possibly from Alexandria, says he. Full of copying errors. – I read on. The fourth and fifth pages blank, too. And so are the rest, the whole book. All blank. – Perhaps the ink has faded. I bring the candle nearer. No the pages are virgin, untouched by nib or quill. – Such a pity you do not understand Greek, says Havelock. This passage particularly fine. Leafs through the crumbling leaves. Ah here it is. – The page is blank. He reads. Long passage of unintelligible Greek. As fine as anything in the Iliad is it not? – Open-mouthed I nod.

A madman clearly. And such a fine organist, too. – I set to work. Hinges rotted, pages friable. But not beyond repair. An hour or two's stitching and all's well again. Nip and tuck good enough for now. – One day, sighs Havelock, one day it will be in print for all the world to see. Think of that. The Margites of Homer, edited by Arthur Havelock D.D., leather bound with gold tooling. Ah think of that, Mr Critchley. Only three thousand years overdue, but worth the wait. Oh well worth the wait. Well back to work. Time waits for no man. Much obliged. – Exit Arthur Havelock.

Enter Matthew Quill. – Heard you were here, he said. Perfect timing. Aeschylus falling apart. Pages all over the place, parchment like dry toast. Can't afford to have it disintegrate now. – Forty plays to edit. Forty! The Sphinx, Europa, Hypsipyle, Niobe, etc, etc, (Enumerates them.) All thought lost. Poor Aeschylus. Tragic figure, killed when a tortoise fell on his head. Bolt from the blue, just like that. – Snaps his fingers and laughs aloud. Tears streaming. – Most unseemly, he says. Shouldn't laugh. Impossible not to, though. The tragic and the absurd never far apart.

Level headed sort of chap. Good humoured, too. Perhaps, I think, I shall ask his advice about Arthur Havelock. – About a man either deluded or fraudulent someone must be told. And Quill more approachable than the Cardinals for sure. – I decide to confide. A word with you, sir, on a delicate matter. – Can't it wait? Very pressed. Oh very well, but first I must share a delicious passage from the Sisyphus. Just transcribed it. Fresh from the Quill as it were. Can scarcely contain myself. Absolutely bursting to tell someone. Let me quote. Long passage of unintelligible Greek. Now peruse for yourself. – Places the book in front of me and points at ... well, at nothing. A blank. I leaf through. Blank after blank after blank. Matthew Quill as mad as Arthur Havelock. Are they all like this?

They were. Over the weeks, months, I got to see them all – the Menander, the Aristophanes, the Origen, the Chaucer. All, all blank. – From their conversations no-one would know it, though. So animated, so proprietorial. – My Homer has this, my Euripides that. My Menander trumps you both. My, my, my. As if they had written them themselves. Which, of course, they had – not out of any desire to deceive but to console themselves. That the world had lost the Margites of Homer and forty plays by Aeschylus was a thought not to be endured. – Did they believe their blank pages fully authored? Undoubtedly. No-one deceived anybody but himself.

Oh there was no end to their uniquenesses. – Every work a masterpiece and every masterpiece a nonesuch. Had to be. Only one copy extant. Well, not even that. Not on paper anyway. In their heads only. That was the way of it. Each man striving to be ahead of the others. – Then one day Arthur Havelock played a wild card – the hapax legomenon. – Do you know the hapax legomenon? No neither did I. From the Greek, you know, meaning a thing said once. A word used once in a book, for instance. A unicum. Some books have several, some only one, some none at all. – My Homer, says Arthur Havelock, has but the one hapax legomenon .– Look of triumph. Others speechless. But not for long. – Within the month Matthew Quill spots two appearances of Havelock's hapax in his Aeschylus and comes up with one of his own. – Soon after St Paul coughs up Havelock's and Quill's hapaxes in his lost letter to the Corinthians. – Other languages join the game. Chaucer and the vernacular saints go to it, hammer and tongs, neck and neck. A hapax apiece, then two, then four, before a miracle play reveals them all and trumps them with six – six! – of its own.

Library in turmoil. Scholars once friendly now bitter rivals. All amity spent. Like misers counting their gold, all hoard their books in private. – And the gold keeps mounting up. Hapaxes all over the place. No vellum or parchment free of them. – Monastic records a fertile source. One day a monks' laundry list out in front, the next a Tudor herbal.

Sandcastles all. No sooner built than washed away. – And the acrimony! The air thick with it, especially after someone discovers a chronicle in mediaeval Welsh. – Uproar. – The cardinals cry foul. Enough, enough. From now on a hapax only counts in Latin, Greek or English. – Universal sigh of relief. Calamity averted. – Or would have been had not a cardinal, the knucklesome one, hinted at a single hapax for the whole library. Only a legend, he said. Probably false. Nay, almost certainly false. Intriguing, though. – Meant it as a jest. Oil on troubled waters, he thought. – Not as it turned out, though. Far from it. All wanted the hapax, the one and only to be theirs. Oh how they longed to say my Homer, my Aeschylus, my Sappho contains the buried treasure. No, don't thank me. Thank Homer, thank Aeschylus. I am but the humble vessel.

There ensued a dreadful time. None dared leave his study for fear of theft or sabotage. Didn't eat for days on end, some of them. Living skeletons. Unwashed, unkempt, beards lengthening. Havelock's a particularly fine specimen, black with ink, but, alas, combustible. – Fell asleep at his labours, catching his beard in the candle flame. A very wick it proved. Fire! Fire! Ran round screaming fire and spreading it too. – The Margites lost in an instant. Up goes Aeschylus – The Sphinx, Niobe, all forty in a whoosh. Up go Menander and Aristophanes, whoosh!, St Paul and Origen, Bede and Chaucer, whoosh! whoosh! Flocks of blackened paper floating on the wind. – Havelock, beard ablaze, jumped into the horse pond, Quill into the very fire. Let me save but one. Please God just one. – Fr Shirley jumped in after. Pulled him out empty-handed. Both singed round the edges. – Cardinals tried to organise a chain of buckets. Too late. The lost books are finally, irretrievably lost. – Fire, flood and conquest they had survived. But Arthur Havelock's beard not. Mehmet the Conqueror not half so lethal.

Except there was no loss because there was nothing to lose. Blank paper only. No loss there.

[Editor's note: Miss Osgood's notes either end here or – more likely – a page has been lost. Not that it matters. It is obvious from the conversation that follows how Jocelyn Critchley's tale ended. Readers may be surprised to learn that there was indeed a hapax legomenon and astonished to learn whose it was. We rejoin Blackwood's narrative in Reigate Station, where the Ebenezer Special, no doubt to the annoyance of Mr Scudamore, has stopped to take on water.]

"But where did the books come from in the first place?" asked Mr Dacre.

"That is a matter of speculation," replied Mr Critchley.

"Then please speculate," prompted Mr Dacre.

"I suspect that some of them started as relics. At the Reformation Catholic families were eager to rescue what they could from the shipwreck of their Church – missals, monstrances and, where they could, books from monastic libraries, feeling no doubt that the passage of monkish hands had lent them a patina of holiness. There was probably a competitive element in this, just as there was in building ever more ingenious priest holes. Some of the books may have been genuine and, who knows, some may lie in obscure corners still waiting to be found. Others – like these – were fakes, empty shells of books included in libraries which no-one was allowed to visit, so that their owners could boast that they possessed the real thing. At some stage someone must have started collecting them, but who assembled them into the library in Romney Marsh remains a mystery."

"And did no scrap of the lost library survive?"

"Oh yes. A single scrap did survive and, when I last heard of it, it had become the subject of heated controversy. Havelock and Quill, singed as they were, were at loggerheads over it before it had cooled from the fire. What excited them was that it was a real word, or, to be more exact, a portion of a real word."

"But if it was all that survived, then it must by definition have been the hapax legomenon they had all been looking for."

"Of course. And that is why they were all so keen to lay claim to it."

"Did you get to see it?"

"Not only did I get to see it, it turned out that I had supplied it in the first place. In my haste to tell you the story of the hapax legomenon, there is one detail I omitted to mention. I had supposed – falsely as it turned out – that the scholars had deceived the Cardinals, persuading them that the objects of their study were what they purported to be. I therefore considered it my duty to expose the deception. Far from being grateful, the Cardinals threatened me that if I breathed a word to anyone else, they would destroy my reputation. Not only would they thwart me in the future, they would persuade the likes of Lord Monson that my bindings were infested with worm and would need to be replaced. In short, if I wished to continue as a bookbinder, I should forget what I had just told them, which was, in any case, quite erroneous. "It is important to remember," said Father Shirley, "that you are a Protestant and do not see with the eye of faith. For those with true vision, all things are visible and all hidden things made known." The Cardinals nodded, adding that now that that had been cleared up there was no reason why we should not continue with the same arrangements as before. My services were essential if the Margites of Homer and the rest were to be restored to the world in their pristine state. So I continued to work for them, but to work as an idle apprentice worked. I skimped on materials. I used cheap glue and thread. I made a point of buying hides only from the most disreputable of dealers, and whereas before I had bound the boards inside the covers with vellum and discarded galley proofs, I now used old handbills. And it was one of these – or a portion of one – that survived the fire. I recognised it instantly. It had been a handbill advertising Dean's Relish, a kind of chutney bottled in Canterbury and widely reputed to cause heartburn. What the scholars were quarrelling over was a scrap of paper with the letters A-N-S-R-E-L-I on it.

"That it was on paper rather than on vellum none of them could deny. Not that that made it any less valuable. Far from it. The Cardinals pronounced it the fragment of an incunabulum, probably Venetian, and all seemed happy to agree. Havelock recognised it as Latin translation of the Margites. Needless to say, Quill disagreed, claiming that it was an Italian translation of the very Hypsipile he had been working on at the time of the fire. One by one the others put in their claims, beginning the process by which Dean's Relish became, amongst other things, the collected works of Menander, a History of Northumbria by Bede and an uncollected Canterbury tale by Chaucer.

"All this happened a very long time ago," concluded Mr Critchley, "and I now think I was wrong to be angry with them. They did no harm and in their way they pointed to a great truth: namely, that the natural condition of all great works is loss. A handful of masterpieces has come down to us, together with rumours of a handful more. But who knows what has fallen into the Void beyond? I refer not merely to unknown works by Homer and the like, but to unknown Homers whose very existence we do not even suspect. One day the last page of the last copy of The Iliad or The Aeneid or Hamlet or Don Quixote or even the New Testament itself will decay, and into the Void will go all the thoughts and feelings that it carried. By patching up these frail vessels I hope to keep oblivion at bay a little longer."

"And do we know who the author of the hapax actually was?" asked Mr Dacre.

"Now there I may be able to help you," I interposed. "His name is Mr Charles Breeze and he is travelling in a third class tub near the rear of the train. He is an advertising copywriter, whose career has, I believe, taken varied forms, though no-one has yet told him that he is the author of half the world's great literature. I think that Mr Critchley should have that honour when we reach London."

4

REIGATE TO LONDON BRIDGE

An Unexpected Passenger Boards the Train
The Duchess of Croydon's Story
We Arrive at London Bridge

It is time now to acquaint the reader with the musical artiste who styled herself the Duchess of Croydon. She was not on Miss Osgood's passenger list, but, having bought a ticket to London, no doubt thought one train as good as another and ours more inviting than most. You will recall that we had made an unscheduled stop at Reigate to take on water. The guard had just raised his whistle to his lips, when there erupted on to the platform a crowd of young swells in the midst of which was a large lady in voluminous skirts and a bonnet with scalloped edges. One of them pointed to our carriage and handed her, together with a wicker hamper, into the compartment. She leant over the side, blowing kisses to her admirers, who returned the compliment by bombarding her with flowers – chrysanthemums, mostly – many of which landed on Miss Binnie and Mme Fontana in a shower of bronze petals. Miss Osgood was about to remonstrate, when *Hengist* emitted an ear-piercing whistle and the 'special', with a rattle of connecting chains, resumed its journey to London.

The lady continued to blow kisses to her admirers until they disappeared from sight. Only then did she squeeze into the seat between Miss Binnie and Mme Fontana and, raising the lid of her hamper, disappeared from view. This was too much for Miss Osgood. She rose to her feet and, with icy politeness, called over the head of Dr leGrove, 'Excuse me, ma'am, might I have your name so that I can check you off on my list?"

The hamper lid remained upright.

Miss Osgood repeated her request, this time standing on tiptoe.

The hamper lid did not so much as quiver.

"Mme Fontana," said Miss Osgood, "please would you attract your neighbour's attention. She must be made to understand that she cannot help herself to any train that happens to take her fancy."

Mme Fontana, who was busy brushing chrysanthemum petals off her shawl, gave the newcomer a sharp tap on the shoulder with her copy of Sir Charles Lyell. Slowly the hamper lid descended and a face, round and fiery, appeared. The cheeks were broad, the teeth widely spaced. The whole was framed by a large bonnet – the largest I think I have ever seen – whose inner surface was lined with peach-coloured silk gathered into folds like the spokes of a wheel. She waved to her fellow passengers with a tinkle of bracelets and was about to return to the hamper, when Miss Osgood, brandishing the passenger list in the air, reached over Dr leGrove's shoulder and prodded her with her umbrella. Still the lady said nothing. Instead she burrowed inside the hamper and took out a white enamel ear trumpet with scarlet roses painted inside the bell.

"That's better," she said, sliding the earpiece inside her bonnet. "Now, was you wanting to talk to me?"

"Indeed I was," replied Miss Osgood. "I wished to point out that you seem to have boarded the wrong train."

"Wrong train?" repeated the bonnet. "Here, this isn't going to Brighton, is it? Anywhere but Brighton. I have nightmares about Brighton. And if you'd been through what I've been through, so would you."

"No, this train is going to London Bridge."

"Praise be. I thought you said Brighton."

Slowly the hamper lid descended and a face,
round and fiery, appeared

"No, you said Brighton."

"Can you blame me after what I've been through? Just between ourselves, I've unpaid debts in Brighton. Boarding houses mostly. Well, that's because I didn't complete my run, you see. Worst audience on the South Coast. Couldn't face the catcalls and the oyster shells. Talking of which, does anyone fancy a custard or a bit of chicken?"

Sensing Miss Osgood's mounting frustration, Dr leGrove tried to take charge of the situation.

"What Miss Osgood means ...," he began.

"Would that be one of the Croydon Osgoods?" interrupted the lady.

"Certainly not," said Miss Osgood.

"Pity. You'd love it there. Lovely people, lovely audience. Genteel, no rowdies. Piece of pie, gentlemen?"

"What," resumed Dr leGrove, "Miss Osgood was trying to say ..."

"Do you not think, Dr leGrove," interrupted Miss Binnie, "that Miss Osgood is capable of saying whatever it is she has to say for herself?"

"Would you mind speaking up?" asked the lady, waving her ear trumpet. "I'm hard of hearing. Now where was I? Oh yes, Croydon. Where I started my career – or, to be more precise, re-started it. Lovely audience. Called me the duchess right from the start and the duchess I've been ever since. You've probably seen me on the bills. By Popular Request, the Duchess of Croydon, Musical Artiste."

"Unfortunately, I have not had the pleasure," said Miss Osgood. "Now if you will allow me to finish. When I said you were on the wrong train, I didn't mean that you were travelling to the wrong destination."

"Oh good. Slice of veal pie, anyone?"

"I meant that this is a private excursion train and that everyone is here by invitation. Not to put too fine a point on it, ma'am, you are trespassing."

"Trespassing?" echoed the Duchess in alarm. "Why didn't you say? You should have said. Of all things I can't abide a trespasser. In

Brighton they'd get forty or fifty gatecrashers a night, regular. No ticket, walked in as cool as you please. Needless to say, they was the ones throwing the oyster shells."

"No-one is suggesting you did it deliberately," said Miss Osgood.

"I should think not indeed. A few grapes, anyone? Very juicy. When's the next stop?"

"London Bridge," said Dr leGrove.

"London Bridge? I only wanted to go to Croydon. Here let me talk to the driver."

Thrusting the hamper into Mme Fontana's arms, the Duchess leaned over the side of the carriage and waved to the driver. Sturdee, taking her gesticulations as a friendly greeting, raised his cap and gave three short blasts on the whistle.

"If you please, ma'am," pleaded Mr Scudamore, "please do not distract the driver. We have already been delayed by the Brighton train."

With a jangling of bracelets, the Duchess shuddered violently.

"I beg you," she said, "do not mention that name in my presence. I shall have it written on my tombstone for all to see. 'Maud Gowlett, Savaged to Death in Brighton, Laid to Rest in Croydon.' Madam," – this to Mme Fontana, whom she had left holding the hamper – "may I trouble you for the wicker bottle? And take a piece of Dundee cake whilst you're in there. No? Anyone else like a piece of Dundee cake?"

"I was about to say, ma'am," continued Mr Scudamore, "that we have already been delayed by the Br – by the train from another railway company – so it is imperative that our journey continue uninterrupted. Whether you welcome it or not, you have our company to London Bridge, where you will easily find a train to Croydon. And since you offer, yes, I will accept a slice of your Dundee cake."

"A genuine mistake, as I am sure we can all agree," said Mr Dacre. "And do you know, I think I might let myself be tempted by a few grapes."

"And I by a slice of veal pie," said Mr Bartholomew.

"What I should like from the Duchess," said Mrs Malachi Brown, "is the story of her life, which I'm sure is a sad one."

The Duchess leaned forward and grasped her hand.

"Thank you, my dear," she said. "You're very kind. I shall be happy to oblige, but only if you think you can bear it. It's not a tale for the faint-hearted, I warn you." – She held out the wicker bottle. – "A drop of something spirituous before we start?"

"If it is all the same to you, ma'am," said Mr Alfred. "I shall seek solace in Sir Charles Lyell, if Mme Fontana would be so good as to lend me her copy."

Mme Fontana was about to pass the book to him, when the Duchess intercepted it, glanced at the title and thrust it into her hamper.

"I know it's taking a liberty," she said, "but looking at you, I'd say you need cheering up. You may not think you need cheering up, but you do. Trust me. I've a nose for it."

From her hamper she produced another book and, with a rattle of bracelets, placed it into the hands of Mrs Malachi Brown, which she enclosed within her own.

"Give that to your husband," she said. "Normally I'd recommend beef tea, but I don't generally travel with it."

Mrs Malachi Brown looked at the book.

"*The Memoirs of Joseph Grimaldi*, edited by Charles Dickens," she read.

Her husband seized the book and glanced at the opening pages.

"Why, this is the autobiography of a clown," he said. "How dare you, ma'am?"

"And it's just what you need," said the Duchess. "Now where was I?"

"You were going to tell us the story of your life," prompted Mme Fontana.

"And what a life it's been," she sniffed, dabbing her eyes with a grubby lace handkerchief. "Triumph and tragedy, tragedy and triumph. I'm not sure I've the strength to begin." She pulled her shawl tight round her and clutched the wicker bottle to her bosom.

"Would a pinch of snuff help?" asked Mr Dacre, proffering an elegant silver snuff box.

"Very kind," she said, "but I'll stick to Duchess Special. I have it made up to an old recipe. One of my Croydon regulars does it lovely."

From within the folds of her shawl she produced an enormous mother-of-pearl snuff box in the shape of the Crystal Palace. When she raised the lid, it played The British Grenadiers, which the Duchess, with much rattling of bracelets, conducted with her disengaged hand.

"Always a favourite of mine. Used to go down a treat at the Britannia in Hoxton. All the swells thought I was singing about them."

"Excuse me, Duchess," said Mr Scudamore, pointing to the snuff box, "but is that not the very Crystal Palace to which we are bound?"

"The very same," she replied.

"Might I ask where you purchased it?"

"Why, in the Crystal Palace," she replied. "Where else?"

There were gasps of astonishment from all those present, including Miss Osgood, who, despite her earlier antipathy to the Duchess, was beginning to warm to her.

"Tell me," she said. "What is it like? Is it as marvellous as they say? What were your favourite exhibits?"

The Duchess, having administered a large pinch of Special to each nostril, held up her hand for silence whilst they took effect. Everyone tensed in anticipation of the ensuing sneeze, which, in the event, was drowned by a violent guffaw from Mr Malachi Brown, who was by now engrossed in the Memoirs of Grimaldi.

"I must say," he exclaimed, "this is damn good."

"Alfred," scolded his wife. "Language."

"The Crystal Palace," said the Duchess wiping away her tears, "is like a huge hamper made of iron and glass. Everything you could possibly want is in it. No-one comes away disappointed. Except me, perhaps, but mine is an exceptional story and even now I'm not sure I wish to share it."

"I say, just listen to this," said Mr Alfred, heaving with laughter.

"Duchess," said Mrs Alfred, "would you be so good so good as to pass him Sir Charles Lyell. I see no other way of keeping him quiet."

"Damn Sir Charles Lyell," said Mr Alfred angrily, "and damn you, Mrs Malachi Brown. "Not another word shall I say as long as I can hang on to Grimaldi, who, I must say, sounds a capital fellow."

"The stage, Duchess," said Mme Fontana, "is yours."

The Duchess of Croydon screwed up her eyes, sneezed loudly and began.

The Duchess of Croydon's Story

I was born between two barrels of herrings on a spring tide, somewhere between Lambeth and Deptford. My father was a lighterman, bred to the river and never happy when he was off it. "Look at me, look at a water rat," he used to say. And you should've seen my mother's face whenever he said it. In her mind the river was a comedown. She'd been born a Cutler and never let us forget it, though what was so special about the Cutlers I couldn't say, since I never got to meet any of them. If, that is, they ever existed, which is, to say the least, problematical. As for my mother herself, depending on her mood, she'd been, variously, a lady's maid, a lady's companion and, when she'd had a drop in, a mistress of William IV, beg my pardon for mentioning it. All of which goes to explain why when my father took me in his arms and declared my birthplace to be Rotherhithe, she raised herself from the deck on one elbow and gasped, "Shadwell". ("More genteel," she explained years later. "Once had a spa.") Well, if it had, it had got lost among the roperies and tanneries by the time I come along. But my father was prepared to humour her. "Anything to keep the old girl happy," he'd say. So Shadwell it was. Me, I like to think I was born in mid-stream, because it was in midstream that I made my musical debut, and this is how it come about.

The night I was born was foggy, a real river fog, one of them that gets in your hair and on your chest. Well, it had obviously got on mine because I started hollering fit to bust. And it's a good job I did. A coal barge bound for Surrey Docks would've run us down if it hadn't been for me. According to my father, the bargee shouted, "Why don't you put the kid on the stage? It's got the lungs for it."

(It, if you please!) Which was kindly meant, I don't doubt, though that's not how my mother took it. "Of all the cheek," she said.

Cheek or not, it was good advice. By the time I was four I was singing for my supper all along the river. Maud Gowlett, the Human Foghorn, they called me. When he wasn't working himself, my father used to hire me out a penny a time to sing in the fog. You may tut-tut, but I've saved lives and cargoes, dozens of 'em, and there's not many can say that. By the time I was fourteen, there wasn't a barge or a wherry that I hadn't foghorned on. As for the watermen, they couldn't keep their eyes off me – and their hands too, though my mother soon put a stop to that, threatening them with Cutlers in high places. "Once they says the word," she told them, "you'll never work again." Offers – respectable ones – come pouring in. It wasn't just the voice. It was the looks. Oh you should have seen me. A rose I was in them days, a English rose.

But as my mother kept reminding me, I was a Cutler and could do better. And I did. I moved up in the world and swapped barges for pleasure steamers. Many's the water party I've serenaded from the Custom House to Margate. Quadrilles on the deck. Songs. Lunch in the saloon. More quadrilles, more songs. Tea and shrimps. Oh them was the days. And in the evenings, on the way home, I'd sit on the deck and sing, and every time we passed another boat they'd cheer. Wherry or steam packet, it didn't make no difference. They'd all raise their hats and cheer. Hurrahs all along the river, steam whistles, spoons and saucepans, you name it. Lovely audience, the river. One of the best.

It couldn't last, though. I had to move on. Move on and move up. I couldn't help myself. It must have been the Cutler in me. So when I was nineteen I left the river and took to the drawing room. Well, it nearly broke my father's heart. To think that any daughter of his should prefer carpet to planks! "Treachery," he said, "black treachery." It was the only time I ever saw him angry. "Give him time," my mother said. "He'll come round." What she meant was that she'd talk him round. And of course she did. "A girl's got to better herself, Gowlett," she said. "She's a Cutler through and through and Cutlers was born to better things."

To begin with it seemed she was right. I arrived at my first swarrée on foot and left in a carriage. At Sir Gideon Trapnell's it was. QC, Inner Temple. Don't tell me you've never heard of him. Well, that makes two of us. But that's where it was, home of, in Bayswater. Chandeliers, lovely carpet. Spotless. Lots of toffs in tails and tiaras and right at the front was an old countess with a lapdog, which yapped when anyone come near. It wasn't long before it set off Lady Trapnell's parrot at the back of the room. Lovely bird, bright red plumage, kept picking up cigar butts and asking for a light. First the pianist give up, then the operatic tenor. That's the artistic temperament for you. Mind you, once the dog and the parrot had got the hang of it, there was no stopping them. "Do something!" shrieks the countess. "Give us a light!" squawks the parrot.

"You," says Sir Gideon, pointing to me, "do something."

So I did. I sang. Sang loud, sang lovely. Bit of opera as I recall. Rossini. I'd got it up special for Sir Gideon. How he loved it! They all did. The countess, Mrs Gideon, all of them, including – and you'll find this hard to believe, though every word is Gospel, cut my throat and hope to die – including the dog and the parrot. Not a bark or a squawk from either. Well, as you can imagine, word quickly got round and what happened at Sir Gideon's soon happened in other houses. People were positively encouraged to bring their animals. One invitation even read 'Price of admission: one pet.' Our very own Jenny Lind, they called me. Not my mother, though. "Welcome to the Cutlers," she said. "Your grandma would've been proud."

I'm sure she would have been, if I hadn't been so stupid as to fall in love. But I couldn't help myself. If you could have seen him you wouldn't blame me. No-one would, not even Grandma Cutler, assuming she ever existed, which, as you know, is open to doubt. Anyway, within a very short while we'd married and I'd ceased to be a Cutler. Handed in my membership card, you might say. Now I expect you're wondering how this all come about. Well, if anyone was to blame, it was the Trapnells. Sir Gideon and Lady T had taken a shine to me, adopted me almost. When they had guests I was the after-supper entertainment and when they went out visiting I was the present for the host. "A little gift for you," they'd say. "The music of the spheres brought to your very hearthrug." It was on one of them sort of visits that I met him. Sir Gideon had been invited into the country to hunt, would I care to go with him? Of course I would. And I was glad I did. Nice house, marble fireplaces, down pillows. And for once there were no pets to bother me, so I thought, "I'll sing for my supper and have an early night." Then one of the guests, horsey type with a braying laugh, pipes up, "I say, Trapnell, why don't we get your little linnet to sing to the hounds in the morning? See if she can shut them up. Pound to a penny she can't."

Well, of course I couldn't. No-one could. Hounds is hounds. I give them
The Roast Beef of Old England, I give them Rossini. None of it worked. Then
one of the women started to laugh – a real dockside cackle and I thought "Hullo,
there's bargee in your pedigree for all your pearls" – and it spread. But they weren't
laughing at me. Oh no. They were laughing at Sir Gideon. So much for your
linnet – that's what they were saying. Lady T looked as black as thunder. And that
was when he stepped forward. He. Archie, my husband, my little Scottish terrier.
"Excuse me, my lord," he said to the host. "If we don't move off soon we shall
lose the early scent." "Well said, Archie," said his lordship. "Out of the mouths
of babes and sucklings, eh? Tally ho, everyone! Off we go!" No-one slapped him
down, even though he was only a whipper-in. Probably all felt guilty at laughing
at me. Anyway, by the time they got back from hunting they'd forgotten all about
it. After dinner I sang and they clapped. All forgiven and forgotten. Only I hadn't
forgotten Archie. As soon as I could I crept down to the servants' quarters and
didn't see my own bed again till morning.

Well, you can guess the rest. A few weeks later we was married. He managed
to nip out between hunts and I between swarrées and hoped no-one would notice.
Well, someone did. The kennelman did. And having ferreted out Archie's secret,
the kennelman told his lordship and his lordship wrote to Archie's stepfather,
telling him the boy had been absent without leave and please would he come and
collect him because he he'd no use for boys of that sort. (Boy! Archie was twenty-
one if he was a day.) Anyway, when I turned up with Sir Gideon a few days later,
he'd gone, snatched most probably. This I got from the kennelman, who caught
me poking round in his kennels looking for Archie.

"Looking for that precious husband of yours?" he asks.

"Thanks to you, yes I am," I says.

"Well," he laughs, "you'll have your work cut out. He's joined the circus.
Up north."

"Circus! He never mentioned no circus to me."

Then it all come out. Archie's stepfather, an ex-convict named McMaster,
owned a circus, though by all accounts not much of one. A few horses, a clown or
two, a freak show. The star turn was a lion named Murdo, an ugly brute with filmy
eyes and a bad temper. Well, this Murdo had fallen out with his trainer, who was
an arm or two short as a consequence, so McMaster was glad to get Archie back

to fill the vacancy. Without him being forced, he'd never have agreed to such a thing. I could swear to that. He'd been carried off, kidnapped, probably with the kennelman's connivance.

There was no time to make my apologies to Sir Gideon, no time for niceties of any sort. I caught the first coach north. It was the end of March and there was still frost on the ground. If I was frozen before we started, with every mile north we went, I froze some more. Two nights we stopped on the way, and when we got to Manchester I was so cold they practically had to carry me to a nearby lodging house. Next morning I was on my way again, this time with the local carrier. With every mile it got colder and with every mile it got blacker. The air was black, the streets were black, and when the carrier stopped, it was at a deserted turnpike in the middle of nowhere. That was it. The road didn't go no further. Well, there was nowhere for it to go to. Just mounds of ash, mound beyond mound, with sometimes a cinder path winding between and sometimes a ditch of reddish water from a local dye works.

In the distance I could hear cheering, so I knew I was close. The trouble was I began to imagine they were cheering Archie, or, worse, the lion. I began to run. Louder and louder grew the cheers. But just when I thought I was nearly there, I found myself on the edge of a canal with not a bridge in sight. I could have wept. I probably did, but my guardian angel was hovering, because just then a barge come by. "Take me over," I says. "What'll you give me?" he asks. Well, that stumped me. I'd spent my last money on my train fare, but then I remembered that I was still in evening dress and wearing Lady Trapnell's earrings. "How about one of these," I asks, "and the other on the way back?" "Jump on board," he says.

And so at last I come to the circus. I've seen Astley's, I've seen Wombwell's, but McMaster's warn't like either. There was a collection of grey tents with a show ring in the middle. According to the posters there was a Bearded Lady, a Three-Headed Dog, a Tightrope Walker, Equestrian Delights Never Before Equalled and a Clown. No superlatives. Just a Clown, so he must have been pretty bad. Top of the bill was a Lion Unsurpassed in Ferocity and a Man Unsurpassed in Daring, who was to enter his cage At Great Personal Risk. It was pretty obvious who that was going to be. I felt sick at the thought.

When I arrived the show had already started. There was a tightrope walker wobbling on a rope between two carts with a crowd of mill hands shouting to her to jump. Behind the tents there were half a dozen nags which must have constitooted the Equestrian Delights and close by them the Clown and the Bearded Lady sharing a drop of something spirituous. As for the lion cage, it was a grand affair with painted wheels and spikes on the roof. All too plain I could see what was going to happen. At the climax of the show they was going to push the cage into the ring and shove my Archie inside with the lion. Or that's what I first thought. But when I looked a bit harder I could see Archie already in there cowering in a corner. From the ring there was a tremendous cheer from the mill hands as the trapeze artist fell off the rope. This, I thought, is my chance. Now or never. I made my way behind the tents, dodged the Clown and the Bearded Lady and ran towards the cage. Now I don't know where it come from, but suddenly, there in front of me, yapping fit to burst, was the three-headed dog.

"Freak shows," interrupted Mme Fontana, "are designed to defraud the gullible. Bearded ladies and three-headed dogs are invariably the product of trickery. I suggest that in reality you were in very little danger."

"On the contrary," observed Mr Malachi Brown, looking up from the *Memoirs of Grimaldi*, "the *lusus naturae* is a well-attested natural phenomenon, inexplicable but genuine nonetheless. But enough of that. Duchess, I heard mention of a clown and my interest was instantly aroused. Pray, tell me more."

"Please ignore him, Duchess," interrupted Mrs Alfred. "I am sure I speak for everyone here when I beg you to continue your story."

There was a polite murmur of assent from the company and a loud "Hear! Hear!" from Dr leGrove.

The yapping of the dog weren't nothing to the fury of McMaster when he turned up. Big man in a swallow-tail coat with brass buttons. Cudgel in one hand and a chain in the other.

"And who the d – are you?" he asked.

I stood my ground.

"I've come for my husband," I said. "I've come for Archie and I won't leave till I've got him."

McMaster's eyes opened wide and for a minute I thought he was going to hit me. Then he grinned.

"Come to think of it, he did say something about a wife, but I didn't take much notice at the time. Let's be having a look at you then." He lifted my chin with the cudgel. "Very nice," he said at last. "The boy's got taste. He ain't got much else, but he's got taste. That I will give him."

"You won't buy me off with flattery," I said. "I've come for Archie and I won't leave till I've got him."

By now a little crowd had gathered – mill hands, the Clown, the Bearded Lady, the horse riders and – last of all because she'd sprained her ankle – the Tightrope Walker. McMaster obviously liked an audience because he give them a big wink and says:

"Tell you what – if you go into the cage and drag him out yourself, you can have him and welcome."

He'd thought I wouldn't do it – and if you'd told me in advance, I'd have thought I wouldn't do it either, especially as Murdo had started roaring, most likely set off by the three-headed dog. But I didn't have time to think. I just said, "You're on. Call off the dog."

"Go on, Mac," shouted the mill hands. "You heard what she said."

Seeing himself trapped by his own promise, he beat each head in turn with the cudgel, wrapped the chain round one of its necks and tied it to a post. Hoping my guardian angel was still hovering, I was just about to climb the steps up the cage, when the Bearded Lady grabbed hold me and whispered in my ear, "Just grab hold of Archie and pull him out. And whatever you do, don't catch Murdo's eye, either of you, or he'll have you. I'm Archie's mother, by the way. Welcome to the family."

Not exactly the mother-in-law Grandma Cutler would have wished for me, I thought, as she scraped her cheek alongside mine.

"But why didn't you stop him going in the cage?" I asked.

"Hold your tongue, woman," growled McMaster to his wife.

"That's why," she said.

"Well, get on with it if you're going," sneered McMaster. "Not afraid, are you?"

Afraid? Of course I was afraid, but I wasn't going to admit it. I climbed the ladder to the cage and rattled the door gently. Archie, who'd been cowering in a corner, looked up. Murdo snarled.

"Archie, my dear," I said, "I've come to fetch you home."

I opened the latch and reached inside to take his hand. Murdo bared his teeth. "Walk out slowly and don't look back," I said.

"Don't be a fool, boy," said McMaster. "If you don't face up to him, he'll have your leg off."

"Don't take no notice of him," said the Bearded Lady who seemed to have recovered her courage. "Looking him in the eye's the last thing you should do. That's the mistake I made with McMaster and look where it's got me."

McMaster shook his cudgel at her. Murdo snarled in sympathy and Archie froze in terror. However hard I pulled he wouldn't budge. In desperation I began to sing. Well, the change was immediate. Murdo rolled over on his back and began to purr.

"Move!" I whispered to Archie. Inch by inch he made his was out of the cage and clicked the latch behind him. There was a cheer from the crowd. He threw himself into my arms and tried to kiss me. I pushed him away. I wasn't having any of that, not after he'd disgraced me in front of McMaster and my mother-in-law. Instead I boxed his ears. Hard.

"What was that for?" he asked.

"For being a milksop," I said. "Now take my hand and don't let go. We're leaving."

Head high, I marched him through the crowd, past the Equestrian Delights, round the tents, across the ring and along the cinder path. To begin with there was silence and I could feel everyone's eyes boring into the back of my head. Then the noise began. A shout or two at first, then a bellow, then a scream.

"Don't look back," I said.

But the din quickly grew. Above the shouting and screaming was the noise I dreaded most – a roaring like a roll of thunder.

"Murdo's out," he said.

"Run," I said. "We're nearly at the canal."

And there, thank God, was the bargee waiting for us, hoping, no doubt, to get his hands on the second earring. But he'd moored badly, given himself too much rope, so the barge had drifted out to the middle of the basin. What my father would have said, I blush to think, and, believe me, I don't blush easy. By now the roaring was close. Well, it was obvious what had happened. Mad at losing the boy, McMaster had opened the cage and let Murdo out. Suddenly I felt Archie let go my hand.

"Pull on the rope," he shouted. "Pull the barge into the bank. I'll hold off Murdo."

That was because I'd cuffed him. He was risking himself to save me. I started pulling on the rope and had nearly hauled the barge into the bank, when the bargee threatened to drop the rope at his end if I didn't give him the other earring first. The cheek of it! But there was no time to argue. I tried to unhook it, but it got stuck in my hair. I tugged and tugged. What seemed like minutes was probably only seconds. At last I got it free and threw it to the bargee. Straight away he starts pulling on the rope and heaving the barge up to the bank.

"Jump!" shouts Archie.

Believe me, I didn't need telling twice. Whilst I was in mid-air between the bank and the barge, I heard a roar, followed the by the snap of jaws and a crunch like ...

And then everything went black, as the train, with a shriek of its whistle, plunged into the Stygian darkness of Merstham Tunnel. Sparks showered down on either side of us and smoke billowed under the awning of the carriage. Miss Osgood shrieked and clutched my hand. Mrs Malachi Brown called out in terror to her husband, who laughed gleefully at her discomfiture. Above the screams from the neighbouring carriages I could hear Dr leGrove intoning something in Latin, whilst Mr Scudamore explained that since the tunnel was 1830 yards long and our speed approximately thirty miles an hour our transit would last a little over two minutes. Although no-one could catch more than the occasional word, the Duchess continued her narration as if nothing had happened and when, some two minutes later, we emerged into the daylight, we re-joined her tale in Brighton, where she was being pelted with oyster shells by a group of holiday makers on the Chain Pier.

... didn't want no gloomy stuff. They was on holiday and wanted cheering up. Well, I wasn't in no state to cheer anyone up. I'd lost Archie, lost the Trapnells and, as for the Cutlers, like I said, I handed in my membership card when I took on the Bearded Lady as a mother-in-law. On my own I was, friendless, penniless.

"Poor soul," exclaimed Mrs Alfred, dabbing her eyes with a lace handkerchief.

"Am I alone in finding this tale familiar?" asked Mr Jocelyn Critchley. "I am sure I once bound something like it for Lord Monson."

How was I to know what Brighton holidaymakers wanted? continued the Duchess. I'll tell you one thing: it was pretty clear what they didn't want. Orpheus' Lament. One verse of that and the oyster shells come raining down thick and fast.

"Ah, I thought so," said Mr Critchley. "Octavo, calf, marbled endpapers."

I should have known when to quit. But I didn't. Maybe one more verse will win them round, I thought. Of course, it only made matters worse. Down come the oyster shells, harder than ever. I was driven right to the end of the Chain Pier, lost my balance and fell in. High tide, too. As I surfaced, I could hear them cheering. "That's the stuff," shouts one. "Let's have more of that." Thought it was part of the act. When the water closed over my head for the third time, I thought, "This is it then, this is the end. And what's more, I don't care." But it warn't the end. The fall had trapped enough air in my skirts to keep me my afloat. I didn't try to reach the shore. I'd given up caring. I just let the tide carry me where it would.

Which is how I ended up on the beach in Hove where I was rescued by a little girl and her dog. Name of Skittles – the dog, that is. Parents had taken a villa for the summer nearby. Family from Croydon. The Osgoods, lovely people. Little girl was called Elsie, in case you were wondering. Became a second set of Trapnells to me, the Osgoods. Only nicer. No airs and graces, no toffs in tiaras. And no parrots neither. Slowly they put me back on my feet again. Back in Croydon they introduced me to saloon bars of the more refined sort. Song and supper rooms they called them in them days. No rowdies and everything done respectable. Bit by bit I spread my wings and moved north, though it was a long time before I could bring myself to cross the river. I kept thinking of the bargee and the earring. In the end I plucked up the courage and, well, if you seen the posters, you know the rest. I've become a legend. Evans Music and Supper Rooms, the Coal Hole in the

Strand, the Cyder Cellars in Maiden Lane, the Britannia Theatre in Hoxton – you name the place, I've sung there. As for admirers, I can't move for them. (You saw what happened in Reigate.) And letters, I get letters. Scores of them. You'd think they'd invented the Penny Post just for me. Which is just as well seeing as I'd lost my family, my real family. Father was run down by a coal barge in the fog and drowned. Mother never recovered and went to join the Cutlers shortly afterwards. As for Archie, I never heard from him again.

"Well, you would hardly expect to hear from a man who had been eaten by a lion," said Mr Bartholomew.

"Eaten by a lion?" echoed the Duchess. "Who said anything about being eaten by a lion?"

"Why, you did," insisted the watchmaker.

"I did nothing of the sort," said the Duchess. "It was McMaster what was eaten by the lion. Murdo just turned on him when he caught up with Archie. When I could bring myself to look he was spitting out the brass buttons and two men were tying him up in a net."

"Then what happened to Archie?" asked Mrs Alfred, evidently disappointed by the turn which events had taken.

"He wouldn't come on board the barge. Said that now McMaster was dead he'd run the circus himself and would start by getting rid of Murdo. 'We could run it together,' I shouted from the barge. 'No fear,' he said, 'not after you boxed my ears the way you did. I reckon I've had a narrow escape.' 'I think so, too,' pipes up the Bearded Lady. 'He's staying this side of the canal. Be off with you.'"

"That," said Mrs Alfred, putting away her handkerchief, "is a most unsatisfactory ending. The one we thought we heard was so much more affecting."

"Take no notice of Mrs Malachi Brown," said Mr Alfred. "She is never happy unless she is wallowing in the miseries of others. It comes of having too few of her own."

As it approached Croydon our train slowed to a walking pace. The Duchess, no doubt hoping that Sturdee was about to make an unpublished stop, rose to her feet and gazed fondly across the meadows at her adopted home. Unfortunately for her – though fortunately for Mr Scudamore, who fretted over any delay, however slight – the signal changed in our favour and we accelerated through Croydon Station in a fine display of steam and smoke. The Duchess waved regally to the crowd on the platform. No-one returned the greeting, most appearing to be more interested in the silver band, which, ignoring Culpepper's earlier injunction, had reverted to popular songs.

"It looks as if I'm going to London Bridge, whether I want to or not," said the Duchess, resuming her seat. "Though now I think about it, that might come in handy. There's a new establishment opening up soon in Lambeth. The Canterbury Music Hall they're going to call it. I thought I'd go over and introduce myself. Never know your luck. When it's finished it's going to seat over seven hundred. Might have been made for me. Hard-boiled egg, anyone?"

"Only eleven miles to go," announced Mr Scudamore as Croydon receded into the distance.

Eleven miles! With our goal in sight, conversation became more animated. According to the Duchess, the Crystal Palace was a vast hamper of iron and glass from which no-one went away hungry. And what riches they all found in it! In the Mediaeval Court Mr Dacre hoped to find samples of stained glass and woodcarving to furnish the parish churches whose improvement he was currently supervising. "Our notions of the Gothic are so superior to those of our ancestors," he said, "that they would surely thank us for improving their work. Posterity will be for ever in our debt." In this he was seconded by Dr leGrove who hoped, among the chalices and chasubles, to find the means to drive away a particularly stubborn manifestation which had resisted his best efforts to date. "But I shall prevail, gentlemen," he said. "I shall prevail. No spirit has got the better of me yet." Mr Bartholomew naturally wished to feast his eyes on the work of the clockmakers – one hundred and thirty in the British section alone – though he also had hopes of winning the £200 prize which Chubbs, the locksmiths, were offering to anyone who could pick one of their locks. The Malachi Browns diverged sharply in their tastes: Mrs Alfred wished most particularly to see an ornamental birdcage, whilst Mr had set his heart on a stuffed Dodo from Mauritius. "Either that," he added, "or an eighty-bladed sportsman's knife from Sheffield." Mr Critchley wished to see the latest in Parisian bookbinding and Mr Scudamore a Viennese dining table designed to seat forty guests and commissioned by no less a person than the Habsburg Emperor himself.

"And what about you, Mr Blackwood?" asked Dr leGrove.

I started at the directness of his question. The object of my journey was, in truth, little more than the journey itself, and that only as an excuse for the tales people might be persuaded to tell on it. To be sure, I had imagined myself sitting at the base of the Crystal Fountain, eavesdropping on the conversations of passers-by, hoping that some at least might contain untold riches, but to this I could not possibly confess.

"I scarcely know, Dr leGrove," I replied. "A four manual harmonium perhaps, or" – I searched desperately for some personal Koh-i-Noor – "or perhaps the latest in printing presses."

"What did I tell you, Mr Dacre?" chuckled Dr leGrove. "Our friend here is something of an author, unless I am much mistaken."

Miss Osgood blushed to the roots of her hair.

"What makes you say that?" I asked, laughing uneasily.

"Instinct, dear sir," boomed Dr leGrove. "Instinct."

I was saved from further embarrassment when, passing though Norwood, Mr Scudamore announced that a mere eight miles of our journey remained.

"Eight miles still to go," remarked Mr Critchley, shaking his head sadly, "and see how the tentacles of London reach out towards us. When I was a child, Norwood was famed for its woods and its gypsies. Now the woods have been replaced by villas and the gypsies driven from their sylvan haunts. Where will it end, gentlemen, where will it end? Mark my words, London will not be satisfied until it has swallowed Tunbridge brick by brick."

"Well, I for one will not complain if it does," said Miss Binnie. "I rejoice in the anonymity of suburbia. Anything is preferable to the prying eyes of Whitstable. Believe me, small town gossip has made Emily's business all but impossible."

"As well it might, Miss Binnie," said Mr Scudamore. "On your own admission, Mme Fontana has been deceiving the gullible. Surely the gossips are entitled to point that out."

"Deceiving the gullible is one way of putting it," said Mme Fontana. "Giving them comfort in their affliction might be another. Believe me, Mr Scudamore, they would not thank you for telling them that they were being defrauded. Truth is an uncomfortable bedfellow in times of sorrow."

The Duchess, who since our transit of Croydon, had been leaning over the side of the carriage with her ear trumpet trying to catch the strains of 'Elsie from Chelsea', now decided that the time was ripe to engage Mme Fontana in conversation. Her offers, first of veal pie, then of snuff, having been rejected, she demanded to know what she and her companion had set their hearts on seeing at the Great Exhibition.

"Nothing," replied Miss Binnie.

"Nothing?" echoed the Duchess.

"Not carpets or tapestries?" asked Mrs Alfred.

"Machinery or furniture?"

"Rock samples or cutlery?"

"Mere trumpery!" snorted Mme Fontana.

It soon became clear that they had no intention of visiting Hyde Park and had used the excursion as an excuse to travel to London cheaply. Once there, they intended, in some anonymous suburb, though not perhaps as far out as Norwood, to seek out premises in which Mme Fontana could conduct her business unscrutinised by neighbours. Miss

Binnie, who thus far had seemed indifferent to the impression which she and her companion had made on the rest of us, evidently sensed a growing mood of disapproval, for she suddenly exclaimed:

"Oh judge us not harshly, ladies and gentlemen. No-one has been harmed by our imposture and, who knows, some good might come of it. Where Emily and I lead other women might follow."

"But in what direction?" asked Miss Osgood.

"Freedom," replied Miss Binnie. "Freedom to own, freedom to earn, freedom to do."

"You speak of 'us'," said Mr Scudamore. "Do I take you are both in the spiritualist line?"

Miss Binnie suddenly looked rather coy.

"Not both, no," she said.

"Might we know what line you are in, Miss Binnie?" enquired Mrs Alfred.

Miss Binnie hesitated.

"Speak up, Binnie," said Mme Fontana. "There is nothing to be ashamed of."

"I am," said Binnie, "a writer of romantic fiction. Some of you may have come upon me under the alias of Minerva Sackville."

"What a capital idea!" exclaimed Mr Malachi Brown. "Now that's something you could turn your hand to, Mrs Alfred. As soon as we return home, I shall lock you away until you have produced a three volume novel so atrociously sentimental that no publisher dare refuse. It's time you started to earn your keep."

"I very much doubt that I have the genius for it," replied Mrs Alfred.

"Who needs genius?" returned Mr Alfred. "You just heard what Miss Binnie said. Any fool can do it."

[Editor's Note: Copies of Minerva Sackville's works are hard to come by. The British Library and the Library of Congress each possess a dozen or so titles, but repeated searches on Abebooks, A Libris and Amazon have not turned up any copies for sale. To satisfy my curiosity I shall therefore have to make

my way to the British Library, which, I must confess, I am in no hurry to
do. That Mrs Alfred failed to take up her husband's offer I can state with
confidence, for reasons which will become clear later.]

By now everyone's attention was taken up by the wonders that
were unfolding on either side of us, as fields gave way to streets,
copses to building lots. Those new to train travel were taken with
the spectacle of houses glimpsed at one moment from above and at
the next from below as the iron road cut through hills and strode
across valleys on stilts of brick.

"I remember the time," sighed Mr Bartholomew, "when from
the top of the stage coach one could reach out and grasp the hands
of people leaning out of their first floor windows. Now one can only
peer down their chimneys or contemplate their truncated upper
halves from below. For this we have the railways to thank. Not only
have they synchronised time, they have eliminated distance and
smoothed out space. A horseman or a coachman has to respect the
lie of the land, flat or rugged as it may be. In its impatience the
railway strides through it or over it, its passage eased by gunpowder
and pickaxes."

Soon houses were joined by workshops and foundries, dairies
and abattoirs. A brewery slid past, a knacker's yard, a steam
laundry. Donkey carts, wheelbarrows and cattle choked the streets,
blocking the passage of the ominbuses from whose rooftops passengers looked at us enviously as we sped past unimpeded. Into
canyons of blackened brick we plunged, round thickets of chimney
pots, past lines of grimy washing, through smells of escaping gas
and ancient fish, drains and stables. On either side rose sounds
of hoof and harness, pick and shovel. An unattended pig snuffled
among vegetable peelings in the gutter. In a doorway festooned
with game, a poulterer saluted a clergyman shepherding a party
of children into a church hall. A feral cat attacked a carcase in a
butcher's yard. Such was the teeming ant colony into which we
were now drawn. At Bermondsey we were joined by the viaduct

which carries the railway over three miles of marshy ground to Greenwich and there, over to the east, we caught our first glimpse of ships at anchor in the river.

Lit by a fitful sun, London lay like a distant promise. Ahead and to our left, the dome of St Paul's rose above a cluster of roofs and spires; to our right a forest of masts and rigging towered over Surrey Docks. In Tooley Street Mr Dacre wished us to observe St Olave's, which had been restored following a recent fire, whilst Mr Critchley was keen that we should note the nearby Grammar School, whose Head, Dr Mackenzie, had commissioned a Letters of the Younger Pliny from him only last year. As for the Duchess of Croydon, she picked up the remains of a chrysanthemum from the floor and threw it out of the carriage in the direction of Rotherhithe.

"My birthplace," she said, wiping away a tear.

A mile to go, half a mile, a quarter. By now spires, masts and domes had been swallowed by the approaches to London Bridge Station. We sidled past coaches and locomotives, water towers and coal bunkers, signals and turntables, coming to rest at last beneath one of the three great canopies that make up the terminus of the South Eastern Railway.

Part Two

5

LONDON BRIDGE TO PIMLICO

London Bridge Station
The Old Swan Pier
The Bugler's Tale of Red Spangle and Mr Henry (Part Two)
An Alarming Incident
The Watchmaker's Tale of The White Elephant Club
Harrison's Hostel
On the Omnibus
The Inventor's Tale of The Devil's Coachman
The Actor's Tale of The Mantle of Kean

At Sturdee's invitation I climbed on to the footplate of the
locomotive the better to see and be seen, for I had arranged
to meet my party at the head of the train. What can compare
with the hurly burly of a London station? Such tumult of voices,
such shrilling of whistles! What a scramble for departing trains!
What a shoal of top hats and bonnets, caps and derbies bobbing on
the tides that flow through the barriers and swirl round the coaches.
And what a tide! Here are newspaper vendors weaving in and out
of the crowds, porters bent double under trunks, cabmen discharg-
ing last-minute passengers, oilmen greasing axles, scourers searching beneath seats for forgotten umbrellas. Over there a porter
drags a leash of pointers towards a guard's van; close by a country

gentleman watches anxiously as a parcel of saplings is strapped to a carriage roof; from the Dover train a Frenchman and his wife, conspicuous in Parisian finery, alight in an avalanche of luggage; in the cab rank a mother of two haggles over a fare. Every train whistle makes someone's heart beat faster – the felon fleeing from justice, the debtor absconding from his debts, the soldier about to join his regiment, the schoolboy returning to school. In that vast crowd all are surely there – all those and many more, more than imagination can compass or eye discern. So many untold stories, so few Osgoods to harvest them all!

"Only think," said Miss Lark, who, at Sturdee's bidding, had joined me on the footplate, "that less than six hours ago we were in Canterbury, and now, as if by miracle, we have been plucked from all that is familiar, and set down here in the beating heart of the metropolis. We are truly blessed, Mr Blackwood; we are truly blessed."

"We are indeed, Miss Lark," I replied.

From their remarks as they gathered round the locomotive, others clearly thought so too. There were, however, those like Turpin and Malachi Brown who insisted that our safe arrival had less to do with miracles than with human ingenuity and that we should count ourselves fortunate – blessed was altogether too strong a word – that we had emerged from the shadows of superstition to live in the kindly light of science.

Miss Osgood stationed herself by the locomotive, notebook in hand, identifying the white rosettes as they arrived. Miss Binnie and Mme Fontana, with a cursory nod in my direction, hurried past and were swallowed by the throng. They were followed by Mr Critchley, who had arranged to stay with an egyptological friend from the British Museum. He hoped that our paths would cross in the Crystal Palace, but if they did not, then he looked forward to renewing our acquaintance on the journey home. So saying, he took his leave. Although she was not, strictly speaking, a member of the party, the Duchess of Croydon took her departure in grand style, inviting

Sturdee and the fireman, now that the journey was done, to share a drop of something spirituous with her. After that she bade a fond farewell to everyone else, including those in the tubs whom, of course, she had never met. Nan Foxley was surprised to find herself warmly embraced, Beamish to find himself the recipient of Dundee cake, Purselove of a chicken leg and Breeze of a boiled egg. None, however, was more delighted than Stumps, to whom she gave a half a quartern loaf and the dregs of the wicker bottle, and none more startled than the Saturnine Stranger into whose hand she thrust *The Memoirs of Grimaldi*, having first snatched it from Malachi Brown's.

"Beg pardon," said the Duchess, "but I'd say he needs it more. If you're short of something to read, try this."

From Culpepper's pocket she plucked his well-thumbed copy of *The Pilgrim's Progress* and handed it to Mr Alfred. "I don't know what it is," she said, "but it come from a man of the cloth, so it must be improving. As for you, dear," she said to Nan, "I should put your bonnet on. You'll find it chilly on the river."

And with that, she took her leave, though not before extracting an apple from the depths of her shawl and pressing it into Culpepper's hand.

"Last of the crop," she said. "Resist it if you can."

Several others in our party had found beds elsewhere. The Malachi Browns, for example, had been offered hospitality by pteridological friends in Chelsea, whilst Dr leGrove and Mr Dacre had been invited to stay with Dr Blomfield, the Bishop of London, at Fulham Palace. Since both these destinations lie upstream of Pimlico Pier, it was agreed that the separatists should travel with us on the same steamer. Mr Scudamore, who was to stay overnight at Lady Rippledale's town house in Bloomsbury, made his apologies and reported to the first class carriage, whence he helped extract her ladyship and Miss Tintsford, of whom I caught no more than a glimpse, so great was the press of people on the platform.

Miss Osgood having accounted for all the white rosettes (as well as for the Saturnine Stranger, who refused to wear one), I signalled to George Costello to sound the charge. At the call of the bugle, the crowds on the platform stood aside to allow us free passage out of the station, Beamish and Dr leGrove leading the way.

"I should keep quiet about this when we return to Canterbury, if I were you, Blackwood," said Mr Meek, who never tired of reminding us of his close connection with the military. "I suspect that the use of military bugles on railway stations is against Queen's Regulations and, quite possibly, against railway by-laws."

"Don't be such a bore, Meek," said Purselove. "Think of young Costello as the Pied Piper, leading us through the mountain to Hyde Park by way of Pimlico."

"All the little boys and girls," quoted Miss Lark,

"With rosy cheeks and flaxen curls,

"And sparkling eyes and teeth like pearls,

"Tripping and skipping, ran merrily after

"The wonderful music with shouting and laughter."

"It has been a long time since I had rosy cheeks and flaxen curls," remarked Miss Osgood sadly.

"Or I teeth like pearls," sighed Mr Ezard.

"I must congratulate you on your knowledge of Mr Browning's poem," said Purselove to Miss Lark. "He wrote it for the son of my old friend William Macready. I was fortunate enough to be present when he read it to the little chap for the first time."

"Did I overhear you say that you knew William Macready?" asked Mrs Malachi Brown.

"Know him, ma'am?" asked Purselove. "Why, I played Banquo to his Macbeth at Drury Lane."

"How thrilling! Did you hear that, Alfred?"

"More to the point, did you ever meet Grimaldi?" demanded her husband.

"A little before my time, sir, I'm afraid," replied Purselove.

"Or the great Edmund Kean?" persisted Mrs Alfred.

"That I never met the great Edmund Kean is one of my greatest regrets," said Purselove.

"Well, that's life for you," said Mr Alfred: "none of us gets what we want, however badly we want it. Wouldn't you agree, Mrs Alfred?"

Mrs Alfred would not agree and told him that since his remarks were clearly directed at her, she would not stay to have her feelings wounded further. Off she flounced and offered her assistance to the newly bonneted Nan Foxley, who was busy trying to persuade Gabriel not to jump off the platform on to the tracks.

"Believe me, Blackwood," said Malachi Brown, "it is deeply frustrating to live with a woman who chooses – deliberately – to misunderstand the most light-hearted of remarks. Into what desperate courses I might one day be driven, I dread to think. Now where has the man in the muffler gone? I want my copy of Grimaldi back."

With cries of wonder and delight our party emerged into Tooley Street. Readers who suppose that Purselove exaggerated when he compared George Costello to the Pied Piper must remember that some fifty persons were following in his wake. Thus far I have named only those with whom I had spoken personally. In fact there were over three hundred excursionists on the train, of whom perhaps a sixth had elected to stay at Harrison's Hostel in Pimlico. Of that fifty, I already knew a good many (including the bandsmen), though the reader may be relieved to know that I do not intend to widen the circle of his acquaintance further. With the exception of Lady Rippledale and Miss Tintsford, whom I came to know more fully on the return journey, our cast of characters is now complete.

Before descending the steps to the wharf, we paused on London Bridge itself to drink in the sights and sounds of the capital. Although it was a fine October day, there was a thick canopy of smoke over the city and several members of the party struggled catch their breath. Of these, Mr Bartholomew and Mr Ezard were perhaps the worst affected, though even they – albeit in short gasps – could not but express admiration for the bustle of lighters and cutters, docks and cranes that enlivened the prospect.

Gabriel's animal spirits, never kennelled for long, were stimulated still further by the sight of the river. Oblivious to danger, he dashed between the carts and carriages, pointing excitedly downriver to crowded wharves and jetties and upriver to where the new Parliament buildings were beginning to rise above the arches of Westminster Bridge. Even Culpepper, gazing at the shipping in the river, was impressed. "Go to the ant, thou sluggard," he quoted: "consider her ways and be wise."

"I always make a point of doing so," replied Dr leGrove. "Nonetheless, one cannot help wishing that the ants of our capital city conducted their business a little more cleanly. The fetor of the river is quite unbearable."

And indeed it was. Seven miles of putrid fermentation produced an overwhelming stench of corruption and decay. No carriage crossed London Bridge with its windows open, no driver omitted to bury his nose in his muffler. Far from being the silver ribbon of the poet's imagination, the Thames was a midden, whose greenish waters blended the outpourings of soap boilers, slaughter men and bone grinders with the personal effluence of a million Londoners. At low tide the river deposited its bounty on the mud where it was picked over by 'mudlarks', who carried off their reeking trophies with whoops of delight. Even as we watched, a dead cat floated under the bridge. "And there's another!" shouted Gabriel. "Ginger tom by the look of it." Dodging between the carriage wheels, he dashed to the opposite parapet to watch the ginger tom continue his stately progress towards Greenwich.

"Is it not shocking," asked Turpin, "that some ninety million gallons of sewage are discharged into the river every day?"

"Think of all those chamber pots!" exclaimed Mr Breeze.

"Think of all those poor chamber maids!" exclaimed Nan.

"Who counted them all, I wonder?" asked Miss Lark.

"Does it matter?" asked Dr leGrove primly.

"Well, somebody must have," pursued Miss Lark, "or they wouldn't have come up with a figure of ninety million gallons."

"But what is truly shocking," continued Turpin, "is that my proposals to suspend a perforated pipe under every bridge in order to spray the river with rose water were dismissed out of hand by the Metropolitan Board of Works."

"I think," said a voice, "that this is hardly a subject for mixed company."

Everyone looked at the speaker in surprise. It was Stumps. I could scarcely believe my ears. Was this the Stumps whose boorishness had so offended Culpepper? Apparently it was. And was this the Culpepper, who now laid his hand approvingly on Stumps's arm, who had wanted him thrown off the train? Apparently so. Seeing my astonishment, Beamish took me to one side and said:

"My dear Blackwood, I think you will find that Stumps is not the man he was. After you left us, he became subdued – one might even say docile – and by the time we reached Reigate, had assumed a look of such childlike helplessness that even Gabriel began to feel sorry for him. No, Stumps is not only not the man he was: he is not the man we took him for. All that talk about Jack Cade and the Chartists was mere braggadocio."

"But how do you account for the change?" I asked.

"Timidity," he replied. "He has a highly developed organ of Cautiousness above the right ear. This I discovered in a re-examination of his skull at Penshurst. If you will forgive a familiar expression – there are no ladies within earshot – he likes to crow on his own dunghill, but now that we are on the biggest dunghill of all, namely London, his courage fails him. The nearer we approached, the more his courage leaked away. During the passage of Merstham Tunnel, he clung to Culpepper like a child. Gabriel, needless, to say, leaned over the side and tried to touch the walls. Mark my words, Blackwood, as we approach Canterbury on Wednesday evening, you will see his courage return. If it does not, may I never go hatless again."

I was unable to pursue the subject further, for at this point I was approached by Miss Osgood and Mrs Alfred who demanded to hear the end of the Tale of Mr Henry and Red Spangle.

"Pray do let us hear the end," said Mrs Alfred, "for although I was not present for the first part, Nan has told me with such feeling that I simply must know what happened."

"Can't you guess?" said Nan. "Let me tell you."

By now Ezard and Miss Lark had joined us.

"Aretmis's marriage to Norris was a profoundly unhappy one. Tertius went away. The only comfort left to her was Mr Henry in his glass case. Every day she dusted it herself – no maidservant was allowed anywhere near it – and as her sorrows deepened, the feathers fell off one by one by one."

"What did I tell you?" whispered Beamish in my ear. "Bumps of Amativeness and Ideality. This confirms my original diagnosis."

"I disagree," said Miss Lark. "What happened was surely this …"

By now the storytellers were beginning to attract a crowd which was spilling out on to the road and proving a danger to passing traffic.

"Ladies and gentlemen," I said. "This is neither the time nor the place for storytelling. Let us take our places on the steamer, where all can take their turn at finishing the tale. George, would you please lead off. Blow, bugle, blow!"

George's bugle rang out, but if it set the wild echoes ringing, they were lost in the rumble of traffic. We crossed the bridge and descended the steps to the Old Swan Pier, where we paid our pennies and boarded the PS *Haberdasher*, a steamer of the Iron Boat Company. We were fortunate in being among the first on board, for the vessel quickly filled up and we were forced further and further into the prow, where, if we were short of elbow room, we were at least close enough to hear each other. This was just as well, for no sooner had the deck hands cast off, than there were calls for George to finish his story.

First, however, there were the alternative endings to consider. Nan had already given us her version of loveless marriage and moulting birds. Miss Lark's version also featured a loveless marriage, though her Norris was not so much unfeeling as brutish. According to her, Artemis sought first safety, then solace in the arms of Tertius, who, at her instigation, challenged his rival to a duel. That both were killed satisfied Culpepper and leGrove, who insisted that vice should never be rewarded, but horrified Mrs Alfred, who considered that a loving heart should be. Other versions were less problematic. In Costello's Tertius did what any red-blooded man would do: namely, joined the army, fought and died in his country's wars and was buried in a foreign field. In Ezard's Artemis commissioned a portrait of Mr Henry, which broke loose from its frame one day and flew out of the window when Tertius happened to be passing. Turpin, on the other hand, was only interested in the rope works and Stumps in the Sportman, who, in his version, was attacked by Red Spangle's successor and died of severe lacerations shortly after.

"And serves him right," concluded Stumps, "for profiting from such a barbarous sport."

Culpepper nodded approvingly.

"How odd it is," remarked Miss Osgood, "that none of you men is interested in Artemis. Your versions are entirely without feeling."

"And all the better for it," said Costello.

"Then I'm afraid the true ending will prove a great disappointment to you, father," said George, "for it is one of the saddest things I ever heard and yet at the same time one of the most joyful"

"Oh do tell," said Mrs Alfred.

"Yes, do," echoed Nan and Miss Osgood.

"Be a decent fellow and put them out their miseries," said Purselove. "We shan't get a moment's peace until you do."

The Bugler's Tale of Red Spangle and Mr Henry (Concluded)

It is hard, resumed George, to say who suffered the greater loss, Tertius or his father. True, The Sportsman continued to supply fighting cocks to his regular customers, but the income he had earned from Red Spangle now belonged to Mr and Mrs Norris – or would have done if Red Spangle had retained his old form. Without The Sportsman to cheer him on, the bird seemed to lose his fighting spirit. Not even the silver spurs to which his new owner treated him could revive it, and within a few matches he was dead, thrown out on a dung heap in Whitehaven, a bloodied mass of flesh and feather.

Rumour reached Tertius that with the death of Red Spangle, Norris, had not only lost his taste for the cockpit, but, under his wife's influence, had turned against the sport and joined the abolitionists, donating money to their cause and speaking at public meetings. As for The Sportsman, he was distraught at the news of Red Spangle's end. "To think that Red Spangle died in vain!" he sobbed. "To think that he lies in an unmarked grave, unmourned, uneaten ..."

"Uneaten?" echoed Tertius.

"He'd have made a good Sunday lunch, with cold cuts the next day and soup on the one before that. Better that than that the rats should have had him. Where's the honour in that? 'Tis a bitter blow, Tertius, and I have thee to thank for it. If I was the man I once was, I'd knock you down, strong as you are. Dammit, boy, I will knock you down. Put up your fists and fight, you dog."

The Sportsman adopted a pugilistic stance, danced a few steps round the room, struck the edge of the table and collapsed in his chair, gasping for breath and calling for brandy. Tertius helped him into bed, where, after a rambling confession in which he admitted, first, to fixing this match and, fourth, to fixing that and then, third and last, to bilking this client and, finally, to defrauding that. After which, fifth (or was it second?), The Sportsman closed his eyes and sank into a stupor from which he never recovered. In that same year of 1835, there perished not just The Sportsman but the noble art of cockfighting, for Parliament, encouraged by the Norrises and thousands like them, passed the Cruelty to Animals Act and suppressed it for ever.

"If only it were true," muttered Stumps piously.

After his father's death Tertius kept poultry and took up falconry. The book which he had given to Artemis and inscribed so fondly had been found by Gilpin at Urmiston New Place and returned to him. For months he could not bear to open it, but eventually decided that rather than return Endymion to the wild, he would put the bird to good use and teach himself the noble art of falconry. It made sense, too, for if the bird could supplement what Tertius caught with rod and gun, then he would be worth his keep. Bird and master made rapid progress, and in the fine weather few were the days they did not roam the fells together.

When he was twenty-seven, Tertius took Endymion to hunt at Urmiston New Place. By now his circumstances were severely straitened, but however much hunger threatened, nothing, he vowed, would induce him to part with the bird. As he put Endymion through his paces, he saw Artemis ride into the sheepfold, together with her husband and a boy of about seven years old. It was clear that they had been watching him for some time. As Tertius raised his hand in greeting, Endymion launched himself into the air and swooped on the party opposite, much to the delight of the boy who stood up in his stirrups and pointed excitedly. Endymion returned to Tertius, followed by Artemis, who splashed across the stream to greet him.

"Artemis," he began.

But Artemis was not listening, for by now her attention was wholly fixed on Endymion, who had abandoned his perch on Tertius's wrist and settled on hers. She looked at him for a long time, and when, at last, she returned him to Tertius, her hand rested on his for several seconds. Was this, he wondered, her way of indicating that that she recognised that this was the bird with which he had hoped to prevent her from becoming Mrs Norris? He was sure that it was.

"What do you call him?" she asked.

"Endymion."

"As you could see, my boy was much taken with him."

There was a shout from the sheepfold and Norris waved his hat.

"I am summoned," she said.

"Are you happy, Mrs Norris?" he asked.

"As happy as woman with a falcon in a glass dome, a flourishing rope works and an ailing husband can be."

"Ailing?" asked Tertius, trying hard to suppress the eagerness in his voice.

"I taught Mr Norris to despise cockfighting and love poetry," she replied. "Mr Wordsworth is an occasional visitor. Secretly, though, he longs for the old ways, but does not have the courage to tell me. It is taking its toll on his constitution."

Norris left the sheepfold and rode to the edge of the beck.

"Ask how much he will take for the bird," he shouted to his wife.

"Tell him," replied Tertius, "that Endymion may not be bought."

Sadly, he turned his horse's head and rode slowly back to Keswick.

A year passed. Tertius sold his poultry and moved into a hovel. He took such work as came his way – filling potholes, hay trussing, dry-stone walling and the like – but never once did he think of selling Endymion. One day he received a visit from Gilpin, who, resplendent in top hat, frock coat and side whiskers, looked every inch the modern man.

"Rather different, I fancy, from when you first saw me in tricorn hat and ruff, Mr Howgill," he said. "As you can see, I have prospered since I came down from the hills."

"And as you can see, Mr Gilpin, since my father died I have not. No, spare me your condolences. We were not close."

"As to my business in coming here," Gilpin continued, "the Widow Norris instructs me to tell you ..."

"Did you say the *Widow* Norris?"

"Did you not know? Her husband died in the Autumn. He had, I believe, been ailing for some time. After his decease, she appointed me manager of the rope works in Carlisle. Since when, if I may say so, the business has prospered as never before."

"And the Widow Norris, what of her?"

"She most especially wishes to speak to you on an urgent matter and begs that you will receive her the day after tomorrow. I am led to understand that a light lunch would be acceptable."

In the past nothing would have pleased Tertius more than to have provided Artemis with a lunch, light or heavy; now he was horrified at the prospect. The hovel in which he lived had an earth floor; the chimney smoked; and the table on which he was to serve the meal rested on bricks, the legs having been fed in six-inch lengths to the fire during the previous winter. Tertius had nothing to pawn, but by offering to mend a wall here and unblock a drain there, he was able to borrow a hearthrug, a table (with cloth) and two place settings. Though the results hardly amounted to respectability, they were enough to indicate that Tertius aspired to respectability without being able to provide it. As to the light lunch itself, its composition cost him sleepless nights, but just before the second midnight he had a sudden inspiration, after which he fell into a profound sleep and did not wake until dawn.

Mrs Norris seemed neither distressed by the meanness of the hovel nor gratified by Tertius's attempts to disguise it. As soon as she had finished eating, which in truth was not long after she had begun, the portion she had been given being so small, she announced the reason for her visit.

"My boy is sick," she said, "and like to die. On his behalf I have come to solicit a gift. In his delirium he keeps asking for your falcon. I have placed Mr Henry at the end of his bed, but Mr Henry will not serve. So powerful is the liking that he has taken to Endymion, I believe he might recover if he were to have the bird or even the promise of the bird. I acknowledge that you owe me nothing and that I have no right make a claim on your generosity. Nonetheless, as a mother I am compelled to do so. Will you let him have Endymion?"

"Artemis, I cannot."

"I will pay any price you ask."

"That is not what I meant."

"Then you refuse?"

"I would gladly give him Endymion if I were able to do so. I repeat: I cannot. It is beyond my power."

"Ah, now I see: you have returned him to the wild."

"Worse than that. We have just eaten him."

She stared at him dumbfounded. For the first time the full force of his devotion struck her and when, at her request, Tertius told her the story of how he had acquired Endymion and of the sacrifices he had had to make in order to do so, she felt ashamed and wished to make amends.

"I hope that doesn't mean that he's going to marry her," remarked the Corporal.

"I do so hope it does," said Nan.

"So do I," drawled Purselove, "and that they go to live at Urmiston New Place where they all contract consumption from the damp and perish miserably – all except Gilpin, who haunts the place still as the mad old retainer. This is a play in which I have acted many times."

"On the contrary," replied George, "Gilpin did indeed return to Urmiston New Place, but with orders to turn it into a weekend retreat for admirers of Mr Wordsworth who flock to the Lakes in search of the picturesque. As for Tertius, he took over the rope works and now supplies rigging to the Royal Navy."

He looked mischievously at his father and added: "So successful is he that I should not be surprised to find samples of his work at the Great Exhibition."

"And Artemis?" asked Nan.

"The last I heard she had turned plump and plain after the birth of her sixth child. In recent years she has taken up spiritualism in the hope of contacting Mr Henry. As for the boy, he made a full recovery. His mother saved Endymion's bones from her plate and gave them to him. For a long time he kept them in a box under the bed along with his lead soldiers. When he left home to join the army, the maidservant threw them on the fire. At any rate that was what he told me when we were last in barracks together, though I must confess he has a reputation for telling tall stories."

Nan and Miss Lark disliked this ending of the Tale and would have insisted on their own had not an alarming incident occurred. Gabriel had not joined the rest of us in the prow of the steamer, but tried instead to clamber up on to the paddle boxes. No sooner had he been dislodged from one than he crossed the vessel and began to climb the other. Eventually, the master, having more important duties to attend to, admitted defeat, contenting himself with an occasional grimace in the boy's direction. Undeterred, Gabriel proceeded to imitate the Master's hand signals. Now for those of you unfamiliar with the workings of penny steamers allow me to explain. There is no bell or telegraph connecting the Master to the Engineer; instead a lad of thirteen or fourteen stands on the engine room hatch and translates the Skipper's hand signals into shouted commands such as 'Full ahead!' or 'Half astern!' At first Gabriel tried to give his own signals, but finding them ignored, joined the call boy on the hatch and started shouting instructions to the Engineer. The steamer began to lurch violently – now to port, now to starboard, now ahead, now astern – causing nearby vessels to scatter in all directions. Though the call boy managed to dislodge him from the hatch, Gabriel fought back. In the ensuing tussle, he was driven first up against the ship's rail and then, despite heroic resistance, over it into the river, where, by great good fortune, he landed in the bottom of a passing skiff.

"Gabriel!" shrieked Nan.

"Man overboard!" gasped Ezard.

"Full ahead," signalled the master to the call boy.

"Full ahead!" shouted the call boy to the Engineer.

"Stop!" shouted Miss Lark, waving her handkerchief.

"Do something!" begged Mrs Alfred.

"Do you have any practical suggestions?" asked her husband.

The Saturnine Stranger took off his hat and waved it at Gabriel, who waved back cheerfully, already at home in the skiff and apparently unconcerned to be heading downstream. George Costello blew his bugle, whilst his father bellowed to the boy in his best parade ground voice to make for Pimlico.

Ignoring the notice which said 'Do not Speak to the Man at the Wheel', Culpepper clambered on to the bridge and confronted the Master.

"You must turn round the ship," he ordered. "I know nothing of the boy's parents, but I am certain they would have expected the adults in the party to see that he came to no harm."

"The boy's a Jonah," replied the Master. "He's better off overboard."

"But we cannot simply abandon him," objected Culpepper.

"Oh but we can," replied the Master, "and we shall. Look, the skiff's already under London Bridge, and in case you hadn't noticed, this is an above-bridge steamer. Everything below is out of bounds."

"But ..."

"Don't blame me: I don't make the rules. Now get off my bridge."

Culpepper looked so utterly crushed when he descended the ladder that the others flocked round to learn what the Master had said.

"He refused," said Culpepper, "simply refused to turn the ship around. I feel this deeply, very deeply. Though I know nothing of this boy, he is as much a part of my flock as the rest of you. I feel that I have let him down badly, and in so doing have let you all down. We must pray that the poor child comes to no harm."

"Amen," said Dr leGrove.

"Hear, hear!" said Purselove.

"Chin up," said Breeze.

"You know, Culpepper," said Turpin, "there was no need to ask the Skipper to turn the vessel around."

"No need?" retorted Culpepper. "No need? On the contrary there was every need."

"You misunderstand me. These steamers are built to operate from both ends. There is no fore and aft, no prow and stern, only fore and fore and prow and prow. All he had to do was to reverse the engines."

"Why did nobody tell me this before?" demanded Culpepper starting up angrily.

"My dear fellow," said Dr leGrove, restraining him gently. "Do not distress yourself. Even if we were to reverse direction this very instant, we could not hope to find him. The boy's fate is no longer in our hands. We must trust to a higher power than our own to keep him safe."

At this advice there was much nodding of heads, and though Culpepper himself could clearly see the sense of it, it did not abate his anguish one jot. So wretched, so dejected was he, that everyone forgot Gabriel and offered him their sympathies instead. Mrs Alfred must have spoken for many when she wished aloud that the Duchess of Croydon were still with them. The Duchess would have known what to do, she said; she would have had some remedy, some palliative in her hamper. It was Mr Dacre who came up with the cure.

"Listen, leGrove," he said, "why don't we take our friend here to Fulham Palace? The Bishop is the very soul of hospitality and likes nothing more than a spot of company, especially if it's clerical. We can all pray for the boy in the Bishop's chapel."

"A splendid notion," replied Dr leGrove. "What do you say, Culpepper?"

Culpepper's expression brightened. He was clearly tempted.

"I say he should go," I urged. "I hate to see him in such low spirits and a night or two at the bishop's would revive them."

"Off you go," said Purselove. "Like some gouty old colonel about to take the waters at Bath."

"But what about the rest of my flock?" asked Culpepper.

"No disrespect, old man," said Breeze, "but I'm sure we could spare you for a couple of days."

"It was not you I was thinking of," retorted Culpepper. "It was Mr Stumps."

"Stumps?"

"Stumps?"

"Don't worry, Culpepper," said Beamish. "We'll look after him and see that he comes to no harm."

Culpepper put his arm through Stumps's.

"No," he said, "my mind is made up. I will not abandon him."

It was at this point that Dacre, unwilling to abandon one splendid notion, came up with a second that was, if anything, even more splendid than the first.

"Look," said Dacre, "why don't we take Mr Stumps along with us to Fulham?"

"To the Bishop's?" asked Miss Osgood.

"Why not?" continued Dacre. "The last sermon I heard him preach was on the subject of Dives and Lazarus. I think he'd be rather tickled if we turned up with a real life Lazarus."

"Do you know," chuckled Dr leGrove, "I think he would. I really think he would. His Grace is a man who loves to find parables in everyday life. He will surely not turn one away from his own door. Who knows, Mr Stumps, you might find yourself the subject of a sermon rather than the target of one. Mind you, you will have to be on your best behaviour."

"No elbows on the table."

"No drinking tea out of the saucer."

"What a wonderful opportunity!" said Nan. "Clean sheets, spotless table cloths, warm water to wash with. Oh, how I envy you. Mr Stumps! You will go, won't you?"

"I don't know," said Stumps, "whether to be to be overjoyed or terrified."

This vision of white linen and warm water was brought to an end by the rapid approach of Westminster Bridge. Mr Meek started up in alarm.

"We shall never fit beneath it," he cried.

"Do not be afraid," said Turpin. "You will observe that the funnels of river steamers are hinged."

No sooner had he spoken than the call boy climbed on to the roof of the engine room and, with practised nonchalance, lowered the funnel on a pulley so that it cleared the bridge at the last minute with inches to spare. As soon as we were upstream, he pulled it upright, but not before clouds of black smoke had issued from its base, spreading out across the passengers on the deck. When it cleared, a remarkable spectacle lay before our eyes.

In the smoky air the new Houses of Parliament rose like an enchanted vision from the waters. From the riverside frontage the scaffolding had all but disappeared, save for where, in a few niches, masons were adding portcullises and Tudor roses.

"I feel like the Lady of Shalott floating past many-towered Camelot," said Miss Lark.

"Except that the towers are as yet little more than stumps," observed Mr Dacre. "Look at them: the Victoria Tower scarcely clears the roof top and the Clock Tower has barely left the ground. One would have expected them to rise *pari passu* with the chambers, growing, as it were, with equal dignity, each lending grandeur to the other."

"There is no hurry," said Mr Bartholomew. "The Great Clock remains uncommissioned and long may it remain so."

"Do you not approve of it?" asked Miss Osgood.

"I abominate the very thought of it," replied the watchmaker. "Imagine it: a tower over three hundred feet high, each side bearing a dial twenty-three feet in diameter and housing a bell that will be heard half way across the city. All dissident voices, all clocks with a mind of their own will be silenced. And that, of course, is the point of it."

"But isn't a dissenting clock one that is simply wrong?" asked Mr Breeze.

"Not a bit of it," replied Mr Bartholomew. "Time is the new tyranny. It is the railways that have carried the dogma of correct time to the four corners of the kingdom on guards' watches. Rightly speaking, Plymouth should be fifteen minutes behind London and it is only the tyranny of Greenwich Meantime that has forced it to submit. And its loss, let me tell you, has been keenly felt. It was a generous, forgiving sort of time. The people of Devon were under no compulsion to take their orders from it. If they wanted to take them from the parson or the squire instead, then that is what they did, and if a local farmer or innkeeper disagreed with the parson or the squire, then he set his clocks to please himself. It is said that there were villages on Dartmoor where half a dozen different times were in operation and people chose the one that suited them best. Not, of course, that they had to adhere to the one. Local carriers knew that a three hour journey might take three hours or two or five depending on where one started and where one ended.

"There were as many local times in those days as there were cheeses. A Cheshire here, a Wensleydale there and no two Cheshires or Wensleydales alike. Such was the happy state of affairs that existed in this country until the Railway Clearing House decided that Greenwich Meantime was the only time fit for use. Oh, I remember it well. Every day a messenger was sent to all the London clockmakers from Greenwich with the correct time. None of us escaped; all were visited. Those who valued their businesses placed a card in their windows guaranteeing that their time was the genuine article. I refused. My trade fell off. That was why I took myself to Tunbridge, where I fight a lonely battle against the encroachment of correct time."

"Yet you still managed to catch the train," observed Turpin.

"A free-born Englishman should be allowed to decide the time for himself," insisted Mr Bartholomew. "Only Caesars and pharaohs inflict the correct time on others. For me the ideal timepiece would be an hourglass containing grains of different size, so that from moment to moment time seems to pause, to hesitate, to hasten – to behave, in fact, very much as we experience it."

"Whatever the size of the grains, the number remains fixed," said Culpepper. "One cannot make more time than is actually there. The years of our life, as the Psalmist reminds us, are but threescore years and ten."

"Amen to that," replied Mr Bartholomew. "Though we cannot create infinitudes of sand, we can savour individual grains and rejoice that each is different from every other."

"'Time travels in diverse paces with diverse persons,'" quoted Purselove. "'I'll tell you who time ambles withal, who time trots withal, who time stands still withal…'"

"You missed who time gallops withal," murmured the Saturnine Stranger under his breath.

I caught his glance. He raised his eyebrows sardonically and for a moment I had the feeling that I had seen him before, but where or in what circumstances I could not recall. He turned his back and the moment of recognition passed. I was about to ask Purselove for whom Time stood still withal, but found that Mr Bartholomew had begun a tale and that Miss Osgood, pencil and pad concealed behind her reticule, was about to set it down.

The Watchmaker's Tale of the White Elephant Club

B efore the coming of the railways, Time spoke in many tongues – the Devon burr, the Irish brogue, the Welsh lilt – and when Greenwich tried to silence them, there was open revolt. Across the Tamar, Cornish flags fluttered in protest; in Plymouth and Brixham tainted clocks were stuffed with seaweed by angry Devonians. Not that it made any difference. From Land's End to John o'Groats, Greenwich swept all before it. But across the country – even in London itself – clubs sprang up which, within their four walls, remained true to the old ways. There was a Cornish Club where the clocks ran slow and where there was a separate room for Scillonians where the clocks ran even slower. There were Devonian and Irish Clubs, not to mention a Welsh Club where the clock, which came from a chapel where the sermons were interminable, ticked with funereal slowness. Time is in our very blood. Change the flow of it and you change the sense of what it is to be ourselves.

Such was the subject of a conversation I once had on a coach from Plymouth to Exeter. My travelling companion was a certain Edwin Broadfold, a ruddy-faced Cornishman who described himself as a clergyman-turned-upholsterer. "Mine is a poor parish among the tin mines," he explained, "and a man must supplement his income as best he can. You will not have heard of it. It is often cut off in winter and no two clocks tell the same time. One might almost say they are at VIs and VIIs." He drew the Roman numerals in the air with his forefinger and wheezed with laughter at the sight of them.

By now the coach had left Postbridge and was labouring up Dartmoor, which rolled away on either side in monotonous waves of heath and furze. If ever there was a place where time ambled withal, it was surely there. In those days the railway had reached only as far as Exeter and my companion and I were hastening to catch the train, he to Bristol, I to London. So slow, however, was our progress that it was impossible we should reach the station that day and unlikely the next.

"What do you say," he asked, "to breaking our journey at the New House? With night coming on we shall be lucky to make Moretonhampstead before ten and I cannot wait that long for my supper. As I recall, there is a clock with a painted face in the parlour – Father Time with his scythe, no less – which I am sure will amuse you."

The matter was decided for us when the coachman announced that one of our horses was lame and that he would go no further than the New House, which was then some two or three miles distant on the top of the Moor. We could all transfer, he said, to the coach which came up from Tavistock at first light. Eager for supper and a seat by the fire, we descended from the coach and, leaving our luggage strapped to the roof, set off on foot.

In truth, the New House is a poor place, but never was sight more welcome after I had struggled up to the crest of the Moor with Broadfold on my arm. Some half dozen guests were seated round the peat fire in the parlour – carriers, tin miners, a scattering of benighted travellers – and they readily made room for us whilst we waited for our supper. In due course we were joined by the coachman, who reunited us with our luggage and demanded his share of the fire. For a while we smoked our pipes in silence, listening to the heavy tick of the clock, until the landlord summoned us to the table. Broadfold ate a hearty supper and, when presented with the reckoning, threw up his hands in mock despair, confessing he had not the means.

"It is a weakness of mine," he said, "that I give way to my stomach before I consult my purse. But you will not be the poorer. I can make it up to you in other ways. What would you say, for example, to a good Lenten sermon – one of my best, made quite a stir in Cornwall – or, perhaps, a set of cushions for the oak settle? Cotton broadcloth, floral pattern. Just the thing."

The tin miners were all for the cotton broadcloth but not the sermon; the landlord was tempted by neither.

"Then, alas, I am unable to pay," sighed Broadfold.

"And I," said the landlord, "am unable to offer you a bed for the night. I'll thank you, master parson, to be on your way."

Though my excursion into Devon had all but emptied my purse, I could not bring myself to see Broadfold turned out on to the Moor.

"Give me the reckoning," I said to the landlord. "I will pay. Perhaps the Rev Broadfold will reward me with a cushion or two, not to mention the Lenten sermon."

"This is handsome of you, Mr Bartholomew," beamed Broadfold. "I will indeed reward you. And not just with cotton broadcloth. What do you say to chenille? No, I insist. I have a fine bolt of chenille at the rectory. Very well then, chenille it shall be. And as an earnest of my good intentions here is a story. And, no, landlord, you may not listen. I owe you nothing. My friend has paid the reckoning. It is to him my dues are owed.

"Several years ago," he began, "shortly after Mr Brunel had built his railway to Bristol, I travelled to London to be shown the sights by an old school fellow who worked as a clerk at Lincoln's Inn. Barney McQuaid had always been in advance of his years. At twelve he took to smoking a pipe, at fourteen dismissed religion as an old wives' tale, and at sixteen insisted that Bonaparte had been the greatest man of the age. As you may imagine, my parents disapproved of our friendship and did their best to discourage it.

"Despite their disapproval, I continued to correspond with him after he moved to London, and, whenever I found myself in town, was happy to be shown the sights by him. On one such visit, he asked me, when we had visited the Tower and St Paul's, if I should care to dine at his club.

"'Club!' said I. 'Isn't that rather grand for a lawyer's clerk? I should have thought Whites or Boodles rather beyond your pocket.'

"'This is no Whites or Boodles,' said he. 'Indeed, this is no ordinary club.'

"'Then I'll wager it charges no ordinary fee,' I laughed.

"At this he looked uncomfortable and changed the subject, proposing instead a visit to the Egyptian Rooms.

"'No, no,' said I, my curiosity having been piqued, 'I want to see this club of yours.'

"'Very well,' he said. 'But do not concern yourself about the fee. I shall pay my dues when the time comes, every last penny of them.'

"It would be easier to tell you where his club was not rather than where it actually was. It was not in St James's or in Mayfair or any other fashionable quarter, nor was it, as far as I could see, in a disreputable one, but how we got there, how long it took us or how far we walked I cannot now recall. Wragglestone Street was a gloomy thoroughfare where the gas lamps remained lighted even in the middle of the day. The houses were of the genteel sort, but neglected, their paint peeling and their railings rusted. In degree of shabbiness the club was no different from its neighbours, though it was remarkable for its shape. It was a tall, thin building that looked as if it had been forcibly inserted between the adjacent houses. So narrow was it that a man with outstretched arms could surely have measured its breadth. A short flight of steps ran up to a narrow front door, before which sat a beggar, his tin bowl perched on his knees. Of that grey and lifeless street he seemed to be the only inhabitant. We squeezed past him and McQuaid led the way inside.

"The geometry of the building defied expectation. By means of flying freeholds it thrust arms into neighbouring houses, plundering space apparently at random. There was even a grand staircase with a white rope across the bottom step and hanging from it an ivory plaque on which was painted: Senior Members Only. Having signed the visitors' book, I was shown into the ground floor lounge, where my companion and I were greeted by the other members who surprised me by their youth and vitality, qualities rare in clubmen. Indeed, they might have been more vital still had anyone thought to open the windows. Not only was the air blue with cigar smoke, but the glass was thick and gnarled, allowing only a greyish trickle of light into the room. Perhaps the most curious feature of the furnishings – and remember, sir, I am an upholsterer as well as a man of the cloth – were the chairs and wall panelling. Take the chairs. There aren't many coverings I cannot name, but in this I met my match. It was clearly some kind of hide and looked very much like vellum, at least as far as the colour was concerned. But the texture was thicker and softer, the surface deeply creased. As for the chairs themselves they were so deep they seemed to swallow their occupants whole. Few had legs long enough to touch the floor and most had to make use of footstools which were covered in the same material as the chairs, as indeed were the walls below the dado which ran round the room at shoulder height.

"'You seem baffled, sir,' said a voice. From the depths of his armchair one of the members pointed his pipe at the mysterious integument. 'Well, you're not the first and I doubt you will be the last. What would you say to elephant?'

"'Elephant?' I said.

"'More to the point, what would you say to white elephant?'

"'Which is why,' said a voice from another fastness, 'the club is known to its members as The White Elephant Club.'

"'But where ...?' I began.

"'Where did we acquire so much white elephant skin? Ah, none of us knows the answer to that – unless it's the Club Secretary. You could always ask him.'

"'If you can find him.'

"'Indeed. A man could grow old in the search.'

There was much knowing if uneasy laughter at this.

"'At least,' said a voice from another elephant-lined nest, 'let me tell you why we are called The White Elephant Club. To Buddhists the white elephant is a sacred beast. It is said that when the King of Siam wishes to ruin one of his ex-favourites he gives him a white elephant. It is a gift that no man has the heart to refuse, even though he knows that the expense of keeping such a beast – so delicate in its tastes, so prodigious in its appetites – will ruin him. So a white elephant is a gift that is both a blessing and a curse. Does that make things a little clearer to you?'

"'Not really,' said I.

"'Nor to me,' laughed the story teller. 'Nonetheless, it is the story that we always tell newcomers to the Club. It is a tradition. But enough of this. Your host is neglecting you. He has not even offered you lunch and surely it must be lunch time.'

"From the depths of the armchairs came a rattle of watch chains.

"'And there is always an excellent lunch on Tuesdays,' continued the storyteller. 'Partridge, if we're lucky.'

"'I thought it was Monday,' said another voice. 'In which case it's likely to be neck of mutton.'

"'Monday!' said a third. 'Is it not still the weekend? Shall we not have Sunday roast?'

"From beyond the gnarled and knotted glass, I heard a faint metallic sound like the striking of a distant church clock.

"'Ignore it,' said McQuaid. 'It's the beggar's tin bowl. When he nods off, it falls from his knee and rolls down the steps on to the pavement. It happens regularly. You could almost set your watch by it.'

"Of that lunch that day I can remember little, save that the conversation concerned debt – gambling debt mostly – an affliction with which most of them were familiar and about which they remained cheerful, even dismissive. What stands out in my memory, however, is an incident which occurred as McQuaid and I were leaving. We had just collected our coats, when two policemen burst through the door and seized a man who had been talking to the porter. In vain did he brandish his pocket watch and protest that he had been there some twenty minutes. The policemen would have none of it and were about to remove him when the sergeant caught sight of the clock behind the porter's desk. Calling off his colleague, he apologised and backed out of the door, where he collided with the beggar on the step and sent his bowl flying. When I looked to McQuaid for an explanation, he mumbled something about having to be back at work and explanations having to wait. He led me back to Chancery Lane, where we parted on good terms, promising to meet next time I was in London.

"Thus ended my first visit to The White Elephant Club. It was some months before I found myself in London again, where I arranged, as on the previous occasion, to meet with my friend. He was full of high spirits and had clearly been looking forward to telling me how much his prospects had improved since I last saw him. Not only had he been promoted within his Chambers, but at The White Elephant Club he had recently been elected to the Senior Lounge.

"'And to what does that entitle you?' I asked.

"'Deeper armchairs, thicker panelling, longer lunches,' he replied.

"'Not to mention a higher subscription, I'll be bound,' I said.

"He looked embarrassed and tried to change the subject, asking me whether I should prefer to visit the Zoological Gardens in Regent's Park or the horse riding at Astley's.

"'On my last visit,' I reminded him, 'you promised to explain why two policemen tried to arrest one of your members.'

"'That was a most unfortunate incident. Had the porter been more vigilant it would not have happened.'

"'But it did happen and I am still owed an explanation.'

"'Very well,' he said reluctantly. "'Know then that in the Club we live on borrowed time. We surround ourselves with furnishings – the chairs, the panelling – which seem to draw its sting. Don't ask me – don't ask any of us – how the trick is done. Only the Secretary knows that, and perhaps not even he. In the Junior Lounge the effect is less marked. The days last a few minutes longer, an hour or two at most, depending how long one spends there and how deep one's armchair. Members often speculate – jestingly, of course – on the criminal possibilities of such an arrangement. Imagine what Derby Day would be like if one knew the outcome of the race before one placed one's bet. Of course, it could not happen. One would have to couple Greenwich time to White Elephant time for the length of the transaction and that, as far as we know, is not possible. One criminal possibility remains, however: namely, to commit a crime in the outside world and rush back into the Club to establish an alibi. And what alibi could be better than being investigated for a crime that has yet to happen? That is what you witnessed on your last visit. The man in question was a former member who had been expelled from the Senior Lounge for ungentlemanly conduct. We suspect – as did the police – that he was responsible for a jewel robbery shortly before – or after, depending on whose time you use – he entered the Club.'

"Soon we found ourselves in Wragglestone Street again, though how we got there I could not begin to describe. Apart from the beggar on the doorstep, it was, as on the previous occasion, completely deserted. Now in most colleges the Senior Common Room is staider, greyer than its junior counterpart, but in the White Elephant Club the opposite was the case. Although – perhaps even because – the chairs were deeper and the panelling thicker, the members of the Senior Lounge were more youthful, more schoolboyish than their counterparts downstairs. According to McQuaid, the latter were mostly middle-aged men with younger wives to whom they wished to remain attractive. The Senior Lounge, however, was home to a more rakish set. Here were men who borrowed extravagantly with no thought of paying back, men who spent their nights in vice and who faced the onslaught of time in the armour of borrowed youth. Here were men who resembled Georgian rakes, men whose amusements were ruinous to their pockets and their health – or would have been had not the time-retardant padding of the Senior Lounge protected them. These were the men in whose company Barney McQuaid now revelled. Lunch was a raucous affair, involving a good deal of food throwing, and was followed a game of leapfrog over the furniture. After brandy (large quantities of it) and cigars (the largest I had ever seen), the company settled down to whist, but the stakes were too high for me, so I made my excuses and left. This time McQuaid did not accompany me to the front door but waved goodbye from an armchair so deep that he was almost lost to sight.

"Several years passed, years in which I failed to secure a rich parish in the Home Counties and had to settle for an impoverished curacy in Cornwall. So dreary was it – and is it – that I felt – and feel – the need to break away from time to time. Which is why I took up upholstery. My father had taught me the rudiments and there was no shortage of customers in the parish. When my bishop complained, I quoted the Parable of the Talents to him, at which he chuckled and said that though he would turn a blind eye, he doubted that the archdeacon would. Well, I quickly silenced the archdeacon with a nursing chair for his wife, who was expecting their fifth child, after which I set to work on my own account and very successfully, too. A set of cushions would buy me a week in a cottage by the sea, a horsehair sofa a few days in London. It was on one of these sojourns in the capital that I decided to renew my acquaintance with Barney McQuaid. It wasn't simply that I valued his services as cicerone, but that I was genuinely concerned for his well-being. As a pastor I should have liked to rescue him from the perpetual youth into which he had strayed.

"I decided to call on him in Lincoln's Inn, where I was informed by no less a person than the Head of Chambers himself, that McQuaid had resigned his position and left no forwarding address. That was all he knew, no point in further questioning, case dismissed. And with that I was shown the door. I had not walked more than a hundred yards along Chancery Lane when I heard footsteps behind me. It was McQuaid's successor as barrister's clerk.

"'Here,' he said, pressing a roll of paper into my hand. 'Take this. No questions, if you please. Take and read. One day, about three years ago, McQuaid failed to turn up at work. We have never seen him since. Then just over a week ago, I found this' – he indicated the roll of paper – 'We have all, it seems, had a most fortunate escape.'

"He hurried off. I unrolled the paper and found to my astonishment that it was ... was ..."

During the latter part of the tale Broadfold's head had begun to descend slowly into his nest of chins.

"Well?" I asked impatiently. "What was in the paper?"

Broadfold began to snore gently. Given that I was unlikely to get any more sense out of him till morning, I called for a candle and climbed the stairs to my room, where I tumbled into bed fully dressed, for the sheets were none too clean and smelt of damp. For some time I lay awake wondering what was in the rolled paper until, lulled by the slow tick of the clock in the parlour, I fell into a profound sleep.

It was after eight when I awoke. I hurried downstairs to find the house astir with passengers from the Tavistock coach, which had left some twenty minutes earlier. On the fireside settle there was no sign of Broadfold and, on asking after him, I found that he had already breakfasted and set off on foot, having instructed the landlord to add his ham and eggs to my reckoning. Although I was annoyed at being cheated of the end of the story, of more concern was my immediate predicament. I had missed the coach from Tavistock and there was no other that

*Lunch was a raucous affair involving
a great deal of food throwing*

day. Fortunately, the driver of the Plymouth coach declared his horse sufficiently recovered to continue our journey, albeit, he warned me, at a slower rate.

We had not gone far when we came across Broadfold sitting on a milestone. He greeted the coach eagerly, expecting to climb aboard, but I instructed the driver to drive on, determined to make Broadfold work for the breakfast he had consumed at my expense.

"Now," I said, lowering the window and leaning out, "what about the end of the story? You must earn your breakfast, my friend, before I allow you in the coach."

No longer in his first youth, Broadfold struggled to keep up with us. The debt was repaid in short instalments, punctuated by pleas to be allowed to board the coach. I remained firm: a debt was a debt, I insisted, and must be paid in full. And in its fashion, Broadfold's debt, supper and breakfast, was paid. I shall spare you the gasps and wheezes which accompanied it and tell it as he might have told it had he had breath enough to speak in complete sentences.

"The paper which the clerk delivered into my hands was a handbill headed Murder. I cannot now recall all the details, but a coroner's jury having returned a verdict of Wilful Murder of Sir Marcus Tresham, Her Majesty's Government was offering Fifty Pounds for any information leading to the arrest of Barnaby McQuaid, formerly lawyer's clerk of Lincoln's Inn. No wonder they had wanted to disown him. I felt I wanted to disown him myself, to expunge all trace of him from my memory. That he should have descended to this! At that moment, I could not decide whom I blamed more – McQuaid for letting himself be led astray or the Senior Lounge for leading him. I caught the first train back to Cornwall, eager to embrace its familiar dullness and vowing never to leave it again. Shortly after my return I received a letter ... Do you think I might climb aboard the coach? I am finding it rather hard to keep up."

"When you have told me what was in the letter."

"The letter was from McQuaid. Needless to say, it did not contain a forwarding address. In it he admitted to killing Sir Marcus, but entirely by accident. Are you sure I cannot come aboard the coach?"

"First you must pay for your breakfast. Ham and eggs was it not?"

"It was, I believe, something of the sort."

"How many eggs?"

"Two, three. The exact number escapes me."

"Let us say five – for which the contents of the letter is surely a small price to pay."

"Not five. I utterly refute five. Will you not re-consider? No? Very well, but I warn you I may not stay the course. McQuaid, you may remember, had always changed the subject whenever I raised the question of his subscription to the White Elephant Club. In his letter he returned to it. He had, he said, made several unsuccessful attempts to contact the Secretary in order to find out what he owed. He had been brought up to live frugally and did not wish to be presented with a bill he could not pay. One day he made his way to the top of the building where the Secretary was said to have his office. No-one answered to his knock, so McQuaid opened the door in order to leave a note on the desk. The time-retardant furnishings were present in such quantity that he felt he was being smothered. Not a surface had been left uncovered. Floor, walls and ceiling, even the long case clock, were layered deep with it. Time, he felt, had not simply been slowed but reversed. On the desk a grey cat watched him struggle across the room and, when he stretched out his hand to leave the note, opened wide its yellow eyes and bared its teeth. McQuaid turned and fled. He hurried downstairs, his speed accelerating as the elephant skin thinned out on the lower floors. By the time he reached the front door he was almost running. He erupted from the building and fell over the beggar, whose tin bowl clattered down the steps on to the pavement."

"Two eggs so far," I said.

"Only two?" he panted. "May I not come aboard the coach?"

"And a rasher of ham," I added. "I will allow you that. But the last three eggs you must pay for."

"To his astonishment the beggar asked him why he was hurrying. Still overwhelmed by the choking atmosphere of the Secretary's office, McQuaid was glad to confide in someone. When he had finished, the beggar said, 'Fetch me my bowl and I will tell you something to your advantage.'"

Broadfold laid his hand on the window sill of the coach.

"Which was?" I asked, brushing his hand away.

"That the Secretary was never to be found in his office, that he never failed to claim his dues and always collected them when his victims least expected it. Worst of all, the dues were payable not in money but in time, and the interest rates were extortionate. For every hour that the Club had arrested, four, five, often more, were demanded in return. No wonder, then, that members were reluctant to talk about their dues, for in many cases it meant confronting their own mortality. Those in the Senior Lounge who had preserved their youth in aspic faced the possibility of becoming septuagenarians overnight."

"Three eggs," I said. "So what did Barney do when he received this warning?"

"He fled. I don't know where. Here, there, anywhere – it didn't matter. Everywhere he went he felt that he was being followed. On land, at sea, at home, abroad, in fields, in streets, he could not – or so he felt – shake off his ghostly pursuer, who was as inescapable as his own shadow."

By now the coach was passing the stone circles on Shapley Common. The day was bright, the skylarks were singing and the gorse stretched away in a blaze of yellow on either side. The coachman cracked his whip exuberantly and began the descent into the combe at a sprightly trot.

"He was never still. He never stayed more than a day in any one place. Sometimes he would rise in the middle of the night and move on, thinking to shake off his pursuer in the dark. At all times he went armed."

Broadfold's voice trailed away. I leaned out of the window and saw him doubled up beside the road, gasping for breath. I called to the coachman to stop and walked back to him.

"Much as I might wish it," he gasped. "I cannot walk another step."

"Consider your debt forgiven," I said. "You may join me in the coach and, when you have caught your breath, tell me how Barney McQuaid came to kill Sir Marcus Tresham."

I helped him into the coach and waited until he had recovered his strength.

"Well?" I asked.

"He eked out a miserable existence. One day a meat porter at Smithfield, another a crow scarer in Dorset. And when no employment was available, he resorted – the shame of it! – to pilfering. One day he returned from the country, seeking refuge in the anonymity of London. It was November and the fogs had begun to creep up from the river. He had spent the night in a sailors' lodging, which he had left at first light, hoping to find a few days' work in the docks. Somewhere in the wharves and jetties near the Custom House, a figure, hand outstretched, emerged from the mist as if he had been expecting to meet him all along. It was

Sir Marcus Tresham. Now Tresham had been one of the most dissipated members of the Senior Lounge, one who openly mocked McQuaid as an upstart lawyer's clerk. And here he was, down by the river as if by appointment. It was the moment McQuaid had been dreading. Here, surely, was the Secretary, hand outstretched to receive his dues. McQuaid turned to run, but Tresham seized him by the sleeve. In the struggle, McQuaid managed to extract his revolver from his pocket and shoot his assailant at point blank range. This much he told me way of self-extenuation in his letter. He had no intention to kill, none at all. It had been an accident, manslaughter at worst. Wilful murder it was not."

"And did you believe him?"

"Not at first. Later, when he had explained more fully, I came to understand – more fully perhaps than he did – what had happened."

"So you met him again?"

"He appeared at my door. I was re-seating a chair or writing a sermon – I forget which – when a figure with white hair and a face as creased and leathery as... as ...."

"Elephant skin?" I suggested.

"Precisely," he said. "I was not unused to such apparitions. Recently discharged sailors would often appear at my door – as they would at the door of any parsonage – and beg a meal or a night in an outhouse. I would always send them round to the kitchen and was about to do so in this case, when the figure reached out and took my hand. 'Edwin,' he said, 'am I so changed that you no longer recognise me? I am Barney McQuaid of Lincoln's Inn.'

"His sufferings had aged him beyond recognition and I found it hard to believe that this was indeed my old school fellow. But as his tale unfolded, my doubts began to fade – reluctantly at first, I confess – until I became convinced not only of his identity but of his innocence.

"'You are indeed innocent,' I told him, when he had finished, 'of the premeditated murder of Sir Marcus Tresham. That I see plainly. But you are also innocent – that is to say, ignorant – of the ways in which others have used you.'

"'But I have been ever on my guard,' he protested. 'Too much so, which is how the tragedy occurred. But I have cheated the Secretary. You cannot deny me that. At least I have not let *him* creep up on me unawares.'

"'On the contrary,' I replied, 'he has had no need to creep up on you unawares, because he has never left you for a single moment. He has been with you in your fear and in your flight. You have burned up your youth, consumed it utterly, in your frenzy to escape. Simply by telling you that payment would be demanded when it was least expected, the friendly beggar ensured that you were filling his bowl from that moment on. He has deceived you, my friend, by telling you the plain truth.'

"'Are you suggesting,' asked McQuaid, 'that the beggar and the Secretary were one and the same right from the start?'

"'Perhaps. Or perhaps the Secretary used the beggar as he used you, as both victim and agent.'

"'Victim I own to, but agent I refute.'

"'Has it not occurred to you that in shooting Tresham, you might have been acting as the Secretary's debt collector? From what you have told me of his long membership of the Senior Lounge, it seems likely that his debts had exhausted his ability to pay. Because you were warned in advance that payment would be demanded when you least expected it, you thought to cheat the prophecy and in so doing brought about its fulfilment, not just for you, but for Tresham also. It was a bad bargain, freely entered into and unfreely enforced.'"

By now the coach was clattering through the streets of Moretonhampstead, and Broadfold, his tale concluded, wondered if we might have lunch at the White Lion before taking the Exeter coach.

"You know, Broadfold," I said, "I begin to find your shamelessness endearing. Perhaps it is a good job our ways are shortly to part."

"I only thought to mention it," he said, "since the lunch at the White Lion is said to be amongst the best in the county. Perhaps I can tempt you with a postscript to the tale of Barney McQuaid"

The boiled fowl was tolerable, and the potatoes, if somewhat waxy, were superior to those met with in most coaching inns, as were the cabinet pudding and the custard in which it swam. When he had finished, Broadfold called for two glasses of negus and when I objected to his presuming on my generosity still further, assured me that the drinks were at his charge, since he had found a few stray coins that had fallen into the lining of his coat.

"I promised you," he said, when the steaming glasses of negus were set down before us, "an end to the tale of Barney McQuaid and the White Elephant Club. I wish it were a happy one, or even a sad one. The truth is that it is neither, for his fate remains a mystery. He knew that the price he had paid for cheating time was too high and, were he to be caught, would be higher still. Nonetheless, he determined to confront the beggar and insisted that I accompany him. We had difficulty in finding Wragglestone Street, not because he had forgotten the way, but because it had undergone such an astonishing transformation that we failed to recognise it. The houses, which before had shut out the world, had now opened themselves to it. Blinds had been raised, curtains drawn. On window sills geraniums glowed in pots. A maidservant was beating a rug draped over the railings. Two children played with a puppy in the street. As for the White Elephant Club, it was nowhere to be seen. Where it had stood, wedged between two terraced houses, was a narrow garden with flowering borders and a cherry tree in full blossom. McQuaid paused outside, nonplussed. A cat with yellow eyes sat in the gateway. As McQuaid tried to cross the threshold, it bared its teeth and hissed.

"At that moment a policeman, no doubt on a routine tour of the neighbourhood, entered the street from the other end. McQuaid took to his heels and ran. That was the last I ever saw of him. Though I keep a close eye on the newspapers, I have never heard of his being arrested. One day I hope he will pause in his endless flight and turn up again on my doorstep. By now his sufferings will be greater than ever: the Garden of Lost Youth has for ever been denied him and he must know that he has no-one but himself to blame. Would you care to share another glass of negus with me, Mr Bartholomew? I have just found another sixpence in the lining of my coat."

Our journey together continued as far as Bristol, first on the coach to Exeter and afterwards on the train. What we talked of I cannot now remember, and it matters little since it forms no part of this story. Although we exchanged addresses and promised to correspond, in the way travelling companions often do, I did not expect to hear from him again. Some months later, however, I received a parcel. It was from Broadfold and contained four beautiful green chenille cushions. I have them in my parlour still, where they are much admired by visitors. Well, that concludes my tale – or rather Edwin Broadfold's tale – of the White Elephant Club, though I, too, have a postscript to add. I wrote to him thanking him for his generous gift and pointed out that though the cushions were welcome they were only a part of what he had promised me and that he still owed me the Lenten sermon. I wrote, of course, in jest. I am no fonder of Lenten sermons than the next man.

To my surprise, he wrote back by return. "Dear Bartholomew," he wrote, "did you not realise that the tale of Barney McQuaid and the White Elephant Club *was* the Lenten sermon? My debt – as all debts must be – is fully repaid.

Mr Bartholomew's tale had taken us past the new Houses of Parliament, past the Millbank Penitentiary, where time must indeed have ambled withal for the inmates, past the floating hotels moored at Vauxhall, past the feculent outflow of the Tyburn, past wharves and jetties, stairs and staithes, until we came at last, with a piercing blast of the ship's whistle, to Pimlico Pier. There we bade farewell to the Malachi Browns and the clerical party. From the jetty I watched the shrunken figure of Stumps huddled between the two clergymen and waved to Mrs Alfred who had resumed hostilities with her husband as soon as Nan's calming presence had been removed. The master semaphored to the call boy, who shouted Full Ahead to the Engineer, the paddles churned, and soon the *PS Haberdasher* and its passengers were silhouettes against the westering sun.

Bugle sounding, George Costello led the way into St George's Square, where we gathered on the lawns to be registered in Miss Osgood's notebook. By now the light was beginning to fade and the lamplighters, prompted by the grimy haze which had settled on the river, had begun their evening's work.

"Then that is everyone accounted for," concluded Miss Osgood, shutting her notebook with a snap.

"Except for young Gabriel," prompted Nan.

"Poor child," sighed Humphrey Ezard.

"May he rest in peace," exclaimed Purselove.

"Amen," added Breeze.

"Amen fiddlesticks!" retorted Mr Ezard with surprising vehemence. "You should not say that unless you mean it."

"Hear, hear," said Mr Turpin. "It is ungentlemanly to joke over so serious a matter. Anything might have happened to the child. It doesn't bear thinking about."

"En avant, mes amis," I cried, hastily changing the subject. "George, sound the bugle if you please. Miss Osgood, allow me to carry your bag."

Now for those of you for whom that summer of 1851 is a faded memory or perhaps not even a memory at all, let me say a little about our destination. In order to prevent landlords from taking advantage of their guests, the great excursionist Mr Thomas Cook had persuaded Mr Thomas Harrison of Pimlico to turn his furniture depository into a hostel where visitors might be cheaply and decently lodged. For one and threepence per night up to a thousand residents were to be provided with bed and bedding, soap and towel. A decent breakfast was to be had for 4d, a good dinner for 8d, and for a further penny per item, the visitor might have his boots blacked, his chin shaved and his infirmities treated by a surgeon who attended every morning at nine. The dormitories were partitioned into cubicles, and, in order to prevent pilfering or drunkenness, janitors patrolled the gas-lit corridors day and night. If the necessities of life had been provided for, the luxuries were not neglected either: there was a large smoking room in which a band played every evening, gratis, and on top of the building an observation platform from which visitors might enjoy uninterrupted views of the river and the city.

Thus much I had gathered from my correspondence with Mr Cook, who had kindly agreed to share with the Ebenezer party a facility which he had established for the convenience of his own customers. That he had agreed to do so was due to the efforts of Serafina, whose family were, as I have already mentioned, aristocrats of the temperance movement and well known to Mr Cook. Garlands, our rivals, could offer nothing to match this.

Burdened with carpet bags and travel cases our party shuffled into Ranelagh Road. The first sight of Harrison's Hostel brought forth gasps of wonder and dismay – dismay because the place looked like a huge warehouse, which of course it was, and wonder because of its sheer size. Occupying over two acres it was built round three sides of a large courtyard, whose fourth opened on to the river.

"This is refreshingly industrial, I must say," remarked Purselove sourly.

"Makes one rather envy Stumps," added Breeze.

At that moment, an omnibus, one of several employed by Mr Cook to convey guests to Hyde Park, rattled into Ranelagh Road. Hardly had the passengers alighted than the Ebenezer party crowded round, demanding to know whether the Exhibition had lived up to expectations, whether the Koh-i-Noor, the Crystal Fountain, the lard vase, the daguerreotypes and the rest were the marvels they were reported to be. I marvelled at the ease with which my companions sought out their own kind. Within a few minutes Nan was deep in conversation with a parlour maid, Miss Lark with a governess, whilst Costello was comparing medals with a veteran of the Peninsular campaign. Turpin had even struck up an acquaintance with a blacksmith, who asked admiringly after the Travelling Topper.

Though tired and footsore, the newcomers, who had arrived from Bradford on one of Mr Cook's excursions the previous day, were eager to show their souvenirs and share their impressions.

"Don't trust the pies," said one.

"Or the sandwiches," said another.

But these were rare dissenting voices. There were more do's than don'ts, starting with 'Do admire the Spode and the Minton' and 'Be sure not to miss the boilers and the fabrics' and continuing with:

"The ploughs, the statues ..."

"The Queen on horseback, Venus and Cupid ..."

"So wanton!"

"The penny buns, the ices, the altar cloths and the spittoons ..."

"The soap and the small arms ...

"Oh clever Samuel Colt!"

Thus, on to the surface of Ranelagh Road, the Crystal Palace poured forth its treasures, item by item, until one of the Bradford party, overcome by thirst, proposed continuing the conversation inside over a cup of tea.

[Editor's Note: I propose to make a cut here. In the manuscript there follow several pages in which Blackwood casts a hotelier's eye over the interior of Harrison's Hostel and calculates the likely income from a thousand beds, breakfasts and suppers and what sort of profit it would amount to. The answer, as Blackwood shrewdly foresaw, was none: Harrison went bankrupt shortly afterwards. As for members of the Ebenezer party, some, he notes, retired to their cubicles for a nap, some made for the dining room with their new friends from Bradford, whilst others climbed up to the lantern to admire the view. We re-join Blackwood an hour or so later. He is sitting on the top of an omnibus in Regent Street, together with Purselove and Breeze, Meek, Beamish and Turpin, all eager to catch a glimpse of the Crystal Palace, even though it is now closed for the day. The traffic is at a complete standstill. Between the immobilised hansoms and growlers, broughams and chaises, the crowds – most of them visitors from the Exhibition who are making their way back to the West End – jostle against the stationary vehicles, causing them to rock violently.]

Although Beamish was happily employed in gazing down on the heads of passers-by, Purselove and Breeze, frustrated by the slow progress of the omnibus and still rattled with Turpin for deprecating their callousness towards Gabriel, began to grow restless. In the course of our journey, I had noticed that Purselove and Breeze were much amused by the Travelling Topper, so much so that I had suspected each of daring the other to turn on the tap and give its inventor a good drenching. And now, stranded on top of an omnibus in the middle of Regent Street, they sought relief in Turpin-baiting once more.

"Tell me, Mr Turpin," began Breeze disingenuously, "are you by any remote chance related to …"

"Or descended from …," interjected Purselove.

"The celebrated highwayman of the same name?"

"Because if you are," continued Purselove, "you might be interested to know that I have played him to packed houses on more than one occasion. My last performance in the role brought me the greatest ovation of my career. A piece of burning wadding flew out of my pistol – no bullets of course, safety of the public always the first consideration – and set the curtain alight. Never saw a house empty so fast. Audience stood in the street and watched the theatre burn down. Marvellous show, they said. Bravo! wouldn't have missed it for the world! After that, I look on all Turpins as friends, especially if the celebrated Dick was one of their ancestors. Is the celebrated Dick one of yours, Mr Turpin?"

"No," said Turpin.

"Bother!" said Purselove.

"But," continued Turpin, "I once met a coachman who was held up by his great grandson – several times, in fact. So much so that they became firm friends, though that was only after the highwayman had retired."

"Retired?" echoed Breeze.

"That's a new one," laughed Purselove. "That's the first I ever heard of a retired highwayman"

"He had no choice," said Turpin. "None of them did. Turnpikes and enclosures robbed them of their hiding places. Out they crept, like earwigs from under stones, cursing the march of science. Oh, how the coachmen laughed! At last, they thought, we'll have the roads all to ourselves. And for a while they did. But it didn't last. Within twenty years most of them were driving London omnibuses if they were lucky or farm carts if they weren't. And that's the way it goes. That's the march of science. It devours everyone – highwayman and coachman today, bargee and lamplighter tomorrow. As for the day after, who can say? Engine driver and station master, I shouldn't wonder. You all look surprised. Why should they be spared? Why should any of us be spared? The march of science has no favourites."

"So what happened to this coachman of yours who befriended a highwayman?" asked Breeze.

"Was he arrested for aiding and abetting a felon?" demanded Purselove.

"Or transported for conspiring to steal Her Majesty's mails?"

"And if not, why not?"

"If you'll let me get a word in edgeways," replied Turpin, "I'll tell you. It's a cautionary tale and one which Mr Culpepper would have approved, for in the end the friendship of a highwayman proved more deadly than his enmity."

If the tale that follows contains more of my words than of Turpin's, then that is because I have set it down from recollection, having had no transcription of Miss Osgood's from which to work. I do not, however, think I have misrepresented him, though given his experiments with a story-telling machine, details of which I shall describe in due course, I do not think he would have objected if I had.

The Inventor's Tale:
The Devil's Coachman

Have you ever wondered what happened to the stagecoaches that used to ply the turnpikes and fill the inn yards? he began. I don't mean the miserable affairs that you still see in country districts; I mean those thoroughbreds of the road with their red wheels and brass lanterns and beef-faced coachmen, those whirlwinds of wood and leather and horseflesh. Well, I'll tell you what happened to them. Wheel by wheel, bolt by bolt, they were scattered to the four winds, ending up in carts and cabinets, beds and alehouse benches. Not long ago I came across the Royal William – a fine coach, a regular on the Poole run – turned into a henhouse. There it was in the middle of a nettle patch, with a cockerel perched on the roof where the guard used to sit. I dismounted from my horse and leant on the field gate, hearing once more the coachman's horn and the jingling of the harness.

"A melancholy sight, isn't she?" said a voice at my elbow.

"She is indeed," I said, immediately falling into the habit of referring to the Royal William as a she. The speaker was a common carter who had stopped his wagon in the road beside me.

"I'm not much of a one for showing my feelings," he continued, "but I don't mind admitting that I shed a silent tear when I had to part from her."

"You drove her?" I asked.

"Rain and shine for more'n twenty year," he replied. "As you can see, I've come down in the world since then."

"You have indeed, my friend," I said, "and I should not blame you if you wished to the devil all those inventors and engineers who brought you to this pass."

"Good of 'ee to say so," he rejoined. "But for the calamity that befell me, I blame no-one but myself. And if other coachmen want to blame me for the calamity that befell them, then I'd have to say it was only right that they should."

"How come?" I asked.

"If you care to ride alongside me, I'll tell you," he said.

"Better still," I replied, "I shall tie my horse to the tail of your cart and sit on the bench beside you."

"My name," he said, when I had secured my horse and climbed up on to the wagon, "is Alfred Pelham. There are still inns where they remember me, though if you mention my name, be sure to call me Pellmellham, because that's how I was known in my prime. Ah, what a wonderful thing one's prime is! No turnpike keeper kept me waiting at his gate; no innkeeper watered his beer; no ostler mixed his oats with chaff. No, sir, no-one got the better of Pellmellham, neither man nor horse, though I do admit to be being worsted by a lion on one occasion. We were passing the Winterslow Hut on the Salisbury run. A menagerie had set up camp for the night in a field next to the inn. You may know the place, sir: drivers used to stop there to take on extra horses for the climb up Three Mile Hill. That night, though, my team was running well, so I thought I'd manage without the extra legs. Well, we swept past the inn in fine style, horn blowing, whip cracking, but before I knew what was happening a beast leapt out of the darkness and threw hisself at the leading horse. Hullo, thinks I, what's all this? Must be a rabid dog. So I shouted to the guard to shoot, but either he was asleep or he'd forgot to charge his weapon, one or the other, I never found out which. I jumped off the box, seized a carriage lamp and lashed out with my whip. But the harder I lashed, the more it stood its ground. I held up the lantern and got the shock of my life. This warn't no dog; this was a lion with its teeth in the flanks of my outside leader, fine horse, name of Pomegranate. You should have seen me move. I was back on the box in a flash. He wasn't done with me, though. He was all set to spring, but at that moment the keepers appeared with nets and drove it back into the inn yard."

"Well, I'm sure it did your reputation no harm," I said; "after all, you did challenge the beast, even though you thought it was a dog."

"I lost count of the free suppers I had, often from complete strangers, though not, as it happened, from the menagerie. You'd have thought that they'd have stumped up, seeing the money they made out of it. There were posters everywhere. 'Come and See the Lion that Attacked the Salisbury Coach.' And people did, in their hundreds. No-one blamed me. Said I'd acted up heroic in the circumstances."

"It seems to have been a happy accident all round," I said, "except for poor Pomegranate."

"That's me all over," he beamed. "When accidents befall me, they're generally happy – with one exception which we'll come to shortly, though even that appeared happy at the time. As for Pomegranate, he made a full recovery and was back in harness inside the month. Now take another case. Take the highwayman on Bagshot Heath. I had to pinch myself when he first rode out of the trees. To look at him you'd have said he was more Turnip than Turpin. No tricorn hat, no silver spurs, no 'Stand and deliver'. No mask neither, just a top hat pulled down low over his eyes with a bullet hole in it for bravado. You could see the moon shining through it like a silver penny. 'This man,' says I to myself, 'is new to his trade. Someone's put him up to this. Look at the way his pistol is trembling. The only thing that's in danger here is his horse's ears.' So I put on an extra turn of speed, gave him a flick of the whip and sent his pistol flying into the bushes. The last we saw of him he was on his hands and knees scrabbling around in the brambles."

"Being a hero was obviously becoming something of a habit of yours," I remarked.

"That wasn't the only thing that was becoming a habit," he said. "A few days later it happened again. Same place, same man. Only it warn't his pistol

I clipped this time: it was his hat, bullet hole in the middle, that one. Well, it wasn't long before the coaches were full of sightseers, who felt cheated when he didn't show up. What they wanted – especially the young ladies, who'd been reading the penny dreadfuls – was an 'encounter'. 'Please, coachman,' they'd say, 'could you make sure we have an encounter?' and 'Please, coachman, could you make sure he relieves us of our valuables. We do so want to be plundered.'"

"And were they?" I asked.

"Only because we stopped and begged him to," he replied. "And it obviously gave him such pleasure to oblige. His face was a picture. Mind you, their so-called valuables didn't amount to much. Fake pearls, broken watches, George III pennies, stuff dredged out of the bottom of drawers. It didn't stop 'em pleading and sobbing, though. You never heard the like."

"Let me guess," exclaimed Purselove, his hands clasped across his bosom. "'For the love of God, sir! Not my grandfather's signet ring! Take it and may my grandmother's curse go with you and yours for ever!'"

"How did you know that?" demanded Turpin. "It was me that Pelham told the story to, not you."

"Theatricals, Mr Turpin," replied Purselove, "theatricals. As I remember the young ladies were keener to surrender their honour rather than their valuables. And speaking as Turpin – Dick, that is, rather than your good self – I was quite ready to take them at their word."

"Shame on you, Mr Purselove," said Beamish. "You would not have said that in the presence of Mr Culpepper and the ladies. Mr Turpin, pray continue. I wish to know what happened to the highwayman."

According to Pelham, continued Turpin, he simply disappeared. Perhaps he found the attentions of the ladies too insistent – one of them even brought a silhouettist to cut a portrait of her handing over her purse – but whatever the reason, he disappeared from his haunts, though not entirely from the story."

"It was many years before I saw him again," Pelham told me. "I'd come in off the Salisbury run and was having supper – veal pie, parsnips, taties – at the White Bear in Piccadilly, when a well-dressed man sat himself at my table and looked me in the eye.

"'Remember me?' he said.

"'I don't think I've had the pleasure,' I replied.

"'Maybe,' he said, 'that's because it wasn't a pleasure, not at the time anyway. Now, would this help you remember?'

"He took a hat off the peg on the wall behind him and, setting it on the table, slid his hand inside and poked a finger out through a hole in front.

"'Now,' he said, 'does that do the trick?'

"It certainly did. I sat back and took a good look at him. With his silk weskit and garnet ring, he was looking a lot smarter than when I last saw him. 'Whatever made you do it?' I asked. 'Anyone could see your heart warn't in it.'

"'Bailiffs,' he said. 'First they took the overmantel; then they helped themselves to a brace of clocks; finally they threatened the wife's baubles. That's when she put her foot down. Turpin, she said, this has got to stop.' – ('Turpin?' I said. 'Any relation of ...?' 'Great grandson,' he said.) – 'Turpin, you've got to do something. Pawn something, rob a coach. I'm not letting them take my baubles. Them's heirlooms. Well, you can guess the rest.'

"'Why have you come to tell me this now?' I asked.

"'Because you,' he said, 'are a prince among coachmen. Known for it. All along the road people talk of Pellmellham as a man who can face down lions and cutthroats (meaning me and, to tell the truth, I rather glory in the appellation, little as I did to deserve it); a man who can drive his passengers through fire and flood and bring them out unsinged and unsoused; a man, in short, whose services friends of mine are willing to pay good money for. What would you say to fifty guineas?'

"I must have looked uneasy, because he laughed and said, 'You need have no worries about these friends of mine. They're what you might call respectable gentlemen in a hurry. Or they will be next Wednesday. And that's where you come in. Next Wednesday evening they will arrive in Salisbury on the Bridport coach. Next morning they need to be in Bristol by nine sharp. Come lion, come tempest, they must be there and you're the man to get them there. Here's twenty guineas on account' – he placed a leather purse on the table – 'and the rest on arrival in Bristol.'

"I picked up the purse and shook it.

"'Count it,' he said. 'It's all there and it's all honestly come by.'

"'And will you be of the party?' I asked.

"'Alas, no. Like Mercury, I merely bring messages from the gods. Once I have persuaded you to agree, my part in the affair is over. Now, Mr Pelham, will you do it? If the night is fine, you will have earned an easy fifty guineas; if foul, then you will have earned an increase in reputation – if such a thing is possible.'

"I was in need of a little flattery just then. One or two of the young drivers had started to fancy themselves as swells and had put it about, some of them, that my lion was a dog and my highwayman a hired player. What's more, some people had started to believe them. What I needed was a triumph, and a death-defying dash to Bristol, especially if the weather was bad, might just do the trick.

"On the day appointed it had started to blow early. Several coaches had pulled over for the night, so the inn yard of The Three Swans was full before the Bridport coach arrived. Round the fire there was a huddle of outside passengers trying to get warm and a group of inside passengers calling for hot toddies to keep out the cold. In the snug the coachmen were swapping tales of wind and flood, and with each new tale the waters rose a little higher and the gale blew a little stronger, until no-one would have been surprised if Noah himself had walked in. On one thing they were agreed: that it would be madness to venture on to the roads on such a night.

"It was past ten when the Bridport coach arrived, disgorging its sodden passengers into the parlour. Their driver, too, was keen to tell his tale of wind and flood. In Dorchester the coach had been struck by flying tiles and in the open country it had taken to the fields where fallen trees had blocked the road. In Blandford the guard had begged the driver to pull in, but the four gentlemen inside – my gentlemen – had urged him to go on. They had a coach waiting for them in Salisbury, they said; it was vital they go on. If only he knew how much depended on it, he would not hesitate. So the driver, ignoring the protest of the outside passengers, pulled his great coat about him and the coach plunged on.

"'A coach is waiting for them here in Salisbury?' said one coachman, looking round the room incredulously. 'What madman is going to drive it on a night like this?' 'And who are the madmen who want to be driven?' asked another.

"I was about to confess to being the madman in question, when the four gentlemen appeared in the doorway. In an inn full of squabbling passengers, there was a strange calm about them. Their linen gleamed, their boots shone and their hats were perpendicular, which, on a night when steeples were toppling, was a remarkable thing to see. Long after the falling tiles and trees had been forgotten, it was the hats, like an orderly row of chimney pots, that people remembered most.

"One of the four, a short man with a heavy watch chain, lit a cigar, blew a great cloud of smoke into the snug and said, 'Which of you is our man? Which if you is the one they call Pelham?'

"Until that moment I hadn't said anything to the other coachmen. I'd hugged the fire and kept mum, but now I stood up and, eyeing the young swells, announced, 'That's me. I am Pelham.'

"Well, you should have heard the outcry, the protests, the cries of 'madman!' But behind it all you could sense the admiration, the envy.

"'That's me,' I repeated. 'I am Pelham, also known to my fellow coachmen – with I hope admiration and affection – as Pellmellham.'

"'Then, Mr Pelham,' said the man with the cigar, 'it is time we were on our way. Remember, Bristol by nine o' clock sharp and the fifty guineas is yours.'

"At that moment a gust of wind smote the inn like a great fist. Bricks crashed down the chimney and into the hearth, flinging sparks and smoke into the snug.

"'This is madness!' cried a carter from Blandford, a pious man who carted dung for a living.

"'You shall not go!' cried a drayman from Ringwood.

"'Seize him someone!' cried a carrier from Cranborne, too timid to do any of the seizing himself.

"'Lock him in the cellar until he comes to his senses!' cried the guard from the London mail coach, catching hold of my sleeve.

"Now this guard was the one who had been asleep on the job when we were attacked by the lion at the Winterslow Hut all those years before. To be crossed by such a man was more than my pride could bear. Shaking him off, I climbed up on the table.

"'I have given these gentlemen my word that I will deliver them to Bristol by nine tomorrow morning,' I declared. 'And may the devil take anyone who tries to stop me!'

"'That's right,' shouted the dung carter, 'call on the devil and much good may it do you.'

"By now my blood was fairly up, I can tell you.

"'If the devil can help me keep my promise,' I shouted in a moment of bravado, 'then I shall receive him with open arms.'

"More bricks and mortar fell into the hearth.

"'You wouldn't dare,' said the Blandford carter.

"'I am Pellmellham,' I declared. 'I fear neither man nor lion, no, nor the devil himself. If he can help, then let him and welcome. Gentlemen – I turned to the gentlemen in the perpendicular hats – it is time for us to go.'

"Now whether the devil had been hiding in the chimney, I don't know, but there was another mighty roar and a cartload of rubble tumbled down the chimney and spilled out into the room. In the smoke and confusion that followed, I made my escape.

"My four gentlemen were standing by the coach, their hats upright, their luggage in the yard beside them. I say luggage, but, apart from the odd carpet bag, it looked like a collection of leather drainpipes tied together with cord. I'd have given anything for a peep inside. All I could think of was fishing rods, though why anyone should want to drive through a hurricane to go fishing in Bristol was beyond me.

"The devil was in that storm. In the city he pelted us with tiles; out in the country he pulled apart hayricks and flung them in our faces. We fought our way, inch by inch, to Wilton and when we got to Wilton a watchman told us to go back. 'The river's over in a dozen places,' he said; 'no-one's going to Bristol that way tonight.' 'Then I'll go another way,' I told him. 'I am Pelham and I am going to Bristol tonight.' 'What other way is there?' he asked. 'I'll find a way,' I said and as soon as I had said it, it came to me what way that was. For a moment my heart misgave me. Only for a moment, though. 'I am Pelham,' I said to myself aloud and turned the horses back to Salisbury. With the wind right behind us, we were soon clattering past the inn we'd started from. One of my gents, obviously recognising where he was, stuck his head out of the window and shouted, 'Nine o' clock sharp, mind.'

"'Nine o' clock sharp,' I repeated and turned the horses north.

"Yes, I turned the horses north. Across Salisbury Plain. To be sure there's no shelter for twenty mile, but then there's no river to flood and no trees to fall.

With the wind and rain coming up in great sweeping gusts from the west, it was all I could do to keep the coach on the road. Up on the Plain the turnpike runs from east to west, but the north-bound roads are little better than tracks which the carters turn into mud. And it's a mercy they do, for the moon, when there is one, picks them out like a shining ribbon. With luck you can follow it – or you can if the wind will let you. The further out on the Plain we went, the harder it blew and the harder it blew the slower we went. After an hour or two, we were so mired in mud and buffeted by wind that we were almost at a standstill.

"'Nine o' clock sharp, mind,' shouted the gents at regular intervals.

"'Nine o'clock sharp,' I replied with a crack of the whip.

"But no crack of the whip could drive the horses faster – or even drive them at all. There came a moment when the wind fought us to a standstill. We lost the moon and with it the muddy ribbon that guided us. I hadn't even the heart to say, 'I am Pelham'. I was about to admit defeat when I remembered my boast in the inn: that if the devil could help me keep my promise, I'd welcome him with open arms. So I shook my fist at the swirling blackness and shouted, 'Now's the time to keep your promise. Get me to Bristol and you can take from me whatever you want.' Some might say that for fifty guineas I was selling my soul cheap, but you'll notice that I didn't actually mention my soul. I hoped he might take something else. After all, what was my soul to him? He already had thousands. Well, he must have heard, for there was a sudden calm and the moon sailed out from behind a cloud. On either side there were rocks piled on top of each other, reaching up to the stars. At first I thought we were in a ruined building. And in a way we were. We had come to rest in Stonehenge, right in the middle of the stone circle, and mighty strange it was. Silver ribbons stretched all over the Plain, but within the stones not a blade of grass stirred. We must have stood there some minutes, whilst the horses got their breath and I fell to thinking about the druids who built the place. Maybe it was them who had answered my prayer and stilled the storm. Who can say? All this went through my mind as we stood there in the moonlight. Suddenly there was knock on the roof of the coach.

"'Nine o' clock sharp, mind,' said a voice.

"'Nine o' clock sharp it is, sir,' I replied and whipped up the horses.

"As soon as we rolled out of the circle of stones, the wind started up again. Only this time the wind was just wind, and the rain just rain. We rolled across

Orcheston Down and into Lavington, where the roofs were intact and the chimney pots still standing. From there we made our way round the edge of the Plain to Warminster and so back to the Bristol road. Soon we were thundering along, dodging fallen branches and sending up showers of spray as we hurtled through the puddles. At daybreak we reached Bath, where a few bleary-eyed servants stared at us in disbelief. In Keynsham an early market cart swerved in horror and stray cats scurried for cover. All along the Bristol road that morning a dozen stories were born of a ghost coach that rattled through the empty streets in the half light. Some said it passed in silence, others that it made a noise like thunder; some even threw in a ghostly coaching horn. But all agreed it was white as frost. And no wonder. In our struggle to cross the Plain, the wind had blown a fine spray of chalky mud over coach and horses, not to mention yours truly. Only the passengers, snug in their wood and leather box, escaped.

"As we stopped outside the Guildhall in Bristol, a crowd had gathered on the opposite pavement. Word seemed to have spread. But if they were expecting ghostly passengers to emerge from a ghostly coach, they were disappointed. Out stepped four smartly dressed gentlemen looking none the worse for their night's buffeting. Their linen was fresh, their neckties knotted, their top hats perpendicular. No sooner had they stepped on to the pavement than a nearby clock struck nine. All four opened their pocket watches, glanced at each other and nodded.

"'Well done, coachman,' said one. 'You have earned your fee. We shall not forget you.'

"'And you,' said another, 'will be unlikely to forget us.'

"'Not a chance of that, sir,' I agreed.

"'And now, if you would be so kind, we should like the leather tubes taken upstairs. The committee is waiting for them.'

"I gathered an armful of drainpipes and carried them up to a large room where a group of smartly dressed gentlemen sat round a big table covered with papers. I placed the drainpipes in the middle and stepped back, hoping that they would open them so I could see what was inside.

"'And the rest, if you please, coachman,' said a whiskery gentleman with a double row of seals on his watch chain.

"I ran downstairs and was handed the rest of the drainpipes by the four gentlemen who were still standing by the coach.

"'Excuse me, sir,' I said, my curiosity getting the better of me at last, 'might I take the liberty of asking what's in these here tubes? I had thought they might be fishing rods, but you don't go fishing on a mahogany table with a lot of gentlemen in tail coats.'

"'Fishing?' echoed one.

"'That's rich!' laughed another.

"'Prime!' said a third.

"'These fishing rods,' said the fourth gentleman, 'are drawings. These fishing rods are cuttings, bridges and tunnels. These fishing rods are carriages and locomotives. In short, coachman, these fishing rods are the Great Western Railway. Or will be, when we have persuaded the gentlemen upstairs to put up the money. Yes, coachman, if we can make our case to their satisfaction, you can say you helped make history tonight. Without you this might never have happened.'

"When he had finished, he handed me a purse.

"'Here's your money, coachman, I shall not forget you. Remind me. What did you say your name was?'

"'Pelham, sir.'

"'No, the other one, the one that you like to be known by.'

"'Pellmellham, sir. And if you don't think it too bold, might I enquire after yours?'

"'My name,' he said, lighting a cigar, 'is Isambard Kingdom Brunel.'

"So that's how the devil collects his dues – a mail coach here, a turnpike there, a wheel, a shaft. That's why the Royal William ended as a hen house and why hundreds of coachmen like me have become common carters. As for the coach I drove to Bristol, well, that came to an even sadder end."

"How come?" I asked.

"After the night ride, no-one could get it clean. Even when the mud had been scraped away, no-one could scrub the white off it. We tried re-painting but the white still came through. Worse than that, you couldn't get horses between the shafts. Neither bran nor the whip could get them in. 'That's Pelham's pact with the devil,' people said. 'The coach is cursed.' It wouldn't have been so bad if it had been my coach. But it wasn't: it was one I borrowed. In the end the owner refused to take it back. I couldn't really blame him. After all, who wants a horseless coach? So I had to buy it from him. And do you know how much it cost me? Fifty guineas."

"The devil giveth and the devil taketh away," I said.

"Not entirely," he replied. "You see, I did come out of the affair a shilling better off. That was what the Great Western Railway gave me for it."

"What on earth did they want it for?" I asked.

"They took the wheels off of it and turned it into a platelayer's hut for workmen to keep their tools and play cards in. It's still there, still covered in white. You can go and see it. I often do. I can't help myself. Of the two, though, I still think the Royal William has the more dignified retirement."

I had noticed earlier that Turpin was a man with a strong sense of his own worth, and when he had finished his tale he doffed the Travelling Topper (not without difficulty) and gave a little bow. Beamish, Meek and I applauded enthusiastically; Purselove and Breeze, on the other hand, seemed quite unmoved, the one polishing his pocket watch, the other tossing up coins and catching them in his hat.

"You know, said Purselove at last, "all that talk of coachmen has put me in mind of Astley's. What say we make our way to Lambeth to see the horse-riding?"

"An excellent notion," added Breeze. "Nothing is going to move here for hours."

"You must excuse me," replied Beamish, who had already begun to descend the iron rungs on the outside of the omnibus. "I have just seen two clergymen pass by, hatless. Bald, too. Such an opportunity. It would be a crime to miss it."

Following his quarry, he was soon lost in the crowd.

"I haven't eaten since breakfast and I refuse to go anywhere without a bite of supper first," announced Meek. "Does anyone care to join me? We can continue on foot to the Crystal Palace afterwards."

"No, Astley's for me," replied Purselove. "I've set my heart on it."

"Me too," said Breeze. "Lead on, Macduff."

"Banquo, actually," said Purselove.

To the evident relief of Turpin they, too, descended the iron rungs and were swallowed by the crowd.

"I noticed a chop house back in Sloane Square," said Meek. "Let us try our luck there."

Uncomfortably aware that I had promised Serafina to confine myself to Mr Harrison's eightpenny suppers, I followed Meek, persuading myself that if he could come up with more Uncle Jack stories, especially if set in far-flung corners of the Empire, then the investment would have been worth it. It wasn't. Both Meek and Turpin, as I quickly discovered once we were seated in Chaplin's Chop House, had expensive tastes and, try as I might to steer the conversation towards the exploits of Uncle Jack, Turpin kept steering it back to the submarine cable which had just been laid between Dover and Calais. This device, he assured us, would change the world for ever – and for the better, too.

"How come?" asked Meek.

"By allowing nation to speak unto nation," said Turpin, "by allowing man to speak unto man at the click of a telegraph key. I foresee an age of universal brotherhood, peace on earth and good will toward men – and all of it brought about, not by priests or prophets, but by engineers."

"Steady on, old chap!" protested Meek. "Aren't you running a bit ahead of yourself? Dover to Calais is twenty-five miles at most. On a fine day they can even see each other."

"But the telegraph will not stop at France. In time it will reach to the four corners of the earth."

"Even across the Atlantic?" I asked.

"I do not see why not," replied Turpin. "The three thousand mile cable does not yet exist, it is true, nor the ships to carry it, but they will, Mr Blackwood, they will. Today's miracle is tomorrow's commonplace object."

Here was my opportunity. By considering the possibility of over-land cables to India and Africa, I hoped to direct the conversation towards Meek's various Uncle Jacks, though by the time I succeeded we were half way through the dessert, and the catch, when I finally landed it, was disappointingly small. The big fish had undoubtedly been the tale of Uncle Jack and the Nizam and that we had already devoured. I left Chaplin's Chop House with my pockets empty and without a story to show for it. In low spirits I followed the other two through the now half-deserted streets to Hyde Park. We talked desultorily of this and that – though of what exactly I cannot now remember, except that sub-marine cables kept appearing regularly – until we reached the Prince's Gate, where a small crowd had gathered round a coffee stall. Nearby a print seller, his wares arranged on the inside of an upturned umbrella, was still doing a brisk trade in engravings of the Exhibition.

Behind him, silent and mysterious, rose the Great Hive itself, its delicate tracery gleaming like frost ferns on a window pane. It is said of Melrose Abbey that to see it rightly you must see it by moon-light, and the same may justly be said of Mr Paxton's glass trinket case. Though crammed with the marvels of the age – pianos and ploughs, tapestries and turbines – no marvel could match the palace itself. Here, if ever, was a vision from the Arabian Nights: its walls floated like a vapour above Kensington Barracks, a hundred moons reflected in their myriad panes, its filigree of iron girders reaching up to the stars. To Christian and Hopeful, the sight of the Heavenly City at the end of their pilgrims' progress could not have been more glorious than this.

"A thousand and sixty iron columns, thirty miles of guttering, nine hundred thousand square feet of glass," began Turpin.

"And a partridge in a pear tree," I interrupted, irritated by having the spell broken by brute mathematics. "Tell me, Turpin, can you not bring yourself simply to marvel? Why must everything end up as numbers?"

"Things don't end as numbers," he replied: "they begin as numbers. Numbers are what things are made of."

When we had gazed our fill, I led the way back to Pimlico, Turpin entertaining Meek with tonnages of iron and acreages of glass. As we turned into Lupus Street, we collided with Beamish, whose eyes were burning with excitement.

"I have just spent a most remarkable evening," he announced. "The implications for phrenonological science are immense. First, I attended a dog fight, – I mustn't say where, illegal you know – immediately followed by a rat baiting in Great St Andrew's Street."

"In the company of two clergymen?" I asked in astonishment.

"Those two clergymen were not clergymen at all but, as I suspected from the start, sportsmen. No clergyman of my acquaintance has such highly developed organs of Combativeness and Acquisitiveness."

"Then why were they dressed as clergymen?"

"To throw the police off the scent. First they took me to a dog fight ..."

"Did they know who you were?"

"I made no secret of it."

"Yet they still took you along as if you were an ordinary punter?" Beamish looked a little sheepish.

"There was, I confess, a price to pay. They asked me to feel the bumps on the fighting dogs before they placed their bets."

"And did you?"

"I went through the motions. It seemed the least I could do to thank them for their co-operation."

"And did it work?"

"The odd thing is, it did. Where the organ of Destructiveness is situated in human beings – a little above the right ear – so, too, it seems, is it situated in dogs."

"That must surely have been pure chance."

"One would have thought so. But afterwards they took me on to a rat pit in Great St Andrew's Street and I repeated my success there. My two false clergymen won all their bets."

"Did they make you feel the rats' bumps as well?" asked Turpin.

"They asked but I did not oblige," replied Beamish. "I draw the line at a rat."

It was at this point that Meek remembered an Uncle Jack story, featuring a distant forebear – quite possibly mythical – who began life as a rat catcher's apprentice. The story was only a fragment and what had happened to the ending nobody knew. According to a family joke, the rats had eaten it.

Before he had the chance to tell his tale we found ourselves outside Harrison's Hostel. Through the open door the sounds of a band issued from the smoking room. A single figure, her shawl wrapped tight about her, sat on a cane-bottomed chair outside the front door. It was Nan.

"Not enjoying yourself with the others, Nan?" I asked.

"Not while Gabriel is unaccounted for, Mr Blackwood," she replied. "I prefer to wait. Earlier Miss Osgood kept me company, but she has now retired for the night."

"Then let me relieve you," I said. "Perhaps Meek would care to smoke a last cigar with me."

"By all means," said Meek.

"Under normal circumstances I would offer to keep you company," said Beamish, "but the prospect of extending phrenology into the animal kingdom is so remarkable, so dazzling, that I must write up my notes whilst the details are still fresh."

"And I," said Turpin, "must go and remove the Travelling Topper. Apart from an hour in the chop house I have been wearing it all day and it has given me a headache."

"Meek and I will be quite sufficient to watch for the boy," I said, "though I must warn you, Nan, that the doors are locked promptly at eleven. After that Gabriel must take his chance."

[Editor's Note: It is clear that Blackwood was glad to have Meek all to himself, so that he might hear undisturbed the Tale of the Rat Catcher's Apprentice, little of it though there was. Since Blackwood repeats the fragment to Turpin on

the return journey in the course of a conversation in which the latter proposed
to invent a machine for mass producing stories, I shall therefore jump to a
point later in the evening when Purselove and Breeze return from Astley's.]

Later that evening when the Canterbury party had retired to bed
and I was sitting on the steps of Harrison's Hostel smoking a last
cigar with Mr Meek, Purselove and Breeze joined us. They had
been, they said, to Astley's to see the horse-riding and, yes, they
didn't mind admitting it, they had taken in a gin shop or two on the
way home. But it was not of Astley's that Purselove wished to speak,
but Turpin.

"Of course one shouldn't do it," he began, "but it's hard not to
poke fun at Turpin. Not for anything he's done, though God knows
his hat is ridiculous enough, but for his smugness."

"I quite agree," said Breeze.

"And what especially irritates a fellow is his assumption that he has
the future in his bones, that where he leads the rest of us must follow."

"Whether we wish to or not," added Breeze.

"Precisely."

"Perhaps he does have the future in his bones," I suggested;
"perhaps he really does see further ahead than the rest of us."

"I doubt it," returned Purselove. "Take my word for it, the future
is going to look very much like the past. The same old tale of love
and war, greed, spite and stupidity. Oh there may be a few more
pipes and wires, I grant you, but I doubt if the essentials will change.
I certainly hope not. If we cease to be greedy and lecherous, there
won't be much call for plays and without plays I shall be out of a job –
which, as it happens, I am anyway, but like all actors I live in hope, Mr
Blackwood, I live in hope. All the same, Breeze and I shouldn't have
mocked Turpin on the omnibus the way we did. It was ungenerous

and uncalled for. I may be shallow, Blackwood, but I'm not ungenerous. I wouldn't want you to think that I'm ungenerous."

And to my astonishment he burst into tears. When I offered him
my handkerchief, he seized it eagerly and made a melodramatic
performance of wiping his eyes and nose.

"Here," I said, "have a cigar. Compose yourself."

"The trouble is, Blackwood," he replied, taking the proffered
cigar, "most actors are shallow creatures and hate themselves for it.
They want nothing more than to feign passions which they cannot
feel themselves. Why do you suppose they are so eager to play
Othello and Lear? Envy, that's why."

"Surely not."

"Envy pure and simple. Those of us who live on the surface envy
those who inhabit the lower depths. What is it Lord Byron says?
'The great object of life is sensation – to feel we exist, even though
in pain.' It is when we are appropriating the pain of others that we
feel most fully alive."

"More so than when you are suffering on your own account?"

"Let me tell you a tale," he said. "Tell? What am I saying? Let me
act it for you. Here then, is a drama of the grand passions performed
for you by someone who has learned to feign what he cannot feel."

Purselove threw his cigar under the wheels of a passing cab,
stepped into the road and began to declaim. Soon heads appeared
in the upper windows of the Hostel and of the elegant houses opposite. A chestnut seller abandoned his brazier at the corner of Lupus
Street; a pieman set down his tray, a chair mender his sheaf of cane;
a barrel organist fell silent; a lamplighter pitched his ladder against
a street lamp and climbed up to secure a better view.

The Actor's Tale of the Mantle of Kean

Tom Supple's mother always claimed that her son was a born mimic. Before
he could walk, he'd mimic the cat stalking a bird. When he was old
enough to go to church, he'd mimic the parson giving the sermon; when

he went to school he was thrashed for mimicking the teacher; and when he came
to man's estate, was thrown out of the counting house for aping the Chief Clerk.

"You, sir," said the Chief Clerk, a faded Regency buck who still rouged his
cheeks, "should have been an actor – to the which degraded profession I have no
doubt you would have been an ornament. Now vacate your stool and depart."

An actor! Now there was an idea. Why had he not thought of it before? But
where to begin? Well, an agent is always a good place and, after many enquiries,
he was recommended to a certain William Bellamy who lived above a tobacconist
in Bow Street. There he was supplied with a letter of introduction to Mr Bradley
Bowles, the well-known actor manager, whose Parnassian Players were preparing
to tour the Far West, where there were large numbers of people eager – or so he
said – to be acquainted with his Othello and Richard III. If the tour was successful,
Bellamy told him, it could be the making of him.

"Who's Othello?" asked Tom.

Bellamy buried his face in his hands.

"Such unpardonable ignorance," he groaned.

"Such delightful innocence," said Bellamy's daughter Blanche and blew Tom
a kiss.

Mr Bradley Bowles could see at once that Tom had not in him the stuff of
which tragic actors are made.

"Your forte," he informed him, "is low farce. I can see it in your face; I can
sense it in your whole demeanour. We start rehearsing tomorrow. Nine sharp at
the Little Standard Theatre in Bishopgate Street. Do not be late. Apply yourself,
learn from your elders and betters, and, who knows, you might, might – I put it no
higher – have the makings of a comic actor."

Tom had more than the makings of a comic actor: it quickly became clear
he was the finished article. In Taunton and Truro, where farces alternated with
Othello and Richard III, he was an instant success. In London and in Liverpool he
was saluted in the street; on omnibuses and steamers he was hugged by strangers.
For the first time in his life he had money in his pocket and, if truth be told,
rather more than was good for him. He sent a regular allowance to his mother
and love tokens to Blanche Bellamy. These she disclosed to her father, who was
not displeased, having always, he said, believed that Tom was destined for great
things. "If only he would give up the farce," he sighed. "The trouble is, he's grown

too fond of the money. One day, though, he may see the error of his ways. I live in hopes, my dear, I live in hopes."

Tom's popularity was resented by his fellow actors. Why, they asked, should a boy, a mere boy fresh from the counting house, be crowned with the laurels that should have been theirs? What made it worse was that he was a mere farceur, a clown without a decent Hamlet or Othello to his name. And then there was the question of bespeaks or benefit nights. Every couple of years or so leading members of the company were allowed a bespeak by Mr Bowles. To their dismay, Tom was allowed one in his first twelve months. Soon their smouldering anger became a naked flame. One evening they marched to Bowles's lodgings, chanting 'A benefit night is ours by right! A benefit night is ours by right!' until the neighbourhood dogs howled in sympathy.

Bowles, who had temporarily abandoned his lofty plinth to play Malvolio, appeared at his bedroom window in yellow stockings villainously cross-gartered.

"My masters, are you mad?" he demanded. "Have you no wit, manners nor honesty but to gabble like tinkers at this time of night?"

This, of course, inflamed tempers still further, none more than Sam Garrow's, who, until Tom's arrival, had been Bowles's second fiddle, playing Iago to his Othello and Buckingham to his Richard. When Bowles was indisposed, he was even allowed – ah! such a privilege – to step into his master's shoes, a change of footwear he hoped to make permanent when Bowles retired. "And pray God make it soon," he would murmur. His wife prayed otherwise, not because she opposed her husband's advancement, but because she knew that the moment he put on Bowles's shoes he would apply them to Tom's posteriors and kick him into the street. And if that were to happen, such were her feelings for the boy, she knew she would have no choice but to follow. Tom's attentions, which in truth were no different from the attentions he showed to other ladies in the company, she mistook for signs of affection, as did her husband, though he was cautious enough to keep his feelings to himself. No, Tom's real affections lay with Blanche Bellamy, who had been following his progress eagerly from above the tobacconist's in Bow Street. She would paste the press cuttings of his provincial tours into a large scrap book, which they would peruse together whenever he was in town. At accounts of this or that performance, she would clap her hands in glee and tell Tom how clever he was. Her father, on the other hand, was less impressed. "What does it all amount to, Tom?" he would ask. "A comic policeman here, a suspicious husband there with not a Shylock or a Brutus in sight. Fame and money are all very well, but what about art? Is there no Edmund Kean in you, no theatrical Vesuvius waiting to erupt? You may have the money to keep my daughter in the comfort to which she aspires, but that is not enough. From a son-in-law I want greatness. Until you have a Hamlet or, at the very least, a Banquo under your belt, you have not my consent to marry her."

Tom had not sought Bellamy's consent to marry Blanche – or Blanche's for that matter – though he had many times been on the brink of doing so.

"Do you hear me, Tom?" demanded Bellamy. "No theatrical peaks, no daughter."

He remembered what Bowles had said to him at their first meeting: Apply yourself, learn from your elders and betters. Well, Tom would do precisely that. For the first time, he began to observe Bowles in the great tragic parts, and it was not long before he had got Othello and Richard, Hamlet and Brutus off by heart. Here, then, were the peaks he must climb and Bowles must help him climb them. But Bowles was far from sympathetic.

"You're no tragedian, Supple," he said. "You've not the gravitas, the grandeur. The cobbler should stick to his last and yours is low farce. Why change? There's money in it for us both."

But Tom persisted, until at last Bowles gave in.

"Very well," he said. "Hecate in Macbeth. But mark, that's my limit."

So Tom played Hecate in a reedy treble which excited a great deal of mirth in the company, all of whom – with the exception of Fanny Garrow – rejoiced to see him overreach himself. Tom did not send Blanche the press cuttings for her scrapbook, but neither did he give up.

Purselove had begun by telling his story as raconteur, but as it gathered pace, he disappeared inside his characters like a hand inside a glove puppet. His movements became more animated; he assumed voices and mannerisms with astonishing virtuosity. If his audience of piemen and chair menders fell under his spell, they put up a spirited resistance first. Whenever Purselove approached, they backed away, fearing that they, too, might be swept up in the drama and be scorched by what they could already feel was going to be a calamitous ending.

TOM: I beg you.

BOWLES: You reduced a noble tragedy to farce. The audience was still sniggering when I made my entrance four lines later. My 'How now you black and secret midnight hags' – a line into which I poured a lifetime's experience – went quite unheard.

TOM: I beg you.

BOWLES: No.

TOM: I shall leave and set up on my own.

BOWLES: You have not the capital.

TOM: I shall find it. I am quite determined.

BOWLES: Very well, Supple. This is my final offer. When we take The Moor of Venice to Drury Lane, you shall be my stand-by. Garrow will not like it. Garrow hopes one day to see me crushed by falling scenery or laid low by an apoplexy, so that he can step into my shoes. I only make this offer, because the stage manager at Drury Lane is a capital fellow who would allow no such accident to occur and because I am in the rudest of health and am less likely to die of an apoplexy than Garrow or, for that matter, you.

Let us leave Tom for the moment, said Purselove, and consider Sam Garrow. Whilst his wife was pining for Tom, he had not stood idly by. One evening he followed Tom to Bow Street, noted the brass plate on the door and next day presented himself to Bellamy as an aspiring tragic actor. Bellamy was sympathetic.

"You could not have chosen better," he told him. "In the theatrical profession, there is no higher calling. Would that I could impress that on the young man who hopes to be my son-in-law, a young man good for nothing but pantomimes and low farce."

Thus it was that Garrow learned of Tom's secret. It was a timely discovery. That very day, Bowles had informed him that Tom was to be his stand-by in their forthcoming production of The Moor of Venice. Garrow was, as usual, to play Iago.

GARROW: The boy
Hath leaped into my seat, the thought whereof
Doth like a poisonous mineral gnaw my inwards
And nothing can nor shall content my soul
Till I am even'd with him wife for wife.

Our scene now shifts to The Theatre Royal, Drury Lane. Tom, you may be sure, has been rehearsing his part as if his life depended on it, which he, of course, insisted it did. Where he had impersonated Hecate in a reedy treble, he now cultivates a basso profundo for Othello. But bass or treble, the gravitas will not come and he knows it. He despairs, but even his despair is of the shallowest kind. 'Oh, that I could put a pistol to my head,' he says, but he knows he will do nothing of the kind. It is in this shallow dejection that he shares a bottle with Arnold Frampton, the Under Stage Manager at Drury Lane.

FRAMPTON: Mr Bowles's best days are behind him, though even in his prime, he was not the equal of the great Kean. You are familiar, I presume, with the career of Edmund Kean?

TOM: I have heard of him.

FRAMPTON: Everyone has heard of him. But to have seen him, to have been, as it were, scorched by him, that was the thing. Never has there been an actor like him, nor will be, I doubt, again. From the wings I witnessed his Shylock on the night that made him famous. I saw his Hamlet, his Othello and was blinded by them. A thunderbolt could not have struck the stage with more devastating effect. From my perch I witnessed his drinking, his tantrums, his greatness and his meanness. I witnessed his rise – and horrors! – his fall. That last performance, how can I – how can anyone – forget? He was playing Othello, his son Iago. Instead of the great outburst 'Be sure thou prov'st my love a whore', he flung his arms round his son and gasped 'Speak the lines for me, Charles, for I am dying.' Such was the end of Edmund Kean. It is eighteen years since he died. Since then no actor has possessed his fire. His son is haunted by his father's shade and holds himself in check, as do Young, Booth and our friend Bowles. Macready comes close, but like the rest of them he is afraid to assume the mantle of Kean.

TOM: The mantle of Kean?

FRAMPTON: After his collapse, he was carried home in the Moor's costume, leaving his clothes in the dressing room. The shirt I kept and offer to actors undertaking the great tragic roles. Who knows, says I, but that some spark, some remnant of Kean's electricity may linger in the fabric.

TOM: And do they embrace your offer?

FRAMPTON: They do not. Though all wish to be the next Kean, they fear that the shirt may burn their flesh.

TOM: Then I shall take the risk. If Bowles falls ill and I take his place, then I shall assume the mantle of Kean. If it attracts the lightning, so much the better. I would sooner a few burns than keep a whole skin by playing in farces and harlequinades.

Well, it goes without saying that Bowles suffered a severe attack of gout, continued Purselove. After all, there would be no story if he had not. Nor would there be any story if Fanny Garrow had not given Tom a peck on the cheek for good luck and if Garrow had not seen it and decided to take his revenge when Tom was least expecting it. Before the show, he took him aside and whispered:

GARROW: Look to your lady, Supple. Word has it that her favours have been more widely shared than you suppose. Of course, it may only be rumour, but you know how it is: none of us can stop the vent of hearing when loud Rumour speaks. Sorry to be the bearer of bad news, old chap. Good luck for the show.

Tom retired to his dressing room, his head swimming. He blacked his face and reddened his lips, feeling nothing and everything at the same time. In a daze he allowed Frampton to slip the mantle of Kean over his head. Immediately he felt as Frankenstein's creature must have felt when the mad doctor applied electrodes to his brain. His limbs convulsed, a searing pain ran down his spine, touched the tips of his toes and rose again through his body, issuing from his mouth in a howl which burned his lips and throat. All his senses were suddenly heightened. Colours no longer clung to the surface of things but seemed to emerge from their very depths. The gas jet burned like a furnace. Sounds in the corridor outside smote his ears in in startling harmonies and dissonances, which were simultaneously sublime and terrifying.

Tom allowed himself to be led by Frampton to the wings where the rest of the cast had assembled. There was a gasp when he appeared. Here was the Tom Supple they knew – but a Tom Supple strangely altered. Here, too, was an Othello such as they and the audience had never seen. Garrow, who as Iago had been used to playing opposite Bowles, seemed afraid of his own machinations and barely summoned the courage to plot his master's downfall. It was in the Third Act, in the very place where calamity had struck Kean, that the lightning descended. A movement in one of the boxes caught Tom's eye. He looked up and saw Blanche and her father watching intently, as if assessing his performance. He stumbled through 'Farewell the plumed troop' and when he howled out the line 'Othello's occupation's gone', she dropped her handkerchief onto the stage and blew him a kiss as a sign that her father had finally consented. And with that Tom pounced on Garrow, seizing him by the throat and bellowing:

Villain, be sure thou prove my love a whore –

Be sure of it; give me the ocular proof;
Or, by the worth of man's eternal soul,
Thou hadst better have been born a dog
Than answer my wak'd wrath.

During his re-enactment of the scene, Purselove's voice assumed a new and terrible intensity, as if he, too, had been invested with the mantle of Kean. By now, his audience was thoroughly alarmed, backing away as he advanced towards them, hands outstretched is if in search of a throat to squeeze. And he might have found one, too, had not a cab driver turned into Ranelagh Road from Lupus Street and, seeing a large crowd obstructing the Queen's highway, decided to disperse it by driving through it at top speed. The crowd parted like the Red Sea and the cab passed safely over, scattering spectators in all directions.

"Now where was I?" resumed Purselove, brushing himself down as if nothing had happened.

"You were about to throttle someone," said Breeze.

And so was Tom, continued Purselove. Members of the audience joined the cast in trying to separate them, but to no avail. Finally, Frampton appeared and pulled the shirt from Tom's back. He fell limply to the floor like an unstrung puppet. By now the house was in uproar. The young swells in the gallery cheered first Tom, then Garrow; the ladies in the boxes resorted to their smelling salts. Tom was escorted to the dressing room by Frampton, who restored him to his senses with a glass of brandy.

FRAMPTON: You nearly killed him.

TOM: Never mind him. Did my performance have gravitas? Did it have grandeur?

FRAMPTON: Did you hear what I said? You nearly killed him.

TOM: Who cares? What matters is whether Bellamy thought my performance up to scratch. I must know. Send for him, Frampton.

Enter Garrow, said Purselove, continuing his narration in the form of a stage direction, his shirt open to reveal the livid marks at his throat.

GARROW: Find someone to act for you, Supple, and when you have, get him to make the necessary arrangements. Swords or pistols, it makes no matter to me.

TOM: Nor to me. I have never held a sword or pistol in my life.

GARROW: Hampstead Heath. First light. Don't be late.

Exit Garrow, continued Purselove, enter Messenger Boy

MESSENGER BOY: The Bellamys have left the building, sir.

FRAMPTON: It seems that your friends have deserted you, Supple.

TOM: Will you act for me, Frampton?

FRAMPTON: It looks as if I'd better, for no-one else will.

If they had hoped to have Hampstead Heath to themselves, Tom and Garrow were disappointed. By the time they arrived, the first swimmers had plunged into the Ponds and servants were snatching hurried trysts before their households were astir. Less expected, however, were the duels, three of which were well under way, none of them, it would seem, attracting more than a cursory glance from passers-by.

"Damn," said Garrow. "This is most inconvenient. We shall have to wait our turn."

"And watch three people get killed first?" asked Tom, astonished at his cold bloodedness.

"Don't be a fool," said Garrow. "These are rehearsals. Over there Hamlet and Laertes, over there Romeo and Tybalt, and yonder, unless I'm much mistaken, are Sir Lucius O' Trigger and Bob Acres from The Rivals. Look at Acres's knees knocking. Always a good sign. True professionals always know what to do with their knees."

Tom's had not stopped knocking since Frampton had called on him before first light. Seeing Garrow, Hamlet and Laertes, both perspiring heavily, followed shortly after by Romeo and Tybalt, put away their foils and walked over to greet the newcomers.

"Come for a practice?" asked Hamlet.

"Mind if we watch?" asked Laertes.

"Are you Laertes or Tybalt today?" Hamlet asked Garrow.

"Laertes," lied Garrow.

"It must be ten years since he last did Tybalt," said Tybalt. "And damn good he was."

"So what's been holding you back?" asked Romeo.

"Bowles," replied Garrow. "Bowles is too old to do Romeo, so it's not in our repertoire, nor is it like to be as long as he's in charge."

"I say," said Hamlet, "would you mind cracking on? We've to be at the Lyceum by nine and I do so want to see the master at work," adding to Laertes, "Best Laertes in the business. Watch and learn."

By now Tom had brought his knees under control. Here was hope at last. With such an attentive audience, he and Garrow would have to pretend that they were just rehearsing and, when it was all over, he, Tom, would assure his adversary that, far from rehearsing, he had fought in earnest and that, as far as he was concerned, was the end of the matter.

"Until we have the place to ourselves," whispered Garrow, "remember that you're Hamlet and I'm Laertes."

Tom, trying to remember Bowles's defensive posture in the role, raised his sword. Garrow lunged immediately.

"One," said Tom.

"No," said Garrow.

"A hit, a very palpable hit," said an appreciative Laertes. "Wouldn't you agree, Hamlet?"

"I've seen him do better," replied Hamlet.

Several minutes of unenthusiastic swordplay followed, during which the two opponents circled each other warily, conscious of the other actors' scrutiny. It quickly became clear that the audience was not impressed.

"Come, Laertes," Hamlet urged Garrow. "You do but dally. I pray you, pass with your best violence."

For Garrow this was cue enough to cast pretence aside. He gathered himself for the fatal lunge, but before he could strike, a voice capable of making itself heard from the back of the stage to the back of the gods, shouted:

"Stop! Stop this instant! Don't think I don't know what's been going on behind my back. You have brought disgrace to yourselves and your profession. Above all, you have brought dishonour to the name of Bradley Bowles."

For Bradley Bowles it was. Pushed by the Bellamys, father and daughter, he had arrived in a bath chair unobserved by the two duellists.

"You forget yourselves," he continued. "This is Hampstead Heath, not the streets of Verona or the court of Elsinore. Supple and Garrow, you are both dismissed. One day, Garrow, the company would have been yours, but after this ..."

With a backward flick of his hand he dismissed Garrow's hopes of future greatness.

"And who," sneered Garrow, "will you use for Iago, Buckingham and all the other second fiddles that accompany your cracked Stradivarius?"

"Hello, what's going on?" said Sir Lucius O'Trigger, who had put away his pistols and joined the company. "Have we missed all the fun?"

"If we have," said Bob Acres, "it's because we put duty first, don't we, Lucy?"

"Duty is your middle name, Bob," said Sir Lucius.

"In that case," said Bradley Bowles, "what would you two gentlemen say to joining Bradley Bowles's Parnassian Players? I need an Iago, a Buckingham and an understudy for the great roles, Bradley Bowles himself, alas, though still in his prime, being increasingly prone to the gout. Now, gentlemen, what do you say?"

On hearing his sentence of banishment, Garrow, who had been fighting back the tears, snatched up his sword and with a bellow of rage lunged at Tom, who was saved, not because he was quick on his feet, though quick he was, but because Blanche Bellamy had been quicker still. Unaware that the sword with which Garrow had struck was not a practice foil, she threw herself in front of Tom and received the full force of the blow on her breast. As she fell to the ground, clutching her hand to her heart, the blood streamed between her fingers.

There was a gasp from the audience. The chestnut seller burst into tears; the lamplighter turned down the gas as a mark of respect; and the chair mender beat his breast with his sheaf of cane. Sobbing, Purselove fell to his knees, as if embracing the lifeless form of Blanche Bellamy. For a long time no one moved, until, finally, Breeze asked:

"And what of Tom?"

"Even in the great dénouement," replied Purselove, "Tom was denied the tragic dignity to which he aspired. Blanche was dead, Garrow hanged, but Tom lingered on, living from hand to mouth, and had it not been for his wife …"

"His wife?" asked Breeze.

"Didn't I mention it? He married Fanny Garrow – or should I say she married him? – as soon as she had finished mourning her husband. And had it not, I say, been for his wife he might have been an incurable drunk. But she saw to it that he had clean linen, a cooked breakfast and became, in due course, Chief Clerk in a respectable counting house."

"Let me guess," said Breeze, "where he lived in fear of being mimicked by the junior clerks."

"Quite so. Right from the start Tom's destiny had more in it of farce than of tragedy."

The crowd began to disperse. One by one the casements were shut and the blinds drawn in the houses opposite. Robbed of attention, Purselove quickly reverted to the maudlin state in which he had begun his tale. He sat down in the middle of the road and began to sob.

"Tell me, Purselove," said Mr Meek, helping the actor to his feet, "were you ever offered the mantle of Kean? Figuratively, I mean – or perhaps even literally, if, of course, it ever existed."

Purselove looked startled.

"How did you know?" he asked. "How did you know?"

"And did you accept?" pursued Meek.

"I refused," replied Purselove. "Think of it: I refused the mantle of Kean. Knowing its reputation I was afraid. And as Tom Supple discovered later, I was right to be. Yet how I envy him! He may have ended as a penpusher, but his memory lives on. In the wings, in the green room people still talk of him. I once played Banquo to Macready's Macbeth, but who remembers that now? Not even Macready. Why, only the other day I passed him in the street and he failed to recognise me. Gentlemen, I was offered my chance of immortality and I refused.

> There is a tide in the affairs of men
> Which, taken at the flood, leads on to fortune;
> Omitted, all the voyage of their life
> Is bound in shallows and in miseries.

I missed my tide, Mr Meek, and have been bound in shallows and in miseries ever since."

Breeze took Purselove's arm and helped him up the steps of Harrison's Hostel.

"Time for bed," he said kindly. "And no histrionics or Mr Harrison will turn us out on the street. He keeps a tidy house."

And indeed he did. No sooner had Purselove and Breeze taken themselves to bed, than one of the janitors appeared in the doorway jangling his keys, indicating that if we wanted to sleep in our beds rather than in the street, then we had better come in directly. I threw my cigar butt into the road and, after a last glance downriver, followed Meek indoors. If Gabriel turned up tonight, he would have to sleep in the doorway, but then, I reflected as I settled myself in my cubicle, it was probably what he was used to anyway.

Extract 2

The St Dunstan Press has just sent me the proofs of my tourist guide to Chaucer's Canterbury. Though too late to do anything about it now, I wonder if I was right to start with the visit of Dean Colet to the shrine of St Thomas in 1512. Perhaps I should have started with those earlier pilgrims who were full of faith and frenzy and who were eager to seize everything that Canterbury had to offer – the souvenirs, the scams, the bespoke ecstasies. Colet detested what he saw. When offered one of the rags with which St Thomas was said to have wiped his face, he threw it from him in disgust. When shown the gilded reliquary containing the saint's head, he told the custodian to sell it and give the money to the poor. And when, on passing St Nicholas's Hospital in Harbledown, he was asked by a bedesman to kiss the Holy Shoe of St Thomas, he remarked to his companion, 'They will be bringing the saint's excrements to kiss next.' Though no Lutheran, Colet was a man ahead of his time. In him you sense that, Henry VIII or no Henry VIII, the days of slobbering over relics were numbered.

Forget the censorious Dean. He had come to sneer and was not disappointed. Imagine instead the Jubilee Year of 1420, when a hundred thousand pilgrims flocked to the city, when every inn was full to bursting and every barn, pen or kennel became a dormitory. Imagine the raucous piety, the clicking of rosaries, the cries of hucksters, the wail of bagpipes, the clatter of cooking pots. Nowhere would have been more crowded, more cacophonous than the Chequer of Hope at the corner of the High Street and Mercery Lane. Visitors had to run the gauntlet of stalls offering pilgrim

badges, flasks of martyr's blood, brooches, bells, baubles, figurines, pen-
dants. It was where, in a fifteenth century continuation of the Canterbury
Tales, Chaucer's pilgrims stayed, where the Pardoner tried to seduce the
barmaid and the barmaid outwitted the Pardoner. And now, imagine entering the Cathedral and approaching the shrine past chantries and chapels
glittering with wax tapers, past carved images covered with gems, past
pools of ruby and sapphire light cast by the stained glass. Imagine being
conducted to the Transept of the Martyrdom, where a wooden altar marks
the place of the murder, then being led to the crypt where you are presented first with the saint's hair shirt and finally – the holiness is almost
too great to bear – his martyred skull. From the crypt you are led up to
the choir where hundreds of relics await you – St George's arm, several
hundred skulls, teeth, hands and assorted bones encased in gold and silver.
After touching, kissing, bowing your way past the reliquaries, you are led
up the steps behind the high altar into the Trinity Chapel until you stand
before the holiest of holies (ah!) – the goal of your journey, the object of
your devotions, the shrine itself (ah!ah!) in which lie the bones of the holy
blissful martyr. Up the steps, worn deep by generations of knees and feet,
you climb, singing 'Tu per Thomae sanguinem'. At the top a priest receives
you, then shows the crown of the saint's head preserved in a golden likeness of his face framed with pearls. At a given sign the painted canopy is
hoisted from the tomb and the shrine itself (rapture!) is at last exposed.
With a white wand the priest guides the eyes of the faithful through the
rubies, diamonds, sapphires and emeralds with which it is embossed. Here
is the gift of Edward I, there the gift of Louis VII of France, yonder that of
Henry V. Exhausted by their ecstasies, the pilgrims gaze as the treasures,
richer, more splendid than anything they could have imagined, disappear
from sight as the painted canopy descends. A fine mesh is thrown over the
shrine. The pilgrims surge forward to pin on it gold and silver models of
afflicted body parts, for St Thomas, as Chaucer reminds us, was a saint that
hem hath holpen whan that they were seke.

    Fast forward now to 1538. Henry VIII issues a proclamation: *Therefore
his Grace strictly chargeth and commandeth that from henceforth the said
Thomas Becket shall not be esteemed, named, reputed, nor called a saint,
but bishop Becket; and that his images and pictures, through the whole*

realm, shall be put down, and removed from all churches, chapels, and other places. In 1538 the shrine was demolished, its riches seized and the bones buried – or, if you believe the Pope, burned. But one fragment of bone escaped burial (or, if you prefer, burning) and made its way Hungary where it has been kept ever since in the Basilica at Esztergom. Recently there has been talk of allowing it home to Canterbury for a visit where it will be welcomed, no doubt, with much pomp and incense. Pilgrims will flock to the city once more and Garlands will, if only for a few brief days, become the new Chequer of Hope.

6

THE GREAT GLASS HIVE

Inside the Glass Hive
Lord Palmerston's Tale (as related by Beamish) of Money to Burn
Gabriel's Tale of The Other Palace

To Nan the Koh-I-Noor proved a cruel disappointment. There were never fewer than two hundred people in the queue and when, finally, she was allowed by the policemen into the enclosure, she could barely see over the heads of those in front. Flanked by two lesser brilliants, the great diamond lay in a gilded cage, where, like a chicken on a spit, it rotated within a ring of gas jets. If these were designed to light hidden fires within, they failed utterly. The stone refused to scintillate. Its depths were murky, its surface dull. Cheated of the long awaited ecstasy, Nan left the tent and took herself to the Crystal Fountain, where she had arranged to meet Miss Osgood. In failing to bring away a memory she could treasure, she found her thoughts returning to Gabriel, despite her determination, for this one day at least, to keep them at bay. Although she had read Serafina's copy of *Oliver Twist*, she refused to believe that Gabriel would fall prey to the first Fagin whose path he crossed. As one who lived in the streets, surely he was too worldly wise for that. But Canterbury streets were not London streets, and his pride in being able to survive in the one might have led him to disregard the dangers of the other.

All this she confided to Miss Osgood, who later confided it to
me in order that I might apprise Serafina when we returned to Canterbury. Miss Osgood herself, meanwhile, had met with no such disappointment in her tour of the Exhibition. Though not generally
given to ecstasy, she was prepared to make an exception in the case
of the Osler Brothers' Crystal Fountain, and in the event found her
faith amply rewarded. Columns of pale pink glass rose, tier upon
tier, from a stone basin to a height of over twenty feet. At the centre
was a hollow shaft, splayed at the top, from which water issued in
broad petal-like jets, before thinning first to a spray and then to a
mist, which glittered, rainbow-hued, in the sun.

*[Editor's Note: So begins Blackwood's chapter on the Great Exhibition – or,
to be more accurate, how I have begun it on his behalf. For the most part,
his account of the visit consists of notes, few of which are longer than a
paragraph and many less than that. His papers include notebooks, tickets,
receipts, letters written after the event, together with pages torn from the
official catalogue and the* Illustrated London News.

*Although he did not plan it, the day on which the Canterbury party
paid their visit – Tuesday 7 October – was the busiest single day of the entire
exhibition when over a hundred thousand people passed through the turnstiles.
Blackwood was shocked by the sheer size of the crowd, complaining of 'an
intolerable press of people' at the South Entrance and of 'the great mêlée' within
the Crystal Palace itself. He notes groups of charity school children, the girls in
white collars and straw bonnets, the boys in blue gowns and yellow stockings; he
notes whole congregations shepherded by their parsons, country folk arriving at
the Prince's Gate in farm carts, Life Guardsmen strutting in their scarlet tunics,
families herded by fathers in top hats – almost certainly new – of every make
and colour. He notes lost children, millhands in clogs, draymen, Billingsgate
porters, clerks released from the counting house, coal heavers, sailors, parlour
maids and potboys. Individuals catch his eye, too: the railway guard with silver
letters on his uniform collar marshalling his party with a railway whistle; the
lady in the crinoline getting stuck in the turnstile; the pickpocket greeting an
old acquaintance with one hand whilst emptying his pocket with the other.*

These, he notes, are shilling people, the ones who flock to the shilling days, the ones for whom this is indeed a world of wonders, where every taste is catered for and every interest satisfied. And they are also, many of them, Bradshaw people – people who have mastered the railway timetables and who will doubtless consult them again to take their families to the seaside or the races or, in due course, follow the Crystal Palace to its new home in Sydenham. There cannot, he writes, be a town or hamlet in the kingdom that has not emptied out its people on to trains and despatched them to London, where they have congregated in queues of half a mile or more in Hyde Park.

How long his party had to queue it is impossible to say, but let us imagine that they have at last passed through the turnstile and entered the palace. A page torn from the Illustrated London News *gives us the sights that met their eyes:]*

Hurried but not impatient, we pass through richly gilded iron gates and the full glories of the transept burst upon our view, heightened and magnified by the narrow dimensions of the external roof and vestibule. A vast hall is before us, lined on either hand with sculptured forms. In the centre rises, like some fantastic stalactite or splinter from an iceberg, a transparent crystal fountain, glittering with all the colours of the rainbow, which, towering from a solid base up to a point, pours down upon an overflowing crystal basin in an unceasing stream with a delicious bubbling sound. Beyond the fountain stands a chair of state – a throne of crimson and gold commands the grand avenues, both east and west. On the left of the throne, at the head of the eastern avenue, the great Indian diamond, the Koh-I-Noor, glitters in a gilded cage or prison. Other statues, another fountain of huge spouting stone tritons, a mass of broad-leaved tropical plants and lofty, smooth-barked palm trees, another pair of gilded gates and over all a mighty elm, spreading its full-leaved branches far and wide and touching the very summit of the lofty roof complete our first impression of the scene. Our eyes travel to the semi-transparent roof with its delicate arches of blue and white

spider-like bracing lines; then they rest upon the pendant tapestry above the galleries, the rich carpets and brocades; and follow the crimson lines of gallery rails, till they weary with the luxuriance of colour, animate and inanimate...

[Editor's Note: To this catalogue of wonders it is worth adding a paragraph scribbled – as are many of the observations in Blackwood's notebooks – in pencil, suggesting perhaps that it was made in situ or later at Harrison's Hostel:]

Signs of autumn apparent not just in Hyde Park, but inside the CP itself, where the giant elms shed their leaves on the boarded floor and are trapped beneath the ladies' skirts, despite efforts of sweepers to remove them as they fall. Having been shut out for most of the summer, Nature determined to find her way back in. The roof, though a marvel of engineering, not wholly successful in keeping out the wind and rain. Panels streaked with algae; in upper galleries buckets and umbrellas, v. discreetly placed, protect exhibits against leaks which do not officially exist. Down in the transepts a few late wasps inspect discarded sandwich wrappers and deep in the barrel of a cannon a sparrow has made her nest.

[Editor's Note: Despite the crowds, Blackwood somehow manages to catch glimpses of many of his party. These appear in his notebooks as follows:]

MEEK gazes in rapture at vase sculpted from mutton fat. So hot is it, a wonder it has not melted long ago. Runs his finger round the frieze to test the sharpness of the carving, then licks it when he thinks no-one looking.

EZARD sits listlessly on rim of Crystal Fountain. Do not try ice cream, he tells me; it tastes like pomatum. He vomits into his hat.

In N. Gallery STUMPS is having his eponymous stumps examined by Major Little, proprietor of Limbs Lost in Action,

Hands a Speciality. Close by the SATURNINE STRANGER discusses different qualities of hemp and jute with a rope-maker from Deptford. From snatches of overheard conversation I gather that in his walk of life, whatever that may be, breaking strains are critical.

In the nave BEAMISH hard on the heels of a hatless gentleman to whom others doff their hats. Evidently someone of consequence. Later I learn from Breeze that it is no other than Lord Palmerston, or, as Purselove with beastly familiarity insists on calling him, 'Pam'.

At the bookbinder's CULPEPPER fondles a finely bound Pilgrim's Progress. I know that strictly speaking, the exhibits are not for sale, he tells the owner, but perhaps in my case you might, ahem, make an exception. O felix culpepper!

TURPIN discussing with a Mr Joseph Burch of Bright & Co, Manchester, the manufacture of printed fabrics using a punched card system. This young man, he tells me, has invented a remarkable system which, in a spirit of scientific co-operation, he is willing to let me adapt for other purposes. And what do you intend to mass manufacture using Mr Burch's punched card system? I ask. Stories, he says, and taps the side of his nose, enjoining me to secrecy.

[Editor's Note: Another notebook contains more fully developed exchanges, in the recording of which I imagine Miss Osgood must have had a hand. In the following, for example, it is hard not to imagine her hovering within earshot, pencil at the ready:]

By rolls of calico Scudamore hails me. Blackwood, he says, let me introduce Miss Tintsford, Lady Rippledale's companion.

No disrespect to Miss T, I reply, but what of Lady Rippledale herself? Surely I should be presented to the lady before the companion.

Lady Rippledale glowers at me from her invalid carriage, then waves her stick at the crowd.

Savages! she shouts.

Ignore her, says Miss T, extending her hand. (Green silk gloves – matching fringes on her shawl – tall woman, statuesque.) She didn't know she was coming to a shilling day.

Then why didn't you bring her to a five shilling day? I ask.

Why didn't you organise your excursion for one? she retorts.

(Lofty manner – more lady-like than her ladyship – fine bones – even her freckles become her.)

The fact is, says S., we thought it would be good for her to see that shilling folk can conduct themselves as well as their betters.

If not better than their betters, adds Miss T.

Filth! says Lady R., prodding a discarded sandwich paper with her stick.

Honoured to make your acquaintance Lady Rippledale, I say, holding out my hand.

Take it away, she shouts.

You're wasting your time, says Miss T. She can't hear you and if she could she wouldn't listen.

Quality folk never do, says S. That's their secret.

And who are you? demands Lady Rippledale.

Percy Blackwood, my lady. Proprietor of the Ebenezer Temperance Hotel in Canterbury.

What did he say? she asks Miss T.

He says he's one of those temperance people.

Temperance people? I wonder they let them in. Jacobins, the whole pack of them. Or do I mean Jacobites? One or the other anyway.

Shall we continue, Lady Rippledale? asks Miss T.

Well, we certainly can't stay here surrounded by these odious people.

Where shall we go to escape them? asks Scudamore.

Suddenly she becomes kittenish, lays a claw on S's arm.

You choose, Henry. Surprise me. Thrill me. Take me where you will, carry me off to your castle on the hill.

(Thinks she's back in Brighton in the Prince Regent's time, confides Miss T. It happens all the time.

Doesn't Henry find it embarrassing?

He's inured to it by now.)

Shall we try the Sèvres, my lady? asks S.

A capital idea. Sèvres is something of a favourite with us, isn't it, Rose?

If you say so, replies Miss T.

That's settled then. The Sèvres it is.

Before they disappear into the crowd, Scudamore turns and says, We've just come from the Sèvres. She's forgotten already.

No she hasn't, remarks Miss T. She just does it to vex me.

[Editor's Note: Other fragmentary glimpses, with or without Miss Osgood's help, follow:]

By the basin of the Crystal Fountain I find Mr Critchley, who is eager to share with me not just the conversations he has had with his egyptological friend, but the sandwiches which the friend's housekeeper has made for him.

My friend, he says, has few interests beyond hieroglyphs and food, whereas I eat very little. You would be doing me a service if you were to share them with me.

Whilst we eat, he tells me that earlier he encountered Malachi Brown examining Colt repeaters in the American Section. What use firearms might be in the collection of ferns he could not imagine. Perhaps, I suggest, he is troubled by vermin. In that case, he replies, why does he not use poison like everybody else? Any reputable apothecary would be happy to oblige. No, there is something troubling about Mr Malachi Brown, something – and I speak in the bookbinding sense – unhinged.

Are you suggesting he may lose his covers? I ask.

Precisely, he says. And then we shall see what we shall see. Of our other acquaintance, I have seen only Dacre and leGrove. You will not

be surprised to learn that they were in the Mediaeval Court, where I
suspect they mean to spend the entire day. I greeted them, but they
ignored me, being deep in conversation with a man I took to be Mr
Pugin. An admirable man this Pugin, no doubt, but as an antiquarian, I deplore the damage done by his followers. Thomas Cromwell
at his most vigorous was not half so destructive. Why, only the other
day I was summoned to a country parsonage near Sandwich to repair
a Venetian incunabulum – Tasso's Gerusalemme Liberate, engravings
by Carracci, very fine – when what should I find but a gargoyle acting
a doorstop and a Norman font as a horse trough? Aha, I thought, Mr
Dacre has been at work. And indeed he had. Oh, the parson couldn't
praise him highly enough. The past is all very well in its way, he said,
but if it does not behave as it should, then it must be tutored rigor-
ously until it does – which is why we need men like Mr Dacre. Sometimes, Mr Blackwood, I come close to despair; I really do.

*[Editor's Note: Perhaps the most remarkable documents concerning
Blackwood's visit to the Great Exhibition – though neither, as it happens,
was written on the day itself – are a handful of letters, the first of which I
shall include here. In the days before the photocopier, many people, Blackwood
and his wife among them, would keep handwritten copies of their letters for
reference. It is from one of these, written by Serafina to her friend Agnes Miller
in Herne Bay, that we first learn of a scandal that had obviously set tongues
wagging in Canterbury:]*

My dear Agnes,

Thank you for your kind enquiries after my health. I should like
to tell you that I have resumed my walks in the Old Palace Gardens
and my attendance at evensong, but, sad to say, I have done neither.
I should like, too, to tell you that confinement to my room has
revived my spirits, but if anything it has depressed them further.
The green wallpaper and fabrics with which Percy thought to calm
my nerves have become oppressive and enervating. Even the presence of Palmerston has become irksome. To be sure, he has all the

gifts one could wish for in a parrot: his memory is retentive – up to thirty words, Percy thinks – and his articulation good. I must confess, however, that favourite lines from Sir Walter Scott lose their savour after repetitions that can last all afternoon.

You ask me if I have heard the news of Miss Lark's elopement. Not only have I heard it, I was amongst the first to know, but, having been enjoined to secrecy, was unable to share it. Percy saw Miss Lark and her inamorato arm in arm in the Crystal Palace, and although he greeted her, she affected not to know him, but walked straight past and was swallowed in the crowd. He confided in Miss Osgood and later, when they returned to Pimlico, she persuaded the warden to unlock Miss Lark's cubicle. It was bare, all her belongings having been removed. On the pillow there was a note which said 'Miss Biddlecombe has done with the proprieties for ever', a reference, apparently, to a tale which she had told the company on the way to London. Back here in Canterbury, the Latimer family kept the secret to themselves, hoping desperately that Aurora might return to Devaux Lodge – provided, of course, that she was respectably married. Others, needless to say, were less forgiving. Once the secret was out, a large number of people confessed to being unsurprised by what had happened, citing the pressed flowers in her prayer book, the amount of lace at her cuffs, the pink ribbons in her bonnet, etc, etc, as evidence of dubious moral character. Who her husband is – assuming him to be her husband – or how she came to meet him are alike unknown, though he is rumoured to be in the engineering line, to which he was introduced by Mr Stephenson the Younger.

The elopement of Miss Lark was not the only little drama to which Percy was witness in the Crystal Palace. Among the visitors that day was no less a personage than the Duke of Wellington. Once word had spread that he was in the building, the crowds gathered to catch a glimpse of the great man and, when he approached, parted to let him pass. At one point in his progress, he was greeted by Corporal Costello. (I am sure you will recall him: he is the Irish bootmaker who never stirs abroad without his medals and who drove his son to join the Buffs – much, I am told, against the boy's inclination.) The Duke was clearly annoyed by the Corporal's effrontery and barked out a perfunctory greeting. He would no doubt have been content to leave it there, had not Costello presented his son, George, who, at Percy's bidding, had brought his bugle along with him in order to lead the Canterbury party though the crowds. Catching sight of the boy's instrument, His Grace, who, as you know, is given to forthright language when provoked, demanded to know what the d — the boy was doing with a valuable item of military equipment and whether he knew he had committed a serious breach of military discipline. Angry voices were raised against the Costellos, but, fortunately for George, the policemen thought they were directed against the Duke himself and hurried him from the building. As you may imagine, the boy was mortified, as indeed was Percy, who was the unwitting cause of his discomfiture. The Corporal, on the other hand, was quite unabashed, and, since his return to Canterbury, has been favouring his customers with accounts of how he and the Duke had shared their memories of old unhappy far off things and battles long ago. George, in the meantime, lives in fear of a summons from the Regimental Quartermaster.

[Editor's Note: Serafina's letter goes on to tell of Percy's encounter with Miss Tintsford and Lady Rippledale, but since her account adds nothing to that of her husband, I shall omit it. Later in the afternoon, no doubt with Miss Osgood acting as amanuensis, he visited the Mediaeval Court, where he found Dacre and leGrove deep in conversation with Augustus Pugin.]

LeGROVE: Ah, Blackwood, there you are. Let me introduce you to Mr Pugin, whose clock tower we all admired from the steamer.
DACRE: And to whose completion we all look forward.
PUGIN: I am delighted to make your acquaintance, Mr Blackwood.
DACRE: Mr Pugin, it seems, has received visits from two of your Canterbury pilgrims.

LeGROVE: From the Rev Culpepper, who strongly disapproved of what he considered to be the overwhelmingly Catholic tone of the Mediaeval Court...

DACRE: The rood screen he singled out for particular opprobrium.

LeGROVE: ... and from Mr Turpin. He of the Travelling Topper.

PUGIN: You would be astonished by how many madcap schemes are shown me for my approval. Most of my female visitors seem to have been writing novels which feature ruined abbeys and have looked to me to supply the architectural details. Worse, one visitor even asked me to design a ruined abbey as a present for his wife.

DACRE: I find that rather charming.

PUGIN: Then there was the Catholic gentleman who wanted an Elizabethan house complete with a priest hole and, if possible, two.

LeGROVE: Did he ask for a ghost as well?

PUGIN: He most certainly did.

LeGROVE: That does not surprise me. It has happened to me on a number of occasions. Rich industrialists are very keen on them, I find. They assume that when I remove manifestations, I must in some way save them, imagining, perhaps, that I have a cupboard of bottled specimens which have been temporarily withdrawn from service. Is it possible, they want to know, to de-exorcise them? Nothing too disturbing, of course, or too destructive. What they want is something melancholy, well-behaved and, if possible, festive. No, what you say does not surprise me, Mr Pugin. We live in an age of make-believe where nothing is valued unless it is dressed up to look like something else.

[Editor's Note: If there was more to this encounter, it has either been lost or was not notated by Miss Osgood. Before they parted, she initiated a curious conversation, which Blackwood thought important enough to record in his own hand – probably later in the day or perhaps even when they got back to Canterbury:]

Has it occurred to you, Mr Blackwood, says Miss O., that most explanations are really stories in disguise?

Miss O. and I had just left the Mediaeval Court and were making our way to the see the exhibits of the German Zollverein. My thoughts being full of Dr leGrove's bottled poltergeists, I did not respond, but she persisted.

I have noticed that when asked about their inventions, exhibitors invariably tell a story – about how they encountered such and such a problem, how the solution came to them in a dream or at a garden party, about how they slew the giants of envy and despair, wooed a rich patron and were admitted in triumph to the Crystal Palace.

Why, you make it sound like The Pilgrim's Progress, I said.

Deliberately so. I exaggerate, of course, but the comparison stands. And here is another. My father was a beekeeper and was convinced that the dances which the bees performed in the hive were really a form of storytelling.

Surely not. What would they tell each other stories about?

Who can say, though I am sure that their adventures among the flowers are full of dangerous rivalry and quests for buried treasure.

You seem to be suggesting that there is no essential difference between the tales of the bees and those of Dr leGrove or Stumps or Costello.

Perhaps I am. I do not know who nick-named this place the Glass Hive, but the name was well chosen. Listen to the voices around you. In one form or another they are nearly all telling stories. It seems we cannot help ourselves.

[Editor's Note: We next meet Blackwood taking tea with Mr Scudamore in the North West Gallery. The account is in his own hand, suggesting that by this time Miss Osgood had wandered off independently.]

Have they let you off the leash? I ask Scudamore.

If only her ladyship were so accommodating, he sighs. No, she is visiting the ladies' Halting Station. I fear she may be gone for some time.

Was the visit to the Sèvres a success?

Not as big a success as the visit to the Halting Station. We have divided the day between the two. Her ladyship is charmed by porcelain of both varieties and intends to invest in both when she returns home.

[Editor's Note: A last glimpse, this time a more protracted one. Though I have placed it late in the day, there is no reason to suppose that it belongs there rather than at an earlier time. In the American section, Blackwood observes Bartholomew and Purselove, The one, it is clear, has come to admire, the other to find fault.]

After my remarks about the tyranny of time, you will no doubt think me out of sympathy with the present age, says Bartholomew. And in many ways I am. All the same it is hard not to admire the Americans for their sheer ingenuity. Look at their sewing machines, their stone cutters, their typewriters, their mechanised harvesters – all designed to take the drudgery out of everyday life.

Not to mention Col. Colt's revolvers which have no doubt been designed to take the drudgery out of killing, replies Purselove.

Tell me, Mr Purselove, did you ever play Malvolio?

Alas no, why do you ask?

Because the part would have suited you. What is it Olivia says to him? That he is sick of self-love and tastes with a distempered appetite? Something of the sort. I am not sure about the self-love but you are certainly guilty of the distempered appetite. Shake off this shallow cynicism. Look around you. Do you find nothing to admire?

Why yes, the vacuum coffin that keeps its occupant fresh until the relatives arrive for the funeral. A capital idea, absolutely first class.

America is a continent. No doubt the device answers to a long felt need.

If America is a continent, then why does it exhibit so little? Oh, its devices are ingenious, I grant you, but why are there so few of them? Why is there so much empty floor space? Manchester alone has twice as much to offer.

Unnoticed by Purselove, an American exhibitor who was presiding over a brick-making machine, had been taking a close interest in his remarks and, in so doing, had become so red of face that he looked as if he were about to burst.

You may scoff at what we have chosen to exhibit, he declared, but men of good will and understanding will rather marvel at what we have chosen not to exhibit. I refer, sir, to those virtues that make the United States superior to the rest of the world. I refer, sir, to universal suffrage, to our schools and churches, to our sense of godliness and enterprise, to our love of freedom. These are the things of which we are justly proud – more so indeed than any of the trumpery on display here in this vast cucumber frame – for these are the things that distinguish us from the rest of the world. And if we must make a choice, we would ten thousand times rather stand fast in education, happiness and morality than in manufactures and so-called fine arts.

By now a small crowd had gathered. When the American had finished his peroration, Purselove clapped loudly, declaring it to be a fine speech – as fine, indeed, as any he had heard outside the theatre – and wondered why the speaker had omitted to mention other fine old American institutions such as slavery and cattle stealing.

Purselove's remarks served to increase the American's boiler pressure still further. With a roar of fury he seized a revolver from Colonel Colt's stand and levelled it at Purselove's head. The crowd gasped and shrank back. At that moment Ezard appeared from nowhere, his hands trembling, his eyes feverishly bright and, with astonishing coolness, turned the barrel of the gun aside and gently detached it from the American's grasp.

Do not hurt him, he said. He is a good man and means no harm. His worst vice is addiction to irony, which he thinks funny and supposes – wrongly – that everyone else will, too.

D — your irony, retorted the American All I ever hear is irony. Everywhere I go I'm told you mustn't mind him, he's being ironic. Why can't you guys just say what you mean and speak out like real men?

One day, sighed Ezard, we may grow out of it, but not, I fear, in my lifetime.

Then it could be sooner than we think, said the American unironically.

[Editor's Note: A last entry. In Blackwood's papers is another page torn from the Illustrated London News. Four days after the Canterburians' visit, the Great Exhibition closed its doors. The great elms were shedding their leaves, the nights were drawing in, and, since there was no artificial light in the Crystal Palace, opening hours would have had to have become shorter and shorter. Winter journeys on unheated and unlit trains, even for passengers wearing the Turpin Topper, would have become less attractive as the weeks passed. No, the Great Exhibition, as Prince Albert had foreseen, was a summer phenomenon and now the summer was all but over. It was time to bring down the curtain.]

This day closes the Great Exhibition of 1851, ran the article. This marvellous Palace of Crystal with its varied and splendid repertory of skill and ingenuity, of art and science, which for the last six months it had exposed to the view of millions of admiring spectators is to be shut henceforth against all except those interested in the dispersion of its treasures. In the course of a few days the work of dismantling will begin. A new bustle and excitement will succeed to the roar of the applauding people who rushed in such astonishing numbers to its fairy avenues. The pleasure seekers will disappear – the equipages of the wealthy will no more block up the approaches – the humbler vehicles of the people will cease to deposit their living cargoes at its doors – waggons and carts will supersede them – and the hoisting of heavy goods, the creaking of cranes and pulleys and the rumble of heavy wheels will for many weeks to come render Hyde Park and its purlieus a scene of even greater animation than it has been since the memorable 1st of May.

Thus fades and perishes, grows dim and dies
All that the world is proud of.

[Editor's Note: To which Blackwood has added in pencil 'The cloud-capp'd towers, the gorgeous palaces, the great globe itself shall dissolve and leave not a rack behind.' But he was wrong. The Crystal Palace did not dissolve, but within a short space of time was re-incarnated in Sydenham and, though it burned down in 1936, its ghost lingers still in the name of a football team.]

[Editor's Note: The following letter must have been written after Blackwood had returned to Canterbury. I include it here because it records a conversation (as reported by Beamish) that Blackwood witnessed – but did not himself overhear – between Lord Palmerston and the Poet Laureate, Lord Tennyson. At least, that is what Blackwood has convinced himself that he witnessed. Palmerston we may be fairly sure of, but in my view Blackwood is too eager to identify his companion as Tennyson. Of course, one can see why he might wish to do so. The letter is essentially a sales pitch, in which he tries to interest a publisher – another Blackwood, by the way – in a tale that many readers would find offensive. To claim the Poet Laureate as its original audience, not to mention Lord Palmerston as its author, would perhaps go some way to making it more palatable.]

Lord Palmerston's
Tale of Money to Burn

My dear Blackwood,

    Though I doubt the enclosed story will shock you, it will, I think, surprise you. I make no apologies for it. If it is salacious, it is only mildly so and will not offend those who do not make a profession of being offended. Since few such subscribe to Blackwood's, it must be published – if it be published at all – elsewhere. And that is where I should welcome your advice. Should you know of anyone who might be interested, please bait your hook with the subject matter without revealing the twists and turns of the plot. You might also mention that the story is likely to be true and that its author is Lord Palmerston, no less. Now that startled you, did it not? You did not know that I numbered the Foreign Secretary among my acquaintance. Would that I did, my dear Blackwood, would that I did! I came across the tale by chance and should you be able to interest any of your friends in publishing it, it might be wise to conceal its true authorship.

By now I hope I have sufficiently whetted your appetite to learn how I came by it. Know then that an acquaintance of mine, a phrenologist by profession, recognised the Foreign Secretary during a recent visit to the Crystal Palace. Now my friend – let us call him HB – was less interested in the exhibits than in the cranial peculiarities of the visitors. As you will know, his lordship is a recognisable figure and most visitors doffed their hats as he passed, prompting him to doff his in return, with the result that it was more often off than on. HB could scarcely believe his luck. Here was the perfect opportunity to study the mental proclivities of the Great Pam himself. He therefore followed close and, in so doing, overheard the tale that Pam, in between hat doffings, told his companion. (HB did not pay much attention to the companion, since he kept his hat undoffed, but suspects that it might have been the Poet Laureate, Lord Tennyson. In my re-telling I have taken the liberty of referring to him as Tennyson throughout.) Now although I have said that I believe Pam's tale to be true, I should add a caveat: this tale was told to me by HB, who heard it – or rather overheard it – from Pam, who had himself learned it, as you will hear, from the British Consul in Venice. This tale, which is already three tellers deep, I now pass on to you.

Pam began, as all story tellers should, with a picture. Imagine, he told his companion, a January day in the Piazza San Marco. It is snowing and San Giorgio di Maggiore is scarcely visible across the water. A crowd of Italians, shielded from the cold by thick cloaks, has gathered round an enormous cauldron in the square, from the four corners of which, snow-covered cannon point inwards. Through the swirling flakes steam launches flying the Austrian flag appear. All lie low in the water, weighed down by huge bales wrapped in sailcloth. At the quayside the bundles are loaded first on to hand carts and then thrown into the cauldron, where a fire is already burning. Flames leap skyward as bale follows bale. The Italians are not allowed to approach the bonfire or the carts, yet the show, for that is clearly what it is, is being staged for their benefit.

"Forgive my interrupting," says Pam's companion, "but you have not yet told me what it was that they were burning."

"Money," replies Pam.

"Money?" echoes the other.

"Or, to be more precise, *moneta patriottica.*"

"Patriotic money?"

"The very same. Until the upheavals of 1848, the Italians were obliged to use the zwanziger; then, when they threw off the Austrian yoke – alas, all too briefly – they printed their own money, *moneta patriottica*, the burning of which was to signal the totality of their defeat. Having crushed their armies and hanged their leaders, their masters insisted on humiliating them still further by burning their money – every note of it – millions of lire – till not one single, solitary scrap of paper was left."

"And did they succeed?"

"No. They thought they had. After the fire had burned itself out, the Austrians tipped the ashes into the Lagoon and threw the cauldron after them. And that, as far as they were concerned, was the end of the matter. Life slowly returned to normal. Cholera fled to the outlying districts; the zwanziger reappeared in the shops; La Fenice performed Rossini; and the palazzi on the Grand Canal – or such as had been left unscathed by the Austrian shelling – opened to a brilliant company. There Austrian officers, Hungarian countesses, Polish uhlans and Russian archdukes flocked to balls and soirées where it was considered bad taste to mention the events of 1848.

Everything was the same, yet nothing was the same. Deep in the harmonies there was an untuned string. It was a Hungarian countess – the Deputy Governor's wife no less – who first noticed it when she spied an emerald brooch hidden beneath her parlour maid's apron. Italian, of course, the girl – all the servants were – and as such had no business wearing or owning such a thing.

"So how did she come by it?" asked Tennyson – let us assume that it was he – "Did she steal it?"

"That's everyone thought. But the girl denied it. It was all Ercole's doing. Ercole had given it to her. She had refused, absolutely refused, but Ercole had insisted."

"Ercole?"

"Betrothed, inamorato, seducer. Accounts vary. What was clear that having laid hold of one treasure – Lord knows where – he thought he'd use it to lay hold of another, namely hers."

"I'm not sure I follow you, my lord."

"Don't be such a humbug, Tennyson: you know damn well what I mean. And so did Ercole when they put it to him. Rifling the girl's treasure he confessed to – boasted about even – but the brooch was different. You should have heard him protest his innocence. The brooch was honestly come by, paid for by the sweat of his brow. Oh, how he had worked, how he had slaved!"

"It must have cost him a fortune. Was he rich?"

"Rich? He varnished gondolas for a living. As for costing the earth, do you know how much he paid for it? A lira."

"Don't you mean a zwanziger?"

"No, I mean a lira."

"Just one?"

"Just one."

"Tell me, my lord, how do you know all this?"

"I'm only telling you what our man in Venice tells me. Now our man's despatches are damned dull, so from time to time I have to ask him to ginger them up a bit. It can't be that hard, I tell him, in a place teeming with whores; there must some juicy morsels you can feed me. And he did. This was one of them, stuck in the middle of a dreary piece about troop deployments. Anyway, all that is by and by. What matters is the lira note with which Ercole paid for the brooch."

"*Moneta patriottica?*"

"The sole survivor of. This note now started appearing everywhere. Hardly a day went by without a report reaching the Governor, and with every sighting it seemed to have doubled in value. To begin with, its purchasing power was modest – a cure for gout, a lace bridal veil, a pair of duelling pistols. Slowly it increased – a sacred relic or two, a quattrocento altarpiece – until finally a Carpaccio and a Titian were rumoured to have changed hands, even, would you believe, a palazzo on the Grand Canal. And as the circulation of the note increased, so, too, did the sighting of the Italian tricolour. Only glimpses, mind. Little flutters of red, white and green on balconies and roof tops, no sooner seen than spirited away. Hardly

an insurrection, but enough to show that the flame of '48 had not quite been
snuffed out.

Word of this reached the Minister in Vienna, who ordered General
Gorzkowski, the Governor of Venice, to seize the offending note with all haste.
Marshal Radetzky, the conqueror of Italy, was due in Venice in time for the
Carnival ball and must at all costs be spared embarrassment. "Revolution,"
wrote the Minister, "I do not fear – that is over and done with for now – but
embarrassment I do. Whatever happens, we must not be made to look ridiculous,
especially as the Marshal's guests are said to include a Russian archduke or two.
See to it that nothing grotesque occurs." Gorzkowski, who read the Minister's
letter during a game of billiards, thought the danger absurdly exaggerated and
summoned his Chief of Police, one Ignaz Peitsch.

"I'm handing the case to you, Peitsch," he said. "It's a heavy responsibility.
Don't bungle it. Now if you'll excuse me I have to dress for the opera. I'm sharing
my box with a French Vicomte and a German Herzog. You will appreciate that I
need to look my best, especially for their wives – did I mention the wives? – who,
just between ourselves, are a pain in the arse. Well, good luck. I'm sure you will
manage splendidly."

Unappealing in appearance and manner, this Peitsch was a conscientious
dullard, who would do unquestioningly whatever he was told to do. First, he
sent for Ercole, only to find that Ercole had disappeared. Next he sent for the
maidservant, only to find that she, too, had fled, taking Ercole's bastard with her.
New owners of old masters, not to mention duelling pistols and bridal veils, were
questioned, but to no effect. No, came the invariable answer, the Titian had always
been in the family, the duelling pistols were an heirloom and the cure for gout –
oh, such a relief! – had been paid for in good, honest zwanzigers.

Gorzkowski grew impatient – but only because the Minister in Vienna had
grown impatient – and ordered Peitsch to redouble his efforts. Radetzky's visit was
imminent. The matter must be cleared up before his arrival. Was that clear? Dammit,
the note couldn't be that hard to find when every Italian in the place seemed know
where it was. As if to confirm the urgency of the matter, gondolas loaded with old
masters and classical statues were seen making their way along the Grand Canal.
Nothing seemed safe – not the stones underfoot, not the bells from the Campanile,
not even, according to some accounts, the horses of St Mark. But of all the rumours,

the most alarming was that of the Exploding Gondola. Like all good rumours it seemed to have no source. Everyone who passed it on had heard it from someone different. Depending on which version you believed, the one lira note had fallen into the hands of violent republicans who had purchased a gondola, or gondolas – take your pick – and filled it (or them) with gunpowder which they meant to explode during Radetzky's visit. The note was no longer a thorn in the side of the authorities, but a dagger aimed at the heart of Austrian rule.

Peitsch had convinced himself that the blow would fall at the Palazzo degli Emilii, where Radetzky was to host a Carnival Ball. Paid informants confirmed his suspicions as to the target and told him to look out for the gondola with the five-toothed comb at the prow. On the night of the ball, the streets were full of masked revellers, many in Commedia costumes. Here were Arlechinos and Columbinas, Balanzones and Pantalones; here were pimps and pickpockets, tumblers and whores all plying their trades. Boats festooned with lanterns jostled for space on the canals, so that it was impossible to tell a gondola from a batella, let alone a five- from a six-toothed comb. With such a press of bodies around him, Peitsch found himself unable to steady his pocket telescope for long enough to identify individual vessels. Suddenly, he caught a flash of red, white and green on the far side of the flotilla. Yes, there it was. A black gondola, low in the water, making its way past the gilded fireflies that swarmed round the palaces on the Grand Canal. Peitsch jumped into a police galley and, breaking out the Austrian flag at the stern, ordered the crew to give chase. And what a chase! Aware that he was being followed, the gondolier darted in and out of the narrow channels which opened off the Grand Canal and where the cholera had lingered longest. So nimble did his quarry prove that Peitsch would have lost him had not one of his men on the Ponte degli Scalzi leapt over the parapet and landed in the vessel. As soon as the galley drew level, Peitsch jumped aboard and exposed the cargo. As he had expected, it consisted of barrels lashed together with rope. Having first ordered his men to dowse their torches, he opened the first and gingerly pushed his finger inside. Sure enough, it was full of powder, though it did not, he was disappointed to find, smell like gun powder. A second barrel and a third yielded the same result. One by one he opened them all, only to find the same contents in each.

"Well?" demanded Peitsch, scooping up a handful of powder from one of the barrels, "What is this?"

"Flour, signior," announced the gondolier. "I deliver to the city's bakeries."

The crowd on the bridge applauded tumultuously. This was better than Carnival, better even than the opera. The laughter, it was said, could be heard as far away as the Palazzo degli Emilii, where Radezky was entertaining his guests amid baroque splendours of white and gold.

It was some weeks before Peitsch dared show his face in public. Fortunately, Vienna seemed to have heard nothing of the affair, the Radetzky ball having passed without embarrassment. But it was only a temporary reprieve. They were bound to learn the truth sooner or later and, as it turned out, it was from Peitsch himself that they learned it. One day he received a letter informing him that the lira note was to be sent to Vienna under military escort. In his reply Peitsch had to confess all. True, he had failed to secure the note, but his vigilance had protected Radetzky and his guests – here he thought to drop in the name of a Russian grand duke or two – from republican outrage and that, surely, was what really mattered.

Vienna disagreed. If Peitsch could not do the job, then he must make way for someone who could. In two months' time the Emperor Franz Josef proposed to visit Venice. When he did so, the note must be in Austrian hands. Did Peitsch think he was up to the task? Peitsch assured them that he was: His Majesty, he promised, need have no fear. But no sooner had he made the promise than the horror of his position struck him. What had he done? Why had he made promises he could not keep? A religious man who began each day on his knees, he decided that the answer lay in prayer. He would work his way through the city's churches in alphabetical order, hoping that among the Andreas, Bartolomeos and Caterinas he might find at least one saint willing lend a sympathetic ear. One day, whilst he was praying in San Sebastiano's, he was tapped on the shoulder by a man in the pew behind him.

"You look troubled," said a voice. "Perhaps you will allow me to help you."

Peitsch turned round. A small man with a cherubic face and pebble-thick spectacles stared back at him unblinkingly.

"You are impertinent," said Peitsch. "How could you possibly know what troubles me?"

"You are looking, are you not," persisted the stranger, "for something which constantly eludes your grasp, something worth almost nothing and at the same time worth nearly everything."

"If you are referring to the *moneta patriottica*," replied Peitsch, "then it is your duty to refer anything you know to the authorities."

"And if I do not?"

"I could have you arrested."

"Then you would never find it. At present I am indeed the owner of the note, but its whereabouts is known to others. If you arrest me, it will disappear before you can lay hands on it. Even now we – or rather you – are being watched."

Peitsch glanced round the church. Though he could see no-one, he decided to take the threat seriously.

"What do you want for it?" he asked. "I have no old masters, no statues, no palazzi to offer."

"It might be more accurate to ask whom do I want."

"Did you have someone particular in mind?" replied Peitsch, thinking perhaps that he was angling for the release of political prisoners.

"Yes, Herr Peitsch," replied the little man. "You."

Peitsch, who knew his Goethe, feared that he was being offered some kind of Faustian bargain.

"My soul," he said, "is not for sale."

"I would not dream of taking your soul. That would be blasphemous and vulgar. No, no, I will settle happily for your hand."

"My hand?"

"In marriage."

"To whom?"

"My daughter Venetia."

Under normal circumstances, Peitsch would have had the man arrested and taken to police barracks for questioning. But he hesitated. Not only might it be ineffective, worse, it might be sinful. Consider: he had prayed through the alphabet from Agnese to Sebastiano for help in finding the note and now the prayer had been answered. This, surely, could be no coincidence.

"There are, of course, conditions attached," continued the stranger.

"How could there not be?" asked Peitsch, uncertain whether to be angry or grateful.

Of course the conditions were impossible and Peitsch laughed aloud when he heard them. He was to marry Venetia, without first having met her, in that very church, and only when the ring was safely on the girl's finger, would the note be handed to one of his men in full sight of the congregation.

"Congregation?"

"A manner of speaking only. In front of witnesses, yours and mine. Half a dozen at most. Well, Herr Peitsch, what do you think of my proposal? No, do not answer now. You are about to tell me that you cannot make bargains with enemies of the state, that it is my duty to hand over the note to the authorities. That, of course, would be Peitsch the policeman speaking. When you have had time to reflect, Peitsch the man may think differently. I shall return here to San Sebastiano's a week from today to hear your reply. Good day, Herr Peitsch."

With that he rose from the pew and, nodding to the sacristan who had just appeared from the vestry, slipped out of the church.

"Who was that?" Peitsch asked the sacristan. The sacristan was not sure. He would have to ask the priest. The priest, when he eventually found him, wasn't sure either but thought it might be Signor Ventolini. Or was it Venturini? Something like that anyway. Or perhaps he had the wrong man. He really couldn't be sure.

It was clear to Peitsch that if he wanted to talk to the stranger again, he would have to keep the appointment the following week. In fact, he surprised himself by wanting to do so anyway. At first he simply wished to recover the note, but as the week wore on he found himself thinking about Venetia. Perhaps she, too, was an answer to his prayers, for he had despatched enough of them asking for a wife and had given up hope of ever finding one. What was more, she came as part of a bargain and would not therefore need wooing. Of his shortcomings of appearance and manner Peitsch was all too well aware, so the proposed arrangement would suit him well. If only he could meet her – or, better still, observe her from afar. But that was impossible, for if he could not trace the father, he had no means of finding the daughter.

On the evening before his interview with Ventolini, he had an astonishing stroke of luck. He was investigating a suspected nest of republicans in one of the fever districts, which was bordered by a stagnant canal and where decayed gondolas lay keel uppermost in the mud. At the end of a cinder path lay a group of low and filthy houses and in one of them, through a gap in the shutters, Peitsch glimpsed a couple having dinner. Within the circle of lamplight he could see their faces quite clearly. One was Ventolini, the other a young woman in her early twenties. Her black hair, which rested on her bare shoulders, was dressed in ringlets in the English fashion; her complexion was olive, her hands long and elegant. If, despite the squalor of her surroundings, Venetia was every inch the lady, Ventolini was scarcely every inch the gentleman. He was dressed in a threadbare tail coat, napkin tucked under his chin, elbows resting on the table. From what Peitsch could see, he was angry with the girl who was serving at table, pointing to the stains on her apron and the dirt under her fingernails. Venetia, he seemed to be saying, would be ashamed to appear in public in such a disgraceful state. Peitsch stood by the window transfixed. When he had gazed his fill, he retreated into the shadows and walked away. Even before he had reached the end of the path, he knew he was in love, that he would meet Ventolini on the morrow and agree to his every demand. For form's sake, however, he must feign a little reluctance. After all, there was still the matter of the lira note. If he agreed too enthusiastically to the marriage, the note might be withdrawn from the settlement. Mindful of his duty, Peitsch resolved to be firm.

"Tell me," he asked Ventolini the next day, "why do you want me to marry your daughter? I am flattered, of course, to be thought as valuable as a Titian or the Horses of St Mark, but even I must ask myself whether I am worth so much."

"I wish my daughter – she wishes it herself – to make a respectable marriage and who is more respectable than the Chief of Police? A count or a general would be too ambitious, but a policeman – even an Austrian who has the ear of the Governor – ought to be well within our reach. Not that the advantage will be all hers. She will make you a good wife, one whom you will be proud to be seen with in public."

"When may I see her?" asked Peitsch.

"Not until the wedding," replied Ventolini. "She insists on it."

"But ..."

"There is no point in objecting. She will not change her mind."

"So she is stubborn," said Peitsch, remembering not to appear too eager.

"Only in matters of personal vanity. She fears you will not find her desirable and might withdraw your consent. That is why she insists on another condition: that she will not lift her wedding veil until the ceremony is over. Only when you are invited to kiss the bride will you see her face. I assure you, Herr Peitsch, you will not be disappointed."

"And the note?"

"As soon as the ring is on her finger you will have your note. Now, all that remains is to agree a date."

"I can see that this is going to end badly," said Tennyson. "Surely he should have smelt a rat."

"Why should he? He desperately wanted the girl and he desperately wanted the note. By this stage he'd lost his sense of smell."

"So he failed to secure either?"

"Quite the contrary: he secured both."

"Then there was, so to speak, no rat to smell?"

"Oh, there was, but not until later. The wedding went entirely according to plan. When the bride lifted her veil, he didn't find he'd been tricked into marrying the scullery maid or the servant who had waited at table. True, she looked a little older and more heavily made up than he had expected, but still exquisitely desirable. And when the ring was slipped on her finger, the note was handed to his lieutenant as agreed. No, Ventolini kept his part of the bargain to the letter."

"Then the disaster occurred on the honeymoon. Let me guess: either she was unresponsive or he inattentive."

"Not at all. The honeymoon exceeded his wildest expectations and, if you will excuse me, I shall refrain from specifying what those were. When, a fortnight later, he returned to his duties in Venice, his subordinates remarked that he looked sleek and self-satisfied, if not downright smug."

"Nemesis is hovering somewhere near. I can feel it."

"Nemesis struck at the opera. Peitsch and Venetia had spent their honeymoon at Bad Ischl in Upper Austria. Apart from a handful of witnesses at the wedding, no-one in Venice had seen them together in public. Peitsch decided, therefore, that Venetia must be launched on to the public stage as soon as possible. Rejecting several invitations to soirées as being too small for what he had in mind, he chose instead the first night of Semiramide at La Fenice. As a reward for his seizure of the lira note, which he was to hand to the Emperor personally the following week, he was allowed, as a mark of special favour, to use the royal box. Delaying their entrance until the house was full, Peitsch and Frau Peitsch took their seats, conscious that the eyes of the whole house were upon them. Conversation stopped; heads turned. In the box opposite, Gorzkowski, flanked by two Russian archdukes, turned his opera glasses on them. In other boxes, graf and gräfin, herzog and herzogin followed suit. There was a gasp. Then someone laughed. Like a forest fire, the laughter spread, first among the undergrowth in the rear stalls, then among the brushwood of the upper gallery, until finally it took hold among the mighty limbs and trunks of the fashionable boxes. La Fenice was ablaze. Roars of laughter swept the audience and when, at last, it abated, someone stood up in the stalls and, pointing to Venetia, shouted 'Whore!' As if in a dream, Peitsch watched his wife rise to her feet and, in a voice coarsened by a thousand street brawls, shout back, "A whore, yes, and the best you've ever had. And you!" – she pointed to the box opposite – "And you!" – a graf shuddered – "And you!" – all the colour drained from a herzog's face – "and you and you!" By now the laughter had given way to an angry tumult in the body of the theatre. But Frau Peitsch's voice would not be quieted. From beneath her skirts, she drew a red, white and green tricolour. "Viva Venezia!" she shouted. "Viva Venezia! e viva la Serenissima!"

"Quite a bargain, don't you think?" asked Lord Palmerston. "Such a comprehensive humiliation of the oppressor and all for a lira. Of course, it was all hushed up. No word of it appeared in the newspapers and it was generally understood at balls and soirées that it was never to be mentioned. But something on that scale simply cannot be contained. It will leak out in whispers and rumours for years to come. What made it worse was the Venetia wasn't even Ventolini's daughter – who, by the way, he enjoyed humiliating by making her serve at table – but his mistress."

"What happened to poor Ignaz Peitsch?"

"He was found floating face down in the Lagoon several days later."

"Murder?"

"Suicide. Poison apparently. And do you know what the apothecary charged him for it?"

"A lira?"

"Or to be more precise the lira."

"And was that the last of it?"

"There have been no recent sightings, but our man believes that the note was sent out of Venice and entrusted to Italian patriots abroad. Mazzini perhaps, or Garibaldi, who knows?"

"And what happened to Venetia? She returned to the streets, I imagine."

"Despite the Fenice affair, the visit of His Imperial and Royal Apostolic Majesty proceeded as if nothing had happened. There was to be no suggestion that anything was amiss. Everything must appear as normal. "

"And did it?"

"Not entirely. There was alarm one afternoon when the Emperor gave his bodyguard the slip and headed out of the Grand Canal in a gondola with a woman who looked remarkably like Venetia. Once word got out, a dozen police boats set off in pursuit led by a steam launch containing his entire bodyguard."

"And then?"

"Our man isn't sure. When the gondola returned – hemmed in tightly by police boats – the Emperor was on his own. He was heard to say that he had taken a gondola because he wished to have a few precious minutes to himself. In the middle of a busy schedule one must always seize such moments and cherish them. And now, he concluded, he would proceed with the rest of his engagements as planned."

"So everything was the same, yet nothing was the same."

"It would appear so," said Lord Palmerston. "That is what our man thinks and so do I."

Well, there you have it: an eminent author, an eminent audience and a tale likely to offend the parson as much as it disappoints the connoisseur. (I refer, of course, to the sort of connoisseur who frequents the premises of Mr Smith in Holywell Street.) What is to be done? In my present straitened circumstances, I am loath to waste it, but a whore is a whore and there is no disguising the fact. It is odd, is it not, that one is so used to being accosted by them in the Haymarket that one scarcely notices them, whereas their absence from the pages of fiction positively clamours for attention.

I remain, yours, etc,

Percy Blackwood

[Editor's Note: Among Blackwood's papers three other documents relate to October 7, though all were written sometime after the events to which they were refer. The first is a letter from Serafina Blackwood to her friend Agnes Miller in Herne Bay; the other two are cuttings from the Kentish Gazette. None tells a complete tale in itself, but from them a complete tale might be inferred. Serafina was no stylist. Much of the dialogue in her letter is written

in reported speech of the he-said-she-said variety: this I have edited to make it more palatable to the modern reader. Though I have taken liberties with the style, I have taken none with the content. Here, then, is the story of what happened – or is alleged to have happened – to Gabriel, the boot black, much as Percy must have related to his wife when she finally managed to drag it out of him.]

My dear Agnes,

You may remember that in my last letter I described the adventures – perhaps I should say misadventures – of Miss Lark and Corporal Costello in the Crystal Palace. What I did not describe, because I was not then aware of, were the even more remarkable adventures of young Gabriel, the boot black from the Christchurch Gate. During the steamer journey from London Bridge to Pimlico Pier, he had fallen overboard and was rescued by a passing skiff. The Rev. Culpepper, our chaplain, was deeply distressed by the loss, as was Nan Foxley, our parlour maid, both of them fearing that the boy was lost for ever and neither of them knowing whom to turn to for help, other than to God, to Whom you may be sure that Culpepper applied himself most earnestly. That his supplications might be the more effective, he even took himself to the Bishop of London's private chapel in Fulham.

Just how effective they were, you may judge for yourself. On the evening of the second day, the Canterbury party, fatigued by their exertions in the Crystal Palace, had retired early for the night. Percy was awakened by one of the janitors banging loudly on the door. Angrily he demanded to know what was so urgent that it could not wait until morning. The janitor persisted, saying that there were people – important people – who insisted on speaking with him and whom it would be imprudent to refuse. Throwing on his overcoat, Percy ventured into the corridor. By now others were stirring and soon the passageway was full of women in curl papers and men in shirt sleeves. Cyril Purselove, the out of work actor, appeared in a green silk dressing gown embroidered with

Shakespearean characters and Albert Turpin, the inventor, in a an oil-stained nightshirt.

Beckoning them to follow, the janitor led the way to the front door. There, looking uncommonly pleased with himself, was the missing boy. Culpepper's prayers, it seemed, had been well and truly answered. Two men in livery accompanied him and, behind them, parked in Ranelagh Road, was a carriage bearing the royal coat of arms.

"Is this one of yours?" asked one of the men, his white-gloved thumb and forefinger holding up the boy by the collar.

"Well, he was," said Purselove, "but does that oblige us to take him back? I hope not, though I must say he looks a little cleaner than when we last saw him."

"That's because I am," remarked the boy, cool as you please.

"Gabriel!" shrieked Nan, who had just appeared in the corridor. "Where have you been?"

Pulling off the shawl with which she had covered her night shirt – one of mine, much patched, but still substantial – she threw it round the boy's shoulders.

"Why, you hair is still wet!" she exclaimed. "Surely you can't have been in the river all this time. When did they pull you out?"

"No-one pulled him out of the river," said one of the flunkeys.

"Nan!" ordered Miss Osgood, arriving on the scene with a blanket. "Cover up this instant. You are scarcely decent."

"He's been given …," continued the flunkey.

"Forced to have…," corrected his companion.

"A bath."

"A bath?"

"I have," said Gabriel.

"He smells as if he has," said Nan, sniffing.

"In which case the return journey should be easier on the nostrils," said Purselove. "And thank God, say I."

By now everyone was trying to talk at once: Nan to find out what had happened to Gabriel, Miss Osgood to insist on modest dress,

Purselove to quote Shakespeare and the janitor to shepherd people back to their rooms. It was Percy who finally restored calm by signalling to George Costello to blow his bugle. George put the bugle to his lips, but perhaps remembering the Duke of Wellington's admonition, thought better of it. But the mere gesture was enough and the clamour subsided.

"Gabriel," said Percy, taking the boy by the shoulders and looking him in the eye, "will you please tell us what happened to you? We have all been sick with worry."

"He hasn't for a start," said Gabriel, pointing to Purselove.

"Guilty as charged," replied the actor.

"Never mind him," continued Percy. "Tell us where you have been."

"Pussy cat, pussy cat, where have you been…," began Gabriel.

"Will you please give me a straight answer?" demanded Percy.

".... I've been up to London to look at the Queen."

"For the love of God," said Percy, who is never in the best of tempers when he has just been roused from sleep, "will somebody try to get some sense out of this boy?"

Nan knelt down in front of him and took his hand.

"Gabriel," she said, "won't you tell us where you have been? We thought you were drowned or kidnapped or run over or robbed."

"What of?" asked the boy.

"Or fallen into bad company," added Miss Osgood.

"The parson has been praying for you," continued Nan.

"Much obliged to him," said the boy.

"So where have you been?" persisted Nan.

"Pussy cat, pussy cat …"

"Oh don't start that again," said Percy.

"What he's trying to tell you," said one of the flunkeys, "is that he spent the night in the Palace."

"Crystal or Buckingham?" asked Breeze.

Breeze's quip seemed to annoy the two flunkeys, who had a proper sense of the respect due to them by their inferiors and since that included everyone present, persons who had to stay in shilling-a-night hostels falling into that category by definition, a particularly large debt was owed. What, they demanded to know, tugging their epaulettes, did the gentleman suppose those were or, more important, what that – that being the royal coat of arms on the carriage door – was.

"But ..."

"But how did he get in? I wish I knew. But get in he did, the Lord knows how. Some say he climbed down the chimney."

"He does look like a chimney sweep's boy," added the other flunkey.

"Some say that he pretended to be a tradesman's boy and came through the tradesman's entrance."

"He could pass for a tradesman's boy."

"Or he could simply have knocked at the Equerry's Door in James Street and walked straight past the night porter into the Palace. It's happened before."

"What we don't know," continued the other flunkey, "is where exactly he spent the night. There were sightings in the Marble Hall ..."

"The Grand Staircase ..."

"The Blue Drawing Room ..."

"The Throne Room. Even ..."

"Oh surely not," gasped Miss Osgood, as he hesitated.

"... even in Her Majesty's bedchamber. But that is just a rumour."

"Almost certainly."

"There was such a chase as you wouldn't believe. And what a field there was! Domestics, gardeners, coachmen, scullery maids, footmen. The Lord Chamberlain gave the tally ho! and off we went. Into, under, over, forward, back ..."

"State rooms, bed rooms, still rooms, cellars ..."

"Eventually we ran him to ground in ..."

"...of all places..."

"The Throne Room, under the throne itself, if you please."

"The actual throne," nodded Gabriel.

"What did you do when you caught him?" asked Nan.

"The Lord Chamberlain gave him a good thrashing."

"I've had worse," said Gabriel.

"Then we gave him a hot meal."

"I've had a lot worse."

"And a bath."

"With soap."

"And brought him here."

"In a carriage," said Gabriel.

"Don't get above yourself. It might have the royal arms on the door, but it's only the brougham the housekeeper uses to go to Fortnums."

Giving Gabriel a valedictory cuff round the ear, the two flunkeys marched out of the hostel, their white-gloved fingers under their noses as if they had been visiting a particularly malodorous workhouse. As soon as they had gone, the janitor slammed the doors and slid the bolts.

"To keep you in," he said to Gabriel.

"Pooh!" said Gabriel, "that wouldn't keep me in if I wanted to be out nor out if I wanted to be in."

Alarmed by this last remark, Nan decided that although a cubicle had been reserved for the boy, he should not, in view of his recent exploits, be left unattended. She therefore proposed that he should sleep on the floor of her own cubicle, whose doors she would keep securely locked until morning. Miss Osgood objected on grounds of propriety, Purselove, mockingly, on grounds of hygiene.

"But I've had a bath," protested the boy.

"It takes more than a bath to erase a lifetime in the gutter," replied Purselove.

"How would you know?" exclaimed Nan angrily. "You've never been there."

"The better class of pauper, of whom I account myself one, tends to favour garrets rather than gutters," replied Purselove. "In the end it comes down to a choice between fleas and rats, and I go for fleas every time."

But Nan was not to be silenced with facile witticisms.

"You haven't said one word to show that you're glad he's back," she continued. "Not one word! He might have been murdered, kidnapped or drowned and all you can do is hold your nose and complain that he smells bad. So would you if you'd had the life he's led."

Taking Gabriel by the hand, she marched him off to her cubicle. The other bystanders now began to disperse, hurried on their way by the janitor. When they had gone, Purselove burst into tears, confessing to Percy that he was a shallow creature whose unhappiness frequently expressed itself – often against his will – in wounding cynicism. If there was anything he could do to make amends to the boy – anything – Percy had but to say the word. And with that promise he pulled his silk dressing gown about him and returned to his cubicle.

As Percy followed at a distance, a cubicle door opened and Mr Beamish, the phrenologist, put his head out.

"Bumps of adhesiveness and combativeness," he whispered loudly; "plain as anything."

"In Purselove?" asked Percy in surprise.

"No, no, the flunkeys. Now if you will excuse me, I must go and make notes whilst the impression is still fresh."

When I wrote to you earlier, I did not include the story of the runaway boot black, because I did not then know of it, Percy having omitted to tell me. Nor would I have known of it had not Miss Osgood called to ask my advice in the matter of the stolen spoons. It seems that some items of cutlery and a tankard – only pewter but, like the cutlery, stamped with the royal insignia – were discovered on the boy's person during the steamer trip back to London Bridge. Percy and Nan, who made the discovery, had clearly intended to tell no-one about it, and in this they seem to have had the blessing of the Reverend Culpepper. To be sure, he admonished the boy and quoted the eighth commandment at him – he could hardly have done less – but advised against informing the police. In the boy's safe return, he had seen an answer to his prayers and could not, he said, believe that God had delivered the boy from harm only to have him end in prison. In a man of the cloth such a conclusion is unpardonable. On this Miss Osgood and I are agreed and have resolved to bring the matter to the committee, who have, if they see fit, the power to remove him from the chaplaincy of the Ebenezer Temperance Society. As you may imagine, my siding with Miss Osgood has occasioned much bitterness between Percy and me. For now Nan remains at the Ebenezer, though under sufferance. Should a suitable situation occur elsewhere, I shall urge her to take it.

Yesterday Miss Osgood and I, after much soul searching and prayer, placed the matter before the police. The boy will appear before the magistrates next week.

I thank you for your kind enquiries after my health. It is, I am pleased to say, much improved. Yesterday I managed a turn round the Old Palace Gardens, followed by evensong at St Peter's. I thank you, too, for asking whether my strength is equal to running a busy hotel, to which the answer must be yes, not because my health is as robust as I should wish, but because the hotel continues to be less busy than it should be.

Yours etc,
Serafina Blackwood.

[Editor's Note: The story is taken up by the Kentish Gazette of November 15, 1851, in which appears the following account of the Canterbury Quarter Sessions.]

The Quarter Sessions of the City and Borough of Canterbury were held in the Guildhall on Thursday before the Recorder, Mr John Deedes Esq. After some preliminary remarks on the nature of their duties, the Recorder noted that the number of prisoners was gratifyingly small and therefore had the satisfaction of advising them that their labours were unlikely to be protracted. Mr Horace Culver was chosen Foreman of the Jury.

[Editor's Note: The Recorder went on to enumerate the cases before the Jury, concluding with that of Gabriel Stokes, bootblack, for 'stealing one pewter tankard, one knife, fork and spoon (unmatching) and one pepper pot, all bearing the arms of Her Majesty, from Buckingham Palace.' Mr Tyrell appeared for the prosecution, Mr Cobb for the defence.]

MR TYRELL: Would you tell the court how the items in in the indictment came into your possession?
STOKES: They was given me.
MR TYRELL: Far from being given you, I put it to you that you stole them.
STOKES: Do you now?
MR TYRELL: I put it to you that you broke into the Palace with the sole intention of helping yourself to whatever you could find.
STOKES: Steady on.
MR TYRELL: And that you were prevented from stealing further items by the timely action of the Palace staff.
STOKES: I didn't steal. I've never stole. I was given.
MR TYRELL: Oh? And by whom?
STOKES: By the Queen.
RECORDER: Did I hear you say the Queen?
STOKES: You did.
MR TYRELL: Would you please describe the circumstances in which Her Majesty gave you the items in question: to wit, one pewter tankard, one knife, one fork, one spoon (unmatching) and one pepper pot in Sheffield plate.
STOKES: She took me on her knee.
RECORDER: On her knee? Where was she sitting when she took you on her knee?
STOKES: On her throne, where do you think?

RECORDER: Did she have her crown on?

STOKES: No, she took it off and give it to Prince Albert what was sitting on the floor alongside of her.

RECORDER: Princes do not sit on floors.

STOKES: This one did.

MR TYRELL: And when you were seated on Her Majesty's knee, what did you talk about?

STOKES: This and that. She wanted to know what it was like to live in the streets.

MR TYRELL: And what did you tell her?

STOKES: I told her about kipping in cellars and doorways, picking meat off old bones, fighting cats for fish heads …

MR TYRELL: Yes, yes, we know all that.

STOKES: No you don't, no more'n what she did. That's why she asked me.

MR TYRELL: And how did Her Majesty respond to your tales of destitution?

STOKES: She give me a hug.

RECORDER: Are you asking us to believe that the Queen of England actually embraced you?

MR TYRELL: With respect, Your Honour, it is important not to lose sight of the indictment, which is for theft. (*To Stokes*) At what point did Her Majesty reward you with the items in question?

STOKES: She didn't, he did.

MR TYRELL: Prince Albert?

STOKES: That's the one. When I'd finished, he said, 'You poor boy. Your story has touched me to the quick. I don't want you to think of me and the wife as being as hard-hearted as some of your tormentors what you've described to us. Have a few items to remember us by.'

MR TYRELL: And he just happened to have these items on him, I suppose?

STOKES: The tankard he did, but the others he had to ring the bell for.

At this point the Recorder adjourned the court for lunch, warning the jury that, owing to the unexpected complexity of the case, it might continue for a second day.

Mr Tyrell began the afternoon session by asking the Recorder if he might make a statement. He had, he said, taken advantage of the lunchtime adjournment to procure a copy of The Times for the day in question. He read aloud as follows: 'Edinburgh 7th October. Her Majesty arrived from Balmoral yesterday evening at eight o'clock. She was enthusiastically received by the inhabitants of the city in her progress to Holyrood Palace, from which she will start this morning at half past eight o' clock on her way to Lancaster, Liverpool and Manchester.' So much, he concluded, for the sympathetic hearing which she was alleged to have given the defendant. In view of the overwhelming evidence, he would not be calling further witnesses.

Mr Cobb began the case for the defence by announcing that he would not call the accused as a witness, since, as the jury would already have noted, the boy did himself no favours in that particular role. He was, said Mr Cobb, a child with an unusually vivid imagination and a tendency to confuse mere imaginings with actual facts. This was evident not only in his account of his dealings with the Queen but also from his descriptions of life in the gutter. For the record, the boy lived with his widowed mother in conditions of respectable poverty. Mr Cobb intended to produce a witness who would put beyond doubt the truth of the defendant's claims insofar as they related to the charge. He therefore asked for one Mr Clarence Bolton to be sworn in as witness.

MR COBB: Mr Bolton, you are, I believe, a footman in the service of Her Majesty.
MR BOLTON: I have that honour, yes, sir.
MR COBB: From your affidavit I see that you were on duty in the Palace on the night in question.
MR BOLTON: That is correct, yes, sir.

MR COBB: How did you learn that there was an intruder in the Palace?

MR BOLTON: Word came down from the Lord Chamberlain's office that there was an interloper and that we were to scour the Palace from top to bottom.

MR COBB: Which you did with some success, I gather, for it was you and a colleague ...

MR BOLTON: Jim Croker ...

MR COBB: Quite so ... for it was you and Mr Jim Croker who finally ran the boy to ground – 'ground' in this case being the Throne Room.

MR BOLTON: And not just the Throne Room, sir, but under the very Chair of State itself.

MR COBB: What did you do when you apprehended him?

MR BOLTON: Gave him a good thrashing, sir.

MR COBB: And then?

MR BOLTON: One of the maidservants gave him a bath.

MR COBB: And then?

MR BOLTON: All the other servants took pity on him and gave him a hot supper in the servants' quarters, where he favoured us with his life story and a very sad one it is.

MR COBB: And after supper?

MR BOLTON: Everybody, including the Housekeeper, a woman at whose breast one does not normally expect to suckle the milk of human kindness, decided to let him take a few keepsakes from the kitchen. Gewgaws, trifles, nothing of any value.

MR COBB: Enumerate them, if you please.

MR BOLTON: One knife, one fork, one spoon, one pewter tankard and one pepper pot, as named in the indictment.

MR COBB: Was the Lord Chamberlain informed of this act of charity?

MR BOLTON: One does not inform the Lord Chamberlain of any-thing; one only makes him aware.

MR COBB: The difference being?

MR BOLTON: That if he likes what you tell him he chooses to be informed, and if he does not, he chooses to turn a blind eye.
MR COBB: And in this case he chose to turn a blind eye?
MR BOLTON: As did the royal chaplain and the equerries.
MR COBB: Thank you, Mr Bolton. That will be all.

The jury brought in a verdict of Not Guilty. Before ordering the boy's release, the Recorder reminded him that although he had been found Not Guilty of theft, a very different verdict might have been returned had he been charged with either perjury or breaking and entering. He had had a lucky escape and should reflect carefully on his good fortune.

[Editor's Note: Alas, Gabriel's good fortune did not last long. Also contained in the Blackwood papers is another newspaper report, this time of the Easter Quarter Sessions of 1852. There, wedged between the cases of Annie Phillips, seamstress, who had a penchant for stealing watches, and James Lawlor, tinsmith, who was in the habit of receiving them, was the case of Cyril Purselove, actor, for impersonating a royal footman. The Recorder stated that the impersonation was tantamount to forgery, and, since forgery was a transportable offence, the prisoner would, if found guilty, face a sentence of seven years transportation to Australia. When asked how he wished to plead, the prisoner unhesitatingly replied 'Guilty and proud of it.'

Before sentencing him, Mr Deedes asked him if he had anything to say. Purselove stated that throughout his acting career he had longed to play one of the great Shakespearean roles. In vain had he waited to be cast as Macbeth or Hamlet or Brutus; in vain had he waited to prove himself a worthy successor to Mr Kean. Against all the odds he had hoped, nay believed, that Fortune would one day favour him. So strong, so insistent was this belief that he neglected all other endeavours; it was, he said, as if he had been corrupted by hope. And when at last Fortune did oblige him with a leading role, it was so far from what he had hoped for that he did not know what to make of it, or even whether to accept it. Yet accept it he did and he had never regretted his decision. No role could have given him as much satisfaction –

not Henry V, not Romeo, not the Prince of Denmark himself – as that of the Queen's footman. He did not regret taking the part, and if it were offered to him again, he would accept without hesitation.

Pity poor Purselove. On the hulks and, later, on the long voyage to Australia, I like to think he kept his panache, pacing the deck in his flowered waistcoat or lying in his hammock in the dressing gown embroidered with Shakespearean characters. Yet perhaps he has no need of our pity. Our last glimpse of him in the archive is on a theatre bill from June 1855:

Following Last Year's Sensational Debut

THE PURSELOVE PLAYERS

Open the Winter Season with

THE TRAGEDY OF MACBETH

In which the Role of the Tyrant will be taken by Mr Cyril Purselove

that of his wife by Miss Annie Phillips and that of Duncan by Mr James Lawlor

When Shall Wee Three Meet Again?

In the Drill Hall, Fremantle, July 23 – 4 August 1855.

By this time Purselove must have become a ticket-of-leave man. Whether he returned home at the end of his sentence or pursued his theatrical career in the more fruitful pastures of New South Wales and Victoria, I have been unable to discover. Nor have I been able to discover whether it was on his own initiative that Purselove appeared in the witness box for Gabriel, or whether Blackwood and Nan, who seem to have grown close following the breach with Serafina, talked him into it. One can almost hear them urging him to do a great right by doing a little wrong. It would, of course, have been more heroic had he acted without prompting, but if, as I suspect was the case, he took his punishment without naming his accomplices, then that would, perhaps, have been the most heroic action of all.

As for Gabriel, the scent goes cold after his acquittal, though not perhaps stone cold. A search of the archives, local and national, produces three possibilities:

Amongst the transports on the voyage to Western Australia is a G Stokes, no age or occupation given;

Amongst the dead of the great Staplehurst railway accident of 1865 is one G. Stokes Esq, chimney sweep;

The accounts for the Royal Household, now held at Windsor, record payments in 1853 and 1854, to 'GS, page boy'.

So which was he? The transport, the crash victim or the page boy? Or was he none of the above? In the absence of further evidence there is no way of knowing. The reader will have to supply the ending, sad or happy according to taste, for himself.]

Part Three

Part Three

7

LONDON BRIDGE TO CROYDON

I travel First Class
The Lady's Companion's Tale of The Arcanum
A Shocking Revelation
Mr Scudamore's Tale of The Boy Butler
An Unscheduled Stop

Our party was in low spirits as it assembled next morning on Pimlico Pier. Many had found it hard to sleep after the previous night's excitement and most were aware in themselves of a void where, until yesterday, months of eager longing had been. All those hopes, all those yearnings which had sought realisation in the Crystal Palace had now been fulfilled – or disappointed – and there was nothing to take their place. The transcendent moment had come and gone; the pilgrims had entered the Celestial City, gazed their fill and been shown the door. And now, gathered on the pier under a grey London sky, they wished they could escape their cold Wednesday and follow Miss Lark into an unending Tuesday, where all desires would be satisfied everlastingly.

If the party was more subdued on the return journey than on the outward, it was also bulkier. Pockets bulged with keepsakes, overcoats with purchases that doubled the size of their wearers. Since the steamer had already taken on passengers – the Bishop of

London's guests among them – at Chelsea and Fulham, it was with difficulty that our party squeezed abroad. Consequently we were dispersed about the deck, so that if Mr Bartholomew offered further reflections on the new clock tower or Turpin on improved paddle wheels, I did not hear them. What I did hear, though from afar, was an altercation between Miss Osgood and Nan about some items which the latter had found earlier that morning in Gabriel's pockets and which the former alleged had been stolen from Buckingham Palace. Since Culpepper was on hand to restore the peace, I saw no reason to intervene and, buttoning my coat against the cold, leaned against the rail to enjoy the unfolding spectacle of wharf and creek.

[Editor's Note: Blackwood is surely being disingenuous here. We know from Serafina's letter to her friend in Herne Bay – summarised at the end of Part 2 – that this episode divided the Canterbury party and led to a breach not only between Blackwood and Miss Osgood but ultimately between Blackwood and his wife. Serafina's version of events, which is presumably a re-heated version of Miss Osgood's, suggests that Blackwood took Nan's side and was supported by Culpepper. We shall never know precisely what was said, since Blackwood's fragmentary notes stop here and do not resume until the Canterbury party gathered at London Bridge Station, where it was joined by the Malachi Browns, Mme Fontana, Miss Binnie and Mr Critchley. The Fulham party, consisting of Dr leGrove, Mr Dacre, Culpepper and Stumps, were, as we have seen, already on the steamer when the others joined it at Pimlico.]

Having urged Miss Osgood to take her place in the second class compartment with Dr leGrove and his contingent, I was hesitating whether to follow her when I was approached by Mr Scudamore with an invitation from Miss Tintsford to join her and Lady Rippledale in the first class compartment.

"Her ladyship insists," he added.

"That is most gracious of her. I am very flattered."

"Don't be. She refers to you as that 'odious Jacobin' and wants to keep an eye on you so that you don't foment revolution."

"What on earth makes her think that I would want to do that?"

"Temperance societies, trade unions, Chartists, the Cato Street conspirators – she makes no distinction. As far as she is concerned, a man who belongs to one belongs to all."

I was about to protest that it was Serafina who was the zealot and not I, when Miss Tintsford called from the window of the carriage.

"Hurry, Mr Blackwood. Hurry, if you please. The train is about to depart."

A glance at Sturdee, who was still eating his sandwiches, revealed that the train was about to do no such thing; nonetheless, as a cure for my indecision, Lady Rippledale's invitation could hardly have been bettered. Followed by Mr Scudamore, I climbed aboard and, sliding the brim of my hat under the ribbons which were stretched across the ceiling for the purpose, settled myself opposite Miss T.

As we waited for the train to start, the talk turned to Lady Rippledale's town house and of her insistence, at ruinous expense, on having it ready for use at a moment's notice, even though she rarely stayed there and always seemed to find fault when she did. Packed with the spoils of her ancestors' Grand Tours, the house in Cavendish Street was, by all accounts, as chilly and unwelcoming as a morgue. Canalettos, marble busts, Roman bronzes, lacquered chests, majolica vases – Mr Scudamore loathed them indiscriminately, whilst Miss Tintsford's especial hatred was reserved for the contents of the china cabinet.

"That dinner service …," growled Miss Tintsford.

"Ah, The Arcanum," sighed Lady Rippledale.

"…will be the death of me. Every time we stay in Lady Rippledale's town house, I feel a strong desire to throw open that cabinet and smash every cup and saucer in it."

"Twelve coffee cups with scroll handles," announced Lady Rippledale, "twelve coffee cups with lyre handles."

"In every chip, every crack, every missing item …"

"Twelve tea cups with scroll handles, nine tea cups with lyre handles …"

"... is written an episode in her deplorable family's history – her father's family, the Erpingtons, that is, not her husband's."

"The oldest earldom in England. Older than the Talbots, older than the Beauforts. Fifteen manors, thirty-two quarterings, twenty-six soup plates ..."

"And a partridge in a pear tree," murmured Mr Scudamore, who had evidently wearied of this litany of soup plates and armorials long ago.

"No-one knows exactly when it came into the family," continued Miss Tintsford, "though it is said to be the work – even the masterwork – of the great Böttger himself." Seeing my puzzled look, she explained: "Surely you have heard of Johann Böttger, Mr Blackwood, the trickster who was locked in a cellar by his master until he discovered the secret of alchemy, only to emerge having mastered the secret of porcelain? I thought everyone knew the story. Shame on you."

"Tradition has it that it arrived on three carts packed in goose feathers," said Mr Scudamore.

"Four!" corrected Lady Rippledale crossly.

"Three," said Mr Scudamore, "and I doubt it was even that many."

The Lady's Companion's Tale of The Arcanum

I had not been in her ladyship's service many weeks before she introduced me to The Arcanum. Think of it, she said, not as a dinner service – though the Queen herself surely possesses no finer – but as a shoal or flock. If a cup or plate goes astray, somewhere in the mass of painted foliage and fruit a petal will drop, a bloom fade or a scroll uncoil. You may laugh, Mr Blackwood, but it is what her ladyship believed and, as far I know, still does. Her devotion to it is unwavering. For her the Erpingtons are The Arcanum, The Arcanum is the Erpingtons. In its cracks and flaws is inscribed the history of her family. Tantrums, drunkenness, madness have taken their toll, and, as the traces of their folly have accumulated, chip by chip, they have tried to pass off the imperfections as honourable scars. A missing cream jug – thrown at a countess by her husband – became a gift to the Prince Regent "because he admired it so". A chip on the rim of a tea cup – hurled in retaliation at the earl by his wife – was christened the "Archbishop Chip" because "His Grace caught the rim a glancing blow with his pectoral cross. We like to think that whoever drinks out of it is particularly blessed."

Sir Geoffrey Rippledale would not have it in the house. "Blessed?" he used to say. "The damn thing is hoodoo; it carries misery with it wherever it goes. Look at your family: drunk, disgraced, syphilitic and, with you, extinct." It was true. Lady Maud is the last of them and, as you may have guessed, childless. Whether she was infertile or he impotent I cannot say. The fact is that there is no issue of their exhausted loins, no child to carry forward her line or his. In France they would have perished in style beneath the guillotine. Here they have just been hollowed out by debt and the pox. That was why her ladyship could make no better match. Without a dowry, the best she could hope for was a booby squire who rode to hounds once a week and snored through the sermon on Sundays. And with Sir Geoffrey Rippledale that is exactly what she got. With him came a manor house by the village pond and a house in Cavendish Street, both quite handsome in their way, though hardly a substitute for Erpington Purlieu.

Erpington Purlieu is the family home in Bedfordshire. Not much of it remains now. The oaks for which it was famed were sold for ship building, and the park, which had been landscaped by Capability Brown, was quarried for stone by the Midland Railway – the very railway that now runs through the garden. For her, Erpington Purlieu is the lost paradise, the Eden from which she has been driven by the sins of her family. As for the Rippledale properties, she utterly despises them ...

"Detestable hovels!" interjected her ladyship.

... in the same way she despises me. In her befuddled state she thinks that is I who have reduced her to the squalor in which she now lives – even though it is a squalor that comprises a house in Cavendish Street and a manor as fine as any in Kent. But it was not always so. The beginning of our acquaintance was a happy one – or as happy as the acquaintance between the daughter of a tradesman and the last of the Erpingtons ...

"Fifteen manors, thirty-two quarterings, twenty-six soup plates ..."
"Ignore her," said Mr Scudamore, "or she'll start itemising the cups and saucers."

... the last of the Erpingtons can be. Her husband had just died. She was feeling sorry for herself and for a time I felt sorry too. She told me the sad tale of Erpington Purlieu, of how it was being sold, brick by brick, to pay off the family's debts. How those debts had arisen she did not say, hinting only at treachery and bad faith on the part of others. Would I like to see the place? she asked. Very much, I replied. Then we must go soon, she said – next week or next month, before the railways dig up the grounds. So we did. And not a moment too soon, for there were still treasures at Erpington Purlieu – Böttger's masterpiece among them – and the navvies had not yet built their hutted encampment in the park. We arrived to find the Chief Engineer and the Chief Surveyor, both no doubt presuming on their rank, drinking tea out of The Arcanum in the dining room. I laugh to think of it now, but at the time I joined with her – shame on me! – in blaming the servants. I even applauded when she threw a saucer at them. After they had gone, we spent the afternoon combing through all the surviving pieces – hundreds of them – for signs of sympathetic repining. And we found them. Or thought we did. A fading rose here, a hairline crack there. How she wept! How I wept, too, at least until she turned on me. Why had I cheered her on? she asked. Why had I not restrained her? Here was a very different Maud Rippledale from the one I had known. But the lapse was a temporary one. Her good humour soon returned and she offered to show me round the house. Note the damp stains on the Chinese wall paper, once the pride and joy of Lady Priscilla. Politely I noted. Remark the ormolu clock, its main spring – alas! – broken, the gift of a Comte de Pellelieu who had sought refuge here from the French Revolution. Politely I remarked. Note this, remark that, witness the other. We visited Nanny Barraclough's room and the nursery where generations of Erpingtons, herself included, had been taught the rudiments of gentility. And Nanny Barraclough herself? I asked. She shrugged. She couldn't rightly remember. Servants came, servants went; one couldn't keep track of them all. But surely a governess was different? Not particularly. A governess was a servant, and a servant was, well, just a servant.

And a lady's companion? I wondered, but forbore to ask, lest I should discover that I, too, was just a servant.

We became frequent visitors to Erpington Purlieu, so frequent, in fact, that her ladyship kept a special carriage with the Erpington arms on the door and a coachman in livery. Little by little we entered that world of make-believe in which you now find us. The Arcanum was put to use once more. To our invitations – afternoon tea, dinner, even a hunt ball – few replied and fewer attended. But those that did, Mr Blackwood, those that did! Pray God you never see the like. Here were living skeletons who could not descend from their carriages unaided and who had to be pushed, propelled or heaved into place at the table. Servants fed those who could not feed themselves and such was the shaking of palsied hands that you couldn't hear yourself speak for the rattle of cup on saucer. Afterwards we gathered up shards of The Arcanum from the table and the floor and counted the damage. Not that it mattered: as far as her ladyship was concerned, nothing was amiss. For the duration of the party she, along with her guests, was in the first flush of youth, jostling to catch the Prince Regent's attention at Brighton.

But once the navvies arrived everything changed. The living skeletons were jeered, their carriages jostled. It was the French Revolution all over again, said one painted lordling, and he for one did not intend to go the way of the Comte de Pellelieu, conveniently ignoring the fact that he *was* the Comte de Pellelieu, who had fled the Terror clutching his ormolu clock and taken root in Bedfordshire. After that, the living skeletons shunned the place and her ladyship ordered its treasures, The Arcanum among them, to be transferred to Cavendish Street. For months Erpington Purlieu lay open to the weather. The Chinese wall paper peeled from the walls, jackdaws nested in the ball room, until finally Lady Maud was forced to admit defeat and sell it to the railway company who converted it into a goods shed. As for Nanny Barraclough, not one brick of the nursery survived to remind us that she had ever existed.

Once Erpington Purlieu was lost, the make-believe became more important than ever. One day her ladyship handed me a letter. Take it to the post without delay, she said. It is most urgent. She had not sealed it, so, naturally I opened it and read. You will, I hope, commend my frankness in telling you this, Mr Blackwood, even if you cannot condone my fault – but then I doubt it was a fault, since I was only doing what her ladyship intended. Well, what other explanation could there be? She, who is so secretive by nature, would scarcely have handed me an unsealed letter if she had not intended me to read it. Or, indeed, to reply to it. Which I did, entering into the spirit of the thing as I had entered into the spirit of the ridiculous charades at Erpington Purlieu. I became her admirer – on paper, at least – and later her lover. At times the salacious details of our conduct, as related by her ladyship, quite shocked me – remember, Mr Blackwood, I am the daughter of a respectable tradesman – but as the shock wore off I began to delight in my own salacious imaginings and marvel in my own ingenuity. We coupled in the most unlikely of places and in what I can only imagine – for I am no authority on such matters – the most unlikely of ways. – (Don't look so pained, Mr Scudamore. Why don't you talk to her ladyship? Occupy her thoughts, divert her attention. After all, it's why she invited you back into the first class carriage.) – In time her ladyship's lover was discarded in favour of others – sometimes several at once – each with a title, each introduced to her by her many non-existent brothers, whose friends they were. (Her brothers, by the way, all made brilliant marriages, their wives proving remarkably fecund, each producing enough sons to guarantee the Erpington name and keep Nanny Barraclough busy for years to come. This last detail you may be sure I insisted on.) In our letters Erpington Purlieu was re-born as a place of intrigue and fashion, a place where The Arcanum was in constant use and gathering cracks by the day. On at least two occasions her ladyship received dazzling offers of marriage which she had to refuse, if only because they would have taken too much explaining away to those who knew her as the mere relict of a country squire.

In our everyday conversations, her ladyship and I never confessed to writing to each other. Officially I was not even supposed to know that she was receiving the letters I had composed on her behalf. If there were rules to our little game, we never discussed them, nor even admitted to each other that there was a game. But there were rules, as I discovered to my cost when I broke the first of them: namely, that since one's station in life is God-given, one must not try to rise above it. God forbid that I should try to better myself! Have you ever considered what it is like to be a lady's companion? To have no life of your own but always to be towed along in the wake of someone else's? To have someone else decide how you will spend your day, what time you will rise, what time go to bed, where you will go, what you will read? – in short, to be an attendant planet to some bright star whose light you are paid to reflect? If ladies could resort to make-believe, then so, too, I thought, could ladies' companions. So I penned a letter of my own. In it I became the daughter of a clergyman who had received a proposal of marriage from a country doctor – nothing too grand, you will notice, my ambitions were all within bounds – and who had asked for time to think it over. Would I, I asked, be allowed my own parlour? Would I be allowed a lapdog, a piano, a dancing master, green wall paper and a parrot with a large vocabulary? If so, then my answer would be yes, yes, a thousand times yes. In the event, my answer was neither yes nor no. Her ladyship completely ignored me. I had thought she might be amused by my little game. I began to grow uneasy. Was she, I wondered, offended by the suggestion that I might want to leave her? Was I being presumptuous in aspiring to a parlour of my own? Her silence continued. Even the flow of letters from her to her lovers dried up. Over tea, which was always served on The Arcanum, we exchanged only routine pleasantries. An unpleasant atmosphere formed, a miasma of rancour and suspicion. Having no correspondence to attend to, I was at a loss to occupy my time. In the end I could stand it no longer. I penned a second letter, apologising for my greed, saying that I could never forgive myself for replying to his proposal with a shopping list. How mercenary he must think me! I implored forgiveness and stated that parlour or no parlour, parrot or no parrot, my answer must be a heartfelt yes. Please, please, I begged, write to me by return. Next day I received a reply. It was not what I had expected. For a start, her ladyship wrote to me, not as to the clergyman's daughter, but to the rakish – and wholly imaginary – cousin with whom, off and on, she had been conducting an affair for years. This dissolute Erpington was a famous quarreller. He had been bound over, expelled from his club and disinherited by his father. This was the confidant to whom Lady Maud now turned for advice. What punishment, she demanded, would he advise for a servant who had abused her trust, disregarded her authority and scorned her pedigree? For such a one what punishment was fitting – or indeed adequate? Loss of privileges, confinement to his quarters – I laughed aloud at the 'his', which was the flimsiest of disguises – or horsewhipping? Or worse?

"Worse?" I echoed.

"Isn't it obvious?" demanded Miss T. "She meant murder."

"There you exaggerate," I replied. "She is no more capable of murder than you or I."

Miss T stared hard at me.

"I think you will find your confidence misplaced," she said. "In the meantime let me complete the story."

Our meals together became tests of will. Although we ate and drank in silence, the air was full of silent voices, shrieking and snarling. The loathing was palpable. Even The Arcanum felt it. In the middle of one silent exchange, when the currents of mutual hatred were particularly strong, there was a loud crack as her tea cup broke free of its handle and smashed to the floor. She sat there, little finger poised, a thin question mark of porcelain gripped between thumb and forefinger, as if nothing had happened. The next day a cream jug suffered the same fate, the day after a sugar bowl. Now I am not suggesting that the Arcanum was bewitched – it is far more likely that it had been damaged in transit from Erpington Purlieu – but I am suggesting that that she, like the rest of her class, believed she could bend the world to her wishes, could rearrange objects, even people, through sheer force of will. Not for nothing had I heard her speak admiringly of Russian aristocrats, of how they owned their serfs and could trade them like horses. Oh how she wished she had been born a subject of the Tsar! What bliss to live in a world where one could reconfigure nature as one chose, where a shaft of hatred directed at a servant might smash a teacup as surely as a bullet!

Out on the platform a bugle sounded. The Silver Band burst into life with 'Elsie from Chelsea'. All down the train there was a slamming of doors; then, with a blast of the guard's whistle and a rattle of connecting chains, the Ebenezer 'special' pulled away from London Bridge Station, a plume of smoke rising to the roof before spreading out sideways and obscuring the adjacent platforms. A porter touched his cap; a small boy pretended to conduct the band with his sister's parasol; a clerical gentleman perched on an upended trunk looked up from his book and frowned at the disturbance. Taking advantage of the noise of departure, Miss Tintsford leaned forward confidentially, took my hand and directed it to her reticule.

"Do not be afraid, Mr Blackwood," she said. "Put your hand inside and tell me what you feel. Ignore the other two. They are deep in conversation."

Uneasily I did as I was bid.

"Well?" she asked.

"Why, it's a revolver!" I exclaimed.

"Of the latest design. I purchased it whilst I was in London. And can you guess why I am carrying it?"

"If you fear for your safety, I am sure your fears are misplaced. Lady Rippledale is too frail to harm anyone."

"Oh, it is not to defend myself that I carry it. I intend to kill her."

I withdrew my hand from the bag in horror.

"You cannot mean it," I said. "I do not believe you capable of such a thing. In any case, if you really were serious, you would not have told me of your intentions. You cannot expect me to be silent if she were to be found dead of gunshot wounds."

Miss Tintsford laughed.

"Rest assured," she said, "I have no intention of going to the gallows for her. No, no, I shall take her abroad, well away from English jurisdiction, and dispose of her there. Italy, perhaps, or Switzerland. Somewhere with plenty of ravines, rocky roads and mountain torrents."

"Why do you not simply leave her?" I asked.

"That is what I sometimes ask myself," she replied. "But I am bound to her in ways you will never understand. I have never been in love, Mr Blackwood – nor, I suspect, has her ladyship, except on paper – but I have been blessed with a perfect hatred. Few men and women can say as much. As a passion it is as all-consuming and self-less as its opposite. What is it Lord Byron says?

'Now hatred is by far the longest pleasure;
Men love in haste, but they detest at leisure.'

And so it is with Lady Maud and me, Mr Blackwood. We detest at leisure, have done so for many years, but the consummation, so long postponed, is fast approaching."

[Editor's Note: In order to complete The Lady's Companion's Tale, I need to interrupt Blackwood's narrative, which continues at this point with Mr

Scudamore's tale of the Boy Butler. After it, the train made an unscheduled stop at Croydon, during which Blackwood transferred to the second class carriage in circumstances which I shall leave him to explain in due course. When the train finally stopped at Tunbridge, Mr Scudamore approached him as he was transferring from the second class carriage to the tub and asked if he might have a quiet word. At this point I leave Blackwood to continue the story in his own words.]

"Ah," said Dr leGrove, catching sight of Mr Scudamore, "are we to take it that her ladyship has expelled you from the first class carriage again? And if so, might we know the offence for which you have been banished?"

"You will notice," said Mme Fontana, "that we have not joined the queue for tea, Mr Scudamore. Even though you have deserted us, we continue to follow your advice. I trust it is still sound."

"Would it were not, ma'am, though I very much fear that it is," said Scudamore. "Now, Mr Blackwood, might I have a private word?"

Since I had intended to join my friends in the tub for the last part of the journey, I took my leave of Dr leGrove and the company in the second class carriage and stepped down on to the platform, closely followed by Mr Critchley and the Malachi Browns, all of whom were leaving the train at Tunbridge, as well as Miss Osgood, who intended to follow me into the tub, our recent disagreement notwithstanding. As peremptorily as I dared, I asked her to go ahead and inform Beamish, Turpin and the rest that I should be joining them shortly.

"Well?" I asked Mr Scudamore, as soon as she had gone.

"Whilst you were talking to Miss Tintsford, her ladyship confided to me what I had long suspected."

"And what was that?"

Mr Scudamore lowered his voice still further.

"On the outward journey you may remember that I was somewhat troubled by my exclusion from the first class carriage. Dr leGrove concluded that I was sulking because I had fallen out of favour. Believe me, this was far from being the case. By now, I am sufficiently used to Lady Rippledale's caprices to be untroubled by them. No, what troubled me was what she might do in Merstham Tunnel without my being there to prevent it. It was my fear that she would try to kill Miss Tintsford, whom she clearly detests. My fears were not groundless. During our conversations earlier, she revealed to me that she has purchased a small pistol and intends to dispose of her companion during their forthcoming visit to the continent. 'I've committed every sin a person can commit apart from murder,' she told me, 'and before I die I should like to commit that too'."

"Would it surprise you to learn that Miss Tintsford harbours similar ambitions?" I asked him.

Mr Scudamore looked genuinely shocked.

"You astonish me," he said.

"She revealed them to me whilst you were talking to her ladyship. She, too, has a pistol and, as for the scene of the crime, favours Switzerland or Italy."

"Why, this is monstrous," he said.

"I am not so sure. If either of them were really serious, I doubt if they would have told us. No, I think it far more likely that they are indulging in another elaborate game of make-believe. Confiding their secret intentions to a third party has more to do with vanity than a thirst for blood."

"I wish I could believe you," he said. "I cannot speak for Miss T, but her ladyship means every word she says. And I will tell you why: when they go on their travels, she intends to take the Arcanum with them."

"Come now," I objected, "she has not the mental capacity to conceive of such a scheme or the physical strength to carry it out."

"Do not be deceived, Mr Blackwood: she is as not as far advanced into her dotage as she would have you believe."

"In that case," I replied, "her powers of impersonation must indeed be remarkable."

The guard's whistle brought our exchange of confidences to an
end and we parted, he to prevent a murder, I to harvest the tales of
the tub. As he made his way back to his carriage, the crowds who
had been bilked yet again of their refreshments at the coffee stall,
surged round him in their eagerness to regain their seats.

*[Editor's Note: Had Blackwood ever organised his papers with a view to
publication, it is doubtful that he would have included the story of Miss
Tintsford and Lady Rippledale. A libel action brought by either party would
have ruined him and although the disappearance of the two protagonists,
as described in the following letter, appears to have been permanent, there is
no way he could have been absolutely sure they would not return. And then
there is the question of Scudamore. Would he have wanted to expose him to
suspicion? I doubt it. In Scudamore Blackwood saw an honourable man
who acted for the best, as the following letter shows. It dates from 1853, two
years after their conversation at Tunbridge, and in it Scudamore brings the
tale as near to a conclusion as it is ever likely to have.]*

Dear Mr Blackwood,

You will remember our conversation on the platform at Tunbridge. Though
I cannot be entirely sure, I fear that your optimism regarding Lady Maud and her
companion was misplaced. Shortly after we returned from London, her ladyship,
with the active collaboration of Miss Tintsford, began planning a Grand Tour, to
take in Venice, Florence, Rome and Naples. She wished, she said, to follow in the
footsteps of her ancestors and to marvel, as they had marvelled, at the wonders of
antiquity. In this she was seconded by her companion. Since neither of them had
shown the remotest interest in the wonders of antiquity before, I was naturally
suspicious.

I will not describe to you the particulars of our journey through France.
Although we travelled by train, we took with us her ladyship's coach secured to
a flat wagon at the rear. Rain or shine – and he endured extremes of both – the
poor coachman had to remain on the driver's box throughout the journey. The
Arcanum, or at least a large selection from it, travelled with the guard and it was my

duty to inspect it at regular intervals for damage. Any separation from the ladies, however brief, caused me great anxiety, and nowhere more so than in our transit of the Alps. Her ladyship insisted on the Mont Cenis Pass, because that was the route into Italy that her ancestors had favoured. And what a route it is! From start to finish one is entirely in the hands of the muleteers. First, they dismantled the carriage and distributed the parts, along with the crates containing The Arcanum, across the backs of twenty mules. Then the ladies were swathed in fur blankets and helped into litters, each of which was carried by eight sturdy mountaineers. As for the coach driver and I, we were given mules, told to keep an eye open for wolves and left to cope as best we could. The mountaineers set off at a trot and soon disappeared from sight. My mount refused to keep up and attached itself to the rear of the mule train carrying the dismembered coach. You may imagine with what anxiety I scrutinised the ravines and precipices, the crags and cataracts. I will not describe to you the discomforts of crossing the Alps on mule back, nor share with you the glories that the poets write of, though they were there in equal measure. We saw no wolves, no bloodstains in the snow; heard no screams or gunshots; nonetheless, it was with great relief that I arrived in Bardonecchia to find the two women demanding to know why I had taken so long and insisting that the coach be reassembled without delay.

From Piedmont we proceeded to Venice, where our arrival caused a stir when the barge carrying the coach capsized and tipped its cargo into the Lagoon. It was rescued and for several days stood drying out in St Mark's Square under the watchful eye of the coachman. Far from being grateful to its rescuers, her ladyship upbraided them for not retrieving the tea cups and fruit bowls which had foundered with it.

It was in Venice that the ladies and I began the game of cat and mouse which continued through our continental tour until the last calamitous day on Mount – but no, I must not anticipate: everything will be revealed in its proper place. Early one morning I went to call on the women, only to find their rooms empty. This was the moment I had been dreading. One of the maidservants in our palazzo had heard them instructing a boatman to take them to Torcello. Securing a boat of my own, I gave chase. Every moment I expected to see a body (or even bodies) in the water – her ladyship's most likely, but possibly also that of the boatmen whose silence Miss T had failed to buy. (You can see how lively my imagination had become.) It was with more than a touch of disappointment, therefore, that I found them calmly viewing the frescoes in Santa Maria Assunta, looking no different from the other tourists who had gathered there.

A week later the same thing happened in Florence. An early departure, a moment's panic, a chase (always, please note, at my own expense), a discovery that all was well, followed by a feeling of disappointment of which I never ceased to be ashamed. In this case they had left our villa beside the Arno and taken a carriage up to Fiesole in order to enjoy the view of the city at first light. 'What could be more natural?' their smiles seemed to say, 'what more delightful?' I am convinced that each knew the other's intentions and suspected that I knew, too. But what was remarkable was the rejuvenating effect that the prospect of murder had had on them. The frisson of danger had put a spring in their step, a sparkle in their eye. Lady Maud had given up all pretence of being in her dotages and T all pretence of being bored to death. Even more remarkable was the fact that they seemed genuinely fond of each other. I say 'seemed', though I began to doubt there was any seeming about it. Mutual loathing had worked a miracle. I relaxed. Early morning disappearances no longer alarmed me. I began to think that I had been imagining things, though had I been a superstitious man I should have been alarmed by the number of cracks that were appearing in The Arcanum and by the pallor of its blossoms.

As I have said, I lowered my guard, though I should have known better. When, one day in Naples, I found that they had gone for one of their early morning jaunts, I was not alarmed. I ate my breakfast alone on the terrace and enjoyed the prospect of the bay all the more for knowing that I should not be summoned by her ladyship's bell. It was only when the domestica told me that the ladies had set off for Pompeii that I decided to investigate. It was just possible, I thought, that the sight of all those calcified bodies might revive thoughts of murder. So I hired a cabriolet – again at my own expense – and hurried to the site. Imagine my horror to find that not only were they not there but, according to other visitors, had never been there at all. Perhaps the domestica had been wrong and it was to Herculaneum that they had gone. Thither I hurried, but no, there was no trace there either. I had been tricked. All my fears, my suspicions came flooding back. And as if to echo my growing disquiet, there was a distant rumble and the ground shook beneath our feet. 'Vesuvius,' said a guide to his party of visitors. 'No cause

When we arrived at the crater we found a
gilded table laid with The Arcanum

for alarm, it happens all the time.' I returned to the villa, hoping to uncover some clue to their destination. And open on her ladyship's desk I found it. It was the diary of a Grand Tour that one of her ancestors had made and the page lay open at an entry from July1789. I have it in front of me as I write:

Today I upheld a family tradition and invited my new-found acquaintance to dine off The Arcanum, not in the grounds of our villa, as they had expected, but on the crater of Vesuvius. And let us, said I, all wear red silk in honour of the fiery god who dwells within the mountain. But might it not tempt fate? asked a timid contessa; might it not incur his wrath? Let it, I said; I care not. I have braved worse – which was not strictly true, but as the only Englishman in the company I could scarcely say otherwise. No, I said, my mind is made up and we shall dine on Vesuvius – and we shall dine in red silk or perish in the attempt. Let the litters be ordered.

So thick was the stench of sulphur, most of us were retching long before we reached the crater. The timid contessa, whose litter was directly in front of mine, vomited into a lace handkerchief which she handed it to a maid servant who was walking alongside. As for the bearers, how they sweated and strained, how they gasped and groaned! Tantivy! tantivy! I cried to encourage them, but to little effect. They plodded on sullenly as before. When we arrived at the crater we found a gilded table laid with The Arcanum. Overcome by the reeking air, one of the servants in the advance party had fallen into the crater and had had to be rescued by one of his fellows. Although the sulphur had robbed us of our appetites, we kept up an appearance of gaiety, though in truth our smiles were somewhat forced. The rascally Neapolitan from whom we had hired the litters had promised us that we had little to fear from La Muntagna, as he called it, that she was docile as a lapdog, that her frolicsome days were over. But the rogue lied – La Muntagna was no lapdog, but a she-wolf, snarling, hissing with displeasure from a thousand fissures and like to stifle us all with her foul breath. For form's sake we braved it as long as we could, watching with silent horror as the gold leaf blackened on the teacups. We were about to descend, when a horseman galloped up the path, whipping his horse to the utmost of her strength – so much so that when they reached the summit, *the horse collapsed, upsetting the gilded table and tipping several items of the Arcanum into the crater. Imagine my dismay when I recognised the horse as Thistle, on whom I had ridden all the way from England, and the rider as my man Jerome. What the devil do you mean by this? I asked; have you no consideration for Thistle – who, by the way, had now expired amid the remaining crockery – or for The Arcanum or for the comfort of your master's guests? Damn you, sir, damn you. And I struck him across the cheek – only a glancing blow, but enough to tip him over the rim into the crater, where he hung giddily, clutching at a rock directly before me. I rested my foot gently on his fingers. Well? I said. I am awaiting an answer. Jerome looked up at me, his face green with nausea. I thought you should hear the news, sir, he replied; Naples is abuzz with it. Well? I repeated, pressing my foot a little harder. The Bastille, he gasped, the Bastille has fallen. The guests looked at each other in horror; the timid contessa swooned. With a bellow of rage I stamped my foot, causing Jerome to lose his grip and tumble into the crater, whence I have no doubt the other servants would have helped him to safety when they, too, had recovered from the shock.*

Of the two I did not know who was in the greater danger – Lady Maud or Miss T – but at least the former's intentions were now clear. I ordered the driver of the cabriolet to hurry to the foot of the mountain, where, as I had expected, I found the Erpington coach and its driver. He had, he told me, delivered The Arcanum and the two ladies into the hands of Italian porters some hours earlier and had been ordered to wait until they returned. It was with the greatest difficulty I persuaded him to leave his post and climb the mountain with me.

By now the weather had changed. Cloud had swallowed the upper half of the cone, so that the higher we climbed the more we breathed in the sulphur which it had trapped. We could feel, too, the restlessness of the volcano, which hissed and rumbled its displeasure with every step we took. Shortly after we entered the cloud we met with the litter bearers, whose rapid descent nearly swept us from the path. In broken English they explained that they had left the two English women taking tea on the edge of the crater and when they, the bearers, had insisted that they descend, the air not being fit to breathe, one of the women had produced a revolver and threatened to shoot them. 'Be off with you', she said, 'be off with you.

Take the litters with you.' Having caught their breath, the bearers continued their rapid descent, exclaiming 'Pazzo! pazzo!' until the fog swallowed them once more. The coachman was all for following them to safety but I insisted we continue to the summit. We had almost reached it when a single shot rang out. Only one, I am certain that there was only one. The coachman insists on two, but that was only later when he had taken refuge in the taverna. No, Mr Blackwood, there was but a single shot: on that I am prepared to take my oath. What was not in doubt was what we found at the summit. Our lungs burning with the sulphur, we broke through the cloud just short of the crater to find ourselves in brilliant sunshine. A gilded table and two gilded chairs stood on a terrace of flattened ash; scattered around and below them were fragments of china. Of The Arcanum, of Böttger's master work, not a single piece remained intact. Handles, spouts, shards of plate and bowl littered the inner slopes of the crater. As for the ladies, they had vanished completely. No sign of them remained – not a bloodstain, not a shred of clothing to show that they had been there, not even a spent cartridge case. I say 'case' in the singular, because I insist that there was but the one shot. But who fired it and who – if anyone – was struck by it, I really cannot say. Later that year, a body, partly preserved by volcanic ash, was discovered within the crater. It was that of a young male dressed – in so far as they could tell from the surviving rags – in eighteenth century costume, though whether that sheds any light on the disappearance of our ladies, I very much doubt.

On the table in front of me is a fragment of saucer that I rescued from The Arcanum. I chose it for the brilliance of its foliage and gold arabesques. During the time it has taken me to write this letter, the colour has faded completely. As I sign off, I find myself looking at a shard of greyish white porcelain, the colour of old bones.

I remain, sir, your sincere and troubled friend,

Henry Scudamore.

[Editor's note: As I have already indicated, Scudamore's completion of his colleague's tale occurred partly during a conversation at Tunbridge Station and partly in a letter which Blackwood received two years later. These fragments

I have pieced together to make a whole, though in so doing I have leapfrogged over Scudamore's tale of The Boy Butler, which I now restore to its rightful place between Miss Tintsford's confession and the emergency stop at Croydon.]

"Her ladyship," began Mr Scudamore, "has often told me how much she envies me. The duties of a servant, she says, are as nothing compared with the difficulties of maintaining a high station and a noble name. This is a delusion under which many of her kind labour. Many of them honestly believe that riding to hounds and spending winters in Bath is more onerous than polishing floors or peeling potatoes. I retort that it is a pity that they cannot change places with us for a day to feel the difference for themselves."

"You should have told her your tale of the Boy Butler, Henry," said Miss Tintsford. "That would have shown her that changing places is not without its dangers."

"That," replied Mr Scudamore, "is precisely what I was about to do."

Mr Scudamore's Tale of the Boy Butler

Let us call him Burton. Just good old, plain old Burton. If he had a Christian name we do not need to know it. No-one called him by it – not Lord and Lady Delaunay, not the servants, not even the great aunt whom he visited every Easter at Broadstairs. It goes without saying that the Delaunays, for whom he butlered were not Delaunays at all, nor, for that matter, were they the Earl and Countess of Bletchley with a country seat in Buckinghamshire and a town house in Bedford Square. A whiff of scandal hangs over this tale and I wish to save all concerned from embarrassment.

If Burton had a weakness, it was for the occasional wager. Though it scarcely amounted to a habit, it was, nonetheless, a chink in his moral armour, an armour that was otherwise thought to be impenetrable. Among butlers he was, everyone agreed, a prince. Masters, servants, everyone said so.

The Earl of Bletchley, on the other hand, was as easy-going as Burton was punctilious. He lived for pleasure – the chase in particular – and rarely troubled his sons or his servants with petty rules. He loved japes and jollity, horse play and buffoonery, but only when he had initiated them and his wife was out of the way. To him the instruments of pleasure were sacred. Thus he hid his cigars from the boys and was the only person to possess a key to the tantalus in his study. This rankled with Burton, who resented the implication that he might be a tippler on the sly. Now a tantalus is always a challenge to servants and this was no exception. Many were the plots that were hatched to open it, most of them fantastical and none with any chance of succeeding. But one eventually did and, to everyone's astonishment, it was Burton who proposed it.

Enter, at this point in the story, Arthur Croker, the head groom. One day over lunch Croker, having backed a 50 to 1 outsider at Newmarket, proposed a wager of five pounds to anyone who could open the tantalus and drink a glass from each decanter. "Very well," said Burton, "I accept the challenge, not because I covet his lordship's brandy, but because I have been slighted. I have a copy of every key in the house except one. That omission is an affront, a slap in the face. There must be a way into the tantalus. Honour demands it. Now let us pray."

This conversation took place before lunch and no servant was allowed to lift knife or fork before Burton had said grace. Not otherwise a religious man, Burton was very keen on grace. Custom and propriety demanded it, he said. Most of the prayers were of his own composition, all were lengthy and some - like today's - were in Latin.

"Amen," said Croker loudly at the end, his mind full of Burton's boast. "And how do you propose to do it?"

"The trick," said Burton, blowing on his soup, "is to gain his lordship's consent without his knowing that he is giving it."

"And how do you propose to do that?"

"I have not yet decided."

After lunch Burton retired to his pantry and locked the door. Croker returned to the stables, wondering if his five pounds were safe. He had made the offer confident that they were: now that Burton, of all people, had taken his wager, he was not so sure.

Next morning Burton carried the post up to Lord Delaunay and asked if he might have a word.

"Fire away," said his lordship.

"From time to time," said Burton, "the rector calls on us below stairs. On his last visit he happened to mention an old custom – mediaeval, I believe – in which a boy was crowned bishop for the month of December."

"What ever for?"

"To commemorate the Holy Innocents, and, in the words of Holy Scripture, 'to put down the mighty from their seats'."

"Holy Scripture, eh? Can't quarrel with that."

"Indeed not, my lord."

"And what did this boy bishop actually do?"

"Preach sermons, order the clergy about, ride a donkey about the cloisters. According to the rector it was the source of much merriment."

"Sounds a splendid idea," said his lordship. "Someone should revive it."

"Odd that you should say that, my lord. One of the servants – Croker, I recall – suggested that we should do precisely that. Only not with a boy bishop, but with a boy butler – and not for a month but just for a day."

His lordship's eyes lit up.

"A boy butler? What a capital scheme!"

"That's what I thought, my lord. Of course, we should have to choose the right boy, one who would enter into the spirit of the thing without overstepping the mark."

"Had you anyone in mind?"

"I thought Ned Croker, the groom's son, might do very well, my lord."

"A clever lad, by all accounts."

"Impish, too."

"Then let's do it. Hang it, why not, Burton? Life in the country is insufferably dull at times. Lady Delaunay won't like it, but I'll win her over. You'll see."

This was more easily said than done. For years, Lady Delaunay had fretted about lax morals below stairs, supposing the maids to have too many followers, prayers before meals to be neglected and grooms to be often drunk. Why she should think this, never having caught anyone red-handed, was something of a mystery, but think it she did and no-one could talk her out of it. So when her husband proposed making a boy butler for a day, she received the idea coldly. After several hours of furious argument, during which Lord Delaunay reminded her repeatedly that it was a wife's duty to obey, she finally gave way, agreeing not to oppose his wishes, provided that she was allowed to eat her meals in silence and take no part in the absurd charade that was to be enacted around her.

Meanwhile below stairs, Ned Croker was fitted – at his lordship's expense – with a miniature butler's outfit and rehearsed in a series of faux pas which were calculated to charm rather than offend. He proved an apt pupil. Not only were the Delaunays not offended, but declared themselves charmed, quite charmed by a day which had begun with his cleaning the silver with saddle soap and ending with his serving the courses at dinner in the wrong order and the last course, which should have been brandied fruits, not at all. In reply to his lordship's enquiries, word came up from the kitchen that it was past the butler's bed time and that he had retired, worn out, for the night. At the news Lord Delaunay and his sons guffawed loudly and even her ladyship was forced to conceal the tiniest of smiles in the napkin which Ned Croker had earlier referred to as a 'serviette'.

On the stroke of midnight, when the rest of the family were in bed, Lord Delaunay summoned Burton to review the day's events.

"I must say," said his lordship unlocking the tantalus and pouring himself a drink, "I haven't enjoyed a jape so much since we kidnapped the chaplain at Eton. Devil of a fuss. Good fun, though. We must do it again sometime – boy butlering, I mean, not kidnapping the chaplain."

Burton judged his moment carefully before venturing his next remark. It was important not to appear too eager.

"The servants thought it a tremendous jape, too, my lord," he said. "They even went so far as to suggest ..." He hesitated.

"Well?"

"A foolish thought, my lord. Too foolish to mention. I'm sorry I brought it up."

"But hang it, Burton, you can't just leave it there."

"Well, my lord, one of the footmen said wouldn't it be diverting if ... No, really, I can't."

"If what?"

"If you and I were to change places."

His lordship stared into the depths of his glass.

"Her ladyship wouldn't like it. Her ladyship wouldn't like it at all."

"Indeed not, my lord, Forgive me for mentioning it."

"But what a jape it would be, eh? You here for a day and me down stairs misbehaving with the servants. I can see it all. Hang it all, Burton, let's do it."

Burton had judged his moment well. His lordship was tiring of the pleasures of the chase in the country and longing to resume them in Bedford Square.

"Very well," replied Burton. "But be prepared for things to go wrong."

"Oh, they won't. Look at today. It went like a dream."

"But it could have been a nightmare."

"Don't be such a bore, Burton. Shall we say this time next week?"

Lord Delaunay emptied the glass and locked the tantalus.

"This time next week, my lord."

Plain Mr Delaunay got off to a disappointing start. He thought he would surprise his wife by taking her tea. He asked cook to show him the trick of it, as well as the complicated business of making up a tray. After several stops to catch his breath, he found himself outside her door. He knocked and entered.

"What are you doing here?" she demanded. ""You know I don't allow you in here before lunch."

"I've brought your tea, milady."

"Don't be ridiculous, Charles," she said. "I have told you that I have no intention of playing this silly game. If you want to dress up and make a fool of yourself, then that is your affair, but don't expect me to join in. And if Burton expects that I shall treat him with the deference which he thinks his due, then he is in for a nasty shock."

"And if I command it?" Lord Delaunay asked, briefly resuming his old self.

"Command it, Delaunay?" she replied, addressing his new one. "Who are you to command me? You forget yourself. You are, after all, only the butler."

Lord Delaunay picked up the tray and marched out of the room in a huff. He returned to the kitchen and, not quite knowing to do next, took himself to the butler's pantry, a room which, he now realised, he had not entered before, Burton always having received him on the threshold whenever he called.

Delaunay ventured inside. It was sparsely furnished. Over the mantelpiece there was an oleograph of the Queen and Prince Albert. On a shelf were arranged tins of silver polish, bottles of linseed oil, a wick trimmer, the wine log with every entry dated by Burton and countersigned by his lordship, a brass bell and an ivory-handled corkscrew. In the corner was an iron-framed bed covered with a tartan blanket. The pillow, his lordship noted, was white as snow and hard as stone. But what attracted his lordship's attention most was a padlocked cupboard. Padlocks suggested hidden treasures, even guilty secrets. To his irritation none of the keys on Burton's ring fitted the lock. Burton, blast him, had not played fair. He was about to give up when he heard footsteps in the corridor outside and, opening the door, found Croker and his son about to disappear into the kitchen.

"Croker," he called, "do you have a key a key to the cupboard in the pantry? Burton omitted to give me one."

"I can't say I do, Mr Delaunay" – his lordship winced at the ease with which Croker called him Mr Delaunay – "but I do have something better – my boy Ned. I've frequently to give him a hiding for going in places he's no business going. Still, he's a useful chap to have in an emergency. And this, I take it, is an emergency?"

Delaunay had by now convinced himself that it was. After a few minutes prodding and poking with a clasp knife, the young cracksman succeeded in forcing the lock and the door swung open. Delaunay tipped him sixpence and dismissed the Crokers from the pantry.

The hidden treasures seemed to consist entirely of books, most of them scuffed from constant use. He took them out of the cupboard and stacked them on the table. An Eton Latin Grammar (loose in the hinges, probably second hand), a Liddell and Scott (newish, but shiny with use, ditto), an Iliad, a Caesar's Gallic Wars, a Virgil ... A Virgil! Hah! What memories that brought back! What scrapes, what japes, what romps, what larks! Oh, the hampers and the scrimmages, the fixtures and the fisticuffs! Yes, Virgil, too, was a fond memory, though he would never have admitted to liking him at the time. The opening he was particularly fond of. How did it go? *Arma virumque cano* – something, something – *fato profugus laviniaque venit*. Arms and the man I sing. Stirring stuff. A good egg, Virgil. He had surprised himself by how much he had remembered. For that he had Beaky Benfield to thank who had thrashed a daily portion into him at Eton. He skipped ahead to where Burton had inserted a bookmark. Ah, Dido. He'd always had a soft spot for Dido. So, too, it seemed, had Burton. A bit histrionic for his taste; all the same he wouldn't have minded a bout or two with her on the quiet. And the underworld bit, where was that? Ah, there it was. *Facilis descensus Averno*, etc. Fine stuff. Told Beaky Benfield that whatever Virgil may have said the way to hell was far from easy; he knew, he'd been looking for it all term. Beaky had given him six for this cheek.

And there were other surprises in the pile of books. A Euclid, Ruskin's *Modern Painters*, Carlyle's *French Revolution*. To Lord Delaunay it looked very much as if Burton had been trying to educate himself in his idle moments. Now there was a fine thing! A butler trying to best his betters! There were friends of his who would have sacked their butlers for such presumption. But he took a more enlightened view. Knowledge was the spirit of the age. He was all for it. Why shouldn't butlers read Euclid or stable boys *The French Revolution?* Though on second thoughts it might be safer if the butlers read *The French Revolution* and the stable boys Euclid. And what was this? *Vestiges of the Natural History of Creation* by Anon. He opened a page at random and read: "Full of rude energy and unregulated impulse, the inferior mind no more requires a superior nature to act as its master than the superior nature require to be surrounded by rough elements on which to exercise its gifts as a tutelary power." Well, the Crokers and their like probably had little enough need of him, though whether he and his ilk could do without the Crokers was hard to tell. Quite possibly not. Seating himself in Burton's armchair, he turned to *Vestiges* and sought further enlightenment.

If his lordship had been vexed by the absence of a key, Burton was irritated by the presence of one. Not the key to the tantalus – that he had already tried, though he had delayed the opening of the decanters until Croker was there to witness it – no, this was an unfamiliar key, a key which, from the polish on it, looked as if it was in constant use. Every other key on his lordship's key ring he could account for; this one was a mystery. Worse, it was a rebuke – further proof, in fact, that Lord Delaunay did not wholly trust him. This continued to rankle. And there was another consideration, too. To play the lord, he must know all his lordship's secrets and, by God, know them he would. If he had to search the house from top to bottom, he would find the lock to which it fitted, and he would start, here, in his lordship's study.

The gong had sounded for lunch before he found it. Concealed behind Fordyce's *Sermons* was the lock to a hidden door upon whose panels his lordship's bookshelves were attached. At a touch they swung open and Burton found himself in a small book-lined recess lit by a skylight concealed on the leads. He was astonished. How could he have overlooked a hidden space in a house where he had worked for nearly twenty years? More astonishing still was the nature of the books. After a cursory glance, Burton realised that he had stumbled across what is euphemistically known as a gentleman's library. Here were *The Lustful Turk*, *Nunnery Tales*, *The Priapic Scriptures*, *Miss Coote's Confessions*, *The Voluptuary's Miscellany*, *Curiositates Eroticae* and many more. Lying open on a small table was *The Mermaid and the Octopus*, finely bound and copiously illustrated. For several minutes he gazed, spellbound (though disapprovingly), at a cat's cradle of writhing limbs and tentacles ...

"Mr Scudamore," I interrupted, "Certain details are best left unspecified, especially when there are ladies present. May we hurry over this part of the story and re-join Delaunay in the butler's pantry?"

"May we do no such thing," said Miss T. "Don't be such a prude, Blackwood. The days when I might have been shocked by such a thing have long since gone. For which, of course, I have her ladyship to thank."

"Pigs!" exclaimed Lady Rippledale. "Look at them! Wallowing in filth!"

I was about to agree, albeit in more measured terms, when I realised that she was pointing out of the carriage window to a small abattoir next to Hatcham Iron Works.

"In any case," continued Miss T, "Erpington Purlieu was no stranger to such literature. How do you suppose that I, a respectable tradesman's daughter, was able to conduct such a libidinous correspondence with her ladyship? Without Aretino's *School of Whoredom* I couldn't have imagined more than a peck on the cheek and neither, I suspect, could her ladyship.

Let us re-join Burton at lunch, continued Mr Scudamore, which turned out to be every bit as bad as her ladyship had feared. Not only was Lord Delaunay more inept than Ned Croker, but her sons, Gerard and Gervase, having their father at their mercy, were taking full advantage of the situation. From soup to dessert – or rather from jelly to pigeon pie, since that was the order in which the courses were served – it was 'Delaunay, do this' and 'Delaunay do that' until the poor man was quite exhausted. Dishes were summoned from the kitchen and returned untasted simply to make him run up and down stairs and, when he tried to send a footman in his place, was told to treat his underlings with more consideration. The game only came to an end when Burton, who was shy of checking their young lordships, suggested that Delaunay's legs were not quite as young as theirs and did not take as kindly to stairs. Lady Delaunay toyed with her food primly during lunch, but, true to her promise, kept her thoughts to herself.

When, finally, Lord Delaunay descended to take lunch with the servants, he found them all seated at the table waiting for him.

"Don't wait for me," he said. "Tuck in."

"What about grace?" asked cook.

"Grace?" echoed his lordship.

"Mr Burton always says grace."

"Oh, phooey to grace," replied Lord Delaunay. "I'm starving."

There were murmurs of approval all round the table. Lord Delaunay smiled benignly. He was certainly having a better time of it than Burton, who had looked decidedly ill at ease dining with his betters. No, better to be a déclassé lord than an ennobled butler. Not only was he enjoying the respect of his peers, but there was an afternoon of Virgil to look forward to and, since there was a Liddell and Scott to hand, he might even try a page or two of Homer. He found himself thinking quite fondly of Beaky Benfield, who had obviously done a better job than either of them had supposed at the time. In the meantime, the pigeon pie was really rather good, as, in their turn, were the jelly and the cheese. Say what you like, he thought, a day which had begun inauspiciously was turning out rather well.

That was not, of course, how Lady Delaunay saw it. She had kept her end of the bargain scrupulously. During lunch she had held her tongue, allowing her sons to abuse their father without check. But that did not mean she condoned it. Far from it. She wanted the madness to end forthwith. She simply could not endure another meal under the present rules of engagement. Before her anger had chance to cool, she wrote a note and, summoning her two sons, charged them to deliver it to their father in the butler's pantry. "Under no circumstances are you to open it," she told them, "but when he has read it, you are to do everything he tells you. And remember, however much he may pretend otherwise, he is your father and should be obeyed."

"She says I'm to teach you a lesson you won't forget," said his lordship, when he had read the letter.

"What for?" asked Gerard.

"For being disrespectful at lunch."

"But you're only the butler, pa."

"Not according to this note."

"Does that mean you're going to whack us?"

"No," said his father, "I'm going to teach you a different sort of lesson. We're going to read Virgil together."

"But Virgil is rot, pa," said Gervase. "Everyone at school says so. Well, not the masters obviously, but ..."

"I should hope not. Who are the masters these days, by the way?"

"There's 'Shrimp' Potter ..."

"He teaches Euclid ..."

" 'Daisy' Trubshaw, who supervises prep ..."

"Tries to ..."

"Beaky Benfield ..."

"Good Lord!" exclaimed Delaunay. "I had no idea Beaky was still alive."

"Only just, though he still has a strong right arm."

"Whack!"

"One day, you'll be as grateful to Beaky as I am. Now let's start with this passage here."

And it was at that moment that the Rev. Norbert Penrose MA (Oxon) put in an appearance. He had arrived at the house not knowing quite what to expect, but whatever it was, it certainly wasn't the sight of the butler and his two sons translating Virgil. As newly appointed curate, he had decided to introduce himself to the local gentry, not because he was a snob – anything but – but because he had long suspected that the morals of the idle rich were looser than those of the hardworking poor. And here, it seemed, was the proof of it. A sermon, one of his best, began to form in his mind.

"Allow me," he said, "to congratulate you on your initiative. I take it these are your sons, sir?"

Delaunay nodded.

"My name," continued the clergyman, extending his hand, "is Norbert Penrose MA (Oxon), the newly appointed curate of St Grimbald's. And you, if I might make so bold, are?"

"Burtons," said Gervase Delaunay. "Butler Burton," – pointing to his father – "Burton Major, Burton Minor."

"And do you like Virgil, young man?"

"My brother and I think he's a very ..."

Gervase struggled for an epithet.

"... a very manly writer," added Gerard.

"That's it," said Gervase. "He's a very manly writer, ain't he, pa?"

Delaunay nodded. "Manly is the word," he said.

A whole sermon on manliness popped into the Reverend Penrose's mind fully formed.

"I am sure the Reverend Penrose has no wish to spend more time than is necessary among the servants," said Lord Delaunay. "Let me take you to his lordship."

"I would not dream of disrupting the good work," he said. "One of the maidservants will show me the way."

Burton, too, had received a visitor after lunch, though scarcely an unexpected one. In order to claim his fiver, he needed to have the opening of the tantalus witnessed by Croker. The business done, he opened the door of the hidden library and beckoned Croker to follow.

"Have you seen what's in here?" he asked.

Croker, who had remained in the study, hoping to snatch a glass or two from the tantalus unobserved, replied that, yes, of course he had, since it was he who had put them there in the first place.

"You?" asked Burton, reappearing in the doorway.

"What I mean is that I fetched them for him, the books, you know. Well, most of them, anyway."

"You mean you actually went into shops – and I presume there are shops which sell such things – and asked in cold blood for *The Lustful Turk* and *Miss Coote's Confessions?*"

"It was more discreet than that. I was told to go to a certain address in Holywell Street where a parcel would be waiting for me and that I was to collect it and bring it to his lordship."

"So you never actually saw what was in the parcels?"

"Oh, yes, I got Ned to undo them. He's very good at that – and at re-parcelling, too. His lordship never suspected a thing. My main worry wasn't that he would find out, but that Ned would read the books – which is why, between unwrapping and re-wrapping, they never left my person."

"But if you knew all along that there was such a library, why didn't you tell me?"

"You never asked."

Imagine for a moment that you are a dagurreotypist. You have set up your apparatus in Lord Delaunay's study to capture the scene for posterity. Through the lens you see Croker, one hand on the tantalus, sitting in his lordship's armchair. He has just lit a cigar. In his green frock coat and high-waisted pants, he looks quite the country gentleman. Opposite him, in the doorway of the secret library, Burton holds up *The Mermaid and the Octopus*, open at one of its more lurid pages. In his tasselled riding boots, he, too, might pass for a country gent, were it not for the illustration he is holding up. In the middle of the daguerrotype, however, there is a blemish, a blur where a young clergyman has advanced into the room, recoiled in horror and retreated hastily towards the door. Unfreeze the scene and it continues thus:

Penrose opened and closed his mouth several times before he could bring himself to speak.

"Does her ladyship know about this?" he enquired at last.

It was an awkward beginning, but Penrose did not know what else to say.

"Just what I was asking his lordship myself," said Croker. "I didn't beat about the bush, but asked him straight out, man to man, 'What if my sister were to find out? What if she were to stumble upon your squalid little collection by accident? What then, eh? She is a sensitive, refined girl – I still think of her as a girl – think what the shock might do to her.'"

"Did I understand you to say your sister?" asked Penrose.

"I am her ladyship's brother, Viscount Legerdemain," continued Croker, christening himself after the 50 to 1 outsider he had backed at Newmarket, "And whom do I have the honour of addressing?"

"The Reverend Norbert Penrose MA (Oxon), recently appointed curate of St Grimbald's."

"Well, Norbert Penrose MA (Oxon)," said the Viscount, rising to his feet and putting his arm round his reverence's shoulder. "I'm sure we are agreed that this should go no further. Her ladyship must know nothing of it, nor must the boys."

Penrose nodded fervently.

"Now you have my word that the books will be destroyed. Of course, it will have to be done discreetly. We can't throw an entire library on to the bonfire and hope no-one will notice. The books will have to be consigned to the flames a few at a time."

"Might I make a suggestion?" said Burton, entering into the spirit of the thing. "Burton the butler has a large locking cupboard in his pantry. Perhaps the books might go there, pending their destruction."

"And the books, which I believe Burton keeps in there, might find a temporary home on the empty shelves up here," said the Viscount.

"That seems an admirable idea", said Penrose, "though I fear the butler will feel the loss of his books keenly."

"Indeed he will," sighed Burton.

"I encountered him on the way here," said Penrose. "He and his son were hard at work with their Latin lessons. That is how boys should be brought up."

"That it should come to this!" said the Viscount. "That gentlemen should look to their servants for example! What an age we live in, Mr Penrose MA! what an age we live in! May I suggest that you return to St Grimbald's and pray that his lordship might return to the paths of virtue and that my sister might not know that he ever strayed from them."

"Amen to that," said Penrose.

"Let me see you to the park gates."

"There is no need for that. I rode here. My horse in the stables."

"Then let me see you to the stables."

Once he had seen Penrose off the premises, Croker headed for the butler's pantry. He marched in without ceremony, ejected the boys, who regarded their deliverance from Virgil as heaven-sent, and told his lordship what had happened.

"I don't care if some confounded parson knows about the books," said his lordship, "but I do care about Burton. Whatever will he think of me?"

"Don't worry about him, my lord. A temporary exchange of books will keep him happy."

"And what if the parson talks?"

"He won't."

"You seem very sure of that."

"His silence is easily purchased. I took the liberty of slipping the *Curiositates Eroticae* into his saddle bag when I accompanied him to the stables. Even as we speak my boy Ned is writing an anonymous note – full of the misspellings which come naturally to him – apprising the rector that his curate has some unusual reading matter in his saddle bag. I think we shall find that the Reverend Penrose will shortly be taking up a curacy very far from here."

"Well done, Croker. But why the *Curiositates*, of all things?"

"I thought it a kindness, my lord. If he is caught with it, he can always claim that he was trying to improve his Latin."

"You think of everything, Croker. However can I repay you?"

"I shall think of something, my lord; I shall think of something."

As the clocks struck midnight, Burton and Lord Delaunay returned to their quarters to reflect on the day. For neither had it lived up to expectations, though there had been compensations of a sort: for his lordship a re-acquaintance with Virgil, for Burton a fiver from Croker. But there were regrets, too: Burton was grieved by the loss of his library, Lord Delaunay embarrassed by the discovery of his.

On the stroke of midnight the maidservant, who was taking Lady Delaunay her hot milk, found a neatly wrapped parcel on the mat outside her door. She put it on the tray and took it in to her ladyship. Later, when she had dismissed the maid and drunk the milk, her ladyship opened the parcel. It was a book entitled *Miss Coote's Confessions* by Z, a novel by the look of it. She opened it and began to read.

As the clocks chimed midnight throughout the rectory, the Reverend Norbert Penrose MA (Oxon) fell to his knees. He had stayed up late to finish his sermon on manliness among the labouring classes and was now ready for bed. "Almighty God," he prayed, "unto whom all hearts be open, all desires known and from whom no secrets are hid, cleanse the thoughts of our hearts." There was a tap on the door. "Penrose," said the rector's voice, "would you care to step outside. I should like a word with you."

The London season has begun. In the largest house in Bedford Square every window is ablaze with lights. The Earl and Countess of Bletchley have invited a distinguished company to dinner and a small crowd has gathered to watch it arrive. And what a company! Bedford Square has not seen its like for many a year – Lord and Lady Paramount, Sir Cedric (recently appointed Attorney General) and Lady Ibbs, The Honourable and Mrs Everard Plume, Mr Horace Stackhouse, the American railroad magnate, Archdeacon and Mrs Podmore, Count Zopido, the Piedmontese Ambassador and alleged author of privately printed erotica, a couple of colonels and many, many more. Carriage after carriage arrives, each bearing a more distinguished coat of arms than the last, but illustrious as the guests may be, they are here to honour one man and he, as it happens, the last to arrive. To the watching crowd's surprise, he arrives in an ordinary cab and is greeted by the Earl himself. It is Beaky Benfield, who has just announced his retirement from Eton after fifty years of pummelling Horace and Virgil into the noddles of reluctant schoolboys. After dinner, his lordship hopes to show Beaky his newly installed library, partly to reassure him that his pummelling has borne fruit and partly to seek his advice. His lordship has decided to take up his seat in the House of Lords at last and wants to model his maiden speech on Cicero and Demosthenes.

Meanwhile the Delaunays' country house has been shut up for the winter. Dust sheets have been spread over the furniture, carpets raised for beating, chandeliers lowered for cleaning. Most of the staff have accompanied the family to London. One of the few to remain is Croker, who from time to time dresses up as Viscount Legerdemain and spends the day browsing in the gun room or lounging in Lord Delaunay's study, where he helps himself from the tantalus, for which he now has a key. He is there on the evening of the dinner in Bedford Square. At about 7.30, he consults his watch, a gold hunter purchased with the winnings from his equine namesake, and murmurs, "About now I should think."

Outside the dining room in Bedford Square, Lady Delaunay calls for quiet and informs guests that owing to the sudden indisposition of their regular butler, they have had to call on the services of a substitute.

"A boy, in fact," she says. "He is only fourteen, but I think you will find him not inexperienced."

A hand squeezes her fingers. She looks up and catches Count Zopido's eye. He smiles faintly. She squeezes the hand back.

Meanwhile, Burton, having been made redundant for the evening, finds himself outside the Argyll Rooms, where, had he not read about them in his lordship's library, would have been astonished by what he found. Forewarned and thus forearmed, he decides – cautiously – to enjoy himself.

8

CROYDON TO TUNBRIDGE

An unexpected change of compartment
The Medium's Tale of Lady Milo and the Dollymops
The Ecclesiastical Architect's Tale of Crockford's Commotions
Concerning Stumps and the Bishop
We take leave of our Tunbridge friends

Mr Scudamore had scarcely finished his tale – assuming, that is, that he had not intended us to follow Burton into the Argyll Rooms – when there was a shriek from *Hengist* and a furious application of brakes, which threw Lady Rippledale across the compartment into his lap. We appeared to have stopped in Croydon Station, though our carriage, which was next to the locomotive, had come to rest somewhat forward of the platform. Hearing screams and shouts from further down the train, I jumped down on to the track and made my way towards the seat of the commotion. I had just begun to climb the ramp when the whistle blew, the crowd on the platform dispersed and the train began to move forward. I ran alongside, but it gathered speed rapidly and had I not grasped a hand that was extended to me from a second class carriage, I should have had to resign myself to a long wait on Croydon Station. I was pulled through an open door and, when I had had a chance to recover, found myself among familiar faces.

"Welcome aboard, Mr Blackwood," said Dr leGrove, releasing my hand. "You are just in time to hear Mme Fontana's story."

"If I might be permitted to catch my breath first," I gasped.

"And whilst you do so," said Mme Fontana, "I should inform you that Dr leGrove has just doubted my fitness for the work I have undertaken – not my personal fitness, you understand, but that of my sex in general. Encounters with spirits, he says, are best left to men like himself. And this, you will observe, despite my having admitted that the only spirits I try to raise are those of my clients. You may consider me a fraud – and I make no bones about it, I am – but my clients would not thank you for exposing me and, were I to give up, they would seek solace elsewhere. Dr leGrove knows this but still thinks that as a woman I have no right to be meddling with the Other Side. Perhaps he thinks that as a woman I have no right to be practising fraud either and that that, too, should be left exclusively to men. Yet do we not read in our newspapers every day of women convicted – even transported – as accomplices, fences, decoys? I put it to you, if women can be partners in crime, may they not be mistresses of it as well? Well, it might surprise you to learn that in one case at least they are. Which brings me to my tale, so, if you have sufficiently recovered your breath, Mr Blackwood, I shall begin."

"I am out of breath," I replied, "because I had to run for the train, though why it stopped at Croydon so suddenly I cannot explain."

"A body on the line," said Mr Critchley.

"Alive or dead?" I asked.

"Oh, very much alive, according to the porter," said Mr Bartholomew.

"Male or female?"

"Female," said Mr Dacre, "or so we were led to believe."

"Did I understand you to say that your story concerned crimi-nals?" interrupted Miss Osgood, who had begun the return journey in the second-class carriage, presuming that at some stage I would join her there.

"And spirits," said Mme Fontana.

"Mannerly ones, I hope."

"Mannerly enough, though one cannot expect criminals, even when they are women, to be entirely ladylike."

"Could you not make them so?"

"And belie the facts? I think not. You must take the rough with the smooth, Miss Osgood, however little of the latter there may be."

The Medium's Tale of Lady Milo and the Dollymops

Though my client did not act like a lady, she still called herself one. "A Lady Milo to see you, mum," announced the maidservant.

"Does she look like a lady?" I asked.

"Too many baubles," said the maidservant.

"Well, does she sound like one?"

"Too many cuss-words."

"Does she look as if she has money?"

"Jingling with it."

"Then show her up."

From her title to her green turban, Lady Milo was every inch the manufactured article. She wore the clothes of a lady without the restraint of one. There were too many frills and flourishes, too many baubles at wrist and throat. Round her shoulders she wore a fur stole, the head and feet still dangling, the pelt matted and worn.

"My business," she began, "is crime." – She pronounced it 'crame.' Having awarded herself a title, she had evidently felt the need of the vowels to go with it. – "Housebreaking mainly. I have a dozen girls working for me, none over thirty, none under seven."

"Seven?"

"Seven year old girl chavies can squeeze through tighter windows than any boy. None of them drinks, none of them blows. None. No dollymops, no judies. But some of them ..."

"Excuse me, but why are you telling me this? How can you be certain that I shall not go to the police?"

"Because there's no way of hiding from you what I need you to do and because if the pigs show up, you will hear from us. None of my girls blabs." – She pronounced it 'blebs' – "We shall know it was you."

I am not, as Dr leGrove will testify, easily intimidated. I can hold my own. Metaphorically speaking, I can bite and scratch, but so, too, could Lady Milo. And there I do not speak metaphorically. And not just bite and scratch, but worse, much worse. She frequently had resort, she told me, to a sand-filled stocking nicknamed The Chaplain. So I was, let me be frank, intimidated.

"As I say," she continued, "none of my girls blabs, but some can't leave the men alone. No fines, no beatings, not The Chaplain himself, will cure them of it. Which brings me to the present catastrophe." – or, as she had it, 'cetestrophe' – "One of my girls has moved on and I need to have words urgently."

"Can't you write?"

"Don't be a fool. She's dead. Time is running out. I need to have words now. No excuses. Draw the blinds, cut the cards, do whatever you have to do, but fetch her now."

What was I to do? It was The Chaplain if I refused. To create a convincing fraud requires preparation and even if I had had time to prepare, Lady Milo would soon have found out that I had deceived her. I made excuses. I tried to postpone the séance. Not only would she not be persuaded, she became more threatening; she kissed the animal she wore round her neck on the nose, murmuring, "If she gives the answer we're looking for, there's money in it for her, isn't there, Rumpus. If not ..."

She tugged sharply on Rumpus's tail, causing him to open his jaws in a silent snarl.

"What do you want to know?" I asked, trying to sound confident in my ability to produce satisfying answer.

"Ask her which is the jerryshop."

"I beg your pardon?"

She placed a pawnshop ticket on the table.

"This is the ticket. Which is the shop?"

"I don't understand."

"You don't need to. Just ask the question."

But I did need to understand. Without knowing the reason for the question, I could not hope to fabricate an answer. In desperation, I mumbled some hocus pocus about astral projections and insisted that they could not be hurried.

"Well, this time they'll have to be," she said. "If it helps, I'll tell you this much. Fences and cracksmen are always separate. On steals, one sells; the two never meet. What isn't known can't be blown. This one - no dollymop, I promise you - emptied a dressing table in Caldicott Square. Luggers, rings, baubles, all gold, very nice, and sewed them into a fox fur which she took to the jerryshop. That's how we do it; that's how the game is played. She hands me the ticket, I hands the ticket to the fence, the fence picks up the goods and unstitches the fox. No names, no traces. Nice and tidy."

"But not this time?"

"How could it? Her man hit her. Not enough to wound, thinks he, but strong enough, as it happens, to kill. I'm so sorry, he says, so very, very sorry. No doubt he was. Handing over the mortal remains, he even shed a tear. The girl we dumped. Him too. Captain Arrow he called himself, though I doubt he'd ever seen the inside of a uniform. Well, he's shot now, fired off into the mud at Tilbury. The ticket - the jerryshop ticket - I have, but not the name of the adjective shop. Now that I need to know because the ticket's got tomorrow's date on it."

She pushed the ticket to the middle of the table, where, catching the heat of the lamp, it curled at the edges.

"So where" - pointing at the ticket - "where is it?"

For you to understand my predicament, I must reveal a few tricks of the trade. Six to eight is the ideal number for a séance. We all sit at a heavy mahogany table holding hands; the lights are dimmed; and, after a few twitches and groans, I announce that I am through to the Other Side. Clients are then free to put questions to the spirits, who respond by knocking on the table - once for no, thrice for yes. The table is supported on a stout centre leg which flares out towards the base and rests on four wooden claws. The leg, as you may have guessed, is hollow. Beneath it, under the floor, there is a small chamber which conceals Astrid, my assistant. When a question is asked, she inserts a rod into the leg and taps on the underside of the table. Described thus, it sounds soulless and mechanical, but there is an art to it and Astrid is a true artist. She has at her disposal a variety of rods, some pointed, some blunt, some metal, some wood. Some have a sponge on the end, some a wire brush. You would be astonished at the variety of effects she can produce. A no can be peremptory or regretful, depending on the device used; a yes hesitant or joyful. These replies can be further enhanced by bells, gongs and even – if the subject met death by drowning – the splashing of water in a bucket.

For all this I need time to prepare, but Lady Milo had insisted on an immediate reply, as if I were some kind of telegraph office, so I had no alternative but to resort to joint cracking. Now those who specialise in this form of deception practise regularly, whereas I, though once proficient, had not tried it for many years. Yet I had no alternative. Lady Milo had threatened me: I could not refuse. I led the way to the consulting room and prayed to God that my joints would not fail me. We sat at the table and she, perhaps suspecting some trickery, grasped my hand tightly. The disablement of my knuckles left me only knees and toes to reply with. Fortunately, my toes proved to be on good form and gave crisp answers to each of Lady Milo's questions. One by one she worked her way through all the pawnbrokers in the Mile End Road, with which she was obviously familiar and from which she had taken her title. "Was it Bogle Brothers?" she asked. "Was it Lorrimer's? Was it Freeman's? Was it Eastwood and Son?" To each I gave a single crack. Sooner or later, I knew that I should have to give three cracks for yes. But when? "Was it Finbow's? Was it Shadlock's?" When would I have to commit myself to what would almost certainly be the wrong answer? The decision forced itself on me soon after we left the Mile End Road. My toes were starting to tire. I doubted I had three cracks left to give.

Was it this, was it that? The interrogation was relentless. Suddenly we found ourselves in Cheapside approaching St Paul's. I remembered being stuck on an omnibus only a few weeks earlier and seeing a tall, masculine-looking woman in a pink Bo Peep bonnet come out of a pawnbrokers called ... now what was it called? I could not for the life of me remember.

"Jones and Parsley," said Lady Milo.

Without thinking I replied with three loud cracks, after which my toes collapsed into my boots, utterly spent.

"The bitch!" said Lady Milo. "The stupid adjective bitch. I told her to steer clear of them. Every gonolph and flimp uses them. The pigs know about them.

Jones is not to be trusted and Parsley's most likely a nose. Trusted or not, though, I've got to risk it. Can't afford not to, not with one day left on the ticket."

She rose to her feet with a clatter of the bangles and pulled a purse from her bag. "Here," she said and threw it on the table.

From the clatter of coins I could hear that it was generously filled.

"That's for your trouble," she said, "that and a retainer."

"A retainer?" I said, horrified.

"If you've given me the right answer, I shall want to use you again; if not, I shall be back to recover my money and I might – how shall I put it? – be irritable. And people don't like it when I get irritable, do they, Rumpus?" she said, addressing the snarling head on her fur stole.

Long after she was gone I remained at the table staring into the lamp, too shaken, too exhausted to move. The precariousness of my situation was all too obvious. Lady Milo had only to visit Jones and Parsley to discover that she had been deceived. I had no alternative but to go into hiding. Instructing the maidservant to send me the names of callers to the house, I sought refuge with a cousin in Wales. There, on the slopes of distant Snowdonia, I settled down to ride out the storm. But there was no storm. Reports from London contained no sightings of Lady Milo, and in less than a month I decided that it was safe to return. Weeks went by, months, and still there was no word from her. I began to look over my shoulder less frequently and dared to feel safe from the attentions of The Chaplain. Then one day she turned up unannounced. How she managed to evade the maidservant I do not know, but she entered my consulting room, Rumpus draped round her neck, and seated herself at the table as if in readiness for a séance. She did not look angry, at least not with me, though her turban on this occasion was ominously scarlet.

"You was right," she said, "though I should have guessed. Jones and Parsley! Who else? None of the Mile End jerryshops was good enough for her. Always went for the flash, though that was only after she went with Captain Arrow and much good that did her. Or him."

I tried to conceal my astonishment that my guess had proved correct and also my dread that she had come with a new demand, insisting on her right since she had paid me a retainer. My fears were fully justified. She had come with a new demand and, as before, insisted on an immediate answer.

"Another casualty," she announced, "and all her own fault. Fell through a
skylight and broke her neck. This girl – let's call her Harmonia, though she was
anything but – cracks an office. Cash box, pass keys, nice little haul. In through the
sky light, out through the sky light. Done it a hundred times before, only this time
the box is heavy, see – been a good day at the office – and half way up the rope she
drops it. No hiding it, oh no, a peal of bells that one. Every watchman in the district
must have heard it. There's a chase across the rooftops. It's been raining ... No doubt
you can guess the rest. Only you can't, because this time there's a twist. It turns that
she's done this crack before. Same office, the very one. No word to me, no one for all
and all for one: this was one for one, keep mum. Only the week before it was. And
how do I know? From the inquest. The night watchman told the tale. Same lay only
the week before. Skylight, rope, cashbox. The very one. Only she kept it to herself. So
this is my question – where did she hide the stiff? where was the lurk? I want to talk
to her now – and I mean talk. No table rapping. Table rapping's no good, not if you
don't know what questions to ask."

Suddenly she started shouting as if the spirit of Harmonia were in the room.

"How could you do this to me? I raised you up. You was just a common trull,
a hoister, a dipper and I raised you up. Where is it? Where's the stiff, you double-
dealing trollop?"

She seized my wrist across the table.

"You," she said. "Get hold of her."

I did not know what to do. I adopted my trance pose, not because I hoped to
summon some non-existent spirit, but because I wanted time to think.

"Well?" she asked.

I sat silently, staring unblinkingly into space.

"Well? Well?"

"She won't answer," I said at last.

"Then try harder."

I intensified my stare.

"Well?"

"Nothing. She won't talk."

"But is she there?"

"Oh yes," I lied. "She's there, right enough, shaking her head at me, refusing
to talk."

"We'll see about that," said Lady Milo, rising to her feet. "She's not going to get away with this. I'll be back. I'll bring a friend. She'll open her up. Being dead won't make no difference. She'll open her up."

If Lady Milo had pretensions to gentility, the friend had none. She wore a bowler hat and check jacket, from the breast pocket of which protruded a clay pipe. For the purposes of this narrative I shall refer to her as Adjective, since she had a fondness for that part of speech and one member of it in particular. On this, her third visit, Lady Milo, who wore a black silk turban and had changed Rumpus for something even more alarming, took a back seat and let Adjective do the talking. Adjective declined the proffered hand shake and told me to get on with it, she and Lady Em having got no adjective time to waste.

"Call her up," she ordered.

I professed not to know whom she was referring to.

"What are we calling her?" she asked Lady Em.

"Harmonia," said her companion.

"Right, you," replied Adjective. "Call up Armonia and ask her how she done the crack. And, more's to the point, where she put the goods."

"She might come quicker if you give her a haitch," remarked Lady Milo tartly.

Although Adjective was even more frightful than I had expected, she had not caught me unprepared. Assuming that neither she nor Lady Milo would tolerate Harmonia's refusal to speak a second time, I had laid a false trail, which would, I hoped, persuade them that they were at a cold scent. I did not, however, intend to direct them to it immediately. On her previous visit, Lady Milo had boasted that she would bring along someone from whom even the dead could not hide. This was not just a figure of speech: I could see she meant it literally. Scared as I was, I was curious to see her at work. How, I wondered, did one set about threatening a spirit? It was obvious that I would not have to wait long to find out, for Adjective was in a hurry.

"Right, Armonia," said Adjective, before I had even drawn the blinds, "I know you're there, so let's not waste time. Where is it? Where's the" – well, you can imagine the adjectives for yourselves from now on – "the goods?"

I drew the blinds, turned the lamp down low and, ignoring Adjective's admonitions to get a move on, began to assume a trance-like state. After several minutes, I emitted a faint falsetto squeak.

"Speak up. Can't hear a word."

I repeated the squeak, this time a little louder.

"Still didn't get you."

I had been practising my ventriloquism and now felt confident enough to attempt a sentence or two.

"Cold, so cold," I squeaked.

"You surprise me," scoffed Lady Milo. "I thought it would be quite hot where you was."

"Don't sound much like her," said Adjective. "Too genteel."

I repeated the phrase, this time trying to cockneyfy the vowels.

"Nah, that's not her," said Adjective. "Nothing like her."

Swallowing my distaste, I repeated the phrase with embellishments.

"Cold, so adjective cold," I ventriloquised.

"That's more like her."

"Enough to freeze your nouns off," I added.

"That's her," said Adjective, "that's ... what did you say her name was?"

"Harmonia."

"That's Ar – adjective – monia all right. Now listen, Armonia, you may be dead, but you can't hide. Well, you can, but not your nearest and dearest. Take your boy. Forgotten his name, but it don't matter, we know where his wet nurse lives. Still on the pap, apparently. You're spoiling him. He should be at work, a little plumper like him. I was beggar's bait at half his age. Or that sister, Peg. A bit of a game pullet, I hear. You'd miss her. So would lots of others, her pimp for one."

"I feel most unwell," announced Miss Osgood, rising to her feet. "I need a change of air. Can we not stop the train?"

"I'm afraid that is impossible," said Mr Dacre. "We cannot stop the train at will."

"Perhaps," suggested Dr leGrove, "you would care to hear instead of a particularly stubborn manifestation I once encountered in Edinburgh, where a delicate lady novelist was haunted by the ghosts of characters whom her publisher had edited to extinction. Refusing to be expunged for all eternity, they insisted on inserting themselves into the novel she was writing at the time, thus rendering it, too, unpublishable."

Lady Milo took a back seat and
let Adjective do all the talking

Since this story sounded – potentially, at least – even more alarming than the tale of Lady Milo and Adjective, Miss Osgood resumed her seat and Mme Fontana continued.

"So here's my offer," said Adjective: "Peg can carry on playing the blanket hornpipe, the boy can stay on the pap, you can toon your arp and everything can stay cosy, prowided ...

"Oh do speak proper," said Lady Milo.

"Provided," continued Adjective with a struggle, "you tell me the lurk. That's all I want to know. Just the lurk. If not, I can't answer for what might happen. That boy, for example ..."

Thoroughly alarmed, I improvised a few falsetto squeaks.

"Can't hear a word," snapped Adjective "Put some elbow into it, can't you?"

"Hollybush Court," I squeaked. "Wash house at the end of the yard. Roof half fallen in, that one. Tin cash box under the copper."

"Hollybush Court?" echoed Lady Milo. "Hollybush Court? What was she doing there? She'd no business being there. That's behind enemy lines."

"Not sure about this," said Adjective. "Sounded too genteel. Could be a trap."

"She could play the lady when she wanted to. No, it's her all right."

"Can we risk it?"

"We'll get someone. Peg's pimp, he'll do it."

Now you may be surprised that I was so precise in my directions. After all, if Peg's pimp found nothing in Hollybush Court, then I could expect a return visit from Adjective. But Peg's pimp would not return empty-handed; I was sure of that, having placed a little something there for him to find: namely, an empty cash box with a broken padlock. My aim, of course, was to make it seem as if the proceeds of the first robbery had themselves become the object of a second. The cashbox had been my idea, the hiding place that of a local urchin who occasionally ran errands for me and who knew the Mile End Road intimately. For a small sum he had agreed to conceal the box and, for a further consideration, to refrain from questioning my motives.

Lady Milo and Adjective left in a flurry of imprecations, directed not at me or even at Harmonia, but at the inhabitants of Hollybush Court with whom they had, apparently, long been at odds. I felt not a little pleased with myself. My stratagem would surely see off my visitors and postpone, perhaps indefinitely, a visit from The

Chaplain. Such was my hope; such, indeed, was my confident expectation. Imagine, then my horror when I found that not only had my ruse not had the desired effect, but had in fact produced the opposite: namely, the death of Harmonia's child. At least, I presumed it was Harmonia's child from the padlock. Child corpses are not, alas, uncommon, but a child corpse with a padlock round its neck is something of a rarity. I first read about it in the newspaper. The odd thing was, Adjective expected Harmonia to have read it, too.

"I don't know if you get the noospapers delivered where you are," she said to Harmonia, when she called on me a week later, "but in case you don't, let me read you a little item from The Standard entitled 'Child's Body Found, Foul Play Suspected'."

I shall spare Miss Osgood all the details – which is more than Adjective did Harmonia – save one: round the victim's neck was a broken padlock – a small one, added the report, of the sort commonly found on cash boxes.

Something of my distress must have been apparent in the falsetto squeaks which I tried to pass off as Harmonia's, for Adjective continued, "Don't play the martyr with me, gel; you ain't got no-one to blame but yourself and you won't have no-one to blame if Peg gets the padlock too. You got a week to think about it, so think hard and think careful."

The next day I fled. I abandoned the house in London and fled, first to my cousin in Wales, then to Whitstable, where I have been pursuing my vocation ever since. It is three years now since I established my practice and, all things considered, have done tolerably well. Or had done until last week, when I spied Lady Milo and Adjective alighting from a train. You may imagine my dismay, my horror. All my fears of The Chaplain which I had thought safely buried surfaced with a sickening rush. I have taken out a lease on a new premises in London – far from the old ones, you may be sure – and shall shortly be moving my belongings there. I have no wish to be found in a ditch with a padlock round my neck.

Miss Binnie was sceptical about these sightings. According to her, Mme Fontana had been seeing Lady Milo and Adjective get off every London train for the last three years.

"They dog her footsteps," she said; "they haunt her dreams; waking and sleeping, they never leave her. But that they have tracked her down to Whitstable seems to me unlikely. As hardened criminals, they must surely have more urgent matters to attend to. If she feels haunted, it is because she feels guilty. Not, I tell her, that she has anything to feel guilty about. She never willed the death of Harmonia's child or that of her sister Peg."

"Peg?" echoed Dr leGrove.

"Oh no!" cried Miss Osgood.

"God forbid," said Mr Critchley.

"Mme Fontana," said Dr leGrove, "I think you owe us an explanation. The death of Peg is too serious a matter to pass over in silence."

"Very well," replied Mme Fontana. "About Peg's death I can tell you very little. What I can tell you is how I came to hear of it, if only to prove that I was as surprised as everyone else. Our local rector commissioned a séance to prove to his clerical friends that spiritualism was a gigantic fraud. 'Exclude the gullible,' he said – by which he meant my usual clientèle – 'replace them with sceptics and the deception will be quickly exposed. I will provide the sceptics, you the manifestations. Will you agree to such a test?' Since refusal would be tantamount to a confession of fraud and such a confession an end to my business, I had no choice but to agree. 'Then let battle commence,' he said, 'and may the best man – or woman – win.' In the course of the séance I pretended to make contact with Peg's pimp. To the sceptics this came as something of a shock. If they had wanted the spirits to be counterfeit, they had also wanted them to be respectable – tradesmen, perhaps, or lawyers – so a pimp came as an unpleasant surprise, especially when he revealed the whereabouts of one of his girls buried in the Deptford mud with a padlock round her neck. Since there was no compelling reason to believe the story, and every good reason to dismiss it as distasteful, the reverend gentlemen went home unconvinced. It was only next day when they read The Morning Post that they changed their minds. The paper revealed that the body of a young woman with a padlock round her neck had indeed been found in the mud at Deptford round about the time the séance was taking place the previous day.

"But how could that have been fraud?" demanded Dr leGrove. "Whatever you may have intended, the spirit spoke true."

"I agree that is how it turned out," admitted Mme Fontana, "but, given my dealings with Lady Milo and Adjective, Deptford mud and padlocks weren't hard to make up."

"But what about the timing?" persisted Dr leGrove. "It was exquisite. You could not have known that *The Morning Post* was going to publish the story next morning."

"Chance," retorted Mme Fontana, "pure chance."

"And the first time, when you identified the correct pawnshop – was that chance?"

"Or luck, which amounts to the same thing. In attempting to convince the rector and his friends, I seem – unintentionally – to have convinced you as well, Dr leGrove. It is most distressing. Are there no sceptics to be found on this train?"

But if there were their identity was lost in smoke and uproar as the train plunged into Merstham Tunnel.

"Tell me, Mr Blackwood," asked Mr Dacre as we emerged into the light, "are you fond of music?"

To my right Mr Bartholomew was extolling the delights of sundials to Miss Osgood and Mr Critchley, whilst Dr leGrove was attempting to persuade Mme Fontana that the spirit of Peg's pimp was the genuine article. (Mr and Mrs Alfred, needless to say, had joined opposite camps, she being of Dr leGrove's party, he of Mme Fontana's.) Mr Dacre, by contrast, seemed indifferent to the subject, hence his attempt to broach a different one altogether.

"Fond enough," I replied; "indeed, when I was younger, more than fond."

"More than fond," he repeated. "How wonderful that must be! For myself I have no ear for music. In church after church I see people ravished by Bach or Mendelssohn and envy them their bewitchment. The nearest I can come – in imagination, at least, – is the glass at Chartres or the vaulting at King's, or" – he hesitated – "or the smell of cigar smoke."

"Surely you cannot be serious."

"About the cigar smoke? I was never more serious in my life."

I waited for further explanation, but Mr Dacre was in no hurry to oblige. For several minutes he gazed at the unfolding landscape.

"The church in Merstham," he said at last, pointing to a spire rising from the trees, "is dedicated to St Katharine of Alexandria and contains some curious fragments of Romanesque carving. Beyond it, on the slopes of the North Downs they quarried the stone for the Henry VII Chapel in Westminster Abbey."

"Tell me about the cigar."

He began by recalling Dr leGrove's story about the haunted manuscript in Edinburgh.

"I have heard him tell it many times before," he said. "It is one of his favourites. In it, you will recall, a delicate lady novelist is haunted by the ghosts of characters – horse stealers, pimps, pickpockets and the like – whom her publisher had expunged on grounds of taste and decency. And in the editor, whose busy blue pencil consigned whole lives – some real, some fictional – to oblivion, I see some-thing of myself, Mr Blackwood. I edit the excesses of a coarser age – the gargoyles, the green men, the fantastical bench ends – ; I erase daubs from walls, delete improprieties from roof bosses, and ensure that infant Jesuses are well swaddled and crucified ones punctured no more than is necessary. A Christian church, Mr Blackwood, should proclaim the gospels in plain stone and instructive glass."

"Then you see yourself as something of an evangelist?"

"By no means. What I do is not informed by belief. I have no belief – or none at present, though I live in hope. No, what I do is purely a matter of aesthetics. I am guided entirely by good taste, Mr Blackwood, which is the nearest thing I have to a moral and spiritual compass. Which brings me, at last, to the cigar."

"Ah, I wondered when we were coming to that."

But we were not to come to it yet. Behind us voices rose in anger as the debate about Mme Fontana's spirits grew ever warmer. Dr leGrove was trying to overwhelm Mr Malachi Brown by sheer weight of example. Manifestations that he had encountered in every corner of the British Isles were pressed into service. What about Exhibit A in Limerick? he asked. Or Exhibit B in Orkney? Not to mention the disturbing cases of X and Y in Gateshead and Ipswich? Mr Malachi Brown was having none of it. Had an impartial observer been present in Limerick or Orkney – or Timbuktoo for that matter – he would undoubtedly have produced a rational explanation for the symptoms that Dr leGrove had described.

"The trouble with sceptics," confided Mr Dacre, "is that they are rarely sceptical about the right things. Take the case of Peg's pimp. What we should be asking is not whether he belonged to this world or the next, but whether Lady Milo and Adjective ever existed in the first place."

"What are you suggesting?" I asked.

"I am suggesting that someone who is a self-confessed fraud might have more impostures up her sleeve than she is prepared to admit. Nor can I help seeing a resemblance between Lady Milo and Adjective on the one hand, and Mme Fontana and Miss Binnie on the other – not perhaps as they are, but as they might wish themselves to be. Now, about the cigar."

"Are we speaking of a real cigar," I asked, "or an allegorical one?"

"Now that," he said, "must be for you to decide, though if you were to offer me a fine Havana at this very moment I should not refuse."

The Ecclesiastical Architect's Tale of Crockford's Commotions

L et me introduce you, he began, to my hero, a man so indecisive, so colourless as scarcely to deserve a name. But a name he must have, for a hero without a name would be like *Hamlet* without the Prince. I have compromised, therefore, by naming him after his club, or at least the club in which he spent most of his time, for he belonged to several and owed money in all. Let us refer to him then as Crockford, and it is coming out of Crockford's that we first meet him on a hot July day a little earlier in the reign of their present Majesties. He has lost fifty pounds at whist, not by the standards of the club a large amount but large enough to cause embarrassment should his father find out. For a while he wanders aimlessly. He loiters in Regent Street, tries on shoes in the Burlington Arcade, admires the carriages in Pall Mall. If only, he thinks, he were not so addicted to play, so beset by regular losses, he might be riding in one himself. The heat is oppressive. The humid air traps the smells of coffee dregs and horse sweat; in florists' windows carnations droop in enamelled buckets. And it is outside a florist's – Blanchards in the Strand – that we first meet the cigar.

It was clamped between the teeth of a sandwich man whose boards, fore and aft, advertised a revivalist meeting in the Coal Exchange. Now under normal circumstances, Crockford would not have given the man a second glance, but to his astonishment he found himself following in his wake as if he had been taken in tow. And all the while the scent of the cigar grew stronger and stronger, obliterating the rank smells that had offended him earlier. It was pungent, exotic, enticing; it stirred in him yearnings he did not know he possessed and to which he could not put a name. He followed the thread of smoke to the Coal Exchange, where a preacher was haranguing a crowd of lost souls who responded to his peroration with alleluias so heartfelt, so contagious that he could not but join in. Oh the frenzy of it, the joy, the zeal! Who that morning, when he left his club, would have predicted that he would be swept along by such a tidal surge of gladness – alleluia! alleluia! – and that before the afternoon was over would have hosanna'd himself hoarse? And as his ears drank in the alleluias, the scent of the cigar grew ever stronger in his nostrils, even though the smoker himself had disappeared. Nor did it leave him when the meeting ended. For many days he could smell it on his clothes, in his whiskers, in the nap of his hat. No washing, no brushing would dispel it and though he never met the sandwich board man again, the taint of his cigar was ineradicable. Time and again Crockford returned to hear the Word proclaimed from the makeshift pulpit. But it was neither the preacher, nor his message that kindled the energy in his soul: it was the cigar. As long as its scent lingered in the folds of his clothes, on his skin, in his hair, his soul would not be still, would not be satisfied.

Alas, it faded as suddenly as it had come. He woke one morning, expecting to find the eager smell on his pillow, but it was no longer there. A little of it lingered in the seams of his gloves, the fold of his handkerchief, but his coat and hat had resumed the smells of the streets – the oyster shells, the coffee dregs, the horse sweat. Out of habit he made his way to the Coal Exchange, where all he could smell were the unwashed bodies of the congregation and the uncleanness of their linen.

Quickly he stepped outside into the street. He felt no regrets; if anything, he felt liberated. What had seemed a lacerating expression of joy now seemed both oppressive and – there was no denying it – faintly ridiculous.

"Why, Crockford," said a familiar voice; "it is Crockford, isn't it? Where the devil have you been all these weeks?"

It was a whist-playing acquaintance from one of his clubs. Crockford greeted him warmly, and when his friend suggested a game of cards followed by lunch at the Ship and Turtle, he accepted without hesitation. And why not? For once in his life he could afford it. Having lived frugally for several weeks he was in funds. For what remained of the summer, he resumed his normal life, doing the round of the clubs, where, to his surprise, he won more than he lost and so had no embarrassing confessions to make to his father.

Autumn set in with sulphurous fogs and, as if prompted by the weather, his winning streak deserted him. Once more he found himself wandering the streets, his nostrils assailed not by coffee dregs and horse sweat, but by soot and smoke. He sought refuge in St James's Park, only to find the gardeners burning fallen leaves. Wrapping his muffler round his face, he hurried back into the city where he paused to admire a display of chrysanthemums outside Blanchard's. And it was there, in exactly the place he had been captivated before, that he fell victim again. A whiff of cigar smoke, a handbill thrust into his hand and he was once more in thrall, not this time to religious revivalists, but to the Chartists, the English Jacobins, the very people who threated to overturn the established order and set the tumbrils rolling. What would they think of him at the club, he wondered, if they knew he was about to throw in his lot with the hooligans who, ten years earlier, had had to be crushed by the army in Newport? Why, he would be blackballed in an instant, excoriated, despised. But he did not care. As he inhaled the smoke from the cigar, he embraced his pariah status with glee.

That first day he would have been hard pressed to say what it was he felt this new-found passion for, but as pamphlet followed pamphlet and oration oration, he became daily more committed to the cause. The Charter and nothing but the Charter: that was the great goal. Once the working man was properly represented in Parliament, all other social reforms would follow. He became prominent in the movement. At Feargus O' Connor's bidding he handed out leaflets in his club and was duly expelled; and at Ernest Jones's, he offered his father a Chartist newspaper and had his allowance cut off.

Early in the following spring, the movement was given new impetus by the revolution in Paris. The smell of insurrection permeated everything. A new petition was begun. Six million signatures! was the cry. Six million signatures and no power on earth could resist the Charter. April 10 was the date fixed for it to be presented to Parliament. From all over the capital Chartist groups were to converge on Kennington Common: one was to march down Tottenham Court Road, one from Stepney, one from Russell Square. The prospect threw the government into a panic. The Duke of Wellington was ordered to defend the capital; the royal family withdrew to the Isle of Wight; Downing Street was cordoned off by troops. As the day approached the smell of cigar smoke strengthened in Crockford's collars and cuffs; in the house it nestled in the cushions and curtains, the sheets and pillow cases. Where the sandwich man's cigar had filled him with a fierce joy, an urge to swell the chorus of hosannas, the Chartist's filled him rage, not on his own behalf, but on behalf of the working man, the urban poor, the dispossessed and disaffected. He was impatient for change. Oh that April 10 were here and the world begun anew!

When at last April 10 dawned, he drew the blinds and gazed out on a sea of wet roofs. He buried his nose in the curtains, where the cigar smoke, catching the taint from his clothes, had embedded itself most deeply. But there was nothing there – no smack, no tang, no taste, nothing but a faint smell of soot. Nor was there anything in the sheets and the curtains. The cigar smoke had gone and, with it, the revolutionary spirit. He felt it leave him, descending through his limbs and oozing out through the soles of his feet. He looked up at the leaden sky, down at the wet pavements and gardens and found himself wondering what was for lunch at his club, before remembering that he had no club, having been blackballed from all of them and rightly so. Today might or might not be a day when history was made, but to him it was a matter of complete indifference. Let others man the barricades: he would stay at home.

By early afternoon he had relented enough to go out, not out of revolutionary fervour, but out of simple curiosity. Apart from the soldiers guarding public buildings, the streets were eerily quiet. He wandered along the routes of the morning's processions. The shops were shuttered, the pavements plastered with wet handbills and the stubs of innumerable cigars. At one point in his wanderings he had to step aside as three hansom cabs swept past bearing the six million signatures of the petition to Parliament. He had expected cheering crowds, but there were none; the cabs rattled through empty streets and disappeared into New Palace Yard unapplauded. Throughout the afternoon he wandered through unfamiliar streets until he was well and truly lost. By now it was raining harder than ever, so he took shelter in the porch of a nearby church and observed the dejected Chartists returning, soaked to the skin, from Kennington. Whatever zeal they might have set out with had given way to sullen resignation. Eyes fixed on the wet pavements, they shuffled back hopelessly to the hovels from which they had emerged.

It was as if his commotions had belonged to someone else and, though he could recall their consequences, he could not recall their exhilaration. Then one day, the veil lifted, not by much, but enough to allow a brief resurgence of flame and colour. He was at a dinner party, one of the many to which he had been invited by club members eager to welcome him back into the fold. Now that he was judged to be free from contagion they were curious to know how he had acquired such passions and what it felt like to be in their grip. These of course were the very questions he was unable to answer. So unsatisfactory were his explanations that his hosts suspected he must be hiding something or even that he was not as fully recovered as they had supposed.

On this particular evening the ladies withdrew, leaving the gentlemen to their port and cigars. Instead of keeping his guests at the table, the host, who was a diamond dealer in Hatton Garden, picked up a box of Havanas and, telling them they would have to earn their smokes, led them to a room at the top of the house.

"Welcome, gentlemen," he said, "to my den. I should like to say that it is my favourite room in the house, but that would be premature, since the carpenters and decorators only finished here last week and I am yet to learn whether it lives up to expectations. If you would care to help yourselves to a cigar, I should like to give you a little tour of my treasures."

One by one the gentlemen lit their cigars and listened dutifully as their host introduced them to the collections in the vitrines which surrounded them. From time to time he would open a case and pass round an object, together with a pocket lens so that its beauties might be the more admired. Thus jewelled snuff boxes, medals, shoe buckles and Tudor miniatures made their way round the room to polite murmurs of approval before being returned to the velvet cushions on which they rested. And all the while the cigar smoke grew thicker and thicker. Crockford was curious to see if he was still vulnerable to its effects. He was not. Or at least not in the same way. A succession of gemstones – topaz, agate, beryl, garnet, cornelian – passed beneath his eyes. As he gazed at the garnet through the pocket lens he felt an sudden ecstasy of pure colour. It was over almost before it began, a promise unfulfilled, but a promise nonetheless. He detected similar vibrations in the chrysoprase and the agate and even, albeit somewhat fainter, in one of the miniatures.

"Mr Crockford," said his host, "you're not smoking."

He held out the cigar box.

"Very well, if you insist," said Crockford, taking a cigar.

"I do. We can't have you being different from the rest, can we? Those days are behind you, I trust."

Crockford's various ecstasies had been carried on the cigar smoke of others. Throughout his commotions it had never occurred to him to smoke himself, fearing that to do so might calm the frenzies to which he was prone or, worse, increase them to the point where they became unendurable. Now he relented. For one thing it seemed impolite to refuse; for another he half hoped that if he smoked a cigar himself his commotions might be restored. It did neither. First he coughed and then, as the smoke settled in his lungs, he felt nauseous and had to rush downstairs and out into the street, his senses in turmoil. When he had mastered the urge to be sick, he collected his hat and coat from the footman, hailed a cab and went home.

So began a long struggle to re-kindle his lost ecstasies through Art. He moved to larger lodgings and began to assemble cabinets of curiosities, beginning modestly with shells and minerals, Chinese bowls and tropical butterflies. Later, having married – and married well, thus regaining his father's favour and doubling his income – he was able to fill whole rooms with his collections, which grew ever more eclectic and grotesque. Gemstones sat alongside birds' eggs, snuff boxes alongside fragments of stained glass. He lived among gorgeous surfaces – silks, satins, tapestries, table tops inlaid with mother of pearl, screens covered with peacock feathers – hoping to catch the afterglow of his commotions. Occasionally, in the fire red of a ruby or the myriad hues of an opal he felt the stirring he sought. But it did not last. After a few seconds the spark would die out. Yet he never gave up. In hothouses he cultivated orchids and tree ferns; in a walled garden he was able to distinguish twenty different species of rose by scent alone. He collected books, not for their subject matter – to which he was largely indifferent – but for rare bindings and unusual fonts. Ever restless, he constantly re-arranged his collections, seeking an elusive perfection, a divine geometry in their ordering. For a while gemstones would share compartments with medals, fossils with silver thimbles. But the perfections thus secured proved to be shortlived – a few days, a few weeks at most before the process of re-ordering would start all over again.

One day he was approached by a craftsman who offered to build him an ivory cabinet in which to store captured sounds. Such a thing, said the craftsman, was not yet possible, but one day it surely would be and then the cabinet could be made to reverberate to whatever sounds were stored within its myriad drawers. One by one Crockford could fill them with everything from the sounds of nature – wind, running water, birdsong – to music and beyond.

"Beyond?" asked Crockford.

"To the Music of the Spheres itself," replied the craftsman. "Not this year, perhaps, nor next, but one day."

"And when I open a drawer of captured organ music, will I be able to hear it? Not with my ears, but with my soul, with the innermost fibre of my being?"

"Only if someone discovers the means to capture it and only if you are disposed – really, truly disposed – to hear. As for the Music of the Spheres, that may be beyond the reach of any of us, either to capture or to hear. But it is important to hope, Mr Crockford; it is important to hope. If I were a mountebank I would promise you these things, but since I make no such promises you may be assured I am not. And if I were a common trickster I would demand the earth, when all I ask is a small annual tribute."

"In what form?"

"Shall we say a yearly box of Havanas until you hear the Music of the Spheres?"

"But that is a commitment without end."

"Almost certainly, but it is a very small price to pay."

Against his wife's advice Crockford bought the cabinet. Every day he opens a drawer to see if he can hear a captured sound. So far he has not dared to open a drawer devoted to music, though once or twice, when he has strained to hear wind or running water, he has caught – or thinks he has caught – the faintest whiff of cigar smoke.

"And am I to take it that Crockford's tale is your own?" I asked.

"How could it be? The great Chartist meeting at Kennington took place only three years ago and I have been following my profession for more than ten."

"Then the tale is false."

"Only up to a point."

"Then a part of it at least is true?"

"Insofar as an allegory is true, I suppose it is. I can never make up my mind."

Mr Dacre proving as elusive as the Music of the Spheres, I decided to quit the pursuit and enquire after Stumps's encounter with the Bishop at Fulham Palace, a subject to which my thoughts had often turned – not without envy – as I lay awake on my hard bed in Harrison's Hostel.

"In return for unlimited brandy and cigars … ," began Mr Dacre.

"Real ones?" I asked.

"I can assure you there is nothing allegorical about the Bishop's cigars. In return, I say, for unlimited brandy and cigars, His Grace gathered enough material for a dozen sermons on the first night and for at least as many on the second. Both men retired to bed well satisfied."

"And his table manners?"

"Deplorable, though when your friend Culpepper tried to correct them, His Grace stopped him, quoting Rousseau on the

Noble Savage. For his part, he said, he found Stumps's uninhibited enjoyment of his food quite delightful and intended, when no-one was looking, to apply himself to God's gifts with similar enthusiasm. It wasn't enough simply to consider oneself a man of the people; one had to act like them – even, on occasion, to eat like them."

"And will he?"

"I doubt it. His Grace is notorious for his sudden enthusiasms. One moment he is all for listening to the Chartists as the voice of the people, the next he is denouncing them as dangerous revolutionists who mean to murder us all."

"When the Bishop was exchanging cigars for sermons, did Stumps oblige with his story of the City on a Hill?"

Dacre did not recall it and asked me to oblige him with a brief account.

"What you have described," he said when I had finished, "does not exactly coincide with the version he told the Bishop, though as I recall there were long sections where Culpepper appropriated the narrative and told it on his behalf."

"Let me guess," I said. "It was a tale in which a Catholic priest urges his congregation of hard-drinking navvies to make poteen."

"And is stopped by an upright, teetotal Anglican who banishes the evildoer from the hilltop and introduces his congregation to the delights of pure spring water," said Dacre. "Yes, you are quite right."

"How did the Bishop respond?"

"As I recall, he poured himself another brandy."

"According to Mr Beamish, to whom you sat opposite on the steamer, Stumps will revert to his former belligerency as we approach Canterbury. It is all a question of being on the right sized dunghill apparently. Too large and he won't crow, too small and he won't stop."

"I must confess," said Dacre, "that I had never thought of Fulham Palace in those terms – and neither, I suspect, had the Bishop."

"Beamish is convinced he is right and has pledged never to go hatless again if he isn't."

"Judging by the weather," said Dacre, indicating the sky, "he must be praying that he is wrong and that you will hold him to his promise.

I, too, had noticed with alarm that the sky had darkened and though it was only mid-afternoon, was threatening to hurry the October day to a close. And now, as we passed through Penshurst, the last station before Tunbridge, heavy drops began to fall, from the force of which we were protected by the canopy of the second class carriage. The promise that I had made at London Bridge to my companions in the tub – namely, that I would end our excursion as I had begun it, in their company – I now began to regret. There was no escaping it. I had given my word and could not in all honesty go back on it. To be drenched in the tub was my bounden duty.

Meanwhile, Mr Critchley and the Malachi Browns were fastening their coats in preparation for our arrival at Tunbridge. Dr leGrove promised to recommend the bookbinder to Mr Alford, the Dean; Mr Bartholomew urged the departing passengers to resist the tyranny of Greenwich Meantime; the Malachi Browns quarrelled about whether they could afford to take a cab at the station; and Mme Fontana shocked everyone by telling the Tunbridge party that she would be delighted to organise séances for them in her new premises and would offer a reduced rate for parties of six or more.

This was too much for Dr leGrove, whose patience had been tried not just by Mme Fontana's shameless confessions of fraud, but by her refusal to acknowledge a genuine manifestation when one had been thrust upon her.

"Surely," he protested, "you cannot forget that both on the outward and the return journeys you have insisted on the fraudulence of your activities. Now you expect us to ignore everything you have said and act as your dupes. Fie on you, Mme Fontana, fie on you!"

Dr leGrove's fieing met with loud applause from the rest of the company. Far from being abashed, Mme Fontana stared back

defiantly, though her riposte was drowned by the squeal of brakes as
Sturdee brought *Hengist* to rest in Tunbridge Station.

*[Editor's Note: Blackwood's account of the arrival at Tunbridge breaks off
at this point, though readers will already know that it was at Tunbridge
that Mr Scudamore confided to Blackwood his fears about Lady Rippledale's
intentions towards her companion. Of the consequences of those intentions,
an account, albeit an inconclusive one in the form of Mr Scudamore's letter,
has already been given.*

*We re-join Blackwood and Miss Osgood, whose relationship was by now
strained by their disagreement over Gabriel, as they climb aboard the tub for
the final stage of the journey.]*

9

TUNBRIDGE TO CANTERBURY

I re-join my old friends in the tub
The Parlour Maid's Tale of The Elves and the Dressmaker
Mr Turpin's Fabularium
Drama at Paddock Wood
The Bailiff's Tale of The Jackdaws' Wedding
The Daguerreotypist's Tale
The Saturnine Stranger Unmuffles
The Saturnine Stranger's Tale
The Parson's Tale
We arrive in Canterbury

Despite the rain, the passengers, most of whom had huddled together on the rear-facing seats, were in remarkably good spirits. Turpin, Beamish and the rest greeted Miss Osgood and me warmly. So, too, did an unexpected addition to the company in the form of the Duchess of Croydon. Seeing my astonishment, Beamish, beside whom I squeezed myself on the bench, grasped my hand and assured me how delighted he was to see me.

"Our new arrival," he said, indicating the Duchess, "has rather dominated the conversation. Poor Turpin, who has been eager to share his thoughts on the Great Exhibition, has scarcely been able to get a word in edgeways."

"But how does she come to be aboard the train in the first place?" Miss Osgood asked Beamish in a loud whisper. "She is no more entitled to be on the return journey than she was to be on the outward one."

"She stopped the train," was the reply.

"I do not quite understand," I said.

"You remember our unexpected delay at Croydon?"

"How could I forget? I was nearly left behind on the platform. But how did she manage to stop the train? One cannot hail a train as if it were a cab."

"One can, though on the whole one chooses not to. She, on the other hand, chooses to be the exception to every rule. She just stood between the rails and waved her umbrella. It was with the greatest difficulty that Sturdee managed to stop in time. Even now she refuses to acknowledge the danger she was in."

During her sojourn in London, the Duchess had clearly had time to replenish her hamper. Though lavish in the distribution of pastries and pies, she directed most of her bounty towards Stumps, dropping titbits into his mouth and wiping his chin clean with her handkerchief. Of the belligerency that Beamish had predicted, there was no sign; on the contrary, he was giggling like a child and whispering sweet nothings in her ear trumpet.

"I fear," whispered Purselove, "I very much fear that our Chartist friend is in love. Among the elderly the tender passions are not a pleasing spectacle. One thinks of Sir Lucius O' Trigger and Mrs Malaprop – or worse, Falstaff and Doll Tearsheet."

"If that is the case," said Breeze, "then she has snatched the prize from under Culpepper's nose."

Poor Culpepper! His dilemma was plain for all to see. If he interfered, he risked losing his influence with Stumps; if, on the other hand, he failed to interfere, he was certain to lose it anyway. A penitent sinner is a feather in the cap of any clergyman and a penitent railway navvy a whole plume of them. A rash intervention now might jeopardise everything. But what if – and the thought must surely have occurred to him – what if he were to set his sights not just on an adult baptism, but on an adult baptism followed by a wedding? Would not two sacraments on the same day make the Archbishop sit up and take notice, especially if the wedding were to be conducted – an absurd thought, but not impossible – by Stumps's old friend the Bishop of London?

Despite the failing light the band continued to play manfully. For the most part they played popular airs, but when the rain strengthened they resorted to military music, hoping to raise the morale of those exposed to the weather. Though most of us sat with our backs to the rain, causing us to squeeze five or six to a bench meant for four, the Costellos faced unflinchingly forward. From time to time they were joined by Mr Meek, who liked to think of himself as a supporter of all things military. And if our brave lads, as he called them, had decided to make a stand against heaven's artillery – "Artillery?" said Corporal Costello. "Pooh! This is only small arms fire" – then he considered it his duty to join them. When the squalls of rain pressed hard against the forward-facing infantry, however, his stoicism deserted him and pleading some excuse – grit in his eye, water getting behind his watch glass – he squeezed into the bench opposite.

The Costellos had two other forward-facing allies in Mr Ezard and the Saturnine Stranger, who found themselves sitting on the same bench, the one wringing the rain from his collar and cuffs, the other clutching his black box tightly to his chest. The latter, who had shown little interest in those around him on the outward journey, appeared to be much taken with the Duchess and she, in between feeding titbits of cake to Stumps, seemed flattered by his attention. From time to time she would wave a piece of pie at him, which he, without saying a word, would accept and place, untasted, inside his black box.

"Something spirituous?" she would ask, holding out the bottle. Had he been able to put that in his black box, too, he would surely have accepted, but when she made it clear that a swig was the limit of her generosity, he declined with a wave of his hand.

Meanwhile, the rain continued to fall, a strong South East-erly driving it into our faces and, though there was a blossoming of umbrellas all along the train, most of them did not survive the violent gusts for long. There was little any of us could do except turn up our collars and summon our fortitude, which, in my case, was in short supply since I had left my hat suspended from the ceiling of the first–class compartment. But there was one person, other than perhaps the Saturnine Stranger, who was not only indifferent to the weather but who positively relished it, and that person was Turpin, whose Travelling Topper had come into its own at last. Replenished with hot water from a coffee stall at London Bridge, it sat on his head steaming slightly where raindrops fell on its outer casing.

Of all the pilgrims to the Crystal Palace, it was perhaps Turpin who came away most fulfilled. Beneath the Topper a dozen ideas, ingenious and absurd by turns, were fermenting. From time to time he tried to share his schemes with Beamish, who responded by describing the phrenological riches he had encountered in the Crystal Palace, and since Beamish was the more voluble of the two, there were more cranial bumps than iron flanges in their conversa-tion. To Turpin my arrival was therefore something of a godsend: here at last was a sympathetic ear into which he could pour his newly concocted schemes. So eager was he that they tumbled out, one after another – fantastical notions most of them – ranging from self-cleaning garden rakes to adjustable horseshoes. But what seemed to engage his attention most was the possibility that the Jacquard loom, whose movements are controlled by a series of punched cards, could be adapted to tell stories. This idea had been suggested to him some years earlier by Ada, the Countess of Lovelace, whose husband had commissioned him to design a water feature for their home at Ockham Park in Surrey. The Coun-tess, who had assisted Mr Charles Babbage in the construction of his celebrated Difference Engine, was of the view that intelligent machines might one day be made to compose music and even write stories. At the time Turpin had thought the idea absurd, but, having watched Mr Burch's punch cards control a Jacquard loom in the Crystal Palace, he had changed his mind. "For," said he, "a story is not unlike a fabric in that it consists of a series of repeated patterns which results from the gradual elimination of choices."

This thought was rather lost on me, but there was no chance to question it further, for Gabriel, who had been asleep with his head on Nan's lap, now woke and demanded to be fed. Fortunately, his wants were quickly satisfied from the Duchess's hamper; his demands for warmth, on the other hand were not, so he burrowed down into Nan's lap again and asked for a story. Though quick to oblige, Nan might have chosen more wisely. The story she chose pleased no-one, not even Gabriel who fell asleep again almost immediately, and certainly not Turpin, into the works of whose story-telling machine it threw a large spanner.

"Once upon a time," she began.

"Ah, a fairy tale," said Turpin. "A classic beginning. Opens up some possibilities, closes off others."

"There was a poor seamstress who lived by an open drain."

"O dear!" exclaimed Turpin. "This will not do, this will not do at all."

"Like many seamstresses, she had come down in the world, having known happier times as a governess – if, that is, the lot of a governess can ever be thought a happy one when the most she can hope for is not to be ignored by her employers or ill-treated by her pupils."

"This is a reversal of fortune story," said Turpin. "I can feel it coming. A fall from happiness, a period of misery, a happy accident – a lucky encounter, perhaps, or a valuable discovery – leading to a brilliant marriage and a life of good works. Such a pity about the drains. I would advise against drains in a story of any kind."

Turpin's commentary, which was whispered in my ear – or as close to my ear as the Topper would allow – never faltered throughout Nan's tale, especially as it proved increasingly resistant to categorisation. In the end, Turpin declared that any tale that could not be transferred to punched cards had no business being called a tale at all. In the meantime, I shall set down *The Elves and the Dressmaker* with fewer of Turpin's interruptions than was actually the case and let the reader decide for himself whether or not his verdict was a just one. And since Miss Osgood's notebook was now too soggy to use, the words in which I set it down will be more mine than Nan's.

Nan's Tale of The Elves and the Dressmaker

Although it ends beside an open drain, she said, my story begins with a trim carriage drawing up outside a house in Regent Street. Outside, there is nothing to indicate that it is a place of business; but inside, the floor-to-ceiling mirrors, the ebony counters, the tables with bolts of velvet tell a very different story. So, too, does the French lady in the silk dress and lace cap with ribbons that descend to her feet. In first-rate houses she is what is known as a *magasinière*, and, although she does not own the business, she is its public face, especially to people of quality.

Lady Crampton has clearly been expected. As she ascends the stairs, she is bowed and bobbed to every step of the way. The proprietress, who has been waiting on the first landing, greets her by name and enquires politely after lord this and lady that, before handing her on to the *magasinière*. The serious business of the visit now begins. Lady Crampton examines the fabrics carefully, enquiring of the French lady which will impress by daylight and which by candlelight, which with pearls and which with rubies. Très charmant this, says the French lady, mais pas si charmant that, opines her ladyship. When at last she makes her choice, she decides that, although she came to order one dress, she might as well make it two. She is then shown into a succession of rooms, each magnificent as the first, each a treasure house of shawls and mantles, laces and linens. There is much to tempt her and she quickly succumbs. When at last her ladyship has been bowed out to her carriage, the *magasinière* summons the First Hand from the work room and places the order. The First Hand in her turn summons the brougham (with powdered footman) and visits the client in her own home to take her measurements, like a surveyor staking out the plot.

"The green velvet is not urgent – shall we say two days from now? – but the ball gown I must have by tomorrow evening," says Lady Crampton. "No later than six. Can you do it?"

"We may have to send for the elves," replies the First Hand, who dreads to think what the girls in the work room will say to the short notice.

"Elves?"

"It is a saying in the work room, my lady. When an order is needed urgently, we pretend that it is a task for the elves."

"A reference to the Elves and the Shoemaker, I presume?"

"Indeed, my lady."

"Well, tell your elves to be punctual, or that is the last order they will get from me."

The First Hand was right: the work room is not happy to learn that Lady Crampton's ball gown is a job for the elves. They grumble a lot, the girls in the work room, even though they know that, compared with other seamstresses, they are well fed and, at twelve pounds per annum, well paid. What is more, their dormitory is well ventilated and they are required to sleep no more than two to a bed. Ah, sleep! If only they could be paid in sleep! They already have three dresses to finish for the next day and, even with help from the elves, will struggle to finish a fourth, let alone a fifth. They are resigned to staying up till the small hours, but the Crampton order will rob them of the morsel of sleep remaining to them. But at least they will not go hungry. At four o'clock the girls will be given bread, butter and tea – as much as they can drink – after which they will work till ten, when a supper of cold meat and cheeses will fortify them for the task ahead.

Between tea and supper an elf arrives in the shape of Ma Finbow's Arthur.

"Any skirts for Rattles Yard?" he asks the porter.

(Outwork always takes the form of skirts. Bodices and sleeves, where the needlework is more intricate, are kept in house.)

"Any skirts today?" the porter asks the First Hand.

"Four," says the First Hand, depositing four roughly cut out skirts, including Lady Crampton's ball gown, across his outstretched arms. "Tell the boy the skirts need to go in at nine sharp and if they're not here by then, Ma Finbow gets no more work from us."

"Tell Ma Finbow that if they're not here by nine," says the footman, handing the skirts to the visiting elf, "you'll get no more work from us."

If Lady Crampton could have seen Rattles Yard, she might have been prepared to wait a little longer so as to have her dresses finished in Regent Street. If she could have seen the cabbage stumps, the overflowing slop pail on the landing, the saucepans, the frying pans, the stumps of brooms, she would certainly have been more patient. But she has not seen any of these things, supposing – if she gave the matter any thought to at all – that the elves were as pampered as she imagined her own servants to be.

The garret to which Arthur delivers his precious cargo – unsmeared, unsplashed and unsullied by the passage of Rattles Yard – is about twelve feet square with a window near the ceiling. In the centre is a deal table around which half a dozen red-eyed, hollow-cheeked girls are seated. They grumble a lot, these girls, more than their counterparts in Regent Street, but, then, they have a lot more to grumble about. Pay for a start. Eight pounds per annum they would have thought generous, twelve pounds (the going rate in Regent Street) the stuff of dreams. And then there is the tea. Far from being available in unlimited quantities, the leaves have to be quite exhausted before they are thrown away. As for the bread and butter, or, to be more precise, the bread (for there was no butter), that, too, is a source of complaint, not because it is in short supply, but because the local baker ekes out his flour with alum and plaster. About their mattresses – straw, one to a girl, dry if she's lucky enough to be by the chimney breast – there is only one complaint: namely, they do not see enough of them.

"Four skirts to go in at nine o' clock?" says Ma Finbow, when Arthur hands over his cargo. "I've already got two for nine and we're struggling with them."

"Do we know who the dress is for, ma?" asks one of the girls.

"And when she wears it to the ball, will she know who made it?"

"Or care?"

"What am I going to do?" asks Ma Finbow. "If we don't deliver on time, we get no more work from Regent Street."

"Sounds like a job for the elves, ma."

Right on cue – for that is how things happen in fairy tales – ("Some fairy tale!" grumbled Turpin) – there came a knock at the door.

It would surprise Lady Crampton to learn that even elves need elves from time to time, though it would surprise everyone in Regent Street still more. They think that they alone are clever enough to have acquired them; it never occurs to them that Ma Finbow might cheat by having them as well.

And now an elf – a sickly, shrunken elf in the early stages of rickets – presents himself at the door, asking for skirts. Ma Finbow hands him two, including the one for Lady Crampton's ball gown.

"Give her these," she says, "and if they're not back by eight sharp, she gets no more work from this house." It pleases Ma Finbow to refer to her garret as a 'house' and woe betide any of her girls who fails to do the same.

"And do these latest elves have elves, too?" asked Purselove.

"The chain of elves goes on until you can't find anyone to work for less," replied Nan. "Lady Crampton would have paid twenty pounds for her ball gown, of which the owner of Regent Street would have taken twelve, the French lady four, the First Hand and the girls (between them) two pound ten shillings, Ma Finbow and her girls one pound eight and sixpence, leaving one and sixpence for the elves at Stacks Court.

"What's all this about prices?" demanded Turpin. "You can't have prices in a fairy tale. Treasure, yes, pieces of gold, yes, riches, wealth untold. But pounds, shillings and pence are definitely against the rules."

"Even elves have to eat," said Nan. "Only in fairy stories can they afford to work for nothing."

"Where does the former governess fit in?" I asked.

As I said, she lived by an open drain – or, to be more precise, above it. If you held a candle close to the gaps in the floor, you could see bubbles in the heaving broth below, or catch phosphorescent scraps of rotten fish rising to the surface. Hers was the meanest room in the meanest tenement in Stacks Court, a yard that was home to several hundred people, half a dozen pigs, which roamed freely in and out of the houses, and a wide variety of trades, among them wood turners, tinkers, second-hand clothes dealers, fish smokers and canary breeders.

Although she lived in the most miserable hovel in the Court, she was the least crushed of its inhabitants. Her proud bearing had earned her the name of the Countess.

("Ah, a fairy tale is still possible," whispered Turpin. "Take away the fish heads and the pounds, shillings and pence and you might still squeeze it on to a punched card.")

Not only did she not resent this, she rather gloried in it, telling anyone who would listen how she had been governess to children of Lord and Lady Plumridge and how she was dismissed following false accusations of theft. Had she been wiser, she might have protested her innocence less, since most of her neighbours were – or had been – in the thieving line and proud of it.

"Well," she asked the rickety elf, "has Ma Finbow got anything for me?"

"Two skirts for ten o' clock sharp," said the rickety elf, "or you don't get no more work from her."

Now whether the rickety elf had said eight or ten – or even two or three – was not clear, he having in addition to a deformity of the bones, a deformity of speech as well as a deformity of the ear, which meant that he had either misheard what Ma Finbow had said or had wrongly conveyed it to the Countess. But whatever he had intended, she heard it as ten and was pleasantly surprised, for though she would have to sew through the night by rushlight, she might be able to snatch an hour's sleep before setting to work.

"When ... when ...," stammered the elf.

"When do you get paid?" asked the Countess. "When I get paid. And when do I get paid? When Ma Finbow gets paid, though who pays her, how much and when, I don't know, much as I should like to. Now give me the skirts and be off with you."

Unnoticed by either of them, the end of Lady Crampton's ball gown scraped across the floor and briefly skimmed the surface of the drain through a gap in the floor boards. So inured was she to the smells of the ditch over which she lived, the Countess noticed nothing amiss. Settling herself in her rockerless rocking chair, she draped the two skirts over her knees and fell instantly asleep.

It is against the rickety elf that Ma Finbow directs her fury when he presents the skirts at ten the next morning.

"That's the last work the Countess gets from this house," says Ma.

And of course the First Hand says the same (with added vehemence) to Ma Finbow's Arthur when he delivers the skirts at half past ten. Since the Countess and Ma Finbow are cheap – none cheaper in fact – it is doubtful that these threats will be carried out. Regent Street, however, is more vulnerable. There are plenty of fashionable houses, each with its own supply of elves, that drift in and out of favour with the well-to-do. All things considered, though, it is doubtful whether Lady Crampton will carry out her threat. After all, the ball gown is only half an hour late, the Regent Street girls having foregone a further hour's sleep to finish it. It is much more likely that she will use the delay to pay less than she agreed. Invariably a late payer, she is often, when an excuse offers itself, a short payer. And so it proves in this case: the twenty pounds she had agreed to pay – (**"Oh dear! prices again,"** said Turpin) – turns out to be fifteen.

"And not a penny more," she says, secretly pleased with her bargain. "Because of your idleness, I nearly missed the ball". Which is quite untrue. Her ladyship has had plenty of time to prepare for the ball, where her new gown has been much admired.

"My dear, you must give me the name of your dressmaker."

"But of course. And take a word of advice: don't let them overcharge you. Drive a hard bargain. They'll respect you all the more for it."

Lady Crampton's bargain is keenly felt among the elves. Everyone has to settle for less. The proprietress of Regent Street takes nine pounds, the French lady two, the First Hand and the girls (between them) one pound seventeen and six, Ma Finbow and her girls one pound two and six, leaving nothing for the Countess, who has to borrow at extortionate interest from the canary breeder to tide her over until Ma Finbow sends more skirts to sew.

Cholera came to Belgravia unannounced, letting itself in quietly through the back door. In fact, it arrived so discreetly that it was possible to pretend that it hadn't arrived at all. Only one person of consequence – and her maid – was a victim and two deaths hardly constitute an epidemic. So the dinner parties, the at-homes and the balls continued, though for the rest of the season there were gaps at table where guests had taken themselves off to the country and it was noticeable that there were fewer takers for the waltz, dancing in long sets having enjoyed something of a revival. Great care was taken to ensure that the story did not find its way into the newspapers, though an outbreak in Stacks Yard was widely reported and generally blamed on the effluvia of pigs, canaries and rotting fish heads. None of the score or so of victims was named, though one was believed to be an idiot boy who ran errands for local tradesmen.

If anyone could have made a connection between the two outbreaks, it was Ma Finbow, for though she never knew the final destination of her work, she knew who came before her in the chain and who after. Had she known of the death of Lady Crampton, she would almost certainly have blamed the Countess. Had the Countess not delivered the dress late, Ma Finbow would have been able to check it, as was her custom, for bugs and stains, thus halting the cholera in its tracks. Of course, she could not have imagined the maidservant folding the dress and then, with unwashed hands, pouring her mistress a glass of water from the bedside carafe. But the exact mechanism mattered less than exposing the culprit. And that was the Countess. Oh, there was no doubt about it, she would have said, no doubt at all. It was the Countess who was to blame.

Nan's tale was not well received by her fellow passengers. Some found it distasteful; others no doubt thought it impertinent of a parlour maid to visit cholera – the pauper's plague – on her betters. With each passenger huddled against his neighbour for warmth, the conversation now fragmented, Beamish telling Purselove about the latest investigations into the Prince of Wales's skull and Breeze dismissing rumours that there had been irregularities in the accounts of the Glee Club. On the bench behind (or rather in front, since we had all turned our backs to the wind) I heard Mr Meek and the Costellos discuss military catering, whilst Mr Ezard shared with the Saturnine Stranger his fears that the wet plate collodion process was about to supersede the daguerreotype, and, were that to be the case, M Louis Daguerre would have lived and died in vain. The Saturnine Stranger did not reply. Undaunted by the rain – perhaps because she was wrapped in shawls that made her swell to twice her size – the Duchess of Croydon continued to ply Stumps with pastries, strewing crumbs all over his waistcoat. In the corner seat at the front end of the tub, Culpepper struggled to read a finely bound copy of *The Pilgrim's Progress*, shielding it from the weather with his shovel hat. Since the rain had made notetaking impossible, Miss Osgood had put away her notebook and was hectoring Nan about her bonnet, urging her to put it on, whilst Nan was equally insistent on leaving it off lest the rain spoiled it.

Miss Osgood's note taking, together with its subsequent abandonment, had not gone unnoticed by Turpin.

"I could not help observing how busy Miss Osgood had been on your behalf until the weather forced her to put away her notebook," he remarked.

"Perhaps you should invent waterproof paper," I replied, trying to change the subject.

"That is a most excellent idea. I shall make a note," he said. "But to return to Miss Osgood. Unless I am much mistaken, she has been harvesting tales for your granary ever since we left Canterbury, has she not? Confess, Mr Blackwood, confess."

Sensing that he was more amused than offended, I admitted that what he had said was true and, in response to further questioning, offered him a partial account of my grand scheme. Of course, I omitted all mention the Ebenezer's debts, pretending instead that such income as Miss Osgood and I hoped to earn from publication would be devoted to temperance charities and other good causes.

"In that case, Mr Blackwood," he replied, "I should be honoured to offer you the services of my fabularium."

[Editor's Note: The fullest account of Turpin's fabularium is to be found in the letters that he and Blackwood exchanged on their return to Canterbury. To convince Blackwood of the practicality of his invention, he asked to borrow The Rat Catcher's Apprentice, the fragment that Meek had narrated to Blackwood outside Harrison's Hostel. Turpin was confident that he could extract a variety of endings, each perfectly conclusive yet at the same time radically different. To this request Blackwood readily agreed and sent him the fragment, which, since it was not notated in shorthand by Miss Osgood, has obviously been 'worked up' by him from his own memories of it.]

The Rat Catcher's Apprentice

We are all familiar with the key above the locksmith's door, the Highlander outside the tobacconist's, the carboys in the apothecary's window – so familiar that we tend not to notice them. But in a back street in York there was a sign which no-one could ignore. Gentlemen would tap it with their canes, boys throw stones at it. It was a brass rat, suspended by its tail from a bracket and fitted with a clockwork motor which the owner of the shop could wind from an upper window. At the time our story begins the rat had not rotated for many a year and few alive could recall having seen him do so. He was known locally as Nebuchadnezzar, though who had given him the name and why, no-one could say. His carcass was pockmarked where stones had struck it; his ears were flattened, his nose blunted. But if Nebuchadnezzar was in a sorry state, so, too, was the shop. The windows were filled with rusting tins of poison and traps of every shape and size. Above the door a faded sign read Ephraim Spindles, Rat Catcher-in-Ordinary to His Majesty King William IV. This last claim was almost certainly false, but since Ephraim Spindles and William IV were long dead, no-one saw fit to challenge it.

He was succeeded by his son Jacob, who was every bit as shiftless as his father. That Spindles had survived at all was thanks, first, to his wife, then, after her death, to his daughter Angelica. It was she who put fresh rats in the display traps and hung dried ones in a line stretched across the window. It was she who charmed the customers – never, they said, was poison served by so fair a hand – and made sure that her father kept the appointments she had made for him. Whilst he spent his days in sewers and cellars, she minded the shop and kept house.

One day, when she was filling stone jars with poison, a sombrely dressed gentleman entered the shop and introduced himself as the Archbishop's Chaplain. He was, he said, in charge of the domestic arrangements at the Palace. In whatever he decided, His Grace was sure to concur. Which brought him to the purpose of his visit. Rats. Rats everywhere. In the stables, in the cellars, even – not a word to anyone, mind – on the main stairs. Might she be able to help? Spindles would be honoured, she told him, and despatched her father to Bishopthorpe without delay. So delighted was the Archbishop with his efforts, that he recommended Spindles to all his colleagues, who, in turn, praised him from their pulpits, so that that he was soon in demand all over the diocese.

Now a man who is rat catcher to the Archbishop of York has no need to advertise. Nevertheless, Angelica sent Nebuchadnezzar away to have his mainspring renewed and his ears straightened. Out went the faded signboard with its absurd boasts about William IV and up went a card announcing that Spindles' many satisfied customers included JPs and ministers of religion. Of course, she had to smarten up her father first. She steamed out the dents in his hat, dyed his waistcoat scarlet and bought him a bottle green coat into whose lining she sewed a whole warren of pockets for his ferrets. But Angelica's boldest innovation was to persuade her father to take on an apprentice. Jacob was not getting any younger, and for the first time he was genuinely overworked as distinct from merely saying so. Reluctantly he agreed. Enquiries were made. A boy was found, and, since this is a story about Meeks, the boy was, of course, a Meek.

You will recall that Meeks come in two varieties: stay-at-home Gilberts and dashing young Jacks. The new apprentice being a Jack, Angelica decided to re-name him Archie, partly because he was from the Scottish branch of the family, and partly because she thought clerical customers might baulk at having their rats exterminated by a mere Jack. She need not have worried. Archie was a great success, especially when he asked them to bless his ferrets before use and sprinkle his traps with holy water. Such was the demand for his services that Jacob retired to the sewers, whilst Archie busied himself with the infestations of gentlefolk.

As his apprenticeship drew to a close, Angelica and her father began to fear for the future. What would happen to them if Archie set himself up as a rival and stole the vicarages and manors, leaving them only the sewers and the tanneries? If, as they feared, he drove a hard bargain, they were prepared to offer him a junior partnership. But Archie wanted more, much more. Not only did he want a half share, he wanted Angelica's hand in marriage. Angelica and her father were horrified, but concealing their distaste, asked for time to consider the proposal.

"You have until tomorrow," he said.

"Whatever are we to do?" asked Angelica as soon as they were alone.

"You could marry him."

"I'd sooner die."

"If you refuse he'll leave and take all our best customers with him."

"Then good riddance to them," she said. "And him. I'm off to bed"

But next morning, to the surprise of Archie and her father, who had resigned himself to losing his protégé, Angelica came up with a proposal of her own.

"If I were to offer a challenge," she told Archie, "a challenge in which I don't think you can possibly succeed, then I would not, technically, have refused you. If you win, I agree to marry you; if you don't, then you will stay at Spindles as a journeyman. Is it a bargain?"

"It depends on the challenge."

"In the bowels of the city there lives a rat before whom all other rats bow down. Drain dwellers bring him tributes, poets with perfumed whiskers flatter him with odes. Few have seen him. From time to time a rumour spreads that he lives in some forgotten crypt or in the roots of the city wall. The truth is that no-one knows. It is sometimes said that there are rat runs deeper than we know of, royal highways that lead to a den where he lives in kingly state, holding court and receiving tribute from rats black and brown. You have a year to find him and bring him to me, dead or alive. For a year I shall wait. If you succeed, I shall marry you; if you fail, then I am free to marry whomsoever I choose and you shall stay a journeyman at Spindles."

"And how will I know this King Rat?"

"He has a golden tail."

For several moments he hovered in indecision. She saw how it was: vanity pricked him on, prudence held him back.

"If you wish," she said, "we can have a notary to witness the bargain."

"In that case I accept."

When the bargain had been signed and sealed and Archie and the notary had departed, Jacob Spindles turned to his daughter and asked:

"How come I have never heard of this King Rat when I know every cellar and rat run in the city?"

"Because," said Angelica, "I have just invented him."

[Editor's note: Here ends the fragment of The Rat Catcher's Apprentice *that Blackwood sent to Turpin. A lengthy correspondence now ensues, much of it taken up with Turpin's assurances that although a machine to generate tales on demand was some way off, it was nonetheless theoretically possible. His basic idea seems to have been that stories fall into categories*

– myth, folklore, romance and so on – categories that license certain possibilities and exclude others. Thus a story that begins 'Once upon a time' may permit talking animals or magical objects, but exclude bullion robberies or mundane domestic details. A choice of category, then, limits possibilities and each choice within that category reduces possibilities still further, the art of story-telling being to spring surprises when all the options seems to have been exhausted.

Readers will recall that Turpin had once discussed with the Countess of Lovelace the possibility of adapting the Jacquard punch card system for the manufacture of stories. It seems that on his return to Canterbury he set about building just such a machine. He called it 'Lovelace', after the Countess, and though it has not survived, details of it were registered with the Patent Office. Turpin's aim was to eliminate the writer. What he envisaged was a system in which publishers would visit a 'fabularium', where they would be presented with a pattern book, from which they would choose a genre and within that genre steer their characters through a series of rewards and hazards until they reached some kind of closure. As they made their choices, they would dictate them to an operative who would transfer them to punch cards. These cards would then be taped together and used to summon what Turpin called 'plot particles' from a huge bank of story components which he had had set up in moveable type. The labour involved must have been enormous. At the time of the correspondence with Blackwood, Lovelace was still in its infancy. Only a few dozen stories – including fairy tales from Perrault, Hans Anderson and the brothers Grimm, Lamb's Tales from Shakespeare, The Arabian Nights and Ovid's Metamorphoses – had been broken down into their constituent parts, but many more were planned. 'Not until the whole libraries have been broken up into plot particles and set up in type will Lovelace be able to dispense any kind of tale on demand," he told Blackwood, anticipating by a hundred years Roland Barthes' notion that there is no such thing as originality, only quotation. Blanks were left for the customer to fill in the odd descriptive detail, as well as the names of people and places. Eventually, Turpin assured Blackwood, it would take no longer to write a story than to read one and, once customers had familiarised themselves with the pattern book, less time even than that. Whether Lovelace ever achieved this happy state, we simply do not know, but since Turpin was a man given to sudden enthusiasms which quickly evaporated, it is doubtful.

As I have said, the correspondence between Turpin and Blackwood represents Lovelace in an early stage of development, when what we would call its database was very limited. What follows are extracts that indicate the directions in which The Rat Catcher's Apprentice *was taken by Turpin's machine.]*

Dear Blackwood,

   I received The Rat Catcher's Apprentice yesterday and set Lovelace to work on it immediately. As I see it, the story leaves off at a point where it could have continued in several different directions. Of the main possibilities I select five:

1. Myth: Gods, heroes, slaying the monster.
2. Folk tale: Riddles and curses, supernatural helpers, talking animals, talismans, love triumphs, the guilty punished.
3. Burlesque. As in 1 or 2 above, but inflated to the point of absurdity.
4. Romance: Heroine issues challenge, the quest, bouts of knight errantry, helpers and hinderers, constancy rewarded.
5. Autobiography: Rats to riches, technical challenges overcome, triumph of the will, girl won round, domestic detail allowed, prices a possibility.

   Since Lovelace's style is not at present all I would wish, I enclose a summary of the plot particles it has selected from Categories 1 and 4.

   No 1 starts with the arming of the hero and the hero's sacrifice of a favourite ferret. Hero enters the labyrinth, is befriended by a young female rat who guides him through the drains and cellars. Finally, he confronts the monster, and, finding his weapons ineffective, strangles it with his bare hands and cuts off its tail in triumph, intending to nail it over the door of the shop. Far from being grateful to his helper, he hands her over to Angelica, who poisons her and hangs her up by her tail in the shop window.

No 4. Hero given an impossible challenge. Sets off on his quest, slays dragons and other undesirables, having first liberated captives from their clutches. Three temptresses confront him. Two he resists, but to the third he succumbs, whereupon she disarms him and delivers him to the King Rat who is not only expecting him but has prepared a box in which to imprison him. When Archie protests that the box is too small, the monster assures him that even he can fit into it and squeezes inside to prove his point. Archie slams the lid shut, having first cut off his tail which he carries home in triumph. As he lays it before his lady it turns into gold before her very eyes.

As you can see, Lovelace supplies plot particles, which at the moment are fairly rudimentary, but throw in some names and an adjective or two and you have the makings of a fine tale. Of course, the system needs further refinement; all the same, I am sure you will agree with me, that for a first assignment Lovelace has acquitted herself well.

I remain, Sir, your obedient servant,

Augustus Turpin

[Editor's Note: It seems that Blackwood did not care for either version, not that it really mattered, since in another letter he describes how, in a recent conversation with Gilbert Meek, he had told the tripe dresser about the fabularium and two the endings which Lovelace had supplied. To his surprise, Meek objected that neither was anything like the official one, of which, as it happened, he had recently been reminded by a member of his family. Blackwood's letter to Turpin concludes:

You identified five roads down which the tale might proceed: myth, folklore, burlesque, romance and autobiography. But there was a sixth – social satire – and this was the one the Meek family chose. One of their Jacks had made a fortune in glue boiling and tried to lord it over them. First, he got himself elected to several Edinburgh clubs, then he applied for a coat of arms, sat for a portrait by Wilkie and finally married a baronial castle in Perthshire, appropriating his wife's ancestry and tartan in the process. It was at this parvenu Jack that the tale was directed. I now offer you the definitive ending, not in summary form, but in a version fit, I hope, for eventual publication.

The Rat Catcher's Apprentice
(The Official Ending)

Once Archie had departed Angelica promptly fell in love with the young man across the street. He was of sound family, his father owned a thriving business and his prospects were good. Neither he nor Angelica saw any reason to delay the wedding, though Jacob urged caution. It would do no harm to wait a year, during which her suitor could only grow richer and she more beautiful. And there was also, he reminded them, the small matter of the contract with Archie.

"What if he does return before the year is over?" she replied. "He can't bring the prize with him because there is no prize to bring."

"Granted," replied her father, "but you will be revealed as a promise breaker, and the business may suffer. Our clergy customers would not like it."

But Angelica's case was strengthened by Archie's continued absence. Months had passed without anyone having set eyes on him. And with his disappearance the moral obligation seemed to weaken, so that, in the end, Jacob modified his objection and ruled that if nine months passed without any sightings, Angelica and Archie should be free to marry.

The wedding was a modest affair, though still grander than Angelica had expected or deserved. The groom's side of the church was packed with wealthy tradesmen, whilst she had had to borrow her bridesmaids from the tobacconists across the street. She felt the disparity keenly. As soon as she was married, she promised herself that she would put rat killing behind her: Jacob would be provided for, the shop sold and Nebuchadnezzar melted down for scrap. As she stood at the altar rail, the vision of a more genteel life passed through her mind.

"I require and charge you both ...," began the rector.

She imagined herself in her very own parlour with her very own piano.

"... as ye will answer at the dreadful day of judgment ..."

Or, better still, conducting her first at-home in her very own drawing room.

"... that if either of you know any impediment why ye may not be lawfully joined together in Matrimony ..."

Or even riding to hounds.

"... ye do now confess it."

There was a brief pause, then a single word rang out like a pistol shot.

"Wait!"

Everyone turned to peer down the aisle. Advancing slowly up the nave was Archie. Slung ghillie-fashion across his shoulders was the body of an enormous rat, its tail a ribbon of shining gold.

From the altar, Archie denounced Angelica's betrayal to the entire congregation. He revealed the promise she had made, the challenge she had issued; he spoke of the dangers he had braved in cellars and drains, of the privations he had undergone and of the horrors he had seen. Finally, he described in shocking detail how he had confronted and killed the giant rat, whom, naturally enough, he had named Nebuchadnezzar. Angelica's vision of the good life evaporated.

If the first wedding was irrecoverably lost, Jacob was determined that the second should be prevented. He called in fresh lawyers to scrutinise the contract, insisting that there must be a loophole somewhere. No, replied the lawyers, the notary who had drawn up the contract had done his work too well for that: the Lord Chancellor himself could not find fault with it.

The lawyers having failed him, Jacob applied to Archie. But Archie was immovable. He had won his prize fairly. Nothing would persuade him to give it up. It was his by right.

Angelica had no alternative, therefore, but to tell him the truth.

"Know then," she said, "that I lied to you. King Rat did not exist. I made him up. To save myself, I invented him. He was a figment of my imagination, nothing more. It is impossible that you should have killed him."

Archie, to whom the revelation came as no surprise, had his answer ready. No matter that her rat was imaginary, his was real. Whether or not the contract was made in bad faith did not matter; he had carried out his part of the bargain to the letter. There was further resort to lawyers, but the lawyers were unanimous: a rat of a particular character had been stipulated and the rat thus stipulated had been delivered. Ergo there were no grounds for a challenge in law. All that remained was for Jacob to persuade Angelica to give in. "After all," he said, "Archie may not make such a bad husband. And the business will flourish, you may be sure of that."

And of course it did, though not in ways that Jacob approved. Shortly after his marriage to Angelica, Archie shut the shop in York and, when Jacob objected, forced him to retire.

"York has had its day," he told Jacob. "We have done our job here too well. There are richer pickings elsewhere."

He opened up branches in Beverly and Hull, where there were rats aplenty – enough, he assured the Spindles, to keep them all in comfort for years to come. He was right. A trickle of comforts soon appeared, shortly after becoming a flood. Once a parlour and a piano had been the limit of Angelica's ambitions; now she longed for an orangery and a carp pond. But her wants were modest compared with Archie's. Trade was so brisk that within a few short years they were able to move from villa to manor and from hall to castle. From the College of Herald he acquired a coat-of-arms – *per fess gules and argent in chief three rats heads erased of the second* – which he applied to every surface of his many mansions. It perched over doorways, glowed in stained glass, glinted on the silver, gleamed on cups and plates and rippled on flags. From Edwin Landseer he commissioned a portrait of himself in Highland costume, his foot resting, not on a fallen stag, but on a giant rat. In the Gun Room and the Library, on mantel pieces and on pedestals, he placed glass cases filled with triumphs of the taxidermist's art. Rats, their postures stiffened by sawdust, stared out of glass cases, all of them clearly labelled with the dates and circumstances of their demise. In corridors and on landings, rats' heads protruded from shields, row upon row of them, broken only by the occasional pastel of a favourite kill. And as his corridors lengthened, so, too, did the rows of rats' heads on the walls. The same went for mantelpieces and glass cases, and for windows and stained glass shields. All was in such exquisitely bad taste that visitors rather marvelled at it than condemned it. Secretly, no doubt, they despised it. But whatever they may have said to each other in private, they dared not criticise publicly or shun Archie's hospitality. They could not afford to. Not only did he suppress their vermin, he put his name to their bills, for the country gentry whose company he now sought were habitually spendthrift.

When Archie finally realised his architectural ambitions in the form of a castle (mock baronial with Tudor flourishes), he decided to build a tomb for Nebuchadnezzar. Sprouting a great many crockets and finials, it was the last word in parvenu vulgarity. One entered through massive oak doors into a vaulted interior paved with encaustic tiles, all of them bearing Archie's coat of arms. Lancet windows filled with strawberry-coloured glass cast a rosy glow over an effigy of Nebuchadnezzar, forepaws clasped as if in prayer, brass tail trailing over the edge of the plinth.

Angelica did not protest at the extravagance – that would have been futile – but pointed out that since Nebuchadnezzar had been buried many years before, disinterment might prove distasteful. Archie was dismissive. The lead-lined coffin had already been recovered and its occupant found to have been as fresh as a daisy. As to extravagance, would she deny him his triumph? He would do as he wished and she would have to put up with it. There was to be a grand ceremonial opening, and she, as hostess, would be expected to attend.

As the rows of rats' heads lengthened in the corridors, Archie's affection for his wife, never strong, diminished. By way of clothes, carriages and creature comforts, he denied her nothing. She had only to ask and he would shower her with furs and fabrics. But his favours were all material; all he required of her was to be the receptacle of his bounty, nothing more. She had wanted a child, and though he was keen to have a son and heir, he always told her that he would attend to it when the time was right. Somehow, though, the time was never right. There was always a race horse to train, a billiard room to refurbish.

"But when?" she asked.

"Before long," he replied, "I hope to be Deputy Lord Lieutenant. Something might be possible before then."

As it happened something was possible sooner than either of them had expected. He was astonished as she when she informed him that a son and heir might be joining them in the New Year.

"But that's when I hope to assume the Deputyship," he protested. "I had it confirmed this morning."

As Angelica's belly swelled, so, too, did her husband's schemes for his term of office. One day he received a letter from Her Majesty's Secretary informing him that the Queen's German cousin was to visit the County and that it was customary, the Lord Lieutenant being indisposed, for his Deputy to accommodate the royal visitors.

"But that is impossible," said his wife. "The dates of his visit are the dates of my confinement. You will have to refuse."

"Nonsense," said Archie. "We shall seal off the East Wing. You can be confined there. He'll never know."

"You mean I can be banished there."

"It will be for your own good."

So furious was the argument that the servants heard it below stairs. Afterwards, she put on her bonnet and shawl and went outside to take the air. She wandered for while in the grounds, for the first time getting lost in the maze which enclosed a topiaried figure of Nebuchadnezzar. Having extricated herself with difficulty, she turned her steps towards the tomb. On impulse she pushed open the door and went in.

To her surprise someone was already there. In the strawberry light she made out an extraordinary figure, who wore a crushed top hat and a belted blue gown with a pewter badge on the sleeve. From his shoulder hung a hessian satchel and from his hat a cluster of faded ribbons. But although she was surprised to find him there, she knew immediately what he was. Archie had told her about gaberlunzie men, or King's beadsmen, whom he remembered from his Scottish childhood. They were a tribe of licensed beggars, who wore a pewter badge as a sign of their calling and carried hessian satchels into which they packed the fruits of their begging. Most were harmless eccentrics who circulated local gossip. A few were said to have magical powers and a very few actually did. According to Archie, there were secret glens in the Highlands where divination and other lost arts were practised. A handful of gaberlunzie men knew their way into them and were familiar with taghairm, gramarye and other eldritch practices. Few were left, fewer still made their way south of the Border.

"Who are you and what do you want?" she demanded.

"Tae see the fine tomb Archie has built for – what d'ye call him?"

"Nebuchadnezzar."

"Nebuchadneezar," he chuckled. "A fine name, an unco fine name. Worth a raik for the name itsel'. Weel, mebbe that, and to see the bairn as weel."

"Bairn?" echoed Angelica in alarm. "What bairn?"

"Will ye listen to her! 'What bairn?' Dinna ye play the innocent wi' me, young leddy."

At that moment Archie appeared in the doorway. He showed no surprise at finding the old man and had clearly been expecting him.

"Angelica," he said, "leave us. What the old scoundrel has to say concerns me alone. Go!"

Angelica fled from the tomb and climbed the steps to the terrace. At the top she turned to look back. Through the open door she could see the two men arguing furiously. The beggar kept gesticulating towards the tomb and then, in a gesture he clearly meant her to see, he went to the door and pointed at her, whereupon Archie seized him by the collar, intending no doubt to throw him off the premises. But the older man was the stronger of the two and flung Archie to the ground. In a voice that carried to the top of the steps, he let forth a string of invective, or perhaps a curse, in what Angelica presumed to be Gaelic, before picking up his hat and satchel and walking away.

Later, Archie, looking a little the worse for wear, came to her sitting room.

"The old scoundrel I neither expected nor wanted to see," he said.

"What did he want?"

"He came to collect his dues, but I would not pay him."

"But what can you possibly owe him?"

He sat down beside her and took her hand.

"Angelica, we have deceived each other. You invented a prince among rats so that you would not have to marry me; I produced one – or rather, the appearance of one – so that you would. But mine was no more real than yours. It was an illusion, a conjuring trick."

"But the tomb?"

"Empty."

"And the lead coffin?"

"Full of stones. I paid for an illusion that lasted a few minutes only."

"How was the trick done?"

"In the remotest glens, there are still people who know how to do such things and the old gaberlunzie knows how to find them."

"So it is to him that you owe all this? House, horses, position. Me."

"And it was to collect his dues that he came," he replied.

A terrifying suspicion began to form in her mind.

"His dues?"

"I promised him anything he wished and a time of his choosing. But he will not have the child. That I promise. I refused him. That is why he struck me."

"It would have been better for us both," said Angelica sadly, "if we had never left York."

If Archie had been discomfited by the gaberlunzie man's visit, he did not remain subdued for long. Soon he was busy with preparations both for the royal visit and for Angelica's confinement, neither of which was to be allowed to trouble the other. After the visit of the gaberlunzie man, Angelica did not find it easy to recover her peace of mind. Her dreams were troubled, her thoughts uneasy. There was, she felt, a force at work in the house, a force that manifested itself in a thousand minor vexations – candles that smoked, falls of soot and, everywhere, an inexplicable smell of heather.

On the day that Prince Leopold arrived, Angelica went into labour. She was dimly aware of a clatter of hooves, a crunch of wheels on gravel and from her window she could see the flag of Saxe-Coburg fluttering from a distant turret. For his part, the Prince was kept well away from the East Wing and was in no danger of straying into the drama taking place there. On his tour he was invited to admire the rats' heads in the corridor, was shown the Landseer portrait of Archie in the dining room and had to be rescued from the maze, though not before he had been introduced to its topiaried occupant. The trouble began in the tomb. In the strawberry twilight, the Prince was convinced he saw the effigy of Nebuchadnezzar twitch. Now it does not do to contradict a prince, even a minor German one, and when Archie diplomatically suggested that it was merely a trick of the light, His Highness was gravely affronted.

"With my own eyes I saw him move," he insisted. "With my own eyes, I say. Take me away from this place. I have had already too much rats for one day."

But if he thought that by being shown to his room his troubles would be at an end, he was mistaken: they had scarcely begun. Prince Leopold was standing before the mirror in his dressing room combing his moustaches, when he saw the rat in the glass case on the mantelpiece tapping the glass as if he wished to be let out. He and his valet listened and watched in horror as the creature began to nibble at the putty which held the glass panels in place. Quitting the room with moustache half-combed, he made his way to the dining room, determined to confront his host. In the corridor he was joined by others of his entourage who had had similar experiences. Suddenly one of the ladies screamed. A large rat whose head had been mounted on an escutcheon now eased itself – shoulders, torso and tail – out of the wooden shield and slithered down the wall on to the floor. Other rats were on the move, too. One by one they squeezed out of their escutcheons and began running down the corridor. By now there was panic among the royal party, some running this way, some that. But whichever way they ran they were met by a fresh army of rats who had freed themselves from cases and frames elsewhere. On the threshold of the dining room His Highness paused, paralysed by fear. Above the mantelpiece, the rat in the Landseer portrait was struggling to acquire a third dimension and free himself from the gilded frame for which Archie had paid fifty guineas in Bond Street. Archie had stationed himself at the entrance of the dining room, but was swept aside by the tide of rats which now converged on the banquet laid out on the table. Whilst the rats plundered the tureens amid a chaos of overturned decanters and broken china, the guests tried to fend them off with whatever missiles came to hand – serviette rings, salt cellars, mustard pots and roast potatoes.

Suddenly, as if someone had waved a wand, the commotion ceased. Residents and dignitaries froze. From far off, from high up in a distant part of the building came a scream, a long unwavering note that lasted fully half a minute, before the chaos and din took up from where they had left off.

Archie freed himself from the clutching hands of his guests and ran as fast as he could down the corridor, past rows of empty glass cases and uninhabited escutcheons, to the door which opened into the East Wing. Pursued by any army of rats, most squeaking in what seemed like high-pitched Gaelic, he ran up the stairs two at a time, until he reached his wife's chamber. He threw open the door in time to see the midwife lift a bundle of swaddling clothes from the bed. From its folds hung a golden tail.

The long drawn-out scream recalled Angelica to her senses. Sitting up, she looked round her. Everything was as it should be – clothes folded on the chair, pitcher on the wash stand, hair brushes on the dressing table. Downstairs she could hear Jacob raking out the ash from the stove. Out in the street, horses' hoofs and hobnailed boots on cobbles announced the start of the working day. She dressed hurriedly and made her way down to the parlour, where her father and Archie were already waiting.

"Well," asked the latter, "have you considered my proposal?"

"As I understand it," she replied, "you will leave if I refuse you and stay if I don't."

"That is correct."

"In that case," she said, "the answer is no. Now, if you will excuse me, I must go and wind Nebuchadnezzar."

[Editor's Note: Turpin seems to have taken the rejection of his endings personally. He scribbled a note to Blackwood, thanking him for the 'official' ending and promising to add it to Lovelace's database. The tone of the note is peevish. Just because an ending is 'official', he complained, doesn't necessarily make it right. From a single point of departure a story might go in more than one direction and reach any number of destinations. It is only when people try to own stories that particular versions become definitive. Most tales, he observed, are like common land where all can graze unsupervised. Only when the land has been enclosed are its limits defined and trespassers warned off. Folk tales and myths, on the other hand, have no owners and no-one patrols their boundaries. That was why he had favoured them.

It is doubtful whether Lovelace ever got beyond the experimental stage. What Turpin excelled at was gadgets, easy to design and quick to make, leaving him free to move on to new schemes before he got bored. Lovelace, by contrast, was a long-term project, requiring patience and money, neither of which he possessed in sufficient quantity. All of which is a pity, because he was probably a better literary theorist than he was an inventor. As far as I can tell, no self-cleaning garden rake or heated topper ever made it into production, but the ideas that stories are complex structures of memes bound together by concealed codes has kept many an academic in tenured comfort throughout the twentieth century. He approached literature unsentimentally, as an engineer. For him it was a series of mechanisms, to be taken apart, examined and reassembled in new and interesting ways.

I said earlier that beyond an application to the Patent Office, Lovelace has left no traces. I have since come to believe that this may not be entirely true. A few weeks ago I attended view day at a Canterbury auction, where I noticed a job lot of items from a printer's workshop. Among the fonts and matrices, there was a form, i.e. a page made up in movable type. Even though the type was reversed, two words leapt out at me: 'Archie' and 'rat'. I put in a successful bid for Lot 27 (Letterpress, items various) and carried it off to my cellar where I placed it alongside the Blackwood archive. I cannot prove it, but I believe that I possess the only surviving fragment of Lovelace. Turpin must have gone on experimenting with it after Blackwood had rejected his mythic and folkloric endings. Still in heroic vein, he has Nebuchadnezzar escaping from a dockside warehouse with Archie in hot pursuit. Once on the quayside the rat shakes off his pursuer by boarding a ship. And the name of the ship? The Matilda Briggs. Its destination? Sumatra. I stared in astonishment. Could it be that the giant rat to which Angelica's imagination had given birth had somehow emerged from Arthur Conan Doyle's pen half a century later, thanks to a string a of intermediaries now lost to us? Could it be that the Giant Rat of Sumatra, that story for which in the words of Sherlock Holmes 'the world is not yet prepared', could have been Nebuchadnezzar? Of course, this is pure speculation, probably even wishful thinking. But there is one other link, albeit a weak one. Conan Doyle is known to have named the Hound of the Baskervilles after his favourite font – Baskerville Old Face. And the font of my Lovelace fragment? Why, the very same.]

The Duchess of Croydon was so enchanted by the attentions of Stumps that she failed to alight at Tunbridge and only awoke to the fact when the train made an unexpected stop at Paddock Wood. Needless to say, she was all for insisting that Sturdee reverse the train up the track, and in this she was seconded by Stumps, who, as a former railway navvy, should have known better. Their pleas were lost, however, in the drama which now unfolded. No sooner had we stopped than a small, rosy-cheeked man in a check waistcoat scrambled into our tub and greeted Mr Breeze by name. Breeze, who had been engrossed in Beamish's report on the Prince of Wales's cranial abnormalities, sprang to his feet in alarm and, opening the door furthest from the platform, leapt down on to the track, where he was seized by a square-faced man, also in check waistcoat, who had clearly been expecting him.

"My apologies, ladies and gentlemen," said the rosy-cheeked man to the astonished company. "A small matter of some pounds, shillings and pence owed by this gentleman. Excuse the dramatic entrance, all too common in our line of work, I'm afraid. Well, it's off to the sponging house with you, Charles", he continued, pulling Breeze back into the tub and snapping a pair of handcuffs on him. "Mrs Sturridge is preparing your old room even as we speak. Everything spick and span, warming pan between the sheets, piano tuned, fresh cheese in the mousetraps. No comfort neglected, no effort spared."

"And no expense either by the sound of it," said Purselove. "This will cost you dear. I wish I could help you, my dear Breeze, but my pockets are as empty as yours."

"Do you mean that people have to pay to be imprisoned for debt?" asked Miss Osgood.

"Indeed they do, ma'am," replied Mr Sturridge, "especially if they wish to be incarcerated in comfort. Lowther, over here, if you please," he added, directing the square-faced man to sit so that Breeze was wedged between them on the bench facing us.

"But that is absurd," persisted Miss Osgood. "If you charge people for their keep, how can they ever hope to be free?"

"If you can't earn enough from peddling Fossett's Electuary and Dean's Relish," suggested Purselove, "why don't you return to your old trade of retrospective destinating?"

Breeze looked uncomfortable.

"Surely it's worth a try," continued Purselove. "There must be thousands of people who long to have their pasts re-written. Take me. I'd pay good money – if I had it – to strike out all those Banquos and Horatios and have them replaced by Hamlets and Macbeths."

"The truth is," said Breeze, "there never was such a trade. I made it up."

"Made it up?" repeated Purselove.

"What I mean is," said Breeze, "that I retrospectively destinated myself. I was, you might say, my only customer."

With a whoosh of steam and a shower of sparks, *Hengist* hauled the Ebenezer 'Special' out of Paddock Wood. By now the October twilight was drawing to a close. Buildings and trees were visible only in outline, and the band, unable to read their music, stuttered to a halt in a series of discords and incomplete phrases. Turpin, who was usually too preoccupied with his own projects to take much notice of what was going on around him, was eager to return to the subject of stories, to which, as he kept reminding me, he brought an engineer's eye.

[Editor's Note: The reader will remember that the earlier part of this conversation has been omitted in favour of the later correspondence between Blackwood and Turpin which sets out more clearly the principles according to which Turpin constructed his Fabulorium.]

At the mention of stories, Mr Sturridge, who, together with Lowther and Breeze, was now little more than a silhouette, pricked up his ears. Why, he said, if the gentleman opposite brought an engineer's eye to the telling of tales, he, Sturridge, brought a bailiff's.

"Debt," he continued, "is a great provoker of stories. Stories as excuses, stories as self-extenuation, stories in which everyone is to blame except the teller. Mrs Sturridge lends a sympathetic ear and afterwards writes them down in a book One day we hope to publish a collection entitled *Tales from the Sponging House*. When the goose has laid enough golden eggs to fill a volume or two, we shall retire on the proceeds."

Inwardly I cursed that Miss Osgood had had to put away her notebook.

"Perhaps," I said, "you would care to share one of the golden eggs with us."

"By all means," he said. "What do you say, Lowther? Shall we give him Mr Springham and the Absconding Bank Clerk or Mr Barrington and the Accursed Heirloom?"

"Why not," replied Lowther, "give them Mr Cornelius and the Lady Cornelia?"

"The very thing!" replied Mr Sturridge. "Instructive, too. We would all do well to heed its warnings. Now Mrs Sturridge and I like to think of our visitors as guests. And if they are guests on compulsion that still does not make them prisoners. How could they be? A sponging house, whatever people may say, is not a prison. It may, I grant you, be a step on the road to one, but it is still only a step, not the whole journey. Only when a man has been admitted to the Marshalsea or the King's Bench can he truly be called a gaolbird. And some gaolbirds, let us not forget, are actually birds – birds, that is, of the feathered variety. Some are free to come and go as they please; others are kept behind bars and taught to sing. And wonderful songsters they make. I knew a man, scene shifter at The Adelphi, who tried to teach a linnet to sing an aria from *Lucia di Lammermoor.*"

"Did he succeed?" asked Purselove.

"He thought he did. 'Listen to that,' he'd say. 'Listen to that. Can you hear it? That's *Regnava del Silenzio*, that is'."

"And was it?"

"No, but that didn't stop him thinking it was. That's how it is with prisoners. They hear what they want to hear and never hear what they don't. A marvellous organ, the human imagination: one never ceases to wonder at it. Why, they send out their starlings or their pigeons on a trip and pretend they've gone on it themselves. 'Off you go,' they say. 'Take yourself off to Margate or Brighton and tell me all about it when you come home.' Best of all is Derby Day. 'Five guineas on Orlando or Merry Monarch and ten if you can

get fifteen to one.' For many of them it's like going on an outing
without leaving their cells."

"For those who combine well-developed Ideality with weak per-
ceptive faculties I imagine it is," observed Beamish.

"And where do Cornelius and the Lady Cornelia fit in?" I
prompted.

"Will you tell it, or shall I?" Mr Sturridge asked Lowther. "It's
your story. It's you what told me."

"And a prisoner what told me – a Mr Turnbull, hired out toy
boats on Hampstead Ponds – so it's no more mine than yours."

"Much obliged, Lowther," said Mr Sturridge, who had clearly
intended to tell it all along. "Here, then, is the story of Mr Cornelius
and the Lady Cornelia – often referred to as *The Jackdaws' Wedding* –
as told to me by Lowther and as told to Lowther by Mr Turnbull of
Hampstead Ponds."

"And as told to Mr Turnbull of Hampstead Ponds," Lowther
reminded him, "by the jackdaw what lived on his window sill in the
King's Bench."

The Bailiff's Tale of
The Jackdaws' Wedding

L et us leave the Lady Cornelia till later – if she was a lady, which I doubt – and
start with Mr Cornelius. Oh, he was a plain mister all right; there was no doubt
about that, even though he had relations who lived in an imposing Tudor
chimney at Hampton Court. They kept regular mealtimes, bathed in ornamental
ponds and even had a riverside retreat at Chertsey. But if Mr Cornelius didn't have
class, he had movables and plenty of them – earrings, coins, cufflinks, spoons –
which he stored in a hollow tree in the grounds of Chiswick House. Now jackdaws'
morality is confusing to outsiders. Though they think of nothing of stealing, they
do not refer to it as such. The words 'rob', 'pilfer' and 'thieve' do not exist in their
vocabulary. Goods are never 'stolen' but 'relocated', and relocated goods are never

'loot' or 'plunder' but 'movables'. Such euphemisms suggest that though they admit to doing no wrong, they must, at some deeper level, feel that they are.

On the whole, jackdaws prefer the shiny religions. They like candlesticks and chalices, bells and silver buckles. Most are Anglicans or Anglo-Catholics, and only in rural Wales, where chapels outnumber churches, do they become Methodists as a last resort. Anglicanism is, in any case, a largely Gothic affair and Gothic churches are rich in perches from which to spot unguarded movables. As luck would have it, in Cornelius's local church – St Mary's, Mortlake – there was a broken pane in the clerestory which allowed him to keep an eye on the collection plate and listen to the sermon, which he always enjoyed, even when he found it baffling.

One Sunday he arrived to take up his position, only to find it occupied by a lady jackdaw with the most splendid plumage he had ever seen. From bill to tail she was an exquisite succession of blacks and greys. Politely Cornelius enquired of the newcomer whether she intended to stay long and, if not, at what point in the service she intended to leave. She would, she said with a tilt of the head, very much like to hear the sermon, the visiting preacher being a great favourite of hers. To which he replied, he would be willing to cede his place to her on condition they meet afterwards in an outdoor tea room where he could particularly recommend the cake.

"Ah, cake!" she sighed, flicking her tail up and down. "What will I not do for cake! My mother, the Duchess, always says, 'Cornelia, cake will be the undoing of you'."

"Pardon me, but did you say 'Cornelia'?"

"Why, don't you like it?"

"On the contrary, I think it a very sweet name, the more so as mine is 'Cornelius'."

"'Cornelius?' I have never much cared for the masculine version. Perhaps if I call you 'Mr Cornelius', I shall get used to it."

"And until you do, I shall call you 'Lady Cornelia'."

"'*The* Lady Cornelia', if you please. It's old-fashioned, I know, but my mother ..."

"The Duchess..."

"Precisely, the Duchess, always insists on it."

And that was how it began. So uplifting was the sermon and so excellent the cake, their courtship got off to a flying start. Mr Cornelius took her on a tour of his favourite rooftops and ledges; she introduced him to her favourite trees and gardens. From the outset it was clear to Mr Cornelius that she did not approve of his acquaintance, nearly all of whom were in trade, whereas hers were more genteel and lived above Palladian mansions or in parkland trees, their nests exquisitely furnished with movables of every description.

At the Lady Cornelia's insistence, he renewed his acquaintance with the Hampton-Corneliuses and spent many a happy hour with them, eyeing the carriage folk and learning to identify their coats of arms. Though proud to mix in such circles, Mr Cornelius was uncomfortably aware of his lack of breeding. He wanted the Lady Cornelia to be proud of him and not to have to make excuses for him behind his back. But if he lived in daily fear of humiliation, life with the Lady Cornelia was worth it. He was besotted with her – with her appearance, her voice, her refinement, her definite article. And what was more, she could read. She had been brought up in a walnut tree in Chelsea, a venerable specimen in a garden belonging to an invalid lady whose companion would sit in its shade and read to her. By following the voice and the words on the printed page she quickly learned how the trick was done. She could repeat by heart whole portions of *The Pickwick Papers*, several verses of the *Lady of Shalott* and almost the whole of *Jorrocks's Jaunts and Jollities*, which was a particular favourite of the invalid lady, who had it read to her over and over again.

From time to time it occurred to Mr Cornelius to ask himself why, of all people, she should have bestowed her affections on him. The answer should have been obvious. (It certainly was to his friends.) The Lady Cornelia was greedy and, like the Hampton-Corneliuses, who lived far beyond their means, indigent. At first she was grateful for small tokens of affection – earrings, silver buttons and the like – but she soon began to make demands of her own, demands which, especially after their engagement, began to tax his ingenuity.

"And why should they not?" she asked when he complained. "True lovers glory in such trials; they do not complain. You should read more poetry, Mr Cornelius; you are too bourgeois."

By way of cure, Mr Cornelius submitted to having Mrs Browning's *Sonnets from the Portuguese* read to him, though he had first to relocate them from the bedside table of a young lady in Rosemary Gardens. Although he knew the house well, he had never called at night before and knew all too well the risk he was taking. But the poems were not enough for the Lady Cornelia. She wanted more; she wanted the silver-backed hairbrush and tortoiseshell comb which had lain beside them on the bedside table as well. Now it is a rule among West London jackdaws not to visit the same place twice in succession. It is partly a matter of risk, partly a matter of etiquette. One doesn't wish to abuse the generosity of people who leave their windows open or their valuables lying about. Among Mr Cornelius's friends, it just wasn't done. Or hadn't been until the Lady Cornelia decided that it ought to be.

"Superstitious nonsense! Nobody believes that sort of thing any more," she scoffed. "You must move with the times, Cornelius."

She was right: he must. It would be hard to disregard the rules of etiquette, but no doubt he would get used to it. He would visit and re-visit the house in Mortlake until the dressing table was bare. Now to visit a dressing table once is dangerous, to visit it twice doubly so. As for third and fourth visits they are foolhardy in the extreme, especially when made in the dark. Having removed Mrs Browning without mishap, he returned for the tortoiseshell comb and, again, escaped undetected. It was the silver-backed hair brush that proved his undoing. It was heavier than expected and fell from his claws with a crash, waking the sleeper and scattering the objects on the dressing table all over the floor. The house was quickly roused, though by the time the master had fetched his shotgun Cornelius was safe on a distant rooftop, out of range and out of earshot.

For weeks afterwards there was not an open window to be found in Rosemary Gardens. Tradesmen withdrew their displays from the pavements; perambulators were stripped of rattles and teething rings. To jackdaws Mortlake became a desert. Those who had obeyed the rules were furious; they rounded on Cornelius and drove him from the neighbourhood. It would take years, they said, perhaps generations, to restore the partnership of man and bird in West London.

The Lady Cornelia was unsympathetic. If her Cornelius had been ostracised by fellow-tradesmen, so much the better. They didn't deserve him. He was well rid of them. In the meantime he would have to move. She therefore persuaded the Hampton Court relations to lend their weekend retreat in Chertsey, whilst she was preparing her trousseau and Cornelius was assembling the marital home in the tree she had chosen.

Jackdaws do not go in for long engagements. But Cornelia and Cornelius were exceptions, partly because she had presented him with such a long shopping list, partly because her relations kept adding to it. Ah yes, her relations. She had made it clear from the start that her widowed mother, the Duchess, and her unmarried sister, the Honourable, were to live with them. They depended on her; she was all in all to them. They would not hear of her leaving them. No, she would not hear his objections. She was adamant: if he took her, he took the Duchess and the Honourable too. True, she was forced to concede that one nest would not be strong enough for all four of them; nonetheless, she clung to her original demand, so that Cornelius was forced to construct and furnish a dower house in the lower branches of the marital tree – a mighty oak in Windsor Great Park with a fine view of Eton College. It would not have been so bad if the Duchess and the Honourable had been grateful. But they weren't. They complained endlessly – about the draughts, about the colour scheme, about the noise made by the neighbouring rooks. On no subject were their complaints shriller than that of soft furnishings. Mr Cornelius had proposed lining the dower house with moss stripped from the royal mausoleum at Frogmore.

"Moss?" they scoffed. "Moss might do very well in the circles in which you move, but it is hardly *comme il faut* in ours. Velvet, if you please, or cretonne if you must."

Thanks to an upholsterer's swatch which had been left on an unguarded work bench, he was able to oblige, though that did not silence them for long. In the end, he refused to have anything to do with them and informed the Lady Cornelia that if they wished to communicate with him it would have to be through her.

In the meantime the latter had plenty of demands of her own. She must have a set of apostle spoons and a silver sugar caster; she simply had to have a Japanese fan; she insisted on a pair of brass nutcrackers, a soup ladle, a pearl-handled paper knife. As time went by, her demands became not only shinier but heavier. Why she needed a paperweight – or a bust of Prince Albert or a Doulton creamer – he never discovered, but it was clear that she would not take no for an answer. But there were limits to what he could achieve. She had set her heart on a cut-glass punch bowl – "It will make a wonderful bath; every bird in the Park will be green with envy", she said – but in the end even she had to accept that it was beyond his strength to lift the item in question. That, of course, did not stop Duchess and the Honourable from complaining loudly.

"We were promised full sanitation," they said, "and now we're being palmed off with a muddy puddle behind the Stables. It is really too humiliating."

Since the incident in Mortlake, Mr Cornelius had done very little re-locating himself. Instead, he had drawn on his reserves and bought whatever he needed from jackdaws who specialised in the kind of baubles favoured by the Lady Cornelia. She had been right: his heart was in trade. He had been born and brought up in it. For the movables themselves he felt no particular attachment. "What's in a buckle or collar stud?" he would ask himself; "why, nothing at all compared with the thrill of the deal." Nonetheless, as he emptied the hollow tree in the grounds of Chiswick House, he began to feel uneasy. Day by day he watched them go – salt cellars, nail files, hatpins in a steady stream. Came the day when he had nothing left to sell, though even when the Lady Cornelia demanded a clock he dared not tell her that he no longer had the means to acquire one.

"Don't be alarmed, Cornelius," she had said. "Nothing grand, nothing fancy. A gentleman's repeater would be ideal, though a lady's lapel watch would do at a pinch."

As it happened, one of his former colleagues possessed just such a watch and would have been prepared to trade it if Mr Cornelius had had anything to trade it with. But he hadn't. His reserves were exhausted. He even took himself to Eton College, where he hoped to snatch one of the young gentleman's timepieces from a study windowsill. But the young gentlemen seemed to have been expecting him and had kept their windows shut. It was hopeless. He was at his wits' end. Worse, the Lady Cornelia was beginning to lose patience.

"I'm not naming the day," she told him, "until we have a home fit to live in and no home is fit to live in until it has a clock."

By now the marital nest was so full that some items would surely not be missed. But which? Which baubles had she shown little interest in despite her keenness to have them? His eye lighted on *Sonnets from the Portuguese*. No-one would miss Mrs Browning, would they? It had been weeks now since she had read to him. What if ...? He paused, scarcely able to believe the boldness of his own idea. What if ...? But no, it was too risky. And yet ...

Next day Mr Cornelius approached the jackdaw with the lady's lapel watch and offered him some pieces of paper.

"These," he said, "are all the rage in Lombard Street. They are called promissory notes. In exchange for one of these you give me goods to the value stated on the note and I undertake to pay you back with interest by the date specified."

"And what if you fail?"

"Now that is the beauty of it. If I fail, then there is a second party nominated in the bill" – he named Sir Sampson Skinner, a well-known jackdaw who lived on the roof of the Mansion House – "who is obliged to pay both interest and principal on my behalf."

No jackdaw, especially one in trading circles, likes to be thought stupid, so the other bird took the paper and pretended to study it. Whilst he stared uncomprehendingly at the lines 'How do I love thee! Let me count the ways', Mr Cornelius leaned over his shoulder and read 'On demand I Mortlake Cornelius promise to pay so and so goods to the values of such and such with interest thereon from this date at the rate of twenty per cent per annum. Co-signed Sir Sampson Skinner Bart.'

And that was how the Lady Cornelia got her clock and Mr Cornelius a date for the wedding. From then on, it was he who set the pace. To every extravagant suggestion she made, he capped it with another. To every complaint of the Duchess and the Honourable, he responded with a glittering bauble – a serviette ring, a silver thimble – until the complaints dwindled to grumbles, the grumbles to scowls and the scowls to grudging murmurs of approval.

As preparations for the wedding gathered pace, the *Sonnets from the Portuguese* shrank to almost nothing. Of the forty-four with which he had started, there were barely half a dozen left. Not only were jackdaws eager to part with their movables, they even began to trade the pieces of paper for other pieces of paper. A page of Mrs Browning with a nominal value of, say, ten guineas might find itself traded for half as much again. 'I see thine image through my tears tonight', a long-dated sonnet, set a new record when it doubled in price and doubled in price again when the jackdaws of Runnymede expressed an interest.

Rumours of the trading frenzy in West London eventually reached the ears of Sir Sampson Skinner himself on the roof of the Mansion House. Sir Sampson was a very serious bird who knew the worth of his colleagues down to the last brass button and was not best pleased when a jackdaw he scarcely knew tried to sell him a piece of paper.

"What's this?" he barked.

"It's called a promissory note," replied the other bird, "and was issued by a Mr Cornelius of Windsor Great Park. He was lent ten guineas, but has to pay back the principal over five years at twenty per cent per annum. The debt is guaranteed by the co-signee, but since you appear to be the co-signee anyway, there's no danger to you if buy it."

"The co-signee?" echoed Sit Sampson incredulously. "Give it here."

The other bird handed it over. Sir Sampson studied the paper closely.

"Repeat what you've just told me," he said.

The other bird, who could see that Sir Sampson was deeply impressed, obliged with a résumé of the bill.

"That's what I thought you said," retorted Sir Sampson. "Now let me read you what it actually says:

> Belovèd, thou hast brought me many flowers
> Plucked in the garden, all the summer through
> And winter, and it seemed as if they grew
> In this close room, nor missed the sun and showers.

Well, what do you have to say? Do you think you can make a fool of me?"

A sudden gust of wind snatched the paper out of Sir Sampson's grasp and blew it away towards the river. Sir Sampson did not attempt to rescue it.

"Well?" he asked.

"But ... but...," stammered the other bird.

"But you didn't know I could read? Is that what you're trying to say? If I weren't convinced that you were utterly stupid, I'd suspect you of fraud. But you're not bright enough. Summon all the jackdaws from Lombard Street. I want to see them immediately."

"Shall I tell them what for, Sir Sampson?"

"Tell them we're going to Windsor."

The wedding, so long delayed, of Mr Cornelius and the Lady Cornelia, which took place on the roof of St George's Chapel, coincided with the changing of the guard. ("I insisted," whispered the Duchess to her neighbour. "Left to Cornelius, it would all have been so drab.") But even without the red coats and marching feet the ceremony would have been impressive. An elderly jay, who wore a silver-plated decanter label round his neck and who was generally known as 'the Bishop' on account of his purplish feathers, officiated with great style. A choir of linnets sang 'O for the Wings of a Dove'; a Hampton-Cornelius recited a poem by Catullus; and the bridesmaids, who had been inattentive throughout the rehearsal, managed not to fidget during the vows. It was, everyone agreed, a beautiful service, and many a dutiful tear was shed on the bride's side of the roof.

Meanwhile, Sir Sampson and the Lombard Street jackdaws had stopped to refresh themselves in Kew Gardens, where they were fortunate enough to find the remains of a family picnic, which included a cheese sandwich and a slice of Victoria sponge. It was impossible to resist. Afterwards, Sir Sampson, who from his perch on the Mansion House had grown notoriously fat on the leavings of Lord Mayors' banquets, suggested that they all take a nap on the Pagoda before continuing to Windsor. The Lombard Street birds agreed. The flight was proving longer than expected and none of them was in his first youth. In any case, the whole thing was probably a wild goose chase, some damn silly notion of Sir Sampson, which would probably amount to nothing when they got there.

Whilst the investigating party rested at Kew, the wedding party had removed from St George's to the Great Park, where it was invited to admire the dower house and the marital nest. A flock of starlings had been hired at great expense – two sonnets and a title page – as outside caterers. They had scoured the tea houses, bakers and bird tables of Eton and Slough and produced a feast of unimaginable magnificence. Whilst the guests ate, drank and marvelled at the bibelots and baubles, the choir of linnets sang sweetly in the branches overhead.

"We liked him right from the start," confided the Duchess to one of the Hampton-Corneliuses whom she was showing round the dower house. "Such a sweet fellow and so besotted with our dear Cornelia."

"Would that I had been so lucky," sighed the Honourable, who had always had difficulty in attracting suitable mates.

"Your time will come, my dear," said the Duchess, "Your time will come."

A finch appeared on the edge of the nest.

"Come quickly," he said. "The Lady Cornelia is going to read some poetry. It's not to be missed."

When they arrived, the Corneliuses' nest was already festooned with birds. Every surface, every rim, including that of the clock, had become a perch. None of the wedding party could read, so a poetry recital was a rare treat. To Mr Cornelius's horror, the Lady Cornelia announced that she was dedicating the recital to her dear, dear, husband and would read some of Mrs Browning's *Sonnets from the Portuguese*, a work which conveyed, as no other, the depth of her feelings for him.

"And when I have read we shall cut the wedding cake," she said. "Now pass me the copy if you would, my dear."

To be saved from disaster by disaster is scarcely a blessing, yet that was how it felt to Cornelius, at least until the extent of the greater disaster became apparent. Several things happened simultaneously as three new groups of actors appeared on the scene. From the West the outside caterers were flying in the cake. They knew a baker in Eton who left his cakes, already sliced, out in the backyard to cool before carrying them into his shop. As soon as he had disappeared indoors, eight starlings descended and carried it off, one to a slice, intending to reassemble it on the floor of the Corneliuses' nest. As they reached the edge of the Great Park, they saw approaching from the East a flight of unfamiliar jackdaws, who were croaking angrily and gesticulating towards the reception. Their whole aspect was so menacing that the starlings, fearful for their safety, dropped the cake and fled. The third party consisted of their Highnesses the Princess Alice and the Princess Helena, who were enjoying an afternoon drive with their new nanny. They already had completed two circuits of the Park and were now approaching the Corneliuses' tree at a smart trot.

"Parker," said Nanny Trubshaw to the coachman, "why do you suppose there are so many birds in that tree?"

Before Parker could reply, a slice of fruit cake struck him full on his cockaded hat. There was worse to follow. Two nut-laden slices fell straight into the nest whose floor, already weakened by the weight of guests, not to mention the accumulation of movables, gave way, releasing a sudden cascade of treasures into the carriage beneath. Scissors, snuffers, brooches, buckles, coins, medals, tweezers, pen nibs, cuff links and a horse brass descended in a glittering shower.

"Why, here's my silver thimble!" exclaimed the Princess Helena, as it fell in her lap.

"And my cornelian brooch," exclaimed the Princess Alice as it plopped into her hand.

"And Dapple's birthday horse brass," exclaimed Parker as it bounced off Dapple's rump.

"Why, I do believe this is my lapel watch", exclaimed Nanny Trubshaw, picking it off the floor of the carriage. "It was a present from my late uncle, the Provost of Balliol."

"But what about all these other treasures?" asked the Princess Alice, indicating the Aladdin's cave which had descended on them.

"I'll tell you what we'll do," replied Nanny Trubshaw. "We'll put them in the dolls' house when we get back to the nursery and ask the dollies what they think."

"I think that is a capital plan," said the Princess Alice. "But not a word to Bertie and Affie."

At the first sign of trouble most members of the wedding party fled. A few headed for the dower house, which had not shared in the general ruin, but were repulsed by the Duchess and the Honourable, who were determined to defend their treasures, come what may. The Lady Cornelia was led away weeping to Hampton Court. As for Mr Cornelius, he was surrounded by the Lombard Street birds and led back to London. This time the party did not stop at Kew Gardens.

"Where are you taking me?" he asked.

"To the King's Bench," said Sir Sampson Skinner." And may you rot there for ever and a day. Promissory notes indeed! And such ghastly poetry, too!"

"Which is where I made his acquaintance," said Lowther, "or rather made the acquaintance of Mr Turnbull of Hampstead Ponds, who claimed to have had the story from Mr Cornelius himself, though I ought to warn you that Mr Turnbull was said to have been driven mad by his losses in the great crash of '46."

But Mr Cornelius existed all right. All his gloss had gone. His eyes were dull, his black feathers grey and his grey feathers grizzled. He'd sooner walk than fly. Flying was strictly for business, by which I mean he was allowed out during the day – carefully supervised, of course, by the Lombard Street birds – to forage. Anything he found he had to hand over to his creditors. He told Turnbull – or so Turnbull told me – that on present progress it would take him until 1900 to pay off the debt.

When he wasn't flying, he would stump around the yard with the other prisoners, who poured out their troubles to him, though it was to Turnbull alone that he confided the story of *his* downfall. What grieved him most was not his own folly, but his wife's failure to visit him. That the Duchess and the Honourable had refused came as no surprise – came, indeed, as something of a relief – but that his wife, whom he had never reproached for his misfortunes, should stay away grieved him deeply. All the same, he never gave up hope. One day, God willing, he would be solvent again and free to leave the King's Bench. In the meantime, he consoled himself by remembering the good times they had had together – going to church, laughing at *Jorrocks's Jaunts and Jollities*, watching the river at Chertsey. Best of all, he imagined himself reciting to her. For he could now read, and for that he had to thank Mr Turnbull, who whiled away the long evenings by reading *The Ingoldsby Legends* to an illiterate cellmate. Thus by following the words on the page as someone spoke them aloud, Cornelius had learned to read in exactly the same way as his wife.

Unlike that of the lady in Chelsea, Turnbull's library was limited to the one volume, which Cornelius got to know almost off by heart, 'The Jackdaw of Rheims' being a particular favourite. More to his taste, however, were the share certificates which Turnbull kept under a brass candlestick on the mantelpiece. They were a revelation. They were not promissory notes: they were money. Or as good as. *This is to certify that the holder of this Certificate is duly registered with the such and such a railway company as the owner of one share of £10.* Ten pounds! Why, fifty or more would clear his debts; he could be free again, free to attend church with Cornelia, free to read poetry to her, free to rebuild their nest in Windsor Great Park. True, he felt a twinge of conscience in relieving his friend of his certificates, but in human terms they were clearly worthless. They must be, or he would not be in the King's Bench. If only he could persuade Sir Sampson, whose word was law in Lombard Street, that the shares were the next best thing to hard cash, then his worries were over.

"And what have you got for me this time?" asked Sir Sampson who was holding court with his cronies on the Mansion House roof when Cornelius called. "*In Memoriam? Paradise Lost?*"

The cronies chuckled dutifully.

"Money," said Cornelius.

"Money?" replied Sir Sampson. "I'll believe that when I see it."

But to everyone's astonishment – including, most probably, his own – he did believe it. In fact, it was just what he had been waiting for. Trying hard to contain his glee, he read the share certificate several times, scratched his head thoughtfully and finally pronounced himself satisfied.

Scissors, snuffers, brooches, buckles, coins, medals, tweezers, pen nibs, cuff links and a horse brass descended in a glittering shower

"Find me fifty more of these," he said, "and you can consider yourself a free man."

A more impetuous bird would have carried off Turnbull's certificates in a single snatch, but misfortune had taught Cornelius caution. One by one he moved them from under the candlestick and hid them in a disused chimney above the punishment block. It was several weeks before Turnbull noticed how depleted the pile had become.

Turnbull had invested the profits from his Hampstead Ponds business in railway shares. After the Great Crash of '46, which had bankrupted him and thousands like him, the shares of genuine railway companies had slowly recovered and rewarded those who had clung on to them. The shares of fraudulent ones, on the other hand, were, of course, worthless and incapable of recovery. Needless to say, it was in shares of this kind that Turnbull had invested. But just as Cornelius consoled himself with dreams of freedom, Turnbull consoled himself with dreams of recovery. One day, he kept telling himself, all his railways, however unpromising, would be built. In their share certificates were invested his hopes for the future. And now they were gone, Heaven only knew where. That evening it was with particular vehemence that Turnbull read the passage from 'The Jackdaw of Rheims' where the Cardinal curses the jackdaw who stole his ring:

> He cursed him in eating, he cursed him in drinking,
> He cursed him in coughing, in sneezing, in winking;
> He cursed him in sitting, in standing, in lying;
> He cursed him in walking, in riding, in flying;
> He cursed him in living, he cursed him in dying ...

That night a terrible gale blew up from the South West. It capsized ships in the Channel, swept unimpeded across Salisbury Plain and the Surrey Heaths, ravaged the New Forest, toppled towers and turrets and pummelled London with a fury that shook the city to its foundations. It tore the rigging from ships in the river, wrenched scaffolding from buildings, uprooted trees in royal parks and stripped slates and chimney pots from roofs, among them slates and chimney pots of the King's Bench.

At the first crash, Turnbull rushed to the window and saw the chimney from the punishment block fall into the yard, releasing what looked like a flock of white doves, which were swept over the roof tops and far away. A freak gust hurled one of them against the window where it flattened itself against the pane. It was a piece of paper. He leaned out and caught it. It was a share certificate for ten pounds. He kissed it and clasped it to his heart, before putting it back in its place under the candlestick. Thank God! Hope was not dead after all. To be sure, it was only ten pounds, but it would grow and grow. Money always did. If you had enough of it – or even the promise of it – you could always make more. It was all a matter of confidence.

He looked forward to sharing the good news with Cornelius.

"Why is it," asked Mr Ezard when Lowther had finished, "that so many stories resemble fire crackers, in which the author lights the fuse and steps back to await the bang? Oh, the fuse may be long or short, I grant you – we may even be led to think it has gone out altogether – but the explosion is inevitable, as is our failure not to be surprised by something we expected all along."

"But a gale," objected Lowther, taking Mr Ezard's observation as a criticism of his tale, "is hardly an explosion."

"Not literally perhaps," replied the daguerrotypist, "but metaphorically it is, as is the bottom falling out of a nest or an outbreak of cholera. And let us not forget that we began this excursion with a suicide, followed by a murder."– He glared accusingly at Costello and Stumps – "As for Jahandar's seventeen-gun salute, what was that if it was not an explosion – seventeen explosions, in fact? For myself, I dislike loud bangs and wish that stories did not so rely on them. I am no writer, but from time to time I scribble down ideas, and, if I have yet to produce the plotless story, I have at least succeeded in eliminating explosions. And for that the world should be grateful."

"On the contrary, sir," replied Turpin, "the world will not be grateful in the least. The world will not thank you for removing the very thing it pays good money to read. When my fabularium is in full production I shall refund any customer who considers my bangs deficient in quantity or volume."

"Then you will forgive me, Mr Turpin, if I do not become one of them. My constitution is delicate and I fear the effect on it of so many violent assaults."

I could see that Turpin was disappointed in Ezard, whose embrace of the new had led him to regard the daguerreotypist as a kindred spirit. But if his disappointment showed, Ezard was too feverish to notice and retreated into his private miseries once more. Poor Ezard, his days among us were clearly numbered. That much must have been clear to all, not least to the Saturnine Stranger, his neighbour, who took a close interest in his sobs and groans whilst refraining from gratuitous expressions of sympathy.

[Editor's Note: Few traces remain of Ezard's earthly existence. The parish register records his birth and death, but little else. If there was a Mrs Ezard, she has left no mark. There is no reference to his business in trade directories of the period and no daguerreotypes survive bearing the name of his studio. His great ambition – to re-constitute as a daguerreotype the engraving that killed his father – remained, we must presume, unfulfilled. But in the Blackwood archive there is a bundle of papers – stained possibly by damp, possibly by chemicals – which may represent the nearest thing we have to a last will and testament. It is a story entitled Notes from a Rainy Country *and if not exactly plotless, it contains no explosions, literal or metaphorical; indeed, the plot such as it is, centres on the absence of them. I cannot be sure that it is Ezard's, though it is certainly in a different hand from anything else in the archive, and if it is Ezard's, I cannot be sure how Blackwood came by it. The tale consists of fragments which may represent a first draft, though, given Ezard's embrace of modernity, may equally represent an experiment in form. The order in which the fragments is printed is not the order in which I found them but the order in which they seem to make most sense. Of course, there is another possibility altogether: that the fragments were never meant to have an order and were to have been shuffled at each successive reading. If*

that were indeed the case, then Ezard's embrace of modernity might have been tighter than Turpin could ever have imagined.]

Notes from a Rainy Country

Fragment 1 The Royal Proclamation

KING: I, Afasius the Fifth (or possibly Sixth), by the Grace of God King of Upper and Lower Epluvium, Lord of the Dikes and Causeways, Grand Fowler of the Marshes and a lot more besides, which I can never remember, do hereby command a ... a ... What's the word, Mnemonicus? ... Well?

THE MNEMONICUS: I forget.

KING: Can anyone help the Mnemonicus?

COURTIER: Jubilee, Your Majesty.

KING: Do hereby command a Silver or Golden Jubilee – no-one can agree on the colour – to celebrate the twentieth year of our reign.

COURTIER: With respect, Your Majesty, twentieth is neither Silver nor Golden.

KING: Do you hear that, Mnemonicus? You must try harder or you could find yourself out of a job.

THE MNEMONICUS: Impossible, Your Majesty. It's hereditary.

KING: So it is, I'd forgotten. Anyway, to continue: Do hereby command a Jubilee of some sort to celebrate the twentieth year or so of our rule.

THE MNEMONICUS: But not if it rains. That is the custom.

KING: Then pray God for a fine day.

THE MNEMONICUS (*aside to COURTIER*): A heavy downpour would save us all a lot of trouble.

Fragment 2: Conversation at an Inn (1)

EPLUVIAN 1 (*reading aloud from the newspaper*): Black to move. Rook to Queen's Bishop 4. The King is still playing the British Ambassador, I see. Same moves as last time. And the time before.

EPLUVIAN 2: I don't know how you remember.

EPLUVIAN 1: It's all here in last year's Weekly. Or last month's. One or the other. They forgot to date it.

EPLUVIAN 2: There wasn't a Weekly last month.
EPLUVIAN 1: That settles it then.
EPLUVIAN 2: How's your damp?
EPLUVIAN 1: Still rising. And yours?
EPLUVIAN 2: Spreading.

Fragment 3: Extract from Arthur Benjamin's Popular Guide to the Kingdoms of Transcarpathia:

Vol IV Epluvium

Knowledge of history, court ritual, forms of religious and civil ceremony is vested in the Mnemonicus, an hereditary office which has been in the same family for generations. The Mnemonicus has the final say in all such matters and has the authority, enshrined in the constitution, to overrule challenges from individuals who presume to think differently. To prevent official memories being contaminated with deviant ideas, the Mnemonicuses have traditionally looked no further afield for their wives than first cousins or even, should no first cousin be available, to aunts and step sisters. The results of this inbreeding are, alas, all too evident in the present incumbent. Poor physique and enfeebled mental powers must surely be the product of exhausted loins and end in cretinism. The constitution, insofar as I could get the Mnemonicus to explain it to me, contains no provision for an alternative bloodline.

The official religion of Epluvium, if it can be said to have one, is Lapsed Catholicism, by which it is not to be understood that Epluvians were once Catholic but have ceased to practise, but that they are happy to practise as much of their faith as they can remember, memory lapses down the years having emptied it of any content. Most can manage the opening lines of the Credo, but stall after that, mumbling the rhythm of the words, though the occasional phrase will surface, 'confiteor in unum baptisma' being one of the most popular, probably because it is connected, as are so many things in Epluvium, with water.

Like most other buildings, churches are lacking in colour. Epluvians seem never to have mastered the art of making dyes permanent. The sun has leached the colour from stained glass windows and priests' vestments. Most church roofs leak and the water dripping from the ceiling, together with the damp rising from the ground, has obliterated the paintings with which church walls were once covered. Umbrellas are a common sight in churches. I have even seen a celebrant conducting mass from beneath the shelter of one.

Fragment 4: Conversation at an Inn (2)

EPLUVIAN 1 (*studying the newspaper*): There's talk of a heatwave.

EPLUVIAN 2: There's always talk of a heatwave. Or a drought.

EPLUVIAN 1: I blame the shepherds. They have so few sheep to look after, they spend their time starting rumours about the weather.

EPLUVIAN 2: What happened to all the sheep, I wonder?

EPLUVIAN 1: I never thought to ask. (*Looking at the newspaper.*) White to move. Pawn to Queen 3.

EPLUVIAN 2: Who's playing?

EPLUVIAN 1: Still the King and the British Ambassador.

EPLUVUIAN 2: Does he know he can't win?

EPLUVIAN 1: Who, the King?

EPLUVIAN 2: The British Ambassador

EPLUVIAN 2: By now he must. They say he feels quite at home here.

Fragment 5: The Archbishop of Pomonia's Easter Sermon

Of the Seven Deadly Sins we must account at least one a virtue. I refer, of course, to Sloth. To speak of it at length, however, would be self-defeating, so I shall refrain. In the name of the Father, Son and ... and ... the Other One. Amen.

Fragment 6: Extract from Tacitus' De Origine et situ Epluviorum

In winter young men of the most warlike tribes begin the day by plunging into frozen rivers, often having to break the ice with ceremonial axes. No male can be accounted a man unless he has wrestled a Carpathian bear to the ground and cut out his heart with the short stabbing knife with which all young males are presented at puberty. Failure to do so may result in a withdrawal of the knife and a temporary banishment to the women's quarters where they may be forced to scour dishes and thread beads. When they are not fighting other tribes, young warriors spend the time in feasts and banquets, where drunken brawls, often resulting in serious injury, are encouraged by tribal elders. In the neighbouring province of Dacia legionary commanders count the Epluvians as amongst their staunchest allies in defending the frontier against barbarians.

Fragment 7: The King and the British Ambassador Play Chess (1)

KING: Your sheep must be a great comfort to you, Sir Charles.

AMBASSADOR: Unfortunately, I have not a ram or a ewe to my name, Your Majesty.

KING: Nor I. Wolves, foot rot, idle shepherds have all taken their taken their toll. The Mnemonicus tells me it is foolish to worry. The Kings of Epluvium, he says, never measured their wealth in sheep. How they did measure it I have no idea. Neither has he, though he thinks it might have been in shipbuilding.

AMBASSADOR: But Epluvium has no coastline.

KING: That's what I tell him. White to move. Bishop to Queen 3. Check.

Fragment 8: Extract from the Journal of
the Westphalian Philological Society

(Volume III June 1837)

Not only does Epluvium lack the railroad and the telegraph, it lacks the words for them. The National Academy has announced that it sees no need to include in the dictionary words for things which have yet to appear, any more than it sees the need to retain words for things which no longer exist. It has therefore decided to exclude from its lexis words such as 'steamship', 'cable' and 'locomotive', though it allows Epluvians to use the Latin equivalents – Epluvian being generally regarded as a Latinate tongue – should they find it unavoidable. (There are, needless to say, no Latin equivalents for 'steamship', 'cable' and 'locomotive'.) The exclusion from the dictionary of many words which relate to forestry and sheep farming, on the other hand, because those industries are largely defunct, has proved more controversial and been widely ignored.

The National Academy sees it as a duty to keep the Epluvian language as simple as possible. Invoking the principle of portability – i.e. the notion that the language should contain no more words or grammatical constructions than the average citizen can carry in his head at any one time – it seeks constantly to reduce the number of nouns, grammatical constructions and even, it is rumoured, letters in circulation. Future tenses had been eliminated on the grounds that there is no need to refer to what has not yet happened, as have adverbs and prepositions indicating convergence – 'to', 'towards', 'onwards', 'forwards' and so on – on the grounds that they are, in some unspecified way, un-Epluvian. The Academy is said to be working on a scheme to reduce the number of letters in the alphabet, not by eliminating the least used, but by removing two per year, one from either end of the alphabet, until a core of a dozen or so remains. Unfortunately, programmes like this cannot be announced in advance, for to do so would require the use of the proscribed future tense.

Although Epluvians are law-abiding people, they have also very poor memories. Thus their willingness to observe the rulings of the Academy is usually nullified by their inability to remember what they were. This observation applies to Academicians as well.

Fragment 9: The King and the British Ambassador Play Chess (2)

AMBASSADOR: Might it not have been forestry? Your oaks could build an entire navy.

KING: Impossible. There is not a sharp axe or saw in the kingdom, not a blade, a hinge, a spade that is not red with rust. In Epluvium metals no longer shine. Look at my guards – not an unrusted sword or breastplate between them. The Jubilee parade will make me a laughing stock.

AMBASSADOR: Check

KING: How can it be check when I have lost my king?

AMBASSADOR: I merely sought to hurry things on a little.

KING: What for? We've all the time in the world. Sometimes I hope it rains to be spared the humiliation of including rusty soldiers in the grand procession. It preys on my mind constantly.

AMBASSADOR: Regarding the wealth of the Epluvian kings, might it not have been rhubarb? They say it grows plentifully in the South.

KING: Do you have rhubarb on your estates, Sir Charles?

AMBASSADOR: I have neither rhubarb nor sheep.

KING: England sounds a wretched country.

AMBASSADOR: Nonetheless, I wish one day to return.

KING: That I cannot allow, at least not until you have beaten me at chess.

AMBASSADOR: But how can that be when half the pieces are missing?

KING: Then we must pray for a miracle.

Fragment 10: The Legend of St Pomona
(from Butler's Lives of the Saints Vol XIII)

The Voivod of the Outer Marshes, who had earned his country's gratitude for defending it against the Ottomans, had a daughter named Pomona whose hand was sought by suitors from the furthest reaches of Dacia, Pannonia and Epluvium. Though she would have been happy, if not eager, to marry any one of them, her father refused his consent, telling her that he had dedicated her chastity to God, Who had rewarded him with many a victory against the pagans. She, who had no desire to be chaste, married in secret with a Pannonian general to whom, in the fullness of time, she bore nineteen children. In penance, her father dressed himself in animal skins and wandered into the mountains where he was attacked by wild beasts and died blessing the bear that devoured him. Though revered locally as a saint, Pomona was refused canonisation by the Pope, who, to the outrage of most Epluvians, bestowed it on her father instead. Notwithstanding the Pope's endorsement, no shrine has ever been erected to him, whilst prayers are regularly offered to his daughter, who is revered as a saint, especially amongst the rhubarb growers of the South. The capital city, Pomonia, bears her name.

Fragment 11: Extracts from the
Journals of Miss Lavender Broadhurst

April 2: Thompson says she will not be bullied into going. I tell her that she has never refused to be bullied before, so I shall continue to bully her until I get my way. She tells me the journey is dangerous. What is life without risk? I ask her. Sir Charles is probably dead, she counters, which is why neither we nor the Foreign Office have heard from him in three years. I reply that if we have not heard from him in three years, then it is more important than ever to find out what has happened to him. To this she has no reply. I sense she is weakening. I play my trump card. Now that father is dead, I tell her with the hint of a sob, Uncle

Charles is my only living relative, and it was my father's dying wish that I put into his hands the ivory chess set with which they played as boys. In what amounts to a declaration of surrender, she informs me that I am a beast and that it will take a week to pack her trunk. We leave tomorrow morning, I tell her. I intend to sew a hundred gold sovereigns into my petticoat and pack all my belongings – viz. a change of clothes, my father's duelling pistols and a flask of powder (Dupont's Diamond Grain, if there is any left in the gun room) – in a carpet bag. My violin will travel, as always, in its own oilskin.

May 6: I have lost Thompson to a circus in Debrecen. Ungrateful wretch. She has been my companion these ten years and has endured my tantrums and caprices – not, to her credit, without complaint – only to desert me before my great adventure has properly begun. What is more, she has deserted me for a lion tamer with a cast in one eye. It is hard to say which of them has the worse bargain: the groom, who takes a bony spinster with a bristling moustache to his bed, or the bride, who takes to hers a man whose greatest pleasure in life is goading a lion with a broom. Well, I am well rid of her. She begs me to stay until the wedding and would esteem it a great favour if I would play the violin for the dancing afterwards. I decline.

*May*16: Et in Epluvium ego. Watched by two customs officers, who decline to challenge me, I cross into Epluvium, soaked to the skin but eager to greet the inhabitants of this strange country. They, it seems, are less eager to greet me. As soon as I approach they retreat into their houses and watch me fearfully through holes in the walls. The first inn along my route shuts its doors against me, but I am in no mood to be ignored and, despite the rain, unwrap my violin from its oilskin and play an irresistible polka. The door remains obstinately shut. Well, thinks I, if I can bully Thompson with my tongue, I can bully you with my polka, so I continue playing. After about half an hour the inn door opens and the landlord, wearing a nightcap, asks me to desist since his guests are trying to sleep. In the middle of the afternoon? I ask. It is the custom, he replies. Will you give me food? I ask. I need food; my horse needs food. If I give you food, he says, will you stop playing? Reluctantly I agree. After an interminable delay, the landlord brings out a bowl of gruel – the thinnest I ever saw – , and an ostler, irritable at having been

roused from sleep, a bucket of mash for the horses. If that does not give him the
bots, I remark, peering into the bucket, nothing will.

May 23: Viewed from the crumbling causeway across which I ride, Pomonia
presents a sorry sight. Either it is sinking into the surrounding marsh, or the
waters of the marsh are rising to engulf it. It is walled, but here and there the walls
have collapsed, allowing blackened water into the fringes of the city. Faded flags fly
from what I take to be the Royal Palace and the Cathedral, and between ordinary
houses are stretched lines of equally faded bunting.

At the main gateway I am stopped by a customs officer, who steps out of a
rat-infested wooden cabin – also decked with colourless bunting – and points to
my violin in its protective oilskin. He takes it from me and beckons me to follow
him inside, where he and a colleague unwrap the parcel. They are, needless to say,
baffled by the contents. Violin, I tell them. Music. Tra-la-la. I offer to play to them
but they hold it beyond my reach. Angrily I insist on seeing the British Ambassador,
but it is quite hopeless: they have no English and I no Epluvian. My attempts to
engage them with such smatterings of German, Romanian and Hungarian as I
possess increase their suspicions further. For the first time I begin to feel alarmed.
Though they are are too lethargic to be threatening, they clearly have no intention
of giving me my violin back. Then I have an inspiration. I fall to my knees and
clasp my hands as if in prayer. In a Catholic country, such as Epluvium, there must
be priests who can speak Latin and though my Latin was never good it might (with
added gestures) suffice. And so it proves. Legatus britannicus, I demand when the
priest arrives. He is obviously fresh from mass, for there are wine stains on his
vestments. After an exchange of increasingly frantic gestures, it dawns on him what
I want. He sighs, shakes his head wearily and beckons me to follow him to the
domus legati britanniae.

When I arrive, not only does Sir Charles not seem pleased to see me, he seems
not to know who I am. My presence, he says, when I introduce myself, will make a
lot of extra work for the servant. As for Lady Broadhurst, she is in no condition to
help anyone, having taken to her bed long ago.

"My Aunt Maud ill?" I exclaim.

"I did not say that," he replies. "I merely said that she had taken to her bed,
which is not the same thing at all."

"But I must see her at once," I insist.

"You will do no such thing," he retorts. "You will wear her out. And now, if you will excuse me, I shall retire early. It has been an exhausting day. The servant will make up a bed and show you to your room."

I, too, retire supperless to bed at an absurdly early hour, not because I am tired, but because, having unpacked there is nothing else to do. My room in the British Embassy has two kinds of damp: rising and falling. It is only a matter of time before they meet. The sheets and pillows feel damp, likewise the old copies of The Morning Post which line the chest of drawers into which I empty the contents of my carpet bag. There are books on a shelf beside the bed, but when I open them, the pages tumble out on to the floor. Before I blow out my candle, I peer through the window into the darkened streets of Pomonia. Few are the Epluvians burning the midnight oil – not that it is midnight or anything close. I am strongly tempted to go out into the street and play a Scottish reel on my fiddle. And it is then – Oh God, have I fallen into the Epluvian habit of forgetting already? – that I remember that I have left my beloved fiddle in the customs post. I blow out the candle and listen to the rain falling on the roof.

May 24: Proof that not everything moves at a snail's pace in Epluvium comes next morning in the form of an invitation from the Palace. Their Majesties King Afasius and Queen Marmonia, having heard of my arrival, request the pleasure of my company at lunch and that of the British Ambassador, whose name for the moment escapes them. The royal carriage will call for us, quite possibly before lunch. It doesn't, so that when we finally arrive at the palace the royal couple are half way through their rhubarb crumble.

"What kept you?" they ask. "Your dumplings will have gone cold."

Having gone supperless to bed, I wolf down the cold dumplings as soon as they are placed in front of me.

"Steady on," says the King, "you'll get indigestion."

"When His Majesty gets indigestion," says the Queen, "he takes to his bed for days."

"Your Majesty," says Uncle Charles, who always wears a topper and tails when he visits the Palace and who is more recognisably his old self when he does so, "will be pleased to learn that my niece has brought me a present."

"But did she bring their Majesties a present? It is customary, you know."

This last speaker is the Mnemonicus, a vacant-looking figure with filmy eyes and a white beard into which a great deal of lunch has found its way. On the journey to the Palace Uncle Charles has warned me that he is likely to be there. Though his all-important memory has left him, his cunning, Uncle Charles warns me, has not. At present it is being directed towards preventing the Jubilee on which the King has set his heart.

"Not exactly," I tell him, "but Uncle Charles intends to share the present with His Majesty regularly. It is a chess set with all its pieces intact."

There is an embarrassed silence.

"Then you will be leaving us?" the King asks Uncle Charles.

"Do you not like it here?" asks the Queen. "Is our hospitality not good enough for you?"

"At any rate you won't think of going before the Jubilee, will you?" the King asks Uncle Charles. "I was counting on your support."

"If," adds the Mnemonicus, "there is a Jubilee. Which, the weather being what it is, there won't be."

"Oh, but there must be a Jubilee!" I exclaim. "Rain or no rain, there must be a Jubilee. You need one, Epluvium needs one. It is desperately overdue."

"The bunting has lost all its colour," says the Queen.

"The guards' weapons are red with rust," sighs the King.

"The band's instruments are terribly out of tune."

"And a twenty-one gun salute ..."

"... or even a nine-gun salute ..."

"...would be highly dangerous. The canon hasn't been fired for years."

"You can use my duelling pistols," I tell them.

"But what about the band?"

"I shall play my violin."

"And the bunting?"

"I shall tear up my spare dresses."

"But the weather," protest their Majesties, "what about the weather?"

"Yes, what about the weather?" echoes the Mnemonicus.

"Bother the weather!" I say. "Rain or shine, sun or sleet, let us have a Jubilee."

King Afasius and Queen Marmonia look at each other nervously.

"Why not ?" asks the Queen.

"Do you think we dare?" asks the King, then turning to me adds, "Would you really help us?"

"On one condition," I reply. "You must order the customs officers to release my violin."

"Consider it done," says the King leaping to his feet.

"You will rue the day," says the Mnemonicus, slumping further into his chair. "Believe me, you will rue the day."

Fragment 12: Memorandum from Dr James Temperley to the Superintendent of the Warwickshire County Asylum

You ask for news of progress in the Broadhurst case. There is, I regret to say, none. She refuses to leave her room if the sun is shining and to enter it unless the walls are running with damp. If I offer to play chess with her, she agrees only if half the pieces (including the kings and queens) are removed before we start. If I offer her *Blackwood's Magazine* or *The Cornhill*, she pushes them away and demands something less likely to keep her awake at night – or, for that matter, during the day. Half-jokingly I suggest Fordyce's Sermons; half-seriously she accepts, whilst adding that what she really craves is the Journal of the Westphalian Philological Society. The case is baffling. Only when I interview the lady who committed her will I be able to make sense of it. Until I learn more of Miss Broadhurst's history I shall be unable to restore her to health.

Yours,

James Temperley FRCS

Fragment 13: Letter from Mrs Honoria Kertesz (née Thompson) to Dr James Temperely FRCS

My mistress and I were on close but not always friendly terms. She would no more think of embarking on one of her madcap adventures without me than I would think of letting her go on one alone. Since the days of our companionship, our roles have been reversed. It is I who have become the adventuress, having mastered the art of tightrope walking in Nepomuk's travelling circus, and she who has withdrawn into herself and become – by temperament at least – an Epluvian. No doubt I should blame myself for allowing her to cross the Carpathians unaccompanied, but to do so would be to regret the strange turn my own life has taken – I refer of course, to my marriage to Mr Kertesz and my mastery of the high wire – and that I cannot in all honesty do.

The purpose of her visit was to place in the hands of the British Ambassador to Epluvium the chess set which her father, the Ambassador's brother, had left him in his will. At least, that was the stated purpose of the visit. And the real one? Recklessness, restlessness, impatience with the commonplaces of daily life. She had, too, a genuine curiosity, which she shared with her uncle's masters in the Foreign Office, about his failure to write home. Was he, she wondered, indisposed, or had he, as the Foreign Office suspected, been 'Epluvianised'. The latter possibility was, apparently, an occupational hazard, and the former, other than in personal terms, of little consequence to the Government, most of whose members (including, it was rumoured, the Foreign Secretary himself) would struggle to find Epluvium on the map.

Having much else to distract me, I scarcely noticed Miss Lavender's departure from Debrecen, but later, when the time came for us to move into our winter quarters, I began to worry about the dangers she might have exposed herself to. With the support of my husband, I persuaded the circus owner, Mr Nepomuk, to let us take some of the animals, including César the lion, into Epluvium as a travelling menagerie. "Think of it as a reconnaissance," I told him. "If there is sufficient interest in a half-circus, then it will be worth our while taking the whole show across the Carpathians in the spring."

Since there was no lack of them in the Epluvian forests, we left the bears behind, and, thus, accompanied by zebras, monkeys, a rheumatic ostrich and César, we crossed the mountains. The Epluvians were neither amused by the monkeys nor intimidated by the lion. Every animal we produced was met with blank indifference. We began to take risks. We let the monkeys loose in village inns in order to advertise our show. (Some, needless to say, absconded.) Led by our ostrich, whose greying plumage we restored with boot polish, we paraded through village streets, unobserved by all except the children. Finally, my husband in trying to rouse in the spectators some semblance of interest lost three fingers to the lion, who was as resentful as the audience at being roused from his torpor. "A few more digits won't make much difference," he said before he fainted; "he's already helped himself to most of my toes. Leave me here in the inn. Go on to Pomonia. Do what we came to do: find Miss Lavender and bring her back."

Finding Miss Lavender was easy, bringing her back near impossible. First, the British Ambassador would not admit me, informing me from an upper window that he was in no state to entertain visitors. In his travelling cage César growled fiercely. "Now that," I told His Excellency, "is the true roar of the British lion. You should be ashamed of yourself. I demand to see my mistress." To reinforce my demand I released one of the monkeys, which scrambled up the drainpipe, pulled off his nightcap and flung it into a puddle. With great reluctance, he agreed to let me in, eventually appearing at the front door in top hat and night shirt.

"Welcome," he said feebly, "to the only patch of British sovereign territory in Epluvium."

"Then this," I informed him, "is where we shall keep the animals. Do you have a courtyard?"

Such was my arrival in Epluvium. With the mundane details of our accommodation and that of the menagerie I shall not detain you, nor with my interviews with Miss Lavender, who refused to leave her room and out of whom I could get no sense. Next day Sir Charles and I were invited for lunch at the Palace. I offered to take the ostrich and the monkeys, thinking that they might amuse their Majesties, but my offer was refused. During this and subsequent visits I managed to piece together what had happened, not so much from Sir Charles or their Majesties, but from various courtiers, chief among them the Mnemonicus, the half-senile court functionary to whom the rest seemed to defer. What I think happened is this. Against all precedent, my mistress persuaded the King to overrule the Mnemonicus and proceed with the Jubilee, rain or shine. She would tear up her spare skirts to provide bunting for the palace; she would lead the band with her violin; and, the royal canon being in no state to fire, she would give the twenty-one gun salute with her duelling pistols. At the prospect, their Majesties were rejuvenated. They banned dumplings from the menu; they ordered the palace roof to be replaced; they commanded the city walls to be repaired and the marsh causeway to be raised. If they could have ordered the rain to stop, they would surely have done so. In horror, the Mnemonicus confronted them. The Jubilee must on no account proceed, he told them. Such an event was unprecedented. Behind their backs he appealed to his cronies. He ordered the Archbishop to deliver his sermon on sloth, twice, thrice a day if necessary. Never mind the paradox, he told him: this was no time for casuistry. He ordered the cooks to restore dumplings to the menu, and when their Majesties accused him of attempting a coup, he accused them of betraying five hundred – or was it a thousand? – years of Epluvian history. But for the first time in his life, no-one listened to him. Bother history, said the Queen. For a while it seemed that my mistress and their majesties had triumphed. People began talking about an Epluvian spring. Sir Charles, too, showed signs of animation and even hinted that Lady Broadhurst might be getting up soon.

And the Jubilee? In the end Epluvium defeated them. Some blame the disgraced Mnemonicus and his cronies, but I think it was the damp, rising and falling as ever. In the general excitement, the servant at the Embassy decided to wash her skirts before they were turned into bunting. All the colours ran and the bunting ended up a yellowish-grey. There was worse to follow. When at last Miss Lavender's violin was delivered from the customs post, she tore off the oilskin, only to find that the strings had snapped and that rats had devoured half the body. She felt the music for the Jubilee slipping through her fingers in a stream of sawdust. Even more humiliating, when the King ordered her to fire the twenty-one gun salute with her duelling pistols, she found that damp had found its way into the flask of Dupont Diamond Grain and turned it into a solid lump. She fled, weeping from the Palace, fled back to the room in the British Embassy, from which I with great difficulty and, yes, not a little force extracted her.

Later I learned that the Mnemonicus and the Archbishop took their revenge on those who had forced the Jubilee on them. They confined King Afasius and Queen Marmonia to the Palace and force fed them boiled cabbage. When the British Ambassador arrived to play chess with the King, they seized the new set he had brought with him and tipped half the pieces into the marsh. Sir Charles returned to the Embassy and took to his bed.

It was obvious that the cure for his kingdom's sickness must be a drastic one and that it was we, the circus folk, who would have to administer it. When the menagerie had passed through the customs post and was safe on the causeway, we forced the officers to close the gates of Pomonia behind us, but not before we had opened César's cage and released him into the city. And there, in the pouring rain, the steam rising from his back, he wanders, growing hungrier by the hour. Sooner or later, the citizens of Pomonia will have to come out and fight, which will be the making of them, or stay locked in their houses, where they will eventually starve. Epluvium will have seen nothing like it since the beast shows which the Romans staged in an arena which has long been swallowed by the marsh.

Fragment 14: Conversation at an Inn (3)

EPLUVIAN 1 (*studying the newspaper*): Black to move. Rook to Queen's Bishop 4.
EPLUVIAN 2: Same gambit, same players.
EPLUVIAN 1: New set, same pieces apparently.
EPLUVIAN 2: Any news of the lion?
EPLUVIAN 1: Lives on rhubarb crumble in the Palace and has become quite a favourite, I hear.
EPLUVIAN 2: Aren't they supposed to be quite fierce?
EPLUVIAN 1: Lions?
EPLUVUIAN 2: No, courtiers.
EPLUVIAN 1: Only when they don't get what they want.
EPLUVIAN 2: And what do they want?
EPLUVIAN 1: To be left alone, I imagine. Just like the rest of us.
EPLUVIAN 2: Amen to that.

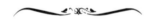

After Staplehurst we entered the Valley of the Shadow of Death. The station had come and gone in a flash. But how we had envied those standing on the lamp-lit platform! How we had longed to join those sitting by the waiting room fire! Alas, the vision had quickly faded. Out of the darkness we had come, into the darkness we must return. And then, somewhere between Staplehurst and Headcorn, we stopped. All that was visible was the red light of a signal and the fire of the locomotive reflected off the smoke billowing from the chimney. By now it was raining harder than ever. Passengers huddled together closely for warmth, and, where there were umbrellas, more intimately than decorum would normally have allowed. After we had sat motionless for several minutes, conversation began to falter, shrinking first to single sentences, then to monosyllables and then dying out altogether. We listened in silence to the sounds of the night. A screech owl cried; someone sneezed in a neighbouring coach; *Hengist* hissed impatiently. But there was another sound which flowed in and around the others – the sound of running water. The Ebenezer 'Special' had come to rest beside a river, or possibly above one, for when the fireman opened the firebox door a brief splash of light was reflected on the water below.

"This," announced Turpin, "is the viaduct above the River Beult. Brick piers, cast-iron trough girders resting on timber baulks. That is not how I would have built it."

To most passengers the identity of the river was a matter of indifference. All they knew was that they were marooned in open country between Staplehurst and Headcorn and that the rain was falling faster than ever. They wished they could sleep away the next few hours and wake in Canterbury, but, that being impossible, they retreated instead into their private misery. Or would have done had not a sudden interruption, a call to arms, rung out from a wholly unexpected quarter. George Costello, who had been facing into the wind and rain alongside his father, now stood up, blew a brief bugle call and demanded everyone's attention.

"We can sit in the darkness and shiver," he announced, "or we can try to divert ourselves. Might I suggest a little game? Many of us have brought back souvenirs from our visit. What say we pass them round in the dark and try to guess by touch alone what they are and to whom they belong?"

Soon objects began to circulate – a paperweight, a card case, a book with an embossed cover, a thimble, a watch guard – and at the end of each round George invited suggestions as to the identity of the object and its owner. The first was not difficult, nor yet the second. But one object defied all attempts to place it. It was fibrous and appeared to be plaited. The ends were tufted and coarse, even sharp, to the touch, like the ends of a ship's cable. None of the other objects had done a single round before being identified, yet this continued to circulate in complete silence. Either no-one recognised it, or, more probably, no-one was willing to own up to his deepest fears about it.

"Don't be bashful," said a voice. "Speak up."

The voice was thin and precise, poised somewhere between mockery and menace, and though unfamiliar – for it surely belonged to no-one in the tub – many thought they recognised it. One after the other they blurted out the name of someone of whom they stood in awe or of whom they were afraid.

"Old Nosey," cried George Costello, afraid that he was being called to account for his unauthorised bugle call.

"John Knox," said Culpepper.

"Prince Albert," said Gabriel.

"Sir Gideon Trapnell," said the Duchess of Croydon.

"Uncle Jack," said Meek

"Monsieur Daguerre," gasped Ezard.

But it was none of the aforementioned and no sooner had the name passed their lips than they knew whose voice it was, even though they had never heard it before. It was as if, in his silences, we had all conducted imaginary conversations with him, conversations which, on our part, consisted mostly of confessions and, on his, of accusations. It was, of course, the voice of the Saturnine Stranger. None of us could see him, and I fancied, foolishly, that the darkness in his part of the tub was deeper than elsewhere.

"Well?" repeated the voice. "Speak up."

"Boiled egg, anyone?" asked the Duchess. "It's the last one. Don't fight over it."

"I don't mind if I do," said the mysterious voice.

There was a delay whilst the boiled egg found its way into my hand. The feel of a hardboiled egg in the dark, especially when shelled, is deeply unpleasant. More unpleasant still, however, was the feel of the hand into which I passed it, not because it felt different from the egg but because it felt exactly the same.

"It looks very much," said the Saturnine Stranger, when he had placed the egg in his black box and shut the lid with a snap, "as if my box is full to bursting."

"And as if my hamper," said the Duchess of Croydon sadly, "is empty."

"I know who you are," said Gabriel.

"You do?"

"Yes, I've blacked your boots."

"Not in Canterbury. I never have my boots blacked in Canterbury."

"No, in Maidstone. Last year. Outside the jail."

"Ah, then you might be right. I always like to go to work looking my best."

"So do the people what go to watch. That's why I went. Bootblacks do a good trade on a hanging day."

"And you," said the Stranger, "you are the boy who stole the Queen's spoons. Well, perhaps one day you and I may become better acquainted."

Thus the Fourth Seal was opened. And I looked and, behold, a pale horse and his name that sat upon him was Death. Perhaps I should not have been surprised. On the steamer to Westminster he had asked the question which Purselove had omitted to answer: namely, 'For whom doth Time gallop withal?' To which the answer, as I later learned, is 'With a thief to the gallows, for though he go as softly as foot can fall, he thinks himself too soon there.'

"You may be wondering," he continued, "why I passed round a length of rope – Italian hemp, by the way, a thousand pounds breaking strain – and why I have dozen other such – different fibres, different breaking strains – in my box."

"I'm sure I speak for others," said Purselove, "when I say I have no curiosity on the subject whatsoever."

"You certainly don't speak for me," said Turpin. "Rope making is a particular interest of mine."

"Nor for me," said Costello. "I've seen too many hangings in Spain to be squeamish."

"I think we should hear the truth," said Nan, "however painful."

"Then let me introduce myself. When I am on duty, I am Thomas Quillam, when at home I am someone else entirely – someone who keeps bees, perhaps, or enjoys the races, or teaches his children their catechism, or beats his wife on Sundays. Who knows? But whoever I am, I leave Thomas Quillam at the door when I become that other self. If authors can hide behind a pseudonym, so can hangmen."

"Are you then ashamed of what you do?" I asked.

"Indeed no. I am the public hangman for the County of Kent and proud of it. Proud of it, but not, alas, delighted by it. By which I would not have you believe that I disapprove of public executions. Far from it. To see an approved villain turned off is always a joy – provided, of course, that he (or, less frequently she) is despatched with taste and delicacy. And there's the rub. You have no doubt heard of William Calcraft, our leading hangman. He is the Nelson, the Wellington of public executioners. He has the ear of home secretaries and prison governors. As long as his word is law, we must persist with the Calcraft short drop – two foot six of it on a good day, less on a bad. And on a two foot six drop a man – or woman and, yes, he's despatched plenty of them – simply chokes to death. There's no art, no science in that. In short, Calcraft is a botcher, a bungler, a strangler. No wonder the crowds don't like him. That doesn't stop them from turning up, of course – they wouldn't miss an execution for the world – but it doesn't mean they like what they see. And what they see is strangulation, so slow in some cases that he has to pull on the victim's legs to finish the job. Where's the dignity in that?"

"But what's the alternative?" asked Corporal Costello.

"The alternative," suggested Culpepper, "would be to abolish public hangings altogether. These distasteful spectacles should be kept behind prison walls."

"There would be a public outcry," said Quillam. "Think of all those excursion trains that would have to be cancelled. Think of all those pies that would remain uneaten ..."

"Think of all those boots that would go unblacked," added Gabriel.

"...all those bottles of ginger beer that would remain undrunk or perhaps never even bottled in the first place. Next to Derby Day, there is nothing the working man likes better than a public hanging."

"Mr Stumps don't, do you, dearie?" said the Duchess of Croydon. Stumps grunted non-committally.

"That's because he's never seen a good one," complained Quillam. "A good hanging should be a pleasure to all parties – the hangman, the prison warders and, above all, the crowd."

"What about the victim?" asked Purselove. "Don't his feelings matter?"

"Or hers," added Nan.

"Although the victim is not there to enjoy himself," replied the Quillam, "he should at least be allowed the satisfaction of knowing that he – and let us assume that it is a he – is a source of pleasure to the many."

"And how are these new, tasteful hangings to be carried out?" asked Beamish.

"By means of the long drop. We can calculate the force exerted on the neck by multiplying the weight of the criminal by the length of the drop. Too short and he will choke to death, too long and he will be decapitated. But the right length will break his neck" – he snapped his fingers – "and cause instant death, to the great satisfaction of all parties concerned."

"So the lighter the criminal, the longer the drop?" asked Turpin.

"And consequently the more expensive," added Quillam. "Women are thus likely to be a greater burden on the state than men, especially if one were to use Italian hemp, a sample of which – five eighths diameter, long fibres, silky to the touch – you have just handled for yourselves. A fourteen stone man – Mr Blackwood, for example – would require an eight foot drop, whereas Mr Purselove, whom I judge to be half a stone lighter, would require another two inches. To distract us from our present miseries, might I propose a new game? I shall name one of the present company and the first person to guess the correct drop will be the winner."

"But how would we know who was right?" asked George.

"I have been observing you closely throughout our journey and have compiled a little table. You may trust me. I am never wrong."

"But how can you see to read your table?" asked Miss Osgood. "It's pitch black."

"I don't need to see it. I know it off by heart."

"Ugh!" exclaimed Miss O. "I can already feel myself choking."

"Only if you end up as one of Mr Calcraft's subjects," joked Quillam. "In which case your last thoughts will be 'Would to God they had listened to Thomas Quillam! Quillam was a man before his time'."

"Eight foot six," said Turpin.

"What is?" I asked

"My drop," he replied. "I've just worked it out."

"And mine," said Ezard, "would be nine foot six. I should be a very expensive man to kill. But I shall not need to trouble the state. Nature has the job well in hand."

"Look," I said as brightly as I could, "instead of your game, why don't you tell us a story instead?"

The Saturnine Stranger's Tale of The Hidden Music

What would you say if I were to tell you that the piece of rope you touched had actually been used, that a fellow creature had expired on the end of it? Would you touch it again? Or would you protest aloud that you would shun it, whilst secretly hoping to fondle it again in the dark? There is no need to answer, for you would almost certainly be hypocrites if you did. So with ropes, so with hangmen. Publicly we are shunned, privately we are sought out by those who condemn us most. And why? Because most people want to feel the rope, and not a few want to buy it. For the superstitious, there is nothing a touch of it cannot cure – ague, scrofula, epilepsy, even a bad run at cards. But that is not the only reason we are sought out. The curious want to know how the condemned man – better still, the condemned woman – passed his or her final hours, what he thought, what she said. And there I cannot satisfy them. The rope I will happily sell them, the secrets of the condemned cell I cannot, not from any scruple, but because I am no more privy to them than anyone else – unless, of course, prison chaplains choose to divulge them, which they almost never do. Which suggests, of course, that occasionally – very occasionally – they do. To lighten our present darkness, therefore, I shall now share one of these rare confidences with you.

So let us join our man in the condemned cell for the last few hours of his life. For want of something better I shall call him Swan, for I was never told what his real name was. His last meal has consisted of a dozen oysters (a luxury, but in the circumstances worth it) and a pint of porter. The turnkey clears away the shells and places a candle in the empty bottle on the table. Advising the prisoner to get some sleep, he withdraws from the cell and locks the door noisily behind him. His footsteps recede down the passage, his boots ringing out on the flags, until he reaches the door at the far end, which he slams behind him with a loud jangling of keys. When at last all is silent, Swan takes a last look round the room, blows out the candle and listens.

He hears the turnkey slam more doors, hears him enter the guard room and throw his keys on the table, hears him walk to his private quarters, eat his supper, remove his boots, undress. He hears the crackling of the straw in his mattress, hears him begin to snore, gently at first, then cacophonously as he falls into an ever more profound sleep.

And beyond the snoring of the turnkey he hears, in the pitchy blackness where sounds are magnified fivefold, the snoring of the other prisoners; he hears them scratching, grinding their teeth, talking in their sleep. He hears the sounds of mice beneath the floor, of water droplets running down the walls. And his hearing extends beyond the confines of the prison. He hears footsteps on the city pavements, hooves on the cobbles, rats in the sewers; he hears all the sounds of the river, of the tide receding, of water draining from the muddy foreshore, of boats pulling on their cables, of water lapping wooden piers, of oars breaking the surface of the river, of the different turbulences as the Tyburn, the Westbourne, the Fleet and the Walbrook empty themselves, each with its peculiar melody, into the Thames. By now no house, no pub, no theatre, no gentleman's club, no house of disrepute is beyond the reach of his ears as he sits there in utter darkness.

Across the city church bells strike twelve.

But it is not just the sounds of a great city that press up against his ears. The whole nation – towns, cities, villages, hamlets – demands to be heard, a polyphony of factories, farms, canals, shunting engines, furnaces, foundries, hackney coaches, printing presses, laundries, collieries and whatever else does not sleep by night. Burglars, footpads, night-watchmen go about their business unobserved by all but heard by him. He hears gas jets hiss, coins being counted, jugs being filled, pages being turned; he hears the sound of nib on paper, brush on hearth, cup on saucer, foot on stair.

In Manchester, in Bradford, in faraway Belfast the clocks strike one.

And if, in its great slumber, the world of man is audibly alive, how much more is that of the animals. How they scratch and scrabble, buzz and cackle. From kennel and cage, from coop and stable come murmurs of dreamless, instinctive existence. Pigeons coo, foxes bark, mice squeak, frogs croak, all as clearly as if they were in the cell next door. And he hears, this time in his own cell, the sounds of the great animal to which his waking self is shackled – namely, that of his own body. He listens to his own breath, to his stomach digesting oysters for the last time, to his heart beating, to the blood coursing through his veins.

In Liverpool and in Ludlow the clocks hurry on. Two o' clock.

And now his ears attune themselves to the ground itself, to the teeming life below the deepest cellar, to the turbulent lives of moles and maggots, earthworms and earwigs. He hears the whisper of roots as they burrow into rock crevices and between particles of soil. He hears the clay groan beneath the weight of London, the sandstone with the burden of Nottingham, the granite with the mass of Aberdeen. He senses convulsions in the earth's core, in those mysterious regions where earthquakes and volcanic eruptions are assembled.

In the manager's office in Tredegar Colliery the clock strikes three.

Among all this hum of animal and vegetable processes, what does Swan hope to hear? Before I can tell you that, I need to tell you something about Swan. From his dying father he inherited his mother and a trumpet with a dent in the bell. "I leave them in your care," the old man had said. "Guard them well." By playing the one on the street corner and forcing the other, when sober, to take in washing, he managed to hold the workhouse at bay. For a while he was a member of a street band that performed outside pubs, but quit when his fellow-bandsmen agreed to be paid in beer rather than cash. In rapid succession he became accompanist to a performing monkey, an acrobat, a fire-eater and a conjuror. He had to fight off marauding bagpipers and barrel-organists for the best pitches and on one occasion was bound over for exchanging blows with a German oompah band. From this precarious existence he was rescued by the manager of the Adelphi Theatre, who, hearing him perform one day in Piccadilly, invited him to join the Adelphi pit orchestra. It was the making of him. For the first time in his life he had a regular (if meagre) income, together with regular hours of work. It was also the unmaking of him. In devoting himself to one of his charges – the trumpet – he neglected the other, namely his mother, who, taking advantage of his regular absences from home, ignored the laundry and devoted herself to drink. Her health, never strong, soon began to suffer. Unable to afford a doctor, he took time off from the theatre to care for her. His absences did not go unnoticed. How could they? A battle scene without trumpets is an absurdity and the Adelphi staged a great many battle scenes. He was dismissed ... and, well, you can guess the rest. Obedient to his father's injunction, he tried to look after his mother and his trumpet and ended by losing both. To pay for his mother's funeral he returned to the street corners but found them colonised by bagpipers and his old enemies, the German oompah bands. In desperation he was forced to pawn his trumpet and, having failed to redeem it, embarked on a life of petty crime and, when he found that petty crime brought only petty rewards, turned instead to burglary. One night he was surprised by an armed watchman, whom he wrestled to the ground, accidentally setting off one of his pistols, with fatal consequences.

Quillam paused and for a while we, like Swan, sat in complete darkness, listening to the sounds of running water and the faint, indefinable murmurs of life in the surrounding tubs.

"But I do not understand," said Beamish at last, "why this catalogue of misfortunes should make him want to sit in the dark. Was
there a particular sound, a voice, his mother's perhaps, which he
wished to hear, or was he comforting himself with the sounds of
existence in the few hours of it that remained to him?"

You will recall, resumed Quillam, that Swan was a musician. One evening,
when he was playing in the theatre, he had a revelation. There were, he realised,
two kinds of theatrical music. There is the music that the actors on stage can hear
– songs, dances and the like – and with which they interact or join in. But there
is also a music they cannot hear, a music intended for the audience alone. When
tensions rise on the stage, strings quiver; when characters fall in love, violins and
flutes remark on it; when armies clash the brass joins in. Sometimes the music
portends, even warns; sometimes it responds. When scenes change, so, too, does
the mood and it is the entr'acte music that changes it. If the characters on stage
could hear their hidden music, he asked himself, would they behave any differently?
Would they avoid danger, heed warnings, love and grieve more deeply? And was
there, he wondered, a hidden music for all of us? Outside the theatre, beyond the
world of make-believe, was there, just out of earshot, a series of tremolandos and
trumpet calls to warn, to protest, to console? He came to believe that there was.
Beside his mother's deathbed he had listened for it and failed to hear it. When
he embarked on his life of crime, he was too pre-occupied to search for it. Now,
in his last hours he is determined to hear his own hidden music, even though it is
probably playing nothing but a funeral march. That is why he has blown out the
candle and sits in the dark.

One, two, three, four. Four o'clock strikes at the Royal Observatory in Greenwich.
By now he has left the sounds of earth far behind. But what does space
sound like? Who knows, for no-one has been there, and, if they had, there
is nothing to hear, for there is no medium to hear it in. Yet if we could
miraculously flood the gulfs of space with air, we might hear what Swan heard
in his darkened cell – the mighty rumble of the earth's axle like a gigantic mill
wheel, the roar of the sun's furnaces, the hum of Saturn's rings, the bell-like
twinkling of distant stars. At last he hears what he has been searching for. First,
there is a silence, a deep and dazzling silence in which he loses all sense of time.

Then, far off on the very limits of hearing, there is a thin creaking noise like a rusty hinge. It starts off as a gasp, a mere sigh, before becoming a screech, then a scream, followed by a loud crash as of a heavy door being slammed and bolted. Afterwards, there is nothing, no echo, no reverberation. The extinction of light and sound is complete.

Down in the governor's office, the clock strikes five.

Outside there is a loud hammer blow, heard this time by everyone in the prison. The workmen have begun to build the scaffold.

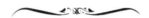

We were recalled to ourselves by a shriek from *Hengist*. This was no hiss of disapproval or displeasure, but a bellow of rage issuing from the depths of its boiler. A glittering column of sparks soared heavenward in defiance of the rain. Most perished in the upper air, but enough rained down on the tubs for the passengers to shield their eyes. Some settled in the brims of hats, some on the bonnet which Nan had put on for the first time since leaving London, a morsel of red-hot soot singeing the ribbon. This time Miss Osgood, though seated next to her, did not interfere, leaving Gabriel to pinch it out with his bare hands.

Inspired by the locomotive the silver band blew a spontaneous fanfare which, though hideously discordant, was as welcome as the Alleluia Chorus. Culpepper, who had listened to the hangman's tale with evident dismay, now rose to his feet and announced in a ringing voice which must have been heard several tubs way:

"I cannot accept that at the end of all our strivings, all our endeavours, a door is slammed in our faces. Comfort ye, comfort ye, my people. Prepare to hear a message of love, of joy, of life everlasting. But first I ask you to join me in an act of contrition. At London Bridge I suffered my beloved copy of *Pilgrim's Progress* to be taken from me and handed to Mr Malachi Brown. I did not protest because I hoped it might soften his heart. That no doubt was virtuous. What happened next was not. I had long yearned for, lusted after, a copy bound in embossed leather and fastened with a gold clasp. In the Crystal Palace I found such a copy. I persuaded the book binder to break the exhibitors' rules and sell it to me. Here it is."

He held it up in the dark. Although we could see only a dull outline, the fake gemstones set in the cover glinted in the light of the sparks that showered down on us.

"Vanity," continued Culpepper, "vanity, vanity, vanity. Shame on you, shame on me, shame on us all. We went as pilgrims to marvel at the wonders of the age, but we come home as shoppers. Each of us went to marvel at his personal Koh-i-Nor or his lard vase, but we come home with the Crystal Palace drawn in poker work. Far from being inspired by the power of the human mind, we burdened ourselves with trinkets. Brothers and sisters, lay up not up for yourselves treasures on earth, where moth and rust doth corrupt and where thieves break through and steal, but join me, this very minute, in a bonfire of the vanities. Now who will follow my lead and cast their baubles aside?"

With that he hurled the meretricious volume out into the night and uttered a loud 'Praise be!' when it landed with a splash in the River Beult. A volley of objects, all of them taken by Quillam from his black box, followed *The Pilgrim's Progress* into the river.

"There you are," said Quillam. "There's my contribution."

"That was very generous of you," I said. "What did you sacrifice?"

"Two meat pies, a boiled egg and *The Memoirs of Grimaldi.*"

"All them things was mine," protested the Duchess. "They all come out of my hamper. What did you take 'em for if you was going to throw them into the river?"

"I was sacrificing them on your behalf," said Quillam. "You should be pleased."

Culpepper was growing impatient.

"Enough of this," he said. "Who's next?"

No-one, it seemed, was next. No-one felt the same guilt over his purchases as Culpepper. All those paperweights and watch guards, all those commemorative plates and thimbles which had earlier been passed from hand to hand in the dark remained firmly in their owners' pockets.

"Looks as if we was on our own, dearie," said the Duchess. "Pity about the book, I thought it looked lovely with all them bits of coloured glass stuck on the cover."

If Culpepper's hopes were dashed, they quickly recovered, for at that moment, the moon appeared from behind the clouds, the rain stopped and, with a loud whoosh of steam and smoke, *Hengist* coaxed the Ebenezer 'special' into motion.

[Editor's Note: Although Culpepper's message of hope has not survived, it is also possible that it has not entirely disappeared. Scattered throughout the Blackwood papers are several scraps, some handwritten, some in Pitman. The latter is not a form of shorthand currently in use and is presumably the Stenographic Soundhand to which Blackwood refers in his opening chapter. So far I have not found anyone who can decipher it.

I believe these fragments are the remains of Culpepper's sermon, though why the original Pitman and the longhand transcript were ripped to shreds is anyone's guess. Perhaps someone tore them up by accident and intended to paste them together afterwards; perhaps Miss Osgood, exasperated by Culpepper's continued defence of Gabriel, tore them up in anger. No less problematic is the question of how and where the sermon was notated in the first place. Even though the moon was shining when Culpepper delivered his sermon, there would not have been enough light for Miss Osgood to take it down in shorthand. But perhaps there was no need, because she had taken it down earlier. In other words, the sermon that Culpepper delivered that evening was one he had delivered before and that Miss Osgood had, with his consent, taken down for practice, probably during a service at the Ebenezer.

All this is, of course, pure conjecture, as is the order of fragments, a selection of which is printed below. Readers should feel free to make what sense of them they can and re-order them in any way they see fit.]

1

freely, and more ...

righteous man of ...

and prayeth, and ...

garment alike in f...

he giveth unto oth...

shook his ...

2

both him and the ...

and the apostle we ...

only believe in the ...

world, but from the ...

what death he shou ...

them with fire, in ..

..exation and the de ...

3

... and provision and victual for him ...

...pensed it, going about the cities and the vi ...

... poor and afflicted, and relieving ...

4

Now ...

which Juda ...

built a pala ...

cities and ...

God and ...

we think

5

succour ...

alone, and that ...

graces and gifts ..,

6

... said: And what is it which thou ...

... that thou wilt grant me. And ...

... shalt ask, I will give the ...

...? And the King ...

... that Christ ...

7

... and said to the merchant: Fear thou ...

... and though shalt indeed be set free ...

... receive life. And the king took ...

... he had determined to flay them ali ...

...sick, and by reason...

... greatly oppressed ...

8

...ed of his friends ...

... for him. And they told ...

...missed to perform but he goeth ...

... giveth to the poor, and teacheth of...

... and doeth many other wonderful things, and ..

...and his cures which are done of him ...

9

Indeed desirest to ...

And forthwith he se ...

With him, saying: I ...

Wouldest pray for ...

That which I have de ...

Of that dwelling for ...
alone, the grace of ...
serve this God who ...
I entreat and s ...
... service, and ...

10
The king answere ...
Convince me by ...
possessions, tha ...
palace which thou...
the heavens? And ...

prison ..

Although the moonlit interval had barely outlasted Culpepper's sermon and although he ended his message of hope with a favourite quotation from Revelation, namely that whoever was not found written in the book of life was cast into the lake of fire, the passengers continued the journey in better spirits than before. By now the Chaplain's apocalyptic outbursts were so routine that they scarcely noticed them. A succession of familiar stations passed, first Headcorn, then Pluckley, and as we paused at Ashford to make way for the Folkestone train, the band, taking advantage of the gaslights, struck up with 'Come Thou Fount of Every Blessing'. Mr Breeze, immobilised between his captors, pulled a face but was too dejected to call for 'Elsie from Chelsea', as he contemplated becoming just another chapter in Mr Sturridge's proposed *Tales from the Sponging House.*

Once we had entered the darkness of the Stour Valley the band lapsed into silence, though by now the passengers were too excited to notice. This was the last stage of the journey, a stretch of rail and river whose landmarks were familiar even in the dark. We thundered over the level crossing at Wye, greeted the lights of Chilham with a half-cheer and those of Chartham with a loud huzzah. Soon

we could see the Harbledown windmill silhouetted against a pale
streak of cloud. More and more pinpricks of light appeared beside
the train; buildings rose up along the tracks and closed us in. From
somewhere nearby came the sound of a barrel organ, together
with bursts of song from a public house. Pigs grunted in a back
garden; steam hissed as a blacksmith plunged a newly shod hoof
into water; a night soil cart rattled over the cobblestones. With a
lack of synchronisation that would have delighted Mr Bartholomew,
clocks across the city struck nine, the last dying away as we rumbled
across St Dunstan's Street, whose puddles gleamed brightly in the
gaslight. Then, with a final squeal of brakes, Sturdee brought us to
rest alongside the platform from which we had departed two days,
twelve hours and three minutes earlier.

    Never had home seemed so desirable. Not Pilgrim himself
entering the Heavenly City can have felt half the joy that the Ebenezer excursionists felt as they stepped down from the train. Nor
were the Shining Ones who met with him harps and crowns greeted
more warmly than we greeted Mr Bowles, the station master, who
ushered us into the waiting room where he had organised a blazing
fire and an urn of hot tea. In an instant our privations were forgotten, our tongues loosened and the souvenirs which had circulated
in the dark exposed to the light of a dozen gas jets. All the commemorative paperweights and mugs, all the medals and thimbles
which had not been thrown in the river were passed again from
hand to hand and admired unashamedly, though Quillam's length
of Italian hemp was noticeably absent, having, like its owner, slipped
away into the night.

    Gratitude makes for strange bedfellows. So thankful for our
delivery were we and so great was the press of bodies round the fire,
that unlikely knots quickly formed within it. Thus Stumps found
himself talking animatedly with Beamish, the Duchess with Culpepper, Purselove with Dacre, George Costello with Miss Osgood,
the Corporal with Mr Batholomew. Even Lady Rippledale paused
on the threshold and, shouted 'savage!' at Mr Meek, before she

was wheeled away to her waiting carriage by Miss Tinstsford and Mr Scudamore, who shook me warmly by the hand and returned the top hat which I had left suspended from the roof of the first-class carriage. Within the groups of conversationalists several little dramas were enacted, unobserved, I suspect, by all but me. When Gabriel produced a silver spoon to stir his tea, Nan snatched it from him so angrily that he spilt the tea over his trousers and began to cry. Breeze, too, must have been close to tears as he encouraged Mr Meek to tell the two bailiffs his Uncle Jack stories, hoping, no doubt, to extend his liberty for a little while longer. For several minutes Sturdee, Turpin and Dr leGrove blocked the exit talking about the next season's flat racing, until Mme Fontana pushed her way into the group to complain that, owing to our late arrival, she had missed the last train to Whitstable. What, she demanded to know, was the driver was going to do about it? Sturdee replied brusquely that it was nothing to do with him, and that I, as the organiser of the excursion, was the man she needed to talk to and, with that, returned to the subject of flat racing.

"And what are you going to do about it?" she asked.

"It looks very much as if you will have to spend the night in Canterbury," I replied.

"And where do you suggest? Inns are noisy, vulgar places. I will not tolerate an inn."

"I know of a small temperance hotel not far away, a little shabby perhaps, but it is neither noisy nor vulgar. I think it would suit you well."

"And what is name of this shabby temperance hotel" she asked.

"Garlands," I replied.

Meanwhile, unnoticed by anyone until Mr Bowles came to lock up later that evening, Mr Ezard quietly breathed his last on a brown-painted bench in the corner.

Having pointed Mme Fontana and Miss Binnie in the direction of Garlands, to whose custom our rivals were more than welcome, Nan and I set off on the last stage of our journey. With home so near,

Palmerston has learned the first two lines of
The Lay of the Last Minstrel *and won't stop,*
even when I cover him up for the night

we made light of the rain, Nan having given up hope of returning with her bonnet as fresh as when she had left two days earlier. Two days! It seemed scarcely credible that we had encountered so many marvels, so many novelties in so short a time.

"Be prepared for a late night," I told her. "The mistress will want to know every last detail before we are allowed to go to bed, though it might be wise to make some omissions. There are subjects best avoided. I refer, of course, to Gabriel. No good can come of letting anyone else know what happened, not, if we are honest, that we really know ourselves."

"It is to be a secret between us then?"

"Indeed it is. We are to be partners, you and I, in a great secret."

To our surprise Serafina was less eager to learn our news than to impart her own. She greeted us warmly. The colour had returned to her cheeks, her eyes were shining and in her manner there was a greater animation than I had seen for many weeks.

"Come and hear, Percy, You, too, Nan. What do you think has happened? Palmerston has learned the first two lines of *The Lay of the Last Minstrel* and won't stop, even when I cover him up for the night."

Seizing our hands, she led us up to her sitting room and pointed to Palmerston's cage.

"The way was long, the wind was cold," came a voice from beneath the night cloth, "The minstrel was infirm and old."

"Such joy, Percy," cried Serafina, "such joy!"

[Editor's Note: After they have warmed themselves at Mr Bowles's fire, our travellers disperse. From time to time they must meet, if only by chance, but we do not know when or where or what they talked about. Perhaps some wonder if Mr Breeze is still the guest of the Sturridges, perhaps some remove their hats as Mr Ezard's coffin passes. As for the Lark scandal, tongues must surely have been wagging, none more than Miss Osgood's. I imagine her accusing Beamish of failing to find the elopement in her bumps and Beamish protesting that he had found it all right but professional etiquette had forced him to be silent. I imagine Dr leGrove having his boots blacked by Gabriel and asking after Mme Fontana, or Nan at Mr Meek's tripe counter reporting the latest sightings of Stumps and the Duchess of Croydon, or Mr Dacre falling out with Culpepper over a proposed reredos in one of the city's churches. Eventually the bonds that tie them weaken. Names and faces are forgotten, outlasted by the souvenirs of the Great Exhibition that adorn mantelpiece and dresser. Do any of them, drinking from their souvenir mugs, ever spare a thought for Percy Blackwood, who, in his search for stories, made the whole thing possible? He certainly did not forget them. His papers are full of cuttings and letters, which offer glimpses into the afterlives of his travelling companions.

Take the Costellos. There is a cutting dated 1855 from The London Gazette *which lists the Crimean War dead of the East Kent Regiment. There, between Peter Farrell Private killed in action on 11 August and Patrick Flynn Private killed in action on 8 September, is George Costello Bugler died of wounds Sebastopol 6 September, buried in Cathcart's Hill Cemetery. Folded round the cutting like a wrapper is a second cutting, presumably from the* East Kent Gazette, *which reads:*

CORPORAL COSTELLO'S DIORAMA OF
THE BATTLES OF THE CRIMEA
SEE THE SIEGE OF SEBASTOPOL,
THE CHARGE OF THE LIGHT BRIGADE,
THE BATTLE OF INKERMAN.
Hear the cannon roar!
Witness the gallantry of our troops!

See the heroes fall!
2d admission, a shilling for parties of 8 or more

On the back of the same sheet is a list of classified ads, one of which has been ringed in blue ink. Headed "Do You Want to See Yourself as Others See You, or Do You Want Others to See You as You Had Always Hoped to See Yourself?", the item continued, "Choose the Destiny that has Always Eluded You. Consult Retrospective Destinator Charles Breeze, 2 Lavender Lane." So Breeze had somehow escaped the clutches of the Sturridges and re-destinated himself, though how he raised the money must forever remain a mystery. Whatever the truth about his debts or about the rumours concerning the Glee Club accounts, it is hard not to be pleased. If he was a rogue, he was just the kind of rogue his clients paid him to turn them into posthumously.

Less cheering is a cutting from 1870 which reports the execution in Maidstone Gaol of Mrs Anne Malachi Brown for the murder of her husband, the eminent pteridologist, Mr Alfred Malachi Brown FRS. Despite what the newspaper described as 'moving scenes' in court as the accused alleged mental cruelty on the part of her husband, the jury found her guilty of murder and condemned her to hang. The prison chaplain, we read, remained with Malachi Brown until ten o'clock on the Sunday night and afterwards retired to rest. By a quarter to six he was back in the condemned cell to administer the holy sacrament. The only persons present at the actual execution were the Under-Sherriff, the Prison Governor, a surgeon, two reporters and the chief warder. Although executions were no longer public, large crowds gathered at the prison gate, and when the black flag was raised above the Roundhouse there were angry jeers and cries of 'Shame!' The executioner is not named, but it is tempting to suppose that it was Quillam, since the report mentions that the execution was carried out by means of the long drop, a practice widely followed in British prisons following the retirement of Mr William Calcraft.

In 1862 an engineer named Chambers wrote an article in The London Journal proposing a rail link between England and France. 'My scheme,' he wrote, 'consists in submerging tubes of suitable dimension and loading them with ballast, whilst at the same time making ample provision for ventilation, light, safety and comfort.' Integral to this plan was a new maritime crane *invented by one Albert Turpin, of whom there is a profile in the cutting from which I have just quoted. The plan, as we know, came to nothing. When the Queen and President Mitterrand travelled through the Tunnel in 1994 it is doubtful if either gave a thought to Chambers, much less to Turpin or to the host of Victorian engineers, English and French, who had proposed such a scheme over century earlier.*

If Turpin's ambitions were doomed to be frustrated, Culpepper's, according to Crockford's Clerical Directory, *were not. A cutting of 1852 reports the wedding of Mr Jacob Jepp, railway navvy, and Maud Gowlett, musical artiste, in the Church of St John the Baptist, Croydon, with the Bishop of London officiating. In his address Dr Blomfield said that no-one should wonder at his role in the proceedings, for it was important that the Church be seen as the friend of the poor as well as the rich, of sinners as well as saints. He was grateful, therefore, to his colleague the Rev Francis Culpepper for inviting him to conduct the ceremony and giving him the opportunity to demonstrate that all are equal in the sight of God, a fact of which the groom, a man of abstemious habits and forthright views, never tired of reminding him. Shortly after – about the same time in fact that the fictional Mr Slope became Chaplain to the Bishop of Barchester – Culpepper was appointed Chaplain to the Bishop of Rochester, with, one hopes, happier consequences.*

More cuttings, more glimpses. One gives a brief account of a talk given by Critchley to the Tunbridge Antiquarian Society on the subject of privately commissioned bindings for Shakespeare's First Folio, the original book having apparently been sold unbound. Another contains a fragment of an article by Bartholomew entitled "Why We Should Renounce the Gregorian Calendar". It begins 'It is two hundred and seventy–three years since the Western Church renounced the Julian calendar and embraced the Gregorian, as a result of which we find ourselves sixty-eight days in advance of where we would otherwise have been. Were we to reverse Pope Gregory's decision we would make ourselves a present of those days which we could live again in the full knowledge of the wrong turnings we had taken.' The rest of the article is indecipherable owing to a mysterious stain that has spread across the paper. Perhaps Mr Meek wrapped a portion of tripe in it before handing it to a customer – to Miss Binnie, perhaps, or Mme Fontana, before they moved to London. Which I assume they did since another cutting contains an advert – admittedly with two large question marks beside it – offering

UNRIVALLED ACCESS TO THE SPIRIT WORLD

by means of Tasseography, Scrying, Pyroscopy and Spirit Rapping
Consult Mme Fontana of Muswell Hill
Satisfied customers include Ministers of Religion and Frustrated Exorcists

Pinned to the clipping is a second advert, this time for a novel entitled The Trials of Amy Redfern or the Paths of Virtue *by Minerva Sackville, Author of* The Chronicles of Elmscott.

Here the paper trail ends, though there are a few fixed points between which the story – largely conjectural from now on – must move. Kelly's Directory, *for example, lists the Ebenezer Temperance Hotel in the 1850s, but not a decade later. A commercial hotel stood on the site under a different name for many years before being destroyed, like most of the other buildings in St Margaret's Street, in the Baedeker raid of 1942. Then there is the matter of burials. Online searches reveal that Serafina, who died in 1859, was buried at Herne Bay, whilst Percy, who outlived her by eighteen years, was one of the first to be buried in the Whitstable Road Cemetery in Canterbury. Nan Foxley survived into the new century and was buried close by.*

The only way to make sense of this is to tell a story, some of which – who knows? – might even be true.

When Violet Osgood turned up a few days later at the Ebenezer, Blackwood expected a renewal of hostilities. But he was wrong. Torn between a desire to see Gabriel punished and a desire to put her shorthand to good use, she cast herself as a peacemaker.

"See," she said, "I come bearing gifts. Shall we set to work?"

She laid the precious notebooks on the table and they began.

It was, of course, impossible to hide the task from Serafina. When she found out that they had been writing up other people's stories – though not, fortunately, before they had finished transcribing them – she was hurt that she had not been told beforehand and angry at what she regarded as theft.

"Leave this to me," said Miss Osgood. "I'll bring her round."

But she didn't. It was Serafina who brought Miss Osgood round, largely because Miss Osgood had used as an example of real theft (as distinct from mere borrowing) the case of Gabriel and the Queen's spoons. Serafina's reaction was so extreme that it re-awakened in Miss Osgood the sense of outrage she had suppressed in order to keep the peace with Percy. The truce was quickly ended. Together they accused him of covering up a crime. It was not to be tolerated, they said. If it was not actually aiding and abetting, it was as good as. For good measure Miss Osgood threw in a few mea culpas of her own. She should never have colluded, never have held back from doing what was right. Her behaviour had been inexcusable. Had it not been for Serafina, she would have continued in error. She owed her a great debt.

Now Serafina did not, in the most literal sense of the phrase, enjoy good health; indeed, she rather despised it, preferring instead the comforts of hypochondria, which confined her to her room with its lowered blinds and poetical parrot. To Percy this was embarrassing and frustrating. Not only had he to make excuses for her, he was frequently denied her company and her bed. So when Miss Osgood made Serafina a present of the Gabriel story, Blackwood was not merely exasperated: he was enraged. The grudges, frets, vexations that had accumulated over the years spilled out in a destructive torrent. They must separate, he said. They must separate without delay.

"But where will you go?" asked Serafina, taken aback by the force of his reaction.

"More to the point," said Miss Osgood, "where can you afford to go?"

"Where I can afford to go is no concern of yours," he retorted and turning to Nan, who had just entered the room, said: "Nan, please find Miss Osgood's cape and umbrella. She is no longer welcome in this house."

With a look of triumph, Nan escorted Miss Osgood out of the room. Percy and Serafina heard the front door slam loudly.

"She might have been wrong to interfere," said Serafina, who had collapsed into a chair, her face white, her hands trembling, "but it was the right question to ask. Where can you afford to go? Because it is you will have to go. My nerves will not allow me to leave."

"Then I shall establish myself in the guest rooms," said Percy. "Two should do it. One for sleeping in, one for writing in."

"But what about the guests?"

"Do we have any?"

"Well, no, but …"

"Then there will be no harm in my taking 11 and 12."

"I have never heard of such a thing."

"Nor have I. Necessity is a hard taskmaster."

In due course Percy acquired a third guest room, number 13, which he proceeded to share with Nan. Such an arrangement was hard to conceal, and when word got about that the proprietor of the Ebenezer was living openly with the parlour maid, such regulars as had remained loyal took themselves to Garlands. In October 1852, a year after the visit to the Crystal Palace, the Ebenezer shut its doors. Serafina went to live in Herne Bay with her friend Agnes Miller, Percy and Nan to live in some lodging house or other, having first been retrospectively destinated as a married couple by Mr Breeze.

If Blackwood had hopes of earning money from the stories, they were dashed when he learned that Miss Osgood had written to Blackwood's Magazine informing them that not only was he no relation of theirs, he had not even written the stories to which he had put his name. It was an act of pure spite, encouraged no doubt by Serafina, who, on learning that Nan was expecting Blackwood's child, vowed never to speak to him again. But it was Serafina who lost most by Miss Osgood's initiative. Denied an income from selling the stories he had gathered, Blackwood was forced to sell the Ebenezer and, such was the law at the time, was under no obligation to share the proceeds with his wife. Instead, he bought the tenancy of The Maypole, a former coaching inn on the outskirts of the city where, as if to make up for his abstemious past, he grew fat and florid. But behind the geniality, there was an emptiness, a void which prosperity and good living could not fill. After hours he would take out the Pitman transcripts and sift through them, like a miser counting his gold. Little by little he added the connecting narrative, completing it just before his death in 1877.

Down through his descendants it passed, down, down, until it fell into the hands of those who either had no interest in it, or who resented the continued *popularity of Garlands, or who simply threw it out because Blackwood's line had expired, or who knew that I was a St Dunstan's author and might make something of it.* Should Mr Blackwood's Fabularium, *as I have chosen to call it, ever see the light of day, I shall appeal to the mysterious donor to identify himself. Or herself. Or themselves. That Blackwood's message in a bottle should have survived its perilous voyage, that it should have washed up on my shore was surely no accident. Someone willed it to happen. And unless they come forward, Percy and Serafina and Nan and Miss Osgood and all the others whose brief candles have flickered in these pages, must remain forever incomplete.]*

From **THE BLOG OF JONATHAN PYBUS
(FORMERLY THE BLOG OF THE SVRS):**

Extract 3

Last night I attended the launch of Bob Critchley's *Fire from Heaven*, the latest in the St Dunstan Press series of pocket guides to Canterbury. You can't fault St Dunstan's for their ambition. They clearly aim to leave no historical stone unturned. Already in the pipeline are coaching inns and the childhood of Christopher Marlowe. Whether they will complete the series before it bankrupts them is anybody's guess. My *Introduction to Chaucer's Canterbury*, which appeared last year, has already turned up in remaindered bookshops.

Fire From Heaven tells the story of the Baedeker raids in 1942. According to Bob Critchley it had been a difficult story to tell. He had struggled to find a narrative thread to stitch the whole thing together. No sooner had he begun to stray from raw statistics – so many lives lost, so many houses destroyed – than the thread began to fray into a hundred different stories, most of them incomplete, some doubtless fanciful. Stories of men on the Cathedral roof throwing incendiary bombs on to the grass below, stories of Archbishop and Mrs Temple in tin hat and night clothes comforting the bereaved, of Hetty the hen trapped beneath the rubble but still managing to lay eggs for the war effort, of gas mains exploding in the streets, of the so-called divine wind that blew many of the marker flares away from the Cathedral, of the barrage balloons borrowed from Exeter, of fireman running the gauntlet of buildings collapsing into the narrow streets, of the cheers which greeted the Flying Food columns, of people sleeping rough in fields and haystacks, of telegrams pouring into the Post Office for news of relatives, of the vast congregation that gathered in the blackened Cathedral to sing O God Our Help in Ages Past.

And what, I asked him, had impressed him most deeply.

-Not, as you might expect, the human stories, he replied, though it was hard not to be moved by the people strafed by fighters in a later daylight raid as they queued to see *Gone with the Wind*, or by the Emergency Controller buried in the rubble of his own house. As for buildings, well, the Cathedral Library was the hardest loss to bear, especially when I heard that Hewlett Johnson, the so-called Red Dean, had boasted to General Montgomery of the size of the crater into which it had disappeared. All those books, all that scholarship ...

-Such loss, such grief, I sighed, quoting something I had read in the Blackwood papers.

-Indeed, he said. Of course, there were other dreadful losses. Whole streets disappeared. Burgate Street, Lower Bridge Street, St George's Street, St Margaret's Street ...

-St Margaret's Street?

-Shops, houses, hotels, the lot. But you asked me what had impressed me the most. I'm almost ashamed to answer. Compared with the loss of life, the loss of the Library, the thing that touched me most is so trivial I scarcely like to mention it. One of the houses destroyed in Burgate Street had belonged to the Rev Richard Barham, author of the *Ingoldsby Legends*. Not much read now, but wildly popular in its day, so much so that there was a plaque on the wall. Nothing of the house survived, but the plaque did. The ARP wardens picked it out of the smouldering ruin next morning. A small example, perhaps, of literature surviving the general ruin.

-It didn't survive the Cathedral Library, though, did it?

-Not everything perished. Some books were rescued and were carried to safety by schoolchildren the next day. But we shouldn't complain. The loss of a few missals and medieval cartularies is nothing compared to what the RAF did to libraries in Dresden and Berlin later. All things considered, Canterbury got off lightly. What was it you quoted earlier?

-Such loss, such grief.

-That was it. What's it a quote from?

-Oh, just something I read in some papers that happened not to be in St Margaret's Street on the night when fire descended from heaven.

Historical Notes

Railways

In 1851 rail travellers to London would have taken the westerly route though Edenbridge and Redhill (then designated Reigate). The modern route, completed in 1868, branches off the earlier one at Tonbridge (commonly spelt Tunbridge until the 1890s) and continues through Sevenoaks and Orpington to London Bridge. Charing Cross, the present terminus of the line, was not opened until 1864.

The Railway Regulation Act of 1844 required the train companies to provide, amongst other things, 'carriages protected from the weather and provided with seats'. But that did not mean that the 'tubs', or open carriages, disappeared overnight. So great was the demand for rolling stock in the year of the Great Exhibition that many tubs were brought back into service and whole trains were made up of them. In his short story *The Fiddler of the Reels*, Hardy describes the arrival of such a train at Waterloo: '... damp weather having set in with the afternoon, the unfortunate occupants of these vehicles were, on the train drawing up at the London terminus, found to be in a pitiable condition from their long journey; blue-faced, stiff-necked, sneezing, rain-beaten, chilled to the marrow, many of the men being hatless; in fact they resembled people who had been out all night in an open boat on a rough sea, rather than inland excursionists for pleasure.'

The River

As a thoroughfare, the Victorian Thames was much busier than the modern one. Engravings from the mid-century show the river so packed with steamers that it is remarkable that they did not collide more often. Steamers were designated above or below bridge depending on whether they operated upstream or downstream of London Bridge.

The above-bridge boats, all of them paddle steamers, belonged either to the Citizen Steamboat Co, the Iron Boat Co or the Westminster Steamboat Co. All the vessels belonging to the Iron Boat Co, on whose P[addle] S[teamer] Haberdasher Blackwood's party travels, were named after City companies. (There were even a PS Fishmonger and a PS Spectacle Maker.) The fare from the Old Swan Pier at London Bridge to Lambeth or Vauxhall was a penny, a tariff which gave the boats their nickname of 'penny steamers.' Most below-bridge steamers, which operated as far afield as Gravesend and Ramsgate, belonged to the Diamond Funnel Company. I have not invented the semaphore communication system between the bridge and the engine room (see Chapter Five); incredible as it may seem, that really was how the boats were directed.

The Thames was not simply a thoroughfare; it was also an elongated cesspool. Although the 'Great Stink', which finally prompted the government to take action, did not occur until the summer of 1858, there had been plenty of lesser stinks before that, Parliament having enacted in the 1840s that all domestic cesspits should drain into the sewers and thus into the Thames. For many of the visitors who flocked to the Great Exhibition, the unexpected horrors of the river must have been as striking as the eagerly anticipated wonders of the Crystal Palace.

The Thames shoreline described in Chapter Five disappeared into the Northern Embankment which Sir Joseph Bazalgette created in the 1860s to contain the sewer which conveyed the waste of homes and factories to Abbey Mills Pumping Station (often referred to as The Cathedral of Sewage) in West Ham. In the *Illustrated London News* there are illustrations of boats moored at a landing stage in front of Harrison's Hostel (see note below), reminding us that before Bazalgette built the Embankment, the riverside was a series of wharves, staithes and malodorous creeks.

Barry and Pugin's Palace of Wesminster was barely half complete when the PS Haberdasher sailed past it. Although the House of Lords chamber had been in use since 1848, that of the Commons was not completed until 1852. The two towers were slow in reaching their present height. Although the foundation stone of the Elizabeth Tower was laid in 1843, the Tower was not completed until 1859, the year in which Big Ben (the name of the bell, not the clock) was installed. The Victoria Tower was completed the following year. An engraving of 1851 shows that the Elizabeth Tower had reached the same height as the main roofline of the Palace, hence Mr Dacre's remarks about the towers being 'little more than stumps'.

Harrison's Hostel

Harrison's Hostel really did exist. Thomas Cook, who, as a temperance reformer, got into the travel business by using excursions to lure working people away from drink, persuaded Mr Thomas Harrison of Pimlico to turn his furniture depository into a hostel for visitors to the Great Exhibition. From Cook's point of view, the venture proved a great success in that it protected ordinary travellers from the extortionate rents being charged by private landlords; from Harrison's, it was a disaster. The hostel bankrupted him. The details of charges and services included in Chapter Five are taken from contemporary sources.

The Great Exhibition

Details of the exhibits – even unlikely ones such as the lard vase, the vacuum coffin and the pulpit with gutta percha speaking tubes – have all been taken from the official catalogue. Palmerston, Tennyson and the Duke of Wellington all visited the Great Exhibition, though not, as far as I know, on the same day. Nan was not alone in being disappointed by the Koh-i-Noor, which attracted long queues and which, despite being displayed within a ring of gas jets, failed to sparkle. The Osler Brothers' fountain was transferred to Sydenham when the Crystal Palace was reconstructed there. It was destroyed in the fire of 1936. Pugin's Mediaeval Court, though much admired, was condemned by many Protestants as being too overtly Catholic. The American display, which did indeed feature the revolvers of Samuel Colt, got off to a poor start because many of the exhibits were late in arriving. What struck many visitors about the American inventions was the extent to which they were designed to take the drudgery out of everyday labour. Such was the influence of the temperance movement, no alcohol was sold within the Crystal Palace and the catering franchise was awarded to Schweppes, who bid £5,500 for it. Public conveniences were a rarity in Victorian cities, but the 'halting stations' designed for the Crystal Palace by George Jennings were soon copied on the streets of London and other cities, not just in Britain but across the world. Finally, Mr Joseph Burch of Bright and Co of Manchester, whose carpet printing machine was the inspiration for Mr Turpin's fabularium, did exist: he was my great grandfather.

Staplehurst Railway Disaster

The Staplehurst Railway Disaster occurred in June 1865, when a group of workmen who had removed the rails from the timber baulks on the viaduct across the River Beult, failed to flag down an express from Folkestone. The locomotive and the leading coach made it safely across the rail-less gap, but the rest of the train displaced the girders which supported the track across the river. Five carriages plunged ten feet into the muddy stream below. Ten passengers were killed and forty-nine injured. One of the passengers in the leading coach was Charles Dickens, who had been reading the manuscript of Our *Mutual Friend* when the accident occurred. In a postscript to the novel, he wrote: 'On Friday, the ninth of June in the present year. Mr and Mrs Boffin (in their manuscript dress of receiving Mr and Mrs Lammle at breakfast) were on the South Eastern Railway with me, in a terribly destructive accident. When I had done what I could to help others, I climbed back into my carriage – nearly turned over a viaduct and caught aslant upon the turn-to extricate the worthy couple. They were much soiled but otherwise unhurt.'

The Baedeker Raids on Canterbury

Although bombs had fallen on or near Canterbury in 1940 and 1941, the raids that caused the greatest damage were part of the so-called Baedeker blitz, which was carried out in reprisal for the allied bombing of Lubeck and Cologne. Its aim, according to a spokesman for the German Foreign Ministry, was to destroy every building in Britain with a three-star rating in the Baedeker tourist guides. The attacks on Canterbury took place on the night of the 31st May, 2nd and 6th June. After the first raid, Hewlett Johnson, the Dean, wrote to a friend: *We had a pretty bad night and Canterbury looks appalling; I think no town has suffered more for its size. 400 shops and business premises and homes quite gone; 1500 more badly damaged; the Cathedral Library terribly smashed ... The loss of life amazingly small, only some 20 as far as is at present known. And only 47 badly wounded cases ...* All the details set out in Pybus's blog have been taken from contemporary sources. It was during a later raid, on October 31 1941, that the people were killed in the cinema queue.

The Palace Intruder

Gabriel's adventures in Buckingham Palace are not completely invented, but were suggested by the case of 'the Boy Jones'. In 1838 a boy was discovered in

Buckingham Palace with Queen Victoria's underwear stuffed down his trousers. He gave his name as Edward Cotton and claimed, astonishingly, to have been born there. Later, he changed his story and said that he had been born in Hertfordshire and had only lived in the Palace for a year. Police investigations revealed that his real name was Edward Jones and that he was the son of a tailor who lived close by. Although he had stolen items from the Palace, he was acquitted by a jury at Queen Square Police Court. He made two further intrusions in 1840, during the second of which he was discovered hiding under the sofa in the Queen's dressing room. For these offences he was sentenced to three months in a house of correction. Shortly after his release he was found in the Palace for a fourth time snacking on food stolen from the kitchens. This time he was sentenced to three months' hard labour. Those interested in the Jones case should read Jan Bondeson's *Queen Victoria's Stalker: The Strange Story of the Boy Jones* (2010). The 1950 film *The Mudlark* is loosely based on Jones's story.

Anachronisms

I admit to two anachronisms, though there may be others I am unaware of. The first is fern mania, a craze which had only just started in 1851 and which reached its apogee in the 1860s. (The word 'pteridomania', used by Mr Malachi Brown, was coined by the Rev Charles Kingsley in 1855.) The second is spiritualism. Mme Fontana would have been more at home in the later Victorian period. Spiritualism, though not unknown at this period – Queen Victoria and Prince Albert attended a séance at Windsor in 1846 – was not yet as widespread as Mme Fontana's tale might imply.

I have also tried to avoid anachronism in language, in that I have not knowingly used any words unavailable in 1851 – with the exception, of course, of 'pteridomania'.

What Else Happened in 1851?

Lord John Russell was Prime Minister – Lord Palmerston resigned as Foreign Secretary in December – The window tax was repealed – Lajos Kossuth, hero of the 1848 revolution in Hungary, arrived in England – The first submarine cable to Calais was laid – Landseer painted *The Monarch of the Glen* and Millais *Mariana* – Ruskin championed the Pre-Raphaelites – Macready played Macbeth for the last time – Marble Arch was moved to its present location from its original site opposite Buckingham Palace – David Livingstone reached the Zambezi – The Derby was won by the 3-1 favourite Teddington and the Grand National by Abd-el-Kader – JMW Turner died – Mrs Bloomer toured Britain advocating the wearing of pantaloons by women.

Six Things I Really Didn't Invent

1) The payment of 'cockpence' to the schoolmaster at Grange-over-Sands for training fighting cocks for matches in the classroom (*The Bugler's Tale*). 2) The messenger who was sent from Greenwich each day to all London clockmakers with the correct time - a practice that lasted until the 1920s (*The Watchmaker's Tale*). 3) The Salisbury lion attack which occurred in October 1816 (*The Inventor's Tale*). 4) The death of Edmund Kean during a performance of Othello in 1833 (*The Actor's Tale*). 5) The burning of moneta patriottica in Venice, though the surviving lira note is my invention (*Lord Palmerston's Tale*). 6) The method of crossing the Alps via the Mont Cenis Pass (*The Lady's Companion's Tale*). 7) The conditions in sweat shops and the outsourcing of components, especially skirts (*The Parlour Maid's Tale*). 8) The controversy over Calcraft and the 'long drop' (*The Saturnine Stranger's Tale*).

Acknowledgements

The author would like to thank Jill Carlisle and Nonnie Hetherington for their help in correcting the text and the London Library for always coming up with the answer regardless of how obscure the question.

Acknowledgement